Chapman and Hall ltd.

Ponce de Leon or the Rise of the Argentine Republic

A Novel

Chapman and Hall ltd.

Ponce de Leon or the Rise of the Argentine Republic
A Novel

ISBN/EAN: 9783337031787

Printed in Europe, USA, Canada, Australia, Japan

Cover: Foto ©Andreas Hilbeck / pixelio.de

More available books at **www.hansebooks.com**

OR THE

RISE OF THE ARGENTINE REPUBLIC.

A Novel.

BY

AN ESTANCIERO.

LONDON:

CHAPMAN & HALL, 193, PICCADILLY.

1878.

CONTENTS.

BOOK I.

THE BABYHOOD OF A GREAT NATION.

BOOK II.

THE PROWESS OF A YOUNG GIANT.

- - - - -

BOOK III.

THE UNKNOWN FUTURE.

BOOK IV.

THE DAWN OF FREEDOM.

PART I.—THE BRIGHTENING OF THE EASTERN SKY.

CONTENTS.

BOOK V.

THE DAWN OF FREEDOM.

PART II.—THE MISTS OF THE EARLY MORN.

BOOK VI.

LIBERTY.

CONTENTS.

GENERAL EPILOGUE.

Al Gran Pueblo Argentino ¡Salud!

PROLOGUE.

THE Argentine Republic drew her first faltering breath in a time of universal tumult. Europe was in a blaze from the confines of Russia to the Atlantic ; the air reeked with blood, the demon of war strode rough-shod over a whole continent, at each step crushing some ancient nation to the dust. The peoples of Europe, down-trodden for ages, rose in their misery and barbarism against their oppressors and wrote out their certificate of Freedom in characters of blood; they asserted their right to be men not slaves, and their voice as that of a mighty trumpet reverberated throughout the earth. In the hearts of the Spanish Creoles of America that voice found an echo.

Spain arrogated to herself unlimited power over the nations she had founded, witting not that they were nations. Though they were of her own bone and her own blood, she knew them not as children, but as bond-slaves, who existed to do her bidding.

The voice of France in the first throes of her great agony sounded in the ears of these bond-slaves, and in secret conclave they whispered one to another, asking one another wistfully, whether they were men and not slaves. To this whispered question for long there was no answer, for Spain was to them as their mother.

Can a mother sin in the eyes of her own child ?

CHAPTER I.

"THANK God I am not a Spaniard."

"Marcelino ! my son ! what new heresy is this?"

"It is no new heresy at all, my mother; it is a fact. Thank God I am not a Spaniard. I am an American, and the day will come when we Americans will show the world that we are men and not slaves."

"Marcelino! Be comforted, my son; it is the fortune of war. You at any rate did your duty, and did not fly till you were left alone. I should have mourned for you if you had been killed. My heart would have been desolate, my son, if I had lost you; now I have you yet, and I am proud of you."

As the stately lady spoke thus, she laid her hands upon her son's shoulder, while he sat gloomily on a low chair; and bending over him, kissed him fondly on the cheek; then, still leaning on him, she raised one hand to his head, running her taper fingers through the tangled locks of curly black hair which covered it. As she thus caressed him, the look of sullen gloom gradually vanished from his face; he looked up at her with eyes the counterparts of her own in their lustrous blackness, but differing from hers as those of an eager, passionate man differ from those of a compassionate, tender-hearted woman.

"Mother," he said, raising his hand to his head, and taking her hand in his own, "sit down and let us talk, for I am going."

"Going! at such a time as this!" answered she, drawing a stool towards her, and seating herself on it beside him, still resting with one hand upon his shoulder, and leaning upon him.

"Yes, mother, going. There will be no more fighting here now, our citizens do not like that work, they told us so to-day pretty plainly when we tried to make them stop and meet the English in the suburbs."

"Going! but where will you go?"

"Anywhere where I can be of more use than here. I cannot stop to see the disgrace of my native city. To-morrow the English will march in in triumph, with their flags flaunting in the air, and their music playing before them. They will march through these streets of ours I tell you, mother; the English flag will fly from the flagstaff in the fort to-morrow, and Buenos Aires will be an English city. Our Buenos Aires, my mother, will be an English city, an English conquest."

"To what God sends there is nothing but resignation, Marcelino."

"God has nothing to do with it, mother; Spain has decreed that we are slaves and not men. Had we been men, do you think a handful of English could take a city like this ? "

"They took us by surprise, when we were not ready for them. Wait till Sobremonte has time to collect troops, he will soon drive them back again to their ships."

"Sobremonte ! If you had seen him at the fort to-day, mother, you would not have much hope from him. The most helpless old woman would have been as much use as he was to-day. The only man to whom we can look now is Liniers. Sobremonte and all the rest will give up their swords and swear fidelity to Great Britain to-morrow."

"So your father told me just now, Marcelino ; he says it is the only thing they can do."

"He is a Spaniard, and thinks as a Spaniard ; of course he must go with the rest. Thank God I am not a Spaniard."

"The Spaniards will soon drive the English out again. Huidobro will send troops from Monte Video, or they will send an army from Spain."

"And why should we look to Spain ? Are there not plenty of us to drive away not one thousand but ten thousand English ? But what has Spain ever done for us that we should fight her battles for her ? We have no quarrel with these English ; for my part I should like to be good friends with them ; but give up my country to them, and let them rule over us—never!"

"No, we will never do that, Marcelino ; but you spoke just now of Liniers. What can he do ? "

"He is a brave man, and a soldier ; with the few troops he had he beat off the English when they tried to land at Ensenada ; so they came nearer, and landed at Quilmes, and our army fled from them like sheep. If Liniers will head us we will soon get enough paisanos together to drive these English into the sea."

"Sobremonte will not permit him to do anything of the kind. What can gauchos do with their lassoes and boleadores against troops?"

"Liniers is not a Spaniard, he is a Frenchman, and would care very little for Sobremonte if he had men behind him ; and men he will have for the asking, that I can promise him."

"All that is nonsense, Marcelino ; you must not go away, you must stop here with me, you will ruin yourself with these strange ideas. Do not leave me ; promise me that you will not go away."

So talked a mother and a son together in the city of Buenos Aires on the evening of the 26th June, 1806. An army of invaders had landed on the coast, and was now encamped close to the city ; the soldiers of Spain had fled before them. On the morrow these invaders proposed to themselves to march into the city, and to take possession of it in the name of the King of Great Britain.

Marcelino Ponce de Leon was the eldest son of one of the Spanish grandees, who ruled over the Vice-royalty of Buenos Aires ; but his mother was a Creole, the daughter of a Creole, and Buenos Aires was his native city.

About the year 1780, Don Roderigo Ponce de Leon left Spain for Buenos Aires in the employ of the Spanish government. Don

Roderigo was a scion of the noble house of Ponce de Leon, whose great ancestor, his namesake, the Marquis of Cadiz, is famed in song and story as the chief of those mighty warriors whose valour crushed for ever the power of the Moors in Spain. He it was who captured the fortress of Alhama, the first victory in that long series of victories which left Ferdinand and Isabella joint sovereigns of the whole of Spain. A victory chronicled in the *Romance mui dolorosa del sitio y toma de Alhama*, in which the distress and consternation of the Moors is vividly set forth :—

> " Por las calles y ventanas,
> Mucho luto parecia,
> Llora el Rey como fembra,
> Que es mucho lo que perdia,
> ¡ Ay de mi ! Alhama ! " [1]

Don Roderigo was proud of his ancestry, but in the diplomatic service of Spain he had in his youth travelled in France and in England. He had mingled with the young nobles of the Court of Versailles, whose talk was of the rights of man, witting not that they themselves stood in the way of these rights, and would presently be overwhelmed in that mighty flood of revolution which reduced their theorizing to practice ; who talked of liberty as of a glorious dream, and later on stood aghast when their dream became a reality. In London he had met men of sterner mould, who could even smile at the defeat of the arms of their own country, and think it no misfortune, since this defeat had given birth to a new nation, whose constitution based itself upon the will of the people ; to a nation of freemen, who made laws for themselves, who appointed themselves their rulers, and obeyed them willingly. As he walked in the streets of that great city, he found himself among a people who, in comparison with his own people, were free ; among a people who thought for themselves, and who spoke their thoughts openly, none daring to stay their utterance. When he returned to Spain, he looked around him upon the stalwart men and graceful women, whose nationality was the same as his own, and he said within himself, Are not these equal to those others ? cannot they think and act for themselves ? Yet he saw that they were as children, following blindly the behests of such as had authority over them ; then, in spite of the traditions of his class, his heart was sore within him at the degradation of his own country. Out of the fulness of his heart he spoke, and there were many who listened to him, till the great lords, the elders of his family, looking seriously into the matter, saw therein much danger to their own order, and finding that opposition but strengthened those pestilent errors which he had learned in his travels in other countries, they washed their hands of him by procuring him an honourable post in the colonies.

He came to Buenos Aires, and was received with the distinction

[1] " And from the windows, o'er the walls,
The sable web of mourning falls,
The King weeps as a woman o'er
His loss, for it is much and sore.
Woe is me ! Alhama ! "
Byron's translation—last verse.

his own talents and great connexions warranted him to expect, but at first no important trust was given into his hands, and he soon felt that his mission to South America was nothing more than an honourable but indefinite exile.

Before he had been two years in Buenos Aires he married Doña Constancia Lopez y Viana, a daughter of Don Gregorio Lopez. This gentleman was a wealthy Creole who had immense estates in various parts of the province of Buenos Aires, where he reared vast herds of cattle, whose hides and tallow yielded him a very sufficient revenue. The manners and customs of the Argentines in those days were very simple, the harsh restrictions on commerce and on intercourse with the rest of the world preserved them from luxury. When living on one of his estancias Don Gregorio was little better housed and fed than his peons, but he ruled over them with an iron hand ; short of life and death his power was absolute over most of them, for most of them were slaves. His residence in the city was a large rambling mansion, one story high, with flat roofs and large patios. Here he spent most of his time, surrounded by a crowd of dependents of all ages and conditions ; to all he dispensed with a lavish hand, exacting only in return implicit obedience.

Don Gregorio had been twice married, his first wife had left him one son who bore his own name ; the children of his second wife had added their mother's surname to his, and were known as the Lopez y Viana family ; among them Don Roderigo Ponce de Leon had found his wife Constancia. They had lived happily together up to the year 1806, in which this story opens, having three sons, Marcelino, Juan Carlos, and Evaristo, and one daughter, Dolores, who differed greatly in appearance from all the rest of the family, having gray eyes shaded with long dark lashes, and hair of a bright chestnut colour which flowed over her shoulders in broad curls almost to her waist, surrounding her if she stood in the sunshine with a halo of glistening gold. This peculiarity endeared her to her father, who saw reproduced in her the traditional features of the ancient house of Ponce, features which time and intermarriage had almost obliterated in their family.

Though Don Roderigo was an outcast from his own family, though new interests and new ties bound him to America, yet he remained at heart a Spaniard, he felt himself one of the dominant race, and could not look upon a native American as his equal. His haughty manners estranged him somewhat from his wife's family, but recommended him to the then Viceroy, who soon forgot the unfavourable report he had received of him, and advanced him from one post to another, till at the close of the last century many thought that the highest post open to any Spaniard in the colonies would at the next change be his.

About that time there arrived in Buenos Aires a naval officer, who had distinguished himself in the service of Spain, and sought promotion and further opportunity for distinguishing himself by service in her colonies. This man was not a Spaniard by birth. Don Santiago Liniers y Bremond was a Frenchman of noble origin, driven by the misfortunes of his country and his class into foreign service. Of an ardent and lively temperament, with distinguished manners, and a high reputation for military skill, he had the art of gaining popularity wherever he went, and soon became a great favourite with the warm-hearted Creoles of Buenos Aires, and not less so with their Spanish rulers, who entrusted him with some of the highest commands at their disposal.

Between Liniers (he dropped his second surname in America, and is known to history as General Liniers) and Don Roderigo an intimacy sprang up which quickly ripened into friendship. Long and earnest were the conversations they held together concerning the events then passing in Europe. As they talked together the warm aspirations of his youth came back to Don Roderigo, visions passed before his eyes of the glorious future that might yet await him, should Spain follow the example of the other peoples and rise and emancipate herself. That she might do so he believed possible, but he saw that it could only be possible after a fierce struggle, in which he could and would bear an honourable part.

Liniers listened willingly to the warm confidences of his friend, though he was far from feeling sympathy with his ideas, but Don Roderigo found others who did sympathize with him, more especially among the better educated of the Creoles. Before many years passed his opinions were known in Madrid, the favour which had been extended to him was withdrawn, and he found himself a marked man in the country which he had hoped before long to rule. His friend Liniers also fell into disfavour, and from being Commandant-General of the Navies of Spain in La Plata he was relegated to the command of a small garrison at Ensenada, which post he still held at the time of the invasion of the English under Beresford.

Marcelino, the eldest son of Don Roderigo, inherited from his mother much of her pliant Creole nature, and his amiable disposition rendered him a favourite with all those with whom he came in contact, but he had also inherited much of the courageous enterprising spirit of his father, and his character had been further modified by his friendship with a man some few years older than himself, who had been sent to Europe to complete his education and had returned early in the year 1805 deeply imbued with the revolutionary ideas then prevalent in France, where he had spent the greater part of his time during his absence from Buenos Aires.

This friend, Don Carlos Evaña by name, was the only son of a wealthy Creole, who, falling under the displeasure of the Spanish authorities, had died in a dungeon, leaving his then infant son to the guardianship of Don Gregorio Lopez.

Marcelino Ponce de Leon had received what was in those days considered a very superior education, had spent three years at the University of Cordova, was well read in the Latin classics, could speak French fluently, and had some knowledge of English. He had returned from Cordova without taking a degree, when his father had wished him to visit Europe, but Marcelino listened to the earnest entreaties of his mother and remained at home, safe, as she thought, from the contagion of those new ideas which she had been taught to look upon with dread.

Mother and son sat far into the night talking earnestly together, the mother daring not to leave him lest he should go she knew not whither, and finding her influence totally unavailing to turn him from what she considered his mad purpose. So they sat on a cold June night in an uncarpeted, fireless room, in which the darkness was made visible by the dull flame of a shaded lamp; so they sat, wrestling together for the mastery; love and tenderness on the one side, love and reverence on the other, equally fearful of giving pain, equally determined not to yield. As the clock in a distant chamber chimed the midnight hour, the husband and the father stood before them. A well-built man of medium stature, with dark-brown hair and eyes, and with a clear, almost ruddy complexion. His son, as he stood up on his entrance, seemed taller by the head, but was more slimly built.

"Marcelino is going," said Doña Constancia; "he will not submit to these English."

"He may stay and yet not submit," answered Don Roderigo. "Sobremonte has fled; they cannot occupy the whole city, and cannot know who are in it, save those who present themselves. I have orders to present myself and shall do so," he said somewhat bitterly, "but there is no reason why you should do so too, unless you wish it."

Marcelino Ponce de Leon remained that night in his father's house, and the next day he heard the sound of the English trumpets and drums from afar off, but he saw them not.

The next day, the 27th June, 1806, 1500 British troops under the command of General Beresford marched into the city, a city of 70,000 inhabitants, with their drums beating and their colours flying, and took peaceable possession thereof; General Beresford establishing his headquarters at the Fort and hoisting the English flag upon the flag-staff. Most of the local authorities hastened to give in their submission, and Buenos Aires became an English city.

CHAPTER II.

BUENOS AIRES became an English city, and throughout the city there was shame and despair; men exchanged fierce looks one with another, muttering low words in their anger, and women wept. And presently a question went circling round from household to household, at a safe distance from the British bayonets :—

" What shall we do ? "

To this question no man answered, but each one looked to some other who should answer for him.

It was the evening of the third day since the triumphal entry of the British, the badly-lighted and unpaved streets were almost deserted, it was bitterly cold, and a thin drizzling rain was falling. Here and there figures muffled in large cloaks wended their way about the streets ; several such figures passed along the street in which stood the house of Don Gregorio Lopez, and entered by the great double door which stood half open. Beyond the door was a covered passage called a " zaguan ; " from the centre of the roof of this zaguan there hung a lamp, under which a tall negro paced up and down. Each man as he passed the doorway and entered the zaguan paused and threw back the fold of his cloak which covered his face, saying to the negro in a low voice—

" España."

" Pass forward to the second patio," answered the negro to each one.

Each man as he heard the answer replied by a slight inclination of the head, and again muffling his face in his cloak, walked across the brick-paved patio to a second zaguan, where another lamp was swinging. Here he was met by a youth to whom he said one word :—

" Rey."

" Good-night and pass forward," answered the youth.

One after another they passed forward through this zaguan to a second patio, where each man paused till he was accosted by another youth, who led him to a door on the left hand, which he opened, ushering him into a large well-lighted room, with a long massive table running down the centre, and chairs ranged all along the walls.

In half an hour a numerous company were assembled in this room, they had removed their hats, but most of them kept on their cloaks. This room was the dining-room of Don Gregorio Lopez, these men there assembled were citizens of Buenos Aires, invited by him to con-

fer together upon what answer should be given to the question which
occupied all minds—

" What shall we do ? "

Don Gregorio had taken such precautions as he thought necessary
to keep the meeting a secret from General Beresford, and also from
such citizens as were not specially invited.   Those whom he had invited were not only citizens of Buenos Aires but were exclusively
men of American birth.   They walked up and down the room in
couples, or stood in groups conversing together in low tones.

To each man as he entered the room Don Gregorio had extended
his hand in cordial welcome ; as the room filled he passed from group
to group saying a few complimentary words, or asking an adroit question on any subject upon which they might happen to be speaking,
but carefully avoiding the question which had called them together.
Don Gregorio was a stout-built man of medium stature, with short hair
which had once been black, but was now plentifully sprinkled with
gray, he had small dark eyes, heavy eyebrows, and bushy gray whiskers,
his lip and chin being clean shaven.   He wore a coat of brown cloth
with brass buttons, the tails of which sloped away from his hips, till
they came almost to a point behind his knees, his waistcoat came down
over his hips, and was open in front, showing a large frill of the finest
cambric, on each side of which hung the ends of the white lace cravat
which enveloped his throat.   Both waistcoat and small-clothes were
of black cloth, and he wore black silk stockings with massive gold
buckles in his shoes.   He had a strong, deep voice, and looked about
him with the air of one having authority, but his manners were exceedingly affable.   On the present occasion his face wore an air of
great satisfaction ; each question addressed to him he answered in carefully subdued tones, accompanying his words with frequent inclinations
of the head and with approving smiles.

Again the door opened, a youth stepping in announced—

" Don Manuel Belgrano," and a man of middle height, with a
high forehead and a thoughtful expression on his face, which gave him
the appearance of being older than he really was, entered the room.

Don Gregorio, who was at that moment standing in the centre of a
group of his guests conversing with them, swung round on his heel as
he heard the name, leaving the sentence which was on his lips incom-
plete, and walked towards the door with both hands stretched out to
welcome the new-comer.   Conversation instantly ceased ; and as the
name Belgrano passed from mouth to mouth, the hands hidden away
under the cloaks issued forth and clapped themselves together, while
a low murmur of " Viva Belgrano ! " too low to be a cheer, went round
the room.

Manuel Belgrano was at this time a man of mature age.   Born in
Buenos Aires in the year 1770, he had in his sixteenth year gone to
Spain, where he passed several years studying at the University of
Salamanca, and afterwards at Valladolid, but his studies embraced a
wider range of subjects than were taught at these seats of learning. Of
a generous and thoughtful temperament, he had eagerly imbibed the
ideas spread throughout Europe by the French Revolution, had
learned to look upon all men as equal, and to hate all manner of

tyranny and oppression. When he left Spain in the year 1794, he thought only of how he might make his studies of service to his own countrymen. He took with him his appointment as secretary to the "Consulado" of Buenos Aires, a body entrusted with the official supervision of the mercantile relations of the colony with the mother-country, and in this post had distinguished himself by his efforts to ameliorate the effect of the ruinous restrictions which were at that time imposed upon all commercial intercourse. Not content with his official duties, he had further exerted himself to establish a Nautical School, and a School of Design, which under his able supervision flourished rapidly, and promised great benefits to the colony. But his efforts found little support among his own countrymen, encountered great opposition from the jealousy of the Spanish authorities, and both schools were eventually closed by a positive order from the Court of Aranjuez, in which the Consulado was severely censured for having permitted them to be established.

On the occupation of the city by the British army, Belgrano had been summoned by General Beresford to deliver up the archives of his department, but had not only refused to do so but had also refused to give in his own formal submission to the new authorities, saying that he was responsible to the Viceroy, could only receive orders from him, and would rejoin him so soon as he could discover where he had gone.

"You come late, my friend," said Don Gregorio, "but I knew you would not fail us, so I waited for you."

"I had much to do, I was busy with my preparations, for I have no time to lose," answered Belgrano, shaking hands with several friends of his who pressed round him.

"What are you about to do?"

"To fly. You do not know what happened me to-day, I will tell you. When General Beresford first sent for me I obeyed him, and when I refused to give up to him the official seal and the archives of the Consulado, saying that I could only obey an order from the Viceroy, he accepted my excuse and dismissed me with much polite-ness and consideration. I believe he thought that Sobremonte would present himself in a day or two. But Sobremonte has gone off no one knows where, and many of us, as you know, have given in our papers to the English general. This afternoon he sent to me an order to present myself at once. To present myself is to submit. I will not submit, therefore I must fly, and that at once. You, my friends, will judge me. Do I not act rightly?"

"Perfectly! perfectly!" echoed from all sides; and again a low murmur of "Viva Belgrano" ran round the room.

"But before you go you will spare us an hour or two," said Don Gregorio. "You have more experience than many of us who are older than you, and your counsel may be of great service to us."

"Assuredly," replied Belgrano. "I do not see what you can do for the present but just quietly submit; you have——"

"Submit! we submit!" exclaimed Marcelino Ponce de Leon, who was one of those present. "For each one man that they have we can put ten, why then should we submit?"

"They are trained soldiers, and are well armed. Do you know what my men said to me when we got the order to retreat? They said, 'It is well, for this sort of work is not for us.'"

"They said well," said another who stood by, Don Juan Martin Puyrredon by name. "They know what they are worth, your city militia, they do not like the cold steel, and it appears that these English do not waste time shooting at a distance, they like the bayonet better," he added with a scornful laugh.

"Give us time to arm a few hundred paisanos, and the militia may remain in their houses," said Marcelino. "We will drive the English into the river without their help."

"The paisanos are brave men, but they cannot fight against trained troops," answered Belgrano quietly.

"If our men were trained they would stand their ground as well as any men," said another, named Don Isidro Lorea, who was a captain in the city militia.

"They had arms and had nothing to do but to stand still and use them the other day," said Puyrredon, "but they did not even do that. You set to work firing before the English came within range, and then when they came nearer you ran. All the effective resistance that the English met was at the Puente Galvés, where Don Marcelino stopped them for an hour or two by burning the bridge."

"When the English charged them with the bayonet your partidarios ran quick enough," replied Lorea in an angry tone. "And Don Marcelino it appears may thank his horse that he got away at all."

"Don Marcelino bore himself like a brave man," said Don Gregorio, laying his hand upon the shoulder of his grandson, and speaking in a loud voice, which had the effect of putting a stop at once to the dispute. "It matters not now what has been done. What we shall do is what you have done me the honour to come here to discuss quietly among ourselves. Do me the favour, my friends, to arrange yourselves round the room; and, Don Manuel, come with me to the head of the table."

So saying, Don Gregorio walked to one end of the table, where he seated himself in an arm-chair, with Don Manuel Belgrano at his right hand and Marcelino Ponce de Leon at his left; the latter having some sheets of paper and pens and ink before him, while the rest seated themselves on chairs round the room, with the exception of one group who remained standing round Don Juan Martin Puyrredon at the far end.

When all were settled in their places, Don Gregorio rose from his seat, and with many signs of hesitation, for he had never before attempted to make a speech, began :—

"Señores, my friends, I have invited you to meet in my house with one sole object; our city is in the power of foreigners, our Viceroy has fled, such troops as we had are dispersed. What shall we do? Shall we submit to these foreigners, to these heretics who are the enemies of Spain, and of our Holy Church?"

"No, no!" arose in answer from all sides.

"You have all of you read the proclamation of this Beresford, in which he offers us freedom in the exercise of our religion, freedom of commerce, and reduction of taxation, styling himself governor of this city of ours by the authority of His Majesty the King of Great Britain. The advantages he offers us are great; shall we not, then, accept this Beresford as our governor?"

"No, no!" again rose in answer.

"Then if we will neither be bribed into treachery to our legitimate king, nor tamely submit, we must fight and drive these English back to their ships. But it was easier to keep them out than to drive them out now they are in."

"It will be difficult, but we will do it," said Puyrredon.

"It will be done, I doubt not," continued Don Gregorio. "Let us then consider carefully the means we should adopt. As yet the first requisite is wanting to us—not one of us here present is a soldier who has seen service. There is one whom I hoped to have seen here, who has served in Europe, and only the other day showed us that he has not forgotten what he learnt there. With a handful of men he beat off all the English army, with their fleet to back them, at Ensenada, and now he has retired without the loss of one man. You know who I mean—Don Santiago Liniers. My son set off yesterday to confer with him, and to bring him here to us to-night; as yet he does not appear, but even in his absence we may agree to appoint him our chief, and when he comes he will tell us what to do."

At that moment there came a knock at the door, which had been locked when Don Gregorio took his seat at the head of the table; one of those near at hand opened it, and gave entrance to the youth who had acted as usher. He walked up to Don Gregorio, and spoke to him in a low voice.

"Tell him to give his name," said Don Gregorio.

"He refuses, but says he must see you."

"Go you, Marcelino, and see if you know him. He may be some messenger from Liniers."

Marcelino went out, but quickly returned, bringing with him a tall man of middle age, with strikingly handsome features. The stranger entered first, and throwing aside his cloak and hat disclosed the undress uniform of a field-officer.

"Don Gregorio, I kiss your feet," said he, bowing to that gentleman. "Señores todos, felices noches," he added, as he cast a quick, searching glance round the room.

"No fear; all are friends," said Marcelino, as he closed the door.

"Liniers! Liniers!" exclaimed many of those present, as they rose from their seats to bid him welcome, and to congratulate him upon his recent feat of arms, while Don Gregorio left his place at the table and walked towards him with outstretched hand.

"My friend, I am glad to see you," said Don Gregorio. "A number of my friends have come here together this evening to consult upon what measures we shall adopt now that the authorities have either submitted to the English or have fled. You are a soldier; this is not the first time you have seen service; we should be glad to hear your opinion."

"And what do these gentlemen say?" answered Liniers, walking up to the table, and leaning his hand upon it, while an expression of anxious thought came over his handsome features.

"There are some who say that we ought to organize the militia of the city and the partidarios into an army at some safe distance from the city, and then attack the English, and crush them before any reinforcement can reach them. There are not 2000 of them, but to form an army we require a chief."

"And something more too than a chief," replied Liniers, with a complacent smile, "something more than a chief; time is wanting. Do you think one could make soldiers of your militia in a week?"

"What we want in discipline we will make up by numbers," said Don Isidro Lorea. "The other day we had no leader, if we had had one the affair would have been very different."

"We were mustered at the fort, and marched off anyhow," said Belgrano; "what more could we expect than what happened? I agree with you, Don Santiago, time is wanting before we can hope to do anything with the militia."

"Then there are others," continued Don Gregorio, "who say that we should do nothing at all at present, but wait until our Viceroy can collect troops sufficient. There is a strong force in Monte Video, and small detachments are scattered about the provinces."

"And they are the most sensible men," said Liniers.

"I am going to rejoin the Viceroy if I can find him," said Belgrano. "Come with me, Don Santiago, he will give you authority to collect troops."

"Better go to Monte Video," said Marcelino Ponce de Leon; "Huidobro can give you both men and arms. You may be back by the end of the month, and we will have an army ready for you by then."

During all this time there was one man there who had hardly spoken to any. He sat on a chair beyond the end of the table, with his cloak folded round him, his arms crossed over his chest, listening quietly to all that was said, neither assenting to nor dissenting from anything that was proposed, his quick, dark eyes alone showing the interest he took in the discussion. His high, square forehead betokened him a man of powerful intellect, while his pale, olive complexion, and the delicacy of his long, thin hands bespoke him a student. As he sat he seemed to be only of medium stature, and slightly built; now he rose and stood beside the table, stretching himself to his full height, half a head taller than any other man there present, and spoke as follows :—

"Señores, I have listened quietly to all that has been said. Were you Spaniards I would applaud your patriotism, I would praise your brave determination to risk your lives in an unequal conflict against men trained to arms. Were I a Spaniard I would join you, and would think my life well lost could I spend it in thrusting out from my country an audacious invader. But this soil on which I stand is not Spain, neither am I a Spaniard, nor are you, my countrymen, Spaniards. You, I, all of us are Americans, the soil upon which we stand is American soil, the air which we breathe is American air. True we are of Spanish blood, our ancestors were Spaniards, they crossed the ocean and spent their lives in conquering a new world.

We are the sons of those gallant men who built up the seats of new
nations on a new continent; day by day we spread ourselves further
over these wide plains, drawing riches from their luxuriant pastures;
we explore the mighty rivers which bring down to us the wealth of
other provinces; and for whom do we so labour and spend our lives?
For Spain! What has Spain ever done for us that we should spend
our lives in her service? Spain sends us rulers and tax-gatherers, who
live here in plenty and go back to Spain laden with riches for which
we have toiled. Spain forces upon us her merchandise when we
could buy better and cheaper elsewhere, and so robs us of the fruit of
our labours. Spain sends us priests to instruct our youth in knowledge which is of no avail, to prevent the spread of anything like real
education, and to keep our consciences in bondage to a slavish superstition. This is what Spain has done for us up to now, and will do for
us to the end.

"There are men among you who have travelled in other lands as I
have done, who have seen the great uprising of the people which now
shakes the earth. Returning to their own land, they have sought to
do something to enlighten the ignorance of their own countrymen, they
have sought to raise them from the barbarism in which they live. How
have their efforts prospered? They have been reviled as infidels, they
have been stigmatized as rebels, and have been fortunate when they
have escaped fines and imprisonment as dangerous to the State. Why
then should we risk our lives for Spain? This land which our fathers
conquered and we possess is our land, it is nothing but a worn-out
tradition which holds us in bondage to Spain. Give ear to me, my
countrymen, and know that this disaster which has fallen upon our
city is no disaster, but is the first step towards our deliverance. There
are many among you would think it sacrilege to stretch out your hand
and tear down the flag under which you were born, under which you
have lived, but if a foreigner tear it down for you and cast it forth from
our country he in no wise injures you, he does but free us from a
tyranny under which we have groaned for centuries.

"We cannot look upon these English as friends, for they come to take
our country into their possession, but neither need we fear them as
enemies. They could not hold their own colonies in subjection
when they rose against them, although half the colonists were their
friends, as many of you to-day are the friends of Spain. How then
shall they bring us into subjection among whom they have not one
friend to aid them? This enterprise of these English is rash folly
which will recoil upon their own heads, but they may do us good
service in driving out from among us these Spanish rulers who have
too long tyrannized over us.

"Why should we fear these English? Far distant from their own
country, they can but obtain a temporary footing on our soil. Let
these dogs of war, the paid agents of tyranny and misrule, rend each
other in their struggle for a dominion which is not theirs. Let the
Spaniards and the English fight out their quarrel by themselves,
while we steadfastly prepare to assert against either or both our own
dominion on our own soil, the inalienable right of all free-born men
to make their own laws and govern themselves. I have spoken!"

C

As the speaker ceased he struck the table with his hand, and looked round him proudly, as though he would defy any one to dissent from any word he had spoken, and a deep silence fell upon all.

To most there present these words and ideas were entirely new. They had listened in wonder, now they looked one at another in doubt and dismay ; what had been said was nothing less than treason, and they knew not but that in listening, merely, they were themselves traitors.

But there were others there to whom these ideas were far from new, they were ideas which they themselves had cherished, but had hidden in their hearts, saying to themselves that the time had not yet come. Don Manuel Belgrano sat with his elbows on the table, covering his face with his hands. Marcelino Ponce de Leon made strokes on the paper which lay before him with a pen which had no ink in it, ever and anon glancing up at the speaker, and as quickly again dropping his eyes to the paper, while his thoughts wandered to a time not long past when Don Carlos Evaña had told him how he had met in London an exile from Venezuela, who had spoken to him just such words as these.

And there was one there present upon whom these words had a different effect to what they had on any other. This was not the first time that Don Santiago Liniers had heard such words as these ; they carried him back in memory into the far-off past, when he had learned to look upon men holding such opinions as impious in the sight of God, outcasts among men, and had hated them with a bitter hatred, envenomed since then by the losses he had suffered at their hands. In silence he listened, leaning upon the back of a chair ; there was to him a fascination in the sound of that deep sonorous voice which spoke treason in accents of firm conviction. His heart sank within him, and as that voice ceased, a cold shiver, for which he could not account, ran through his frame. He looked up at the speaker, and met the glance of a pair of dark eyes fixed sternly upon him ; again the cold shiver ran through him, he turned away his gaze and looked anxiously around him, eager to note the effect of these words on others.

Then rose Don Gregorio Lopez from his seat, and leaning with both hands upon the table before him, said in a low voice, and speaking with great deliberation—

" My friends, each man has a right to entertain such ideas as he please, but we are not met together this evening to discuss ideas. I am sorry to see that there is much division of opinion amongst us ; it is thus impossible that we unite cordially together in any one plan of action. The object for which I invited you to meet me this evening has thus failed. For my part I say, ' Out with these English !' Those who think as I do will each act as he thinks best, in his own way, to bring about this result.

" Afuera Los Ingleses ! Fueran ! !" was the answer from all sides. After which the meeting resolved itself into groups, in which men talked eagerly together for some minutes, discussing together their several plans, and announcing their intentions. Then the door being thrown open they gradually dispersed to their several homes.

Don Carlos Evaña was one of the last to leave. As he shook hands with Don Gregorio, the latter said to him—

"Ah, Carlos! you boys learn many ideas in your travels, but, believe me, it is at times dangerous to expose them so publicly."

"And believe me," answered Don Carlos, "that the day is not far off when these ideas of mine will be the law of a new nation in America."

As he went out he was joined by Marcelino.

"Will you take no part with any of us?" asked Marcelino.

"To raise again that emblem of tyranny which has been torn down? Not I. Have you so soon forgotten the lessons we have learned together?"

"I have not forgotten them, Carlos; but how shall I think of them when a foreigner rules in my native country?"

"All tyrants are foreigners, Marcelino. When once we are fairly rid of our tyrants then it will be time enough to turn out these English. If it were to gain our country for ourselves none would be more forward than Carlos Evaña."

"Let us turn out the English, and then we will work together."

"You do not know it, but these English are our best friends, Marcelino."

"Such friends are better at a distance," replied Marcelino.

CHAPTER III.

CONCERNING THE DANGER OF FRIENDSHIP WITH AN ENEMY.

THE fort, where General Beresford had taken up his quarters, was an edifice of imposing appearance but of no great strength, situate in the centre of the river-face of the city. Its eastern front, which overlooked the river, was a semi-circular pile of brickwork, rising from the water's edge some sixty feet above the average level of the river, and was pierced with embrasures from which the black mouths of cannon protruded. It was built in the massive style adopted by the Spaniards, but its chief strength consisted in the shallowness of the river, which prevented the near approach of any hostile squadron. In the rear of this semi-circular casemate stood some brick buildings in which the Viceroy and his principal officers had apartments. Beyond these buildings was a flat, open space, which served as a parade-ground, in the centre of which rose the flagstaff, on which the standard of Great Britain had now replaced the gaudy flag of Spain. The whole of these buildings and the parade-ground were surrounded by a low brick wall, which was again surrounded by a wide, dry ditch, crossed in the centre of the western front of the fort by a drawbridge which through a wide gateway gave entrance to the stronghold from the Plaza de Los Perdices.

This Plaza was a wide, open space, about 150 yards across, where the country people daily brought their game, fruit, and vegetables for sale to the citizens; it was thus the market-place of the city. This wide, open space still exists, and is now known as the Plaza Veinte y Cinco de Mayo, but it is no longer used as a market. To the west of the Plaza de Los Perdices, facing the fort, stood two rows of shops, the flat roofs of which were prolonged over the causeways both in front and rear, and resting upon square brick pillars at the edge of the causeways, formed arcades, cut off from the buildings at the north and south the Plaza by roadways, which were the continuations of the two central streets of the city.

Between the two arcades there was an open space crossed by a towering arch of brickwork, having the appearance of a gigantic gateway, which gave passage from the Plaza de Los Perdices to the Plaza Mayor, which lay beyond. These two arcades with the archway were known as the "Recoba Vieja."

The Plaza Mayor was equal in size to the other, and was surrounded by buildings; half the western face being occupied by the "Cabildo" or Government House, a lofty building two storeys high, with balconies projecting in front of the windows of the upper storey, which storey also projected over the causeway in front of the Cabildo, resting upon massive brick pillars, and so forming another arcade, which occupied one half only of this side the Plaza. Half the northern side the Plaza was occupied by the cathedral; the rest of the buildings around were ordinary houses mostly one storey high, those on the south side being also fronted by an arcade which covered the causeway, and gave the name of the "Recoba Nueva" to that side the Plaza.

The centre of the Plaza was unoccupied and unpaved, but carriages and horsemen being restricted to the sides, it was maintained in tolerably level condition, affording a pleasant promenade for the citizens in fine weather. All the buildings in both Plazas were of brick, plastered and whitewashed, the cathedral being surmounted by a mighty dome. The houses had large doorways and windows, but the latter were protected by iron railings.

General Beresford took up his quarters in the fort, where he occupied the apartments of the fugitive Viceroy; British soldiers occupied the casemates and the barracks of the troops, their scarlet uniforms were continually to be seen crossing the parade ground, and were by day plentifully sprinkled about the adjacent Plazas. Most of his troops Beresford cantoned in the houses about the Plaza Mayor; one strong detachment occupied the Cabildo. His enterprise so far had been attended with great success, but he did not disguise from himself that his situation was extremely critical, his force was too small to do more than overawe the city. All that he could do was to strengthen his position as much as possible and wait for reinforcements.

In furtherance of this plan he constructed temporary platforms and planted thirty guns on the parade-ground at the fort, whose fire swept the Plaza de Los Perdices and commanded all its approaches; he drew breastworks across the entrances to the Plaza Mayor, and established a line of outposts, one strong detachment being stationed at the Retiro to the extreme north of the city, where on the high ground fronting the river stood a large edifice which had been built about a century previously by some English slave-merchants, and used by them as a storehouse for their human merchandise. This storehouse had been more recently used as a barrack by the Spanish garrison of Buenos Aires. In front of it there was a large space of open ground some squares in extent; to the north of this open space stood a bull-ring, a large circular edifice very strongly built round an open arena. From this bull-ring the open space in front of the barracks was sometimes named the Plaza Toros, but its more usual name was the Plaza del Retiro.

Further, General Beresford sought in every way to conciliate the good-will of the inhabitants, preserving the strictest discipline among his soldiery, and paying liberally for all supplies. And the inhabitants of Buenos Aires apparently bore him no ill-will, treating him rather as a guest than as a conqueror, inviting him and his officers to tertulias at their houses, and accepting such hospitality as he could offer them in exchange. Conspicuous among the householders for their friendly treatment of the English were Don Gregorio Lopez and his son-in-law Don Roderigo Ponce de Leon.

The Marquis of Sobremonte, Viceroy of Buenos Aires, in his hurried flight from the city had an excuse in his anxiety to save the public treasure, which amounted to nearly a million and a half sterling in bullion and specie. At the Villa Lujan, a country town some fourteen leagues west of Buenos Aires, he was overtaken by a detachment sent by Beresford in pursuit, and fled without any attempt at resistance, abandoning the greater part of the treasure. The British detachment met with no opposition from the country-people either in its march upon Lujan or on its return to the capital, and Beresford, after reserving sufficient specie for the pay and support of his troops for several months, embarked one million sterling on board the frigate " Narcissus," which sailed at once for England.

The ground plan of the city of Buenos Aires resembles a chess-board, all the streets running either perpendicular to the course of the river, that is, due east and west, or parallel with it, that is, due north and south, crossing each other at right angles at distances of 150 varas. The city is thus cut up into square blocks of houses, each block being styled a manzana. Between the two streets which run out westwards from the Plaza Mayor, the two central streets of the city, and ten squares distant from this Plaza, one entire block was left vacant of buildings, and was in those days a mere open space of waste ground.

At the northern corner of the eastern side of this vacant space stood the house of Don Isidro Lorea. Don Isidro was a captain in the city militia. On the morning of the 26th June, when the English were advancing upon the city, he had mustered his men, had marched them to the fort, and had placed himself and them at the orders of the Marquis of Sobremonte. Later on he had marched them into the suburbs, and upon the near approach of the invaders had fled with them in confusion and dismay back to his own home. Don Isidro's ideas on military matters were vague in the extreme ; previous to that day he had never seen a gun fired in anger ; but he was no coward, and when the first effects of his terror had passed over he bitterly upbraided himself for his pusillanimity. Tears had stood in the eyes of his wife, Doña Dalmacia, as she had watched him march away, and she had spent the time during his absence on her knees in a neighbouring church, praying earnestly for his safety ; but when he returned to her safe, sound, and vanquished, then those same eyes looked upon him in utter scorn and contempt, and his heart quailed within him even more than it had quailed at the sight of the British bayonets.

During those days of shame and despair which followed, Don Isidro nourished within his breast wild schemes of revenge and retaliation, and he eagerly associated himself with those who planned together the destruction of the small British force which held their city in thrall.

Yet weeks passed and nothing was attempted. As Don Gregorio Lopez had told them, their first necessity was a leader, and he to whom they all looked as a leader had gone from them. Liniers had gone to Monte Video to seek the aid of Huidobro, who commanded in that city, telling them to make what preparations they could in the mean time, and that he would look to them for help on his return.

It was now the last week in July, a cold, clear, starlight night. In defiance of the orders of General Beresford, and in despite of British patrols, there was much going to and fro in the streets of the city that night; a rumour had gone forth that Huidobro, a man of very different stamp to Sobremonte, had received Liniers with open arms and had at once placed all his disposable military force under his command, and that Liniers was coming back with what speed he could. This news created a great ferment throughout the city, each man wishing to know the certainty of what he had only vaguely heard, and seeking information from others who were no better informed than himself.

The house of Don Isidro Lorea was divided into two distinct parts, the part occupying the corner of the block being used as the almacen (a general store), of which the main entrance looked upon the open ground, while several windows opened upon the adjacent street. The other half was the dwelling house, and had a separate entrance, a massive doorway opening on the waste ground, which gave entrance through a zaguan to a large, brick-paved patio, surrounded by the principal rooms of the household. Three windows to the left of the doorway gave light to the principal room of all, the sala, at one end of which there was a smaller room known as the ante-sala, which was frequently used by Don Isidro as his private office. All the exterior windows of both house and almacen were guarded by massive iron "rejas," bars set in the brickwork, which prevented all clandestine entrance into the house.

On this night the door of the dwelling-house was fast closed, but any one rapping with his knuckles at the door of the almacen would have found it open to him forthwith. Many did so knock on that night, and passing in, went out again by a side door into the patio of the dwelling-house, and thence to the sala, or to the ante-sala, as seemed to them good. The folding doors between the two rooms were thrown wide open, so that the two rooms were as one, and there was much passing to and fro between them. The sala was a large, richly-furnished apartment, with spindle-shanked chairs and tables, and much gaudy frippery in the way of ornament. Here Doña Dalmacia sat in state, with a heavy velvet mantle thrown over her shoulders. She was a stout, handsome woman, something over thirty years of age, but was of that class of woman who preserves her good looks till long past maturity, her complexion being of that clear olive which looks perfectly white by candle-light, while the beauty of her chiselled features and dark flashing eyes age might impair, but would not destroy. Here she sat in state, talking eagerly and proudly with the men who thronged around her—chiefly young men, who had but one thought in their hearts, but one subject upon which they could converse,—the expulsion of the English.

"Ah, Don Marcelino," she said in clear ringing tones, as Marcelino Ponce de Leon entered the room, "I have not seen you for weeks, but I know you have not been idle; tell me what have you done? The day is very near now."

"I kiss your feet, Misia Dalmacia," answered Marcelino, as he bowed low before her. "We have not lost our time; we have collected and armed nearly 1000 men, and they are near at hand when they are wanted. I have come in to hear what is doing, and to you I come first."

"You have done well, for I can tell you something which will rejoice you. Isidro has a note from Liniers dated a week back, he was then leaving Monte Video with 1000 troops, all fully equipped, and has probably by this reached Colonia. Vessels will meet him there to bring him to Las Conchas, so he may be here any day now."

"Viva, Liniers !" said Marcelino; "he will find us ready, and then——" His flashing eyes and clenched hands supplied the hiatus in his words.

"But, Don Marcelino, be cautious yet," said Doña Dalmacia. "We have done what we can to amuse these English, but this Beresford is a crafty fox, and has his suspicions."

"And there are traitors among us who sell news to him for gold," said a short, stout man, who stood near by, Don Felipe Navarro by name, a brother of Doña Dalmacia.

"Yes, you must not let any one know where your men are," added Doña Dalmacia; "only be ready. If Beresford hears of your preparations he will attack you before Liniers can land."

"Let him," said Marcelino disdainfully. "We will be ready for him if he ventures outside the city. We have formed an encampment at the Quinta de Perdriel, if he comes there we will know how to send him back again."

"That is very near," said Doña Dalmacia.

"The less distance we have to march when the day comes the better," answered Marcelino. "But you city people, what have you done?" added he, turning to Don Felipe Navarro.

"Every house will send out a soldier, and every azotea will be a battery when the fire commences," replied Don Felipe.

"We have two cannon hid in the almacen, and plenty of ammunition," said Doña Dalmacia. "Isidro has all his arrangements complete. This house is the headquarters for all the neighbourhood, and when he fires off two rockets, at any hour of the day or night, 200 men will meet here."

A mulatta girl entered the room bearing a silver salver with cups of chocolate, which she handed round to the guests, and as they sipped the chocolate Marcelino listened to many a strange tale about the English. Don Isidro Lorea was very anxious to get rid of the English, but while they were there his tradesman's instincts prompted him to cultivate friendly relations with them. He had never before found such good customers, and in the day-time Doña Dalmacia had frequently parties of officers in her sala, with whom she conversed in very roundabout fashion, finding much amusement in teaching them to suck mate, and gleaning what information she could from them concerning the dispositions and intentions of their chief. Many shrewd remarks she made, and heartily she laughed as she told of the ludicrous mistakes they made in attempting polite speeches to her.

"But withal," she said, "they are not bad sort of people; it gives sorrow to me to think that they are enemies and—heretics."

"Little it matters to me that they are heretics," said Marcelino. "For my part I believe there is more than one way to heaven."

"Your friend Don Carlos Evaña appears very intimate with them," said Don Isidro, who had come from the outer room as they were speaking.

Don Isidro was of short stature and of light, active build, with very clear complexion, aquiline nose, and jet-black hair and beard, the latter falling in glossy waves down on to his chest. His manners were very polished and he had a great habit of gesticulating with his hands as he talked.

"Ah! Don Isidro, buenas noches," said Marcelino, as he turned quickly and gave him his hand; "I thought you were not at home. Yes, I should think it probable that Don Carlos would be intimate with them, but what of that?"

"It is not well that a man should be intimate with the enemies of his country."

"Don Carlos has told us that in this affair he will take no part. He has lived in England and speaks their language well. Doña Dalmacia tells me that you are all doing what you can to amuse them; he is better able to amuse them than any of you."

"We amuse the officers, but the general seems to care little for amusement, he is doing all he can to strengthen his position, and seems to know exactly where to meet us. I tell you, Don Marcelino, there are traitors amongst us."

As Don Isidro said this he stretched out both his hands with the palms upwards and stamped his foot on the ground, looking somewhat defiantly at Don Marcelino. The latter flushed to the roots of his hair, but smiling to conceal his annoyance, he answered in a light tone—

"It may be so, of that kind of people there are always too many. Find them out and shut their mouths for them, that is all the advice I can give you."

"If you and the others would have taken my advice, the Señor Evaña would have been forced to leave the city, and there would be one traitor the less walking amongst us to-day. What does he here, aiding us in nothing, and holding conferences every day with the English general?"

"How!" said Marcelino, now really angry. "Have you yet that absurd idea in your head? I tell you again, Don Isidro, that as I know my own honour so I know that of my friend Carlos Evaña. To walk among you and to tell of your preparations to the English is to be a spy, and if you apply that word to my friend you will answer to me."

"I know you, Don Marcelino, and I know that there is not one man amongst us of a sounder heart than you, but every man is liable to be deceived, and your friendship blinds you to——"

"Isidro!" said Doña Dalmacia interrupting her husband. "Basta! in these circumstances it is not meet that those who are working in the good cause should quarrel."

"The intimate friend of General Beresford——"

"Isidro!" exclaimed Doña Dalmacia, again interrupting her husband.

"Thou also!" said Don Isidro; then shrugging his shoulders, and clapping his hands on his hips, he made a low inclination with his head to Don Marcelino and returned to the ante-sala.

Marcelino returned his salutation with rigid formality; then taking Don Felipe Navarro by the arm he led him to a retired corner of the sala, where he questioned him earnestly concerning the treachery thus plainly imputed to his friend.

"One thing is certain," said Don Felipe, "Don Carlos is very intimate with General Beresford, hardly a day passes but he spends some hours with him, and they have often long private conversations together. We have our spies, and know everything that the English do, but we do not know what the general and Don Carlos find to talk about."

"I will ask him, and you may be sure he will tell me. But from what you say Don Carlos makes no effort to hide his friendship for the English general."

"Not the slightest."

"Then that is proof at once. Spies walk in darkness, and do not go to visit their employers in broad daylight."

"But Don Carlos makes no secret of his opinions. He counsels us to make friends of the English, and openly speaks of freeing us with their help from Spain. That is treason against our lord the king."

"Against the king I say nothing; but Spain is our tyrant, and Spaniards come here only to plunder us. Don Carlos shows his patriotism by his enmity to Spain, and his patriotism is guarantee that he will never prove false to us who are his countrymen."

"But further, he is an enemy to the holy mother Church, he never goes to Mass, and scoffs at the priests; he is an infidel, a heretic —from a man like that one may suspect anything."

"One should suspect no man without proofs," said Marcelino, turning away. Then after taking leave with great cordiality of Doña Dalmacia and of those about her he went on to the ante-sala.

"Don Isidro," said he, "I am going to see my friend Don Carlos Evaña. I shall tell him plainly that he is suspected, and advise him to avoid the society of these English for the present."

"You will not find him," said Don Isidro; "Beresford gives a dinner to-day at the fort to the authorities, and to some of our principal men; naturally his great friend will be there."

"I doubt it," said one of the visitors, who had been talking to Don Isidro; "Don Carlos never goes anywhere where he is likely to meet Spaniards."

"My father will be at the fort," said Marcelino.

"I know he is, and the two Don Gregorios also," said another; "I saw them go together."

"Then I will go and see my mother. I have avoided our house whenever I have been in the city, for I feared to compromise my father."

"You have done well," said Don Isidro. "More than once I have been asked by English officers whether I knew anything of the eldest son of Don Roderigo Ponce de Leon. If you go to-night you will see some of them there, there are always English officers there in the evenings, tertulias are things of every day. As your father will not fight them, Doña Constancia does her part in amusing them."

"Hum!" said Marcelino. "I do not wish to meet any of them until we meet sword in hand."

"No fear," said another; "the officers will be all on duty to-night."

"I will go at any rate," said Marcelino. "I may meet Carlos there, so good-night to you all until *the* day."

But Don Isidro would not let him depart thus coldly, he sprang to his feet, and grasping him warmly by the hand said—

"Before many days we will meet again; meantime, warn your friend that he keep within his own house and I guarantee you that no harm shall come to him."

Marcelino found no difficulty in reaching his father's house, his name was his passport. He walked boldly along the streets, met several patrols of British soldiery, was questioned by them, but was immediately permitted to pass on, as he gave his name, speaking in English, and told them where he was going. As he drew near he heard sounds of music; in the first patio he found several English soldiers muffled in their gray great-coats, unarmed, walking up and down and joking in a rough, good-humoured way with the mulatta girls and negresses, the servants of his father's household.

"What are you women doing here?" asked Marcelino sternly.

"The night is fine, and the Señora permits us to watch the dancing," answered one.

"It is Don Marcelino," whispered another. "What joy for the Señora; I will run and tell her."

"Stay where you are; I want to see who are here first." So saying Marcelino went up to one of the sala doors, and opening it softly looked in.

His mother was seated on a sofa at the far end, conversing gaily with an English officer, whose massive epaulets showed him to be one who held a high command. Other ladies sat about the sides of the room, most of whom had one or two cavaliers in attendance, while the centre of the room was filled with a crowd of dancers, of whom some half-dozen wore the scarlet uniforms of Great Britain. The dance was one of those formal square dances then much in vogue, and a flush of pleasure spread over Marcelino's face as he looked upon the graceful forms flitting to and fro. As he looked there came a pause in the dance, and the smile that was on his face vanished in a frown. At the head of the room, standing conspicuously side by side under the full glare of a chandelier of wax lights, were two upon whom his gaze was rivetted at once. One was a British officer, in the scarlet jacket and tartan trews of a Highland regiment. He had the yellow hair, clear skin, blue eyes, and reddish whiskers of a Lowland Scot. The other was his own sister Dolores.

One looking casually upon these two might have taken them for brother and sister, there was so much likeness between them, but a second look would have shown an essential difference. Dolores Ponce de Leon was remarkable for the small size of her hands and feet, and

for the delicate moulding of her features. The hands and feet of her
partner, though well-formed, were large, and his features were somewhat coarse—there was more of strength than of elegance in his
appearance. No one after a careful scrutiny could have taken them
for brother and sister, they were types of two branches of one great
race, the Anglo-Saxons of Great Britain, the Goths of Spain.

Again closing the door, Marcelino walked away to his own room in
an inner part of the house, saying to the same girl to whom he had
before spoken—

"When these go, tell my mother that I have returned."

When he reached his own room he clapped his hands, at which
summons an aged negro presented himself.

"Ah! Patroncito Marcelino," said the old negro as he saw him;
"so much as the Señora has hoped for you, and no one could tell
where you were. The Patron said you would be back in a few days,
but now it is weeks. In what can I be of service to your Señoria?"

"Have you seen Don Carlos Evaña to-day?"

"I saw the Señor Evaña not half an hour ago, when I went in
with a tray of dulces."

"Go and tell him that I am come, but do not let any one else hear
what you say."

CHAPTER IV.

THE meeting between Marcelino Ponce de Leon and his friend Don Carlos Evaña was very cordial; they embraced like brothers. Then Don Carlos proceeded to question Marcelino concerning all that he had done during the past three weeks. To every question Marcelino answered unreservedly, Evaña listening to him with a tender light playing in his usually stern eyes, and an approving smile upon his lips.

"How I envy you," he said, as the other paused, his face glowing with enthusiasm.

"Why do you not join us? You are more clever and braver than I am. Ah! how willingly I would serve under you. The chiefs we have are zealous enough but very few of them have any brains. I have no experience, but I can see the follies they do; one man like you were worth more than all the rest put together."

"Of all those you have named to me, Don Juan Martin and yourself seem the only ones at all fitted to command," replied Evaña. "Why are you only a subordinate?"

"There is so much jealousy among them, all want to command, so I thought I should set a good example by showing how to obey."

"Would there were more like you," said Evaña, with a sigh.

"There would be one more and one better than me, if you would only join us," replied Marcelino.

"It may not be, I have vowed my life to one work, the Independence of my native country. So long as Spain claims dominion over these provinces I have only one aim in life, and there is only one enemy against whom I will raise my hand."

"Yet, cannot you see, Carlos, that in this struggle with the English we shall train our men and make soldiers of them, and so prepare them for a fiercer struggle which must come later on?"

"What you have told me teaches me, even if I did not know it before, that the worst misfortune which can happen to us is to triumph over these English."

"How so? We shall at any rate gain experience and confidence in our own strength."

"And ignorance of our own weakness; that is the danger I foresee," said Evaña. "It will be painful to me to see my own countrymen defeated by a foreigner, but believe me, Marcelino, it will be the

greatest good that can·happen to our country, if it teach us that success can only be gained by self-abnegation."

"Let the Spaniards then be our teachers, not these English, who are
strangers to us."

"I have talked much with their General Beresford during the last
month," said Evaña.

"So I have been told," said Marcelino abruptly.

"You have been told? My wise countrymen with their childish
plots, and their schemes which any one can see through, object to my
intimacy with the English general. Is it not so?"

"It is, Carlos. Is it well that you should be a friend to the enemy
of your country?"

"I seek to destroy that enemy by making him our friend."

"The English have taken our city by force, so long as they behave
themselves as conquerors we must look upon them as enemies."

"You will find them stern enemies to grapple with. Your preparations only make my work more difficult. Beresford may listen to
reason, but he will meet force with force, and he is well-informed of
all your movements."

"Yes, Carlos, there are traitors amongst us, and it was about that
I wished to talk with you. Do not go any more to visit General
Beresford; shut yourself in your own house, or leave the city, there
are many suspect you."

"Suspect me! And of what?"

"Of being a spy of the English."

"A spy! Me a spy of the English! Can you sit there quietly,
Marcelino, and say that to me?" exclaimed Evaña, springing to his
feet.

"I know you, Carlos, therefore I can sit here quietly and tell you
of it, for I know that it is false. I did not sit quietly when they told
me."

"Who are they?"

"Nay, that I will not tell you, this is no time for quarrels among
ourselves. But I have told them that whoever applies that word to
you shall answer to me for the slander. Yet I ask you for your own
sake to hold no more conversations with the English general. You
only expose yourself to calumny, and your efforts will be all in vain.
We cannot look upon these English as friends so long as they hold
our city."

"Then you will turn them out if you can, and will make enemies of
them, for they will not forgive a defeat. You will give yourselves
back bound hand and foot to the Spaniards."

"Carlos, my friend, believe me, it is too late to reason now.
Liniers is near at hand, and the whole city and province is ready for
a rising. If Beresford had come here offering us friendship and
alliance against Spain we might have joined him, or at least remained
neutral, now it is too late."

"Too late! no, it is not too late yet. I will see Beresford again
for the last time. He knows of all your preparations, for he has his
spies, though I am not one of them, but he makes light of what you
can do, the man he fears is Liniers, and it is against him that he is on

the watch. I will show him that your aid to either side will turn the scale, then perhaps he may decide at once for an alliance with *us.*"

The two friends talked little more together that night, the room door was opened by an eager hand, Doña Constancia and Dolores came in, and in the joy of meeting them again Marcelino thought no more of the projects of his friend Evaña, but spoke only of the speedy expulsion of the English from their city.

The next day, in the forenoon, Don Carlos Evaña left his house and walked through the city to the Plaza Mayor, and thence to the fort, where he enquired for General Beresford. On his way he had met and passed many of his countrymen; sometimes they stood in groups at street corners, or at the doors of almacenes talking together, sometimes they were walking hurriedly along; on all their faces there was only one expression, an expression of suppressed excitement and anticipation. With some of them he exchanged salutations, some of them looked another way, affecting not to see him, none of them accosted him; he felt himself thrust out from among them, he knew that he had no share in the one thought which occupied all hearts, and his heart grew bitter within him.

"A spy!" he muttered to himself, as he folded his cloak more closely round him; "when I do but seek to prevent them forging fresh fetters for themselves. The fools!"

"There goes Evaña to visit the friend," said one, as he turned into a street leading to the Plaza Mayor; and they to whom this man spoke gave him no salutation, and looked after him, as he passed on, scowlingly.

General Beresford was writing, but was not particularly occupied for the moment, and rose smilingly to meet Evaña as he entered his apartment, stretching out his hand to him in welcome. Evaña took his hand somewhat coldly, and laying his hat on a table seated himself.

"You do well to keep your cloak on," said Beresford, walking up and down, and stamping his feet upon the tiled floor. "There is one thing of which you Porteños have no notion, and that is how to make yourselves comfortable in cold weather. Look here at this large, half-empty room without a fire-place, how can you expect a Christian to live in such a room in such weather as this? Why in England the horses are better lodged than you are here. There is not a window that fits tight, and as for the doors, they seem made on purpose to let the wind in instead of keeping it out. It comes in from both doors and windows in little gusts which would give a horse his death of cold, to say nothing of a man."

"Yet we don't die quicker than other people, that I can see," replied Evaña; "our city is noted for its healthiness."

"That you owe to the Pampero, as you call this south-west wind, which clears the air for you about once a month, and a very good wind it is in its way, but of the best things it is possible to have too much. It was awfully cold when I inspected the troops this morning; some of the men looked blue with the cold and could hardly hold their muskets, this wind goes through you like a knife. I don't object to it on the parade-ground once in a way, but I do object to it most decidedly in my own room. I must have something done to these windows, hear how they rattle."

" Unless you make up your mind quickly to some decisive action they will not annoy you much longer," replied Evaña.

" Ha, ha, my friend !" said Beresford; " that is your little game, is it? I thought you looked unusually solemn this morning. That Frenchman of yours, Liniers, is coming with a pack of Spanish curs behind him to pitchfork me into the sea. When may we expect his Excellency ?"

" I think you know when to expect him better than I can tell you."

" Well, perhaps I do, but you see I am not trembling in my shoes yet."

" You are not afraid of Liniers, and you have no cause to fear *him*."

" Then who is this dreadful enemy who is more to be feared than the mighty Liniers ?"

" The people of Buenos Aires."

General Beresford paused in his walk up and down the room and looked earnestly at Evaña, and a grave look came over his face as he slowly answered—

" You mean what you say ?"

Evaña merely bowed his head in reply, and Beresford renewed his pacing up and down, evidently in deep thought. Then pausing again he resumed—

" I know it. This apathy, of which you have spoken to me so much, is a mask. I have sources of information of which you know nothing. I know that these shop-keepers have their deposits of arms, and that hordes of gauchos are assembling outside. It will be necessary to give them a lesson, and yet you would fain have persuaded me that they were my friends."

" They might have been."

" And my allies, too? I want no such allies. Liniers would send them flying with one volley of musketry, as I did a month ago."

" That they fled from you then was because they had no heart in the cause. Why should they fight for Spain ? I tell you that if you fight them again you will find them a much more stubborn foe. Shop-keepers you call them and gauchos !" said Evaña, rising to his feet ; " you will find that whatever be their occupation they are men. The next time you set your bull-dogs on them they will not turn like frightened sheep, but will meet you foot to foot and hand to hand. Do I not know them ? They are my countrymen ! What have you done since you have been here but insult them ? Even your civility and the strict discipline you keep among your men is an insult to them. One does not waste polite speeches on a friend, nor are soldiers kept to their quarters when they are living in a friendly city. You have your outposts keeping watch upon all their movements ; you have your patrols, who prevent free transit about the streets at night. Every means you take to show them that they are conquered; but they know that they are not conquered—they know that they have never measured their strength with you yet. You despise them, but I tell you that if you persist in making them your enemies you will find them more dangerous than Liniers and his Spaniards. They will not drive you into the sea, but they will tear you to pieces where you stand."

"Sit down, sit down, do not get excited," said Beresford quietly. "I am not afraid of the raw levies they can bring against me, but I have no wish to try their strength. What I have done in the way of outposts and patrols is a necessity."

"You are a soldier, and act on military rules," said Evaña, resuming his seat. "If you wish success to your enterprise, you must learn to be a diplomatist as well as a soldier."

"And with whom shall I treat? To whom can I address myself?"

"To the people, in a public declaration that you make war only on the Spaniards."

"Even if I could make such a declaration—for which allow me to remind you that, as I have told you before, I have no authority—my words would be but as words spoken to the wind. Who is there that can give me any answer, or can come forward to treat with me?"

"No one," answered Evaña, with a sigh; "but your words would not be spoken to the wind, they would speak to the hearts of men, and would disarm those who are now arming against you."

"Look you, Señor Evaña, the Home Government knows nothing of this expedition; it is an affair entirely arranged by Sir Home Popham and myself. We have taken your city from the Spaniards, and intend to hold it until we get instructions from England. Our Government has no wish to take possession of this country, but they wish to open these rivers to our commerce. Go you and two more of your principal men to England, and arrange an alliance for yourselves with Great Britain. You will be well received by Mr. Fox; he is an enthusiast about liberty of the people, and so forth. With Pitt you would have had no chance, but there is no telling, these Whigs might like the idea of a liberal crusade in South America, and of serving the Spaniards as the French served us. I do not see why you should not be independent of Spain; you are quite strong enough to stand by yourselves, if you only knew it."

"I do know it, and I know that without our aid you cannot hold our city against Liniers and his Spaniards, therefore I come to show you how you may make an alliance with us."

"You know it yourself, but your countrymen do not know it; they have grown up from childhood with a blind reverence for Spain. Nine-tenths of them would think it treason to enter into any alliance with me, therefore I will not ask it of them; all I ask of them is that they keep neutral."

"To remain neutral would be to forfeit our rights as men. My countrymen will not tamely look on while you and the Spaniards arrange between you who is to rule over us. We claim the casting vote in the dispute. Offer us your aid to achieve our independence, we will treat with you, and you shall be our guest; if you refuse it, you are but a foreigner and an enemy, and we will thrust you forth."

"With whom shall I treat? With you? You have no influence with them; first, because you are little known, and secondly, because you are my friend. With the municipality? Its powers are ill-defined; I could but treat with its members as with private individuals, besides which they are Spaniards. With Don Gregorio

Lopez, or with any other of the wealthy Creoles? What I might arrange with them might be all cancelled by the first popular government you might appoint. No, Señor Evaña, you are a man who has studied much in books, but you have not studied men as I have. I can make no treaty, except with some recognized authority, and no such authority exists among you. A declaration from me as general of the British army it is beyond the scope of my commission to give; but you know my opinion concerning the feasibility of achieving your independence, and I have told you that the Government of Great Britain would be likely to look upon the project with favour, if it were properly represented to them. Now is the time for you to strike a blow for your independence yourselves; turn your armed levies against Liniers when he arrives with his Spaniards, then you will make yourselves my allies, though there can as yet be no treaty between us. You shake your head, you cannot do it! Then allow me to tell you, my friend, that you were born too soon. Men who will not fight for their own freedom are not yet ripe for independence."

To this Evaña answered nothing for a space, but rising from his chair, commenced to walk with hasty strides about the room, while Beresford, seating himself at his desk, took up his pen and went on calmly with some writing on which he had been engaged when Evaña entered. Ten minutes so elapsed, then Evaña stopped in front of Beresford, and laying one hand on the table, said :—

"Can I, then, promise that you will aid us?"

"I can promise nothing officially, personally, there is nothing I should like better."

"Too late! too late!" said Evaña, in a bitter tone. "Our men are eager for the struggle, nothing but an open declaration from you will now give me any influence with them."

"Yea, there is something else may bring them to their senses," said Beresford, laying down his pen. "They were panic-struck when they first saw me, now they have got used to the sight of red coats, and they have got back some stomach for fighting, they want a lesson to cure them of their new mania for playing at soldiers. They have had the folly to collect a strong force of their levies not far from here, right under my nose, as it were, but where they are I do not exactly know. Where are they?"

"Nay, do not ask me," replied Evaña.

"Though you will not tell me I shall easily find it out, and you may tell them, if you like, that I am going to beat up their quarters; but I would advise you to do nothing of the kind, unless you think they would wait for me."

"So that you may massacre them with your disciplined troops."

"There shall be no unnecessary bloodshed, I shall merely disperse them and send them off to their homes, where they will be much more safe than in trying to help Liniers to hoist the Spanish flag on that staff outside there. Plenty of them will die if they try to do that."

"If I can bring six or eight of our principal men here, will you tell them that you will do your best to aid us in freeing ourselves from Spain?"

"I will tell them what I have told you, that I myself would gladly join you if I had a commission to that effect, and that I believe the British Government would receive the idea very favourably. But I tell you now, that you will not get six or eight men to listen to me, whom I would care to speak to."

"Not now perhaps, but they may," replied Evaña, with some hesitation.

"Yes, when they have had a lesson to show them their weakness."

"You will give them that lesson, you say?"

"Yes, but Liniers should be at Colonia by now, if my advices are correct. There is no time to lose if we are to come to any understanding together. Once Liniers joins them, to me all are alike Spaniards."

"Will you promise me that your troops shall not fire upon them?"

"I do not think I shall go myself, I shall probably send Colonel Pack, his orders will be to disperse them. If he finds it necessary he will fire, not otherwise."

Evaña turned from him and walked to the far end of the room, where he stood for some moments at a window, gazing with dreamy eyes out upon the parade-ground, where British sentries in long gray coats paced between the Spanish guns which had so recently changed owners; upon the Plaza de Los Perdices, where the market-people moved to and fro among their stalls; and further yet upon the towers and domes of the churches of his native city.

"The day is close at hand," said he to himself. "This man does not see his danger, though I tell him of it. He will fight like a lion at bay, but that flag with the red and blue crosses will come down, and that hated flag, the flag of tyranny, will go up there again. If there were division among them he might have some chance, and as he says there is no time to lose, even to-morrow Liniers may land and it will be too late, to-day is already the last day in July. Besides, I shall not save them any way, he has spies."

As he said this, his whole frame trembled with suppressed passion.

"Yes, they want a lesson, the fools," he muttered through his teeth. Then turning back to Beresford, he looked him sternly in the face.

"The Quinta de Perdriel, do you know where that is?"

"Yes," answered Beresford.

"There it is that your pupils await you."

A smile flitted over the face of the English general as he bowed in reply. Evaña without another word left the room and walked with hasty strides away to his own home.

CHAPTER V.

PERDRIEL.

Don Carlos Evaña spent the afternoon, evening, and night of the 31st July shut in his own apartments, seeing no one, studying not at all, reading by fits and starts, and knowing nothing of what he read, thinking always. He could not sleep; before dawn he mounted to his azotea, hoping by exercise to weary himself to sleep.

His house stood in the same block as that of Don Gregorio Lopez. As he looked round him he saw a stout figure wrapped up in a thick woollen poncho, standing on the azotea of Don Gregorio's house, he crossed two other houses and went up to him, it was Don Gregorio himself.

"Buenos dias, Carlos," said Don Gregorio; "you are early abroad in spite of the cold."

"Milagro!" replied Evaña; "it is a frequent custom of mine to pass the night in study, and then to breathe the morning air before I go to bed."

"A most abominable custom, my friend," said Don Gregorio. "The night is made dark on purpose that men may sleep, when the sun shines then is the time for all work."

"I find the quiet of night very favourable to study, one is not liable to interruption when all others are asleep."

"That is one of the ideas you have brought with you from the Old World. Like many of your ideas it is out of place in the New."

"My ideas are out of place solely because they are new," replied Evaña; "but the new will be old when their time comes."

"True. Some day you will be as old as I am, Carlos; perhaps, I should say, for if you pass your nights without sleep continuously you will never reach my age. If you ever do, you will know by then that all rapid and violent changes are out of place, not only in the Old World but in the New also."

"Violent changes are at times necessary, Don Gregorio. Without violence change is frequently impossible, and change is one of the conditions of our existence."

"Change is one of the laws of Nature," replied Don Gregorio; "but the changes of Nature proceed gradually. Watch them in the trees; from bud to leaf, from leaf to flower, from flower to fruit, then fall the leaves and the tree rests for the winter. When spring comes again another series of change commences, and from year to year the tree increases in size and beauty."

"Till the day comes," said Evaña, as Don Gregorio paused, "when a storm tears up the old tree by the roots, and it gives place to younger trees. Your simile does not hold good, Don Gregorio; even Nature finds violence a necessity at times to remove some obstruction to her invariable law of progress. These fierce storms which at times sweep over our city cause great damage and suffering while they last, but without them neither trees nor men would flourish."

"True, but Nature does not work blindly, she knows what will be the result of the storms she sends upon us. Do you know, Carlos, what will be the result of the storm you would fain raise amongst us?"

"I do. The result will be the birth of a great nation."

"If the nation is to be, it is born already, but it is not yet strong enough to walk alone."

"And therefore requires assistance," said Evaña.

"We shall know before long what sort of assistance we may expect from your friends the English. I was awakened an hour ago by their trampling along the street; they do not treat us very much like friends."

"Some patrol, I suppose."

"No patrol at all, but an expedition."

"A reconnaissance, probably, into the suburbs."

"A reconnoitring party would not take guns with them."

"Guns!" said Evaña, with an involuntary shudder of apprehension; "what direction did they take?"

"Westward. I have no doubt that they have gone to wake up our friends at Perdriel. Marcelino is there, so, as you may imagine, I am very anxious. It is that has brought me so early to the azotea."

Evaña turned away sick at heart. Marcelino was in danger, the English must anticipate resistance, or they would not take guns with them. Evaña knew the daring spirit of his friend; with raw levies of men, the whole brunt of the fighting, if there were any, would be borne by such as he. He had brought this danger upon him, he had not even attempted to warn him of it. Marcelino had reposed such confidence in him that he had told him of all their plans, and had confided in him as though he were one of themselves, though he had openly refused to join them. He had stood forth alone to defend him when treachery was imputed to him; he had taken as an insult to himself a calumny which was a calumny no longer. Evaña shivered, but it was not with cold, as he folded his cloak more closely round him. Two or three turns he took on the azotea, then going back to Don Gregorio, the two paced up and down for some time in silence, side by side. In thoughts and ideas they were wide apart, but one great anxiety was common to both, and though they spoke no more they were well content to be together, the presence of each was to the other as a mute sympathy.

Presently, as the dawning day broke over the city which lay around them, there came to them from afar off the crackling sound of an irregular fire of musketry, which lasted about ten minutes, when there came the louder report of a cannon, then all was still. As minute after minute passed and there was no further sound of fighting, Evaña breathed more freely.

"It is all over now," said he to Don Gregorio.

"So it appears," replied the elder gentleman.   "Thank God, there has not been much of it."

" I will go and see what has happened," said Evaña.

" Do, Carlos, and bring me word as soon as you return."

Evaña descended at once to his own house, and going to an inner patio where his horse was tied under a shed, he saddled him himself, led him out into the street, mounted, and rode off. As he passed along he saw many men looking out from the doors of their houses, stopping the market-people or the milkmen as they trotted in on their mules and raw-boned horses, and questioning them. He drew rein once or twice and listened to what was said, but the information he thus gleaned amounted to nothing at all, so pressing his horse to a sharp canter he went on more rapidly, had passed the suburbs and was among the quintas, when again he heard the sound of musketry. This time it was no longer the irregular dropping fire of skirmishers, it was the regular file firing of trained infantry hotly engaged, and presently mingled with it came the thunder of artillery.

Evaña drove his spurs into his horse's flanks and galloped on at full speed, but ere he reached the scene of action the firing had ceased, and light clouds of gray smoke drifting away were all that he could see of the recent conflict. Passing a hollow without slacking speed, he was soon on the open ground, and Perdriel lay before him.

Pickets of gray-coated infantry were marching away from him, while beyond the plain was dotted with flying horsemen. Now and then one of these pickets would halt, there was a shimmer of glistening steel as their muskets fell to the " present," there was a flash of fire and a light cloud of smoke, then on marched the infantry as before. Further and further away galloped the horsemen, and Evaña saw that the rout of his own countrymen was complete.

He knew that it would be so, he had said that their victory would be a misfortune, but the sight was not pleasant to him. He felt that he would rather himself have been one of those panic-stricken horsemen, flying for their lives after hazarding them for their country, than be as he now was, a passive spectator of the scene.

He galloped on till he reached the spot where he saw for the first time the immediate result of the " pastime of kings." Around him on the frosted grass lay some threescore of his own countrymen, dead or dying. Some lay peacefully stretched out on their backs or faces as though they were asleep ; some with their limbs doubled up beneath them, and their bodies twisted into strange contortions ; some lay crushed under their dead horses. Some few there were who were sitting up, striving in a helpless manner to staunch the blood from some deep wound which was draining their life away. Forcing his frightened horse to carry him into the midst of this scene of horror, Evaña, his heart wildly beating with a terror hitherto unknown to him, gazed eagerly around looking for something which he felt he could willingly give up his own life not to find, the body of his friend Marcelino. His search was unsuccessful, the bodies lying round him were all those of swarthy, long-haired, coarsely-dressed paisanos. Turning rein, and heeding nothing the cries of the wounded who called wildly upon him for assistance and for water, he again drove his spurs into his horse's flank and galloped to the quinta, which he saw was occupied by British troops.

Two hours before dawn that morning there was a mustering of men in the Plaza Mayor, no drums beat to arms, no trumpets sounded; silently the men took their places in the ranks, each man with his firelock on his shoulder, and his cartridge-box strapped on outside his gray overcoat, but without knapsack. They were in light marching order, and had been told off the night before for some special service which required secresy and speed. There were about 500 of them, and they had two guns with them.

When all was ready the officer in command, who was mounted on a small horse, gave the word to march, and away they went at a quick step along the quiet, darksome streets out westward. Light sleepers were awakened from their dreams by the heavy tramp of armed men, and the rumbling of the wheels of cannon. Windows were opened, and men half asleep gazed forth from between the "rejas" on the long lines of gray-coated figures, who went swiftly by in the darkness, their eyes dwelling more especially with a sort of dreamy fascination upon the sloped barrels of the muskets, and on the polished bayonets which glinted in the clear rays of the stars.

After marching about a mile and a half the detachment emerged from the main city into the suburbs, where the streets were no longer continuous lines of houses, but were bordered by gardens and orchards, then the street itself merged into a broad track, along which here and there, on either hand, stood detached buildings, some of them large, square, solidly-built houses, with flat, battlemented roofs, and with reja-protected windows; but more of them were mere huts of mud and wattle, with thatched roofs and no windows, save perhaps a square hole in the wall closed at night-time by a wooden shutter. When there were no houses there the road was bordered by a shallow ditch, on the inside of which, on the top of the mound formed by the earth which had been thrown out of the ditch, was planted an irregular fence of aloes, whose broad, sharp-pointed leaves presented a formidable obstacle in the way of any intruder. These fences enclosed the gardens of the men who furnished the Plaza de Los Perdices with its daily supply of fruit and vegetables, these thatched houses were their dwellings. Some of them were already stirring as the troops passed, and were busy fixing panniers of raw hide upon the backs of long-eared mules, or filling these panniers with such produce as their gardens could produce at that season. The unwonted appearance of troops marching on the road caused them no surprise; they were men who were not in the habit of being astonished at anything. They paused for a moment in their work to look after the troops, observing one to another—

"The English! What do they, that they get up so early?"

Then straightway resuming their occupations they thought no more of them.

About a mile the gray-coated soldiers marched through these fenced gardens, which joined on to one another, or were separated only by an occasional roadway, till they came to a new region of "quintas,"

which were only gardens such as those they had passed, but on a
larger scale, divided one from another by wide open spaces of pasture-
land. Here they frequently saw horses picketed, or cows lay chewing
the cud, and gazing upon them with soft, sleepy eyes. The road was
nothing but a broad, beaten track running between these quintas, cut
up with deep ruts made by the wheels of heavy carts, but firm under
foot, hardened to the hardness of stone by the frosts of winter. At
some of these quintas boys were already driving up cows from the
pasture towards rows of white posts standing outside the quinta fences,
where other cows were tied, and women were busy milking.

In a hollow the troops were halted. At the head of the column
had marched the light company of the 71st Highlanders, under the
command of its captain, who had two lieutenants with him. As they
halted, the commanding officer rode up to the head of the column.

"Gordon," said he, to one of the lieutenants, "you have been here
before, and know something of the ground. We are close to Perdriel
now, I believe."

"Yes, sir. It is just over the rise lying a little to the left of the
road."

"Take twenty men with you and go forward, and see what you can
make out."

The young officer touched his Highland bonnet, and then with
twenty men, who carried their arms at the trail, marched swiftly away up
the slope and disappeared. In about half an hour he returned alone.

"I have left my men hidden under the fence of a small quinta," he
said. "The enemy are encamped just beyond in the open, to the
left of the Quinta de Perdriel."

"Do they cover much ground?"

"They seem to have a great many horses picketed all about, they
stretch as far as I could see, but they have not many bivouac fires,
and those are close up to the quinta."

"Is the ground all open between here and there?"

"This small quinta where I have left the men is all that is in the
way, and it will hide our approach. On both sides of it the ground
is quite open."

"Have they no outposts or videttes?"

"None that I could see."

"Then the sooner we are on to them the better. Lead on straight
for this small quinta you tell me of."

In low, gruff tones the word "march" passed from front to rear,
and again the small column was in motion, winding along like a gray
serpent up the slope, over the crisp, frozen grass, where each foot-
print left a black mark on the glistening surface, bringing on with it
in the rear of the column the two guns, like a serpent which carries a
double sting in its tail.

The stars had faded away out of the heavens, the eastern sky was
tinged with ruddy gold, birds hopped about in the short grass, or
flew hither and thither chirping a welcome to the new-born day, for
the birds do not sing in Buenos Aires, as this column of armed men,
strong in their discipline, blindly obedient to the command of an
experienced leader, marched swiftly and stealthily towards their prey.

And what was their prey ? A body of men nearly twice their own number, as strong of arm and as stout in heart as they, but men who knew no discipline, and were strangers to the use of arms ; men who knew just as much of war as did their leaders, that is to say, just nothing at all, and thus had no confidence or trust in them, but would perchance follow where they led, if they saw no faltering in them, and had no personal antipathy to them.

As the composition of these two bodies of men was distinct, so also were the objects which had brought them together. The British soldier did his duty, and asked no questions ; he was ready to shoot, stab, or knock on the head any one he was told ; his life was just as precious to him as that of any other man was to that other, but he had sold his services, and his life, if need be, to his native country for a small modicum of pay and a pension, if he lived long enough to earn it. He had nothing to think of but to do his duty blindly, and it was his habit so to do it ; he fought the battles of his native country wherever she liked to send him, and obeyed her implicitly, she being represented to him by whatever officer happened for the moment to be in command of him. To these men who formed this column of 500 soldiers, General Beresford represented the might and majesty of Great Britain ; he had told them to go forth and scatter his enemies with fire and steel, and they intended to do it ; why these other men were the enemies of Great Britain they never troubled themselves to enquire, they did their duty as they were accustomed to.

The men who were now encamped in and about the Quinta de Perdriel were no trained soldiers gathered together to fight the battles of their country, they were hardy yeomen, men whose lives were mostly spent on horseback and in the open air. A cry had gone forth among them that a band of foreigners had invaded their native country, had taken their chief city, and had chased away their Spanish rulers ; men whom they knew had called upon them to assemble and take up arms to drive out these invaders. Such a call had never before been made upon them, but they obeyed it cheerfully, and had come together as though to some festive gathering, their hearts swelling with a strange, unwonted pride. That they had a country which was theirs, and from which it was their duty to drive any foreign invader, was an idea which was quite new to them, their hearts for the first time beat with patriotism.

Their leaders were mostly young men, to whom patriotism was not altogether a novelty, they were eager and enthusiastic, and waited longingly for the day when they might display their devotion to their country by feats of arms, and might seal it, if necessary, with their blood.

Neither of these two opposing forces represented a perfect army ; the distinguishing qualities of both in combination have characterized all the armies of all nations, who have at any time in the history of the world earned for themselves immortal fame by their prowess both in victory and defeat.

As the column emerged from the hollow upon the level plain they heard a confused murmur of voices which came to them from a distance through the clear morning air, the patriot levies were already

astir.   As they drew near the quinta, under whose fence Lieutenant
Gordon had left his men, they heard a shout and saw some of
the Highlanders rush out from their concealment.   The approach of
the column had been perceived by a small party which had passed
the night at this quinta, the horses of which were picketed inside the
fence.   Several men had mounted hurriedly and were now trying to
make their escape.   The Highlanders ran to the tranquera on the
south side the quinta, and stopped their exit by that passage, making
prisoners of two who tried to burst through ; but there was another
exit in the western fence where the hedge had been broken down by
stray cattle, by which others made good their escape, and galloped
off to the main camp.

The column immediately deployed and advanced in line, with one
company and the two guns in reserve.   The Highland light company
on the right, had orders to advance upon and occupy the further
quinta itself, the main body keeping more to the left, where the blue
smoke curling up in long spirals from the watch-fires gave token of
an encampment.

The Quinta de Perdriel was a large enclosure, one half of which
was planted with trees.   The buildings consisted of a large, flat-roofed
house, stretching round two sides of a patio.   Another side of this
patio was shut in by a low wall with an iron gateway in the centre,
which ran in a line with the fence, and the remaining side was
occupied by a confused group of ranchos which stretched back some
fifty yards into the quinta.   The shape of the enclosure was an oblong,
the fence was the usual shallow ditch backed by an aloe hedge, along
which arose here and there the tall stems on which it is said that the
aloe carries a flower once only in every hundred years.   The hedge
was in many places eight feet high and quite impenetrable, but there
were numerous gaps through which a man might easily force his way
if he could scramble up the bank and did not mind a few scratches.
The quinta house and out-buildings stood on the southern face of the
enclosure ; the attacking column approached it from the south-east,
and the encampment lay beyond, outside the western fence.

A horseman rode at full gallop into the patio of the quinta, other
horsemen rushed madly about the encampment ; all shouted the same
warning cry—

" Los Ingleses ! Los Ingleses ! ! "

In an instant all was confusion, men sprang to the backs of their
horses without stopping to saddle, and galloped off to drive up the
horses which were feeding in troops all over the plain ; others seized
their arms and collected in groups, not knowing what to do, and having no one to tell them.   The leaders ran together in the large patio
of the quinta, shouting contradictory orders which no one obeyed.
The doors and windows of the flat-roofed house were closed, and the
iron entrance-gate was shut.   Women crowded into the ranchos, shriek-
ing and dragging their children with them.   Among all this confusion
one man alone preserved his coolness and presence of mind, Marcelino Ponce de Leon, who at the first shout of alarm mounted to the
azotea, and made a rapid inspection of the approaching enemy ; then
descending again to the patio—

"Don Juan Martin," said he, addressing one of the chief leaders, "run you outside and mount all the men you can collect together, while we keep them out of the quinta."

Don Juan Martin Puyrredon mounted his horse, which stood at hand ready saddled for him, and causing the iron gate to be opened galloped off at once; and collecting the groups of armed men, who waited in the open, not knowing what to do, told them to take up their saddles and retreat with him behind the quinta, where by this time a good number of horses had been driven together.

" Now those who have muskets up to the azotea," said Marcelino, as Puyrredon galloped off.

"I will defend the gate," shouted one excited young man, drawing his sword, and giving it a wild flourish in the air, " who will help me?" In a moment he was surrounded by volunteers. Then Marcelino, calling on a number of others by name to follow him, ran off through the trees which surrounded the house towards the eastern fence of the quinta. He was only just in time, the Highlanders were already on the other side, but had halted while search was made for some way of passing through it. A random volley of pistol and carbine shots was the first notice they had of a foe more formidable than thorny aloes.

The captain in command gave the word " Forward !" and Lieutenant Gordon shouting, " Come on, 71st, follow me !" ran quickly over the intervening ground, and picking out the lowest place he could see in the hedge before him jumped clean over the ditch and into the hedge, whence he slipped and fell on his knees inside. In an instant he was on his feet again, and with two or three dexterous cuts with his claymore cleared a way for his men to follow him through the fence; the next moment a blow on the head stretched him on the ground, but ere it could be repeated the Highlanders came springing in through the gap and entrance was won.

Marcelino made one desperate rush with such men as he could get to follow him, to try and drive them back; but his men with their swords and facones could not stand against the muskets and bayonets of the Highlanders, they were beaten off, and Marcelino broke his own sword in the scuffle. As they retired Lieutenant Gordon drew up a few of his men in line, and rushed after them with levelled bayonets, when they fled at once to the shelter of the trees. Here Marcelino again tried to make a stand, but the Highlanders had now cut several passages for themselves through the aloe hedge, and poured in by dozens. In five minutes the light company had the whole of the quinta to the rear of the house in their possession.

Meantime the main body of the British force had driven everything before them in the open, capturing a quantity of arms and horse-gear, and several carts containing provisions and ammunition. They now turned their attention to the flat-roofed house, whence a desultory fire had been opened upon them, threw out skirmishers, who ran up to the ditch and fired upon all who showed their heads above the parapet of the roof or who stood unprotected in the patio or among the out-buildings. Then finding the iron gate fast locked and the key gone, one of the guns was brought up, and at the first discharge shattered it so severely that it was easily pulled down and the troops poured into the patio.

Marcelino, who had retreated to the house and had taken the command there, had withdrawn the men from the azotea, for towards the quinta there was no parapet to the roof, and the light company spread among the trees had them at their mercy. He now turned his attention to strengthening the doors and windows and spoke of holding out to the last extremity, and of allowing the house to be knocked to pieces about his ears rather than surrender, but he had only about forty men with him and their ammunition was nearly all expended. They looked blankly one at another, and as he was but one of themselves they waited only for a pretext to throw off the authority which he had given himself over them.

By interior doors the rooms of the house all communicated, but most of the garrison were collected in the principal room, waiting in gloomy silence for what might happen, marvelling that the English left them so long without molestation. After about twenty minutes of this anxious waiting, they heard again hoarse voices of command and the rapid tramp of marching men. Cautiously opening the shutters of the windows they looked out and saw that only a small detachment was left in possession of the patio, while a strong force of the enemy was manœuvring in the open.

Don Juan Martin Puyrredon having got from Marcelino Ponce de Leon some idea of what to do, did it with considerable energy, and having collected five or six hundred of his men and brought them into something like order, now returned to the scene and at once made a swoop upon the small British force which was drawn up to receive him. The British officer had formed his men in line two deep, with his right resting on the quinta fence, the two guns in the centre in reserve, and a few sections thrown back on his left to guard against any attempt to take him in the rear.

Waving his sword, and riding some two lengths ahead of his men, Don Juan Martin brought them on at a gallop, their sabres and the blades of their lances glistening brightly in the rays of the rising sun, while their many-coloured ponchos fluttered and danced in the morning breeze. When about 200 yards distant he shouted the word—"Charge!" and bowing to his horse's neck and driving in his spurs he dashed at full speed at his enemy. His men answered with a wild yell, and throwing themselves almost flat on their horses' backs broke their ranks and followed him, a disorganized mob of horsemen, rushing at headlong speed upon a slender line of gray-coated soldiers, who stood motionless to receive them, motionless, but quite ready, with their firelocks grasped tight in their hands, their teeth set, and their eyes gleaming with excitement. Scarce fifty yards intervened between them and the foremost horsemen, when from the lips of that one horseman who sat so quietly in his saddle in the centre of the line of soldiery came one low word addressed to the bugler who stood beside him ; the notes of the bugle rang out clear on the frosty air, down went those shining barrels, a flash of fire and smoke ran from one end to the other of the line, and then began again in one continuous roll. At the same time the Highland company who had remained in the quinta, and had been drawn up behind the fence, hidden by the leaves of the aloes, opened a rapid flanking fire upon the horsemen. Horses and men rolled over in dozens. Don Juan Martin Puyrredon was one of the first to fall. His horse was shot under him. Half-stunned and dazed, he staggered to his feet; then one of his men drawing rein beside him, he mounted up behind him, and rode out of the press.

But other brave leaders were not wanting. Shouting words of encouragement to their men, they led them through the smoke right on to the British bayonets; but it was no use, they could make no impression on that stolid line of infantry. If they spurred their horses against the bayonets of the first rank, it only made them an easy mark for the bullets of the second. One strong squadron of them had outflanked the infantry, and wheeled round to attack them in the rear. Upon these the guns were brought to bear, two rounds of canister at short range emptied many of their saddles, and scattered them in hopeless confusion. The struggle did not last five minutes. The level ground around the British position was strewed with men and horses, most of them quiet in death, some few groaning and writhing with the agony of mortal wounds.

Don Juan Martin Puyrredon having procured another horse, rallied yet again a confused crowd of the stragglers and with them made another attempt to take his enemy in flank; but his men no longer followed him with reckless impetuosity; as they saw the gunners again wheel round their pieces to oppose them they turned and fled. Don Juan Martin drew rein within fifty paces of the British bayonets; clenching his hand he raised it and shook it at them in fierce despair, then turned and trotted slowly away. More than one musket came sharply up to the shoulder as he thus defied the soldiery, but the officer in command shouted to them in clear ringing tones—

"Do not shoot him! He is a brave fellow that."

His men echoed his opinion by bursting into a hearty "Hurrah!"

Leaving the artillery and Highlanders in possession of the quinta, the officer in command started at once with the rest of his men in pursuit. Split up into pickets of about twenty men each, they spread rapidly over the open ground beyond the quinta, firing upon any groups who ventured to let them come within range. But the panic-stricken horsemen made no further attempt to molest them. Such groups as attempted to rally, broke up and fled as the infantry came down upon them at the double; in half an hour not a single horseman remained in sight.

Some threescore, dead or mortally wounded, lay upon the plain, five dead men lay on the flat roof of the azotea. The British detachment had two men killed and about a dozen wounded.

The lesson which General Beresford had thought it necessary to teach had been taught by one well experienced in such kind of teaching; whether it had been learnt or not was quite another question.

Meantime, as the first volleys of musketry shook their windows, the garrison of the flat-roofed house had whispered one to another that now was their time to escape. In vain Marcelino prayed them to hold out till Don Juan Martin had driven off the English, they had imbibed a wholesome fear of these English and would not listen to him. They opened a side door and rushed forth; the officer in command of the picket which occupied the patio made no attempt to stop them, they ran at once for the trees and were soon safe from all pursuit. All save one, who stood alone in the open doorway, with his arms crossed over his chest and the stump of a broken sword in his hand, listening intently to the sounds of the fierce contention which raged outside, of which he could see nothing from where he stood.

As these sounds died away his lips closed tightly together, and as the ringing sound of a British cheer came to him through the smoke, which was lightly drifting away over the tree-tops, he threw the stump of the broken sword from him and bowed his head as though he resigned himself to some bitter fate.

" Porkey Oosty no va ? " said a voice close at hand, speaking in very barbarous Spanish, but yet in words which Marcelino could understand.

He looked round and saw a young English officer standing on the paved causeway which surrounded the house, looking curiously at him.

" Will not you stop me ? " answered Marcelino in English.

" Stop you ? no ; our orders are to send you away from here."

Marcelino looked at him attentively, he had seen him before somewhere, presently he remembered where that was. This was the young officer who, to his astonishment and that of his men, had jumped in among them over the aloe fence not an hour before ; also the same officer whom he had seen standing under the glare of the wax-lights beside his sister in his mother's sala only two nights ago.

" You will not stop here, you will go back to the city ? " he said.

" I believe so," replied the officer.

" Then will you do me a favour ? "

" I shall have much pleasure."

" You visit at the house of Don Roderigo Ponce de Leon ? "

" Yes, frequently," answered the young officer, his face lighting up with pleasure.

" I will write a line for Doña Constancia if you will carry it for me."

" Certainly I will," answered the other, who began to have some idea of who he was speaking to.

Marcelino drew a pocket-book from his breast and wrote in pencil a line only to say that he was safe, signing it only with one letter, M. Then tearing out the leaf, he folded it up and handed it to Lieutenant Gordon, saying—

" There is no treason in it, but it may give ease to an anxious heart."

" She shall have it as soon as I can get off," replied the other.

They shook hands cordially together, and Marcelino raising his hat turned away, and walked off deliberately but rapidly through the quinta.

" He is her brother, or I am a Dutchman," said Lieutenant Gordon to himself, as he watched him till he disappeared among the trees ; " and a fine fellow, too ; what a pity we should have to fight those fellows ! "

CHAPTER VI.

As Marcelino left the quinta on one side, Evaña galloped in by the gate on the other. The Highland officer in command knew him slightly, having seen him frequently in company with General Beresford, and seeing his agitation divined the object of his visit, and invited him to dismount.

"Are there any killed here?" asked Evaña.

"Several," replied the officer.

The men were collecting the bodies of the slain from among the trees and from the azotea, and laid them in the patio side by side; some wounded also they removed within the house. Eagerly Evaña scrutinized them one by one as the soldiers brought them forward; as they brought the last his heart gave a bound of joy, Marcelino was not among them.

"There are some wounded outside," said he to the officer; "I will go and see if I can assist them."

"I will send a party to collect them and bring them here," replied the officer.

But without waiting for aid, Evaña remounted his horse, rode back to the scene of horror which lay without, and set to work to aid the wounded to the best of his ability, tearing strips from the clothing of the dead to bind up the wounds of those for whom there was yet hope.

One man he saw lying on his face with a leg hid under the body of his dead horse. As he passed him the man turned his head slightly to look at him; he was not dead. Evaña knelt down beside him to see if he was past all aid; he could see no wound on him.

"Speak," said he to him, "where are you wounded?"

"Leave me," answered the man; "for God's sake, leave me. I am not wounded, but if they know that I am alive they will kill me."

"I am alive, and they do not kill me," said Evaña. "Don't be a fool; the fight is over now, get up and help me with these wounded."

Then taking up a lance-shaft which lay by, Evaña pushed it under the body of the fallen horse, and using it as a lever raised the dead animal sufficiently to let the man draw his leg out from underneath. He staggered to his feet and limped about, his leg was bruised but he was otherwise unhurt.

"Ah! I am lost! Here come the heretics," he exclaimed, as Evaña chafed his leg for him to restore the circulation; then he threw himself again flat on the ground, saying, "Mount your horse and fly while you can."

Evaña looked round and saw a party of Highlanders headed by an officer, and carrying stretchers, coming towards him from the quinta. As they drew near he saw with pleasure that the officer was one he knew, Lieutenant Gordon ; he had met him more than once at the house of Don Roderigo Ponce de Leon.

"Señor Evaña, good morning ; you are well employed," said the lieutenant. "I have come to help you. Most of them appear to be killed, if there are any wounded we will carry them inside."

"There are few," answered Evaña sadly ; then giving him a kick in the ribs, he said to the man lying at his feet, "Get up, you fool, and help us."

The man rose at once to his feet, glaring savagely at the new-comers, but when he saw that they only smiled and looked curiously at him, he set to work very willingly with the rest, and in a short time such wounded as there remained any hope for were removed to the quinta. All the beds in the house were brought into requisition for them, and they were placed in the care of the women and a few men belonging to the quinta who had taken no part in the fighting and had not fled with the rest.

When the wounded were all sent off, Evaña commenced a search among the dead ; they were all swarthy, roughly-dressed paisanos. The man whom he had rescued from the fallen horse knew several of them and told him their names, which Evaña at once took down in his pocket-book, and then enquired of him if he knew anything of Don Marcelino Ponce de Leon, or had seen anything of him that day.

"Is he a tall young man with black hair and a short black beard?"

"Yes."

"Always very dandy in his dress, like one of the city?"

"Yes."

"Then I think I know who you mean ; I saw him yesterday. He was always wanting us to do exercise and was never satisfied, and very much a friend with Don Juan Martin. I did not see him to-day, but there was some fighting in the quinta, perhaps he was there."

"I will go at once and enquire there," replied Evaña, walking towards his horse.

"And what shall I do?" asked the man. "Are you going to leave me here among these?"

"Take your recao and bridle off your horse and follow me ; if I cannot get you another horse I will give you mine."

When they reached the quinta Evaña found many others there who had come from the city to see what had happened, to whom the High-landers were offering stray horses which they had captured for sale. He bought one for two dollars and gave it to the man who had followed him, who lost no time in saddling and mounting.

"Patron," said he to Evaña, as he settled himself in the saddle, "you have saved my life. My life, my services, and all that I have are at your disposal. I am only a poor gaucho, but you have only to speak, and I will do whatever you wish for you."

He still thought that the English had only removed the wounded to the house so that they might cut their throats at their leisure, and that they would have killed him at once had not Evaña been there to speak for him.

"Vaya con Dios," replied Evaña, and as the man galloped off he smiled, remembering that he had neither told him his name nor where he came from, so that he knew not where to apply for his services should he require them.

Evaña dismounted in the patio of the quinta and then went in search of Lieutenant Gordon, whom he found inside the house superintending the arrangements for the comfort of the wounded."

"Señor Gordon," said he, drawing him to one side, "I have come here in search of a friend of mine, who I have reason to believe was one of the garrison of the quinta this morning. I am very anxious about him."

"What was his name?" asked the lieutenant.

"I do not wish to mention his name," replied Evaña.

"Was it the same as this?" asked the other, drawing from his waistcoat-pocket a small piece of paper folded into the form of a letter and addressed to—   La Sra:

Doña Constancia Lopez y Viana.

"No," answered Evaña, as a thrill of joy shot through him; he recognized the hand-writing of his friend.

Lieutenant Gordon looked at him for a moment with a puzzled expression on his face, then—

"Ah! I forgot," said he; "women do not change their names in this country when they marry. Of course, but you recognize that writing?"

"Yes, it is his."

"Then he is all safe, I spoke with him not an hour ago. He went away the last of them all. But it is not his fault that he is safe, if they had been all like him we should not have got in so easily."

"If they were all like him you would not have got in at all," replied Evaña warmly, at which the young officer smiled and shrugged his shoulders.

"Excuse me," continued Evaña, "but that note is to his mother. If you will permit me I will take it to her at once."

A look of disappointment came over Lieutenant Gordon's face, he seemed loth to part with the letter, but after pondering a little he handed it to Evaña, saying—

"Yes, you had better take it, you can go at once, but I may probably be here all day."

Evaña put it carefully into his pocket-book.

"You will not mention his name to any one," he said, turning to go away.

"No fear," answered Gordon. "No one spoke to him but myself, and as he did not mention his name there will be no need to tell it, but probably no questions will be asked."

As Evaña rode out of the gate he met the commanding officer returning from the pursuit, and stopped to speak with him. He recognized him as Colonel Pack, General Beresford's second in command.

"I shall remain here till the afternoon," said the colonel, in reply to a question of Evaña's. "They have carried off most of their wounded with them; those fellows are deuced difficult to unhorse, but we have some here, I believe, and it will be well if you can send me some native surgeon to look after them."

E

This Evaña promised to do, and then started at once for the city at a quick gallop.

At the house of Don Roderigo Ponce de Leon he found all in a state of great anxiety. Vague rumours of a fierce fight that morning, in which the slaughter had been immense, were current among them. Some said that Liniers had arrived in the night, and had been completely defeated; others, that he had cut to pieces the entire English detachment sent to oppose him, and was now advancing upon the city; others, that the English had fallen upon the levies at Perdriel, and had massacred them. Many not belonging to the household were there, seeking information, or giving information upon which no reliance could be placed. Among them Doña Constancia wandered restlessly, listening to all, but believing nothing of what was said.

The entrance of Evaña into the sala, booted and spurred, and flushed with his rapid gallop, caused a general cessation of talk. Taking out his pocket-book he drew from it the folded paper and handed it to Doña Constancia with a reassuring smile.

"Gracias à Dios!" exclaimed she, as she read the few words written by Marcelino. "He has spared my son to me yet again."

Her daughter Dolores, leaning on her shoulder, read the words with her; then throwing her arms round her mother's neck, and hiding her face in her bosom, she burst into tears.

"Yes; thank God that Marcelino is safe," she murmured; "but why should they fight when they might be such good friends?"

Evaña heard the low words, and a tender look came over his usually stern features as he gazed upon her; then turning away he gave Don Roderigo and the others a rapid account of what he had seen and heard that morning. As he spoke Doña Constancia came and stood beside her husband, resting her crossed hands upon his shoulder, while Dolores leaned upon her father with his right arm thrown round her.

"Then Marcelino was not engaged with the cavalry?" said Don Roderigo.

"No; he appears to have been in the quinta all the time. I believe they made some attempt to defend the place. Mr. Gordon spoke very highly of the way he had behaved."

"And the Señor Gordon intended to have brought this note himself?" asked Doña Constancia.

"Yes; and he seemed much disappointed that he was not able to do so."

"You will find him for me, and will bring him here, Roderigo?" said Doña Constancia.

"I will," said Don Roderigo. "We shall hear all the particulars from him. But have you no idea, Don Carlos, where Marcelino has gone to?"

"No; but as their levies seem to be completely dispersed, he will probably wait at no great distance until we see what Liniers can do."

"He will go and join Liniers now, and they will fight again," said Dolores.

"God protect us!" said Doña Constancia. "Have we not already ough of this?"

There was great ferment throughout the city all that day. It soon became generally known that the partidarios under Don Juan Martin Puyrredon had suffered a severe defeat at the hands of the English, but instead of losing heart at the news the townsmen murmured among themselves vows of vengeance, and the name of Liniers passed frequently from lip to lip; in him was now all their hope.

Late in the afternoon many of them were gathered together in the dining-room of Don Gregorio Lopez. Don Carlos Evaña had made another effort to bring them to look favourably upon the English; the only answers he received were fierce threats and upbraidings: the threats he treated with contempt, the upbraidings he suffered in silence.

"Take my advice, Don Carlos," said Don Gregorio Lopez, "leave off talking to us in that strain; your ideas are all very well in your study, here they are quite out of place. However ready we might have been to accept the friendship of the English, the time has now gone by. The sword is drawn and we have thrown away the scabbard."

"There is war between us now, and war to the knife," said Don Isidro Lorea, who was one of those present. "They have attacked us, and have murdered our brothers with their cannon; this question can now only be settled by fire and blood."

"It is folly to talk to us of Spanish tyranny," said another. "Do the Spaniards ever send their men to shoot us and bayonet us when we are asleep? On the contrary, the Spaniards have often shed their blood in our defence, they have made war upon the Indians for us, and their ships destroyed the English pirates who infested the Parana in the days of our grandfathers."

"I have been at Perdriel to-day," said another; "I helped to put the dead into the carts we sent out for them. For each dead man I touched I vowed that I will kill an Englishman. Wait until Liniers comes; if he is strong enough, then we will show them the mercy they showed to our countrymen to-day; those of them who can swim off to their ships may escape, the rest die. If he is not strong enough for them, then we will kill them all the same, but more slowly, with the knife."

"If you had listened to me before, this disaster would never have happened," said Evaña. "The partidarios were armed, therefore their encampment was a challenge. General Beresford does not make war upon peaceable citizens."

"Basta, Don Carlos," said Don Gregorio. "In attacking the partidarios he has made war upon us. We are men; if we cannot fight him we know at least how to die with honour. Come with me, I have something to say to you in private."

Don Gregorio took Evaña with him into a smaller room, and locking the door, he seated himself.

"Do you know what these say of you?" said he.

"Sufficient evil, I make no doubt," answered Evaña.

"More than sufficient, my friend. They say you have reasons for thus speaking in favour of the English."

"Reasons! of course I have. I love my country, and would see her free and great. I know that she can only become so by the help of these English."

" I know you love your country. There are some who say that you love English gold better."

" I know they say that too," answered Evaña, looking straight at Don Gregorio.

" I know you better, Carlos," said Don Gregorio. " But men make traitors of themselves for ideas as well as for gold. To say the least, your frequent interviews and friendship with the English general are not in good taste at this juncture."

" You know the reason why I have sought his friendship, Don Gregorio."

" I do ; but you must now see that it is too late."

" I fear it is."

" I know it is, and I request you as a personal favour to myself to see him no more."

Evaña made an impatient gesture as he answered—

" I have already made a considerable impression upon him, he has even assured me that he would be very willing to join us in a war for our independence, and that the British Government would look favourably upon a project for an alliance with us. Shall I then leave the work half done ? "

" It is not half done ; this morning's work has undone it all. Even I would not now make peace with the English on any condition short of their immediate departure from the country. Listen to one who is older than you, Carlos, and knows much more of his own countrymen than you do. I tell you that all alliance between us and the English is at present impossible. Promise me that you will see him no more."

" What must be, must be," said Evaña with a sigh. " I will not visit him again for fifteen days ; by then we shall have seen what Liniers can do."

" That is well, Carlos ; I am content," said Don Gregorio. " Now I have another request to make of you. For the fifteen days be my guest, I will give you a quiet room, and you shall send for what books and things you like from your own house, for anything that you wish you have nothing to do but to ask."

" You wish me to be your prisoner ; can you not trust me, Don Gregorio ? " asked Evaña sadly.

" Trust you ? of course I do ; your word is better security to me than any prison, you are as a son to me ; I propose this for your own safety."

" What ! not content with calumny, they would assassinate me too ! " exclaimed Evaña.

" I fear it," said Don Gregorio.

" Fear not, against assassins I will trust to my own right arm."

" As you will," answered Don Gregorio, then unlocking the door, he grasped his hand warmly, and they walked out together.

Evaña went straight to his own house, and shut himself up in his own rooms to ponder upon the failure of this scheme, and to devise a fresh one, while throughout the city Don Gregorio Lopez, Don Isidro Lorea, and many others were eagerly consulting together about how they might best assist the operations of General Liniers and avenge the disaster of Perdriel.

CHAPTER VII.

COLONIA is a small town situated on the eastern bank of the estuary of La Plata, right in front of Buenos Aires. In the year 1806 it was fortified, having walls built of massive blocks of granite, and bastions on which cannon were planted.

On the afternoon of the same day on which Colonel Pack dispersed the levies of the partidarios at Perdriel, Liniers reached Colonia at the head of 1000 men, who had been placed under his command by General Huidobro, the Governor of Monte Video. Two days afterwards he embarked with this force on board such craft as he could collect together, and on the 4th August landed at Las Conchas on the other side of the river, some nine leagues north of Buenos Aires.

Volunteers flocked to his standard. In a few days he saw himself at the head of over 4000 men, with whom he marched upon the capital. To the west of the city was a wide, open space of ground, known as the Plaza Miserere, of which General Liniers took possession.

The city remained all this time very quiet. General Beresford found no difficulty in procuring provisions for his men, the shops were open, business went on as usual, and the markets were well supplied; but since the affair of the 1st the English officers had been invited to no more tertulias, and when they adventured to pay complimentary visits to the houses of any of their native friends they were conscious of being received with great coldness by the men, while the ladies were generally invisible altogether. One officer alone found himself an exception in this matter. When Lieutenant Gordon visited the house of Don Roderigo Ponce de Leon he experienced no lack of cordiality, and the ladies especially seemed never to tire of listening to what he could tell them of the black-haired young man who had opposed his entrance to the Quinta de Perdriel, and whom he had not detained when the fight was over.

The city was quiet because it was ready, and only awaited the signal to rise in arms and drive out its conquerors. Every man had provided himself with a weapon of some kind; many of the militia had stolen out at night with their arms and accoutrements, and had joined the force under the command of General Liniers. Don Isidro Lorea had not left town, and was as attentive as ever to his business, but he had always two rockets at hand in one corner of his almacen, his sword

and a brace of loaded pistols lay ever on a small table in his ante-
sala, covered over by some embroidery work of his wife Doña Dalmacia, who had regained all her confidence in him, and was prodigal
of her caresses.

General Beresford was a prey to great inquietude. The dispersion
at Perdriel seemed to have failed altogether in its object ; the city
gave him no trouble, but he knew that the hardy yeomen of the country, undeterred by their defeat, had joined Liniers by hundreds.
Under skilful management their reckless valour would not be thrown
away, and their numbers made them dangerous. Moreover, he had
seen nothing since the last day of July of his friend Don Carlos
Evaña, and on sending to his house to enquire for him he had been
informed that he had left the city. Without his intervention any
attempt to come to an arrangement with the townspeople was impossible. On the 10th he received a summons from Liniers to surrender
at discretion within fifteen minutes. General Beresford did not require
fifteen minutes to make up his mind, he could have only one answer
to such a summons, which was a prompt refusal.

On the morning of the 11th Liniers moved from the west to the
north of the city, and drove in the British detachment which was stationed at the Retiro. Beresford despatched at once a reinforcement
to retake the position, but this force was driven back by a tremendous
fire of artillery and musketry, which was directed upon the troops as
soon as they debouched from the shelter of the streets. After this
Beresford drew in his other outposts, and stood on the defensive in
the two central plazas, where the fort served him as a citadel in case
of a reverse.

Then Don Isidro Lorea buckled on his sword, thrust his two pistols
into his belt, kissed his wife, and taking his two rockets in his hand
sallied out into the open ground in front of his house. There he fired
off these rockets one after the other. Ere their sticks had reached
the ground, doors opened in houses near at hand, and armed and
eager men ran out to join him. In half an hour he had his 200 men
drawn up, the two guns he had hidden in his almacen brought out
and mounted, and waited only for orders to march upon the Plaza
Mayor. But no orders came. Liniers contented himself with the
advantage he had already gained that day, and took his measures with
the greatest precaution. He established a line of outposts which
completely surrounded the British position on the land side, but he
kept the bulk of his troops in the suburbs, and deferred further operations until the next day.

Few of the militia retired to their homes that night, they made
great fires at the street corners and bivouaced in the open air. By
sunrise next morning they were all again under arms and impatient of
the delay, the reason of which they could not understand.

Don Isidro Lorea had planted his two guns at the end of the street
which led from the south side the open space to the Plaza Mayor,
and had told off parties of his men to occupy the adjacent azoteas.
At sunrise he drew up his small force on the open ground and looked
eagerly for the arrival of a reinforcement which Liniers had promised
to send him. An hour he waited ; his men began already to murmur

loudly, when at last a welcome shout announced the arrival of those who were to share with them their task that day.

Don Juan Martin Puyrredon rode in by one street at the head of a column of his fierce partidarios, the yeomen of Buenos Aires: Don Marcelino Ponce de Leon at the same moment rode in by another at the head of another column of horsemen. Marcelino's conduct at Perdriel had won him warm approbation from all who had shared with him the dangers of that skirmish, and Don Juan Martin had made him his second in command. Their losses by deaths, wounds, and desertion at Perdriel were already more than made up by the volunteers who had joined them since.

As they debouched upon the open ground, both columns halted and the two commanders rode forward to speak with Don Isidro. Their consultation was long and somewhat angry; Don Juan Martin wished Don Isidro to take his guns out of the way so that he might advance at once upon the Plaza with his horsemen, but Don Isidro insisted upon leading the column of attack himself, and protested that without the guns it would be impossible to destroy the breastwork which the English had thrown across the end of the street. The dispute waxed warm, but it was at last decided that Don Isidro with his two guns and a small party of infantry should march down the street leading to the right hand the Plaza Mayor, that Don Juan Martin should follow him with his cavalry in the centre of the street, that the rest of the infantry should keep pace with the cavalry along the side-walks, and that Don Marcelino with his column of cavalry should advance by the parallel street one square to the left, and either attempt to force a way into the Plaza for himself or support the other column as he might judge best.

The arrangements were hardly complete ere a spattering fire of musketry was heard from the northern quarter of the city; Liniers was evidently moving though he had as yet sent no orders. At the sound of the musketry the impatience of the men became ungovernable, they were tired of seeing their chiefs talking together and to all appearance wasting their time, they broke up the conference with loud shouts of "Avancen! Avancen!" It seemed as though very little more would have made them break their ranks altogether and rush without leaders upon the enemy. Even the horses of the cavalry seemed to share the general impatience, they curvetted, champing their bits and neighing with excitement.

The signal to march was received with loud "Vivas." Some score men, slinging their muskets, laid hold of the guns and trundled them along. Don Isidro with a small party of his best men marched in front, and close behind came Don Juan Martin Puyrredon, sitting his restive black horse with ease in spite of his plunging, at the head of as fine a body of men as any country in the world could furnish. Tall, square-shouldered, and spare of flesh, they were formed equally for strength and endurance; in the saddle they knew no fatigue, they feared no danger; they were horsemen, to each man his horse was as a part of himself, and being a part of himself was a necessity.

Similar scenes among the native levies were at the same time going on all over the city; everywhere the cry went up, "Avancen! Avancen!"

And Liniers, seeing that his army was getting out of hand, gave the signal to advance, and at once moved with his regular forces from the Retiro upon the central Plazas.

Don Isidro Lorea had the honour of opening the attack; halting his guns one square from the British breastwork, he opened fire with round shot upon the slight defence; the guns were served by eager hands and the fire was rapid, and, in spite of the musketry from the azoteas flanking the breastwork, a breach was soon made. Don Juan Martin Puyrredon wanted no more; shouting to the gunners to wheel their pieces to one side, he waved his sword to his men, and putting spurs to his horse dashed at full speed down the street. His own men and the infantry followed him pell-mell, the British bayonets and clubbed muskets were of no avail against his fiery onset, he burst through the small detachment which guarded the ruined breastwork and made his way to the centre of the Plaza; his men poured in after him, and the infantry forcing their way into the houses on either hand drove the British troops from the azoteas.

At the same time another party of militia, headed by Don Felipe Navarro, had burst into the houses in the block on the south side the Plaza Mayor, and crossing the azoteas now attacked the British troops who were stationed on the roof of the Recoba Nueva. The struggle was a short one; in a few minutes these troops were all either killed or prisoners.

Meantime Don Marcelino Ponce de Leon had advanced with his column to the cross street level with the corner where Don Isidro had planted his guns. Here he halted, and, after a careful inspection of the breastwork which barred his entrance to the Plaza, dismounted half his men and sent their horses to the rear. These men he joined to a detachment of Linier's troops who had advanced thus far by the cross street from the Retiro, and bursting in the doors of the houses on the east side the street, he mounted at once to the azoteas and led them against a British picket posted at the far corner which looked upon the Plaza and commanded the approaches to two breastworks. His Spanish troops poured in a volley at close quarters, then his own men rushed forward brandishing sabres and facones, and shouting wild cries of defiance. The British defended themselves with desperation, and were aided by a heavy fire from the next block and from the roof of the cathedral, where other parties of British troops were stationed, but they were outnumbered ten to one, and in five minutes the few who were not killed or disabled threw down their arms and surrendered.

Marcelino left the troops in possession of the azotea lately occupied by the British with instructions to screen themselves for a space as well as they could from the fire directed upon them from the cathedral, but to concentrate their own fire upon the party of the enemy who held the breastwork, as soon as he should give the signal. This breastwork was merely a line of barrels set on end across the street, topped with a row of sacks filled with sand, to demolish which would be easy if it could be reached. The dismounted cavalry left the azotea and collected in the patio of the house to the right of the breastwork, the door of which opened about twenty yards up the street, while

Marcelino returned, put himself at the head of the rest of his men, and led them on at a trot. As he reached the street corner he waved his sword, it was the signal agreed upon. The Spanish troops sprang from the sheltering parapets, under which they had crouched, and opened a deadly fire upon the British detachment posted at the breast-work; the dismounted cavalry opened the door of the house, poured into the street, and rushing upon the barricade with their facones in their teeth, tore away in a twinkling the sacks and barrels from the centre of the roadway. Marcelino, who was by this time half-way down the square, again waved his sword and put spurs to his horse, his men answered him with fierce shouts and yells, and utterly regardless of the fire directed against them from the azotea on their right, which struck many of them from their saddles, rushed with headlong fury for the opening before them. Don Juan Martin Puyrredon had not spurred his horse fifty yards into the Plaza on one side, ere Marcelino and his column poured into it on the other, while another body of militia charged and took almost unopposed the breastwork which crossed the street beside the cathedral.

The partidarios spread themselves over the Plaza, sabring and lancing the scattered groups of soldiery, who, attacked on all sides, and overwhelmed by a plunging fire from the roof of the Recoba Nueva, strove in vain to re-form their broken ranks. A strong party of the 71st Highlanders drawn up in front of the archway of the Recoba Vieja yet presented a firm front, and kept up a steady fire upon the horsemen as they continued to pour into the Plaza, till the ground in front of the Cabildo was strewn with men and horses.

"A mi! Muchachos! A mi!!" shouted Don Juan Martin Puyrredon, as he saw the deadly effect of this steady fire.

Marcelino brought up a number of his men in tolerable order, and Don Juan Martin joining them with those who had answered to his shout, put himself at their head and charged right upon the centre of the Highlanders. The rest of his men who were spread about the Plaza joined in the general rush, nothing could withstand their onset, they beat down the Highlanders under their horses' feet and galloped over them. A sergeant who carried the regimental colour was cut down by Don Juan Martin, who snatched the flag from his hand as he sank upon the ground, and waved it over his head in triumph.

"Save the flag!" shouted a Highland officer, as he rallied some of his men under the archway.

The men lowered their bayonets and rushed desperately upon the triumphant horsemen; for a moment they drove them back, and the officer springing upon Don Juan Martin, seized the staff of the flag with both hands and almost tore him from his saddle. But Puyrredon still clung fiercely to his prize, and Marcelino, who was close at hand, drew a pistol from his belt and fired. The officer made one more frantic effort to free the flag from the clutch of his foe, then fell back senseless. As he fell, Marcelino recognized in him the young officer who had taken the note from him to his mother on the day of the fight at Perdriel. He sprang to the ground at once, and calling upon two of his men to help him, lifted him up and carried him out of the press.

The success of the Highlanders was only for a moment, they were surrounded, their order was lost, their leader apparently slain; standing back to back and using their bayonets freely, about one half of them forced a passage through the archway and rejoined their comrades in the Plaza de los Perdices.

Meantime in this Plaza General Beresford had had enough to do to withstand the onset of Liniers and his trained troops, aided by swarms of militia and armed citizens, who after desperate fighting had dislodged the British from most of the houses commanding the Plaza, and now opened a galling fire upon them from the azoteas. Beresford saw that his only chance lay in holding the fort until succour could reach him from the squadron. As rapidly as possible he passed his men in at the gate and raised the drawbridge. Some of the reckless horsemen who had captured the Plaza Mayor dashed after him as he retreated, but the fire of the guns on the parade-ground quickly drove them back again to the shelter of the Recoba Vieja.

Liniers lost no time in bringing up all his guns, and covered the azoteas around the Plaza with infantry. For two hours the firing was kept up on both sides, but with little result, when Beresford showed a flag of truce, and the firing ceased. But Liniers refused to enter into any negotiation with him, calling upon him to surrender at discretion.

While Beresford hesitated the troops and levies of all arms poured into the Plaza, hundreds of them sprang into the ditch of the fort, and clamoured for an immediate assault. Then the British flag was hauled down from the flagstaff, the Spanish flag was run up in its stead, the gate opened, the drawbridge was lowered, and General Beresford walked out alone to deliver up his sword to Liniers in token of surrender. Liniers putting aside the proffered sword opened his arms and clasped him to his breast, the air was rent with the acclamations of the multitude, and the British troops drawn up within the fort grounded arms in silence.

The loss of the British in this affair was 400, between killed and wounded; that of the victors is variously estimated, but must have been at least the same number.

BOOK II.

THE PROWESS OF A YOUNG GIANT.

PROLOGUE.

THE first tottering steps of a child, held up by the hands of its nurse, are not strictly speaking steps at all, they consist of a series of kicks with the heels upon the floor, and are in no way conducive to progression. The day that the child first stands alone, the day he first successfully balances his weight upon his feet unaided, is an epoch in his history. Once having learned the strength of his limbs, to use them and to walk is a necessary sequence.

The flight of the Viceroy Sobremonte, the rout of the Spanish troops, left the people of Buenos Aires alone in face of the enemy. They armed themselves, they chose their own leader, they turned upon the enemy and crushed him.

Buenos Aires was no longer a servile dependent upon Spain ; in her hour of trial she had triumphed by her own strength, the trial and the triumph taught her what she knew not before, they taught her that she could stand alone. Having learnt that she could stand alone, she essayed to walk.

Sobremonte had fled to the provinces, he returned with an army, but Buenos Aires knew him not and had already rulers of her own. The city called together a "Congress of Notables;" of these "Notables" only one-fourth were natives, but the Congress acted under the eyes of the people and obeyed their behests. The leader chosen by the people in their hour of trial was again chosen by them in their hour of triumph, and entrusted with the task of forming their rude levies into an army.

Liniers, though he had no such title, became virtually the dictator of Buenos Aires, and Buenos Aires prepared herself to renew the struggle with Great Britain, looking no longer to Spain for protection but trusting in her own strength.

CHAPTER I.

ABOUT three leagues from Buenos Aires, and about half a mile to the west of the great southern road which led to the Guardia Chascomus, stood the Quinta de Ponce. The house was a small one with a sloping roof of tiles and with a veranda running round three sides of it. There were also three smaller houses detached, built of mud and wattle, with thatched roofs. The ground belonging to the quinta was fenced in and carefully cultivated, all round the fence ran a double row of poplars, and many other trees grew about in clumps. The house stood at one corner of the quinta, some twenty yards away from the fence ; all about that corner the ground was laid out as a garden, where flowers grew in wild luxuriance. Within, the house was furnished with great simplicity ; numerous doors and windows shaded by green jalousies provided for ample ventilation ; the veranda and the many trees which grew around it protected it from the glare of the summer sun. It was well adapted for a summer residence, and had been built for that object by Don Roderigo Ponce de Leon, whose family regularly spent there the hot months of the year.

A cluster of similar quintas on a smaller scale stood around the Quinta de Ponce, divided from each other by roads bordered by poplars. Beyond these quintas on every side was open pasture-land, stretching away to the southward in long undulations, dotted here and there by the lonely, treeless house of some native " hacendado." To the north the towers and domes of Buenos Aires could be seen marking themselves clearly out on the horizon, to the south-east at a nearer distance the sun-rays were reflected from the white-walled houses of the small town of Quilmes. This group of quintas formed a sort of oasis, on which the traveller, bound on some far journey into the depths of the treeless Pampa, looked back with a sort of tender gratitude as he passed by, it was his last glimpse of the world of men as he galloped on towards the world of Nature.

It was a sultry evening towards the end of November, the sun had sunk behind a dense bank of clouds on the horizon ; though the sky overhead was yet clear there was evidently a storm brewing somewhere, but the weather occasioned no inquietude to three persons who were sitting under the front veranda of the Quinta de Ponce. These three were Doña Constancia, the wife of Don Roderigo, Dolores his daughter, and Lieutenant Gordon of the 71st Highlanders, who had been their guest since the preceding 12th August—their guest, but at the same time a prisoner of war.

When Marcelino had found, after the fighting ceased that day, that Gordon's wound was not mortal he had him carried at once to his father's house, where under the care of the surgeon of his own regiment he rapidly recovered, but still remained there as a guest, and when in the spring the family left town for the quinta he went with them, hoping in the fresh country air soon to regain his former strength and activity. Marcelino and he were fast friends, and with all the household he soon became a favourite. Lounging there in an easy-chair under the veranda he did not look like a prisoner of war, nor did he feel like one either, talking gaily with the two ladies who were his companions.

Doña Constancia had an embroidery-frame before her, but her daughter seemed to have nothing particular to do, as she sat on a low stool beside her, laughing at some absurd mistake in Spanish which Gordon had just made, for in spite of the best of teaching the young soldier was by no means yet a proficient in the language of the country. No man could wish for better teachers than he had. Doña Constancia, tall and stately, was a model of matronly beauty, and the clear, rich tones of her voice as she spoke sounded like music to the ear; her daughter, much smaller in person, and differing greatly from her in features and complexion, Gordon had already learned to look upon as the fairest specimen of womankind he had ever met. In voice alone she resembled her mother; it was the same voice but much younger, and had a silvery ring in it which at present amply compensated for the want of depth in tone which could only come with maturity.

It is said that the most speedy way in which a man can learn a foreign tongue is to listen to it as spoken by a beautiful woman. Gordon had had ample opportunity of hearing Spanish so spoken, and already spoke it himself with considerable fluency, but not with perfect correctness, and so not unfrequently made ludicrous mistakes, at which Dolores laughed.

Porteña ladies do not generally laugh at the mistakes in language made by inexperienced foreigners, their innate good-breeding makes them very tolerant of inaccuracies; but Dolores did laugh at the mistakes made by Lieutenant Gordon, and her laughter was a sign of the mutual confidence existing between them. Besides which Dolores was very fond of laughing, and Gordon liked to hear her laugh, and to see the merriment lighting up her face and shining in her deep-gray eyes, half veiled by the long dark lashes which fell over them.

"Why do you laugh so much, Dolores?" said Doña Constancia; "I feel sure that when you try to talk English you make far worse mistakes than Mr. Gordon does in Spanish."

"Indeed she does, Doña Constancia," said Gordon, "fifty times worse."

"And then you laugh at me," said Dolores, still laughing; "and it is quite right that you should laugh. If you looked grave and dismal, as if you were some teacher, I should not like it at all, and would never try to speak a word of English."

"I will laugh as much as you like if you will only set to work to learn to read English. I found in my trunk to-day a prize that I will give you as soon as you can read one page of it without making more than three mistakes."

"A prize! Oh! I will be very good and very diligent; but what is it?"

"It is a book."

"An English book?"

"Yes; it is a novel called 'Evelina.' All the young ladies in England read it, and in my country too."

"A novel!" said Doña Constancia, somewhat gravely; "I do not wish Dolores to read novels. I never read a novel."

"You never read a novel, Doña Constancia," said Gordon. "Well to be sure you have no novels in Spanish, or hardly any other books either, that I can see."

"Oh yes, we have," said Dolores. "Papa has plenty of books in town. Marcelino is always reading them, and is always wanting me to read with him. I used to try just to please him, but oh! I used to get so tired. Long, prosy tales about people that I never heard of, nor ever want to hear of; about Cortes and Pizarro, and Boabdil el Chico, and the Duke of Alva, and the King of Jerusalem, and I don't know how many more. Marcelino says that they were once all real people, and that I ought to know what has happened in the world before I was born, but I would rather read those legends of the saints that Padre Jacinto lends me sometimes, though Marcelino tells me that they are all false. Padre Jacinto was very angry with him for telling me that, but Marcelino knows more than Padre Jacinto does."

"Those legends are sanctioned by the Church, Lola," said Doña Constancia, "and so it is very right that you should read them, but you have no need to tell Padre Jacinto what Marcelino says about them."

"Or about him either," said Dolores. "Marcelino says that if he had a house of his own he would never allow a padre to come inside his doors."

"Those are the French ideas that Marcelino has learnt from Don Carlos Evaña," said Doña Constancia sadly. "He will learn better some day."

"But nearly all the young men who are at all clever have just the same ideas, mamma," replied Dolores. "Don Carlos would not speak to a priest, and used to say all kinds of things about them. Padre Jacinto says that if they talk that way and never go to Mass they will never go to heaven when they die, but for my part, if it is only men like Padre Jacinto can go to heaven, I would rather go——somewhere else with Marcelino."

"Hush, Dolores! you do not know what you are saying," said Doña Constancia. "It is getting so dark that I can hardly see to work any longer. Let us walk down the road a little, Marcelino is late this evening."

"Papa said he would try and come out this evening, so I suppose Marcelino has waited for him," said Dolores.

Doña Constancia wore an immense tortoise-shell comb at the back of her head, secured in the thick folds of her luxuriant hair, over this she threw a light shawl of black lace, the ends of which she brought

F

forward over her shoulders. This was the " mantilla," a style of head-dress which suited well the stately beauty and graceful figure of Doña Constancia. Her daughter threw a similar light shawl over her head, but she wore no comb, and her hair, arranged in large plaits, formed a golden background to the interlaced flowers and leaves of black silk which made up the gossamer-like web which she used as a head-covering.

" If your Padre Jacinto could read English I do not think he would object to Dolores reading ' Evelina,' Doña Constancia," said Gordon, as they walked down the road side by side. " My sisters have both read it, and were delighted with it. In fact the book is a present to me from one of them."

" But then he cannot read English. What is it about?" asked Dolores.

" It is about a young English lady, who was brought up very quietly in the country, and describes what she saw and felt in London when she went there for the first time, and about the balls and theatres she went to."

" I am sure then I might read that," said Dolores. " I should so much like to know what the young ladies in England are like. Are they at all like us, Mr. Gordon?"

As the lieutenant looked at the fair questioner, he thought that if they were all like her England would be a very Eden to live in, but he answered—

" There are of all kinds there, bad and good, as everywhere else, but they do not dress with so much taste as you do, and when they walk in the open air they wear hats with feathers in them instead of ' mantillas;' but sometimes they put on most horrible bonnets, which hide their faces, so that one cannot see what they are like."

" How absurd!" said Dolores. " But are they pretty?"

" Oh, yes! There are more pretty girls there than in any other country in the world."

At this Doña Constancia and Dolores both laughed very heartily.

" You say that with enthusiasm, Mr. Gordon," said Doña Constancia.

" I suppose he has good reasons for being enthusiastic," said Dolores. " Does not your heart beat quicker when you think of them, Mr. Gordon?"

" Hardly," replied the lieutenant; " for in spite of all your kindness to me it reminds me that I am a prisoner of war."

" Do not think of that, you will not be a prisoner always," said Doña Constancia. " You will be able to go back some day and see the pretty English girls you think so much of."

" I am very sorry I said that," said Dolores. " But you should not think you are a prisoner when you are with us. You are our guest, not a prisoner, and I hope you will stop long enough with us for me to learn to read ' Evelina,' and then I shall know what the English ladies are like."

They had reached the end of the road between the poplars, and now stood for a space gazing over the open plain which stretched before them for no great distance ere it mingled with the fast-falling shades of night, appearing to mount upwards, as though it were the slope of some hill-side, and to shut them in within a very near horizon. Lieutenant Gordon bent his ear to the ground and listened.

"I can hear them," he said; "they will soon be in sight; but there are more than two of them, and they are galloping very quickly."

"We will stop here, mamma, shall not we? Then they will dismount, and we will all walk back together," said Dolores.

They waited, and presently the footfalls of horses at a rapid pace could be heard by them without bending to the ground. Then out of the darkness appeared four figures, who saw them and drew rein as they came closer.

"Grandpapa and Uncle Gregorio also," said Dolores, clapping her hands..

Two more horsemen came behind, and the first four dismounting gave their horses in charge to these two, who were peons.

"Your blessing, papa," said Dolores, running up to Don Roderigo, and in another minute she was in his arms.

"Your blessing, papa," said Doña Constancia, gliding in her usual stately manner up to Don Gregorio Lopez, who answered a few low words and kissed her gravely on the forehead.

Then there was more kissing and saluting among the others, Gordon having his due share of the latter, after which they all turned to walk together to the house, Don Roderigo leading the way with his wife leaning on one arm, while his daughter clung to the other talking eagerly with him. Marcelino, walking beside his mother, conversed with her in low tones. The other three followed, Don Gregorio the elder occasionally addressing some complimentary observation to the lieutenant, but his son walked on beside them in silence.

When they reached the quinta the whole party halted under the front veranda. The main room of the house, which served both as sala and dining-room, was brilliantly lighted up and the table laid out for supper, and the windows and doors being open a flood of light poured upon them which contrasted somewhat dazzlingly with the darkness from which they had emerged. The four new-comers all wore light ponchos and were booted and spurred. Dolores ran inside to see that extra covers were laid for the unexpected guests, Doña Constancia followed her more slowly; as she went Gordon saw her turn and gaze wistfully upon him; at the same time he noticed an unusual gravity upon the faces of the others, even his fast friend Marcelino seemed anxious not to meet his eye.

"My friend Gordon," said Don Roderigo, turning abruptly towards him as his wife disappeared, "I have an unpleasant duty to perform. We have advices that the British Government on hearing of the capitulation of Buenos Aires prepared at once to send out a strong reinforcement; the British fleet yet remains cruising off Monte Video, there is little doubt that they will make another attempt to take our city. Under these circumstances the "Reconquistador"[1] has determined that all our English prisoners shall be sent into the interior. I have asked for an exemption for you, and have offered to guarantee

[1] A complimentary title given by the people to General Liniers after the victory of the 12th August.

your security, but I can only give that guarantee on one condition : that you pledge me your word of honour that you will make no attempt to escape, that if your countrymen land you will hold no communication with them, and that while you remain with us you will reside wherever I may direct."

Lieutenant Gordon turned pale as he heard this, then flushed crimson, and as Don Roderigo ceased speaking answered at once—

"I can have only one answer, Don Roderigo," he said. "You have all treated me with such kindness that I have never felt that I am a prisoner among you. Your offer to stand guarantee for me is a fresh kindness, for which I can never be sufficiently grateful. I should be a scoundrel and a fool to reject it, so I give you my word as you require. I will make no attempt to escape, and will hold no communication with my countrymen except through you or with your permission."

"Palabra de Ingles?" said Don Gregorio the younger in a harsh voice.

"The word of a soldier and a gentleman," replied Lieutenant Gordon.

"Then you will continue to be our guest?" said Don Roderigo, grasping his hand warmly. "You will always take care that either Marcelino or myself know where you are, and for the present, at least, I will place no restriction upon your movements ; go and come as you please amongst us."

"I am very glad," said Marcelino, coming forward and embracing him ; "I was afraid you would refuse."

The lieutenant, albeit not much accustomed to embracing, responded cordially to his caress, and then the elder Don Gregorio took his hand, saying—

"We will do what we can to make your time as a prisoner pass pleasantly amongst us. Do you think you are strong enough yet for a gallop? If you are, I am on my way to one of my estancias, and invite you to accompany me."

"I shall have great pleasure in going with you, I feel quite strong again now, and have a great curiosity to see something of your life on the Pampas, but I have neither saddle nor horse."

"I will find you a saddle," said Marcelino ; "as for a horse, that can always be found. Leave all that to me ; we will make a gaucho of you before we let you go back to your own country."

Marcelino and Lieutenant Gordon had shared one room between them since they had been living at the quinta. As they retired for the night, so soon as they were alone together, Gordon seated himself on the side of his bed and asked his friendly gaoler—

"Why did you think that I would not give my parole to your father ?"

"I was afraid you might have thought it your duty to lose no chance of rejoining your army."

"My parole does not prevent me from doing all I can to procure my release by exchange; but if you sent me up the country no one would know anything of me."

"Then when the English come, if they take any officer of ours prisoner they will give him back for you ?"

"Probably so."

"And then you would go back to them and would fight against us?"

Gordon hesitated, looking wistfully at his friend ere he answered—

" I should have to do my duty, but do not let us suppose anything like that. Have you heard nothing of your friend the Señor Evaña ? You told me you thought he had gone to England."

" No, I have heard nothing from him since I received that letter from Monte Video that I told you of. If he has gone to England I shall not hear again from him for months."

" General Beresford has declared publicly that he considers it the true policy for England to aid you natives in freeing yourselves from Spain."

" Yes, General Beresford has been very incautious, and has no right to complain that he is now a prisoner at Lujan, instead of being free on parole in Buenos Aires ; many good men are in prison now for listening to him."

" And you think you are not ready yet for independence ? "

" No, we are not. You have met Don Manuel Belgrano at our house in town I think ? "

" A soft-eyed man, with a long nose, and neither beard nor whiskers, who talks English and French ? "

" Yes, that is he. He is now major of the Patricios, and no officer is more active than he is in drilling the men, or more zealous in urging all of us to prepare for another struggle with the English. He is no friend to Spain, yet he says, ' The old master or none at all,' and so say all of us."

" When Sobremonte comes back the first thing he will do will be to disarm your militia."

" Disarm the Patricios and Arribeños !¹ He had better not try to do that."

" He will, you will resist it, and then will commence your war of independence."

" I hope you are not a true prophet; if we strike the blow too soon we shall fail. As I said before, we are not ripe for independence."

" And so long as the Spaniards rule over you they will take care that you never do ripen, so that your hope of independence is a dangerous dream."

" Dangerous it may be, but it is no dream," said Marcelino, rising excitedly to his feet ; " I know my own countrymen and I have faith in the future of my native country. No great work can be performed without danger; there are heroes amongst us who fear no danger; let the dangers come, they will teach us how to meet them. I tell you, my friend, before these black hairs of mine have turned gray you will see the rise of a great Republic on the shores of La Plata."

" In establishing it you will do your share of the work nobly," answered Gordon. " May God help you, for I believe you have a hard task before you."

¹ One of the first measures adopted by General Liniers on assuming the command in Buenos Aires, was to organize the native militia into four battalions of infantry. The first and second battalions were composed of Creoles of Spanish descent, the third was composed of negroes and mulattoes, all natives of Buenos Aires ; these three battalions formed the regiment of the " Patricios." The fourth battalion was composed of provincials, and was known as the " Arribeño " regiment.

"Do you believe there is a God?" asked Marcelino, reseating himself and looking steadfastly at his friend.

"I do, as surely as I see you sitting there before me."

"I think there is too; but I do not think that he takes any interest in the affairs of men."

"That is most illogical," replied Gordon. "In all God's works around us we see the greatest evidence of care and foresight in preparing this world for our habitation, how then shall he care nothing for us who are his chiefest work?"

"I wish I could think as you do. Do you know, one of the first days when you were ill at our house I went in to look at you, you were delirious, I thought you would die, and the thought made me very miserable; I would have done anything to save you and could do nothing. I fell down on my knees by your side, I don't know why, and I prayed wildly to God that he would let you live. It is in moments like that that one feels that there is really a God. When I thought what I was doing I jumped up again to my feet ashamed of my weak folly, but I went away quite happy for I felt sure that you would live. Do you think that God would listen to a prayer addressed to him in that way?"

Tears swam in Gordon's eyes at this new proof of his friend's care for him.

"Those are just the prayers that God does listen to," he answered. "When men can do nothing then they feel their dependence upon God and trust entirely to him. That is simple faith, and is just what God requires of us."

"Some men would call it superstition," said Marcelino.

"You acknowledge that there is a God, and you know that he must be infinitely greater and more powerful than you are, therefore to trust in him is no superstition. To trust in dead men or in ceremonies of man's devising, that is superstition."

"Who shall mark the line between faith and superstition?" asked Marcelino.

"It is impossible to do it, for it is a purely mental line in the mind of each individual. I know Protestants in my own country who carry their horror of ceremonies to such an extent that their worship of God can hardly be considered as worship at all, yet many of them are most fearfully superstitious; and I believe there are good Christians among you who go through all the ceremonies of the Romish Church, whose faith is very slightly tainted with superstition. Yet faith and superstition are quite distinct from one another."

"But your religion is all taken from your Bible, which is a bundle of old books written by the Lord knows who or when. Does it teach you anything about faith?"

"The one lesson which the Bible teaches is simple faith, the rest is mainly historical."

"Some day I will read the Bible, I have one somewhere, Evaña brought it for me from England as a curiosity," said Marcelino. "I should like to know more about this faith you tell me of. If the Bible is really a message from God, as some people say it is, every one ought to read it. If religion is faith in God, then it is a study fit for men and may well be the guiding principle of a man's life."

CHAPTER II.

THE YEOMANRY OF BUENOS AIRES.

"WHAT, Marcelino! are you going too?" asked Doña Constancia the next morning, as she saw her son, after fully equipping his friend Gordon for a journey, getting himself ready also.

"Yes, mamita; and I am very glad you have come to ask me, for I want to tell you why I am going. My uncle Gregorio is going to Las Barrancas to raise a squadron of cavalry, as you know, and I have been trying to persuade grandpapa to let me raise a company of infantry among the slaves on his chacras about the Guardia Chascomus."

"Make slaves into soldiers!"

"Yes, mother. The affair at Perdriel showed me that if we want to beat the English we must have infantry. The Spanish regiments and the militia are sufficient to defend Buenos Aires, but we want troops who can meet the English in the open field. Now the paisanos will not serve on foot, but I think I could soon drill negroes into very fair foot soldiers. If grandpapa will set the example plenty more will give me slaves, and I will raise a large regiment."

"But to put arms into the hands of slaves, that is never done."

"No, and therefore grandpapa says we must keep it secret till we see whether it can be done. Don Fausto Velasquez is on his estancia now, so we are going to ride over from the Barrancas to the Pajonales to consult with him before I do anything."

"I do not like the idea at all, Marcelino. Now that Juan Carlos has joined the Patricios you are surely exempt from service. If you must serve, why did you resign your commission?"

"For the sake of peace, mother. Don Isidro Lorea behaved very well on the 12th August, so now he thinks himself a hero, and wants to have everything his own way in the regiment. Many think that I know more of military affairs than he does, and there was danger of disunion, so I resigned my commission, and I have permission from Liniers to form a separate command for myself if I can find men."

"And you have not told your father?"

"No, this must be a secret for the present. The Cabildo would put a stop to the project if they knew of it, but once I get the men together Liniers will bear me out."

Doña Constancia attempted no more to dissuade him from the idea, and before the sun was two hours high all were ready for the road except Don Roderigo, who remained at the quinta, and who had promised to read "Evelina," and to report upon the book on their return.

The "Casa-teja," and much land lying around, was the property of Don Gregorio Lopez, and was one of his estancias. Here Don Gregorio and his party drew rein a little before noon, and in ten minutes they were seated at breakfast in the principal room.

"You are tired, Don Alejandro," said Don Gregorio to Lieutenant Gordon.

"A little, for I have only been a few times on horseback at the quinta, but in an hour I shall be quite ready for another gallop."

"Yes, and then to-morrow you will be quite knocked up. No, it is well that the old and the invalid keep company together. We will remain here until to-morrow, but my son and Marcelino are in a hurry, so we will let them go on by themselves."

The word of Don Gregorio was the law of his household, so that matter was settled without discussion, and Don Gregorio the younger and Marcelino, after partaking sparingly of the plentiful breakfast which was spread before them, mounted fresh horses and galloped off, taking a peon with them and driving a tropilla before them. They travelled fast, but ere sun-down the storm which was brewing on the preceding evening burst upon them, and they were forced to take refuge in a rancho which stood by itself surrounded by a forest of thistles, some two squares to the left of the road. They received the usual frank welcome of a paisano, and were told to dismount and unsaddle. In ten minutes they were seated on horse-skulls in a smoky kitchen, sucking mate,[1] and safe from the storm which now raged furiously, driving clouds of thistle-down before it and laying prostrate acres of the tall thistles themselves.

Their host was a slim, active man, not so tall as Marcelino, but apparently some few years his senior. His complexion was a bright yellow with a ruddy tinge in his smooth cheeks. His hair, jet-black and glossy, was of very coarse texture, falling down to his shoulders in a scarcely perceptible wave; had it been cut short it would have appeared quite straight. A small black moustache graced his thin upper-lip, and a slight fringe of black hair on his chin did duty as a beard. His eyes, black also, were very bright and in constant movement.

His wife was a young woman of similar complexion but of stouter build, with full red lips and with very white teeth, which she was fond of showing, by smiling whenever she was spoken to, but she spoke very little herself, leaving that part of their entertainment to her husband.

For some time they talked on indifferent subjects; at last Don Gregorio said—

"I often pass this way, but I never remember seeing this rancho before."

"I have only been here two months, till then I lived with my father over there," replied their host with a jerk of his head.

"Are you by chance one of the Vianas?" asked Don Gregorio.

"Just so. I am Venceslao Viana, at your service, Señor, and this is my wife. When I married, my father gave me some cows, and I

---

[1] A word of two syllables—American tea.

have built this place for myself. We were married at the Guardia,
for, as my father said to me, people of family should marry."

As the man said this he threw back his head proudly, and his wife
smiled at her guests, showing more of her white teeth than ever.
They both evidently thought that they had conferred great distinction
upon themselves by marrying, as was in fact the case, for among the
paisanos in those days marriage was a token of respectability and
social standing.

"I call myself Gregorio Lopez," said Don Gregorio in reply, "and
I congratulate you both." ·

"Many thanks, Señor. Don Gregorio of the Barrancas, is it not so?"

"Exactly."

"Then we are in some sort relations," answered Venceslao.

"To me, no; to this one, yes," replied Don Gregorio coldly, and
looking at Marcelino. "I knew that Viana's land lay somewhere
near here, but I did not know that it reached as far as this."

A brother of the second wife of Don Gregorio Lopez the elder,
named Francisco Viana, had married a mulatta, and had by so doing
lost caste with his own family, and had lived ever since in seclusion
on his estancia, so that his existence was unknown to the younger
branches of the family of Don Gregorio Lopez, and Marcelino looked
curiously at Venceslao, wondering how he could in any way be a relation of his.

"I have seen you before," said Venceslao, as he returned his gaze.

"Have you? Where? I have not been so far as this since I was
a boy," replied Marcelino.

"When the English."

"How? Were you with us at Perdriel?"

"Yes. I saw you there every day."

"And after, what became of you?"

"I escaped by a miracle, and came straight back to my father's
house."

"Were you with Don Juan Martin?"

"Yes. I followed him right up to the English, but they confounded
us with shot. Caramba! how the bullets went, phiz! phiz! I shall
never forget it. I missed a stroke at one of them with my lance, and
before I knew what had happened my horse reared and fell over with
me, and caught my leg so that I could not get away. Dios! what
moments those were! it appeared a century. Afterwards, when they
were coming to finish me, there was a tall man, one of the city, who
spoke to them in their own Castilian, so they let me go, and he gave
me a horse, but I did not feel safe till I got back here. Dios mio!
for days I did not know whether I was alive or dead. And you,
where were you that day? You will excuse me the question."

"I was in the quinta all the time."

"Jesus!" exclaimed the wife. "Venceslao said they killed all that
were there."

"They killed some of us," replied Marcelino, "when we tried to
keep them out, but when they got inside they let the rest of us go."

"Look you, what an escape you made! You have never seen them
again I feel sure," said Venceslao.

" I did though. I went off to Las Conchas, and had my revenge at the Reconquest."

" Also you found yourself in that affair? Already you had not enough of them?"

" A patriot never has enough while an enemy treads the soil of his native country."

" A patriot! what is that?"

" A patriot is one who is ready to make every sacrifice for the good of his country, as you did when you risked your life for our country at Perdriel."

" You are mistaken. They talked to us in the encampment about that; but excuse me, I am not a patriot, of that I understand nothing. I went to the war because Julian Sanchez was going, and asked me to go with him. You see he has done me many favours, he is my brother-in-law, and we were always great friends, so that I could not do less than go when he invited me."

" And how did it go with him? " asked Don Gregorio.

" Well. He did not find himself at the fight, he had gone the night before to visit some friends at San José de Flores."

" And afterwards? "

" He presented himself to Don Juan Martin at Las Conchas, but when he found I was not with them he came back to tell my family that I was killed, and here he found me alive."

" The English are coming again," said Don Gregorio.

" You don't say so! "

" True. And there will come more of them this time."

" And all will be to do over again. Look you what heretics they are, that they will not leave us in peace; for my part I abhor them; why did they come here at first? "

" They are at war with the Spaniards," replied Marcelino. " Last year they had a great fight with the Spanish ships on the sea, and the English were the strongest; so now they go about in their ships where they like, and wherever they find Spaniards on the land where they can get near in their ships they come on shore and fight them."

" And that is what they call war? " said Venceslao. " Look you that they are barbarians."

" The same would the Spaniards do to them if they could," said Marcelino.

" And what does that matter to us? " said Venceslao.

" Nothing, until they come to our country; but if they come here, then it is our duty to help the Spaniards to turn them out."

" It may be, but I don't see why. If they only come to fight the Spaniards, why should we meddle? Let them fight themselves alone."

" But if the English beat the Spaniards then they will take our country for themselves."

" In every way that may not be. They would put laws after their fashion, and we should have to talk their Castilian, I could never accustom myself to that."

Beyond the Guardia Chascomus, which was at that time a frontier town held by a small garrison of Spanish troops, there stretches a chain of lakes, running in a southerly direction till they join the Rio Salado. In some places the land around these lakes slopes gently down to the water's edge, so that when they overflow during heavy rains, their waters spread themselves for a considerable distance over the plain. At other places the surrounding land rises abruptly, forming perpendicular cliffs, which are called "barrancas;" probably the highest of these barrancas is not more than forty feet above the general level of the lake; but forty feet is a considerable elevation where the chief feature of the country is one uniform flatness. About half-way between the Guardia and the Rio Salado, the east side of this chain of lakes was for nearly two leagues one continuous line of barrancas; all the land about there, contiguous to the lakes and stretching far inland, was the property of Don Gregorio Lopez the younger, who had inherited it from his mother whom he had never seen. He had placed there an estancia called "Las Barrancas," where he and his father had immense herds of cattle and troops of mares, and a few flocks of long-legged sheep.

The estancia itself consisted of a group of ranchos, in front of which two ombues shaded the palenque, where horses were tied. Behind them was an enclosure of considerable size, part of which was planted with trees, and the rest carefully cultivated by slaves. Some slaves were also employed as herdsmen, but the majority of these mounted peons were freemen, who worked hard for small wages, and who mostly lived in ranchos of their own on different parts of the estate, at great distances from each other. All these freemen provided their own horses, and were skilled from their earliest youth in the use of the lasso and bolas. They almost lived on horseback, and had the greatest dislike to any labour which could only be performed on foot, deeming such work below the dignity of a man, and only fit for slaves.

Many other estancias similarly organized lay scattered about the Pampa, within a day's gallop of the Estancia de Las Barrancas. The limits of these different estancias were ill-defined, their title-deeds being merely a grant of some certain number of leagues of land from the Viceregal Government of Buenos Aires or of Peru. There was yet much land not allotted at all, so that any of these freemen who worked on the estancias, who could get together a few cows and horses, and wished to settle down quietly, could easily find land on which to build himself a rancho and to pasture his animals. These freemen were of a roving nature, seldom working more than a few months at a time on one estancia; but hundreds of them had thus made homes for themselves; to some of them at times government gave grants of the land on which they had settled, and they became proprietors. They were a hardy, simple race of yeomen, who held the dwellers in cities in great contempt, and considered that man's first necessity in life was a good horse. Their amusements consisted of feats of horsemanship, in which horse-racing naturally held a prominent place, in hunting deer and ostrich with their boleadores, or in listening to the long monotonous songs of some "cantor" of their own class, who generally invented his songs for himself, and not unfrequently improvised a fresh one when some incident of the day provided him with a subject. Government was to them a mysterious power, which gave grants of land and imposed taxes. Religion to them consisted in the baptism of children, and in the burial of the dead in consecrated ground; yet they had an unwritten law among them which they observed most strictly, and they had a sort of natural religion, which told them that there was a God and a life beyond the grave.

Among these men, peons or small proprietors, Don Gregorio Lopez proposed to raise a squadron of cavalry, and Marcelino Ponce de Leon proposed to help him in his work by instilling into them the first principles of patriotism.

Don Gregorio met with very fair success, his recruits being left at liberty all the week and meeting every Sunday at the Estancia de Las Barrancas for drill, which to them was a novel amusement. Their chief did not purpose to embody them permanently until the near approach of the English should render their services necessary, but contented himself for the present with selecting his officers and instructing them in their duties, in all which he showed considerable skill. But his nephew instead of being any assistance to him was rather a hindrance.

The sturdy yeomen were accustomed to obey their superiors and to ask no questions, the summons of Don Gregorio they looked upon as a command, to serve under him if they were wanted they considered a duty from which they might ask exemption as a favour, but to which they could not refuse obedience. Marcelino spoke to them of patriotism, and tried to instil into them enthusiasm for the defence of their native country against foreign invasion. Patriotism was some new idea which they did not understand; as for enthusiasm, it mattered nothing to them who had the city so long as nobody took their cows from them. But when Marcelino began to talk to them of the rights of free-born men, of liberty, equality, and so forth, then their shrewd common sense prompted them to argue the point with him.

"If all men are equal," said one of them, "why has the patron Don Gregorio twelve leagues of camp, while I have only 200 cows and have to feed them where I can?"

"And what is this liberty," asked another, "if I have to leave my cows to go and fight these English, who never did me any harm that I know of?"

"Will it be true what they say of these English, Patroncito?" said another; "that they are not people but have tails like the monkeys?"

"Those are lies," answered Marcelino; "the English are men just like we are."

"Then why should they not come here? there is plenty of camp for them which has now no owner."

When Marcelino spoke to them in high-flown words they did not understand him, when he tried simple arguments they posed him with questions such as these. The only effect of his talk was to raise vague, communistic ideas in their minds, and to teach them that they were in some unknown way unjustly treated, which was not at all conducive to the strict discipline which Don Gregorio sought to maintain among them.

Thus passed two weeks, when a peon brought Marcelino a letter from Don Fausto Velasquez of the Estancia de Los Pajonales, telling him that his grandfather had already been some days with him, and inviting him over at once to join in their consultation concerning the arming of the slaves.

Marcelino received the letter in the morning, and sunset found him the guest of Don Fausto Velasquez. His uncle had laughed at him as he bade him good-bye, telling him that he might be a very clever fellow in the city, but that in the campaña he was worse than useless.

"You do not understand our people," he said; "it is necessary to order them, and they obey, but you must not give reasons to them, for they know nothing."

CHAPTER III.

ARMING THE SLAVES.

THE estancia house at Los Pajonales was a large brick building with a flat roof, surrounded by a stockade of posts. There were also three ranchos detached within the stockade, and outside a considerable extent of ground was enclosed by a ditch and cultivated, the negro slaves who were kept for this work having their huts at a distance at the far side the enclosed ground.

When Marcelino Ponce de Leon reached the estancia he was conducted at once to the sala, being met at the door by Don Fausto Velasquez, a middle-aged man, tall and of striking presence, who was dressed with great neatness in light linen clothing suitable to the season, and wore his hair powdered and tied behind his head with a ribbon. Don Fausto bowed low with great formality to Marcelino as he entered, and then taking his hand led him up to his mother, a dignified old lady with silvery hair, who was dressed in black silk and reclined on cushions at one end of a low estrade which ran all down one side of the room. She received him very graciously and enquired particularly after his mother, who had been a great favourite of hers in days gone by; then with an approving smile and a graceful inclination of the head she dismissed him.

Several other ladies were present, all of whom were seated or reclined on cushions on this estrade, some were sewing or knitting, others were sucking mate, which was served to them by two little negro girls. One of these ladies was the wife of Don Fausto, a stout, well-developed woman, with regular features, an exceedingly white skin, and with large, lustrous black eyes, but with a languid manner about her which lessened considerably the effect of their brilliance. She was a sister, many years younger, of the lady who had been the second wife of Don Gregorio Lopez, and was thus grand-aunt to Marcelino, though younger than his own mother. At her feet there rolled a stout, active little boy about five years old, whom she caressed occasionally in her languid way, calling him her "son," her "Justito," who seemed to find great pleasure in vain attempts to prevail upon her to join him in a game of romps.

After being introduced to the other ladies and to two or three men who were present, and after a cordial exchange of greetings with Don Gregorio Lopez and Lieutenant Gordon, Marcelino drew forward a heavy, straight-backed chair, the seat of which was of embossed leather, and placed himself in front of his aunt, whom he had not seen for several years, Don Fausto having resided for that time on his estancia in consequence of some trouble he had had with the Spanish authorities of Buenos Aires. For Don Fausto, though a Creole, was a proud man and a wealthy, and thought himself the equal of any Spaniard, an idea which in those days was apt to bring any free-spoken Creole into trouble. The other men were mostly walking about, sucking mate when their turn came, and occasionally addressing a few words to one or other of the ladies, but the conversation was far from animated.

Other than the cushioned estrade on which the ladies were seated, the room was very bare of furniture, a couple of small tables and a few high-backed, very uncomfortable-looking chairs comprised the whole of it; but upon the walls hung some very choice paintings, several of which were said to be the works of Velasquez, a famous Spanish painter, who was claimed by Don Fausto as one of his ancestors. The art of painting was held in small repute in Buenos Aires at that time; Don Fausto knew nothing of it, only preserved these paintings out of respect for the memory of his father, who had set great store by them, and was both surprised and pleased at the great admiration of them which was expressed by his English guest Lieutenant Gordon. He strove in vain to see any beauty in them himself, but he was proud to see them appreciated by another who came from the Old World.

Marcelino talked long with his aunt, telling her of his adventures in Buenos Aires during the English occupation. As he told of the affair at Perdriel and of the defeat of the English on the 12th August, she caught up her little son in her arms, pressing him to her bosom with unwonted animation, saying as she caressed him—

"Ah, Justiniano, my little son! your mother will take better care of you, she will never let you run away from her, nor fight fierce soldiers who come over the sea!"

"The soldiers, mamita!" said the boy laughing, and patting her cheek with his little hand; "I have never seen a soldier, but when I am big like this one then I will put myself to kill the English. All of them, mamita, all of them."

As he said this he struggled from his mother's arms, and rolling over a cushion, clambered down from the estrade, and running up to Lieutenant Gordon clenched his little fist and struck him on the leg.

"This is one," he said; "some day when I am big I will kill you."

Marcelino rose hurriedly from his chair, and Don Fausto walked quickly to the spot with a look of great annoyance on his face, but Gordon stooping down to the boy lifted him up in his arms and kissed him, saying with a merry laugh—

"When you are as big as I am, my little man, we English will be great friends with you, and will know better than to come here to fight you."

"Thanks, my friend, thanks," said Don Fausto, taking his free hand in both his own. "With years we shall all of us learn a little wisdom."

Justiniano looked wonderingly from one to the other with a finger in his mouth to aid his reflections, then seizing hold of one of Gordon's whiskers he whispered in his ear—

"You no, don't be frightened, you are not one of the bad ones. Always we will be friends."

"Mind you remember that, little rascal," said Marcelino, patting him on the cheek.

"If he ever forgets it you will remind him," said Gordon: then raising the boy to his shoulder he danced with him up and down the long room, the child shouting and tossing his arms about with delight.

Doña Josefina, the boy's mother, had meanwhile sunk back again upon her cushions, following him with her eyes, and seemed to care little whether Marcelino resumed the conversation or not, but there were other ladies there younger than she, who had listened eagerly to what Marcelino had told them of the English invasion, and wished to hear more. The twilight deepened into darkness, the mate-pot ceased its rounds amongst them, lamps were lighted, fresh faces were seen in the room, and others who had been there disappeared, but still Marcelino talked on in glowing, enthusiastic language of the changes during the last sixteen months in the city of Buenos Aires, and of the greater changes which he foresaw in the future. He had often talked thus before among men of his own age and of his own class, and he had seen weariness in their faces, and scorn curling on their lips; he had talked thus to men his seniors in age, and had been treated as a visionary, or had been silenced by a stern rebuke ; but here he found an audience who hung upon his words, who sympathized in his hopes, and saw no folly in his wildest aspirations ; it was an audience of women, of women learned in needlework and household lore, skilled in the art of dressing themselves and making the most of the natural graces to which they were born, of beautiful women who could barely write their own names, who knew little of the world in which they lived, and nothing of the world ,which had passed away. These women were incapable of following out the abstruse reasonings by which at times he sought to elucidate his argument, the illustrations he drew from history conveyed no lesson to their minds, his logic was thrown away upon them, yet they understood him and sympathized with him, and learned from him to believe that their country would one day be a great nation, governed by its own laws, and free from all foreign control.

Several of them joined in the conversation with him, asking him questions, making shrewd observations of their own and deductions from his arguments, some of which were very wide of the conclusion to which he wished to point. One of them, a young girl, plainly dressed, and of very plain features, with a sallow complexion and brown hair, asked him no questions, and spoke to him no word. Listening to him, she had crept nearer till she leaned upon Doña Josefina, resting her folded hands upon her shoulder, and her chin upon them, her thin lips pressed tightly together, and her whole life seemingly concentrated in her large gray eyes.

Marcelino felt her gaze and moved uneasily on his chair, but he continued the conversation without pause till one of his audience, drawing herself up and pressing her hands together, exclaimed—

"Look ! look at Malena !"

"What have you, Niña?" said Doña Josefina.

Malena, raising herself from her leaning posture, heaved a deep sigh, and looked round her in a bewildered sort of manner as though she had just awakened from a dream.

After supper it was the custom for Don Fausto and his guests to repair to the veranda and to spend an hour or two there smoking and talking together while coffee was handed round, but on this evening Gordon found himself alone there before he had finished his first cigar ; after drinking their coffee the others had walked off, Marcelino saying to him as he went—

" Wait for me here."

Don Fausto had invited such neighbours of his, landed proprietors and slave-owners, as resided within a day's gallop of his estancia, to visit him that day for the purpose of discussing together the project of raising a regiment of slaves, which had been started by Marcelino Ponce de Leon. After coffee they assembled together in a small room ; four only had accepted the invitation of Don Fausto. Don Fausto explained to them the purpose for which they were met together, and then left Marcelino to himself to argue his case with them. Marcelino spoke long and eagerly to them, but they looked upon it as a scheme full of danger in the future, and he would probably have given up the idea but for the aid of Don Gregorio Lopez, who struck in to his assistance.

" Our slaves," he said, " are not as a rule hard-worked, they will not lead more easy lives under strict military discipline than they do at present, therefore I do not think a few months' military service will make them any the worse workmen afterwards."

" It will make them better workmen," said Marcelino, " for it will make them more active and more obedient than they now are. The objection I see, which none of you have mentioned, is that they will not give up their present easy life for one of hardship and danger. I do not want unwilling recruits, I want volunteers, and I anticipated more difficulty with them than with you."

" As far as my slaves are concerned you will have no difficulty," said Don Gregorio. " If we defeat the English I will give one in every ten of them who may serve under you his liberty ; that will be reward enough to bring you volunteers."

" If all the proprietors would do that, then I should soon raise my regiment," said Marcelino.

" But I do not see yet why such a step is necessary," said one of the strangers. " With the new regiments, Liniers has sufficient infantry in the city, and in the campaña we can collect thousands of partidarios in an emergency."

" Yes, you can," replied Marcelino, " and they would give very efficient assistance to drilled troops on a field of battle, but they could not stop the advance of an army from the coast, and in the city they would be useless. And again, the militia and the Spanish regiments who are kept embodied in the city will defend entrenchments to the last, but they cannot manœuvre in the open against the well-drilled soldiers of the English. They are only of use to defend the city, so that if the English land again at Quilmes, Liniers has no troops fit to meet them. But if I can raise and drill 2000 negroes, and teach them

G

to march and manœuvre, then Liniers will have a small force upon which he can rely for any rapid movement, and can trust the defence of the line of the Riachuelo to his other infantry, and to the partidarios."

"Two thousand!" exclaimed Don Fausto; "you can never collect 2000 slaves from this district."

"No, I cannot, but if I can commence here with 200, then others will come forward from all the country."

"Well, if Don Gregorio will let you pick fifty from among his slaves I will give you twenty from mine; I will run the risk of some of them being killed."

"Conforme," said Don Gregorio; "the thing is to commence at once; where do you intend to fix your head-quarters?"

"If you will permit me, grandpapa, I should like to establish myself at your large chacra close to the Guardia, the Chacra de Los Sauces. I shall encamp my men on the open ground, and there is a rancho I marked there which will do for me. The commandant of the Guardia has promised me a sergeant and three corporals to assist me in drilling them."

"Agreed," replied Don Gregorio. "Then, gentlemen, if you will promise nothing definite, you will let us hope that when the danger becomes more pressing you will let my grandson seek more recruits among your slaves."

"I will let you have twenty as soon as the wheat is cut," said one.

"Come, we have not done so badly," said Don Gregorio to his grandson; "the thing is to make a beginning."

Marcelino was disappointed to find his idea meet with so cold a reception, nevertheless he returned to the veranda in very good spirits, and met with more sympathy in his scheme from his English friend than he had done from his own countrymen. Don Fausto had promised to call all his slaves together the following morning for inspection by Marcelino, and ere the sun was up the latter was awakened by some one shaking him by the shoulder. Opening his eyes drowsily, he saw his friend Gordon standing by his bed.

"Get up, my friend," said the latter; "if you would be a soldier you must learn to parade your men every morning at sunrise."

Laughing at his eagerness, Marcelino sprang from his bed.

"Why you take as much interest in it as I do," said he.

"Ah! if it were only not against us, I would be the first of your recruits myself."

"The day will come yet," answered Marcelino, "when we shall fight side by side."

Rejecting youths and old men, Marcelino found it easy to select twenty stalwart negroes from among the many slaves who were brought together by Don Fausto for his inspection, but when he commenced to make a speech to them, asking them to show themselves men by volunteering under his orders for the defence of their native country, his host cut him short, and spoke to them himself.

"Boys," said he, "our country has need of your services. Go with my young friend here, and obey him as you would obey me. You are henceforth under military discipline; disobedience or desertion will be punished with death. If you behave yourselves bravely a reward shall not be wanting to each one of you ; to any two of you who may be specially recommended to me by Don Marcelino I will give freedom on your return. To-day you are at liberty to make what preparations you require, to-morrow at sunrise you march."

Several of the "volunteers" looked far from joyful as they listened to this speech, and many of the women collected round burst into loud lamentations as the word passed among them that these twenty had been selected to go and fight the English. Marcelino would willingly have exchanged two or three of them who had families for others of those he had passed over, but Don Fausto would not hear of it.

"The first duty of a slave, as of a soldier, is unquestioning obedience." said he.

"Give them plenty to eat and keep them hard at work, and they will be quite happy," said Don Gregorio. "You have made a good selection, and I believe if you are strict with them you will soon drill them into very good soldiers."

Later on in the day word was brought to Marcelino that one of the twenty had made off from the negro huts towards a dense pajonal about half a league from the estancia. Don Fausto immediately mounted several peons, and started in pursuit. Before sundown he returned, bringing back the runaway, tied hands and feet, on the back of a spare horse.

"There is your deserter," said he to Marcelino ; "I should advise you to shoot him at once, as a warning to the others."

"No, that would be a poor commencement," replied Marcelino. Then summoning the other nineteen, he ordered them to drive four stout stakes into the ground in the form of a square, and to lash the runaway to them by the ancles and wrists with flat strips of raw hide ; after which he told off four of them to keep guard over him till the following morning, giving him food and water as he required, but allowing no one to approach him or speak to him.

During the evening Marcelino visited his prisoner once every two hours, and found his guards always at their posts, till midnight, when, on the runaway promising that he would make no further effort to escape, he told the others to cut the thongs so that he might sleep at ease, but warned him that if he repeated the offence he would shoot him on the spot where he found him.

"I am glad you did not shoot him," said Gordon, who was with Marcelino at the time ; "but with these men you will find it necessary to be very severe."

Next morning at sunrise Marcelino and his twenty men marched away, Marcelino riding, but the men marching on foot, each man with a bundle of spare clothes and provisions, and a stout stick. Don Gregorio and Gordon set off at the same time, attended by peons driving a tropilla before them, and reached the Guardia Chascomus before midday.

The next day Marcelino and his recruits reached the Chacra de Los Sauces, where Don Gregorio had collected the most robust of his slaves from his various establishments round about. From these Marcelino selected fifty, and with the seventy men he had thus under his orders he formed an encampment on some open ground by the edge of the Laguna de Chascomus, and, aided by the sergeant and corporals sent him by the commandant of the Guardia, proceeded at once to drill them into soldiers.

He had not been many days at work ere, greatly to his surprise and pleasure, he received a fresh detachment of recruits, ten stout slaves, sent to him by his father, who also wrote him a letter expressing the warmest interest in his project, and offering him any further assistance in his power.

CHAPTER IV.

STANDING ALONE.

WEEKS passed, busy weeks for Marcelino Ponce de Leon. Every morning at cock-crow the reveillé sounded at the Chacra de Los Sauces, at sunrise the recruits mustered, and the first six hours of the day were spent in steady drill and in long marches. Marcelino had but a dozen muskets which had been lent him by the commandant of the Guardia; a dozen men were detached every hour for instruction in the manual exercise by the sergeant, the rest were instructed in evolutions by Marcelino himself and the corporals. The afternoons were spent by the negroes in the manufacture of accoutrements, and in the routine work of the encampment; at sundown they were paraded again, and sentinels were told off for the night.

Under this discipline the negroes improved rapidly, lost their slouching gait, and some of them showed such intelligence that in January Marcelino selected sergeants and corporals from among them, and advanced his four Spaniards to brevet rank as subaltern officers. Not a week passed but he received some accession of strength by small drafts of slaves from the estancias or chacras round about; at the end of January he had 150 men. At this time he received a note from Don Gregorio Lopez of the Barrancas, telling him that he was going to march his newly-raised squadron inside for inspection by General Liniers, and advising him to accompany him, as, if his recruits would bear inspection, the Reconquistador would probably give him arms for them at once.

It was the second week in February; Don Roderigo Ponce de Leon and his wife Doña Constancia had a houseful of guests at their quinta. The paved veranda round the house had resounded all day with the clanking of sabres and the jingling of armed heels. The Reconquistador and his staff had breakfasted with them that day at noon, after inspecting the cavalry regiment from Las Barrancas and the negro recruits under the command of Marcelino Ponce de Leon. Her military guests had done full justice to the plentiful breakfast Doña Constancia had placed before them, patriotic toasts had been honoured with enthusiasm, cheerfulness and confidence had shone in every face.

The morning inspection had passed off very well, the cavalry had performed some simple evolutions without getting into hopeless disorder; the negroes, now fully armed and accoutred, had marched and wheeled with a rapidity and precision which surprised the general, and had elicited a warm eulogium from Major Belgrano of the Patricios, for whose opinion the commandant of the negroes had a very high regard. All this was very pleasing to Doña Constancia, but nevertheless, now that Liniers and his staff had returned to town, and her remaining guests were chiefly members of their own family, sitting at her ease under the front veranda with her favourite son beside her, she was far from cheerful or happy herself. She had cause for anxiety, one face that she had been accustomed to see almost daily for more than twenty years she had not seen to-day, nor for many days past, the face of her second son, Juan Carlos.

Early in January a detachment of the Patricios had volunteered to proceed to Monte Video to aid in the defence of that city against the English. They had crossed the river too late to take part in the action of the 20th January, in which the Spanish troops had been defeated by Sir Samuel Auchmuty. Since then the city had been invested by land and sea, and whether the Patricios were on their way back again, or whether they had succeeded in entering the city, and now formed a portion of the beleaguered garrison, was as yet unknown in Buenos Aires. Among these volunteers had gone Juan Carlos Ponce de Leon with the rank of lieutenant.

Mother and son found much to talk of, and they talked together sitting side by side, till the long shadows of the trees had stretched themselves right across the open space in front of the house, had climbed up the white palings of the outer fence, shutting them out from the sinking sun, and had then stretched on into infinity until they were no longer shadows at all, but all was one general shadow, the shadow of night. Others came and went in the veranda, some who had had a busy day seating themselves there to rest their weary limbs, but presently lounging away again to some room inside where they could rest yet more at their ease. Others walked to and fro under the shade of the trees in couples, blue smoke curling up from under the wide brims of their hats, and as they themselves were lost to sight under the darkling shade of the foliage, the fiery tips of their cigars yet gave evidence of their presence. Among them Dolores flitted backwards and forwards, having taken upon herself the care of their guests now that the more important of them had gone, and so leaving her mother at liberty and at rest. She was dressed in a white gossamer-like material bound together some few inches below her shoulders by a broad scarlet ribbon, tied behind her in a huge bow with two long streamers. The sleeves of her dress were very short, not reaching down to her elbows, and were puffed out till they looked like a pair of young balloons. Her round white arms were uncovered, and on her head she wore a small straw-hat, also adorned with scarlet bows and streamers, of which hat she was very proud, only wearing it on great occasions, for such a head-dress was rarely seen in Buenos Aires at that time.

This review of the recruits raised by her uncle and brother had been a great occasion for Dolores. During the inspection she had ridden at the left hand of General Liniers in this her gala dress, with the addition of a flowing mantle and gloves reaching up to her elbows. The general had been very polite to her, treating her with great deference and toasting her afterwards at the breakfast as the Queen of the day. In his suite she had also found many other attentive cavaliers, who had found a sure way to her smiles and good graces by lavishing encomiums upon her brother and his negro troops. Among these cavaliers was one who seemed to take almost as much pride as herself in the proficiency of the negroes, but who looked somewhat contemptuously upon the cavalry, Lieutenant Gordon, who was again her father's guest at the Quinta de Ponce. To him General Liniers had been very cordial, and Major Belgrano of the Patricios had ridden beside him all the morning, conversing with him and listening attentively to all his critiques upon the movements and bearing of the recruits. Major Belgrano had not returned to town with the General and his staff, but had accepted Don Roderigo's invitation to remain at the quinta until the following day.

Dolores had also had another cavalier in attendance who had enjoyed the military display even more than she had done, her youngest brother Evaristo, who was yet only fourteen years of age. Mounted on a pony, he had galloped about all the morning, eagerly trying to make himself useful, chiefly succeeding in being always in the way when any rapid movement was performed, but invariably extricating himself with great skill and presence of mind from his difficulties.

"They will ride over that boy presently," said Liniers to Dolores, on one of the occasions. "Who is he?"

"He is my brother," replied Dolores.

Whereupon Liniers, calling the lad to him, complimented him upon his horsemanship, and subdued and rewarded his enthusiasm by appointing him an extra aide-de-camp, and keeping him beside himself till the evolutions came to an end.

Lamps were lighted in the sala, the table was duly set out for dinner, Marcelino and his mother yet sat side by side under the shade of the wide veranda, when the galloping of horses was heard on the road outside. As they reached the quinta gate the horsemen drew rein and dismounted, they opened the gate and two walked up the winding path to the veranda with the confidence of men who were no strangers there. As they drew near one quickened his step and took off his hat as he set foot on the brick pavement. One word only he said—

"Mamita!"

"Juan Carlos! my son!" exclaimed Doña Constancia, springing from her chair and throwing herself into his arms.

At her cry many others came forward from inside and from under the trees, and crowded round Juan Carlos, shaking him warmly by the hand or embracing him, all of them asking him but one question :—

"What news?"

"What matter the news?" said Doña Constancia; "I have my son again, let me look at him."

She drew him into the sala, into the lamplight.

"You look pale, my son," said she, "and weary. These cursed wars! But you are back again!"

"We have been very anxious about you, Juan Carlos," said Don Roderigo. "Since the affair of the 20th January we could not tell what had become of you. I am glad you have come back again, it would have been useless to try to force your way into Monte Video."

"I went to Monte Video, father," answered Juan Carlos sadly, "and I have come back again. That I am here at all I owe to—— Ah! where is he? I thought he had come with me."

He turned and looked out into the darkness. There, unnoticed by any one, leaning in an attitude of careless grace against one of the iron pillars of the veranda, stood a tall man, with his hat thrust back from his forehead, while an amused smile flitted over his sallow features, lighting them up into a kind of stern beauty.

"Evaña!" exclaimed Marcelino, who was the first to recognize him, and ran out at once to seize him by the hand and draw him forward.

"You are glad to see me again, mother," said Juan Carlos. "Then thank him, for to him I probably owe my life, and certainly my escape from an English prison."

"Don Carlos!" said Doña Constancia; "you are back? This is the second time that you have been the one who has given me happiness when I was anxious for my sons. Are you their guardian angel? God bless you for it, I can only give you the thanks of a grateful mother."

"And that is reward sufficient, Señora," said Evaña, as he raised her hand to his lips in courtly salutation. "But I fear that the news we bring will not give equal pleasure to all of you."

"What of Monte Video?" asked Don Roderigo. "What has been done?"

Evaña turned away without answering, leaving Juan Carlos to answer for him.

"You said you came from Monte Video; what has happened?" asked Marcelino of his brother.

"Monte Video has fallen," answered Juan Carlos.

"How? The English have taken the city already!" exclaimed Don Roderigo.

"They opened a breach in the wall close to the sea, and stormed it under the fire of their ships. We had blocked up the gap in the night before the assault, and the defence was rude and cost them many men, but they carried everything before them at the point of the bayonet."

"When was the assault?"

"At dawn on the third."

"And you had entered the city before that?"

"Yes, three days before. We were not at the breach, but were posted near the citadel, and beat off a party that tried to scale the wall, but we were cut off and surrounded by the English before we knew that they had forced the breach. We fired on them, and they would have massacred us but for Don Carlos, who kept them back, and ran in through our fire waving a handkerchief. He told us that resistance was useless, as the English had already captured the Plaza, and had all our positions in reverse, so we surrendered."

"Then you were made prisoner," said Marcelino.

"Yes, but Don Carlos spoke for me, and they let me go on

promising that I would not serve against them any more in this war."

"And Sobremonte, what does he do?" asked Don Roderigo. "He had some force collected not far off, and we expected that he would prevent the English from attempting an assault."

"Sobremonte does nothing."

"And never will do anything," said Marcelino sullenly.

"How many men have the English?" asked Major Belgrano.

"About 5000," answered Juan Carlos.

"They have the city, but they have not yet the campaña," said Don Gregorio Lopez, who had already sent off his recruits to their homes, but who had remained himself at the quinta.

"The campaña, with Sobremonte to keep it, is the same as lost," said Marcelino.

"Henceforward we can only look upon the Banda Oriental as a danger," said Major Belgrano. "The English have now secured themselves a footing on American soil, that is all they seek in Monte Video, but the prize they strike for is Buenos Aires. They will come, my friends, but this time they will find us ready for them. Is it not so, Don Gregorio? Is it not so, Marcelino?"

"It is," answered both together.

"Then courage, my friends," added Belgrano; "you have to-day shown us that we have the raw material amongst ourselves of an efficient army. I have wished to take our militia from their homes and embody them as soldiers. I feel confident that this is the only way in which we can hope to meet with success in a renewed struggle against these invaders, but my counsels are set at nought, and my forebodings are treated with derision. The Reconquistador is a man of experience and shares my opinions, but unfortunately he values his popularity too much to support them. Aid me then, my friends, ere it be too late."

"I would aid you with pleasure if my aid could be of any service," said Don Roderigo; "but the militia will not leave their homes and their families until the enemy land."

"Leave such follies alone, that is what I counsel you, Don Manuel," said Don Gregorio Lopez. "Among streets and houses your militia are all right, but in the open camp they are worth nothing."

"The proper way to defend the city," said Belgrano, "is to meet the invaders when they land, and not to let them see the city at all."

Don Gregorio and the major carried on the discussion for some time, but no one else paid any further attention to the matter, crowding round Juan Carlos as he told of his adventures since he had left Buenos Aires, and questioning Evaña as to where he had been for months past, but not pressing their questions, as he seemed little inclined to satisfy their curiosity.

It was nearly midnight. Marcelino and his friend Don Carlos Evaña sat in an inner room talking earnestly together, seated one on each side of a small table, on which stood a shaded lamp. Both had been smoking, but Marcelino had let his cigar go out, so absorbed was he in the subject on which they conversed together.

"What are you two discussing?" said Major Belgrano, pausing as he passed the open door in company with Don Gregorio Lopez; "you might be talking treason, you look so solemn."

"Something very like treason, according to my friend here," answered Evaña, stretching himself on his chair, and puffing a long jet of smoke from his lips. "Come in; I should like to hear your opinion on the subject, Major, and yours too, Don Gregorio."

"Say no more," said Marcelino, leaning over the table, and whispering to him, "with my uncle there is danger in such ideas; he does not understand you as I do."

"Danger!" replied Evaña laughing; "I should like all the world to listen to me, my opinions are no secret. I see you in your ignorance rushing headlong to destruction; I am no traitor, but a friend, when I try to open your eyes to your danger. What do you say, Don Gregorio?"

"You are among friends here and may speak," replied Don Gregorio, drawing forward a chair and seating himself; "but I know your opinions, and I warn you that you run great danger if you show yourself in the city."

"So will you run danger when you rush with your raw levies upon the bayonets of the English."

"I shall do my duty."

"And I not less so. I have been to England, as I told you, and what I foresaw has come to pass. The English are not a warlike people, but they are very jealous of their military fame, and the affair of the 12th August has raised a storm of indignation. I had interviews with several members of the Government, and got the same answer from them all. Whatever their private opinions may be, they are forced to yield to the popular clamour, which demands the conquest of Buenos Aires in satisfaction for the defeat of their General Beresford."

"And the people of Buenos Aires will deny this satisfaction to the people of England," said Don Gregorio, fiercely striking the table with his clenched fist. "We have defeated and made prisoner one Beresford; let them send ten Beresfords, we will serve them all the same."

"Whatever harm they may yet do us, they have at least done us one service," replied Evaña; "they have taught us our own strength. I know and rejoice at it. Am I not also a Porteño of Buenos Aires? Shall I not glory in the prowess of my own countrymen?"

"Well, it may be so. You are a Porteño and a fellow-countryman, but you sympathize strangely with the enemies of our country. How is that?"

"Spain is our enemy, we have no other."

"And these English then are our friends! They come with their ships and their cannon to break down our walls and to kill the best men amongst us, as they killed Don Pancho Maciel, not a month ago, near Monte Video. Frankly, of friendship of that kind I understand nothing."

"Don Pancho Maciel died in defence of the flag of our tyrants, many more will die as he did if we continue to defend it. To you,

Belgrano, I appeal; you have more influence with the Patricios than any other, your newly-organized militia has the destinies of our country in its hands. Let them tear down that flaunting flag which waves at the fort, and put our own flag in its place, then we can treat with the English and they will be our friends."

"Our flag! We have no flag," replied Belgrano.

"We have none, but we can make one. The day we hoist our own flag we declare our independence and achieve it."

"You deceive yourself, Evaña," said Belgrano; "the time has not yet come. To tear down that flag now would be to kindle at once a civil war amongst us, that flag alone it is that binds us together."

"Your own argument tells against you, Carlos," said Marcelino. "We are the sons of Spaniards, the English people know no difference between us and them. Whatever flag we fight under, they look upon us as enemies, and will not be content till they have trampled us under their feet."

"We have more chance than we had last year," said Belgrano. "We have 8000 trained infantry in the capital, and the campaña will rise as one man when the enemy lands."

"To say nothing of the slaves," said Evaña laughing. "How many of them have you, Marcelino?"

"I have enough to commence with, and I have many promises of more to-day."

"And not one of them has yet fired a musket. Can your Patricios yet fire a musket without shutting their eyes, Belgrano?"

To this Major Belgrano did not answer, and Evaña continued—

"Give up this idea of a foolhardy resistance to an overwhelming force; you are brave men, show that you are also wise, receive the English as friends, and staunch friends you will find them. All their interests drive them to a friendly alliance with us. There is time yet to organize a provisional government of our own, there wants but one step more to consolidate our independence, a separate treaty with the English."

As Evaña ceased the three others looked doubtfully at one another, his words had made a deep impression upon them, for with two of them at least their independence of Spain was second in importance in their eyes only to their freedom from the enforced authority of Great Britain.

"Do you think the English commander would make a treaty with us, and abstain from invading our country, if we had a government of our own?" asked Belgrano.

"I doubt it much," said Don Gregorio.

"Nevertheless, the first step might be taken," said Marcelino. "After this news from Monte Video it will not be difficult to persuade the corporations to depose the Viceroy. Sobremonte has already not one friend in the city."

"Well thought," said Belgrano, rising. "Of this we will speak more to-morrow, and will consult with Don Roderigo."

"These ideas of yours are not so new to us as they were," said Marcelino to Evaña, when they were again alone. "General Beres-

ford and his officers openly declare that the British Government
would cordially welcome an alliance with us if we would declare our
independence of Spain, but they may make peace with Spain any day
and withdraw their help from us.   I can only see danger in such an
alliance until we have some solid organization of our own."

" Do they mix freely with the citizens ? " asked Evaña eagerly.

" They were for two months at liberty on parole," replied Marcelino ;
" but they spoke so very openly that Liniers and the Cabildo took
alarm ; Beresford and Pack and several others were arrested and sent
to Lujan in October, and most of the other officers have been sent
into the interior ; fortunately Gordon has been all the time separate
from the rest, so we have been able to keep him with us.   Several
citizens were also arrested on suspicion of treasonable designs, and
until now there they are, the most of them, in prison.   It is fortunate
that you have been away all these months, or you would have most
certainly been imprisoned.   We gave it out that you had gone to
Paraguay, but you will require to be very cautious."

The following morning Don Roderigo, Don Gregorio, Major Belgrano, and Don Carlos Evaña rode in together to the city.   Before
sun-down the latter had interviews with most of the principal native
residents, and with many Spaniards also.   The result of his propaganda
appeared on the 10th February, when the various corporations of
which the actual Government was composed assembled together and
formally deposed the Marquis de Sobremonte from his authority as
Viceroy and took possession of his seals and papers.

Thus Buenos Aires became for the time *de facto* an independent
Commonwealth, but her Government ruled in the name of Spain, and
one only fear kept the heterogeneous members together, fear of the
English.

CHAPTER V.

THE excitement occasioned in Buenos Aires by the fall of Monte Video, and the favourable report of General Liniers, brought many recruits to Marcelino Ponce de Leon, so that at the end of March he had over 300 men under his command at the Chacra de Los Sauces, but his dream of forming a legion of 2000 men remained a dream, he had to be content with his 300, and spared no pains to make efficient soldiers of them.

Early in March General Beresford, Colonel Pack, and three other English officers escaped by the aid of some friendly Creoles from their prison at Lujan ; three days they remained concealed in Buenos Aires, and then embarked at night in a small boat and sailed for Monte Video. They were picked up on their way by an English cruiser and reached the British head-quarters in safety. General Liniers sent to demand that they should be delivered up to him on the ground that they had broken their parole; the demand was refused by Sir Samuel Auchmuty on the plea that their imprisonment at Lujan cancelled the parole which they had previously given. General Beresford returned at once to England, and to Colonel Pack was confided the command of the garrison of Colonia.

Meantime the English had overrun the western parts of the Banda Oriental, they had garrisons at Canelones, Santa Lucia, and Colonia ; but the country-people remained unsubdued, hovering in small parties about any position held by the British, cutting off stragglers, seriously impeding the communications between the different garrisons, and driving off the horses from their immediate neighbourhood, so that the invaders had great difficulty in mounting their cavalry. In addition to this, various expeditions were sent from Buenos Aires to aid the natives of the eastern province against the common foe ; in particular, a strong force under the command of Colonel Don Calisto Elio, a Spanish officer, which was attacked by Colonel Pack in the neighbourhood of Colonia, totally defeated and compelled to re-embark, with heavy loss both in men and equipments.

So the months passed on until June, when it was reported in Buenos Aires that large reinforcements of English had reached Monte Video, and that the invasion so much talked of would be no longer deferred. This intelligence excited the enthusiasm of the citizens to the utmost ; the militia required no urging to be constant at their meetings for drill, confidence beamed in every face and was spoken by every tongue, no——not by every tongue. Major Belgrano had thrown up his commission in the Patricios, disgusted at the small heed paid to his warnings, and now served on the staff of General Balviani. He did not speak confidently, he said that neither the militia nor the Spanish regiments could face half their number of English troops in the open field.

Don Carlos Evaña lived again at his house, near to that of Don Gregorio Lopez, taking no part in the military preparations and thereby incurring general censure, but passing his days in study and his evenings at the houses of his more particular friends, talking little, but listening much and watching always.

One evening a miscellaneous company, including many ladies, were assembled in the large sala of the house of Don Gregorio Lopez. Many officers in uniform were there; they were the most favoured guests, envied by the men who were in plain clothes, and basking in the smiles of the ladies, who looked upon them as their defenders, and told them so in flattering words. One young officer was more especially selected for attention, he had been absent from the city for months. Slim and active, his uniform displayed to perfection his graceful figure, while his bronzed cheek and erect bearing marked him out as one to whom military duty was a profession, not a pastime, as it was to many of the citizen soldiers around him.

Marcelino Ponce de Leon had marched his men to the Casateja, and leaving them there had come to town to place himself and his command at the orders of General Liniers, deeming his negroes now fit for active service. He had already received his orders, which were to march to the town of Ensenada and to report himself to his uncle Colonel Lopez of the Barrancas cavalry, who had the command of that important station, and whose regiment was spread in detachments along the coast.

One of the ladies present was Doña Dalmacia, the wife of Don Isidro Lorea.

"Come and talk to me, Don Marcelino," said she to him, as he crossed the room and passed near her chair. "I wish to speak to you about a friend of yours."

"Always at your orders, Señora," said Marcelino, seating himself beside her.

"Your friend Don Carlos Evaña is a patriot, so say you and some others who know him better than I do; but for my part I understand nothing of such patriotism. An invasion is coming, all our young men take some part in the preparations except he, he shuts himself up in his house and does nothing. Where was he last year? There are who say he was never in Paraguay at all, but was in England. It is known that there are Americans in London, who have for their own purposes encouraged and even asked the British Government to send out this expedition; probably he knows them, perhaps he is one of them, he was much in London before he came back from Europe."

"Don Carlos does nothing because he thinks resistance is useless."

"And he stirs not a hand to save our city from the dishonour of a second time being conquered by a foreign army."

"He says that its conquest is dishonour to Spain, not to us; in this I do not agree with him."

"I should think not. If we are beaten the loss and the dishonour will be ours. But I have no fear; on the 12th August we had no troops, now we have thousands; we shall win, and the glory will be ours. You will have your part in it, my friend, but as for Evaña— Pish! I am sorry that he is a friend of yours, and a protegé of Don Gregorio; if he were not he would long since have been where such traitors ought to be, in the calabozo."

"Forgive me for differing from you, Doña Dalmacia, but Evaña is no traitor, he is simply an enemy of Spain. If we drive back the English we shall have the glory, as you say, but Spain will reap the reward."

"If! why you say 'if' as though there could be any doubt about it."

"This army which is coming against us is much stronger than the detachment Beresford took our city with a year ago."

"A surprise; now we are ready; 'el hombre prevenido nunca fué vencido.'"[1]

"Evaña says we are not 'prevenido,' our militia cannot face the English in the field, and I agree with him. I have not seen much of the English, but their soldiers are better than our militia. Gordon has told me much about their drill and discipline."

"Do you know I like that English friend of yours," said Doña Dalmacia. "He is very simple, but he is not wanting in intelligence."

"And he is a soldier, therefore his opinion is of more value than that of either Evaña or myself; he says that one English division would be sufficient to rout all the infantry now in the city, in the open field."

"He did not tell me so the other day when he was at my house. He told me that he had been to pay you a visit, and that your negroes were very good soldiers."

"My negroes are not citizen soldiers, Doña Dalmacia."

"But you will not tell me that they are equal to Isidro's company."

To this Marcelino merely bowed in answer, and hastened to turn the conversation.

"But about Evaña, Señora," said he; "I am sorry that you should think so ill of him as to say that he merits the calabozo."

"There are some who would put him there to-morrow but for fear of offending Don Gregorio, and perhaps they may do. I called you to me to tell you so. Several officers of the Patricios met together to-day at our house; Isidro has brought them here, and has asked Don Gregorio to send for Don Carlos Evaña, so that they may question him privately as to where he was last year, and if he was in England what he was doing there. If he refuses to answer their questions they will denounce him to the Reconquistador and he will be arrested to-morrow."

"Many thanks, Señora, for having told me this. If Evaña comes he will at any rate have one friend beside him."

"Don Gregorio is his friend."

"True, but my grandfather does not understand him as I do."

"And you would like to be with him when they question him?"

[1] "The prepared man was never conquered."—*Spanish Proverb.*

"I should," replied Marcelino, looking round. "Where is my grandfather? I will speak to him at once."

"Then I will not keep you longer. Just before I called you, Don Carlos came in. You were so much occupied with the bright eyes of Elisa Puyrredon that you did not see him, and he went away with Don Gregorio and Isidro and some others; you will find them in some other room. Come back and tell me what he says."

"I will not fail," said Marcelino, as he rose from his seat and walked away.

Marcelino learned from a servant that his grandfather and several others were in the dining-room, in consultation, the man said. He found the door of the room locked, but on knocking he was admitted. Don Gregorio sat in his arm-chair with a stern, anxious expression on his face; others sat or stood around him, several of whom wore on the left sleeve a scarlet badge, on which was embroidered in black letters the words 'Buenos Aires;' these were officers in the regiment of the Patricios. In front of them, leaning back in a chair, with his legs crossed, and a scornful smile flitting over his features, sat Don Carlos Evaña.

"Why do you speak to us of the Spaniards? leave them," said one of the Patricios to him, as Marcelino entered. "It is not of them we wish to speak, it is of the English."

"How came you to be with the English when they captured Monte Video?" asked Don Isidro Lorea.

"The thing is very simple," answered Evaña. "I came back from Europe in an English ship."

"And you joined them in the assault, and entered the town with them?"

"I followed them through the breach when they had stormed it."

"Traitor! you took part with our enemies, and yet you dare to come here and live amongst us?" exclaimed Don Isidro.

"Gently, Don Isidro," said Marcelino, who had seated himself beside his friend. "Don Carlos went in without arms, and exposed his own life among them to save the lives of our people. To him I owe that my brother Juan Carlos was not killed that day."

"Gentlemen," said Don Gregorio, "let us not dispute about what has nothing to do with the subject before us. Don Carlos is no traitor to us, and his friendship with the English may be of great service to us. Those who have most experience amongst us nearly all agree that it is almost hopeless to attempt to defend our city against the army the English will bring against us now."

"There is no man amongst us of more experience than the Reconquistador," answered another officer, "and he speaks very differently."

"Liniers," replied Don Gregorio with an impatient shrug of his shoulders, "Liniers is a vain, hot-headed fool. When you shout 'Viva Liniers!' he is ready to tell you any sort of folly. Ask Belgrano, your late major, he will tell you that the English will drive all your battalions before them like sheep."

"What Belgrano says is worth no attention," said Don Isidro. "If things are not done exactly as he wishes, they are all wrong. If we find the English too strong for us in the open we will retreat upon the city, and we will defend it block by block, and street by street. It cost them hundreds of men to storm one breach in Monte Video, here each street-corner will be a breach, and the street itself will be their grave."

"Well said! well said! Viva Don Isidro!" shouted the officers, clapping their hands. Even Evaña smiled encouragement upon his accuser.

"Let us be friends, Don Isidro," said he, rising and stretching out his hand to him. "Our country has need of such as you, and it is to prevent you and others like you from throwing away your lives in a useless contest that I strive to make you look upon the English as friends, and to unite you against our real enemy."

"If you wish us to look upon the English as friends," said Don Isidro, drawing back, "try your persuasive talents upon them and keep them from invading our country. They have the Banda Oriental, let them keep it; but if they come here they are enemies, and the sword alone will make treaty between us."

"They say there is a new general come out to take command of the English," said Marcelino, as Evaña, somewhat disconcerted, reseated himself. "Do you know him, Evaña?"

"His name is Whitelock," answered Evaña.

"He might be more willing than the other to make some arrangement with us," said Don Gregorio, "as he has left England later. From that letter you showed me it seems that Miranda and your other friends in London have not been idle lately. Do you know anything of him?"

"No, I never heard of him before; but doubtless his instructions will be the same as those of Sir Samuel."

"You are known to many of the English, could you not go to Monte Video and prevail upon Whitelock to remain there?" said Don Gregorio.

"Do so," said Don Isidro; "in this way you may make your friendship with the English of some use to us and we shall no longer look upon you as a traitor. Something you will have done, though you care not to risk your life in the defence."

"I am not more careful of my life than other men," answered Evaña angrily, "but I am not fool enough to——"

"Say you will go, Evaña," interrupted Marcelino; "I believe you may possibly do some good, and you can bring us information upon which we can rely. To-morrow I leave this for Ensenada, come with me, and I will manage somehow to get you put across the river."

"Be it so. At what hour do you leave?"

"Probably not before noon, but I will send you word."

"Then adios, Don Gregorio," said Evaña, shaking hands with the old gentleman. "If the English hang me as a spy they will do me less injustice than these friends of yours, who would shoot me as a traitor."

"Neither spy nor traitor are you, Carlos," replied Don Gregorio. "Whether you succeed in averting this war from us or not, I know that you will regard as nothing the danger to yourself. Go, and may God have you in his keeping."

It was nearly midnight when Marcelino reached his father's house.
To his surprise he found the whole household astir, busily employed
dismantling the rooms and packing up clothes, house-linen, and
crockery.   In the sala he found his sister, assisted by Evaristo and
Gordon, collecting the thousand and one articles of ornament and
luxury with which the room was adorned and carefully stowing them
away in a large packing-case.

"Lola!" said he, going behind her and seizing her by the two
elbows, "what is all this about?   Are you going to fly away?"

"Ahi!" screamed Dolores, springing away from him.   "Marcelino,
how you frightened me!   I thought that they had come already and
that I was a prisoner."

"Who are 'they,' that you are so frightened of, and what are you
doing?" asked Marcelino, seating himself on the case and drawing
her towards him.

"Hush!" answered Dolores, laying one finger on her lip and
looking round at Lieutenant Gordon, then stooping over him she
whispered in his ear, "the English. Papa was away all evening,
when he came back he told us to commence at once to pack up
everything, for we are all to go out to the quinta to-morrow."

"But why?" asked Marcelino, laying a hand upon the shoulder of
his brother Evaristo, who had come up to him as he spoke.

"Don Alejandro says a soldier should obey and ask no questions,"
said Evaristo; "so he and Lola and I have been hard at work ever
since."

"You are not a soldier, my fine fellow," said Marcelino.

"Not yet, but I shall be."

"Don't say that, Evaristo," said Dolores.   "You know mamma
does not like to hear you say that.   Is it not plenty that one is a
soldier?"

"I shall go with them to the quinta of course," said Evaristo;
"but when *they* come," he continued in a lower voice, and looking at
Gordon, "then I shall be with you.   Promise me, Marcelino, that you
will send for me, I will do all you tell me if you will only let me be
with you."

"You must stop at the quinta and take care of mamma and Lola."

"There will be papa and Juan Carlos and Don Alejandro."

"And Evaristo too," said Dolores.   "Come, now that you are here,
though it is so late, you shall help me just a little, for we have nearly
finished now."

As they spoke together Gordon had kept away at the far end of
the room.   Rising from his seat on the packing-case, Marcelino went
up to him and laid one hand on his shoulder.

"It is not far off now," he said in a low voice.

"It appears not, but I have asked no questions," replied Gordon.

"Promise me that whatever happens you will stay by them to the
end," said Marcelino.

"I will, so help me God," replied Gordon.

The four then worked steadily on in silence till the packing-case
was full, and all the smaller articles which had been scattered about
the room were stowed away.   Then Marcelino went in search of his

father and learnt from him that advices had been received that day which reported that the bulk of the English forces had been concentrated in Monte Video, and that their number made it hopeless to attempt to oppose their landing on the western shore of La Plata, so that some of the leading townsmen had proposed to entrench the city at once. Rather than run the risk of being shut up in a besieged city, Don Roderigo had determined to remove his family to the quinta, stowing away his furniture in an inner room, locking up his plate and valuables in an under-ground cellar, and leaving the dismantled house in the custody of a couple of slaves.

"I am glad you have so decided, father," said Marcelino. "I shall care less for their cannon when I know that my mother and Dolores are out of reach of their shot. I suppose you will take Don Alejandro with you."

"Yes, in case the English should land at Quilmes or Ensenada, some of their foraging parties may come as far as the quinta, and Gordon may be of service to us."

The next morning a great lumbering vehicle resembling an oblong box upon wheels, which was called a "galera," was drawn up in the street in front of the house of Don Roderigo. It was a capacious conveyance, and had need to be so, for it had a heavy load to carry that day. Marcelino with his two brothers, Lieutenant Gordon, and Don Carlos Evaña formed the escort.

As they left the city a feeling of sadness oppressed them all. What might happen before they met there again? Should they ever again all meet together in the old house?

CHAPTER VI.

THE LANDING OF THE ENGLISH.

THE commission held by Don Marcelino Ponce de Leon designated him as a captain of militia, but having a separate command he was known at Ensenada as the "Comandante de los Morenos." On presenting himself to his uncle he was ordered to encamp his men near to the river-side to the north of the town. The land about there was very swampy, and "paja" grew in great luxuriance; the negroes made themselves little huts with this paja, in which a man could neither sit nor stand upright, but in which he could lie at full length and sleep at his ease, quite sufficiently protected from the night dews or rain. A small rancho close at hand was taken by Marcelino for his own accommodation, and here he spent rather more than a fortnight, always on the alert, and practising his negroes at target-shooting in addition to their regular drills.

On the 26th June his brother Evaristo galloped into his encampment, bringing him letters from the quinta and from the city. Among them was a short one from his friend Evaña, accompanying a sort of circular letter which he had addressed to Don Gregorio Lopez and to several others, leading citizens of Buenos Aires.

"I have done what I can," he said in his letter to Marcelino, "but it is all in vain; the English insist upon the surrender of the city, and their new general, Whitelock, brings with him his commission as Governor of Buenos Aires, with a salary of £12,000 per annum. This Whitelock appears to me to be very inferior to General Beresford both in intelligence and in military skill, but he has some first-class officers with him. Although I cannot join you in defence of the flag of Spain, I sympathize greatly with your mistaken heroism. Would that I could wish you success, but I cannot. Your victory will be a misfortune to our country, and the welfare of our country must with me override all personal feeling. Vale."

Marcelino had filled up many a lonely evening during the past summer and autumn by reading in that book whose chief lesson, as his friend Gordon had told him, was faith. As he read he became more and more convinced that the book was the word of God, and that the lessons it taught were of Divine authority. As he applied these lessons to his own actions, he became confirmed in his opinion that his present course was the right one to pursue. If they beat off the English armament they might thereby forge fresh fetters for themselves, but Marcelino had learnt in this book that to do right and to leave the result to God was the essence of faith. He was satisfied that he was doing right, and that the result would be in some unseen way for the future welfare of his country.

As the bugles sounded the reveillé the next morning, there came a knock at the door of the rancho in which Marcelino had taken up his quarters. He sprang from his catre, and, hurrying on a few clothes, opened the door.

"Adelante," he said, and a negro sergeant stepped into the room.

"Señor Comandante," said the sergeant, "the Señor Lieutenant sends me to advise you that the river is covered with ships, which appear to be coming here."

As the door opened Evaristo had also awakened. As the sergeant spoke he sprang up, shouting—

"The English! and I shall be one of the first to see them. What luck!"

Marcelino rapidly dressed himself, buckled on his sword, and with Evaristo beside him walked up to a small hillock in front of his encampment which overlooked the river, and on which it had been his constant practice since his arrival there to have a sentry at all hours on the look-out. The sentry was still there, wrapped up in a thick, striped poncho, and walking rapidly backwards and forwards. As Marcelino approached he drew himself up, presented arms, and then resumed his rapid walk up and down. On the hillock stood another man wrapped in a large cloak, gazing steadfastly towards the river. As the sentry presented arms he turned and raised his hand to his cap in a military salute.

"Buenos dias, Asneiros," said Marcelino, returning his salute; "it appears that we have them at last."

"So it appears, Señor Comandante," replied the other.

Asneiros was a Spaniard who had formerly been a sergeant in the garrison of Chascomus. He was now first lieutenant of the negro corps, and was greatly trusted by Marcelino. This trust he merited, for he was a very active officer, but he was a rigid disciplinarian and very severe. The negroes obeyed him from fear only; their commandant they obeyed with cheerful alacrity, for his treatment of them, while always strict, showed a constant care for their comfort, and a due appreciation of their efforts to please him.

It was a bright, clear morning. The muddy waters of La Plata, flowing slowly and silently onwards towards the great ocean, broke in rippling wavelets upon the shelving beach at the foot of the hillock. The sun had not yet risen, but the eastern sky was lighted up with the radiance which marshalled his approach. The light-gray clouds which hung low on the horizon lifted themselves like a veil of gossamer tinged with rainbow hues, heralding the advent of a new-born day. Under these light clouds, away across a wide expanse of dark, still water, the line of the horizon was broken by a multitude of dark objects of uncertain form; now clustering together and merging one into the other, anon scattering themselves and losing their identity as they were hidden from sight by the clouds of dawn, changing continually.

Side by side stood the two brothers watching them, neither speaking a word, each communing with his own thoughts, but in manner of thought differing as their natures differed; the one pondering with the far-stretching thought of a man, the other with the careless confidence of a boy eager after novelty; upon both there came a sense of awe which kept them silent. As they stood so watching, the sun arose steadily from behind the line of dark waters, and it was day. Then the line of the horizon stretched further and further away, the dark objects which had broken that line faded, and the first beams of the morning sun fell diagonally upon the white sails of a vast fleet of ships.

As the sun rose, a breeze ruffled the calm surface of the river and swept over the hillock where the brothers stood; at the same moment Marcelino heard a footstep behind him and awoke from his reverie with a shiver. He looked round, his uncle Colonel Lopez stood beside him.

" Will it be they?" asked the colonel.

"Without doubt," answered Marcelino. "But they are far off yet, and it is cold; come, let us take coffee."

Three hours later all doubt was at an end, the breeze, though light, was favourable to the hostile squadron, which came steadily on under easy sail. Again Colonel Lopez with his two nephews and Lieutenant Asneiros stood on the hillock watching it. They understood nothing of naval affairs and could not tell one ship from another, yet even their eyes could see that they sailed on in perfect order, each ship in its own station and keeping at due distance from the one before it. The leading ships were men-of-war of light draught, brigs and gunboats; they had men in their chains throwing the lead continually, but from the confidence with which they advanced in the deep channel, avoiding the shoals, it was evident that their course was already marked out for them. From the gaff of each of these ships waved the white standard, bearing the red cross of Saint George, and from their main trucks streamed the long pennant which marked them as men-of-war. After them came transports crowded with troops, and deeply laden with stores and ammunition, many of them with every sail set, and yet that was only just able to keep their places as marked for them by the swifter, lighter-built men-of-war. These ships carried the red ensign. Beyond them again came larger ships, sloops-of-war, with their ports triced up and guns run out.

As the watchers gazed two of the brigs crowded on sail and, running rapidly in, cast anchor, one nearly in front of the hillock upon which they stood, the other further to the south. Between them lay a long stretch of flat shore, where boats might safely run aground, and where any force attempting to oppose a landing would come under the fire of their guns.

"Against these we can do nothing," said Colonel Lopez, as he counted the guns which frowned from the sides of the nearest brig. "Put your men under arms and march them to the high road."

In half an hour the negroes, with their baggage mules and camp-equipage, marched off under the command of Lieutenant Asneiros; and Marcelino, after seeing them safe through the swamp to the firm ground beyond, returned on horse-back to the hillock accompanied by Evaristo on his pony.

No attempt was made by the invaders to land that day, many of the transports did not come to anchor till nearly sun-down. The negroes were encamped on the high ground about a league from their former station, patrols of cavalry were set to watch the coast all night, and Colonel Lopez took his two nephews with him to his quarters at the village of Ensenada, whence he sent off a despatch to General Liniers, acquainting him with the arrival of the hostile squadron off that place, but stated that as they had made no attempt to land it might yet be their intention to proceed further north and to disembark nearer to the city.

The next morning at daylight all three were again in the saddle, and rode to the hillock from which they had watched the enemy on the day previous. Evaristo was most unusually silent that morning, keeping near to his brother continually and wistfully watching him. Marcelino had hardly spoken to him, but frequently when beside him he had stretched out his hand caressing him, and when he had spoken his voice had a gentle tenderness in its tones which filled the boy's mind with vague apprehensions of misfortune.

In the hollow behind the hillock, close to where the negroes had had their encampment, a body of cavalry was drawn up where they could not be seen from the river. The English ships were now at anchor, their sails either furled or hanging loose in the brails, boats flitted to and fro among them or hung in clusters at the sides of some bluff-bowed transport. One large sloop yet lay some distance off, with her top-sails backed and with lines of small flags fluttering in the air from the trucks of her stately masts. On the gun-brigs and on some of the transports other lines of flags ran up to the mast-heads in answer to these signals. The decks of the transports were crowded with scarlet-coated men, and as the ships rose and fell, swinging to their anchors, the beams of the rising sun glinted on polished steel. Marcelino had seen these red-coats before and knew them again, they were the trained soldiery of England, on the decks of the transports they swarmed by thousands ; but what he had never seen before was an English fleet, and now his gaze was rivetted upon the vast armament, so powerful yet so completely under control. As he looked upon them his face flushed and he exclaimed, heedless that any heard him—

"Ah ! if we had these with us, what need we fear from Spain ? "

Evaristo bent forward on his pony's neck and looked wonderingly at his brother, but Colonel Lopez, who had dismounted, stamped his foot angrily and seemed about to make some hasty reply, when from the far-side of the nearest brig there darted out a long jet of gray smoke, and a few seconds afterwards the dull boom of a heavy gun cut short the words ere they had passed his lips. Down came the lines of fluttering flags from the mast-heads of the large ship outside, then three round balls of coloured bunting ran up in a string to the main truck, and as they reached that giddy height burst open and became three flags ; then from one of the ports on her lower deck there leaped a bright flash, a jet of smoke, and sharp through the maze of shipping sounded the report of the gun which gave the signal for shore.

The roar of that gun echoed in the hearts of the three watchers as

a knell. An infant people had struck down the flag of a mighty nation and had it trailed in the dust; in all the pomp and imposing
majesty of mature strength a nation came to try conclusions once
more with an infant people.

In an instant the open water between the lines of transports was
filled with boats crowded with the red-coated soldiery, the crews of
the nearest ships sprang into the rigging waving their hats and shouting, the soldiers responded by a ringing cheer. Then the stout oarsmen bent their backs, the oars as though moved by one hand took the
water, and swiftly, in long, regular lines, the flotilla glided over the
shallow water to the land.

"Look, uncle!" said Evaristo, pointing to the nearest brig.

Colonel Lopez was at that moment thinking to himself, whether by
a rush of his horsemen upon the boats as they grounded he could not
inflict serious injury upon the foe; what Evaristo pointed out to him
gave him his answer at once. By some means, inexplicable to the
colonel, the brig had been warped round on her anchor till she lay
nearly stem on to the hillock; the brass tompions had been removed
from the muzzles of her guns, and now her whole broadside swept the
low-lying land for which the boats were making.

"Basta!" said the colonel, "we have seen them. Now let Liniers
do what he can with them."

Stooping from the saddle, Marcelino put his arms round his brother's
neck and embraced him.

"You have seen them, now go," he said. "One kiss for mamita,"
and he kissed him again.

"But you, Marcelino! Let me——"

"Mamita waits thee," answered Marcelino, as the soft tenderness
of his face faded into an expression of stern command.

Evaristo answered no more, but throwing his arms round his
brother's neck he kissed him eagerly, then gathering up his reins, he
drew the back of his hand across his eyes and galloped off.

Half an hour later a strong force of the English with two guns had
landed; they were apparently about to make some forward movement,
when Colonel Lopez, who had all this time watched them in silence,
turned to his nephew and said—

"Rejoin your negroes and march by the high road to the Puente
Galvès, there you will halt and await orders from General Liniers, I
will keep these in sight."

Marcelino touched his hat and rode off; the colonel, leaving the
hillock, remounted his horse, and dividing his men into small detachments prepared to keep a careful watch on all the movements of the
invaders.

Two hours after sunrise, on the 1st July, a chasque from Colonel
Lopez galloped through the streets of Buenos Aires at headlong speed;
as he passed along, many shouted to him "What news?"

The stolid paisano answered nothing but galloped straight on, and
only drew rein in the Plaza Mayor, where he dismounted in front of
the Cabildo and enquired for General Liniers.

"Are you a chasque?" asked a young officer.

"I am."

"Where from?"

"From away yonder."

"What news?"

"A letter for the Señor Reconquistador."

"He is very busy, is it anything urgent?"

"I have orders to deliver it immediately, and into his own hand."

"Then follow me."

In a large upper room the members of the Cabildo were met together in consultation. Don Gregorio Lopez was the only native member of that body, and had been only recently appointed, the others were all Spaniards. Don Gregorio had just read to them part of a letter he had received some days previously from Don Carlos Evaña.

"From this letter, Señores," he said, "it is evident that the Señor Evaña considers it impossible that we oppose any effectual resistance to the powerful force which is now coming against us. Resistance will only cause useless bloodshed and expose the city to all the horrors of a sack by infuriated soldiery. He counsels us to surrender the city and then to attempt some negotiation."

At this a low murmur of disapproval ran round the room, and several cried "No! no!"

"I pray you to listen to me yet, Señores," continued Don Gregorio, "though I fear I shall try your patience. We none of us wish to see our country disgraced, but it is well that we shut not our eyes to the peril which hangs over us. We have but one experienced soldier among us, the only troops upon which we can place any confidence are collected here in our city, if in an unequal struggle our general be killed and our troops dispersed we are left completely at the mercy of our invaders."

"True, true," replied Don Martin Alzaga, who, as "Alcalde de primer voto," was president of the Cabildo. "And he who has Buenos Aires has everything; but Buenos Aires is not to be swallowed in one mouthful."

"Last year," said Liniers, starting to his feet, "Beresford took our city by surprise, but he had not everything. In one month our city became a trap, in which we caught him like a wild beast in a net. Now we are ready, and have an army; I for my part wish only one thing, that they may make up their minds to advance from Ensenada upon the city, and so give me a chance of meeting them in the open field. The first army that Buenos Aires has ever raised shall hurl the haughty English back again to their ships in disgrace."

"I do not know whether it will be easy to drive the English back to their ships, but we must defend the city to the last extremity," said Don Martin Alzaga.

"I am quite of your opinion, Don Martin," said Don Gregorio; "but I am sorry to say that I cannot consider the army able to meet the English in the open field. Therefore with all due deference to the greater experience of the illustrious Señor Reconquistador, I beg to submit to you whether it would not be better to turn our attention solely to the defence of the city. The flat roofs of our houses, and the barred windows, make each block a separate fortress; by cut-

ting ditches across the ends of the streets we can in a very few days
surround the city with a continuous line of fortifications, we can call
upon every man in the city to aid in the defence of these lines, and
can direct the whole strength of the troops at once upon the point
which may be most seriously menaced. The chief advantage which
the English have over us is their superior discipline, which will avail
them little in the narrow streets of the suburbs."

At this most of the assembly looked grave ; such a step seemed to
them an admission of weakness, and there was a general murmur of
dissent as Don Gregorio resumed his seat. General Liniers glanced
rapidly round the room, and then with a smile on his face rose to
reply.

"Permit me, Señor Don Gregorio," said he, "to congratulate you
upon the knowledge you have so unexpectedly shown on military
matters, but I do not at all agree with you. So long as I retain the
command in chief I do not intend to let the English approach within
cannon-shot of the city ; if I fall there will be time enough to dig
ditches and fortify the azoteas, in which case, Señores, you know now
where you may find my successor."

"Señores," said Don Gregorio, very calmly, "I make no pretence
to any knowledge of military affairs, but the words I have spoken have
not been spoken unadvisedly. The Señor Evaña has to some extent
studied the science of war. He has surveyed the city, and has drawn
up a plan of defence, which I have with me now. In his letter to me
he adds in a postscript, 'If you still determine on resistance remember
the plan I gave you, that is your only chance.' Now, Señores, I appeal
to you. Why not——"

Here the speaker was interrupted by the entrance of a young officer.

"A chasque from Quilmes for the Señor General," he said.

"Admit him," said Liniers.

The officer stepped back and ushered into the room a slight-built
man of a clear yellowish complexion, with long black hair which
flowed down over his shoulders. He wore a striped poncho, which
covered him completely down to his knees, below which appeared his
boots, each made of the skin from the hind leg of a colt, a boot which
had no seam in it, and was waterproof except where the great toe projected for the purpose of holding the stirrup. He held his hat in his
hand, and as he came forward his huge iron spurs clanked at each step
he took.

"I seek the Señor General Liniers," said he, looking round him
with the greatest nonchalance, and tossing his poncho on to his
shoulder to free his arm as he drew a letter from a pocket in the tira-
dor which he wore round his waist.

"I am he," said General Liniers.

"A letter from the Señor Colonel Lopez."

"You can retire," said Liniers, as he took the letter, "but remain
at hand, I may want you."

Liniers returned to his seat, and did not open the letter until the
man had retired.

"Señores, with your permission," said he, as soon as the door was
closed ; then breaking the seal he opened the letter. As he read it

his face flushed with a proud joy, then rising to his feet he looked steadily at each of the watching faces before him.

"Señores, they come," he said; then as no one answered, each waiting breathlessly for his next word, he continued, "and we, we are ready; I shall at once give orders that the alarm-guns be fired, and then each man to his post. Wait till I have given the order, and then I will read you the letter."

In five minutes an aide-de-camp was walking rapidly across the Plaza Mayor with an order to the commandant of artillery stationed in the fort from the commander-in-chief, and Liniers, taking up the letter from Colonel Lopez, read as follows :—

"La Reduction de Quilmes,
" 1 de Julio 1807,
"à las 7 de la mañana.
"A su Excelencia,
" El General Don Santiago Liniers,
" Excelentissimo Señor.

"As I had the honour to advise Y. E. in my despatches of the 27th June and of each day following, the enemy's fleet anchored near to the Ensenada de Barragan on the 27th, and on the following day landed a large force about half a league to the northward of that town. For two days I have watched them as closely as was consistent with the safety of my men, and have had several skirmishes with their foraging parties and advanced posts without being able with my cavalry to make any considerable impression upon them. As far as I can estimate they appear to be from ten to twelve thousand men perfectly equipped, and with a large park of artillery, but they have no cavalry, or very few. Their entire force is now clear of the swamps, and is echelloned on the high road between this and the Ensenada. Of their intention there can be no longer any doubt; they are this morning marching straight upon the Puente Galves; their advanced-guard is already within a league of this.

"I shall continue myself with my cavalry in observation of their movements, but have despatched the infantry corps under the command of Captain Ponce de Leon to occupy the Puente Galves. Doubtless this officer has already reported himself to Y. E.

"The advanced guard of the enemy, which marches more'than a league in advance of the main body, consists apparently of about 3000 men with four guns.

"I shall this evening concentrate my forces and encamp in the neighbourhood of the Puente Galves, where I shall await orders from Y. E.

"God keep your Excellency many years,
"S. S.,
"Gregorio Lopez, hijo."

"Señores," said Liniers, as he finished reading, "I shall put my-self at the head of the troops and march at once against the invader. I shall do my duty, I feel sure my troops will do theirs; I shall return victorious, or you will never see me again. Meantime I leave to you the care of the city, and trust that you will attend with the utmost speed to any requisition for supplies that I may make upon you."

"Señores," said Don Martin Alzaga, "we are grateful to the illustrious soldier who has just spoken for the confidence he has placed in us. To show our appreciation of his trust, and our determination to aid him to the utmost of our ability, I propose that this Cabildo declare itself in permanent session so long as the danger lasts, and that we devote our time exclusively to such measures as may be requisite for the public safety."

" Agreed! agreed!" shouted the various members, rising from their seats.

The words had hardly passed their lips ere the roar of a heavy gun from the fort shook the windows of the room, and drowned the sound of their voices. They paused, looking at one another, till another heavy gun, and then another, spoke to the startled city, telling the news that they had just received, that the foe was at hand. Then crowding round Liniers, each man shook him by the hand, wishing him God speed. So the Reconquistador went forth from them in proud confidence, to win fresh laurels or a hero's grave.

Scarcely had the echoing voices of the alarm-guns ceased to reverberate in the long, narrow streets of the city, than from every tower in every church there sprang the clanging sound of bells. No peaceful voice was that of these bells calling worshippers to prayer, it was the fierce, rapid clang of alarm calling upon men to hurry forth to battle and to slaughter. Through all the city, into every home and household, rushed this voice of terror, surprising the tradesman at his desk, the artizan at his bench or forge, the student at his books, and the man of wealth amid the luxuries of a life of ease. To all, the roar of the guns and the clangour of the bells spoke one message— ¡ "The foe is at our gates; arm, and go forth to meet him."

The summons, though startling, was expected. Each man left at once his occupation, whatever it might be; the shops were closed, the bench and forge were deserted, the books were cast aside, and the man of no occupation found one which might perchance last him for his life-course yet to run.

Everything had been prepared for this moment; each company of the militia had its own point of rendezvous, each regiment had its head-quarters, what each man had to do was to arm and proceed at once to his station. There was hurry and bustle throughout the city, the usually quiet streets were thronged with groups of armed men pressing eagerly onwards, mothers kissed their sons with tearful eyes, wives strained husbands to their bosoms in one last embrace, but there was no faltering or hanging back. Buenos Aires felt herself strong, and grudged not the blood of her best and dearest in the most righteous of all causes, the defence of home and fatherland, for Buenos Aires was a child as yet, and her childhood was heroic.

Each company of militia as it collected marched off to the regimental head-quarters; the regiments concentrated in the Plaza de Los Perdices, where General Liniers received them, having with him already a strong force of regular troops, comprising almost the entire garrison of the city.

To each regiment was allotted its place in the line of battle, the Patricios claiming as their right the post of honour, at the head of the column on the march, on the right flank in action. About an hour before sundown the whole force was marshalled in order, and marched away through the city and out by the wide, sandy road which led to the Puente Galvés, now the Barraca bridge.

Men, women, and children crowded in the streets through which they passed, gazing upon them in silence, broken only by words of farewell as some well-known face passed by amid all the pomp of military display. Many a tearful eye watched them, many a heart throbbed wildly, but as the eyes looked along those serried files, and glanced at the apparently interminable lines of bayonets, the hearts swelled with confidence. Buenos Aires trusted proudly in the champions to whom she had confided her honour and her defence.

CHAPTER VII.

THE BAPTISM OF FIRE.

DREARILY passed the night of the 1st July with the citizen soldiers of Buenos Aires and their Spanish brethren in arms, who to the number of about 8000, with fifty guns, under the command of General Don Santiago Liniers, the Reconquistador, the hero of the 12th August, had crossed the Riachuelo by the Puente Galvès after nightfall, and had encamped in the open country beyond, there to await the advance of the English upon the city. Tents they had none, baggage little more than each man could carry for himself, and their commissariat was of the most limited extent. The mounted auxiliaries from the campaña, many of whom had arrived at the general rendezvous, had driven herds of beeves before them; many of these beeves were slaughtered, abundant rations of raw meat were served out to the hungry soldiery, but for the cooking of it each man had to trust to his own devices. The hardy horsemen of the campaña were accustomed to such emergencies, they threw slices of the meat into the ashes of their bivouac fires; when the outside of the meat was burned to a cinder they considered it cooked, and devoured it half raw. But the more delicately-nurtured citizens of Buenos Aires could not eat the tough meat with such cookery; some of them had been provident enough to carry small supplies with them, but the majority were dependent upon the ration beef, and suffered accordingly.

Some two hours before midnight a mounted officer, covered from neck to heels in a long cloak, rode through the encampment enquiring for the bivouac of the Patricios, and more particularly for Captain Lorea of that regiment. Captain Lorea, his brother-in-law Don Felipe Navarro, and several other officers were grouped round a fire, talking together in low tones and puffing wreaths of blue smoke into the chilly night air from under the wide brims of their hats.

"Felices noches, Señores," said the horseman, drawing rein beside them.

"Ah! Don Marcelino," said Captain Lorea, starting to his feet; "welcome! Dismount, and tell us what you have seen of these invaders. I hardly thought to see you till to-morrow."

"'To-morrow we shall have plenty to do," replied Don Marcelino Ponce de Leon, dismounting; "so I have come to talk to you now, and to ask you what preparations are making in the city. I have been encamped here for two days, but know nothing of what has been done."

"This will not be new to you," said Don Felipe Navarro, as they shook hands.

"Oh no! Among you city men I feel like an old campaigner. You have much to learn yet, from what I could see as I came along. I fear some of your men will not be in very good fighting trim to-morrow."

"To-morrow is another day," said Lorea. "We shall pass the night badly, but it will pass."

Marcelino then gave them a detailed account of the events of the 27th and 28th June.

"My uncle," he added, "is encamped with part of his cavalry between this and Quilmes, a chasque has just come in from him. He says that the English have already marched a strong vanguard in this direction, but he believes that the main body is yet beyond Quilmes."

"So much the better," said Lorea. "We will beat their vanguard to-morrow and there will be so many the less to fight the day after."

"And what of the city? Have any preparations been made to resist an assault?"

"An assault! There is time enough to think about that. To-day, at a meeting of the Cabildo, your grandfather proposed that the city should be entrenched, and that we should let the English attack us there. Fortunately the Reconquistador was there. Here in the open camp, in face of the enemy, is the proper place for the defenders of the city."

"In any way," said Marcelino, looking gloomily at the fire, "this is not our proper position, with a river and a narrow bridge behind us. We ought to be on the other side the Riachuelo to defend the bridge and the passes higher up."

"Oh!" said Felipe Navarro impatiently, "the Reconquistador knows what he does."

"Don Gregorio had a plan," said Lorea. "According to him our city is much stronger than Monte Video, just because it has no walls."

"I have seen that plan," replied Marcelino, "and I believe that if it were adopted the English could never take our city by assault, every street is a new line of defence. The man who drew out that plan——"

"Your friend Evaña," said Lorea scornfully. "All that he does is well done in the eyes of a Ponce de Leon, and there is no Ponce de Leon among you who is not worth three of him! Bah! we will speak no more of it. How did your negroes stand the march?"

"For them it was nothing. I left them singing round their fires after a good supper; come and see them. I can give you a good cup of coffee to warm you up for the night."

The negro corps, which was known as "Los Morenos de Ponce," was encamped near to the Puente Galvès, almost in the centre of the position occupied by the army; sentries paced to and fro between the watch-fires; round each fire groups of men lay wrapped in their thick ponchos, sleeping soundly; beside each fire stood a row of camp-kettles filled with soup for the early breakfast on the morrow.

At one fire sat Lieutenant Asneiros on a three-legged stool, beside him knelt a tall negro who was feeding the fire, and watching a kettle of water which stood on the embers. Giving his horse in charge to the negro, Marcelino introduced his friends to the lieutenant.

"Here you are quiet enough," said one of the officers of the Patricios; "the rest of the army is too enthusiastic to care much for sleep."

"They know nothing," said the lieutenant. "Good food and sleep are the necessary preparation for hard work."

"For my part," said Don Isidro Lorea, "I rejoice to see the men so joyful. I feel no inclination to sleep, and am only anxious for the moment when I can give the word to fire on the invaders."

"You will give it without doubt to-morrow," replied the lieutenant. "I hope to God that firing may be all we have to do."

"And what more would you have?" asked Don Felipe Navarro.

As the lieutenant only shrugged his shoulders contemptuously at this question, Marcelino answered for him—

"Any man can fire off a musket, but only a trained soldier can manœuvre in face of the enemy."

"What matters it?" said Asneiros; "what will be, will be."

After this they sat or lay on the ground round the fire till midnight, talking cheerfully together of the loved ones whom they had left behind them in the city, sipping coffee which was served to them by the tall negro (who was Marcelino's favourite servant, Manuel), scenting the damp night air with the perfume of their cigars, and occasionally singing snatches of song. When his guests left him, Marcelino wrapped himself in his cloak, threw himself down under a low hedge on a heap of twigs and leaves which Manuel had prepared for his couch, and slept till dawn.

Gaily the trumpets sounded a welcome to the new-born day, the men sprang up with alacrity from their couches on the cold, wet ground, threw fresh fuel on the watch-fires, and crowded round them chafing their hands at the ruddy blaze.

Marcelino, climbing to the top of the hedge under which he had slept, looked eagerly out over the encampment, marked by the blue lines of smoke which hung heavily in the damp air over every watch-fire. The extent of ground it covered made the force collected appear much greater than it really was, and the heart of the young soldier swelled within him with pride and a fierce joy as he looked upon this evidence of the power of his native city.

A fresh flourish of trumpets saluted the rising sun, and then the whole force stood to arms, each regiment in its own encampment, while the aides of General Liniers galloped wildly about, for an immediate movement was in contemplation. The Reconquistador had ridden out at dawn to survey the ground in front of him ; the aides, as they delivered their orders to the commanders of the different regiments, announced that fresh chasques had arrived from Colonel Lopez, that the English vanguard had encamped that night two leagues this side of Quilmes, and must now be close at hand. For an hour there was a great amount of marching and counter-marching, then on a level space of ground intersected by the southern road the whole force was drawn out in line of battle, with guns in the intervals between the different divisions. The extreme right was held by the first regiment of the Patricios, the left by General Balviani's division, and the "Morenos de Ponce" were stationed near the centre of the line. In front of them groups of horsemen were dotted over the plain, while far away on the great southern road was seen a dense column of infantry marching steadily towards them, their scarlet uniforms contrasting vividly in the bright sunshine with the dark verdure of the surrounding pasture-land. This was the British vanguard, under the command of Major-general Levison Gower, numbering some 2000 bayonets.

General Liniers, attended by his whole suite, rode along the line from right to left. Confidence and exultation beamed in his face, and with many a cheerful word he complimented the commanders of the various regiments as he rode by upon the martial appearance of their men. Each regiment presented arms as he passed it, but the negro corps alone received him with shouts of welcome, shouts which were sternly silenced by Lieutenant Asneiros, as subversive of discipline. Marcelino sat on horseback in front of his men, the Reconquistador drew rein beside him.

"What say you?" said he. "These friends of ours arrive late to the dance. Think you that they will force their way through us and gain the bridge?"

"That is more than they can do," replied Marcelino.

"Just so, but they will try it, probably by an attack on my right flank. Your negroes march well; when the action commences I shall send orders to you to make a circuit beyond yon clump of poplars and fall upon their rear. Balviani will support you, but will advance by the road; the success of the movement will depend upon your speed."

"Your trust shall not be thrown away, general," replied Marcelino, dropping the point of his sword as the general rode on; then looking round he scanned the dark, eager faces of his men as they watched the movements of the foe, and he knew that they would not fail him, but would follow him where he led, even into the thickest of that forest of glittering steel.

General Liniers had hardly completed the inspection of his forces, and the British were yet more than half a league distant, when Marcelino saw them halt. They had reached the crest of a lomada, from which the ground sloped gently towards the position occupied by the army of Buenos Aires, and which stretched away westwards as far as eye could reach, running nearly parallel to the course of the Riachuelo. On resuming the march, the hostile column left the high road and turned off westwards, following the course of this lomada.

Liniers, fearing to be taken in flank, immediately commenced a corresponding movement to his right. Both armies thus marched parallel to each other, retaining much their former relative position, but hidden from each other by the rising ground and by the various chacras and plantations which lay scattered about.

The British, marching on the high ground, met with few obstacles to their progress, while the Buenos Airean army had to force its way through swamps and the many water-courses which intersected the low-lying grounds between the lomada and the Riachuelo. Through these swamps the men waded knee-deep in mud; in the water-courses

many of them sank up to their elbows, wetting their ammunition.
After more than a league of this toilsome marching they reached
firmer ground, where the lomada approached nearer to the course of
the river; here they found that the British had again halted behind the
crest of the lomada. Again Liniers drew up his array, and the citizen
soldiers forgot the sufferings of the rapid march and the cold which
pierced them to the bones in their eagerness to close at once with
the foe.

The British screened their movements by the rising ground, but the
gleam of bayonets to the right of their position showed that some
manœuvre was in preparation. Then skirmishers in the dark-green
uniform of the rifles moved rapidly forward on the high ground. An
aide-de-camp from General Liniers came at headlong speed to the left
centre, where stood the "Morenos de Ponce." He delivered an order
to the commandant of that corps. Marcelino, wheeling his horse, addressed a few words to his men, then, waving his sword, the negroes
with a loud shout rushed forward, and, breaking into skirmishing
order, ran swiftly up the slope. The British rifles received them with
a spattering fire, then hurriedly retreated to the crest of the lomada,
and formed in line. A few notes on the bugle and Marcelino had his
men all again together, and, telling them to reserve their fire, led them
on. The dark line of soldiery gave way before them and marched
rapidly off. The negroes broke their ranks and rushed after them
with loud yells.

On the crest of the rising ground Marcelino drew rein, and ——
Where was the British army? Half stupefied, he gazed over the vacant
plain before him. All of the enemy that he could see was this small
body of light-armed riflemen, who were in rapid retreat, pursued by
his own negroes.

"Marcelino! They have gone! They have gone!"

"Evaristo!" exclaimed Marcelino, as he saw his brother, mounted
on his pony, close beside him.

"I told you I would be with you when the fighting came," said the
boy, with a bright smile. "Before day I was up and saddled my pony
and came away. I have watched them all the morning, and I knew
you could not be far off."

"But they? Where are they?"

"They have gone, do not I tell you? There where those quintas
hide the river, the Paso Chico. They have crossed by the pass, and
have marched up the road straight away for town."

"There, Evaristo, over there," said Marcelino, pointing towards the
hollow where the army of Buenos Aires was waiting, drawn up in
battle-array, for the foe who had escaped them; "gallop as hard as
you can to General Liniers and tell him that. Tell him that I have
gone in pursuit."

As Evaristo galloped off, Marcelino put spurs to his horse, and,
rejoining his negroes, urged them on; but, rapidly as they marched,
the British riflemen, who had nothing more than their rifles and cartridge-boxes to carry, out-paced them, and had crossed the pass ere
Marcelino and his negroes reached the river.

Evaristo was not the first to announce to General Liniers the eva-

sion of the English vanguard. Colonel Lopez had also watched
them all the morning, hovering on their flanks and rear, but not venturing to molest them. When he saw them march from their second
position straight for the Paso Chico, he sent off an officer at once to
the general with the intelligence, and putting himself at the head of
such of his cavalry as he could collect around him he drew them up
across the road leading to the pass. One British regiment deployed,
poured in a volley, charged, and drove most of the horsemen pell-
mell across the pass to the other side, dispersing the rest in all directions. Again collecting some of his scattered troops, Colonel Lopez
endeavoured to cut off the retreat of the detachment which had remained on the lomada. But the ground favoured the light-armed
infantry. Instead of following in the track of the main body, they
made at once for a quinta which lay between them and the river, and
bursting through the fences, which were impracticable for cavalry,
reached the pass, and crossed without the loss of one man. The
colonel then led his troopers to the road at a gallop, but on reaching
the river was met by a volley of grape from two field-pieces in position on the far bank. Many of his men fell. He drew back to the
shelter of the poplars which formed the quinta fence, and awaited the
arrival of his nephew.

Marcelino, dismounting when he reached the quinta, led his men
on foot to the edge of the river, just in time to witness the repulse of
the cavalry. The owner of the quinta had a boat moored to a post
about a square down the stream, hidden from sight of the pass by a
bend in the river and the trees of another quinta on the left bank.
Enjoining the strictest silence, Marcelino marched his men with trailed
arms through the quinta to beyond the bend, rapidly passed them
across the river, and took possession of the other quinta without being
perceived by the enemy, who first knew of his whereabouts as from
the shelter of the trees he opened a heavy fire upon the artillerymen
and the light infantry who had halted close at hand. Colonel Lopez,
who had been informed by him of his intention, and who had meantime been reinforced by several squads of cavalry, once more emerged
into the main road, and, at the head of a yelling mob of horsemen,
dashed through the pass. For a moment the capture of the guns
appeared inevitable; the artillerymen defended themselves desperately,
but were completely surrounded by the furious horsemen.

Colonel Lopez, however, by his eagerness to capture the guns,
blocked up the head of the pass, and prevented the passage of half of
his troops, and the riflemen, who were screened by the horsemen from
the fire of the negro corps, rushed upon the disordered mass with
levelled bayonets, forced many of them into the river, and drove the
rest back upon the quinta. The negroes, who were advancing from
the shelter of the trees to the assistance of the horsemen, were thrown
into great disorder by the fugitives, and before Marcelino and Asneiros
could re-form their broken ranks and draw them clear they were
attacked in flank by an entire regiment of light infantry, which was
sent at the double by General Gower to the support of the rifles.

The bulk of the British vanguard had halted about a quarter of a
mile from the pass to rest the troops after their rapid march from the

lomada. General Gower had not perceived the passage of the river
by the negroes, and was taken by surprise at the sudden fire opened
upon his two guns from the quinta. The whole force was immediately
under arms, and one regiment, driving Colonel Lopez and his scattered
horsemen before them, charged upon the right flank of the " Morenos "
at the same moment that the guns opened fire upon them from the
river-side.

" To the quinta, muchachos !" shouted Marcelino.

The negroes faced about and ran for it. Marcelino, catching his
bugler by the arm, followed more slowly, and as soon as the bulk of
them had gained the shelter of the trees the trumpet sounded the
" rally." About half his force obeyed the summons, the rest dispersed
in confusion about the quinta. Despatching Asneiros to collect the
stragglers, Marcelino then spread his men along the fence and again
opened fire upon the English, who replied by one volley, and then
retreated rapidly up the road, taking their guns and wounded with them.

Of the horsemen who had passed the river, hardly any were in sight ;
some had taken refuge in the quinta on foot, many had forced their
horses into the river and had swam across ; of what had become of
his uncle, Marcelino knew nothing for long after.

When Asneiros rejoined him, they paraded the corps once more in
the open and found they had suffered a loss of fifty men in killed,
wounded, and missing.

" We have begun badly," said Marcelino to his lieutenant.

" What would you !" replied Asneiros, shrugging his shoulders.
" Alone we should have done something. But with these others
——Bah !"

CHAPTER VIII.

LOS CORRALES DE LA MISERERE.

ON receiving intelligence of the passage of the Riachuelo by the invaders at the Paso Chico, from which a good road led to the Puente Galvès, General Liniers at once counter-marched to his former position and occupied the bridge, having previously sent off an aide-de-camp with instructions to the Comandante de los Morenos to rejoin him there with all possible speed.

Marcelino left Asneiros to bring on the negroes by the road on the left bank of the river, and galloped off himself at once to confer with the general. He informed him that the English had apparently given up all idea of attacking the bridge, and had marched away by a road which led from the Paso Chico to the Corrales de la Miserere.

General Liniers became alarmed for the safety of the city, and leaving General Balviani's division to hold the Puente Galvès, marched back at once with the rest of his troops, pressing on as fast as the wearied state of the men would permit. The citizen soldiers, and not less so the Spanish regulars, unused to long marches, were fatigued by their unwonted exertions, and dispirited by the unexpected manœuvres of the enemy; they plodded along the muddy road in silence, hundreds of them sank down by the wayside unable to proceed further, and many of the guns, sticking fast in a deep "pantano," were abandoned. On reaching the suburbs of the city they wheeled to the left, and late in the afternoon drew near to the Plaza Miserere. The Patricios, who had some guns with them, followed by the "Morenos de Ponce," had considerably outmarched the rest of the army, and at once took up a position to the east of this Plaza, so as to defend all the western entrances to the city, the negro corps being posted at the south-east corner of the Plaza in a small quinta surrounded by an aloe hedge, in which there were many gaps.

Meantime the British vanguard, which marched upon the city by a more circuitous and much worse road than that by which General Liniers had retreated, had also encountered great difficulties. The river at the Paso Chico was more than waist-deep, through this the men had waded, carrying their cartridge-boxes and the ammunition for the guns upon their shoulders. The 88th regiment, which formed a part of this division, had been for nine months on board ship, so that the men were in no condition to undertake a forced march along roads ancle-deep in mud. General Crauford with the 95th regiment and the rifles pressed on in front, but after marching about a league

from the pass General Gower found it was impossible to bring on his
guns any further, and accordingly left them behind him under the
care of General Lumley, with three companies of infantry, and such of
the men from the different regiments as were unable to proceed.

The Plaza Miserere was a wide, open space of ground beyond the
suburbs of the city, and was distant about two-and-a-half miles due
west from the Plaza Mayor. This space was at that time surrounded by
detached quintas, and was a centre from which many roads branched
off in all directions. It was used as a slaughtering ground by the
butchers who supplied the city, and at one side were large corrales
where cattle were penned previous to slaughter. These corrales, being
formed of rough posts strongly bound together by transverse beams
tied to each post by thongs of raw hide, formed an excellent stockade.

In spite of the detachment of a division to hold the Puente Galvès
and the numerous stragglers, Liniers had yet under his orders, when
he reached the Plaza Miserere, more than double the number of men
comprising the entire British vanguard, and spared no exertion to reinspire his troops with confidence; but the greater part of them were
yet entangled in the narrow roads of the suburbs, when the advanced
guard of the invaders under the command of General Crauford debouched upon the Plaza from the west, and took possession of the
corrales.

Without waiting for orders from General Liniers, the artillery
attached to the Patricios, and some other pieces which had been
planted among the quintas on the south side the Plaza, at once opened
a heavy but ill-directed fire of grape and round shot upon the head of
the British column, and the Patricios advancing from the suburbs
upon the open ground also commenced firing.

The sound of the musketry operated with a magical effect upon the
entire force, the men shouted to be led at once against the enemy,
and Liniers gave the order for a general advance.

From every road on the south side the Plaza dense columns of
troops poured into the open space, replying to the slow fire of the
British by rapid volleys of musketry. General Gower had drawn
back his left wing upon the advance of the Patricios, then as General
Liniers in person headed an attack upon the corrales, two regiments
poured in a volley, and led by General Crauford charged the Patricios
with the bayonet, driving them in headlong confusion back into the
western suburbs. The advance of General Liniers had been checked
by a heavy fire from the corrales; he was now charged by the entire
British force, in front and on the right flank. Liniers galloped to
and fro frantically calling upon his men to keep their ranks; but all
was in vain, retreat was impossible, the roads were blocked up by the
rear-guards of the several columns. Many of the men threw down
their arms and fled to the nearest quintas, the destruction of the entire
force seemed inevitable, when Marcelino Ponce de Leon, who had received no orders, conceived it his duty to act without them.

The two regiments which had dispersed the Patricios were in front
of him, advancing with levelled bayonets upon the flank of the main
body. Shouting to his men to follow him, he dashed through the
quinta fence, then forming them hurriedly he opened fire upon the

flank of the advancing British. The two regiments halted, wheeled, poured in a volley at close quarters, and charged. Marcelino's horse fell under him, the negroes set up a shout of dismay; their ranks were shattered, their leader was apparently killed, down on them bore swiftly along a line of glittering steel, threatening to envelope them on both flanks, they turned and fled. In vain Asneiros struck at them with his sword, in vain Evaristo, who had rejoined his brother at the Paso Chico, threw himself in their way, shouting—

"Morenos! cowards! will you leave my brother to be killed by these English?"

They were panic-struck, and fought fiercely with each other for the gaps in the fence which would admit them to the shelter of the quinta. Asneiros, calling two subalterns to aid him, seized the largest of these gaps, and the three with their swords kept back a number of the fugitives.

Meantime Marcelino had sprung to his feet, half dazed but unwounded; the English were close upon him, for a moment he stared wildly round him, then Evaristo galloped up to him.

"Mount behind me, Marcelino," he shouted, shaking his left foot from the stirrup.

The next minute the pony with a double load was galloping away for the quinta, where Evaristo sprang to the ground and Marcelino, galloping after the fugitives, succeeded in rallying some threescore men, whom he led back to the fence and joined to those whom Asneiros had stopped and had already drawn up under shelter of the aloe hedge. The English had halted, and were apparently about to renew their attack upon General Liniers, when the negroes opened fire upon them from the hedge. With a loud cheer 800 red and green-coated soldiery rushed upon the frail barrier which hid the remnant of the "Morenos de Ponce," burst a way for themselves through it, or ran in by the undefended gaps. There was a minute of wild confusion, the negroes firing at random upon an enemy who outnumbered them five to one, and who attacked them from all sides. Marcelino, now on foot, and his officers tried to draw them away from the hedge, and to fall back upon some outhouses in the rear of the quinta, but the movements of the English were too rapid, the retreat soon changed into headlong flight; about forty of the negroes, being cut off and surrounded, threw down their arms and were made prisoners. At the far side of the quinta, Marcelino made another attempt to rally his men, but was at once charged by a party of the enemy.

"Surrender!" shouted the officer who led them.

Marcelino had lost his sword when his horse was killed under him, he stooped and seized the musket of a negro who had fallen at his feet mortally wounded, and beating aside the bayonets of those nearest to him, tried to force his way through them; the next moment he was beaten down by the butt-ends of their muskets and trampled under their feet as they rushed on in pursuit.

When Marcelino had rallied his men in the quinta, he had called his brother to him, and telling him to remount his pony, had given him into the care of his servant Manuel, telling the latter to go off with him at once straight for the city. The negro took the pony by the bridle and led him away, but on reaching the cross-road behind the quinta by an open gateway, Evaristo refused to go any further, and drawing tight his rein sat there in the saddle watching the last struggle of the " Morenos de Ponce."

" Vamos !" said Manuel, as the fugitive negroes came running past them.

" No ! no !" said Evaristo, still tightly holding his pony by the head. " Oh ! my brother, even yet I can save you !" he cried, as he saw Marcelino's last desperate effort, then twitching the rein from Manuel's hand, he urged his pony back through the gateway, and was close to his brother when he fell, trampled to the earth under the feet of the furious soldiery. But Manuel on foot had kept pace with him, and now springing up behind him wrenched the reins from him, and holding him fast in his arms, turned the pony's head and galloped off, and neither spoke nor slacked his pace until he had reached the house of Don Gregorio Lopez, where he set the boy down, half dead with sorrow and excitement, and went back himself in search of his master, whom he had small hope of ever seeing again alive.

The " Morenos de Ponce " were utterly routed and dispersed ; Marcelino had sacrificed himself and his men, but he had saved the army of General Liniers from destruction. A deadly fire from the Corrales de la Miserere had checked the advance of the main body of the army, the charge of the British infantry had driven it back in hopeless confusion into the roads by which it had debouched upon the Plaza ; had the flank movement of the two regiments under General Crauford been uninterrupted, the retreat of the greater part of the army would have been cut off. As it was, General Liniers lost eleven guns, and was driven from amongst the quintas into the open camp, far away to the left of the road by which he had advanced. Night closed in and prevented further pursuit by the victorious enemy. Almost broken-hearted by the misfortune which had befallen him, and desperate at the ruin of all his high hopes, the Reconquistador threw himself upon the ground and for hours spoke to no one. About 1000 men lay round him in every attitude of exhaustion and despair ; of the rest of his army he knew nothing, it was dispersed in all directions.

The army to which Buenos Aires had entrusted her honour and her defence had melted away at the first brush with the enemy. Buenos Aires had no longer an army and the enemy was at her gates.

CHAPTER IX.

THE NIGHT OF SORROW.

ALL day the city had been in a state of nervous anxiety, all manner of conflicting rumours were current, every horseman who appeared in the streets was beset by a crowd of eager questioners, men ran to and fro and went from house to house, gleaning what intelligence they could. According to some General Liniers had marched from the Puente Galvès at dawn in search of the enemy, according to others he was yet encamped there and beset by the entire English army. As either hope or fear gained the ascendant, so each man spoke as his hopes or his fears prompted him.

Thus the day wore on; occasionally there was heard the far-off rattling of musketry or the dull boom of a distant gun, but nothing certain was known. Then in the eventide it spread about that the enemy had passed the Riachuelo and was marching upon the city, from the church towers their red-coated soldiery could be seen manœuvring on the open ground of the Plaza Miserere. But where was General Liniers? where were the citizen soldiers who had marched out so proudly to drive those English into the sea? The anxiety of the city became consternation.

Then from the west and near at hand there came again the rattling sound of musketry, interspersed with the frequent booming of the guns. The sound came in gusts, fitfully, now dying away into a feeble treble, the spattering fire of skirmishers anon swelling to a full chord, the regular volley-firing of drilled troops accompanied with the deep bass of the cannon. About half an hour the firing lasted, dying gradually away as the shades of night fell upon the anxious city. What had happened? Men hurried about no longer, seeking news, each sat in his own place, waiting for the news which would surely come.

After night-fall terror-stricken fugitives hurried through the streets, each seeking his own home, each telling his own tale of defeat and ruinous disaster. Then the anxiety of the city, which had become consternation, became despair.

From every household arose the voice of sorrow and of lamentation. Mothers embraced their sons, wives clasped husbands to their bosoms, welcoming them back from deadly peril, but they welcomed them back with tears, and as they listened to their tale a cry of sorrow burst from them, and there was loud wailing over the shame and disgrace which

had fallen upon their native city. And there were households to
which none returned, there were mothers who watched and waited for
sons whom they were never more to see, there were wives who listened
with painful eagerness for a well-known footstep which would never
more fall upon their ears, and who, though they knew it not, were
already widows. Throughout the great straggling city there was
mourning and desolation. And the city was in darkness, and darkness, if it be not rest, is sorrow and despair.

Then up rose Don Martin Alzaga from his seat at the council-table ;
Don Martin Alzaga, president of the Cabildo, of that body which had
now the destinies of the city in its hands. Don Martin had listened
in stern silence to the various reports brought in by members of the
Cabildo who had been abroad in the city in search of news. Of
Liniers himself no one knew anything, but of the fate of his army
there could be no question, it had been shamefully beaten and dispersed by what was, from all accounts, only a detachment of the
invading force ; it was no longer an army, Buenos Aires lay defenceless
before her victorious enemy. Buenos Aires lay defenceless, yet,
though she knew it not, in her defenceless condition lay her chiefest
strength. The overthrow over which she mourned awakened the
heroism innate in the Iberian race, and at the same time inspired the
British generals with an overweening confidence, sure prelude of
disaster.

From the days of Cortes and Pizarro to the present, the Iberian
race has ever shown itself greatest in misfortune. In prosperity cruel,
arrogant, and blind, the Spanish people have, when overwhelmed by
disaster, ever shown a capacity for endurance and a fertility of resource
such as has rarely been displayed by any other. When misfortunes
have fallen upon them, such as would crush other peoples to the dust,
then it is that they first put out their strength and rise superior to all
disaster. The secret of it lies partly in national character, but more
still in this fact, that the strength of Spain lies, not in her great men
and her nobles, but in her people. When Spain was the head of a
mighty empire, her nobles were new men sprung from the great body
of the people, who had carved out their fortunes by their swords ;
their valour and their skill gave Spain the empire over two worlds ;
these men were the representative men of the Spanish people. Since
then, the ruling class in Spain had been gradually and systematically
raised above the people, and separated from them. The people were
taught submission, and learned to see others rule over them till they
lost all care or interest in the aims and objects of their rulers.

At the commencement of the war of succession the Archduke
Charles and his English allies overran nearly the whole of Spain and
took possession of the capital. So again, at an epoch later than this
of which we treat, the armies of Napoleon marched from the
Pyrenees to Cadiz in one unbroken series of triumphs. The great
men of Spain, as imbecile as they were arrogant, invited by their
ignorance the destruction which fell upon them ; the soldiers of Spain,
who were recruited from the people, cared not to shed their blood for
rulers they despised, they fled, hardly waiting for the enemy to attack
them. Then in each case, when all was lost, the Spanish people rose

in their strength and cast out the foreign rulers set over them by foreign force.

Buenos Aires, a colony of Spain, has inherited two of the chief characteristics of the mother-country, pride and heroism. As though they were Spaniards, her native leaders have often shown themselves too proud to learn, and have thus brought disaster upon their country ; when the disaster has come, they have ever met it with the heroism of the Iberian race.

Don Martin Alzaga was a true son of Spain, he had supported Liniers in his rash determination to face the veteran troops of England with his militia and half-drilled levies, he had scoffed at the idea of taking any further measures for defence ; the blow had now fallen, Buenos Aires lay at the mercy of her enemy. All evening Don Martin had sat in his chair, listening in silence to the long chronicle of disaster ; as each said his say and sat down, his spirits rose within him, and in his brain he revolved rapidly all that had been before said concerning the defence of the city. If Buenos Aires must fall, then let the enemy have nothing more than ruins over which to triumph.

Such were the thoughts of Don Martin Alzaga as he rose from his chair at the head of the council-table and spoke as follows :—

"Señores, a great disaster has befallen us. Our army is destroyed, we know not what has become of our general-in-chief, the illustrious Señor Don Santiago Liniers ; in his absence the responsibility falls upon us. There is now no time for vacillation, we must look our danger straight in the face, and, if it please God, we shall yet find a way for our deliverance. We have now no army, but the dispersed soldiers are flocking back to the city ; we have yet guns, muskets, and men, why then should we despair? I look upon many a downcast face, I have heard from many of you words of sorrow, as though hope were gone from us ; from what you relate, the whole city is given over to lamentation. True it is that we have suffered a great disaster, but shall one blow suffice to subdue us? Are we not Spaniards? Is not this Buenos Aires of ours the first city on the great South American continent? Are we not the same men who not a year ago forced an entire English army to capitulate, although they were established in our citadel and had taken our city from us? Let us cast aside this depression and this unmanly sorrow, and join heart and hand together in the great work which it has fallen upon us to perform. Let us show ourselves worthy of the trust which the illustrious Reconquistador placed in us when he marched only yesterday against the foe. Let us rouse the citizens from the stupor of despair into which they have fallen, let us reunite our dispersed soldiery, and to-morrow again show a firm front to the arrogant enemy who assails us. To-morrow this enemy, exultant with his transient success, will doubtless summon us to surrender our city ; I, as the chief of this Cabildo, will receive this summons and shall return it with disdain, without waiting to know what terms he may offer ; never shall any treaty for the surrender of our city bear the signature of Martin Alzaga.

"What say you, Señores? Will you show yourselves worthy to be rulers of Buenos Aires? Will you aid me to vindicate the outraged honour of our country?"

Don Martin paused and looked proudly round him, the faces of his hearers, no longer downcast, reflected his own enthusiasm, each eye sought his, brilliant with hope. Springing to their feet they crowded round him, assuring him that they were all of one mind, and that mind was to lay the city in ruins rather than surrender.

"Señores," said Don Gregorio Lopez, "we will entrench the city and defend it block by block against the invaders. Old as I am I encharge myself with the defence of my own quarter."

"Yet you have your plan, Don Gregorio!" said Don Martin Alzaga gaily. "I believe it comes now very much to the point."

"The plan of my young friend Evaña," replied Don Gregorio.

"Let it be whose it may, we will study it together, and we two will decide what can be done with it, but first, Señores, there are other things more urgent. The people are in despair, and night has covered the city with mourning; the first thing we have to do is to raise the spirit of the people. Once that we reinspire them with confidence, we may hope everything from their courage and abnegation, which we all know. Let us disperse the darkness of night with bonfires and illuminations; the sorrow and the shame will give place to enthusiasm."

"Well said," said Don Gregorio Lopez. "The illuminations will also attract the fugitives, who may yet be dispersed about the suburbs. It also appears that General Balviani took no part in the engagement with the English, and is yet encamped at the Puente Galvès with his division; let us send for him at once, and we shall have a nucleus upon which to re-form the stragglers."

No time was lost in discussion, these propositions were at once adopted. Various members of the Cabildo sallied forth to see after the illuminations, and a mounted officer galloped away by the southern road with an order to General Balviani to retire at once upon the city.

Midnight came, the city was one blaze of light. Lights shone from the windows of every house, festoons of lamps hung across many a street; on every open space and at every street corner in the suburbs there blazed huge bonfires, encircling the city with a girdle of flames. The British sentries at the Plaza Miserere looked wonderingly upon these endless lines of fire, and listened anxiously to the rising hum of many thousand voices, which declared the whole city to be astir. That city, since sundown so dark and desolate, so sunken in sorrow and despair, was now a scene of wild excitement and of fierce resolve; men said only one to another, What shall we do? Men sought only for a leader. The defeat of the evening was an affair long past and forgotten; men thought only of the morrow, and of the stern duty which on that morrow they would surely do.

In the midst of all this excitement Balviani's division returned to the city, marching swiftly along the illuminated streets, dragging their guns with them, which guns Balviani had directed to be spiked on receipt of the order from the Cabildo for his immediate return; but to his command the artillerymen paid no heed, harnessing themselves to the guns and dragging them through pantanos and mud, when their wearied cattle dropped with fatigue, while the rain poured down upon them in torrents. Yet in spite of the rain the people crowded round them as they marched along, saluting them with shouts and with many a warm pressure of the hand. Their march more resembled the triumphant entry of a victorious army than the return of the remnant of a beaten one.

Meantime some of the elder members of the Cabildo had been occupied in a careful examination of the plan of the Señor Evaña for the defence of the city. It was improbable that the English would at once attack them, a day at least must elapse before they could bring up their entire force from the Ensenada. But the plan was much too extensive to be carried out in one day, though it was exceedingly simple; they therefore determined upon the adoption of one part of it only: to draw a line including one block of houses all round the two central Plazas; to dig a ditch across the end of every street on this line, throwing up the earth inside, and forming on it a breastwork and a platform for a gun; to garrison strongly all the azoteas on this line, and to station a strong force at each trench. Further, they determined that all the spare arms they possessed should be distributed to such of the citizens as might apply for them for the defence of their own houses, and that all the troops they could spare, after providing sufficiently for the central garrison, should be distributed about the azoteas all round to the distance of ten squares from the Plaza Mayor, and that each block should be placed under the command of some trustworthy officer, with instructions to harass the invaders to the utmost of their power as they advanced towards the centre, but not to attempt to meet them in the streets.

Then a list was made out of the officers to whom was to be entrusted the work of constructing the various trenches, and a second of those who were to command in each block, both within and without the line of entrenchments.

Among these appointments Major Belgrano was entrusted with the construction of two of the defences to the south of the Plaza Mayor. Captain Lorea, with his own company, had charge of the block in which his own house stood, which was considered to be one of the most important outposts; his brother-in-law, Don Felipe Navarro, had command of the block situate to the west of the Church of Santo Domingo; and Don Marcelino Ponce de Leon and his negroes were appointed to the block contiguous to the Church of San Miguel. All these appointments were provisional, for nothing positive was known as yet as to the losses which the army had suffered in the action at the Corrales de la Miserere.

The plan of defence thus adopted was a part only of that sketched out by Don Carlos Evaña, which was modified by the suppression of an exterior line of defence and of sundry details, for the carrying out of which the time was too short. The garrisons of the Retiro and the Residencia, which formed two most important outposts to the north and south of the central Plazas, were to be instructed to defend themselves to the last extremity.

Two hours after sundown on that night of sorrow, Doña Dalmacia Navarro sat alone in her sala, alone and in darkness, save for a lamp which burned dimly in the ante-sala on the writing-table of her husband. So had she sat alone ever since the firing had ceased on the Plaza Miserere, communing anxiously with herself, refusing all attention or sympathy from those who would gladly have shared her anxiety with her, replying only to those who would at times approach her with this one question—

"Yet has no one come?"

And the answer was always, no. Men hurried across the wide, open space before her sala windows and along the adjacent street; eagerly listening, she heard something of the words they spoke as they passed on—these words were ever of disaster, ruin, and despair, and as she listened her heart sank within her. The army was evidently completely beaten; and Isidro and the gallant men he led, she knew them well, they were not the men to fly like frightened boys, they would have withstood the onset of the English even if left alone; and those volleys she had heard, and that roaring of the guns, at whom had they been directed? who had fired them? She shuddered to herself as she thought how she had exulted at the sound, and had pictured to herself hundreds of prostrate foes, stretched in wounds and death on her native soil.

Unable to bear her anxious thoughts in the quiet darkness of her sala, she rose from her seat and went into the ante-sala, drawing her heavy mantle round her with a shiver. She went and sat in her husband's chair, and leaned upon his desk turning over his papers mechanically, scarce knowing what she did. She took up his pen and fondled it in her hands; beside it lay a tinsel pen-wiper, heavily embroidered with beads and gold cord, which she had made for him herself; she bent over it and kissed it, as she had seen him do the day she had given it to him, his saint's day, not two short months ago. Then she looked under the sofa and saw his slippers lying there, and drew them out and laid them beside his chair ready for him when he should come in. Would he ever put them on again? As she asked herself that question a low moan broke from her, she could look at them no longer, she could no longer bear the sight and neighbourhood of all these things which spoke to her of him, and seemed to ask her were they his no more? She left the ante-sala and the dim light, and went back to the darkness of her sala, crouching down on a low chair and burying her face in her hands.

Then there came a footstep and a voice, two voices, both of them she knew. They were safe—her husband and her brother. What mattered defeat and shame, they might be retrieved, but from death there is no return. A wild joy succeeded to her anxious sorrow, she started to her feet; as she reached the folding-doors, her husband stood before her, but oh! so changed. Dripping wet,—for it was raining heavily,—with clothes torn and covered with mud, his face pale and haggard, his eyes deep-sunk in his head; but for his voice she would scarce have known him.

"Isidro!" she exclaimed, opening her arms to him.

But he shrank from her, and, throwing himself upon the sofa, buried his face in the cushions.

"Do not touch me, do not come near me," he said, as she bent over him. "You know not what has happened."

"The English have been too strong for you," said Doña Dalmacia, seating herself beside him, and laying one soft arm on his neck.

" They were few, and we fled from them like sheep, like sheep. We
are disgraced for ever. Never more shall we dare to look them in the
face."

" You are tired ; to-morrow will be another day."

" Ah ! Dalma, if you only knew how they made us march ; all the
blessed day without a morsel to eat and nothing but muddy water to
drink," said Don Isidro, raising himself on his elbow and venturing at
last to look at his wife. What he saw in her face was a tender look of
pity and of sympathy.

" Are you not ashamed of me, Dalma ? " he asked her, with a
brightening eye. " I am a runaway and a coward. Are you not
ashamed of me, Dalma ? "

" You are no coward, Isidro," said Doña Dalmacia, throwing her
arms round his neck ; " you are tired and have eaten nothing ; to-
morrow will be another day."

Don Isidro bowed his head upon her shoulder, and for a minute
there was silence between them.

Don Felipe Navarro, who had come in with his brother-in-law, had
thrown himself wearily into an arm-chair.

" Yes, Dalma, my sister," said he, " to-morrow will be another
day, and we without an army shall have all the invaders upon us.
Those we saw to-day were only the vanguard."

" Without an army," exclaimed Doña Dalmacia, looking round at
him with a fresh terror in her eyes. " Have then so many fallen ?
And the Reconquistador, what has become of him ? "

" Of Liniers I know nothing. We have not many killed, but the
army is dispersed," replied Don Felipe.

" We have no hope now, for there is no confidence," said Don Isidro.
" All the fight was without order ; it may be said that there was no fight.
We were not beaten, we ran away because we did not know what to do."

" So long as it was an affair of shooting," said Don Felipe, " our men
stood well enough, but when they came at us with the bayonet——
Do you know, it is an imposing thing, that charge with the bayonet.
Those English with their smooth faces look like boys, but when they
came at us in a long line close together we felt that they were men.
If we had waited for them the half of our men would have stopped
there for ever."

" Have many stopped there ? " said Doña Dalmacia. " I have heard
heavier firing at a review."

" Of ours we have lost very few," replied Don Isidro. " The corps on
the left, where Liniers was, were all in disorder, and I don't think they
lost many. But I fear me much, Dalma, we have lost a friend."

" Say ! " said Doña Dalmacia, nervously closing one hand upon his
shoulder.

" Los Morenos de Ponce," are almost annihilated."

" Marcelino sacrificed himself and his men to save the others," said
Felipe Navarro.

" It is what one might foretell of him," said Doña Dalmacia, bursting into tears.

" Do not weep, my soul," said Don Isidro. " As yet we know
nothing positive. Felipe and I met some of the negroes after night-

fall, and went back with them to the quinta from which they were
driven. There were many dead lying about, and we carried off a
great many wounded; every house about there is an hospital. We
searched where they said he had fallen—we found the bodies of three
negroes, but of him we could find nothing."

"Always we will hope," said the brave lady, rising and wiping away
her tears. "To-morrow will be another day."

Just then there came a knock at the outer door, and a loud voice
shouted—

"Order from the Señores of the Cabildo. That three lights be
placed in every window and a lamp hung in every doorway."

Again the knock was repeated.

"It shall be done," said Don Isidro, running out himself in answer
to the summons.

At the Quinta de Ponce the whole household was astir before sunrise on the morning of the 2nd July, roused from sleep by the cries of
the female servants and slaves, who had seen Evaristo saddle his pony
and gallop off towards town at dawn. Don Roderigo paced anxiously
to and fro in the sala, his wife covered with a loose wrapper and
with dishevelled hair vainly trying to soothe him.

"Where can that foolish boy have gone to?" said he. "Did he
speak to no one before he went?"

"I can tell you, papa," said Dolores, who came in at that moment,
"he has gone to join Marcelino; he said he would be with him when
the fighting began, and Evaristo always does what he says he will."

"What can he do? a mere boy like him?" said Doña Constancia,
clasping her hands and looking tearfully at her husband.

"Do not cry, Mamita," said Dolores, half crying herself, "God will
protect him as he will Marcelino."

"Who has made you so wise about what God will do?" said Don
Roderigo sharply. "No duty calls him away from us."

As they spoke a mulatta girl came running into the room.

"Oh! Patrona! the English! the English!!" cried she, wringing
her hands.

Dolores and her mother clung to each other in terror.

"Where?" said Don Roderigo, putting himself in the way of the
terrified mulatta, and stamping his foot to bring her to her senses.

"The English Señor, Patron, the English Señor, Don Alejandro,
he has climbed up a tree, and he can see them on the high road.
They go straight for the city, he knows them. Oh! my God! what
will become of us?"

"Silence, fool!" said Don Roderigo; "if they are going to the city
they will not come here."

At frequent intervals all day long Lieutenant Gordon climbed up
into his tree, giving an account of all the movements he saw in the
open country round him. Three hours after the passing of this first
body, which Gordon had calculated at about 2000 men, and which
had marched by the high road leading to the Puente Galvès, there came
a much larger body, which left the road, and crossing camp about half
a league to the south of the Quinta de Ponce, marched round the head-

waters of the Arroyo Maciel and then turned northwards towards the Paso Zamorra on the Riachuelo.

Anxiously the day passed with them all. About noon the sound of cannon and musketry came to them from a direction far to the west of the Puente Galvès, but it soon ceased, and no more was heard till close upon sundown, when it commenced again, dying gradually away as darkness came on. Again Gordon climbed into his tree; over the tree-tops of the quintas about the Plaza Miserere there hung light clouds of white smoke, then night came on, all was again silent; what had happened?

This question Doña Constancia asked herself as she sat in a low chair in the sala. Dolores, seated beside her on a low stool, resting her head upon her mother's knee, asked herself that question also. Don Roderigo, Juan Carlos, and Gordon each also asked himself that question; no one answered it, and they expected no answer till the morrow. They sat in darkness, for darkness was to them rest and relief, hiding from each the anxiety which clouded the faces of them all; and in silence, for each feared to give utterance to his own thoughts. There came a barking of dogs, a trampling of horses' feet, and a confused sound of voices outside; the door opened, a servant came in bearing a lighted lamp and announced, "El Señor Coronel Lopez."

As Colonel Lopez entered the room he bowed gravely to all present, then advancing to Doña Constancia he ceremoniously kissed her hand. They crowded round him in silence, waiting for him to speak, all save Doña Constancia, who sat still in her chair twining her fingers together nervously, and looking eagerly at him. But he spoke not, throwing his hat on to a chair, and fumbling with the throat-buttons of his cloak.

"Say—what news?" said Don Roderigo. "How has the day gone with ours?"

"What news?" replied the colonel. "Little, and what there is is bad. Where can I take off this cloak of mine?" he added, looking significantly at Don Roderigo.

"Come this way," said the latter.

"No, no!" exclaimed Doña Constancia, springing to her feet and clutching him with both hands by one arm. "My son! have you seen him? Quick, tell me, anything is better than this uncertainty."

"Marcelino! yes, I was with him this morning. Since then I know nothing of him. We tried to capture two guns from these English; me they pitched into the river, of him I know nothing."

"No, no! you are hiding something from me; he was with you, what has become of him?"

"I tell you, Constancia, I know nothing."

"He is dead!" said Doña Constancia, sinking back into her chair and covering her face with her hands.

"Uncle," said Dolores in a hoarse voice, "tell all you know. I know that he can't be——" she could not finish the sentence.

"I believe he is a prisoner," said the colonel. "He passed the river with his negroes, and was cut off from the rest. He had no way to escape, I suppose he is a prisoner."

"I saw them," said Gordon. "There could not be much over 2000 of them. Where was Liniers? They said yesterday that he had marched out with all the garrison of the city."

"Liniers talks much, but knows nothing. The English played with him, got behind him, and marched upon the city. I watched them; for my part, I have had plenty of it. What could Marcelino and I do alone? They did not even take one step to support us. It appears that he counter-marched at once when he saw them across the river, and went back to the city; in the suburbs they fell upon him and routed him completely; without doubt you heard the firing two hours ago. We have no army now, and by this time the English have the city. All is lost, and I have come to consult with you," added he, laying his hand on the shoulder of Don Roderigo.

These two left the room together; the others remained, looking at one another in consternation.

"Do not believe him, Doña Constancia," said Gordon, kneeling down beside her. "You have been so good to me, I cannot bear you to look like that. What he has said is simply impossible; I am a soldier and know how these things are done. Marcelino would never have passed the river unless he had supports, and Liniers had five times as many men as those English I saw."

While Gordon with Juan Carlos and Dolores did all they could to calm the anxiety of Doña Constancia, Don Roderigo heard enough from the colonel to fill him with even deeper anxiety than before. Leaving him, he went out, called for his horse, and then returned to the sala, covered from neck to ancles in a large horseman's cloak, and with a brace of pistols in his waist-belt.

"You leave us?" exclaimed Doña Constancia, as she saw him return.

"Yes," said he, bending over her caressingly. "I am not a soldier; while we had an army I left this work to soldiers, now we have no army I shall do my duty as a citizen. Adios!"

So he left them, and Doña Constancia, leaning upon the shoulder of Juan Carlos, said dreamily—

"Father, sons, husband, all that I have, and this is what they call patriotism."

So saying, her knees bent under her and she would have fallen, but that her remaining son threw his arm round her, and supported her in a fainting state to a sofa, where, as she lay, she heard the footfalls of her husband's horse as he galloped rapidly away.

CHAPTER X.

THE COUNCIL OF WAR.

THE morrow came, and it was another day.

At sunrise the drums beat to arms all over the city; again the troops, native militia and Spaniards, assembled at their various head-quarters. Trace of the sorrow and depression of the past night had all vanished; all was again enthusiasm and fierce resolve. On comparing notes one with another, the losses seemed marvellously small after the crushing defeat they had suffered. In some regiments entire companies were missing, but they were probably with General Liniers, of whom nothing was yet known.

It was immediately resolved by the various chiefs that the English should not be left unmolested, and sundry companies were detailed at once for service in the suburbs, while the rest of the forces were employed on the central defences around the Plaza Mayor.

Captain Lorea of the Patricios was the first to march with his company. He marched straight for the quinta which had been held the previous day by the "Morenos de Ponce." Here he found that the English had established an outpost. He at once opened fire and advanced against them, upon which the enemy retired. Then posting his men along the far fence, with instructions to fire on any of the English who should come within range, he renewed his search for his missing friend Marcelino. But the search was again in vain. He could find no trace of him, and the occupants of the quinta could tell him nothing. They had fled when the fighting commenced, and had only returned at midnight.

All day long the firing continued in the suburbs, with loss of life on both sides, but the English withdrew any outpost that was seriously attacked, only to re-occupy it when their foes retreated. So much powder and shot wasted in a military point of view, but not wasted in its effects upon the citizen soldiers, who thus became accustomed to the whiz of the shot, and whose renewed confidence might have melted away in forced inactivity.

There was one corps in the army of yesterday which had no head-quarters in the city, the "Morenos de Ponce." At sunrise they paraded in the Plaza de Los Perdices, under the command of Lieutenant Asneiros, about 120 men, all told. Backwards and forwards through the ranks walked the lieutenant, rigorously inspecting arms and accoutrements, when a horseman drew rein in front of the line. Many of the negroes knew him, and their dark faces brightened up as they looked upon him.

"Morenos!" said he, raising his hand, "we all know how gallantly you followed your brave leader yesterday. The country appreciates your services. Spain, our mother-country, whose flag you have so valiantly defended, will reward them. Your commandant, my son," here the speaker's voice faltered a little, "is absent; wounded or a prisoner, we know not what has become of him. We yet need your services, Morenos; we have an arrogant enemy before us, but the city is yet ours, and we will defend it to the last. You have shown yourselves worthy to follow the lead of a Ponce de Leon. When the struggle commences, if my son be not with you, I myself will take his place. Together we will avenge the deaths of your slaughtered comrades and the loss of your commandant upon the insolent invader."

"Viva, Don Roderigo! Viva!!" shouted the negroes; after which the horseman, waving his hand to them, spoke a few words to Asneiros and trotted off.

About an hour afterwards an English officer with his eyes bandaged, and escorted by a picket of the first Patricios, presented himself to the Cabildo, having been received in the suburbs by Colonel Elio, carrying a flag of truce, and bearing a demand from General Gower for the immediate surrender of the city. The members present glanced curiously one at the other and some laughed. Don Roderigo Ponce de Leon, as the one among them most conversant with English, took upon himself to answer the demand.

"Your general," said he, "deceives himself; he thinks that by his victory of yesterday he has crushed us. He deceives himself. Tell him that our troops are yet numerous and enthusiastic, and that to a man we are all ready to die, if need be, in defence of our city. The hour has now come for us to show our patriotism, and we shall do it."

All the members rose from their seats and bowed with great formality as the officer retired.

As he went, a horseman in the dress of a paisano dismounted at the door of the Cabildo, and announced himself as a chasque with a despatch from General Liniers. He was at once led to the council-chamber, and delivered his despatch to Don Gregorio Lopez, who acted as president during a temporary absence of Don Martin Alzaga.

Don Gregorio read the letter, and then threw it across the table to his son-in-law, saying contemptuously—

"Look at that."

The letter was from General Liniers to the Cabildo, announcing in terms of humility, almost amounting to despair, the complete defeat and dispersion of his army, and stating that he had yet 1000 men with him and awaited orders.

"Just what one might expect," said Don Roderigo, when he had glanced over it and handed it to another member of the Cabildo. "Men of his fiery temperament are ever the most cast down when a reverse comes. It will be best to order him at once back to the city to take command of the defence."

"Give him the command again, when by his folly he has lost us an army?" exclaimed Don Gregorio.

"Just so," replied Don Roderigo. "As we place confidence in him, so will he strive to merit it. He is a soldier, and the men like him : he knows better than any of us what to do. The affair of yesterday will be a lesson to him."

" If we call him back he is at once the chief over us all, and our plan of defence will be set aside."

" That, no ; we have determined to act on the defensive without consulting him, we must tell him that it is to take command of the defence alone that we recall him. What do you say, Señores?" said Don Roderigo, addressing himself to the other members. "Shall we not do better with a soldier to command our troops?"

" Liniers is a daring soldier," said one of them. "The men will forget yesterday when they hear his cheerful voice again among them. When they see him they will remember only that last year he was the hero who forced an entire army to surrender."

In this view all agreed, and Don Roderigo sat down to answer the despatch at once in very few words. As he wrote, Don Gregorio turned to look at the chasque who had remained in the room, looking about him with an air of the most complete indifference.

" I have seen you before, my friend," said he. "Are you not the man who brought from Colonel Lopez the news of the advance of the English upon Quilmes?"

" Just so," answered the man. "The Señor General Liniers took me with him that day, and yesterday I was with him to the end."

" Then you were present at the fight on the Plaza Miserere?"

" Yes, I saw it all, but I do not call that a fight. When they ought to have rushed on them they stopped to shoot, and it was all disorder. But what would you? They were on foot. I, yes; last year I saw a fight further away, beyond the Plaza Miserere. There, yes; there we went on to the top of them like men, but it was all in vain ; in the same, no more, it ended. Look you that these English are the very devil, but have no fear, in some way we shall arrange them."

" Were you with Don Juan Martin Puyrredon at Perdriel?"

" I was, and I escaped only by a miracle. That, yes; that was a fight. When a man is on horseback he is worth three, but these people of the city who go on foot! what would you have?"

" But these English, they were on foot, both yesterday and at Perdriel."

" And among houses and fences. Let them come and seek us in the open camp ; we will teach them."

" It appears that my son has had a warrior among his men."

" Your son, Señor! Who will he be?"

" Colonel Lopez, who was your chief two days ago."

" And your worship, will you be the Señor Don Gregorio Lopez?"

" I am he. And you, what is your name?"

" I call myself Venceslao Viana, at your service, Señor Don Gregorio."

At this Don Gregorio rose from his seat with a grave look on his face and walked away to a window, while Don Roderigo looked up from the letter which he had just finished, and examined attentively the face of the chasque, who appeared somewhat disconcerted at the abrupt termination of his conversation with Don Gregorio.

Then folding up the letter and sealing it with the official seal of the Cabildo, Don Roderigo handed it to Venceslao Viana.

"This to the Señor General Liniers," he said. "But first tell me, have you seen anything of the English to-day?"

"Much, I came right through their lines. There is another army of them crossed the Riachuelo at the Zamorra Pass this morning."

"Then vaya con Dios, and don't lose a minute;" so saying, Don Roderigo opened the door for him, and shaking him warmly by the hand dismissed him, as much surprised at his politeness as at the sudden coolness of Don Gregorio.

"One must be the devil himself to understand the ways of these men who wear coats," said Venceslao to himself, as he mounted his horse. "That old man must be in some way a relation of mine; he will be one of those relations in the city of whom my father never speaks. He would speak to me no more when he knew who I was. And that other! Who knows if he is not a relation also. When one is a man of family one never knows where one may meet relations."

Venceslao was not much given to thinking, and had soon something else to employ his wits on, having to make diligent use of his eyes to escape the scouting and foraging parties of the English. He reached General Liniers in safety and delivered his despatch, which restored the despondent soldier to his usual confident activity. Taking Venceslao as his guide he marched rapidly by cross-roads back to town, exchanging a few harmless shots with a party of English who were advancing towards the Miserere, and at once took charge of the preparations for defence.

That evening, as Venceslao was lounging about under the colonnade in front of the Cabildo, he was accosted by Don Roderigo Ponce de Leon.

"What are you doing, friend?" said Don Roderigo.

"I am waiting for nightfall. There are so many English about that it will be dangerous to go out by daylight," replied Venceslao.

"Go out! And where are you going?"

"To present myself to my chief."

"That cannot be. Here in the city is the place for all good patriots. You have seen fire, we need men like you."

"And what can I do here? Of these manœuvres on foot I know nothing, and my horse will die of hunger."

"Of that have no fear, remain with me, I will find something for you to do."

"With very much pleasure; Señor, I am at your service," answered Venceslao.

"Then go to my house, there you will find plenty of comrades. Go that way," said Don Roderigo, pointing along the face of the Cabildo northwards. "Take the second turning to the left and then go straight on till close to the church of San Miguel. You will see a negro sentry at a doorway, that is my house. The 'Morenos de Ponce' are quartered there; tell Lieutenant Asneiros that Don Roderigo sent you. I shall be there myself later on."

"Hasta luego, Señor Don Roderigo," said Venceslao, mounting his horse and trotting off.

As he settled himself in the saddle he shook his head meditatively and said to himself, " Certainly he must be some relation of mine. Look you, when a man is of family he has duties of which others know nothing. This Señor Don Roderigo must have some claim on my services, for that it is that he sends me. It is necessary then that I obey, so here goes to join the 'Morenos de Ponce.' I have seen something of them, and now that I think of it, the comandante is that young man who was at my house with the colonel months ago, before I made myself a lancer; the colonel said he might be some relation of mine, I will ask him about it."

Here his soliloquy was cut short by his finding the street blocked up by a huge mound of earth, beyond which was a deep ditch. On the mound a party of the Catalan regiment were hard at work raising a stout breastwork and laying down a platform for a heavy gun, which stood in the street behind. On the azotea on each side a sentry paced up and down with his firelock on his shoulder. A Spanish officer stopped him and enquired where he was going.

" I belong to the 'Morenos de Ponce,'" answered Venceslao. "Where are they quartered?"

" Pass," answered the officer, pointing to a narrow passage on the sidewalk. " Four squares from here on the left hand."

Venceslao passed on, found the "Morenos de Ponce," and was soon at home among them, but he did not find the comandante, and his curiosity concerning his relationship remained unsatisfied.

Meantime the news of the landing of the English had spread over the campaña, and the chiefs of the partidarios hastily collected their men together. On the night of the 3rd July messengers from them made their way into the city, bearing letters asking instructions from the Reconquistador. To all the same answer was returned, that the men who had firearms should repair to the city and join the garrison, and that the rest should hover about the rear of the invading army and annoy it to the best of their ability. During the day, and more especially during the night of the 4th July, hundreds of paisanos entered the city, and were spread about in small detachments attached to the different infantry corps. A strong force of them were also embodied and encamped on the Plaza de Los Perdices, where they would be at hand should cavalry be required.

On the 4th, Don Isidro Lorea turned his attention to fortifying his house. He threw open all the windows of both house and almacen, blocking them up for half their height with boxes and barrels, through which he made two loop-holes at each window. On the parapet of his azotea he arranged tercios of yerba and boxes filled with earth, leaving a few inches between each to serve as loopholes. In addition to his own company he had all the men resident in that and the two neighbouring blocks under his command, which raised his force to about 400, all supplied with fire-arms and ammunition. His instructions from General Liniers were, that he should on no account venture into the streets, but was to defend his position to the last extremity.

It was the afternoon of the 4th July, the British army was cantonned all along the western side of the city, the British fleet was at anchor in the roadstead, but as yet no attack had been made. General White-lock with his staff occupied a small country house close to the Plaza Miserere, to which he had been conducted by an American named White, to whom this house had formerly belonged. Mr. White had been for many years resident in Buenos Aires; he had joined the English army at Monte Video, and was frequently consulted by General Whitelock, who placed much confidence in him.

General Whitelock held a council of war that afternoon, all his superior officers being present. The council was held in the dining-room of Mr. White's house; on the table in this room lay a map of the city, on which most of the churches and public buildings were clearly marked, but which was full of inaccuracies.

The council had now sat for nearly an hour; the general, seated in an arm-chair at the head of the table, seemed somewhat ruffled at what had passed. On the faces of many of his officers there was an evident gloom; they had not approved of the plan of attack which had been disclosed to them, but their advice had not been asked, they had been merely summoned to have the plan explained to them and to receive instructions. The troops had been under arms all the morning, General Whitelock having at first contemplated making the assault at midday, but the constant fire kept up upon his advanced posts had decided him to postpone it until the next morning; even he saw the danger of advancing in broad daylight down those long, narrow streets.

But on the faces of some younger officers there sat the smile of undoubting confidence, and many a gay jest passed among them at the expense of the runaway Frenchman and his Creole troops, who, after the signal proof of incapacity which they had given two days before, had yet dared to return a defiant answer to a second summons to surrender their city.

At this moment the door opened, and a tall man with stern, sallow features entered the room.

"Excuse me, General," said he in very good English, but with a foreign accent, "I knew not that you were engaged, I will retire."

"By no means, Señor," said General Whitelock. "Come in and sit down, I thought we had left you in Monte Video."

"I landed at Quilmes this morning, and Colonel Mahon informed me where I should find you."

"Craddock," said the general to an aide-de-camp, "a chair for the Señor Evaña."

"Have you heard of the answer I have received from these citizens of Buenos Aires to my summons?" asked the general as Evaña seated himself.

"I have heard that they refuse to surrender," answered Evaña coldly.

"Refuse! Yes, and in terms which would come well from a victorious army, but not from a defeated mob of militia. See there, read for yourself," added the general, handing an open despatch to Evaña.

Evaña took the despatch and read it. A flush spread over his features as he read the proud disdainful words in which the men of an open city defied the menace of a soldier at the head of a well-appointed army. He glanced at the signatures, and saw amongst them those of Don Gregorio Lopez and of Don Roderigo Ponce de Leon. His own countrymen and the Spaniards joined cordially together in the heroic resolve to defend the city to the last, and for what? For Spain. He sighed deeply as he refolded the despatch and returned it to the general with a low bow, saying—

"Then there is nothing but an appeal to arms."

"And that we need think little of," answered the general. "Perda cuidao, as your people say, the sun will shine for the last time to-morrow upon the Spanish flag in that fort over yonder, and you will have some shopkeeping countrymen the fewer."

"God grant that that flag come down," said Evaña; "too long has it crushed out the soul of my country, but, General, as I told you before, you do not know my countrymen. If you would but have made allies of them, that flag would have come down without your risking the lives of thousands of men in pulling it down."

"It would have given place to some new-fangled flag of a republic I suppose. Enough of that, Señor Evaña, the flag that has to fly there to-morrow is the English flag."

"Then you purpose taking the city by assault?" said Evaña.

"Just so," answered the general; "I intend to give those saucy citizens of yours another taste of the cold steel, it seems that one lesson is not enough for them."

"You will lose many men, General. You have the command of the river, I should have thought a blockade would have been much more certain and would have spared useless bloodshed."

"The calculation of a civilian and not of a soldier, Señor Evaña. What do you say, Craddock? Do you think you would win your spurs by starving them out?"

"I should precious soon tire of that work," answered the aide-de-camp; "besides which you would have to shoot me, General, for I should begin to smuggle provisions into the city as soon as I heard that the pretty Porteñas were beginning to look thin on siege rations."

"Always thinking of the girls, Craddock," said the general laughing. "Well, I can promise you that you wont have to wait much longer before you can begin making love to them."

"He may chance to have his love-making spoiled before he even sees them," said Evaña, bending over the table and examining the map of the city which lay before him.

"Every bullet has its billet," said the aide-de-camp, with a sneer; "the billets of those of your militia seem mostly up in the air from what I hear of their shooting."

During this talk most of the officers who had taken part in the council left the room, but two or three still remained. One of them was a strikingly handsome man of medium stature, with curly brown hair and hazel eyes.

"Perhaps the Señor Evaña would like to know our plan of assault," said this officer.

"Explain it to him, Craddock," said the general.

"We shall keep 1000 men in reserve at the corrales," said Crad-

dock, "besides Colonel Mahon's brigade, which will advance to
the Galvès bridge to-morrow. The rest of the troops we divide into
three columns of attack, which will advance by parallel streets through
the city to the river-side, and will then unite in a combined attack
upon the great square, where we understand the principal force of the
enemy is entrenched."

" I see a great many streets marked on the plan," said Evaña.

" Exactly so," replied the aide-de-camp ; " each column will march
in subdivisions by adjacent streets, which will mutually support each
other in case of need."

" And each subdivision will be separated from the next by a block
of barricaded houses 140 yards long," interrupted Evaña.

" You see, General," said the handsome officer, "he has hit upon
your weak place at once."

" What does he know?" said the general angrily; "fire away,
Craddock."

" In the Spanish cities," continued Craddock, "the churches invariably occupy the most important positions. We have thus fixed upon
two churches upon which the three columns will form their base of
attack upon the centre."

" We have learnt to-day that they are running up barricades in some
parts of the city," said the officer who had spoken before.

" Are they?" exclaimed Evaña eagerly, as he thought of the plan
of defence he had left with Don Gregorio Lopez. " Do you know
where they have placed these barricades ? "

" Near to the principal square," answered the other.

"'There is nothing that we know of to prevent us reaching our first
positions," said the aide-de-camp. "We shall simply march down the
streets musket on shoulder without firing a shot, till we are near enough
to inspect these barricades. We may probably have to batter them
with cannon before we make our second advance. See, these are the
churches I told you of. On the north there is this place, a large convent, I believe."

" Las Monjas Catalinas," said Evaña.

" A convent is always a good place to occupy as a post, it is——"

" Quite in your line, eh ! Craddock," interrupted the general ;
"unfortunately, my boy, you wont be with that column to-morrow."

"'The columns of the left and centre will concentrate upon this
convent after establishing a strong rear-guard at the bull-ring here to
the north of the city," resumed Craddock. " Then in the centre there
is this church, San Miguel I think they call it."

Evaña nodded his head.

" This church stands in the highest part of the city. When the
three columns have reached their stations, we shall march a part of the
reserve upon this church so as to open communications with the attacks from the north and south upon the great square. Then on the
south, where Crauford has the command," said Craddock, nodding to
the brown-haired officer, "we have first a large detached house
surrounded by iron railings."

" The Residencia," said Evaña.

" I believe that is what it is called. Colonel Guard will be detached to occupy this position. Then further on, only three blocks from the great square, we have a large church with a dome and two lofty towers. General Crauford with the rest of the column of the right will form his base of attack upon this church."

"How do you call that church, Señor Evaña?" asked General Crauford.

"The church of Santo Domingo," answered Evaña.

"Crauford takes great interest in that church," said Craddock; "he has been all day on the roof examining it through a telescope, but he can't see much of it from here."

"Crauford wanted to take the city all by himself on Thursday night," said General Whitelock.

"There was nothing to oppose me after I had dispersed the militia and that negro regiment that fought so well," said General Crauford. "If I had not been recalled by Gower I should have marched through the city and captured the fort. I penetrated through the suburbs to the head of a street which Pack told me leads straight to the great square."

"It is a pity you did not," said Evaña; "the city was panic-struck from what I hear; you would probably have captured the fort without firing a shot. To-morrow you will find it a very different matter to march down those long, straight streets."

"We shall lose some men of course," said General Whitelock, "but we shall establish ourselves on both flanks of their principal position, and then you will see that Frenchman will have had enough of it, and he will surrender."

"You know not what you are doing, General," said Evaña; "if you had studied for a year you could not have devised a plan which would have entailed greater sacrifice of life. I tell you that if you carry out this plan of yours, those streets of Buenos Aires will be to you and your men pathways of death."

"Señor Evaña," replied General Whitelock, rising bruskly from his chair, "when I need the advice of so distinguished a *militaire* as yourself be certain that I shall not forget to ask for it."

To this Evaña made no answer, but rising from his seat he took up his hat, bowed formally to all present, and left the room.

"This native friend of ours has somewhat nettled the general," whispered Captain Craddock in Crauford's ear.

"He has," answered the other gloomily, "and the worst is, that what he says is perfectly true. Give me that city and a garrison of 10,000 men, and I defy any 50,000 troops in the world to drive me out of it, even if they had Napoleon himself to lead them, or that new Indian general of ours they think so much of at home, Sir Arthur Wellesley."

"Bah!" replied the aide-de-camp scornfully; "they are only militia and dismounted gauchos, what need we fear from them? As for Liniers, you and Gower showed us on Thursday what he is worth."

Long after nightfall Don Carlos Evaña walked by himself on the flat roof of the quinta house, wrapped in a large cloak which kept the cold from his body, and in thought which made him oblivious to all

that passed around him. He heeded nothing the buzz and bustle
which pervaded all the quinta, never noticed the mounted messengers
who rode forth or came in continually at the open gateway, his eye
looked only on the glittering lights of his native city, his ear heard
only the distant hum which told him that there also all was busy preparation for the conflict of the morrow.

His heart was sad, for his hopes died away within him. He had
crossed the ocean to urge on the despatch of this very expedition
which now menaced his native city. So far success had attended it,
even beyond his hopes, but the result which he desired seemed further
from attainment than ever. Should the struggle of the morrow end
in favour of the English, the result would be merely a change of
masters; instead of serving men of their own race, language, and
religion, his countrymen would serve strangers.

On the other hand, if the English were worsted in their attack upon
the city, then would his countrymen be more than ever attached to
Spain, more quiescent than ever under her most tyrannical decrees.
For the danger and the glory would be theirs, the blood that might
flow would be their blood, the city they had fought and bled to
defend would be their city, saved by them for Spain. Men love ever
those for whom they have done great service and for whom they have
braved great danger.

In either case the dream of a republic of Argentines, of the rise of
a great, young nation on the banks of La Plata, was at an end, and an
Argentine Republic was the dream of Evaña's life.

Therefore Don Carlos Evaña was sad at heart, and the hope of
years died away within him.

Yet his cheek flushed with pride as he thought of the defiant
answer his countrymen had returned to the summons of the British
general. On what grounded they their confidence? Surely the Corrales de la Miserere had taught them plain enough that their troops
could not meet those of England on equal terms! Then Evaña
thought of his own plan of defence.

"If they have adopted it only in part," said he to himself, "the
plan of attack devised by this General Whitelock will give them every
possible advantage."

"Oh! that it were not for Spain, and that I were with you! Oh!
my people," he exclaimed aloud.

His own voice startled him. He looked round hurriedly; no one
was near. He resumed his monotonous walk up and down, and now
his thoughts went back to the council upon which he had intruded in
the afternoon, and he pondered upon the talk he had had with General
Whitelock and the others.

"Such manifest folly," said he to himself. "They all saw it except
that fool of an aide-de-camp. There are good soldiers among them,
how is it that the one who knows least commands them all? Have I
been mistaken in the English? Would their alliance be of no service
to us? No, I have seen them in their own country. The English
are a great people, but there are many fools among them."

CHAPTER XI.

THE Corrales de la Miserere stood in a hollow. On the higher ground behind this hollow stood Mr. White's house and some other quintas; to the east of the hollow the ground rose gradually for more than half a mile till it reached the level of the centre of the city, which extended to within half a mile of the eastern face of the city, when the ground again sloped gently down to the beach. Thus from the Corrales de la Miserere nothing whatever could be seen of the city, save the houses immediately bordering on the Plaza, and the orchards and aloe fences of the suburbs which stretched to the right and left of the position held by the British army. Even from Mr. White's house, which overlooked the suburbs and the nearer quarters of the city, very little could be seen of it without ascending to the roof, from which the towers and domes of the churches were plainly visible, but the city itself appeared only as a wilderness of houses, the lines of the streets being undistinguishable.

The city of Buenos Aires at that time was in the shape of a triangle, of which the river front of the city, about three miles long, formed the base, the apex being at the Plaza Miserere. On the two sides of this triangle clustered the suburbs, cut up at regular distances into blocks by roads which were the continuations of the streets of the city. The city with its suburbs formed thus an irregular parallelogram, but in the suburbs, in addition to the streets, there were many bye-roads, in which a stranger might easily go astray.

The centre of the position held by the British army rested upon the apex of the triangle which formed the city proper; in front of the right and left of this position lay the suburbs.

An hour before daylight on the morning of the 5th July the entire British army was under arms. Each subdivision paraded at the head of the street by which it was to advance into the city. The number of men in each subdivision varied from 250 up to 600 men, the total force comprising the three columns being something less than 5000.

The column of the left. under the command of Sir Samuel Auchmuty, comprised the 38th, 87th, and 5th regiments of the line, and was directed to occupy the bull-ring, the Retiro, and the convent of Las Monjas Catalinas. The column of the centre, under the command of General Lumley, comprised the 36th and part of the 88th regiment, and was directed to establish itself in the houses overlooking the beach, and then combine with the column of General Auchmuty in an

attack upon the centre of the city. The column of the right, under
the command of General Crauford, comprised eight companies of
light infantry, eight companies of the 95th (the rifle corps), and
seventy recruits of the 71st regiment, also the 45th regiment, which
was detailed under Colonel Guard for the special service of occupying
the Residencia. General Crauford was directed to occupy the church
of Santo Domingo. Thus the instructions to the three generals in
command were to establish themselves along the eastern face of the
city, in positions distant three miles from the headquarters of the
army, and separated from it by a wilderness of houses and quintas
swarming with a hostile population. Further than this they had no
definite instructions, save that the capture of the fort and the great
square was understood to be the main object of the attack.

The reserve consisted of the 6th Carabineers; four troops of the
9th Light Dragoons, all dismounted; a part of the 88th regiment;
pickets from all these regiments, which remained in charge of the
knapsacks and great-coats of the men; about forty of the 17th Light
Dragoons, mounted, and such of the artillery as had not been left
with Colonel Mahon at Quilmes.

General Crauford had two light field-pieces attached to his column,
the other columns were without artillery.

Colonel Duff of the 88th regiment had such misgivings as to the
result of the day that he left the colours of his regiment behind him
with the reserve, and, when he advanced before dawn to the head of
the street by which he was to enter the city, he found his regiment so
weak that he sent back for two of the companies which had been left
with the reserve. Before these companies were allowed to join him
they were ordered to take the flints from their muskets and leave
them behind, and Colonel Duff lost much time in trying to provide
them with flints, by searching among the rest of his men for spare
ones. Even so, many of the men of these two companies entered
into action without flints.

The division under the command of Colonel Mahon, which advanced from Quilmes to the Puente Galvès on the 5th July, consisted
of about 1800 men, infantry, artillery, and dismounted cavalry, the
9th and 17th Light Dragoons, and 200 sailors from the squadron, who
had been landed by Admiral Murray to assist in dragging the cannon
through the swamps at Ensenada, where five guns captured from the
Spaniards at Monte Video stuck fast and were destroyed by Colonel
Frazer.

The idea of General Whitelock appears to have been, that by
avoiding the main streets of the city, which led direct from the
Corrales to the Plaza Mayor, and by a rapid march before sunrise,
without firing, through the suburbs and shorter streets, he would
succeed in surprising the principal positions to the north and south of
the great square, which idea, considering that most of these positions
were a league distant from the Plaza Miserere, presumed a great want
of vigilance on the part of the garrison, while all chance of a surprise
was effectually destroyed by the way in which the signal to advance
was given.

As day dawned a salvo of twenty-one British guns on the Plaza Miserere gave the signal. The troops marched at once; each sub-division in column of sections, seven men in line, left its position and disappeared down the muddy roads, hedged by aloe fences, which led through the suburbs. They disappeared, marching along avenues in which they could see nothing either to the right hand or to the left, towards an unknown goal at the end of a long, narrow path shrouded in darkness and in mist.

Liniers had made every preparation for a vigorous defence. In-cluding the regular troops, the three battalions of Patricios, the Arribeño regiment, armed citizens, slaves,[1] and the dismounted paisanos, he had over 15,000 men under his command. The regular troops were concentrated about the defences of the Plaza Mayor, but the militia were spread about on the azoteas all over the city.

The thunder of the British guns roused up at once the sleeping city; on every azotea the troops stood to arms, by every gun stood a gunner with a lighted match. There had been much rain for several days past, now over all the city there hung a thick haze. Men rushed up to the roofs of their houses, and peered anxiously over the parapets into the murky morning air. Then over the whole city there fell a great silence.

Rapidly through the suburbs marched the invading columns, meeting with no foe, scarce seeing any sign of life; then as the haze cleared somewhat away they entered the long, straight streets of the city, long monotonous lines of white houses, with barred windows and parapeted roofs, deserted streets in which was neither life nor motion, streets stretching straight before them with no visible end. Some of the subdivisions encountered cavalry videttes near the suburbs, who trotted away before them, shouting up to the azoteas of the houses as they passed the warning of their approach.

When or where the firing commenced no one knows, but presently these deserted streets sprang at once into fiery life; on each hand the azoteas bristled with armed men who fired without aim into the thick of the moving mass of men beneath them, who still marched swiftly on with shouldered muskets, and fired not one shot in return. When one man fell another took his place, and still the word was "forward." Fiercer and fiercer grew the fire from the parapets of those flat-roofed houses, men no longer crouching under them for shelter, but leaning over the better to select their victim. Losing patience at the tedious task of reloading, casting aside their firelocks, some tore down the parapet itself with their hands and hurled the bricks at the heads of the marching men. Women with dishevelled hair ran about madly on those flat roofs, more fierce, more relentless than the men, urging them on in their work of death, seizing bricks, grenades, or any other missile that came to hand, and throwing them in wild fury at the lines of living men, who pressed steadily on with teeth clenched and glaring eyes, but who still sent back not one shot in return. Rank after rank was broken, men fell by dozens and by scores, and still where each man fell another took his place, still with sloped muskets, and shoulder

---

[1] Many of the citizens had armed their household slaves.

to shoulder, the soldiery pressed on up those pathways of death, where the leaden hail poured upon them like hailstones in a winter storm, and where, as they neared the centre, round shot and grape from the defences of the Plaza Mayor tore through them.

Through all this tempest of fire the well-trained troops held on their way unflinchingly, and every subdivision, or a remnant of it, reached the position for which it marched. The bull-ring, the Retiro barracks, the church of Las Monjas Catalinas, the church of Santo Domingo, the Residencia, and several blocks of houses on the river face of the city were captured and occupied. But round each position so captured crowded thousands of the furious foe, rendered more furious still by the unavailing slaughter they had inflicted upon the invaders.

Then the British troops came to bay, the welcome word was given to load and fire, and in turn their shot poured havoc and death into the dense masses about them. Many a trim soldier of the Patricios fell lifeless on the parapet over which he leaned. Many an honest householder, who had loaded his fowling-piece with ball that day in defence of hearth and fatherland, then fired it for the last time, and fell back upon the tiles which covered his own home, pouring out his life-blood from a mortal wound. Many a swarthy, bearded paisano, threw up his arms as a pang shot through him, and glaring wildly on the unwonted scenes around him, bethought him of the peaceful solitude of his native Pampa, bethought him of his lowly rancho and of the half-naked little urchins who called him father, then sank down with swiftly-failing breath as death darkened those wild eyes for ever. Many a slave who fought bravely with freedom before him as his guerdon then gained equality with his master in the grave.

But, regardless of those who fell, more and more pressed fiercely round every position held by the British troops; those regiments which penetrated into the vicinity of the Plaza Mayor were the most fiercely assailed.

The 88th regiment, in two subdivisions, under the command of Colonel Duff and Major Vandeleur, entered the city by the streets now known as Piedad and Cuyo. After an abortive attempt to capture the church of San Miguel, Colonel Duff marched on, losing men at every step, till he found himself under the guns of the defences of the centre, when turning to the left he burst into and occupied a house close to the Merced Church. Major Vandeleur, after losing half his command, occupied another house about a square further north. But their men were driven from the azoteas by the overwhelming fire of the enemy, and after several hours of unavailing resistance both divisions were compelled to surrender.

General Lumley, with the remainder of his brigade, advancing by the Calles Parque and Tucuman, seized some houses in the last block before reaching the beach and held them with the 36th regiment against furious assaults and a heavy cannonade from the fort until the afternoon.

The column of the left, under the command of Brigadier-general Sir Samuel Auchmuty, advanced upon the northern quarter of the city. The 38th regiment, under the command of Colonel Nugent, at the extreme left of the line, made a considerable detour through the suburbs, and then advanced by a narrow road straight upon the Plaza del Retiro. Here the garrison was strongly posted in the barracks and the bull-ring, with cannon planted upon the open ground, and a large, flat roofed house in front was occupied as an outpost. From this house a heavy fire was directed upon the regiment, causing severe loss; but it was captured by the bayonet, not one of the garrison escaping. Colonel Nugent then attempted to advance upon the bull-ring, but was repulsed by a murderous fire of artillery, upon which he detached two companies to take possession of a house on the high ground overlooking the river, to the north of the Retiro barracks. This operation was successful, and the two companies, leaving the house by a side door, forced their way into the barracks, drove out the garrison at the point of the bayonet, and captured several cannon, all of which but one twelve-pounder were spiked. Colonel Nugent then hoisted his colours on the flag-staff, and opened fire with the captured gun upon the bull-ring.

Meantime Sir Samuel Auchmuty had advanced with the 87th regiment by the Calles Arenales and Santa Fé, thinking that they would lead him to the left flank of the enemy's position on the Plaza del Retiro; instead of which, after a march of more than two miles, he found himself directly in front of their position, and was received by a tremendous fire of artillery and musketry from the bull-ring, against which it was impossible to advance. He accordingly retreated two squares to the right, where the little river Tercero, which flows down the Calle Paraguay, had scooped out a sort of trench, along which he marched his regiment, sheltered from the fire of the enemy, and took possession of a large house and garden on the high ground overlooking the river. Then hearing of the success of Colonel Nugent, he advanced to his support, and at half-past nine, after two hours of incessant firing, the garrison of the bull-ring hung out a white flag and surrendered at discretion.

By this success the British column captured 700 prisoners, thirty-two guns, most of them of large calibre, two mortars, and an immense quantity of ammunition, and secured at once a formidable base of attack, and the means of communicating with the squadron.

The right wing of this column, consisting of the 5th regiment, under the command of Lieutenant-colonel Davie, which advanced by the Calles Charcas and Paraguay, met with but slight opposition, and captured some spiked guns in a cross street. After occupying some houses on the river front Colonel Davie detached an officer with a strong party to seize the church and convent of Las Monjas Catalinas, but Major King of this regiment in attempting to capture another large house was driven back by overwhelming numbers of the enemy.

The right column of attack, under the command of General Crauford, marched upon the southern quarter of the city. The left wing of this column, led by Colonel Pack, about 600 strong, advanced by the Calle Moreno, and penetrated to the last block without much loss, although the Calle Moreno was but one block distant from the defences of the Plaza Mayor. The approaches to these defences had been all night illuminated by lamps hanging in the doorways and windows of the houses; these lamps were still burning dimly in the murky air of the early morning when Colonel Pack halted among the scattered houses which overlooked the beach to the south of the fort. These houses were under the guns of the fort, and offered no position that he could safely occupy. He looked about him; to his left lay a narrow street, closed by a black mound of earth; once over that mound and he was in the Plaza de los Perdices, and by one desperate effort might seize the fort and decide the fortunes of the day. His first step was to detach Colonel Cadogan with his rear-guard to attack the church of San Francisco and so secure his rear. This church stood close to the trench which crossed the Calle Defensa at its junction with the Calle Potosi; the azoteas all round were strongly garrisoned.

Advancing rapidly up the narrow street, Colonel Cadogan brought up a field-piece to blow open the side door of the church, but from the surrounding azoteas and from the earthwork so tremendous a fire was poured upon him that "on a sudden the whole of the leading company and every man and horse at the gun were killed or disabled." He was forced to a precipitate retreat, and bursting into a house in the Calle Moreno took refuge there with 140 men.

Colonel Pack, with the remainder of his command, wheeled rapidly into the Calle Balcarce, and made a desperate assault upon the earth-work which closed the entrance to the Plaza de los Perdices. Over the top of this earthwork frowned the muzzles of two heavy guns, in front yawned a ditch twelve feet wide by six deep. The light infantry rushed up that narrow street straight upon the black muzzles of those guns, while the grape-shot tore through their ranks, and an incessant fire of musketry poured upon them from the azoteas on either hand. They reached the ditch and sprang into it, only to find before them a perpendicular wall of earth twelve feet high, over which they strove to clamber, while hand-grenades, bricks, and all sorts of missiles were showered upon them from above; till seeing no possibility of success, Colonel Pack, who was himself wounded, drew off seventy men, the remnant of his force, and retreated upon the church of Santo Domingo. There he met General Cranford, who had reached that position unopposed, and who at once took possession of the church by blowing open a side door with a shot from a field-piece.

On the extreme right of the British line, Colonel Guard, with the 45th regiment, penetrated through the suburbs to the south of the city, and attacked and captured the Residencia with very slight loss, taking about 100 prisoners. The Residencia was at that time used as a hospital, the wards being occupied by 150 sick, many of whom had been wounded in the affair of the 2nd. It was surrounded by high walls and an iron railing, and was a very strong position. Leaving Major Nicholls with 400 men to hold the Residencia, Colonel Guard then advanced with the grenadier company by the Calle Defensa to join General Cranford. Reinforced by that general with a detachment of light infantry, he then attempted to re-open communications with Colonel Cadogan, but had hardly advanced fifty yards from Santo Domingo when the guns on the defences of the Plaza Mayor opened upon him with grape, and a storm of shot poured upon him from the adjacent azoteas. The grenadier company was swept away, Major Trotter of the Rifles was killed, and he, with the few men left, was forced to seek shelter in the church.

Meantime, on the Plaza Miserere, General Whitelock, surrounded by his staff, walked to and fro, knowing nothing of what had happened, hearing from far off the shouts and cries of the combatants, the incessant rattling of musketry, the frequent boom of cannon. Of those troops who had disappeared in the murky dawn into that great wilderness of houses, not one returned to tell how their comrades fared. The firing was far off on the eastern face of the city to the north and to the south of the Plaza Mayor. Between these points and the Plaza Miserere there intervened a vast mass of flat-roofed houses, which swarmed with armed men. No messenger could penetrate that wilderness. One officer, who was sent off to the right with a few dragoons, returned, saying that to pass onwards was impossible.

The troops of the reserve were all under arms, and surrounded by swarms of native cavalry, who now and then crept near enough to fire upon them, and who watched for an opportunity of pouncing upon any weak party which might venture away from the main body. One party of this cavalry, about 200 men, approached so near that Lieutenant-colonel Torrens, chief of the staff to General Whitelock, was apprehensive of danger from them. Taking with him thirty dragoons, he charged them, drove them before him, and pursued them for nearly a league.

Then about eight o'clock General Whitelock determined upon a further offensive movement upon the centre. Two detachments were ordered upon this service. Three companies of infantry with two field-pieces advanced by the street now known as the Calle Piedad, and a corps composed of the 6th Carabineers and two troops of the 9th Light Dragoons, dismounted, under the command of Colonel Kington of the Carabineers, with Major Pigot of the Dragoons as his second in command, was ordered to penetrate by the next street to the right. This corps had also two field-pieces attached to it. The carabineers were armed with carbines and bayonets, the dragoons had muskets.

The infantry, galled by a heavy fire from the azoteas, forced their way as far as the church of San Miguel, and bursting open the church doors and the doors of several of the adjacent houses established themselves there, filling the tower of the church with marksmen, whose fire soon drove away the enemy from the neighbouring azoteas. The two field-pieces were planted in the street in front of the church, and by their fire drove off a party of the enemy who were advancing upon them up the Calle Piedad.

At dawn Don Isidro Lorea inspected all his preparations and posted his men with great care. At each loop-hole in the barricaded windows of his house and almacen he placed three men, two of whom were to load while the other fired ; his own company of Patricios he stationed on the azotea and took command of them himself. He had barely completed his arrangements when the salvo of British guns gave the signal for the attack. At the report of the guns Doña Dalmacia ascended to the azotea.

"Go! go!" said Don Isidro, as she approached him. "They come! How can I do my duty if thou art in danger?"

"I come but to embrace thee once more," she answered; "I know that thou art brave and wilt do thy duty," so saying she threw her arms round him and kissed him. Then turning to the men she spoke cheerful words to them, encouraging them to do their duty, and passing along the ranks shook hands with many of them whom she had known from childhood. The men answered her words with loud "Vivas," she left them and retired to the security of her own room, but not to rest there in idleness, she knew that fighting would entail wounds and death. With her maids around her she went on with the work from which the report of the guns had roused her—appliances for the relief of the wounded and for the alleviation of the sufferings of the dying.

Hardly had Doña Dalmacia left the azotea than the report of a musket was heard in the suburbs somewhat to the right, then another, then came shouts and cries, and the musketry grew into one continuous rattle, gradually spreading over the whole city to the north and to the south of the Plaza Mayor, but Don Isidro could see no foe approach him, and no musket was fired in his immediate neighbourhood.

Two hours his watch lasted and the partial cessation of the firing told him that the heat of the conflict was over; from all sides came reports of a fearful slaughter of the invaders. Then away in the suburb beyond his position he heard the reports of several muskets, and there was a cry from a neighbouring azotea:—

"They come!"

He moved his men up to the parapet, and stationed himself at the corner, looking up the street out westwards. What he saw was a dense body of red-coated soldiery, with brass helmets, with sloped muskets and bayonets fixed, marching rapidly towards him. What he saw was a miscellaneous multitude of men leaning over the parapets of the houses and firing upon these marching soldiers, or stepping back from the parapet to reload. What he saw were soldiers dropping on their faces as they marched, or staggering out of the ranks and clutching at the bars of windows ere they laid them down on the side-walks to die.

As they issued from the street and emerged upon the open space, the galling fire which had attended their progress died away. The azoteas in front of them and about them were lined with armed men, who waited for the signal from Don Isidro, and Don Isidro stood motionless at his corner watching them. At the head of the column came a troop of stalwart men, marching on with firm step and eyes looking straight before them; in front of them rode a mounted officer, the plumes of his cocked hat had been shot away, blood stained the white gauntlet he wore on his bridle-hand, but stiffly erect he sat in his saddle, and his face was calm as though he knew no anxiety, but his lips were firmly pressed together, and the fingers of his right hand twined round the hilt of his sabre in a convulsive grasp.

Don Isidro was a civilian, but he was also sufficiently a soldier to admire and appreciate the perfection of military drill. Admiration and pity struggled within him against what he knew was his stern duty; his men looked at him in astonishment. The leading troopers were already half way across the open space, when with a shudder he shook himself free from his thoughts, leaped up on to the parapet, waved his sword, and shouted—

" At discretion ! fire ! "

A storm of shot shattered the ranks of those stately troopers, the horse of the mounted officer plunged wildly in the air and fell back over him, the head of the column was completely destroyed, the bodies of the tall troopers strewed the ground on which but a minute before they had marched so proudly. Only for a moment was the march of the column delayed, on it came swiftly as before, men dropping at every step under the fire from the loop-holed windows. They reached the corner, then from the windows of the almacen a rapid flanking fire opened upon them, and fresh assailants, leaning over the parapets of the houses on either hand, met them with a fresh storm of shot. The column reached the corner, entered the street, but went no further, the leading files melted away under that deadly fire. The retreat was sounded, the soldiery retired out of reach of the fire of the Patricios to the back of the open space, where, opening fire themselves, they drove the defenders back from the nearer parapets and obtained a respite.

Meantime the infantry corps had passed on a square further north. From this subdivision came galloping back a mounted officer, his cocked hat and plumes showed him to be an aide-de-camp. He enquired angrily from Colonel Kington the reason of his halt, and of his breaking the general orders by allowing the men to fire. In reply the colonel pointed to the heaps of men, dead and dying, who lay about the street corner.

" I am bringing up a gun. I must take that corner house, I cannot pass it, the windows are all loopholed."

" You know the positive orders of General Whitelock ! Unless you advance at once I shall be forced to report you."

Again the troopers formed in column, again they advanced over ground strewn with the bodies of their slaughtered comrades, their leader marching, now on foot, at their head, the aide-de-camp beside him, a fine-made young man, with the blue eyes and yellow hair of the midland counties, Craddock by name, the favourite aide-de-camp of General Whitelock.

Don Isidro had watched all these manœuvres ; again he reserved his fire till the column was more than half way to the fatal corner, again leaping on to the parapet he waved his sword as a signal, again a storm of shot swept away whole ranks of living men. Colonel Kington fell ; the aide-de-camp reeled in his saddle, let go his reins to press his hand to his side, his frightened horse turned and galloped off, away back through the now silent suburb to the British camp ; his rider, seeing nothing, knowing nothing of where he went, kept his seat till the horse stopped, when he was gently lifted from the saddle, carried into a house, and laid upon a bed. There he lingered till sundown, neither opening his eyes nor speaking, save once, when General Whitelock bent over him and spoke to him.

" Ah, General ! " he said. " Those streets of Buenos Aires, they are, as that Spaniard said they would be, the pathways of death."

Again the column recoiled from that fatal corner, and a gun being now brought up was wheeled into position in front of the door of Don

Isidro's house, at somewhat more than 100 yards distance. The first shot crashed through a panel of the door and did little harm ; the second struck it full in the centre, where it was secured by a heavy cross-bar, shattering the latter and the door itself so much that it was only held by the lower bolts. Two more shots, and the door was a complete wreck. Then the troopers, in open order, again advanced, firing steadily at the Patricios on the azotea, and at the loopholed windows.

Fiercely occupied as each man was at his own post, Doña Dalmacia was the first to notice the shattered door. Leaving her own room she ran across the patio to the almacen, calling upon the men there to bring out boxes and barrels to block up the zaguan. Excited men rushed out into the patio as they heard her voice, not comprehending what she said amid the roar of the musketry. Seeing the open doorway they fired from the patio upon the advancing troops. In vain Doña Dalmacia ran among them, entreating them to block up the entrance at once, they were mad with the fury of the fight. English bullets came amongst them, several of them fell, then Doña Dalmacia, running into the sala, brought out a heavy chair and threw it on its side in the middle of the zaguan. Hardly had she done so ere a bullet struck her in the throat, she fell forward upon the chair, clinging to it with her hands, her blood pouring over the embroidered velvet in a steady stream.

Don Isidro had heard his wife's voice ; calling upon some of his men to follow him, he ran down the narrow stair from the roof; as he set foot in the patio he saw his wife fall.

"Dalma!" he screamed, rushing to her and raising her in his arms. It was the last word he ever uttered. She opened her eyes once, looked upon him with a loving smile, her lips moved, but no words came, he saw she was dead. With one arm clasped round her, he shook the other hand fiercely at the English ; they poured in one deadly volley, and then rushed into the zaguan. Don Isidro fell. shot through the heart, in death yet clasping his wife to him ; their blood, mingling in one red stream, dyed the feet of the furious soldiers as they ran in over their prostrate bodies.

The shouts of men, the screams of women, as they saw Don Isidro fall back upon the pavement with his wife's body in his arms, brought the entire garrison of the house into the patio. From the roof, from the sala, from the almacen men rushed towards the main entrance, beating back the soldiery with clubbed muskets, stabbing furiously with knives, bayonets, or whatever weapon came to hand, while from the azotea the Patricios opened fire upon the zaguan itself. The struggle was sharp but short ; all the English who had entered the patio were killed, the zaguan was choked with the bodies of their dead. Reinforcements poured in from every side, a strong party from the suburbs ventured into the open street and attacked the invaders in the rear ; Captain Buller who had led the attack upon the house had fallen in the zaguan ; again they retreated. The Patricios rushed out in pursuit.

The English, re-forming their broken ranks, attempted to cover their retreat by the fire of their cannon, but from every side poured in upon them fresh hosts of foes. Men fell by dozens; for five minutes the open ground was the scene of a frightful butchery. Then a cry arose among the Patricios, " To the cannon, muchachos ! "

A party of the Patricios, in something like order, rushed with levelled bayonets on the gun ; behind them came a motley crowd—shopmen in their shirt-sleeves, their faces grimy with gunpowder ; half-naked slaves armed with pikes and hatchets ; paisanos, who, wrapping their ponchos round their left arms, threw aside their carbines and drew from their waistbands poniards twenty inches in the blade. The artillerymen were shot down or bayonetted, the gun captured, and the dismounted dragoons driven in confusion back up the street by which they had advanced. Here they were met in precipitate retreat by Captain Forster, an aide-de-camp to General Whitelock, who assisted Major Pigott to rally them. Re-forming them and bringing up the other gun, Major Pigott opened such a deadly fire of grape and musketry upon his pursuers that he drove them back across the open ground and forced them to take shelter in the houses, abandoning the gun they had captured. He then burst open the doors of a corner-house to the west of the open space, took possession of it, and posting a strong party of his men on the flat roof drove off by a well-directed fire all the men on the neighbouring azoteas.

Here he remained all the rest of the day, not venturing to make any further attempt to advance. Throughout the afternoon the Patricios kept up a fire of musketry, but they did not venture to attack him.

All morning the crews of the British fleet, anchored in the roadstead, had looked anxiously from the masts and yards of their ships for any indication of how the day was going. First on the Residencia, then on the church of Las Monjas Catalinas, then on the Retiro, then on the church of Santo Domingo, and at length, soon after ten o'clock, on the church of San Miguel they saw the flag of England waving in triumph. The greater part of the city was already theirs, and it was yet early ; the first part of the plan of General Whitelock had been successfully achieved. As the flag was hoisted last of all on the church of San Miguel the watching sailors greeted the sight with loud shouts of joy, with ringing cheers which were heard even to the shore.

Yes, the first part of the plan of General Whitelock had been successfully achieved, the first positions had been attained, but at what cost ? Fully one third of the troops which had paraded at dawn in full confidence of success were now hors-de-combat. All over the streets of Buenos Aires lay British soldiers still in death or grievously wounded. As yet merely the *undefended* part of the city had been traversed, only one attack had been made upon an entrenched position, and that had been repulsed with fearful slaughter.

Those open streets of Buenos Aires, held only by squads of militia and half-armed citizens, had been to the trained soldiery of England the pathways of death.

CHAPTER XII.

THE AFTERNOON OF THE 5TH JULY.

THE salvo of British guns at dawn on the 5th July roused General Liniers from the soundest sleep he had enjoyed for several days. He sprang up with the alacrity of one who, having a hard task before him, had made every possible preparation and was confident of success. In ten minutes the whole of the troops in and about the Plaza Mayor, were under arms, and every post about the defences of the centre strongly occupied. Beyond this there was nothing he could do but wait in readiness for any emergency which might befall.

When Colonel Cadogan attacked the church of San Francisco he sent out a strong detachment of Spanish infantry to aid the militia, and then took charge in person of the defence of the entrenchment which was so furiously assailed by Colonel Pack. When these attacks were repulsed he turned his attention to the north of his position, where two subdivisions of the 88th regiment had established themselves in two houses about a square distant from each other in the vicinity of the Merced Church. On the azoteas around these houses he massed about 3000 men, chiefly militia and armed citizens, and then directed an attack upon them by the streets and from the beach by strong parties of Spanish troops with artillery. At the head of these troops marched the "Morenos de Ponce," led by Lieutenant Asneiros. The English, driven from the azoteas by the overwhelming fire concentrated upon them, stubbornly held their position till nearly twelve o'clock; Lieutenant-colonel Duff then yielded to the summons of Asneiros and handed him his sword, after having 220 men and seventeen officers killed and wounded. Major Vandeleur, whose loss had been almost as heavy, surrendered immediately afterwards.

After this success, General Liniers repaired to the tower of the Cabildo, and looked forth around him. To the north the English flag waved on the church of Las Monjas Catalinas, and over some houses nearer the river; to the west on the tower of San Miguel, and to the south on the church of Santo Domingo; it was upon this last flag that his gaze lingered. Round each position so held by the foe the azoteas were crowded with armed men, the rattle of musketry was incessant, and the guns from the fort were firing steadily and with sure aim upon those houses near the beach which were held by the 36th regiment.

Calling to him Colonel Elio, his second in command, General Liniers directed him to march with a strong force of infantry and four guns upon these houses near the beach, and upon the church of Las Monjas Catalinas. Then sending for Asneiros, he directed him to return at once with the "Morenos" to his former station contiguous to the church of San Miguel, and to instruct Don Roderigo Ponce de Leon to concert measures with the commander of the Arribeño regiment, which occupied the two neighbouring blocks, for the recapture of that position. Having so provided for the north and west, he then turned his attention to the recapture of the church of Santo Domingo.

The first measure of Colonel Elio was to go forward himself with a flag of truce to the position held by General Lumley. Telling him that further resistance was useless, and informing him of the fate of the 88th regiment, he summoned him to surrender. To this General Lumley returned a scornful refusal, and the firing which had ceased on the appearance of the flag of truce, recommenced with greater fury than ever.

Again Colonel Elio went forward with a flag of truce, and this time with a written order from General Liniers, commanding him to surrender within a quarter of an hour, to which General Lumley replied as before. A strong force of Spanish infantry then advanced by the beach and opened fire with two field-pieces at point-blank range. Lieutenant-colonel Bourne sallied out at the head of fifty grenadiers, drove the infantry at the point of the bayonet back to the walls of the fort, and spiked both guns. At the same time another strong body of infantry which advanced by the streets was met by Major King with a wing of the 5th regiment and driven back with heavy loss.

The loss of the 36th was already heavy, both in officers and men; the ammunition was almost exhausted, the numbers of the enemy increased every moment. After communicating with Colonel Davie, who still held the church of Las Monjas Catalinas, General Lumley determined upon evacuating both positions, and retiring by the beach to the Retiro, where what remained of the two columns of the left and centre concentrated soon after two o'clock, and restricted their attention to securing that position.

On the block contiguous to the church of San Miguel Don Roderigo Ponce de Leon held the command on the morning of the 5th July, having under his orders the "Morenos de Ponce" and about 300 armed citizens and slaves, the adjacent blocks fronting him being held by detachments of the Arribeño regiment.

Lieutenant-colonel Duff, marching down the Calle Piedad in the early morning with his wing of the 88th regiment, had attempted to force an entrance into the church of San Miguel, but the massive door resisted all his efforts to break it open, and the fire of the Arribeños from the opposite azoteas was so destructive that he was compelled to relinquish his attempt and march on, leaving thirty of his men lying dead or badly wounded under the porch.

When a second party of English attacked the church some hours later, Don Roderigo had few men with him. The "Morenos" and the Arribeños had been summoned by General Liniers to aid in the attack upon the 88th regiment, and many of the armed citizens had gone with them. With such as remained under his orders, Don

Roderigo withdrew to the far side of the block, out of range of the
fire of the English sharpshooters. As the English burst into the
church, a large double door further down the street was opened, a
horseman issued from it having a boy behind him *en croupe*, who, instantly setting spurs to his horse, galloped off, while the door closed
behind them.

"Don't fire, men, it is only a boy!" shouted the officer in command
of the English, and the horse carried his double load in safety to the
first cross street.

The horseman was Venceslao Viana, the boy was Evaristo Ponce
de Leon.

On the return of Asneiros, Don Roderigo left the azotea, and descending into the cross street where the "Morenos" were halted,
proceeded to make arrangements with the commandant of the Arribeño regiment for the recapture of the church. In half an hour the
streets to the north and east of the church were occupied by strong
parties of the Arribeños, and hundreds of armed citizens, flushed
with their recent triumph over the 88th regiment, poured on to all the
adjacent azoteas, crouching down behind the parapets, and creeping
nearer and nearer to the British position.

"Now we shall see what you are worth, Morenitos," said Venceslao
Viana, as he galloped up to Don Roderigo with a message from the
commander of the Arribeño regiment that all was ready.

"Adelante! Marchen!" shouted Asneiros, as Don Roderigo gave
him a signal.

Steadily the well-drilled negroes marched to the corner, wheeled
into the street not 120 yards from the British guns, and then with a
loud yell charged straight upon them. Round-shot and grape answered their shout of defiance, and swept them from the centre of
the street, but, spread along the side-walks, they still advanced, firing
upon the artillerymen. The infantry drawn up in front of the church
advanced to the support of the artillery, red-coated soldiers poured
from the houses of the block beyond, of which the invaders had
taken possession. The advance of the negroes was stopped, but the
roar of the cannon had given the signal, men sprang to their feet on
every azotea round about, on every side militia marched into the open
streets. The red-coated soldiery, facing in every direction, kept their
foes at bay with a steady fire of musketry, one gun was wheeled round,
and a shower of grape drove back the Arribeños, who came by the
cross street from the north straight upon the church.

Again Asneiros formed up the negro corps. Don Roderigo himself led them on, waving his hat, and calling upon them to trust to
the bayonet. The negroes answered him with shouts, and rushed on.
Again a shower of grape tore through them. A dozen men fell. The
first to fall was Don Roderigo. Several of the negroes, throwing
down their muskets, ran to him, and, raising him in their arms, carried
him to the shelter of the next street.

Evaristo had seen his father fall, and ran up to him.

"Tata! Tata!" he cried; "speak to me! speak to me, Tata!"

"I am not dead yet, my son," said Don Roderigo. "I think my
leg is broken—a small matter. Run and tell Asneiros—"

"Yet there is one Ponce de Leon to finish these," said Evaristo, running off.

In front of the church of San Miguel, the second house from the corner had a peaked roof, covered with large red tiles. This house, by breaking the line of the azotea, had been a great protection to the English formed in the street below. The adjacent azotea was crowded with armed citizens, who saw with consternation the second repulse of the negroes.

"Cost what it may, we must stop the fire of that gun," shouted a young officer of the Spanish navy who was among them. "Follow me, boys!"

So saying he clambered up on to the roof of the tiled house, and tearing up one of the tiles from the coping threw it at the gunner, who at that moment held the linstock in his hand. The tile struck him on the side of the head, down he fell, and the burning tow dropped under the gun instead of firing it. The citizens gave a loud shout as they saw him fall. Laying down their firelocks, scores of them followed the young officer, showering heavy tiles upon the artillerymen as fast as they could tear them from the roof.

"Ah! Morenitos! are you afraid of a cannon?" said Venceslao Viana to the negroes, as they clustered at the street corner; "follow me, and I will show you how cannon are taken!"

He had already arranged the coils of his lasso in his hand; he now galloped up the street whirling it round his head. A dozen yards from the gun he checked his horse, threw the noose over the breech of the cannon, then turned and drove in his spurs. For a few yards he dragged the gun after him, then it turned over, and the fastenings of the trunnions giving way, he galloped off with his prize, leaving the wheels and body behind him.

"Follow me, Morenitos!" shouted Evaristo, as the gun upset; "yet there is a Ponce de Leon to show you the way."

The negroes yelled, and losing all order, followed him pell-mell; a party of the Arribeños followed them, wild cheers and shouts rose from all sides, the fire from the azoteas was more furious than ever. The negroes drove the English infantry before them from the front of the church and captured the other gun, but were in their turn charged and driven back. but they took the gun with them.

Then the Arribeños again advanced by the cross street from the north, poured in a volley at not more than twenty yards' distance, and charged. The small English force was cut in two, one part made good its retreat to the suburbs, the other, driven into the church by a fresh advance of the negroes led by Asneiros, had no alternative but to surrender.

The officer in command surrendered to Lieutenant Asneiros, his men threw down their arms, the English flag was removed from the tower of the church, and Asneiros won the second sword he took that day.

Meantime General Liniers, as a first step to the recapture of the church of Santo Domingo, completely surrounded the house occupied by Colonel Cadogan, keeping up a constant fire upon the small garrison, till, when he had only forty men left able to fire a musket, that officer surrendered.

Liniers then despatched an officer with a flag of truce to General Crauford, telling him that the assault had failed in all quarters, that the losses of the English had been fearful, that several detachments had surrendered, that he himself was surrounded and completely cut off, and calling upon him to yield himself and his men prisoners of war. To which summons General Crauford returned a decided refusal.

On receipt of this answer General Liniers directed an advance from all sides upon the church, militia and armed citizens swarmed on all the neighbouring azoteas, and their concentrated fire soon overpowered that of the British sharp-shooters who occupied the towers and leads of the church, and forced them to retire.

In front of the principal door of the church was an open space, on which a portion of the light infantry were stationed, screened by intervening houses from the fire of the guns on the entrenchments of the Plaza Mayor, and on the south side the fort. Don Felipe Navarro, who commanded on the block to the west of the church, had just heard of the deaths of his sister and of Don Isidro Lorea ; furious at the intelligence, and seeing the retreat of the sharp-shooters from the towers and roof of the church, he led his men right up to the parapet overlooking the open space, and springing upon it pointed with his sword to the troops below him—

"There they are, muchachos !   Fire upon the heretics !   Fire ! "

The words were hardly past his lips ere a ball struck him in the chest, he fell from the parapet into the street below, dead ere he reached the ground.

But now from every azotea round a deadly fire was directed upon the open space, and the troops, unable to make any effective reply, were withdrawn into the church.

Within the church the British troops were safe from the fire of musketry, but their position was full of danger, the great doors might easily be beaten in by cannon, and then the garrison would be at the mercy of their foes.   General Crauford called together a council of his officers.

Colonel Pack, on rejoining his superior officer, after the failure of the attack led by himself, had counselled an immediate retreat upon the Residencia, but General Crauford could not then see the necessity for any such step, and considered that he was compelled by his instructions to occupy the church of Santo Domingo. Later on Colonel Pack had discovered in the church the flag of his old regiment, the 71st Highlanders, which had been captured on the 12th August. Overjoyed at the recovery of his flag, he had ascended to the roof and planted it on the eastern tower of the church, and spoke no more of the necessity of retreat.   He now brought it down again and repeated his former counsel. But most of the other officers agreed that without a strong diversion in their rear, retreat was now impossible, that to attempt it would result only in a wholesale slaughter of the men.

Then General Liniers mounted a heavy gun upon a neighbouring azotea and opened fire with it upon the eastern tower of the church, at the same time that the guns on the southern side the fort were also turned upon it, with the intention of bringing it down upon the heads of the English garrison.

Until four o'clock General Crauford held out, hoping that General Whitelock might make some effort to relieve him, while not a man of his could show himself at any opening without drawing upon himself at once the fire of 100 muskets, and the base of the tower crumbled away under the steady fire of the cannon. Finding his situation hopeless, he then hung out a flag of truce, the firing ceased, and he surrendered, yielding himself, his officers, and 600 men as prisoners of war, and leaving 100 more, who were too severely wounded to be moved, lying on the floor of the church under the great dome.

It was four o'clock in the afternoon, a wild shout of joy rose up all over the city, Buenos Aires was once more in the possession of her own people. Stern men, who seemed to have no softness in them, wept like children ; friends and brothers rushed into each others' arms, embracing each other in the exuberance of their delight. For half an hour the city gave itself up to the delirium of triumph.

Then while daylight yet lasted those who had been foremost in the strife took the lead in the work of mercy. Bands of the Patricios scoured the streets all over the city, collecting the wounded British soldiers who had so lately been their deadly foes. Where the carnage had been the greatest, where the struggle had been the fiercest, every house became a hospital, and every household ministered to the wants of suffering men. And in many a household there was mourning and loud lamentation over those who were of that household no longer ; in many a house fathers, brothers, or well-loved friends lay moaning on beds of pain ; yet every house was open to the wounded foemen who had brought that sorrow upon them, and upon whom it had so fearfully recoiled. Gentle hands raised them from the earth, bound up their shattered limbs, and held cups of water to lips pale with agony.

Then night once more covered the city with a veil of darkness, the roar of the cannon, the rattle of the musketry, which had been incessant all day, was no longer heard.

The great struggle of the 5th July was now a matter of the past, was already an epoch in the history of a young nation, who recked not as yet that she was a nation. Whose sons had fought under a flag that was not theirs, and who laid the hard-won laurels of victory at the feet of an older nation, looking up to her in loving reverence as to a mother.

So the night passed over, and on the morrow it was another day.

CHAPTER XIII.

THE CAPITULATION OF THE 6TH JULY.

At sundown on the evening of the 5th July, General Liniers presided at a council of the Cabildo; the utmost enthusiasm prevailed. The number and quality of the prisoners they had made, the heavy loss they had inflicted upon the invading army, filled each man with the confidence of certain victory. In this enthusiasm and confidence General Liniers fully shared, and he proposed that terms of arrangement should be offered to the English General for the prevention of further bloodshed. He proposed that on condition of the immediate evacuation of the province all the prisoners should be given up, and that the English should be permitted to re-embark without molestation.

"No, no!" said Don Martin Alzaga eagerly. "By that we should lose the entire fruits of the victory we have won. Let us insist that they also evacuate the Banda Oriental."

"It is impossible that General Whitelock should listen to such a proposition," said the Reconquistador. "As yet not more than half his force has been engaged. To make such a proposition would be to prevent all chance of an arrangement."

"Let it," answered Don Martin Alzaga. "As yet he has not even seen our teeth. Our men were cautious to-day, we did not even know our strength; to-morrow every man will be a hero, we will attack him in his own positions, and he shall not get away at all."

"If we are rash we shall lose the advantage we have gained," said Don Gregorio Lopez.

"Try it, at any rate," said Don Martin, "he can but refuse."

The majority of the council supported Don Martin Alzaga, a letter was drawn up as he had proposed, and despatched at daylight to the Retiro, where it was received by Sir Samuel Auchmuty, who at once forwarded it to the Plaza Miserere, where General Whitelock had passed the night in almost complete ignorance of the events of the day, having had but one communication with Sir Samuel Auchmuty on the afternoon of the 5th, and none whatever with the leaders of the other two columns.

The following is the official translation of this despatch :—

"General Liniers to General Whitelock.

"Sir,
         "The same sentiments of humanity which induced your Excellency to propose to me to capitulate, lead me, now that I am fully acquainted with your force, that I have taken eighty officers and upwards of 1000 men, and killed more than double that number,

without your having reached the centre of my position, the same
sentiments, I say, lead me, in order to avoid a further effusion of blood,
and to give your Excellency a fresh proof of Spanish generosity, to
offer to your Excellency, that if you choose to re-embark with the
remainder of your army, to evacuate Monte Video and the whole of
the river Plata, leaving me hostages for the execution of the treaty. I
will not only return all the prisoners which I have now made, but also
all those which were taken from General Beresford. At the same
time I think it necessary to state, that if your Excellency does not
admit this offer, I cannot answer for the safety of the prisoners, as my
troops are so infinitely exasperated against them, and the more, as
three of my aides-de-camp have been wounded bearing flags of truce ;
and for this reason I send your Excellency this letter by an English
officer, and shall wait your answer for one hour.

> "I have the honour to be, &c.,
> "Santiago Liniers.

"Buenos Aires, 5th July, 1807,
    at 5 o'clock in the evening."

At daylight, on the morning of the 6th, a strong column of British
troops advanced from the Retiro upon the centre, but not venturing
again to attempt the passage of those long, straight streets, descended
to the river-side and advanced by the beach under cover of the fire of
four gunboats, which came close in shore for the purpose of supporting
them. Two squares from the fort they were hotly assailed by the
regular troops and the militia, but after an hour's firing the column
retreated unpursued to its former position. The gunboats continued
their fire for several hours, throwing both round shot and shell into
the vicinity of the fort and the Plaza Mayor, one shell bursting in the
apartments of General Liniers in the fort.

At about eleven o'clock General Whitelock, who was still at the
Miserere, received the above despatch from General Liniers, and returned an answer by an aide-de-camp, after which he himself proceeded
with an escort to the Retiro, there to await the reply.

The following is a copy of this despatch :—

> "General Whitelock to General Liniers.
> "Headquarters,
> "Place de Tauros, 6th July, 1807.

"Sir,
    "I have the honour to acknowledge receipt of your letter.
You do me no more than justice in believing that whatever advances
the cause of humanity would be grateful to me ; and therefore as, from
the extent of the action of yesterday, the wounded on both sides are
dispersed over a considerable space of ground, I would propose that
there should be a truce for four-and-twenty hours, that each might
collect those dispersed on the lines of approach of the different columns.
The ground on which the armies now stand to be the line of demar-
cation, and each to bring the wounded of the other to deliver them
to the respective outposts.

"As to the idea of surrendering the advantages which this army has
gained, it is quite inadmissible, having also taken many prisoners,

captured a quantity of artillery, with all its stores, and gained both its flanks. I leave to your candour the comparison of the relative situation of the two armies.

"I have to lament the circumstance A. D. C. having been wounded; I cannot account for it otherwise than by attributing it to those mistakes which often occur at the commencement of hostilities. I shall take care that nothing of the kind shall happen for the future; but I have to remark that my A. D. C. was fired at the whole way of his approach to your lines on the 4th inst., when I sent him with a flag of truce.

"J. Whitelock."

To this proposition for a suspension of hostilities General Liniers returned a decisive negative, giving the British General only a quarter of an hour for deliberation, and reiterating his previous demand for the surrender of all the acquisitions of the English in the Rio de La Plata.

The quarter of an hour passed, no answer was returned, whereupon General Liniers, with a strong force of the Patricios, supported by a body of regular troops, sallied forth from his entrenchments and advanced upon the Residencia by the Calle Defensa. This position was still held by Major Nicholls with 400 men of the 45th regiment, who charged his assailants with the bayonet, drove them back with heavy loss, and captured two howitzers, with their limbers and ammunition. Later on another attempt was made upon this position, but the attacking column was received with discharges of grape from the captured guns and forced to retreat.

About two o'clock General Whitelock, who was then at the Retiro, sent another officer to General Liniers with a flag of truce, accepting the terms offered by him in his despatch of the previous evening, upon which the firing at once ceased.

Soon after sundown Major-general Levison Gower, with a strong escort of Spanish troops, proceeded through the city to the fort for the purpose of drawing up with General Liniers a formal deed of capitulation, which should be signed on the day following. As he passed through the streets the excited populace thronged round him with fierce shouts of defiance, at times firing into the air, but by the exertions of the Spanish officers who were with him he reached the fort in safety, and was led to the room in which General Liniers was at that moment at dinner, having several of the English officers, his prisoners, with him as his guests. The disorderly crowd, armed with swords and pistols, rushed in over the drawbridge in front of the escort, and forced their way into the dining-room, shouting—

"Señor Pack! Señor Pack! come out, we have something to arrange with you."

It had been represented to the people by the Spanish authorities that General Beresford and the officers who had escaped with him from Lujan, in March, had broken their parole. This, together with his success at Perdriel and Colonia, and the fact of his having been the only English officer who had attacked the entrenchments on the 5th, greatly irritated the populace against Colonel Pack, and they would certainly have wreaked bloody vengeance upon him had they got him into their power.

General Liniers sprang from his chair as the rioters burst into the room, and seizing the foremost by the throat forced them back, going out with them and doing all in his power to pacify them, in which he partially succeeded, but apprehensive of a further attempt, he, two hours later, sent Colonel Pack to the Retiro under a strong escort of Spanish troops.

Two priests, who were dining with General Liniers that evening, also interposed between Colonel Pack and the rioters, and declared that they would lose their own lives rather than permit any harm to befall him.

The following day the treaty of capitulation was signed by Santiago Liniers, Cæsar Balviani, and Bernardo Velasco on the part of the Spaniards; and by General Whitelock and Admiral Murray on behalf of the British, the latter agreeing to evacuate Monte Video within two months.

On the same day the British released all their prisoners, and about 1700 men, many of whom were wounded, were released by the garrison of the city; but the British General was forced to leave about 200 men who were too severely wounded to be moved, in the care of the Spaniards, and it was impossible for General Liniers at that time to deliver up the prisoners captured with General Beresford, they being dispersed at great distances throughout the provinces.

Many of the dead were buried in the places where they fell, in particular those of the left wing of the 88th regiment, which had penetrated the city by the Calle Cuyo. This street acted at that time as a drain to all that part of the city, the roadway near to the beach had been washed away by heavy rains till it formed a deep ditch. After the fighting was over, this ditch was used as a grave, and a new roadway formed over the bodies of the slain. During the process of repaving the city, in the year 1860, the excavations in this street brought to light a quantity of human bones, mixed up with brass buttons and regimental badges. Of these the then British Consul-general, Frank Parish, Esq., took charge, and provided them with more fitting sepulture in the British cemetery.

In a few days the survivors of this expedition re-embarked from the beach below the Retiro. The British flag was driven in disgrace from the whole Viceroyalty of Buenos Aires.

M

EPILOGUE TO BOOKS I. AND II.

THE MONUMENTS AND THE REWARDS OF VICTORY.

THE Plaza Mayor, in which the fierce horsemen of Don Juan Martin Puyrredon trampled underfoot the choicest troops of General Beresford, bears to this day the name of the "Plaza Victoria," in commemoration of the victory of the 12th August, 1806.

Don Juan Martin led his horsemen to victory by the street now known as the "Calle Victoria," which is thus to this day a monument to the prowess of the wild horsemen of the Pampas.

The Calle Reconquista, the street by which General Liniers led his Spanish troops on that same 12th August, is to this day a monument of that feat of arms by which he himself gained the title of the "Reconquistador."

The Calle Defensa, in which stand the church of San Francisco, the church of Santo Domingo, and the Residencia, is by its name a monument to the heroic defence of their city by the militia and citizens of Buenos Aires on the 5th and 6th July, 1807.

The vacant space which early in this century lay in front of the house of Don Isidro Lorea is now a public Plaza, planted with trees, laid out with walks, one of the breathing-places of the great straggling city. It is known as the "Plaza Lorea," and is a monument to the heroic courage and untimely fate of Don Isidro Lorea and his wife Dalmacia.

Twenty cannon-shot imbedded in the brickwork of the eastern tower of the church of Santo Domingo tell to this day of the desperate lengths to which the citizens of Buenos Aires were ready to go rather than yield one foot of ground to a foreign invader. When the tower needs white-washing these cannon-shot are carefully painted black; they speak to all who look upon them of the days when as yet the Argentine Republic was a dream, when an infant people yet in tutelage dared to defy the power of a mighty nation.

Within the church of Santo Domingo, under the dome, hang six colours, the flags of English regiments which laid down their arms, defeated on the 12th August, 1806, and on the 5th July, 1807. One is the flag of the 71st Highlanders, seized by Don Juan Martin Puyrredon with his own hand.

Nearly 1000 armed slaves had taken a part in the defence of the city on the 5th and 6th July. To some of them their own masters gave freedom as their reward. The Patricios raised a subscription amongst themselves, and purchased the freedom of seventy slaves, drawn by lot from all who had been under fire.

When the Mendicant Asylum was opened, in the year 1860, the first admitted into the institution was a worn-out old man, who was son to the twice victorious General Liniers.

The native Argentines found their reward in the knowledge of their own strength, and in the organization of their militia, which they preserved after all danger from Great Britain had vanished, in spite of the opposition of their Spanish rulers. The regiments of the Patricios and the Arribeños were afterwards the nucleus upon which were formed those conquering armies which eventually annihilated the power of Spain in South America.

APPENDIX.

THE COURT-MARTIAL.

THE disgraceful defeat of the second expedition against Buenos Aires roused a storm of indignation in Great Britain. General White-lock was arrested on his return to England, and tried by court-martial.

The Court sat at Chelsea Hospital, and the trial which commenced on the 28th January, 1808, was continued by adjournment to the 15th March.

The Court consisted of nineteen general officers, under the presidency of General the Rt. Hon. Sir W. Meadows, K. B. One active member of this court-martial was Lieutenant-general Sir John Moore, K. B., who as yet recked nothing of the disastrous retreat through Galicia or of the blood-stained ramparts of Coruña.

Nearly all the officers in command of regiments or subdivisions of regiments on the 5th July, 1807, the general officers, and the officers of the staff, besides others connected with the expedition, were examined, after which General Whitelock was called upon for his defence.

The sentence of the Court was, that " Lieutenant-general Whitelock be cashiered, and declared totally unfit and unworthy to serve his Majesty in any military capacity whatever."

Concerning the equity and even lenience of this sentence there can be no question, but in justice to an officer at once incapable and unfortunate it is well to state the principal point in his defence.

In the General Orders issued to the army on the 4th July occurs the following sentence :—

" Each officer commanding a division of the left wing, which is from the 88th to 87th inclusively, to take care that he does not incline to his right of the right wing, that is, Light Brigade and 45th regiment to the left." (Sic.)

General Whitelock in his defence alleged that Colonels Pack and

Cadogan disobeyed this order by their attack upon the church of San Francisco and of the entrenchment, both of which lay to the left of their line of advance, and also General Crauford by his occupation of the church of Santo Domingo, which lay to the left of his line of advance. Had Colonel Pack occupied the church of Santo Domingo, and General Crauford the houses to the rear of that church, they might in the afternoon have retreated upon the Residencia, and the entire column would have been available on the day following.

The chief mistake of General Whitelock seems to have been that he made no attempt to establish a cordial understanding between himself and his officers, seldom consulting them, and listening to the advice of irresponsible men of far less experience. In particular, Colonel Pack, who had resided for three months in Buenos Aires, was never once consulted by that General. The result was that the valour of the troops was thrown away, they were sacrificed by the ignorance and incapacity of their commander, and deep disgrace and humiliation was inflicted upon the British flag.

The name of General Whitelock is to this day a bye-word of reproach in the provinces of La Plata, but there are no grounds for attributing the misfortune to treachery, as it is the common custom of the Spaniards to do. It is an unfortunate characteristic of the Iberian race to attribute all disasters rather to treachery than to ignorance and incapacity.

BOOK III.

THE UNKNOWN FUTURE.

PROLOGUE.

When a child first learns his strength he adventures to walk, and delights in the exercise of his new-found powers; yet in every difficulty he seeks the supporting hand of his nurse, in every trouble he flies for refuge to his mother, he trusts in her and confides in her, obeys all her commands implicitly, questioning nothing. The day comes when neither nurse nor mother is by to aid him, he pauses, trembling at the unwonted solitude, then his spirit stirs itself within him, and he thinks. The day that the child first thinks for himself he has set his foot on the second round in the ladder of life.

Two struggles with the English had taught the Argentine people one great lesson—that in times of difficulty and danger they need look for no help from Spain.

Then the all-conquering genius of revolution set his heel upon Spain. Spain, long tottering, fell, and became a mere appanage to the empire of Napoleon. Spain had kept her children in bondage, now she was in tutelage herself.

Buenos Aires looked around her and she was alone. Her stay and her support was gone from her, but she knew no fear, for her spirit was strong within her. The danger with which she was menaced was a danger no longer—the enemy whom she had fought for Spain was now her friend.

The third expedition, with which Great Britain was preparing to avenge the two defeats she had suffered in Buenos Aires, never reached the shores of La Plata. Troops mustered at Cork, but ere they embarked their destination was changed. In Portugal, under the command of Sir Arthur Wellesley, they won the two victories of Roliça and Vimeira, the first in that long list of victories which is called by English historians the Peninsular War.

CHAPTER I.

AT THE QUINTA DE DON ALFONSO.

It was near the end of August. In a small, barely-furnished room at the quinta where General Whitelock had held his council of war on the afternoon of the 4th July, Marcelino Ponce de Leon lay on a low bedstead reading a newspaper entitled "La Estrella del Sur." It was about the size of a fly-sheet of the present day, very badly printed on very bad paper, and it bore the date "Monte Video, April, 1807." The Comandante de los Morenos de Ponce looked very pale; his left arm was bandaged, and lay in a sling formed by a silk handkerchief, which passed round his neck and hung down in front of him. He was propped up with pillows, and held the paper in his right hand; even turning it and holding it in a position to read was a labour to him.

There came a footstep in the patio outside, a hand was laid upon the latch of the door, Marcelino hurriedly rolled up the paper, and pushed it under the pillow behind him. The door was softly opened, and Don Carlos Evaña walked in.

"It is you, Carlos," said Marcelino; "I thought it was my host, for he has not been to see me to-day. Come and sit down and talk."

"With pleasure, I have come to spend the morning with you. Don Alfonso has gone into the city to meet his daughter, who has been living for the last four years with Don Fausto Velasquez and his family at their estancia."

"His daughter! I did not know he had one."

"Nor I either till yesterday. It seems that while he was in prison Don Fausto Velasquez took pity on his daughter, and she has lived more with his family than with her father ever since."

"But how goes my father?"

"Yesterday he was hobbling about with a crutch—the wound was nothing more than a simple fracture. He says the only thing he has to grumble about is your being here, and he is very anxious for you to grow strong enough to be moved."

"There again, and none of them will come to see me while I am here, not even my mother!"

"Poor Doña Constancia! I can tell you it has cost her many tears, but Don Roderigo's orders are positive. Luckily I followed General Whitelock here, or I don't think they would ever have heard of you till you got well enough to seek them yourself."

"And the English officer who brought me here, have you never been able to find out who he was?"

"I have not the slightest clue to him, except that he was an officer of Craufurd's brigade."

"Well, one is forced at times to accept benefits for which one cannot even give thanks; but God knows who he is, and will reward him."

"Pish!" answered Evaña; "did not you do the same for that English friend of yours, Gordon?"

"The circumstances were quite different. I could not have done less for him, and I have my reward in a valued friendship which will last our two lives. But Gordon, how is it he has never been to see me?"

"He was sent outside after Whitelock's capitulation. The Cabildo only gave up such of Beresford's prisoners as happened to be in the city at the time of the assault; they have kept your friend Gordon for you a little longer. He went to the Pajonales, so I should not wonder if he has come back with Don Fausto."

"Poor fellow! But I should have been very sorry if he had gone without my seeing him again."

"I don't know whether I am doing right in letting you talk so much, but you do look very much better to-day, and your voice is quite clear again. That will be good news for Doña Constancia and Dolores; I shall go and see them this afternoon."

"Who is this Don Alfonso? He has been to me the best physician and the most grumpy host that ever a man had."

"If I tell you his surname you will know at once who he is, then we need talk no more of him, and I will read to you. His name is Miranda."

"Miranda!" said Marcelino meditatively; "Miranda! Is he any relation to the General, Don Francisco?"

"His brother."

"And what has he done that my father should think him his enemy?"

"Have you never heard? It happened before I went to Europe!"

"What happened?"

"I see you have never heard of him before. Strange! Then I suppose I must tell you. You have heard of the expeditions of Miranda for the liberation of Venezuela?"

"Oh yes: you and I have often spoken of them."

"Unluckily for Don Alfonso, who was in England at the time of his second attempt in 1798, he just then determined to return to Venezuela. He had lost his wife, who was an Englishwoman, I suppose that made him leave England. He had never mixed in politics, and knew nothing of his brother's schemes, but when he landed at Carracas he was thrown into prison, and only liberated on condition of leaving the country at once. He came here. Your father had him arrested again, and kept him in prison for more than a year. Your grandfather and Don Fausto Velasquez interfered to get him out, and the affair nearly ended in a complete rupture between your father and the rest of the family. It is generally believed that Don Alfonso revenged himself on Don Roderigo by sending secret information against him to Spain. Whether that is true I do not know, but soon after that your father fell into disgrace, and the two have been deadly enemies ever since. I wonder you never heard of this."

"I remember that before I went to Cordova there was a great quarrel between my father and my grandfather. I have seen my mother cry about it for an hour together, but I never knew what it was about. It must have been this affair, I suppose," answered Marcelino musingly. "How strange of my father! He is very liberal in his ideas. but he cannot see that we in our country have just the same rights that Spaniards have in Spain."

Then Marcelino lay back wearily on his pillows, and a shade of sadness passed over his face.

"I have let you talk too much," said Evaña; "and I should not have told you of this yet but that I thought you had heard before of Don Alfonso Miranda. Let me read to you; I have brought you another paper."

So saying, Evaña drew another paper from the breast-pocket of his coat, and began reading it aloud to his sick friend, every now and then pausing to make comments, and to add observations of his own. Marcelino listened dreamily with his eyes half closed, and a smile playing over his lips for some time, till his eyes closed altogether, and Evaña looking at him saw that he was asleep.

For two hours Evaña sat in silence at the bedside of his friend, listening to his low, regular breathing, looking at him now and then and marking the ravages which sickness and pain had made upon his young face. As he looked an expression of pain came into his own face, he thought of the numbers of his own countrymen in the bloom of their youth, or in the pride of their manhood, who would be struck down even as his own friend here before the dream of his life could be accomplished, before the dominion of Spain could be cast off, and a republic of Argentines take its place among the nations of the world. Of his own life he recked nothing, he had calculated the probable cost of a struggle with Spain, the price of liberty would be counted down in the lives of men, and that his own life would be one of them he thought likely enough, for did not he seek his own place in the very van of the great movement. But that the friends of his youth, who would follow him in the blind generosity of their hearts, fighting for a liberty of which they could not know the value, should fall, that thought was painful to him, and fall they would, that he knew right well.

So passed two hours; again the door opened, and a girl entered, bearing a tray with a basin of broth and some thin slices of bread on a plate.

"Here is your broth," said Evaña, as Marcelino awoke at the sound of the opening door; "let us see if you will leave less of it than you did yesterday."

"I don't intend to leave any of it to-day," replied Marcelino. "But first, Carlos, tell me, that daughter of Don Alfonso's you spoke of, what is she like?"

"I have never seen her," replied Evaña.

"I was at the Pajonales last summer, I must have met her there."

"She has been there for the last four years.

"There was a little girl there they called the Inglesita, I never thought of asking her name; she could not be more than fourteen or fifteen years old. She had a snub nose, and the most beautiful large gray eyes I ever saw."

"That would be her; you appear to remember her very well," said Evaña smiling; "but she must be more than fifteen, those English always look younger than their real age. Her name is Magdalen."

"Magdalen! Malena, I think I heard them call her so."

"That's she, without doubt. So the best thing you can do is to get strong enough to move into the sala, and then the owner of those gray eyes will amuse you better than I can."

"You don't admire gray eyes, you admire black ones, like my mother's or Eliza Puyrredon's; but I can tell you gray eyes are the most beautiful of all, if a sympathetic heart shines through them."

"You have studied them?"

"I have seen one pair which I shall never forget."

"And I also," said Evaña to himself; but he added aloud, "never mind about eyes just now, you can dream of them after you have taken your broth."

When Evaña, covering him carefully up, left the room, Marcelino lay back on his pillows, thinking dreamily of those gray eyes that Evaña's talk had brought back to his recollection. He had never spoken a dozen words to the Inglesita, but she had listened attentively to what he had said to others; he had looked at her, had seen his own ideas reflected in her eyes, and those eyes had haunted him ever since.

Next morning at his usual hour Don Carlos Evaña was again at the Quinta de Don Alfonso. Marcelino's eyes brightened as he took his seat beside him after making enquiries about his progress.

"Never mind about me," he said, "I am twice as strong to-day; but tell me your news, I am sure it is good from your face."

"Good and bad, both; but I don't know whether we need think the bad bad."

"Then the bad first. What is it?"

"Your grandfather has resigned his seat in the Cabildo."

"But that is bad, he was the only Creole those Spaniards thought worthy to sit with them."

"No, it is good. The best thing for us is that there be a broad line drawn between Spaniards and the sons of the soil. The broader this line is the easier will it be for us to tell friends from enemies when the day comes."

"And he resigned of his own will?"

"Yes, but not till he saw that to remain was to expose himself to expulsion."

"To expulsion! after all that he did for the defence of the city! If it had not been for him Liniers would never have been able to rescue the city from Beresford. And after that, who has done as much as he for the equipment of the militia?"

"No one," answered Evaña smiling. "Why you are strong enough to be quite indignant."

"Indignant! I should think I am."

"They only tolerated him so long as he was useful to them," replied Evaña. "I think he has done very well to resign."

" What became of Asneiros when my men were disbanded ? "

" Liniers has given him a captain's commission, but I don't know if he has joined any regiment yet."

" He is a smart soldier, but he is all a Spaniard. Do you know, if there were many Spaniards among us like him we could never have the country to ourselves, they would beat us if we came to fighting."

" There are many Spaniards as good as he," replied Evaña; "but not for that have I any fear. The Spanish system keeps the good men down, that is the weakness of Spain, and that is also the reason why we must free ourselves from Spain. We have many good men amongst us, but nothing can they do so long as Spain and the Spanish system rule over us."

" True. I shall see Asneiros some day, and shall keep my eye on him."

" Well, you have my bad news, now for the good ones. Your friend Gordon has come back with Don Fausto, and is coming with me to see you this afternoon."

" Viva! Yes, that is good."

" You can talk to him as much you like about the gray-eyed Magdalen. She talks English as well as I do, and Gordon and she are great friends."

" And Gordon, poor fellow, will be a prisoner yet for no one knows how long."

" He does not seem to fret about it. Very few prisoners find such kind gaolers ; I am sure I do not pity him."

" What made him go to Don Fausto's estancia ? "

" He had to go somewhere, for if he had been seen by any English officer he would have been claimed, so Don Fausto took him with him when he went back."

" Then was Don Fausto in the city on the 5th July ? "

" Did I never tell you? He came in with a party of peons all armed to the teeth, as soon as he heard that the English had landed. He got into town on the night of the 4th, and without resting a moment set to work to turn his house into a fortification ; a lot of the Patricios went to help him, and there they stood all day waiting for some Englishmen to come and be shot, and not one went anywhere near them."

" I should have thought that was exactly where the English would have tried to go in. Don Juan Martin Puyrredon went by that street on the 12th August, with Don Isidro Lorea to help him."

" They did try, but poor Don Isidro stopped them."

" Don Isidro ! what about him ? How your voice changed when you spoke of him," said Marcelino, raising himself on his elbow and looking earnestly at Evaña.

" It was a slip," said Evaña sadly. " I did not intend to have told you yet, but you must know some day. He was killed, fighting like a hero at the head of his men. Could you wish for a better death yourself fighting for his country in defence of his own home ? "

" And Doña Dalmacia ! what a blow for her ! How does she bear it ? "

" I have not seen her since. He completely beat the English and captured a gun. Don't ask me any more about it; when you are well and strong again we will go all round the city together, and I will tell you all I know of the attack and the defence. But I have something else to tell you now. Your Uncle Gregorio is missing."

"I thought you said he went to the quinta after the fight at the Paso Chico."

"He did, but the next day he went outside, and has never been back. We expected to hear of him from Don Fausto, but no one knows where he has gone."

"Oh, that is nothing! he is always disappearing like that, but he always turns up again. The old game, I suppose, some pair of shining black eyes."

"But it is strange now when all the comandantes are in the city, and he is in command of a regiment."

"Ah, Carlos, you don't understand those things; politics are everything to you, and if you see a pair of bright eyes you don't even notice what colour they are. When my uncle Gregorio sees a pair which smile on him he forgets everything. He always was that way, so they tell me."

"And then, after looking at himself in those eyes for a month or so, he gets tired of them, and goes away, and never thinks of them any more," said Evaña. "Frankly, I cannot understand a man like that, yet I believe there are such men."

"Of them there are many, but you are not one of them. Carlos, therefore you cannot understand my uncle. If ever you love it will be for all your life; you are a tyrant to every one else, but you would be a slave to a woman you loved."

"Therefore I had better never love," replied Evaña; "man was not made to be slave to any, but to be lord over the whole earth."

"But not lord over his own heart, Carlos, that is in no man's power. Proud as you are, your time will come."

"Let me read you some more of the 'Estrella del Sur,'" said Evaña, hastily.

"I have it safe under my pillow, no one has seen it," replied Marcelino. "Ah! Carlos, if the English had only made war upon the Spaniards with these newspapers instead of with cannon-balls, then we could have received them as friends."

"Be it then our work to teach the lesson they have failed to teach," replied Evaña.

CHAPTER II.

THE EPISODE OF THE FAIR MAURICIA.

A FORTNIGHT passed, Marcelino gained strength rapidly, Don Alfonso pronounced him well enough to bear removal, and very readily acquiesced in the desire of Don Roderigo that he should pass his convalescence under another roof. A covered litter, carried by slaves and escorted by Don Carlos Evaña and Lieutenant Gordon, made its appearance at the quinta one fine morning in September. That night Marcelino slept under his father's roof and his pillow was smoothed for him by his mother's hand. The change did him good, a few days more and he was able to spend his afternoons on a sofa in his mother's sala.

Little by little he learnt all the particulars of the struggle of the 5th and 6th July. The sad fate of Doña Dalmacia Navarro caused him deep sorrow, but on the whole he was surprised to learn the small extent of the loss suffered by his fellow-citizens, and his heart swelled with pride as anecdote after anecdote of their bravery and of their tender care for the victims of the fight, were poured into his willing ear.

One afternoon as his sister Dolores, aided by his two friends Don Carlos Evaña and Lieutenant Gordon, were doing their best to amuse him, Don Roderigo Ponce de Leon hurriedly entered the room and requested Don Carlos Evaña to favour him with his company for a few minutes.

"What is there?" asked Marcelino, as the door closed. "My father looked very grave."

"I came in just as he did," said Gordon. "There was a gaucho waiting for him, who seemed very impatient to see him. They went into Don Roderigo's private room together."

"Will it be some news of my uncle Gregorio, I know grandpapa is very anxious about him?" said Dolores.

News about this uncle Gregorio it most certainly was, and news which caused great disquietude to Don Roderigo. While raising his regiment in the preceding summer, Don Gregorio Lopez the younger had made the acquaintance of Don Francisco Viana, the father of Venceslao Viana, and had passed much of his spare time at his estancia, receiving from him much assistance in his recruiting operations. Don Francisco had several daughters, all good-looking, in spite of the dark blood which they inherited from their mother. One of them named Mauricia appeared to the Colonel of cavalry the handsomest woman he had ever seen in his life. He at once fell deeply in love with her, and felt that life without her to share it with him would be a burden

to him greater than he could bear. This sensation was no novelty to
the Señor Colonel Don Gregorio Lopez, it was commonly reported of
him in Buenos Aires that he experienced it at least once every six
months, nevertheless he pursued this new love with all the ardour of
a first affection and prospered in his suit.

The day of the repulse of General Whitelock he made his appearance
at the estancia of Don Francisco, all the men were absent, during the
night he disappeared, and Mauricia went with him. Great was the
sorrow of the family, who knew of his love and had encouraged it. Don
Francisco had seen in the marriage of his daughter with the Colonel a
means of reconciliation with his own family, a matter which he had
much at heart. Search was made in every direction for the runaway
couple, but for long there was no tidings of them, till Venceslao returned
from Buenos Aires, who, being better acquainted than the rest with
the Colonel's habits, before many days had traced them to the
Guardia Ranchos.

So much Don Roderigo told to Don Carlos Evaña as they stood in
an ante-room together, then he added—

"This man insists upon the Colonel marrying his sister at once,
but this the Colonel refuses to do, and he has come in to ask my
intervention in the matter. Now, as you know, Don Gregorio is very
jealous of my meddling in the affairs of his family, and I don't see
that I should be justified in doing so in this instance. But this Mauricia is the niece of my mother-in-law, therefore the honour of her
family is involved in this matter. You have great influence with Don
Gregorio, much more than I have, and I think it would be best for
you to break the matter to him. It will be very painful to him, he
has so carefully avoided all connexion with Don Francisco Viana,
that I believe he would rather see his eldest son dead than married
to one of his daughters."

Evaña did not answer immediately, but stood with his eyes fixed on
the ground, pulling nervously at his moustache with one of his long,
white hands.

"You had better see the man yourself," continued Don Roderigo,
opening a side door. "You will find him in here, and while you
speak to him I will go and consult Constancia."

Evaña entered the room of which Don Roderigo had opened the
door, and saw before him a handsome, dark-featured man, in the
ordinary rough dress of a paisano, seated on a chair, twirling his hat
round between his fingers. The man looked up at him as he closed
the door behind him, then dropping his hat he started to his feet,
exclaiming—

"My deliverer! my preserver! at last I have met you. Always
when I have been in this city since, I have looked for you. Thanks
be to God that I again see you."

"Who are you?" replied Evaña, looking at him in surprise. "I
have never that I know of done you any service, or even seen you
before."

"Already have you forgotten the massacre at Perdriel, where you
dragged me out from among the dead, and saved me when they were
coming to finish us?"

"You are the man that I helped from under a dead horse! I think I remember your face now."

"Yes, I am that man whose life you saved. I am Venceslao Viana."

"You never told me your name, but I am glad that I was able to assist you. Alas! the most of those lying there were beyond all assistance."

"Two minutes more and I should have been like the rest, beyond all assistance, for I knew nothing of their speech, and you spoke for me. You saved my life."

"Hum!" answered Evaña, looking steadily at the eager eyes of the man before him.

"Yes. Señor, I owe you my life," said Venceslao, somewhat abashed by the cold, searching gaze of Evaña. "I owe you my life, and, as I told you then, my services, everything that I have is at your disposal, send me where you will and I will go, tell me anything I may do for you and I will do it."

"Perhaps some day I may need your services," replied Evaña; "then I will apply to you freely, and shall count upon you."

"God grant that it be soon," said Venceslao, as a flush of pleasure brightened his face.

Evaña started, Venceslao had echoed his own thoughts in his ready words. Again he looked searchingly into the bright eyes of the paisano, but he could read nothing more there than the gratitude which prompted a simple nature to acknowledge and repay as he best could a signal service, there was no ulterior thought.

"Sit down," said Evaña, taking a chair to himself. "Some other day we will talk of that. I have come to speak with you on a matter in which perhaps I may be able to help you better than Don Roderigo. Tell me all about this affair between your sister and Colonel Lopez."

Half an hour they sat talking together, during which time Evaña learnt all about the family and connexions of Don Francisco Viana, and much about Colonel Lopez of which he had no idea, for though he had necessarily seen much of the latter he had never been intimate with him. Now he learnt that Don Gregorio Lopez the younger had very considerable influence over all the estancieros in the southern parts of the province, and was looked up to by all the stout yeomanry as their natural chief.

"Then you all knew of the Colonel's love for your sister?" said Evaña.

"Yes, all of us, it was no secret. The Colonel was always at our house when his duties permitted him; he came and went just as he pleased. We are very simple people, and for our friends our door is always open. We thought him our friend, and never dreamed of dishonour."

"But you thought he was going to marry her, had nothing ever been said about it?"

"Said, no, but it was a thing understood. We are not rich as he is, but we have land and cattle of our own, we are people of family, and are not gauchos. My sister Mauricia is very beautiful, and it is not strange that he should love her. Besides, there is already some

N

relationship between us, his father married as his second wife my
father's sister."

"Yes, I know all about that, but your father has been for many
years estranged from the rest of his family."

"What matters that? we are still of the same family. That he
should bring dishonour upon his own relations is what we never
thought the Colonel capable of doing, we esteemed him very highly."

"Then you seek the intervention of his own family to prevent this
dishonour?"

"Just so; he will not see us, not even me, and before proceeding
to extremities we would wish to try every means."

"Before proceeding to extremities! what do you mean by that?"

"Pues! that you know well enough, it is sufficient that I
mention it."

"You would force him to marry her? But how?"

"If he does not marry her there are no longer any terms between
us," said Venceslao, rising excitedly from his seat. "We are a decent
family as is any other family; I am the eldest son of my father, upon
me devolves this duty to avenge the honour of my family, and I have
sworn upon the Holy Cross that my duty I will do, although ten die
and I among them."

"Be calm, man, and sit down, fresh misfortunes cannot cancel the
one you lament. Sit down and talk rationally, I wish to be your
friend."

"Among gaucho-folk this sort of thing is little thought of," said
Venceslao, still standing and gesticulating with his hands, "but
among people of family it is different. The family gives dignity and
privileges to a man, but it also imposes upon him duties. I am
nothing more than a simple paisano, but I am an honest man, and
the honour of my family is dearer to me than my own life, as dear to
me as that of any of the grandees of the city is to him. It appears
that the Señor Coronel thinks little of the honour of his father's
family, to me it remains to teach him that being people of family all
are equal."

Evaña's eyes glistened; that all honest men were equal, and that
rank and wealth were but as tinsel adornments, was one of the leading
articles of his political creed. That many of his own standing agreed
with him, he knew, but he did not know that such ideas would find
any favour among the rough, unlettered denizens of the Pampa. In
thought he peered through the mists of the unknown future, and he
saw a time when the aid and friendship of such a man as Venceslao
Viana might be of great service to him; rising from his seat he went
up to him and laid his hand upon his shoulder.

"There is justice in all you say, my friend," said he, "and to me
you may speak safely, but it is not well to speak your thoughts aloud
in every ear. Be calm, there is no need for us yet to discuss this
between us. I wish to be your friend, and I wish also to be a friend
to Colonel Lopez, I desire that he and you may be friends together
and not enemies. Trust me, he shall marry your sister."

"Ah! Señor, if you can manage that you will lift a great weight
from my heart, and will do me a greater service than when you saved

me from the English. Before this I greatly liked the Colonel Lopez, as a chief I never wish to find one whom I would follow with greater pleasure. This has been a great tribulation to all of us. Oh! Señor, save us if you can, the service you will do us is infinite." So saying, Venceslao reseated himself on his chair and bowing his face on his hands burst into tears, sobbing till his shoulders shook with the violence of his grief.

Evaña took two or three turns up and down the room, then coming back to Venceslao he again laid his hand on his shoulder.

"I am going to see Don Gregorio, the father of the Colonel, he is the only one who has any power over his son, stay here with Don Roderigo till I see you again;" so saying, Evaña turned from him and left the room.

In another room he found Don Roderigo and Doña Constancia, the latter held a handkerchief in her hand and had evidently been weeping.

"You have heard what he says?" asked Don Roderigo.

"He has told me everything," replied Evaña, "and I am going to see Don Gregorio."

"I will go with you," said Don Roderigo.

"No, no," said Doña Constancia; "let Don Carlos go alone. It is right that my father should know of this, but I do not wish that you should have any dispute with him. Such an idea! If you mention it to him he will never speak to you again."

"Constancia says that it is absolutely impossible to think of such a thing as a marriage between them," said Don Roderigo.

"The idea is folly," said Doña Constancia. "That Gregorio should amuse himself with a gauchita, to that we are accustomed, but Roderigo says that they insist upon him marrying her!"

"I fear me, Señora," said Evaña, "that is the only course left open to him. This Mauricia is no gauchita, she is a cousin of your own, Señora."

"Cousin! we recognize no such relationship," replied Doña Constancia haughtily. "What are you going to tell my father, Don Carlos?"

"I am going to tell him the simple facts, he will decide for himself whether he will interfere at all in the matter."

"But you will be careful not to mention to him that these Vianas insist upon him marrying the girl?"

"I shall tell him that also, Señora, and shall do my best to prevail upon him to consent to it."

"Don Carlos!" exclaimed Doña Constancia, clasping her hands and looking at him in astonishment.

"I see nothing so extravagant in the idea, Señora. For years you have all been wishing that Don Gregorio would marry, he is old enough to know what sort of a wife will suit him best."

"Pues! do what you think best, but my father, I know, will never give his consent, and we can never receive her."

"That may never be necessary," said Don Roderigo. "Don Gregorio will live on his estancia, it is the life for which he is most fitted."

Evaña went and saw Don Gregorio, for more than two hours they talked together.

" My son could seek a wife in the first families. Of those Vianas of Chascomus I wish no one to speak to me, for me they are as though they did not exist," said Don Gregorio, as he walked up and down the dining-room in his anger.

But Evaña would speak of the Vianas, and of their existence Don Gregorio was most painfully aware.

" I know what you mean, Carlos," said Don Gregorio ; " though you will not say it plainly to me. You mean that Don Francisco Viana is my equal, that therefore his daughter is the equal of my son, and that he does not degrade himself by marrying such a woman. I deny your premises, and therefore the whole of your argument falls to the ground. By birth Don Francisco is my equal, in everything else he is my inferior; he has himself married a woman not only inferior to him in birth but in race also. His daughter is not the equal of my son, and there is less disgrace to her in their present connexion than would come to my son by their marriage."

" In their own way they are a most respectable family, from all I can hear," replied Evaña ; " and they feel keenly the disgrace which has come upon them."

" Bah ! what matters it, that family ! Bring that man here to see me, Carlos, I will speak to him myself."

It was nightfall before Don Carlos Evaña returned to the house of Don Gregorio Lopez, accompanied by Venceslao Viana. They were shown into a small room in the first patio, and were soon joined by Don Gregorio. Don Gregorio looked hard at the roughly-dressed but handsome man who stood before him ; the dark blood he had inherited from his mother was plainly seen in his skin and in his hair, but his features were of almost classical beauty, and in his face there was a look of intelligence and of fearless honesty of purpose which won upon the old gentleman in spite of his prejudices. Venceslao on his part also carefully scrutinized the appearance of Don Gregorio, and recognized him at once.

" It is the same," said he to himself, bethinking him of the letter he had carried from Liniers to the Cabildo on the morning of the 3rd July. " It is the same, I knew that in some way he was a relation of mine, they all of them seem to be people of ' Categoria,' but not for that shall I yield one inch. The higher the family, the deeper is the stain of dishonour."

" Thanks for having taken the trouble to come and visit me, take a seat," said Don Gregorio, without however offering to shake hands with him. " My son has behaved very badly to your sister, and to all of you ; apparently you have shown him much kindness, and he has requited you most infamously. I am glad you have come to see me, for I have great influence over my son, and will use my utmost endeavour to induce him to make you every possible reparation. I shall write to him, that on pain of my severest displeasure he return your sister at once to her father's house, that is the first thing he must do, then we will see what further——"

" No, Señor ! excuse me," interrupted Venceslao, " that is not the first thing. The first thing he has to do is to make her his wife. after that, if he cares for her no longer, the door of her father's house will be open to her, not before."

"Do me the favour to listen to me. You must be aware that an alliance——"

"Excuse me, Señor Don Gregorio. By the side of a great Señor as you are. my father is but a poor man, but we are an honest family. and of good name. Our honour is as dear to us as your own is to you, and we will not permit a stain to be cast upon our good name by any one with impunity."

"You permit yourself to talk folly, my friend," said Don Gregorio, striving to preserve his calmness. "I asked you here that we might speak together in a friendly manner, and I can excuse much to you, as you have reason for indignation."

"Reason!" said Venceslao excitedly. "You do not know my father. He is a venerable old man, older than you are I think. Your son has brought shame and sorrow upon his head, and would you that I, his eldest son, shall talk of reason! I have well loved your son, and have followed him as my chief, and I wish to save him from the consequences of his own act, or I had no need to have come here."

"What is that you say?" said Don Gregorio, frowning angrily.

"I think it is useless to speak any more," said Evaña, "I see that it can have no good result; I will go to the Guardia Ranchos, and will see Colonel Lopez myself."

Venceslao looked at him gratefully. and rose from his seat to go.

"Not yet," said Don Gregorio, stepping rapidly between him and the door. "You have used words which require explanation, you do not leave this room till I know more of your intentions."

"If the honour of your family is nothing to you, to my father it is more precious than life, and I, his son, know how to avenge any affront to the family."

"My family!" said Don Gregorio.

"I am of your family, and so is my sister Mauricia; the stain is upon you as well as upon us. I have come to appeal to you, as the head of the family; it appears that the honour of the family is to you of small value, I am a man of another stamp, and will know how to take my measures. I will know what measures to take."

"Talk no more in that way, Venceslao," said Evaña; "you forget the respect you owe to an old man."

"It is not alone in respect that he is wanting," said Don Gregorio; "he has used words which require explanation, and I require an explicit explanation before he leaves this room."

"I have spoken clearly enough, and seek to hide nothing," said Venceslao.

"You have spoken of consequences to my son," said Don Gregorio.

"I have spoken; I know my duty, and shall do it."

"You apprehend danger?" said Evaña to Don Gregorio, taking him aside. "Dismiss all fear of that. Those who talk much never do anything. Leave it all to me; as I told you, I will go to morrow to the Guardia Ranchos, and will see Gregorio myself, we shall arrange the matter, but if you interfere with this man it will occasion a scandal. You might write to Gregorio, and I will carry the letter for you."

"No, I will not write, I am too angry to write now, but tell my son that he must submit to any demand they may make upon him, and that I will not see him again until he has completely severed all connexion between himself and this family.

"I will tell him what you say, word for word," said Evaña.

Two days after this, Don Carlos Evaña and Colonel Don Gregorio Lopez sat talking together in the plainly-furnished sala of a house in the frontier town of Ranchos, which is situate about ten leagues to the north-east of the Guardia Chascomus. For more than an hour they had talked together, and it was now near sundown. The Colonel sat leaning back in an arm-chair, with his legs stretched out before him, his hat, loosely set on, completely concealed his forehead, his eyes being just visible under the wide flap. He was smoking, and was apparently more intent upon watching the white rings of smoke, which he now and then succeeded in puffing into the air, than upon the conversation of the Señor Evaña. Everything in his demeanour and attitude denoted careless ease, yet now and then there was a hurried, anxious glance in his eye, which showed that the ease was more apparent than real. Don Carlos Evaña was not at all at his ease, and made no attempt to appear so. He had laid aside his cloak and hat, and walked up and down the room, nervously rolling a cigar between his fingers.

"All that you say to me is in vain, Carlos," said Don Gregorio. "Mauricia is a pearl among women, the more I know of her the more precious she is to me."

"Then marry her, and make her yours for life," replied Evaña.

"And break for ever with my father! no!"

"I gave you your father's message, word for word, as he gave it to me; he insists upon your severing all connexion with that family, as I told you."

"With the family with pleasure; I have done that most decisively already by robbing a daughter from them," replied the colonel, with a hollow laugh.

"And never did you do anything more contrary to your own interests."

"Why do you so insist upon my interests? Granted that I do lose my influence with the paisanage, and that I cease to be comandante, what matters that to you?"

"To me! what can it matter to me? But to you it matters more than you think. The day is not far distant when the comandantes will have the destinies of our country in their hands."

"Ah! always at that old idea of yours—America for the Americans. It seems to me that we fought the English for Spain and not for America. I raised a regiment and worked like a slave for months, because it was my father's wish that I should do so. How have they rewarded my father?"

As Don Gregorio said this all his carelessness disappeared, he thrust his hat back from his forehead, and stamping angrily with one foot on the tiled floor he fiercely repeated his question, "How have they rewarded my father?"

"They despise him, and kick him out from amongst them as though he were a dog," replied Evaña.

"Pues! why then should I be comandante, to drill troops and run upon the fire, if need be, for them?"

"You speak well. But answer me one question. How many Spaniards are there in your regiment?"

"None. What do I want with Spaniards?"

"In the Partido of Chascomus, how many Spaniards are there who have houses and land?"

"Perhaps fifty."

"Then if you have all the paisanos at your back you need fear nothing from the Cabildo if you happened to quarrel with them?"

"In my own partido I am king, and fear no one."

"Answer me yet another question. Who was it that drove Beresford from the Plaza Mayor, and so insured his destruction on the 12th August?"

"Juan Martin Puyrredon and my nephew."

"Another question. What troops drove back the English columns on the 5th July?"

"The Patricios. I am not a school-boy that you should ask me questions that every one knows."

"Well, I will ask you no more. But look you here; you are an American, and are king, as you say, in your own partido. Don Juan Martin Puyrredon, Don Martin Rodriguez, and all the other comandantes are just as powerful in their districts as you are in yours; the strength of Buenos Aires is in the native militia, who obey Don Cornelio Saavedra, everywhere the strength is in the hands of Americans; where the strength is, there the power will go. They have turned Don Gregorio out of the Cabildo, the Spaniards are to have all the power to themselves. Think you that this can last? No, I tell you your father must go back to that Cabildo. You must keep up your regiment, and when the day comes your strength and influence will put him there."

"It may be," replied Don Gregorio, again leaning back lazily in his chair; "but for the present we have other things to think of. You did not come here to tell me that."

"No, but if you marry Mauricia you secure your power and influence. If you do not, your help will never be of any service to your father."

"Tales, my friend, why should I marry her? She is better off here with me now than she ever was before, or was ever likely to be."

"You think so, but I doubt it. She must love you very dearly, or she would not have run away from her home with you. She would be proud to be your wife, now she is to you as your horse or your dog, you can turn her away when you are tired of her. She has sacrificed everything for you, but she has no claim upon you."

"She has more than a claim, she has power over me. She knows that I can refuse her nothing; this house, everything that I have is hers, she has only to ask, and she knows it."

"Has she ever asked you for anything?"

"Never. She is with me because she loves me, and I love her."

"Has she ever asked to see her father, or any of her family?"

" Never. I never speak to her about them, and I never wish her
to see them again."

" Yet she was much attached to them all. Do you think she has
forgotten them?"

As Don Gregorio did not answer this question, Evaña continued—

" Men cut themselves off from their families and form homes for
themselves, but women never forget the homes of their childhood.
It may be a light thing to you to quarrel with your father, but it will
be a sore trial to Mauricia to lose hers, you have blasted her life for
her."

" Folly, man ! Here she has a house of her own, a better one than
she ever lived in before, servants to wait upon her, and nothing to do
but amuse herself."

" Nothing to do !" answered Evana. " Idleness either in man or
woman is destructive of happiness. If she has nothing to do she will
soon be miserable ; she has been accustomed always to have plenty of
work on her hands. If she were your wife she would feel that this
house was hers, and would soon find plenty of work in ruling it for
you. As the head of your household her work would be happiness
to her ; as your wife she would feel herself a queen among her
sisters."

" Since when have you learned to know so much of women, Carlos ? " replied Don Gregorio, laughing. " Formerly you cared for
nothing but books."

Evaña turned impatiently away from him and did not answer,
whereupon Don Gregorio arose from his chair, saying—

" I will go and speak with Mauricia, for her happiness I am ready
to make any sacrifice."

Evaña relighted his cigar and threw himself full-length upon a sofa ;
the cigar was long smoked out ere Don Gregorio returned.

For several days past Mauricia had been less cheerful than 'she
was wont to be. Don Gregorio had noticed this once or twice when
he had come upon her unawares ; he had found her in tears, which
she had striven to hide from him. When he left Evaña he found her
sitting alone with some embroidery work before her, but her fingers
were idle, traces of recent tears were on her cheeks, yet as he sat
down beside her she cast her sad thoughts to the winds, and turned
to greet him with a loving smile.

" Has your friend gone ? " she asked.

" No, not yet. We have been talking of your father, and of the
rest of your family ; he says——"

But as Don Gregorio spoke of her father, all the sad thoughts in
which she had been indulging rushed back to her mind, her colour
faded from her face, and she clasped her hands together, twining her
fingers one over the other, and bowing her head upon her bosom.
About her father and her family she could not speak, and, as Don
Gregorio spoke to her of them slightingly, her heart for the first time
rose in rebellion against him.

" They all loved me," said she sharply, in a tone which Don Gregorio had never heard from her before, " and I have brought sorrow and shame upon them ; what matters it that they are poor ? " As

she said this she hid her face in her hands, and the tears trickled through her fingers.

Don Gregorio did all that he could to soothe her, speaking loving words to her, leaning over her and caressing her; but to all that he said she spoke not one word in return, still hiding her face from him, still struggling in her own way against the remorse which lay heavy on her heart.

"They want me to marry thee," said he, drawing slightly away from her.

At this her hands dropped from her face, she turned and looked full upon him, a wild gleam of joy and hope in her eyes.

"Will they forgive me?" she asked eagerly.

"To my wife they have nothing to forgive," replied Don Gregorio haughtily. "If it is that thou lovest them better than me, leave me; go to them and ask them to forgive thee."

"No, no!" replied Mauricia, again dropping her face on to her hands, "with thee, wherever thou art?"

"Thou askest me not then to marry thee?"

"Do not be angry with me, only love me, and let me always be with thee." So saying, Mauricia rose from her seat, and threw herself on her knees beside him, laying both her hands upon one arm and leaning upon him.

Don Gregorio put his arm round her and bent over her, asking her again—

"Willest thou that we marry?"

But Mauricia still clung to him answering him nothing. Then he took her in his arms and raised her to her feet, and said in a low whisper—

"Venceslao is near here, I go to send him to thy father to ask his permission for thee to become my wife."

With a low cry of joy she threw her arms round his neck, kissing him frantically.

It was a Sunday forenoon, three weeks after this, that Don Carlos Evaña, accompanied by Venceslao Viana, rode up to the estancia of Don Francisco Viana. Many horses were tethered about, and dogs rushed out barking fiercely at them, but no one came to bid them welcome.

"They are at service," said Venceslao, as he tied Evaña's horse for him to the palenque; "would you like to see? It is a thing you will not see on other estancias."

"With pleasure; I am curious to see it."

"It is well worth seeing," said Venceslao, smiling. "There is no Padre Cura can say Mass like my father does."

He then led the way into a large room where the whole household was collected, sitting or kneeling on the ground in rows, the women having small carpets under them, and some of the men had coarse rugs or sheepskins. Don Francisco himself, a venerable-looking old man with white hair, which hung down to his shoulders, and a long white beard, stood behind a small table at one end of the room, reading from a large book which lay open on it before him—the service

of the day. His eye flashed a cordial greeting to Evaña as he entered,
he paused for one moment to bow a mute salutation, and then calmly
resumed his reading.

Evaña took a seat on a chair which stood near the door, looking
with curiosity upon a scene such as he had never before witnessed,
and many a furtive glance was cast upon him by the worshippers,
more especially from the front row, where Mauricia knelt with her
mother and her sisters. Don Gregorio was not present, and Venceslao whispered to Evaña that he had ridden into the Guardia that
morning, and would be back before sundown. As the service ended
all knelt down, bowing their heads, and Don Francisco, raising his
hands, pronounced the benediction ; then as the others rose to their
feet he made his way through them, and came up to Evaña with tears
in his eyes, and both hands stretched out in welcome.

"May God all-powerful and the most Holy Virgin have you ever
in their keeping, and return to you tenfold the benefits you have
worked for us. You have saved a whole family from misery, and have
brought joy and contentment back to our household."

A feeling of shame came over Evaña as he stammered out some
incoherent words in answer, then he said—

"I had no idea you had so large a family. Are all these yours?"

"All," replied the old man, looking proudly round him ; "all are
mine, sons, daughters, and relatives of my wife. I have no stranger
in my household, we are but one family."

Then taking Evaña by the hand he introduced him to his wife and
daughters, who kissed his hands, and the mother, a stout, well-featured
woman, with dark complexion and coarse, black hair, thanked him
and blessed him with many fervent words for having restored her
daughter to her when she wept over her as lost.

"Boys," said Don Francisco, turning to the male members of his
family, "you see this Señor, we owe to him a benefit which we can
never repay ; through fire and through water our lives and all that we
have are at his service if the day ever comes that he need them."

Then he added in a low voice to Evaña—

"Don Gregorio has told me that the day may come when you may
need a few stout horsemen at your back. Look round, you will see
stout men among my household. All are yours when you call for
them."

Evaña remained three days at the estancia of Don Francisco, days
which were held as fête days by the family and their neighbours, and
passed in all manner of rural sports and games. On the Tuesday there
was a grand ostrich hunt, in which over 200 horsemen took a part.
Many were the feats of horsemanship performed, and the choicest
trophies were laid at the feet of Don Carlos Evaña, though the hunt
was nominally to celebrate the wedding of the Señor Coronel Don
Gregorio Lopez and the fair Mauricia, daughter of Don Francisco
Viana.

CHAPTER III.

WATCH AND WAIT.

WHEN Don Carlos Evaña left the estancia of Don Francisco Viana, Colonel Lopez accompanied him for about a league on his way. As he drew rein to turn back, he stretched out his hand to Evaña, saying—

" May God keep you, my friend. If you had not come to see me I should never have married her, and now I know it is the best thing I ever did in my life. Do what you can for me to make my peace with my father. I have written to him announcing my marriage, but have no answer from him. If he will receive me I will go in and visit him at once, but of course Mauricia will remain on the estancia."

In consequence of this Evaña went in by way of the Casateja, having an idea that he might find Don Gregorio there. In this he was not disappointed, but he was much disappointed at the reception he met with. Don Gregorio told him plainly that he believed his son to be the victim of a conspiracy, to which he, Evaña, had lent himself for some unknown purposes of his own, so that the interview between them was highly unpleasant to both of them, and Evaña gave a sigh of relief as he swung himself once more into his saddle, and galloped off for the Quinta de Ponce.

Here also he met with disappointment. He had always been a great favourite with Doña Constancia, but now she received him very coldly.

" And you tell me that it is actually true, Carlos ? " she said. " You stood by and did nothing to prevent it, and gave your countenance to it by being present ? I always looked upon you as one of ourselves, Carlos."

" I have no dearer wish in life than that you should continue to do so, Doña Constancia," replied Evaña. " In what I have done I have acted as I considered that the interests of the Colonel himself demanded. Had I considered my own interests I should have refused to have anything to do in the affair either one way or another. Your father seems disposed to excuse the Colonel and to lay the whole blame upon me. I am content that he should do so if by so doing he learns to forgive his son. But if you blame me I shall feel that I have incurred a very heavy and most unmerited misfortune."

" You are always generous, Carlos," said Doña Constancia, " and I should be sorry to blame you more than you deserve. Your intentions may have been quite right, but you have at any rate shown great want of judgment, and we did not expect that from you. That my brother should commit such great folly is no matter of surprise to any of us, but to papa it has been a very severe blow, and I cannot help feeling angry with you for the share you have had in causing him this sorrow."

If Evaña felt sore at the reception Doña Constancia gave him, he was amply compensated by the cordial greeting of her daughter Dolores, who on this subject held very different ideas from either her mother or grandfather, and declared them boldly, fortified as her own opinion was by the few words which Don Roderigo had said upon the subject.

She, Marcelino, and Lieutenant Gordon were seated under the front veranda when Evaña joined them after his short conversation with Doña Constancia.

"What a time you have been away, more than a month, but you have been well employed, I think," said Dolores, smiling upon him. "Marcelino and I have talked it all over together, and we agree that you have done our uncle a great service, if you had anything to do with his marriage, as they say you had."

"Every one has been wanting Uncle Gregorio to marry for years," said Marcelino, "and now they are angry because he has chosen his wife himself."

"Sit down and tell us all about it, Don Carlos," said Dolores.

Evaña sat down and remained talking with them for nearly an hour.

"I have quite a curiosity to see that Don Francisco," said Dolores ; "he must be like one of the old patriarchs."

"And lives like one too," said Evaña. "His wife and daughters make clothes for the whole household, they spin and weave the wool of their own sheep, and the whole of the outside work is done by the boys, I do not think they have any slaves."

"And he says Mass every Sunday and Feast-day? I don't think that is proper," said Dolores.

"Ask Padre Jacinto," said Marcelino ; "he will tell you that it is very wicked."

"He does not say Mass exactly, at least I think not," said Evaña. "He reads passages of Scripture, and psalms, and prayers, and no Latin, so every one can understand him."

"If Don Fausto will take me out with him next time he goes I will go and see this Don Francisco," said Gordon ; "I should like to hear the service very much."

"We will go together some day when I am strong enough to ride so far," said Marcelino.

"How very ungrateful of you, Marcelino. What would grandpapa say?" said Dolores. "Don Carlos! I have something to tell you. The wonderful French carriage that you sent out to grandpapa has actually been used at last."

"There is some hope for us then yet," replied Evaña. "When carriages are used then we shall begin to be civilized."

"But it was a very special occasion. Grandpapa took Marcelino to the Miserere, and they spent a day with Don Alfonso."

"And how was the medico?" asked Evaña. "As grumpy as ever?"

"Oh no ; all smiles and hospitality," replied Marcelino. "He received me as my grandfather's grandson, and you know he can refuse nothing to Don Gregorio. Gordon went with us, we were both told that the house was ours, and we mean to go again."

"Bravo!" exclaimed Evaña. "Don Alfonso is coming out in a new line. It is something new for him to invite young men to his house."

"You do not call yourself old, do you?" asked Gordon.

"Don Alfonso treats me as if I was," replied Evaña.

"That is because you are so learned and wise," said Dolores, at which speech Evaña looked uncomfortable and the others laughed.

"My paisanita was there too," said Gordon, "so we passed a very pleasant day I can tell you."

"And Marcelino was bashful and dared not talk to her in English," said Dolores.

"She talks Spanish as well as you do, so why should I?" said Marcelino.

"You must ride every day while you are here," said Evaña. "When you are strong enough to ride there she will teach you English better than Gordon can."

"As soon as I am strong enough I shall have something else to do," said Marcelino; "I am going into harness. I suppose you don't know the last news. Juan Carlos is going to Spain and I am to take his place at the Consulado."

"Juan Carlos going to Spain!" said Evaña. "What is he going there for?"

"Papa arranged it all," said Dolores. "As a reward for Marcelino's bravery last year the Council of the Indies sent out to him an appointment 'for his son' to a very high post at Cadiz. Of course it was intended for Marcelino, but he won't go, so papa accepted it for Juan Carlos. We did all we could to persuade Marcelino, but it was no use, I don't think even if you had been here you could have persuaded him, and it is too late now."

"You seem very anxious to get rid of me, Lola," said Marcelino.

"You know I am not. But I can't make out what could make you refuse such an honour as that."

"I may perhaps be of some use to my own country at the Consulado, and Juan Carlos wishes to visit Europe."

"Use! you might be of more use in Spain. Papa says that in a few years you might have been in the council 'yourself, then you would have been one of the rulers of Spanish America, and you might have come here again as Viceroy. Juan Carlos is not as clever as you are, he will never be Viceroy."

"I do not think he will," said Marcelino. "But if I went, who is to command my negroes when the English come again?"

"They are disbanded," said Dolores. "Besides, the English will not come again. Have they not enough with two defeats? Do you think they will come again, Mr. Gordon?"

At this Gordon looked troubled and made no answer, but Evaña answered for him.

"I have lived in England and know the English, I think they will," said he. "You have heard me speak of their game 'the box;' I have seen a man knocked down ten times, and yet get up again all bleeding

as he was and win after all. The English are all like that, to be
beaten is only to begin again."

"It is their merchants," said Marcelino, "who will force them to
continue the war with us. Their commerce is ruined by the conti-
nental system of Napoleon, and they think to make a market here for
their goods with cannon-shot and bayonets."

At this Gordon rose from his chair and walked away under the
trees, and Dolores, looking after him as he went, said sadly—

"It is a barbarity, this war, why cannot we be friends?"

"Our masters the Spaniards will not let us," said Evaña.

"The Spaniards! always the Spaniards," said Dolores impatiently,
then she also rose from her chair and went inside the house.

"So you do not care to be Viceroy of Buenos Aires?" said Evaña,
as he and Marcelino were left alone.

"I think I have as good a chance of becoming Viceroy by remaining
here as by going to Spain," replied Marcelino.

"How so? Everything seems to be falling back into its old
channel."

"With one great difference, that so long as there is any fear of
another English invasion the militia will remain embodied. You
know Liniers, the Spaniards distrust him, for he is a Frenchman, and is
very popular with us Creoles, he knows that his power depends altogether upon the Patricios. Don Cornelio Saavedra is his particular
friend, Liniers does nothing without consulting him; the opinions of
the people are the opinions of Don Cornelio, and he has his way in
spite of the secret hostility of the Cabildo. I tell you, Carlos, we
Porteños are already the rulers of Buenos Aires."

"Then the English are still of some service to us," replied Evaña.
"So long as there is any danger of another visit from them, Liniers
and Don Cornelio will keep up the militia, and the will of the people
will be law, but take care how you say that in the streets, my friend.
What says Don Roderigo?"

"My father expects that the Court of Aranjuez will make Liniers
Viceroy, the danger of another English invasion will make them over-
look all other considerations, but that if Spain should make peace
with England then he will be recalled at once."

"And the militia will be disbanded, and everything be as before,"
said Evaña.

"But in the mean time, months, perhaps years, will pass, during
which we have the power *de facto* in our own hands. Time is working
a pacific revolution amongst us; at last Spain will see that the only way
to preserve her colonies will be to give us the right of self-government."

"Spain give us the right of self-government! Dreams, my friend!
Since when did you get that idea?"

"Since the day when I went with my grandfather to visit Don
Alfonso."

"Ah! my friend, I compliment you upon your new master in
politics," said Evaña, laughing; "Don Alfonso has worked a miracle
with you. Why don't you go to Spain and come back Viceroy?
Tell me, do you really think that Spain will ever consent to leave the
revenues of the country at our disposal?"

"Of course we should still have to pay some of it to the King as our sovereign."

"Yes, but King Charles is not Spain. What would become of the Consulado of Cadiz if they lost the monopoly of our trade? What would become of the lazy Spanish grandees, who draw their revenues from us and do nothing in return?"

"We are the subjects of King Charles as much as they are; if the King consents to be our sovereign just as he is the sovereign of Spain, and lets us have a Cortes of our own, what can the Consulado of Cadiz or the Spanish nobles do against us?"

"You know as well as I do that all Spaniards, from the King downwards, look upon us as their slaves and consider all that we have as their property. From Don Alfonso you can never have got such ideas as these."

"There is Gordon," said Marcelino, interrupting Evaña. "Don Alejandro!" he added, calling to Lieutenant Gordon, "come here and help me."

Then as Gordon returned to the veranda and resumed his seat, he continued—

"You remember the conversation we had with my grandfather and Don Alfonso that day we were at the quinta?"

"Perfectly," replied Gordon.

"Now tell me again what made your colonies in North America revolt against England?"

"Government wanted to tax them for imperial purposes," said Gordon.

"Then formerly none of their revenues went to England?"

"No, the colonial revenues were applied to colonial purposes, but of course they had to pay the English officials."

"And they had their own laws and their own municipal institutions, and would have been perfectly content to remain colonies until now if England had only left them as they were?"

"I believe they would. I don't think that King George had anywhere more loyal subjects than in those colonies until the English Parliament began to tax them by its own authority."

"What the English wanted to force upon the Americans of the United States is what Spain has always forced upon us. Americans had a right to rebel against the English, we have a right to rebel against Spain?"

"I think so," replied Gordon.

"But the Americans would have been content enough with King George if the English Parliament had left them alone, and we would be content enough with King Charles if he would let us have our own laws, as your colonies had before their War of Independence."

"Dismiss any such idea from your mind, Marcelino, it is folly, and you know it," said Evaña, rising to his feet. "Why you should try to believe that we can ever enjoy the rights of free-born men by any proceedure short of an absolute rupture with Spain I cannot imagine."

"But I can imagine it very easily," said Gordon.

Then Evaña, looking earnestly at Marcelino, saw a deep shade of anxious sorrow come over his still worn features.

"Ah! my friend," he said, "I see that you have some reason of your own for wishing that we could achieve our freedom and yet preserve our connexion with Spain, but again I tell you that it is impossible."

"Oh! Carlos, do you not see why it is that I am so anxious to preserve our connexion with Spain?" exclaimed Marcelino.

"I see only that freedom and Spanish rule are incompatible," replied Evaña.

"And my father? Do you never think of him?"

"He is a Spaniard," replied Evaña; then as he spoke the sadness which clouded Marcelino's face was reflected in his own.

"Yes, he is a Spaniard," said Marcelino, "and there are other Spaniards like him, though not many; men of liberal minds, who would gladly see Spain herself free from the rule of bigoted priests and ignorant nobles, who would gladly see the colonies of Spain ruled by their own laws, but they as sternly as any other Spaniards assert the supremacy of the royal house of Spain."

"I wish I could think any pacific revolution possible," said Evaña with a sigh. "But we have power in our own lands now, let us make use of it. Why are you going to the Consulado?"

"My father wishes me to devote myself to the civil service. At present I think I shall be of use there. And you, will you do nothing?"

"I have already done something; I have bought an estancia."

"You! you will never be an estanciero!"

"I never intend to be. But on my estancia I have peons, and my peons will be soldiers the day I want them. I have not lost the month I spent outside with your uncle, I have persuaded him also to do something. That mob of horsemen he had with him at the Ensenada were just of no use whatever, he is going to select about 200 of the best of them and form them into a regiment of dragoons. I have a letter from him to Liniers on the subject; if Liniers will send him arms, and three or four sergeants to drill the men for him, he will do the rest."

"Bravo! before the English come again we shall have some decent cavalry. Don Martin Rodriguez is also raising a regiment of hussars at his own expense among the peons and quinteros in the suburbs. With some drilled cavalry among them to steady them, our partidarios may be of great service in the open."

"Your gauchos, if properly drilled and officered, would make excellent cavalry," said Gordon.

"It is chiefly the want of officers makes them of so little use," said Evaña.

"But tell me, Carlos," said Marcelino, "where is your estancia?"

"It adjoins the land of Don Fausto Velasquez. I have put Venceslao Viana in charge of the place. He will have command of a troop of forty men in Don Gregorio's regiment."

"Then if there be another invasion you will join us, Carlos?"

"If the English come as they did before, to conquer us, then I will be a dragoon, and will lead my men myself against them. Watch and wait, that is all we can do at present; when time lifts the veil from before the unknown future then we shall know against what enemy to turn our arms."

CHAPTER IV.

THE RAISING OF THE VEIL.

"NEARLY a year, mamita, nearly a year," said Dolores to her mother, as they sat together under the wide veranda at the Quinta de Ponce.

"And it seems a long time to you, Lola?" replied Doña Constancia.

"The time has passed quickly, but it seems ages ago. Last year there was always something happening. Marcelino was busy training his negroes, and in town every one was talking of the new regiments, and about what the English were doing in Monte Video, and when they were coming. Now they say the English are coming again, but no one knows when. Marcelino is secretary at the Consulado, grandpapa hardly ever leaves his house, and Uncle Gregorio is always at his estancia outside."

"But we are not left quite alone, Lola; we have one visitor who comes very often."

"Yes, Don Carlos Evaña, when he is not at his new estancia; but now he and Mr. Gordon have been there more than a month, and they said they were only going for a week. But when they are here they never talk politics as they used to do; Don Carlos seems to think of nothing but of his estancia. Papa is the only one who talks of politics now, and he talks only of the Prince of La Paz, and Prince Ferdinand."

"I never thought that you cared about politics, Lola."

"But I like to hear them talk and argue, mamita; it sounds as if it was something important when they are so eager about it, but now they are never eager, any of them. Even Marcelino the other day, when Don Manuel Belgrano was here, did not seem to care anything about what the French did in Portugal, though papa got quite excited about it."

It was nearly a year, as Dolores said, nearly a year since the last invasion of the English, for it was now the month of May in the year 1808, a balmy day for the season, with light, fleecy clouds flitting over the blue vault of heaven now and then hiding the sun. A calm day in which the air was never still, and yet no one could tell from which quarter the wind came. When there was any wind, it came in little gusts, sweeping along the smooth walks of the quinta, creating great tumult and bustle among the dry leaves fallen from the overhanging branches of the trees, so stirring them as though with the intent to garner them up, then straightway casting them down again and leav-

O

in z them, and going sighing away among the tree-tops, mourning over the past glories of the summer.

It was nearly a year since the last invasion of the English, it was nearly time that they came again, if so be that they were coming; and men said that they were coming, and, full of confidence at the failure of two previous invasions, they thought lightly of it; yet not for that did they neglect some needful preparation, and Buenos Aires was stronger now and better able to meet invasion than she had ever been before. So the summer had passed, and the autumn, and the only event of importance that had occurred had been the formal nomination by the Court of Aranjuez of General Don Santiago Liniers as Viceroy of Buenos Aires, raising him at the same time to the rank of field-marshal, to the great content of the Patricios, who looked to Liniers as their own especial leader, and to the general satisfaction of all Porteños.

"Yes, Lola, we have been very quiet all this summer and autumn, but to-day is our last day here," said Doña Constancia.

"And won't Aunt Josefina be glad to see us in town again. Marcelino is stronger now than ever he was, so next month of course she will give that grand ball she has promised so long in his honour; but, ah me! it is so long ago now that he has forgotten what it is to be a hero, and has a pale face and white hands, you would never take him now to be the Comandante de los Morenos de Ponce."

"Then if you think heroes ought to have sunburnt faces and brown hands, you must look for another one. What say you to Don Carlos for a hero?"

"He would make a very good hero, mamita; but he has never done anything yet but gallop about."

"And gallop in to Buenos Aires and back whenever a certain young lady that I know, has fancied that she wanted anything that was to be found in the city."

"He has been very kind to us all the summer; so strange of him, who never seemed to care for anything except his books. But every one seems to be quite changed now, except you, mamma?"

"Yes, Lola, as time goes on every one changes; I see a great change in you."

"In me, mamma?"

"Yes, in you, Lola. Last year you used to be as merry as the day was long; now I often see you sitting with your hands before you quite quiet, thinking to yourself. What do you think about, Lola?"

"Thousands of things, mamma, at times, but generally about nothing," replied Dolores, as a bright flush spread over her cheeks.

"Do you ever think of any one in particular, Lola?"

Then as Dolores did not answer this question, but bowed her head while the long dark lashes fell over her eyes like a veil, Doña Constancia added another—

"Do you think much of Don Carlos Evaña, Lola? He has paid you great attention for months. I never before knew him pay attention to any one."

"To me, mamma?" exclaimed Dolores, looking up with a merry smile.

" Yes, to you, Lola."

" Oh ! mamita, what ideas you do get into that pretty head of yours ! Why Don Carlos talks three times as much to you as he does to me. Next you will tell me that he is in love with me ! Fancy the wisest of men being in love with a foolish, ignorant girl like me ! " So saying. Dolores jumped up from her seat with a ringing laugh.

" Lola ! " said Doña Constancia, " come and sit down again, I want to talk to you, and do not like you to laugh at what I say."

" No, no, no, mamita ! " said Dolores, running off along one of the walks, and still laughing. " I hear horses on the road, some one is coming."

Dolores went up the quinta fence and looked over, then presently she came back and reseated herself very quietly beside her mother, saying—

" They come, mamita, they have gone in by the other gate."

" Who come, Lola ? "

" Don Carlos and Mr. Gordon."

A few minutes passed. mother and daughter sitting in silence together ; Dolores with her hands clasped, looking dreamily out upon the trees, her mother watching her. Then the two whom Dolores had seen coming came, walking slowly up by a winding path together. Dolores rose and went to meet them, smiling merrily at Don Carlos Evaña with a new look of curiosity in her eyes, and holding out her hand to him in cordial welcome. Then after the usual greetings she turned from him, the smile dying away from her face, and the fringes of her eyes hiding them, to give a silent welcome to his companion. Her hand hesitated as she stretched it out towards him, and the flush spreading over her features added a fresh charm to her radiant beauty. Between these two a coldness and constraint had sprung up during the last few months, putting an end to the careless intimacy which had previously existed. Don Carlos had watched them closely all these months, but had spoken no word to any one of what he had seen ; now, though he was speaking to Doña Constancia and held her hand in his, still he watched them with a jealous scrutiny.

An hour later, as they sat together talking of the morrow's journey to the city, and of the gay doings which might be looked for during the coming winter, if so be that the English would only leave them in peace, two more were added to the company, Marcelino and Evaristo, who had galloped out from town together to superintend the removal of the morrow.

" And what news from the Old World ? " asked Gordon, when the messages had all been duly delivered. " Have not my paisanos made up their minds not to come yet ? It seems to me that we have plenty to do in Europe without coming here."

" Great news ! " replied Marcelino, looking eagerly at Evaña. " King Charles has abdicated, and Ferdinand VII. is now King of Spain and the Indies."

" Viva ! Fernando Septimo ! Viva !! " shouted Evaristo, throwing up his hat.

Don Carlos Evaña had been leaning back lazily in an arm-chair, but as Evaristo shouted "Viva! Fernando Septimo," he started upright, clutching both the arms of his chair with his hands.

"He has the French with him, Prince Ferdinand?" said he, almost breathless with excitement.

"He depends upon French assistance," said Marcelino, "and it is rumoured that he is to marry a niece of the Emperor."

"Spain! Spain! how art thou fallen!" said Evaña, in a hollow voice. "Nor Charles, nor Ferdinand, but the Lieutenant of the Emperor, he will be King of Spain. When was it that the 'Moniteur' said those few words of Portugal: 'The House of Braganza has ceased to reign?' As yet only a few months have passed since then. Ere this year run out there will be another line in the 'Moniteur' concerning Spain: 'The House of Bourbon has ceased to reign.' All Europe—— but come, Marcelino, tell me more of this;" so saying, Evaña sprang from his chair, and taking Marcelino by the arm the two walked away under the trees, talking eagerly together in low tones.

"Now, Lola, what do you say?" said Doña Constancia. "Has Don Carlos forgotten all about politics?"

"I have something else to tell you, Carlos," said Marcelino, after they had talked long together. "My grandfather has never smiled since the day he heard of my uncle's marriage, he has fallen off greatly; I fear my mother will be much shocked when she sees him. He never speaks of Don Gregorio, but I know he is always thinking of him, and I believe he only wants an excuse to forgive him. It is very hard on you, Carlos, for us to ask you to meddle any more in this affair, after the reproaches you have suffered already, but I think if you could prevail upon Don Gregorio to come in and go straight to his father that he would receive him with open arms."

"I will go at once," replied Evana.

"To-morrow?"

"No, now, this evening."

"There is no need for that, it is nearly sundown, but to-morrow, I shall think it so good of you to do it. And if great changes are at hand, as you say, if you succeed in reconciling Don Gregorio with his father you will greatly increase your own power, with either of them you will be able to do what you like."

"Do not say that. I owe much to your grandfather, and to his son too, to all of you in fact. I shall bring some happiness back to you, let me think that I do it from gratitude only, from no ulterior motive. It is a rough road to tread, this road that I have chosen, demanding sacrifices at every turn; love, friendship, even honour itself must be trampled under-foot by one who devotes himself to ambition. Let me think that I can do a service to my best friends without any selfish motive."

"What can be more noble and less selfish than your ambition, Carlos? You seek the freedom of your native country, and are ready to sacrifice yourself for her sake."

"Myself, yes. Ah! if that were only all! But wait here, I will rejoin you in a minute."

As they spoke they had walked back to the front of the house, and Doña Constancia called to them—

"We are going to walk up the road to take one more look over the Pampa, will you come with us?"

"In one minute, Señora," said Evaña, walking away towards the back of the house.

Evaristo found himself something else to do, but the rest were soon afterwards walking together up the road between the long lines of poplars, Doña Constancia walking in front with Marcelino and Lieutenant Gordon, while Don Carlos Evaña and Dolores came behind. Doña Constancia walked quickly, so that these two were soon left quite by themselves. At first they talked of the news brought out by Marcelino, Dolores trying her best to incite Don Carlos to some vehement expression of his political opinions, which were well known to her, but she tried in vain, his enthusiasm seemed to have quite evaporated during his talk with Marcelino, and his thoughts seemed to be far away, and bent on some quite different subject.

"You are very happy, Dolores," said Evaña; "why should you care anything for Spain or for Spanish affairs?"

"Spain is papa's country," said Dolores; "I love everything that papa cares for."

"Your father loves you very dearly, Dolores, you are very fortunate, every one you have near you loves you."

"Yes, I am very fortunate, and very happy, with papa and mamma and my brothers and so many aunts and uncles and cousins to care for, and who all love me, I am very happy, I ought to be," said Dolores, unconscious that in so saying she reopened an old wound in the sensitive nature of her companion, who had none of whom he could so speak, and who, having none, all the more deeply felt the need of them.

"Yes, you ought to be happy, and you are, but no one in this world can be always free from sorrow and trouble, not even the most happy; to all there comes a time when they feel the want of something more than the love of those who have always been dear to them; some trouble comes to them, in which the support and aid of some firm friend may be of great service to them. Would you value the friendship of one who, while you are happy in the love of all about you, would never intrude a thought or a wish of his own upon you, but, if you were in trouble and in need of any help that he could give, would leave everything to serve you, and seek a reward only in the pleasure it would give him to aid you in any way?"

Dolores looked up at him in surprise as he paused for an answer; she had never felt the need of such friendship, and hardly thought it possible that she ever should do, but as she saw the eagerness in his eyes her own fell before them, she stammered out some words in reply, she hardly knew what, and Evaña went on—

"I know you do not love me, Dolores," he said; "you never will love me as you love your father or your brothers. We have seen much of each other during the past few months, but circumstances may very likely interfere between us so that we see much less of each other in future. It would be a great consolation to me to know that sometimes you will yet think of me, and that if some who are dear to you speak evil of me, you will not condemn me in your heart unheard, but will think of me as a friend who would make any sacrifice to serve you. Will you not let me be your friend, Dolores?"

"My friend, oh! yes. Why not? We have always been friends, and you are Marcelino's best friend, he often says so."

"Yes, Marcelino and I have known each other long and intimately, and nothing will come between us to interrupt our friendship, but with you and me it is different; already I see a cloud rising between us which may drive us far apart, our ways in life are separate, but will you not promise me, Dolores, always to think of me as your friend, whatever happens?"

"You are my friend, and mamma's and papa's and Marcelino's, and to grandpapa you are as a son."

"I know all that, and I value their friendship and their kindness to me, but some of them may learn to think me unworthy of their friendship, and you may do so too; but will you not promise me, as I have asked you, always to think of me as your friend, whatever happens?"

There was a plaintiveness in Evaña's voice as he asked this which startled Dolores, looking up again at him she saw his face flushed, and an eager, imploring look in his eyes such as she had never seen before.

"Promise me that, Dolores," he continued, taking her hand in his. "To you it may seem unreasonable and unkind that I should fear any interruption to our friendship, but I know the value of what I ask from you, I know that if you promise me you will keep your promise, whatever happens; I know that you will always look upon me as your friend."

Then Dolores knew that Evaña loved her; ignorant and foolish as she had said she was beside him, yet she knew now that he loved her, and she knew also that he never would tell her so in words, never seek her love in return. A strange mixture of fear and regret filled her heart, for she knew that she could never love him as he loved her, though he was well worthy of her love, and in that she could not love him she pitied him all the more. And she feared she knew not what; she had always looked up to him as to one much wiser than herself, and now he spoke of some unknown cause which might interrupt the friendship she had always felt for him; her hand trembled in his firm grasp and she burst into tears.

"Do not cry, Lola," said Evaña, using for the first time that dear, familiar name by which she was known to those who were nearest and dearest to her; "do not cry, if you are angry I will importune you no more, I will suffer anything rather than see you sad."

"No, no, I am not angry," said Dolores, making a strong effort to keep back her tears. "I will promise what you wish, I know that you are my friend, and always will be."

"And will be, whatever happens, Lola."

"Yes, whatever happens I will never doubt you, and will think of you only as my friend."

"And as your friend you will ever trust me, and will seek my aid without hesitation or scruple if the case should ever arise in which I may be of service to you or yours?"

"I will, just as Marcelino does."

"Just as you trust in Marcelino, that is what I mean. God bless you, I shall go away very happy, as happy as I ever shall be."

"Go away! are you going? Where to?"

"I am going back again outside, I shall probably not return for a month or two."

"But you are not going now?"

"Yes, now at once. I only wished to speak with you, and win that promise from your own lips before I went. My horse is coming, I shall wait for him there beyond the fence where Doña Constancia is standing."

"You were always wise, now wiser than ever before," said Dolores, stepping closer to him and laying her disengaged hand upon his arm. But Evaña shrank from her as though this mute caress were a pain to him, and they walked on side by side until they emerged from between the rows of poplars out upon the open plain, and rejoined the others who there awaited them.

"Mamma," said Dolores, "you promised me that I should see the sunset, but there will be no sunset for us to look on to-night."

Far away on the western horizon there lay a bank of dull gray clouds, behind which the sun had already sunk. From behind these clouds sprang diverging rays of orange and gold, stretching up over the gray sky almost to the zenith, and tinging all objects upon which they shone with the reflection of their brilliance.

"No, we shall not see the sunset," said Gordon. "That cloud is a veil which hides him from us, but if it were not for that cloud we could not look steadily upon the western sky, the sun would dazzle our eyes, and we should see nothing. Is not this that we can look upon more beautiful than any sunset?"

"It is the sunset all the same," said Dolores, "only that the sun is wanting."

"The sun has been kind enough to hide himself behind that cloud for your sake, Lola," said her brother, "so that without dazzling your eyes you may see how he can paint the sky. In the most beautiful sunsets of summer you never saw anything so beautiful as this."

"No, I never did," said Dolores.

Just then the servant of Don Carlos Evaña rode up to them leading a saddled horse by the rein.

"Don Carlos! your horse?" said Doña Constancia.

"Yes, Señora," replied Evaña; "I have urgent business outside, and shall leave as soon as you turn back to the quinta."

All except Dolores looked at him in surprise.

"Why not remain till to-morrow?" said Marcelino.

"I have a fancy to gallop through the night," said Evaña.

"The sooner you go the sooner you will be back," said Doña Constancia.

"Look, Don Carlos," said Dolores, "there is something for you to see before you go. Was there ever anything more beautiful than this?"

The gray cloud had lifted itself, disclosing one bright spot of fire on the far horizon, the last gleam of the departing day. As the cloud rose it seemed to dissipate itself, mingling its gray tones with the golden radiance of the setting sun, tempering the brilliance of those broad bands of glory which stretched over the western sky, melting them as it rose over them, absorbing them into itself, then with them vanishing away.

Then the bright spot of fire sank down out of sight, and straightway the place so lately filled by the gray cloud became one mass of brilliant light. Two broad bands of rich vermilion, with one band of yellow gold between them, parallel to the horizon, hung like a gorgeous canopy over the resting-place of the sun.

"See, Don Carlos!" said Dolores; "the flag of Spain! See, when Nature seeks to array herself in her most glorious dress how she chooses the colours of the most glorious of the nations."

"The cloud has risen from the face of the setting sun," replied Evaña, "and I see the emblem of Spain before me sinking after the sun into the darkness of night. That sky is as a prophecy, giving to all of us an insight into what will shortly come to pass."

"Buenas noches, Don Carlos, and a pleasant journey to you," said Doña Constancia laughing. "Come with me, Mr. Gordon; we will go back and leave these politicians to prophesy and discuss the future as long as they like."

Removing his hat, Evaña shook hands gravely with her and with Gordon; then, as they walked away, he turned again to Dolores.

"Yes," he said, "I see the flag of Spain painted on the sky in all its gorgeous colours, where but a few minutes ago there hung a dark, gray cloud. That cloud was as a veil hiding from us the unknown future; the veil has risen, and we stand face to face with the future, now no longer unknown to us. The news we have heard to-day is but news of the first step in the rapid downward course of Spain. Other news shall follow, which shall stir our hearts to their inmost depths, till we wake to the full knowledge that we are a free people. The genius of revolution shall set his foot upon Spain, shall crush our tyrant in the dust, and in crushing him shall break our chains for us for ever."

"God grant it," said Marcelino; "then may we live in peace ourselves, Spaniards and Americans alike citizens of a new nation."

Clinging to her brother's arm, Dolores looked in wonder on them both. There was silence for a space as the three stood side by side gazing on the western sky, where the gorgeous colours of the sunset faded gradually away, merging themselves into the gray tints of the evening twilight. So they stood for a space, each occupied with his own thoughts, each interpreting to himself as his desires led him the prophecy of the setting sun.

Evaña took the hand of Dolores in his own and raised it to his lips, saying but one word—

"Remember."

"Always my friend, whatever happens," said Dolores.

Grasping Marcelino by the hand, Don Carlos Evaña stood for one moment as though he would speak, his lips pressed tightly together, and the signs of deep emotion on his face. Then laying his other hand upon the shoulder of his friend, he bent forward and kissed him.

"My brother," he said; then turning from them he mounted his horse and slowly rode away.

Brother and sister stood silently side by side looking after him till the gray shades of the falling night closed around him, when Marcelino bent over Dolores and kissed her, putting his arm round her, and led her away back between the rows of the tall poplar trees to the quinta.

"Marcelino," said Dolores, as they drew near to the quinta gate, "are men who are born to be great also always born to be unhappy?"

Marcelino divined much of what was passing in his sister's mind, but not all, and to her question he gave no answer in words, but again bent over her and kissed her, and from that day forth brother and sister felt that there was another tie between them, but about the evening on which they two had looked together upon the setting sun while Evaña had expounded for them the prophecy of the clouds they never spoke.

When Dolores thought of it she thought but of one word—Remember; and Marcelino from that night forth looked no longer upon Evaña as his dearest friend, but as his brother.

CHAPTER V.

NEARLY two months passed, it was the 4th July. In the large sala of the house of Don Roderigo Ponce de Leon, Lieutenant Gordon stood by himself near a window, looking out dreamily into the street, a shade of sadness and of deep anxiety on his face. Don Roderigo had just left him, after a short conversation in which he had spoken many kind words to him, and had announced to him that he was no longer a prisoner of war, that he was released from his parole, and was free to go wheresoever it pleased him.

Don Roderigo had expected that his news would have been received with an outburst of joy, and so had taken it upon himself to make the announcement to him, for he had a kindly feeling for the young officer who had been so long his guest, and he felt a pleasure himself in telling him what he thought would give him pleasure. He was thus somewhat surprised when he saw the colour fade from his cheek, and at receiving answer only in a few incoherent words in acknowledgment of his great kindness.

His release was not unexpected by Lieutenant Gordon, the course which affairs were taking in Spain had shown him that the war between Spain and Great Britain was already virtually at an end, there could not be much longer any pretext for detaining him as a prisoner in Buenos Aires, and, once free, his duty called him far away. He himself had taken no step to obtain his release, had said no word to any one of his anticipation; now that the release came he thought only of its immediate consequences, and these consequences were to him painful, the announcement of freedom was to him as a sentence of banishment.

As he stood there by the window, sadly communing with his own thoughts, footsteps again approached him; he turned and saw Marcelino coming towards him with both hands stretched out, his face beaming with smiles and words of congratulation on his lips, but the words died away as Marcelino saw the sadness in the face of his friend. Then Gordon smiled and said—

"You come to congratulate me and you find me sad, most prisoners rejoice when they see their prison doors open for them, but is it strange that I cannot rejoice? I have had you for my gaoler and my imprisonment has been one long holiday."

"We have done our best to make it pleasant to you."

"That you have, all of you. I know that in the future I shall look back upon my prison as the dearest spot upon earth."

"We shall be sorry to lose you and shall miss you much, but have not you promised me that it shall only be for a time?"

"I have, and if God give me life I will keep my promise. When my own country needs my sword no longer then I will come back and aid you in the great object you have at heart."

"That object is surely well-nigh attained already. Spain fighting for her own liberty will hardly deny liberty to us."

"I wish I could think so, but I fear you will not become a free people without a sore struggle, and one which will entail much sorrow upon yourself."

"I know of what you think, it has caused me many a sleepless night for months past. You think of my father?"

"Yes, Don Roderigo is a man of very liberal opinions, but when the struggle commences he will remember only that he is a Spaniard."

"But he and many other Spaniards would gladly yield to us a share in the government of our own country, that is all we ask from Spain, we do not wish for absolute independence."

"You do not, for your father's sake, but others who have no such tie to Spain will be content with nothing short of complete independence. That Spain shall ever yield to you rights which she denies to her own sons is a dream, my friend. A year ago that was your opinion also."

"It was," said Marcelino sadly.

"You know that you have my sympathy in every trouble that may befall you," continued Gordon. "I wish I could remain and share your troubles with you, but in your chief trouble I cannot help you, I cannot even advise you. You will have to choose between your duty to your country and your duty to your father, look to God and your own conscience, they alone can guide you in each difficulty as it arises."

"God help me then, for if you cannot advise me I know not who can."

Then came the sound of feet tripping over the soft carpet towards them, and Dolores, with a bright flush on her face and a smile on her lip, came to present her congratulations to the newly-released prisoner of war, but her speech stopped short as she looked upon the grave faces of the two, and she hardly listened to what Gordon said in return, but laying her hand upon her brother's arm she said—

"What makes you sad, Marcelino?"

"We are losing a friend, Lola," said Marcelino, forcing himself to smile. "Is it not natural that I should be sad?"

"Yes, it is not strange, but he is not going now?"

"In three days I believe," said Gordon. "Don Roderigo tells me there is an English man-of-war at Monte Video, and I must lose no time in returning to my duty."

"Three days!" said Dolores, the colour fading from her cheeks.

"But he does not regret his imprisonment among us, Lola," said Marcelino softly, "he will not forget us when he is back in his own country."

"Forget! never!" said Gordon. "These last two years have been the happiest in my life so far. Wherever I go I shall look upon this country as my second home, and shall long for the day when I can return to it and to you."

"Then you will come back?" asked Dolores eagerly.

"That is my firm purpose. As yet I am only a subaltern and must rejoin my regiment, but when the war is over I shall come back; I shall have one great joy if the 71st has the luck to be ordered on active service, that in my next campaign I shall be fighting for you and not against you."

"Do not forget to say that in your speech at the banquet to-morrow," said Marcelino. "Are you clever at making speeches?"

"I never made one in my life," replied Gordon.

"Then if you do not prepare one you will simply say two words and sit down again, and every one will be disappointed."

"I hope I shall manage to say something more than two words, I ought to after all the kindness I have received, but of a set speech I am incapable."

"Without preparation that is very probable; but if I were to write down for you some hints, you could easily make them into a speech. You may safely say things that none of us dare to say, such as I have often heard you say in intimate conversation. You will be the only Englishman present."

"That is a fact, and I will speak out boldly as an Englishman just what I think, but in preparing my speech some hints from you might be of service to me."

"I will go and write them out for you at once," said Marcelino, and turning from them he left the room.

Dolores and Lieutenant Gordon being left alone stood together at the window for some minutes without speaking. Dolores was the first to break the silence.

"You are sorry to leave us, Mr. Gordon," she said; "but it will give you great joy to see your own family again."

"It will. You who have never been away from your own people cannot tell the joy there is in meeting again those you love after a long absence," replied Gordon.

"But I can understand it, remember how long Marcelino was away from us; I was quite a little girl when he went to Cordova, but I used often to think of him and wonder what he would be like, and then when he did come back I was so proud of him. Your sisters are thinking about you now as I used to think about Marcelino."

"I dare say they are, for this was my first experience of foreign service. I had no idea that I should come here when I left England, for we were sent to the Cape of Good Hope."

"What things you will have to tell them! If you had never been ——if you had not stopped with us you would never have known what it is to gallop over the Pampa."

"And more than that, I should never have known you as I do know you. They know already what kind friends I have found here, how fortunate I have been. When I reach home I shall never be tired of talking to them about you."

"They will be glad to have you back again, but they will not care to hear much about us. Marcelino has told me how in Europe they think that all South Americans are savages."

"They will soon learn to know better when I tell them about you, and about Doña Constancia and Don Roderigo and Marcelino, and about all of you. And about your houses, and about your tertulias in the evenings. They will learn to think much of you, my sisters would be ready to love you if they only saw you. My mother knows your name already; in her second letter she asked me a great many questions about you."

"But you will not stop long with them, will you? If the English send an army to Spain you will go and fight for Spain against Napoleon."

"If my regiment is ordered there I shall go with it. Would you be glad to hear that I was fighting for Spain?"

"I should. Will not you be proud to fight for Spain?"

"You look upon Spain as your own country; then if I fight for Spain I shall think that I am fighting for you. If the 71st is not sent to Spain I will exchange into some other regiment and go there for your sake, if an English army does go. If I were in Spain you would often think of me. I am only a subaltern with little more than my sword to depend upon, but when the war is over and we have beaten Napoleon out of Spain then I shall come back here, for I shall never forget Buenos Aires, and shall think of you every day till I come back again. Promise me that wherever I have to go you will not forget me."

"Oh! of that there is not the slightest fear," said Dolores, in a low, eager voice, which sounded in Gordon's ears as the sweetest music, and the memory of which remained with him for years after, while an ocean rolled between them.

"My time is very short here now," he said, in a tremulous voice; "perhaps we may never be alone together again before I go, and years may pass before I am able to return. You have promised that you will not forget me, that you will think of me while I am far away; will you not give me some still sweeter hope? Will you not let me hope that when I return I shall find you as you are now? Will you not let me centre all my hopes for life in you?"

"When you reach your own country you will find some one for whom you will care much more than you can ever care for me," said Dolores, in a very low voice, while the long, dark lashes fell over her eyes, and she bent her head, gazing upon the ground.

"Never," replied Gordon earnestly; "I never met any one whom I could love as I love you, and I never shall."

As he spoke he stepped nearer to her, and took one of her hands in his own.

"I know not what life is before me," he continued, "but one little word from you encouraging me to hope would gild that life so that I should shrink from no toil or hardship which might bring me nearer to you. Will you not bid me hope, I ask no more."

To this Dolores answered nothing, but the taper fingers of her hand twined round his with a gentle pressure, which sent a thrill of proud joy through his whole frame.

Again the door opened, and in came Doña Constancia, smiling, and stretching out her hand to Lieutenant Gordon.

"I have come to congratulate you," she said, apparently unconscious of the excitement which was only too manifest in his face. "You are going from us, and we shall miss you very much."

Long the three sat together talking of the future, Gordon again and again reiterating his resolution to come back and make Buenos Aires his home.

The next day there was high feasting at the house of Don Gregorio Lopez. His dining-room was very large, but there was barely room for the numerous guests assembled. It was a political banquet in celebration of the first anniversary of the defeat of the English army, which had attacked the city under the command of General Whitelock. The Viceroy, Marshal Don Santiago Liniers, with many of his principal officers, was present; also the leading members of the various corporations which formed the government, together with the commanders of the various regiments, both of the Spanish troops and the militia; also others who held no official position, but were there as personal friends of their host. Among these there was one who, among the crowd of brown and blue uniforms, profusely embroidered with gold lace and bullion, was conspicuous by his plain scarlet coat, and the gay tartan plaid which hung gracefully from his shoulder. It being a political banquet there were no ladies present.

The banquet commenced an hour before sundown; after about two hours Don Gregorio rose from his seat, and in a short complimentary speech proposed the health of the Viceroy, the hero of the 12th August, 1806, and of the 5th and 6th July, 1807. The toast was drunk with enthusiasm; then Liniers replied at greater length and proposed "The Junta of Seville," now the virtual government of Spain and the Indies, on account of the imprisonment by Napoleon of the ex-king Charles IV. and his son Ferdinand. To these followed many other patriotic and complimentary toasts; and then there was a short pause, during which each man spoke with his neighbour in low tones, till Don Manuel Belgrano, after receiving a nod of acquiescence from Don Gregorio, rose to his feet and proposed the "Morenos de Ponce." His speech was a short one, but it elicited a long one from Don Marcelino in acknowledgment of the toast. For Marcelino was proud of his negroes; and as on the 5th July he had not commanded them he could expatiate freely upon their gallantry on that occasion without laying himself open to an accusation of vanity. He told many anecdotes about them, illustrative both of their devotedness and of their simplicity; several of these anecdotes excited peals of laughter, and when he at length sat down he was applauded by a vehement clapping of hands, the Viceroy himself setting the example.

Then Don Roderigo Ponce de Leon rose to his feet:—

"Señores," he said, "we this day celebrate the first anniversary of our great victory over the English. We do right to celebrate this victory gained by a colony of the old and glorious kingdom of Spain over the well-appointed army of a great and valiant nation. We are proud of the victory we gained on the 5th July, 1807, but I know that you will all join with me in the wish that we may never gain another. The war between England and Spain resulted from the insidious intrigues of the usurper who, not content with seizing for himself the throne of France, seeks to make kings and princes of all the low-born adventurers who surround him, seizing for them by fraud and violence the thrones of every kingdom in Europe. Thank God, the mask of friendship by which he has deluded Spain has at last been torn from him, we have seen ere it was too late the abyss into which he would have led us. England, Austria, Prussia, and Russia have in vain striven to stay the advance of his victorious standards, but at last his usurpations have raised against him a foe who will trample them in the dust. Spain, unconquered Spain, has risen up against him. The Spanish people have risen as one man against Napoleon, and Spain will be the graveyard of his ruffian soldiery. We have seen and acknowledge the errors which led us into hostilities against England, we have stretched out the hand to her in friendship, she has clasped it in forgiveness of the past. We forgive the destruction of our navies at Trafalgar, she forgives the wholesale slaughter of her soldiery in the streets of this our city. England and Spain are now firm allies, together we shall reconquer the territory the invader has already wrested from us, and shall bring back in triumph our rightful king.

" No, Señores, we wish for no more victories over the English, the English are our friends and sworn allies. We who witnessed the fight this day one year ago, who saw how dauntlessly the English advanced under a hailstorm of balls which strewed our streets with their dead ; we who saw how small parties of them, cut off from all succour and hemmed in on every side, yet held out for hours refusing to surrender ; we who saw them on that day know how to appreciate the valour of such brave allies. We rejoice that they are no longer our foes, they are now our friends, and as friends and allies we welcome them to fight beside us in the cause of every people. We have seen them as they are, and know that they are worthy to fight side by side with the indomitable soldiery of Spain.

" Señores, fill your glasses and join me in one more toast to our friends the English ! "

Again with loud " Vivas " every man rose from his seat, and every eye was turned towards the place where Lieutenant Gordon sat in his scarlet coat, the sole representative there of the new-found friends of Spain. As the applause ceased he rose and spoke as follows :—

" Señores, it is with many mixed feelings that I rise to thank you for the warmth with which you have received the toast which has just been proposed to you by my kind friend Don Roderigo, whose guest I have been for two years. Two years ago the fortune of war made me your prisoner ; thanks to Don Roderigo, and to others of you from whom I have received unvarying kindness, these two years have been to me as one long holiday ; I cannot look upon you as my gaolers, I cannot fancy that I ever did look upon you as my enemies, your kindness to me will make it impossible for me ever to think of you otherwise than as dear friends. When I am far away, I know not where, in the service of my own country, I shall look back upon Buenos Aires as the spot where I have passed the happiest years of my life. I came here knowing as little as Englishmen generally do of Spain or of the colonies of Spain, I was a soldier, my country was at war with Spain, and I came here to do her bidding, to fight as I thought against Spain. I came here as an enemy, the chances of war made me your prisoner, among you I have lived ever since.

"Living among you I have learned to know you, and to think it the greatest of all misfortunes that England and you should look upon each other as enemies. Living among you I have learned that Buenos Aires is not Spain, and that in fighting against Buenos Aires England fights against a country which every interest binds to her in firm friendship and alliance. Most of you by race and language are Spaniards, many of you were born in Spain, but this country is not Spain, those who live in this country cannot long remain Spaniards. In the Old World we live fettered by the trammels of worn-out traditions, but here in the New World the very air is redolent of freedom. Unarmed, often alone, I have galloped for days over your boundless Pampa, I have shared the hospitality of great landowners, whose possessions exceed the limits of many an English county, and have also often been indebted for a night's lodging to the kindness of some lowly herdsman; from both the reception was the same, a frank welcome, an offer of everything I could require, and no question asked as to whence I came, or when or whither I would go. Galloping north, south, and west over the trackless Pampa, meeting nowhere with any obstacle, finding everywhere frankness and open-handed hospitality, I have felt the blood course through my veins with the joy of unrestricted freedom. I have gazed around me to the very verge of the far-off horizon, seeing nothing which could prevent me from galloping on and on whithersoever my will might lead me, and have known for the first time in my life the proud feeling of absolute independence.

"This liberty, which has been to me but as a brief holiday, has been to the majority of the men of this country the leading influence of their life. These immense plains which you call the Pampa are peopled by a hardy race of yeomen, who have grown to maturity in an atmosphere of freedom; from their earliest boyhood they have been accustomed to think and act for themselves, they have been trained in self-reliance, the trammels of the Old World are to them unknown, liberty is with them the very essence of their life. And you who live in the city also feel the impulse of this all-pervading influence. Obsolete laws and customs fetter you and check the growth of the genuine instincts of your nature, but you breathe the free air of America; around you stretch those boundless plains which speak to you whenever you look upon them of the nothingness of man in face of the immensity of Nature. No man, whether he be a Spaniard, an Englishman, or a Frenchman, can live long surrounded by these influences without feeling that in the sight of God all men are equal. It has therefore caused me no surprise to find here men who, in ideas and modes of thought, resemble the most advanced philosophers of Europe.

"The liberal ideas, which carried to excess have been a scourge to France, driving her to seek for peace under the iron rule of a military despot, have yet their foundation in great natural truths; these truths are taught to you by every influence which surrounds you. Thus the men of this land, though colonists of Spain, are yet a separate people. In coming here to fight against Spain we forced you into hostilities against us, and raised up for ourselves an enemy where we might have found our firmest friend. Spain alone is powerless against us, but twice have we been foiled by a colony of Spain.

"A colony is an infant nation; the day will come when in the maturity of your strength you will take your place among the nations of the world. If in your infancy you have by your valour humbled the pride of haughty England, that place will surely be in the foremost rank. England at peace with Spain is now no longer your enemy, and will be the first to stretch out to you the hand, and welcome you into the great family of the nations.

"England and Spain have now the glorious task before them of setting bounds to the insatiate ambition of Napoleon; in this struggle I hope to have my part, fighting once more under the red cross of St. George, in the most righteous of all causes, the deliverance of a noble people from foreign usurpation. In fighting for Spain I shall feel that I am fighting for you also, and thus in some degree repaying the great kindness which during two years of captivity has taught me to look upon Buenos Aires as my second country.

"Señores, again I thank you for the warmth with which you have welcomed the friendship of old England."

As Gordon resumed his seat, the majority of those present commenced clapping their hands, shouting "Vivan los Ingleses!" and some few added in a lower tone, "The true allies of America."

But there were others, among them the Viceroy, who neither shouted nor clapped their hands, but looked uneasily one at the other, as though they were far from pleased.

Don Gregorio, looking round his table, saw the various emotions depicted on the faces of his guests; he saw a cloud on the usually open countenance of the Viceroy, ill-concealed anger in the faces of Don Martin Alzaga and other Spaniards, annoyance and vexation in the face of his son-in-law Don Roderigo Ponce de Leon; while in the flushed features of many of his younger guests he read a dangerous excitement, which one untoward word might rouse into a storm. Hurriedly he rose from his seat.

"Señores," he said, "Spain has taken upon herself a task which Europe united has failed to accomplish. In this she will need staunch allies, she will find them in the English, therefore fill your glasses once more and honour a repetition of this toast, 'To our friends the English!'"

"To our friends the English!" shouted all the company, rising to their feet, and the toast being duly honoured they left their places and began conversing in groups about the room, upon which Don Gregorio ordered a large pair of folding doors to be thrown open, and invited his guests to adjourn to the sala for coffee, thus preventing the perpetration of any more ambiguous speeches."

From the sala the guests gradually dispersed, many of them being engaged to pass the rest of the night at the house of Don Fausto Velasquez.

"My congratulations on your speech, my friend," said Marcelino to
Gordon, as they left the house together.

"Some of them did not half like it," replied Gordon, laughing;
"but I said nothing that I have not said to you fifty times."

"True, but it would be treason for any of us to speak so before
the Viceroy. The Spanish doctrine is that 'a colony is a slave.'"

"If her colonists were slaves Spain would have lost this colony a
year ago. It takes men to beat us."

"Well, as my father said, we will never beat you again. I never
drank to a toast with more pleasure in my life than I did to his 'To
our friends the English!'"

BOOK IV.
THE DAWN OF FREEDOM.

PART I.
THE BRIGHTENING OF THE EASTERN SKY.

PROLOGUE.

THE thoughts of a youth are as the winds of heaven, which blow where they list, none knowing whence they come or whither they go, yet have they all some certain course and goal. The thoughts of a youth spring from the instincts of his nature, and are turned hither and thither by the ever-varying circumstances which surround him, yet all tend to one end—the development of his strength and character. The youth has but one object before him, to be a man; if he live, the attainment of this object is certain, its value is to him incalculable; manhood is to the youth the gate which opens to him the whole world.

The veil had fallen from before the unknown future, Buenos Aires stood face to face with her destiny. Her chains had been struck from her hands and from her feet, by events of which she could have no foreknowledge; she stood upright in her youthful strength, unfettered, and alone.

But Buenos Aires had looked upon Spain as upon a mother; now that Spain lay prostrate in her degradation she felt her tyranny no longer, she remembered only that she was her mother.

The waves of the sea toss up their heads rushing to and fro, dashing themselves in never-ending succession upon the shingly beach, each wave after its headlong rush sinking back again into the ocean, vanishing for ever, yet does the tide ever march steadily onwards. As are the waves of ocean, so are the thoughts of a youth, vacillating ever, yet ever advancing towards the one inevitable goal. As are the thoughts of a youth, so are the acts of a young nation, which is not yet known to be a nation, vacillating ever, yet ever advancing towards that one goal which is the object of all her aspirations—Independence.

CHAPTER I.

THE quinta of Don Alfonso Miranda was not a pretentious dwelling, nevertheless there were men in Buenos Aires who thought it one of the pleasantest houses in or about the city, in which they could wile away a leisure hour. Among others Lieutenant Gordon, during the last year of his residence in Buenos Aires, had been very fond of strolling out there either on foot or on horseback, and had frequently delighted the owner by telling him that while there he could almost fancy himself back in his native country, and certainly if any flat-roofed house with barred windows could remind an Englishman of England it was the house of Don Alfonso Miranda. Don Alfonso had lived so long in England that he had acquired many of the tastes of an Englishman, he had learnt by practical experience the meaning of the English word "comfort," and had fitted up his South American home with a variety of contrivances for keeping out the heat in summer and the cold in winter, which were complete novelties to the hospitable people who had welcomed him amongst them, and who had befriended his daughter when he fell under the ban of their Spanish rulers.

This house, after his release from prison, he had purchased from an American of the name of White, who had built it for himself, but had special reasons of his own for being glad to find a purchaser in Don Alfonso. This same Mr. White had returned to Buenos Aires in the year 1807, in company with General Whitelock, and was much consulted by that unfortunate officer.

In one of the rooms in this house was a large, open fire-place, where cheerful wood fires burnt in the cold season. When Don Alfonso brought his daughter to live with him she made tea for him in the English fashion, presiding with demure gravity over her porcelain tea-cups, clustered round a tall, steaming urn. This tea-urn and the fire-place were to their native visitors most marvellous innovations, but Don Alfonso had now no greater pleasure in life than to sit cosily in an arm-chair beside his fire on a chilly winter evening, watching his daughter as she so presided at her own tea-table, listening to her voice as she chatted with some chance visitor, and thinking dreamily of his English home and his English wife, now both lost to him for ever. Don Alfonso was himself of rather taciturn disposition, but he liked to hear others talk, and there was no voice he loved to hear so much as that of his daughter Magdalen.

Magdalen was but a very young woman, her teens wanted yet one of completion, but when she returned to the city, after her long visit at the Pajonales with the family of Don Fausto Velasquez, her father thought her quite old enough to govern his household for him. He had fitted up two rooms with great care for her especial use, adorning them with books, pictures, and trinkets which had years ago belonged to her mother, and which he had carefully packed up and brought with him across the ocean for the special purpose of some day bestowing them upon his daughter.

Doña Josefina and her friends found the Quinta de Don Alfonso a very pleasant resort in the warm summer evenings. It stood off a short distance from one of the main roads, separated from it and from the wide, open space which went by the name of the Plaza Miserere by thickly-planted trees.

Where ladies go, there young men are ever sure to follow, so that before her first summer at her father's quinta had passed over, Magdalen had taught some score of young men who had never tasted tea in their lives before, to drink it out of her porcelain cups. Among those who drank out of her porcelain cups this summer there were three who had found special favour in her eyes, Don Carlos Evaña, Don Marcelino Ponce de Leon, and Lieutenant Gordon, for they would now and then speak to her in English; her father having taken care that she should not forget her native tongue, generally speaking to her himself in that language, and she was glad when she could find any one to talk English with. Of English books she had what her friends thought a large collection, and these three friends would sometimes borrow some of these books from her, and talk to her about them after reading them. But one great trouble she had; she had not come at once to the quinta when she returned to the city with Don Fausto, but had remained several weeks with Doña Josefina, at whose house she had frequently met Dolores Ponce de Leon. Between Dolores and her a warm friendship had sprung up, in which there was more than friendship, for each became to the other as a sister, and as sisters they loved each other, telling each other unreservedly the deepest secrets of their hearts, hearts which had as yet known no deep emotion, and in which there were no secrets but such as they might have told unblushingly to all the world. Still they met occasionally at the house of Don Fausto Velasquez, where Magdalen went often, or at the house of Don Gregorio Lopez, where she went less frequently, but to the quinta Dolores never came, saying that her father had forbidden her. The reason of this remained a mystery to Magdalen, for when she had applied in her perplexity to Doña Josefina that lady had spoken to her such words of Don Alfonso that she felt she could never ask any more questions on the subject.

The outside of the house of Don Alfonso differed in one respect from the generality of the houses about Buenos Aires. On the eastern side, which was the front, instead of the usual veranda there stood before the main entrance a wide porch of trellis-work, over which honeysuckle and other flowering creepers climbed luxuriantly, loading the air in the summer-time with the sweet scent of flowers innumerable. The flooring of this porch, on a level with that of the house, was raised some two feet above the level of the garden, from which the approach was by three wide steps. In this porch it was a frequent custom with Don Alfonso to sit with his daughter or with their guests in the warm evenings of the summer and autumn, sheltered from the sun, and gazing through the foliage of the trees upon the green suburbs and upon the white houses of the nearer portion of the city, and farther away upon the summits of the towers and domes of churches.

Magdalen rejoiced with the joy of a young girl whose life so far had been passed amongst strangers, when she found herself at the head of her father's household, and her sweet womanly instincts developed themselves rapidly as she felt that the comfort of others depended upon her diligence and foresight. The household was but a small one, but there was much for her to do in the way of contrivance and arrangement, for Don Alfonso would never buy anything which could possibly be made at home, or which his quinta would produce.

So Magdalen passed the spring, summer, and autumn in great contentment with her father at his quinta; it was now winter, and though she had made frequent visits to her friends in the city, yet she had during all this time never passed one night from under her father's roof until the night of the 5th July, which she spent in very unwonted fashion under the roof of Don Fausto Velasquez, dancing and listening to soft speeches in the spacious saloons of Doña Josefina, which were crowded with all that Buenos Aires could furnish in the way of beauty and distinction.

The number of those having some claim to distinction in Buenos Aires was not great at that time, for until the first invasion of the English under Beresford the modes by which a native of Buenos Aires could distinguish himself were very few. Two English invasions had given opportunities for distinction, and officers of the Patricios and Arribeños who had shown skill or courage were the favoured guests of Doña Josefina on this occasion. Among these officers there was but one Spaniard, a captain in the regiment of the Andaluces. To this captain Doña Josefina showed great attention, introducing him to many a fair partner, whispering to them to pardon his coarse manners and want of address, as he was a protegé of hers, and had been lieutenant of the "Morenos de Ponce."

But of beauty Buenos Aires had enough and to spare. It is said (in Buenos Aires) that when Venus was apportioning her gifts among her sisters she gave pre-eminence in grace and elegance to the Spanish woman, in liveliness and savoir-faire to the Frenchwoman, to the Italian perfection of form and feature, to the Englishwoman a complexion clear as the morning, and so on, some special gift to the women of every race upon earth, but that she forgot the Porteña altogether, till being told of her neglect she took from each woman of every race a fragment of the special perfection of each one of them and bestowed it upon the Porteña, thus creating a race of women unequalled in the variety of their charms in any country under the sun. However that may be, it would be difficult to find anywhere such a collection of beauty as graced the saloons of Doña Josefina on this evening of the 5th July.

Magdalen was not a Porteña, her friends called her the " Inglesita," because England had been her birthplace. She was short in stature, irregular in feature, with high cheek-bones ; her English birth had not even endowed her with a brilliant complexion, but her figure was good, her hands and feet were small, and there was an easy grace about her every movement which was in itself no inconsiderable charm. Throughout this evening she was surrounded by a constant succession of ad-mirers emulous of her hand, and each one as he led her to a seat after a dance lingered near her, wondering to himself what it was that made him so linger.

She spoke little during the dances, for this was the first city ball at which she had ever been present ; the brilliance of the scene somewhat embarrassed her, and many of those who sought an introduction to her she had never seen before. This was her first ball and she enjoyed it greatly, the pleasure which she felt beamed in her face ; joy is infectious and produces joy in those who look upon it, by sympathy.

Her dress was of white muslin, richly embroidered, with a very short body and immense balloon sleeves padded with swan's-down, which stood out round her shoulders but left the greater part of her arms bare. Under this dress she wore another of blue silk, the outer dress of muslin being looped up at the left side with a small rosette of blue silk ; both dresses were exceedingly long in the skirt, sweeping the ground for fully a yard and a half behind her as she walked. Her hair, rising straight up from her forehead, was combed in a fashion much in vogue at that day into one mass on the top of her head, and was sparingly sprinkled with powder ; from the back a few curls fell down behind her ears, and two or three smaller curls lay in careful negligence upon her forehead and temples. She wore a necklace of pearls, from the centre of which hung a small gold cross, and her left wrist was encircled by a bracelet of plain gold.

About an hour before midnight, during a pause between two dances, Magdalen was walking down one of the rooms in company with Lieutenant Gordon, who was repeating to her some of the anecdotes which Marcelino Ponce de Leon had told about his negroes at the banquet not two hours before, when she was accosted by an officer in gala uniform, with the epaulets of a major on his shoulders. She started at his voice as he spoke to her, and then looked up at him with a glad smile, but as her eyes met his they fell beneath their earnest gaze and a warm flush spread over her cheeks. The officer who had addressed her, and whose bright dark eyes were riveted upon her face as he bowed lowly before her, was Marcelino himself.

Marcelino had never forgotten those eyes which had haunted him during the long summer and autumn which he had passed training his negroes, and he had eagerly accepted Don Alfonso's subsequent invitation to visit him at his quinta, but during the many evenings he had passed there since he had never again seen the same look in those eyes, often as he had looked into them in search of it, and he had learned to think of Magdalen as an amiable but very plain-featured girl, with a certain nameless fascination about her for which he could not account. Also, as a girl with a talent for conversation, and a voice to which he could listen for hours with the same feeling as though he had been listening to music.

Magdalen had inherited from her English mother a gift more charming than any physical beauty, and one less liable to fade, that of a most melodious voice. In Buenos Aires, where physical beauty is so general among women, a melodious voice is but rarely heard, and Marcelino had often caused great amusement to his friend Gordon during many months past by his mode of asking him to accompany him on a visit to Don Alfonso.

"Come out with me to the Miserere, and talk to your paisanita for me while I listen."

As Marcelino now looked upon Magdalen, with the girlish joy beaming in her face, he saw once again that same look in her eyes which had haunted him for so long and which he had never forgotten. Her face seemed to him lighted up with a new beauty all its own, a beauty far exceeding all beauty of feature or complexion, the beauty of expression. When she smiled upon him with the glad smile with which she received him, her soul looked out upon him through those large gray eyes, a soul in consonance with the sweet voice he loved to listen to, the soul of a large-hearted, loving woman. To Marcelino she never appeared plain-featured again.

He asked her hand for the next dance, and then instead of dancing they sauntered away to a quiet corner, where they sat down and talked together.

"So Gordon has been telling you about the banquet?" said Marcelino.

"Not much about the banquet, but about the speech you made," replied Magdalen.

"I made! Yes, I did make a speech of a sort; talked about my negroes, which is very easy for me to do; but his was the great speech, did not he tell you about that?"

"Not a word. What did he say?"

"He said one thing, which there are some of us will take care to spread all over the country. He said that a colony is an infant nation."

"You think so, I know. I have heard you say something like it more than once."

"Yes, but not in public, and before the Viceroy. In us poor Creoles it would be rank treason to say such a thing, but just at present an Englishman may say what he likes."

"Then when he goes there will be no one left among you who will dare to speak the truth openly?"

"No one, for a time at least; but the day is coming when all will be able to speak openly just what they think."

"Why not begin at once? I should think it was never too early to speak the truth."

"There you are mistaken; but you must think me very stupid to talk to you about politics in a ball-room, though I have seen you listen when others were talking politics at the quinta."

"I always listen, and then talk to papa about it afterwards. Papa and I are great politicians when we are alone together. I have never seen my uncle Don Francisco, but papa has talked to me for hours about him, though he hardly ever speaks of him to any one else."

"Allow me to compliment you on your dress, I admire the colours you have chosen ; blue and white, are they your favourite colours ? "

"Yes, they are, so I would wear them. Doña Josefina and Lola did all they could to persuade me to wear pink, but I can be very obstinate when I choose."

"And quite right too. I never saw you looking so well before, all the men seem to think so, it was ever so long before I could get a chance of speaking to you."

"That is because you are the hero of the ball, and have so many others to speak to. Does not Lola look beautiful this evening, quite like a little queen ?"

"I think she has spoiled it by the way she has arranged her hair, the peinete [1] does not suit her at all, and I should think it must be very uncomfortable."

"La moda nunca incomoda," [2] answered Magdalen.

"I am glad you have not followed the fashion," said Marcelino, "for the peinete would suit you even less than it does Lola."

As they spoke, a lady of fair stature and of radiant beauty, in the first bloom of womanhood, dressed in pink, and with masses of dark hair falling in silken curls upon her white shoulders, came sailing proudly down the room leaning upon the arm of a young officer ; as she passed near them she turned her brilliant black eyes full upon Marcelino, and bending towards him with a peculiar wave of her fan, said in a low voice—

"Le felicito " (I congratulate you).

Magdalen, who had apparently not heard her words, gazed eagerly after her.

"What a beautiful girl," she said ; "I do not think I ever saw such a beautiful girl. Who is she ?"

"Elisa Puyrredon ; she is sister to Doña Juana de Saenz-Valiente ; some men say that the two sisters and my aunt Josefina are the three most beautiful women in Buenos Aires."

"And what do you say ?"

"I don't know any woman equal in beauty to Elisa Puyrredon."

"But we were talking about my uncle," said Magdalen. "I am so proud to have such a man for my uncle. I think a man who has spent his life as he has, has done more that he may be proud of than the greatest conqueror that ever lived. He has always been beaten ; but even Napoleon, with all the battles he has won, is not near so great a man in my eyes as my uncle Francisco."

As Magdalen spoke her face flushed, her enthusiasm beamed in her large gray eyes, tinging them with a darker colour than was usual to them ; and Marcelino, watching her intently, forgot to speak, till meeting his wrapt gaze she bent her head and appeared intent only upon the figures on her fan.

---

[1] The large comb at that time worn in Buenos Aires as in Spain, generally made of tortoiseshell, and sometimes two feet in width.

[2] The fashion is never uncomfortable.

"Then you think that a man who devotes himself to the welfare of his country, even if he fail and be proscribed and banished, has not spent his life in vain?" said Marcelino.

"In vain, no! Good work is never done in vain."

"You will miss Gordon very much."

"Indeed I shall, and so will you; but he says he will come back again, and I think he will."

Magdalen spoke this last sentence in a peculiarly confidential tone, raising her fan as she spoke, and looking over the edge of it at Marcelino, but the glance and the tone were alike thrown away upon that gentleman.

"He promised me long ago," replied he, "that if we have to fight for our freedom he will join us; but now I think we shall win it without fighting, the French are doing that for us. He likes the country, so some day we shall have him back again. What will you do without him? You will have no one to read English to you in the porch next summer."

"Poor me! but it was very seldom he did read to me last summer. I think he likes galloping about better than reading. Last summer he was always in a hurry to get away, and his gallops were always in one direction."

"Yes, the traitor! he was always taking me to the Miserere in the afternoons, and then leaving me to find my way back by myself."

"Yet I never saw you angry with him for deserting you."

"The time passed so pleasantly that I never missed him till it was time to go back. You cannot think how I am wishing for the long days to come again."

"Papa likes the winter best."

"Yes, he likes to sit at his fireside while you make tea for him, but we Porteños like the open air better. For me the most pleasant place in any season is where you are."

"A compliment! You know that I do not like compliments," answered Magdalen, with a look of annoyance.

"I did not intend it as a compliment," said Marcelino.

"When men say things like that it sounds to me as if they were mocking one. There are some men who are always doing it, and it is so annoying. You have never said anything like that to me before."

"I never said a word to you yet that I did not mean. Do you not like to hear the truth spoken to you?"

"Yes, even if it be unpleasant."

"And I like to speak the truth when it is pleasant to do so; when it is not I prefer to keep silent."

"If you never speak anything but the truth to me we shall always be good friends, and I shall know how to interpret your silence."

"Then we are good friends now, for I have never said a word to you that is not true. I am going away, and I do not know when I shall be back. I should be very sorry to go away leaving you angry at anything I had said to you."

"You are going away! Where to?"

"To Rio Janeiro. I arranged it this morning. If the captain of the English frigate which is at Monte Video will give me a passage

I am going with Gordon, so I shall not lose him so soon as you will."

"He does not know, at least he said nothing of it to me."

"No, I have not told him yet. No one knows but you and my father."

"Poor Dolores! she will be quite lonely, losing both you and Mr. Gordon at once."

"Not so lonely as you generally are. She has always plenty of people about her. If she saw you more often she would miss us less. Could not you come and pay Aunt Josefina a visit of a month or so, I know she wants you to do so?"

"And leave papa all alone! Impossible!"

"Then I will tell you what to do. Come and spend one day every week with Aunt Josefina. Lola often tells me that she wishes she could see more of you than she does."

"Does she? Oh! I am so glad. I shall be here all day to-morrow till the evening, and then every Wednesday morning after this I will come in and spend the day with Doña Josefina. I am sure papa will let me if I ask him, and when I have a fixed day for coming then Lola will come too."

"Then when I come back the Wednesdays will be an established custom, and I shall think that I have done something to give you a pleasure by suggesting it. Every Wednesday while I am away I shall think that you and Lola are together, and when she speaks of me you will think of me for a moment, and will remember that I am thinking of you."

CHAPTER II.

IN August there came an emissary from the Emperor Napoleon to
Buenos Aires. Viceroy Liniers received this Frenchman very affably,
and the two held conferences together of which none knew the purport; but why this Frenchman had come was no secret to any one
in Buenos Aires. He came on behalf of the Emperor Napoleon to
invite the colonies of Spain to follow the example of their mother-
country, telling them that Spaniards desired no longer that Bourbons
should reign over them, but had welcomed with joy a new king whom
he had chosen for them, his brother Joseph.

But Buenos Aires had heard of this new king, Joseph, before this
Frenchman had come to tell her of him, and knew that those Spanish
nobles and courtiers who had crowded round Murat at Madrid, and
had welcomed the new king whom Napoleon had sent to them, were
not the Spanish people. Buenos Aires knew that the Spanish people
would have no foreigner for their king, and that the Central Junta
established at Seville proposed to rule Spain and to make war upon
Napoleon in the name of Ferdinand VII., who by the abdication of
his father was the legitimate King of Spain, although both he and his
father were now prisoners in France, and were said to have renounced
their rights in favour of the new king, Joseph.

Buenos Aires had no great cause to love Spain, and her reverence
for her was fast dying out, yet still she looked upon Spain as her
mother, and her spirit rose in anger as she heard of her degradation.
Men went about from house to house and stood in groups at the
street corners, talking eagerly one to the other, questioning one another why it was that this Frenchman was hospitably entertained in
their city, while Spain lay prostrate at the feet of Napoleon, who had
sent him? Then they remembered Liniers also was a Frenchman,
and their wrath was kindled against him; and when sundry Spaniards
came amongst them, striving with soft speeches to still their indignation, telling them that the question was not theirs, but was Spain's,
that Spain would decide for herself and for them, they thrust them
out from among them with scornful words.

On the 15th August Liniers made a proclamation to them, counselling them to moderation, showing how the destinies of a colony should
follow those of the mother-country, but that while the struggle went
on they should for their own sake hold aloof. But neither to him
would they listen, and throughout the city the ferment was great.

Then on the 21st August Liniers gave answer to the emissary of Napoleon, and justified himself in the eyes of the men of Buenos Aires by proclaiming with all due formality and military display Ferdinand VII. King of Spain and the Indies.

It was evening on this 21st August, the roll of the drums was long since hushed, the regular troops had retired to their barracks, the militia to their homes, the quietude of a winter night had come down over the city. The streets were almost deserted, yet here and there men might be seen issuing from their houses, and wending their way through the darkness to the house of Don Gregorio Lopez. Each man as he reached the door of this house looked cautiously round to see that he was alone, then struck one smart rap with his knuckles upon one of the panels of the door, and bent his head to listen. From the inside there came one rap in answer, upon which he struck twice rapidly in the same place as before, and the door opened. In the centre of the zaguan hung a lamp, which threw its rays directly on the face of each man as he went in; under this lamp stood a tall negro. Each man as he entered the zaguan waited till the door closed behind him, then said to the negro one word—

" Patria."

" Buenas noches y pasa adelante," replied the negro, stepping to one side and leaving the passage free.

Each man crossed the first patio and entered a second zaguan, where three young men stood in silence, waiting till he should speak. To them he also spoke one word—

" Libertad."

Upon which one of them led him across the second patio, and ushered him into the same large room in which Don Gregorio had held another secret meeting more than two years before, some few days after General Beresford had taken possession of the city.

Some days previous to the proclamation of King Ferdinand, and while the excitement of the city was at its greatest, Marcelino Ponce de Leon had returned to Buenos Aires. His trip to Rio de Janeiro had been a pleasant one, but he had there met with a certain Don Saturnino Rodriguez Peña, a Porteño by birth, who had inspired him with a great idea. Big with this idea he hurried back, and after an interview with his grandfather sent messengers in every direction, summoning the friends of Don Gregorio Lopez to meet at his house on the evening of the 21st August. One of these messengers galloped out by the southern road and returned on the day of the meeting with Don Carlos Evaña and Don Gregorio Lopez the younger, whose father had received him with open arms when he had visited the city in May, soon after the sudden return of Don Carlos Evaña to his estancia.

About nine o'clock a numerous company was assembled, then the door of the dining-room was shut, and Don Gregorio took his place at the head of the long table, the rest seating themselves on chairs or standing in groups about the room.

Don Gregorio rose from his seat and looked round him, pausing ere he spoke; a proud smile beamed on his face; as the rest looked upon him this smile was reflected in their faces and many of them clapped their hands.

"Señores," said Don Gregorio, as the applause subsided, "it is with pride and pleasure that I look round on you who have come here at my invitation. It brings to my remembrance, as it will to many of you, an evening more than two years ago when we met together as we do now. These two years have been years which will be for ever memorable in the annals of our country." Here Don Gregorio was interrupted by "Vivas" and clamorous applause; when silence was restored he went on :—

"These two years have worked a mighty change amongst us. We have learnt in times of difficulty and danger to trust to our own strength and our own ability, and we have found that we have both strength and ability within ourselves. In former times we looked to Spain to protect us in danger, and we obeyed without question the mandates of the rulers she set over us. In these years Spain has been unable to do anything to protect us, yet have we defended ourselves successfully. We turned out the Viceroy sent by Spain as our ruler. and have now a Viceroy of our own selection, to whom we look as the representative of our legitimate sovereign. But our sovereign himself is in prison. cut off from all communication with us, to whom then shall we look as to the source of the authority which we obey?

"During the last two years ideas and wishes have grown up amongst us which were formerly unknown, it is for the discussion of these ideas that I have called upon you to meet me this evening. One such idea my grandson Marcelino has asked my permission to lay before you."

As Don Gregorio resumed his seat. Marcelino Ponce de Leon rose in the midst of an ominous silence, and in a carefully-prepared speech disclosed a plan for bringing the Princess Carlota, sister of King Ferdinand and wife of the Prince-regent of Brazil, to Buenos Aires to rule over the provinces of the Rio de La Plata as queen.

During his speech he was frequently interrupted, and as he sat down the confusion rose to a tumult. Most of those present laughed at the idea as absurd. and some in no measured terms expressed their indignation. When the uproar had partially subsided, Don Gregorio Lopez again rose to his feet and said—

"Señores, it is with my entire approval that my grandson has laid this proposition before you. I think it well worthy of careful consideration by all of us, but I doubt much whether it would be received with favour by our Spanish rulers."

"Our Spanish rulers!" shouted Don Carlos Evaña, springing indignantly to his feet, "our Spanish rulers! they are the men who are to decide this and every other question for us! Spain has fallen, and with Spain the one check which existed to protect us from Spanish rapacity; in place of being the slaves of a great empire we are now the slaves of a handful of Spaniards. Who are these Spaniards that they should come among us and arrogate to themselves the possession of all authority? Do not deceive yourselves, my countrymen, we, the citizens of this country, have inborn rights which no Spaniard, no king, or Bourbon, can take from us. There is no longer any question of Spain or Bourbons, we are the people, and the time has come for us to demand our rights as men. What shall we do to claim and take possession of these rights of ours? That is the question which is now before us.

Q

"To you, Don Gregorio, as the man of most influence among us ; to you, young men, who wear the uniform of our victorious militia, the rising hope of our country, I address this question, that you take it into your serious consideration, but I ask you not for your answer, that answer it is not for us alone to give, that answer must come from an entire people, and shall ere long be spoken on the house-tops in the full blaze of the sun."

Then, as Evaña sat down, burst forth from the younger members of that assembly a storm of applause, and Valentin Lopez y Viana, the youngest son of Don Gregorio, raising his hand in the air, shouted "Viva la Patria !" a cry which found its echo in every heart there present, and which ere long reverberated from south to north over an entire continent, rousing enslaved nations into the bold assertion of their rights as men.

There was no more discussion of this or any other question ; with many there present the influence of Spain was yet paramount, they might shout "Viva la Patria," but the Patria was to them a dream, and Spain was a dread reality, and treason against Spain was a fearful crime, entailing fearful punishment ; they were only too glad to take any pretext for opening the doors and seeking the shelter of their own homes.

In deep chagrin Marcelino left the house in company with Don Manuel Belgrano, the only one who had shown any warm sympathy with his project.

CHAPTER III.

SEVERAL WAYS OF LOOKING AT ONE QUESTION.

It was the evening after the one on which Don Gregorio Lopez had held a secret conference with his friends as narrated in the preceding chapter. Don Alfonso Miranda in a loose dressing-gown and slippers sat in an easy-chair at his fireside. On the wide, open hearth logs of wood burnt and crackled cheerfully, throwing out showers of sparks when they were touched.

Opposite to Don Alfonso, in another easy-chair, sat Don Carlos Evaña, holding in his hand a tea-cup which had just been refilled for him by the small white hands of Magdalen Miranda, who sat near to him at a round table, in the centre of which hissed a huge brown urn. At the far side of this table, with the urn between him and the fire, sat Marcelino Ponce de Leon, holding a silver tea-pot under the spout of the urn, while Magdalen with her hand on the tap let just so much water run into it as she judged sufficient for one more cup of tea.

"You did not tell us anything about that, Don Marcelino," said Magdalen.

"No," replied Marcelino, looking across the table at Don Alfonso.

"Don Carlos, you see, trusts us more than you do," replied the young lady, with a slight toss of her head.

"It is not want of trust that kept me silent. But secrecy implies danger; to admit you to the secret admits you to the danger also."

"Among sixty! Did not you say there were sixty, Don Carlos?" asked Magdalen.

"Yes; and the secret of sixty is not much of a secret," answered Evaña.

"I do not see why it should be a secret at all," said Magdalen. "The Princess Carlota could not be queen without the consent of her brother. Did you see her when you were at Rio?"

"Yes, Gordon took me with him to a ball at the British Embassy, and she was there for about half an hour."

"What is she like?" asked Magdalen, but before Marcelino could answer Don Alfonso turned towards him and asked him abruptly—

"You were at the British Embassy, did you speak with Lord Strangford?"

"Yes, he took me to one side and asked me a great many questions about this country and about Whitelock's affair."

"Did he mention my name to you?"

"Yes, and seemed curious to know what you were doing here. I told him as little as I could of you."

"Right, quite right," replied Don Alfonso, turning back again to the fire.

"You have been several times in the city while I was away," said Marcelino.

"I make it a custom to go every Wednesday to see Doña Josefina," replied Magdalen, bending over her empty tea-cups and arranging them on a small tray.

"To one person you give great pleasure by so doing," said Evaña, in a low voice.

"And that one is myself," said Magdalen. "When are you going out again to your estancia, Don Carlos?"

"Some time next month," replied Evaña. "Are you tired of giving me tea in your English fashion?"

"Not at all, I like trying to civilize you proud Porteños, who suck mate through tubes one after the other, and yet think yourselves the most polished people on the face of the world."

"You go often to your estancia, Don Carlos?" said Don Alfonso, rising from his chair.

The playful smile vanished from Magdalen's face as she heard her father speak, there was something in the tone of his voice which she had seldom or never heard before. As she looked up at him she saw that his lips were white, and his face set as though he were a prey to some unseen terror. She had risen from her seat to summon her maid to remove the tray and urn, but as she looked at her father she sat down again, clasping her hands together.

"Since I purchased the place I have spent nearly half my time there," replied Evaña.

"You do well, but you would do better to spend all your time there," continued Don Alfonso. "I have heard that when you are there you pay more attention to men than to beasts, and think more of your horses than you do of your cattle."

"Yet I have more cattle than either men or horses," replied Evaña evasively.

"Listen to me, young men, both of you," said Don Alfonso. "One of you buys an estancia and gives away his cattle to any men who will join a regiment with which he has nothing whatever to do; the other gets three months' leave of absence for a voyage of pleasure, meets in Rio Janeiro a man whose hatred of Spain has driven him into exile from his own country, and then hurriedly returns before his leave has half expired. Then both of you are present at a secret meeting and report that the subject discussed was a project for supplanting our rightful king by his sister. At this meeting there was much talking, but nothing was resolved upon, each man spoke his own thoughts. Now I know that if Don Manuel Belgrano and Don Carlos Evaña spoke their thoughts they would say something very different from this insane project of bringing a queen to reign over us."

"I assure you, Don Alfonso," said Marcelino, "that Don Manuel Belgrano is much in favour of the idea."

"It may be so," replied Don Alfonso; "but when men meet in secret to speak their thoughts what they speak is treason. I do not ask you of what you spoke last night, I do not wish to know, but I

will tell you what neither of you know. When I left England ten
years ago I was a hale, strong man, now look at my white hair and
my weak, trembling hands. I am an old man before my time; I should
have died, and my daughter would be an orphan, but for the kindness
of men who knew nothing of me save that I was in misery. Ten
years ago I thought myself a rich man, now I am poor, as you see.
All this is the result of the reckless folly of other men, for whose
faults I have suffered. You talk of patriotism and love for your
country, do you ever think of the misery your wild schemes may
bring upon others? The day I landed at Carracas six men, of whom
four had been the friends of my youth, were put to a shameful death,
hung, drawn, and quartered; when I asked why, they spoke to me of
my brother, and because my name was Miranda they thrust me into
a dungeon, loaded me with irons. and would doubtless have taken my
life also, but that I was rich and could bribe my gaolers. I know
nothing of my brother, and of your schemes I will know nothing either,
can you not leave me to enjoy in peace the little that is left to me?"

As Don Alfonso spoke, jerking out his words in abrupt sentences,
his face became nearly livid, and his hands trembled so that he could
hardly grasp the arms of his chair as he sat down again. Marcelino
covered his face with his hands, and Evaña sat motionless biting his
moustache, which was a way he had when he was angry. Magdalen
looked from one to the other with an expression of deep pain on her
face : then as her father sat down she drew out a low stool from under
the table, and placing it beside his chair she seated herself upon it,
and taking his hand in hers patted it softly, caressing him as one
would soothe a child when in trouble.

Then Marcelino took another chair in front of the fire, and strove
to change the current of their thoughts by cheerful talk, but Evaña
replied only in monosyllables, and Don Alfonso spoke not at all, sitting
there moodily in his arm-chair gazing at the fire. Marcelino and
Magdalen talked together almost in whispers, speaking to each other
at random on any subject which came uppermost, Magdalen still
holding her father's hand in hers. Thus half an hour passed over,
when Evaña rose to his feet and said—

" It is late, let us go."

" Remember what I have said," said Don Alfonso, " I wish to
know nothing of your schemes."

Then, without looking at either of them, he waved his hand and so
dismissed his two guests.

Magdalen accompanied them to the porch, looking wistfully out
into the night as they put on their cloaks and hats; as they shook
hands with her she whispered softly to Marcelino—

" Something has happened to annoy papa, I knew it."

Marcelino and Don Carlos had their horses tied under the trees,
they mounted and rode slowly away. Until they were squares from
the quinta neither of them spoke. Then said Don Carlos in a musing tone—

" See you how two men of the same birth and blood may differ?"

" Don Alfonso is certainly a very different man from his brother
as you have described him to me," replied Marcelino.

"Originally he was of much the same character," said Evaña;
"but the easy life he led in England has enervated out of him the
stern energy which distinguishes Don Francisco, and his imprisonments here and at Carracas have completely cowed what spirit he
had left. He is a sample of the effects of Spanish tyranny, of which
I have seen many; the good in him has been crushed out of him, and
he has become what you have seen to-night, a drivelling coward, and
at the same time he is dangerous, for he is both treacherous and
revengeful."

"Knowing what he has suffered, I think it was unwise of you, Carlos, to say anything to him of the meeting last night. You could
not suppose that he would take any part with us."

"I did hope that he might, his name alone would be of great
service to us, and I spoke with a purpose. I have received a letter
from the General, I believe he has also written to Don Alfonso, I
wanted him to tell me."

"What does the General say?"

"Very little, and in very guarded words, but I know what he
means. He means that the time has come, and that after our
triumph of last year, Mexico, Venezuela, Chili, and Peru all look
to us to give the signal. Your idea of giving us a queen in the
Princess Carlota will not find much favour from him if he ever hears
of it."

"But you will not oppose it?"

"I do not think I shall have any need to, it will fall through without my interference. Look here, my brother, between us there must
be no secrets."

As he spoke Evaña edged his horse nearer to Marcelino, and laid
one hand on his shoulder.

"You have started the idea, be content, leave Belgrano to carry it
out if he can. As Miranda says, the time has come; all that I have
done so far is preparative, now I am going to begin my work—join
me."

"And your object?"

"A republic."

"We are not yet ready for complete independence."

"So long as Spaniards rule over us we shall never be more ready
than we are now."

"How do you propose to begin?"

"I wish to form a small secret committee of men who are ready
to dare everything for the accomplishment of our one object."

"Have you spoken to any one else of it?"

"You are the first."

"Then let me be the last also, Carlos. We are so strong that we
have no need of any secresy, what we want is publicity to educate the
people into a knowledge of their own rights and of their own power.
To form a committee as you suggest is the first step towards a conspiracy, and will give a pretext for forcible measures of repression,
which can only end in civil war. Let us openly demand that half
the seats in the Cabildo be given to Creoles, and that Creoles be
henceforth eligible for any post under government."

" And then we will throw open our ports to the world and invite the English to come and trade with us?"

" Just so. With our own men in every corporation all necessary reforms are possible."

" And Spaniards are going to give up their monopolies and let us introduce all manner of innovations, and be brothers to us so long as we let their flag fly at the fort, and shout 'Viva La Reina!' or 'Viva el Rey!' which ever it may chance to be."

" They will submit to necessity."

" When they see it they will, but until we show it them they will never see it. No, my brother, we must first assert, seize by force, if necessary, the power of governing ourselves, we must first appoint a government of our own, then we may safely welcome all Spaniards who choose to join us, and give them equal rights with ourselves. If we content ourselves with asking as privileges for what are our natural rights, they may yield them to us now that they have no strength to struggle against us, but it will only be to take them back again so soon as they find themselves strong enough to do it."

While Don Alfonso and his two visitors were speaking in their way of the meeting of the previous evening, the same subject was under discussion from a very different point of view in the private apartments of his Excellency the Viceroy. Marshal Liniers had also two visitors that evening, Don Martin Alzaga and Don Roderigo Ponce de Leon.

The precautions taken by Don Gregorio Lopez had prevented unfriendly intrusion, but had by no means sufficed to keep the meeting itself a secret. Don Martin Alzaga had heard of it beforehand, and had warned the Viceroy, counselling him to use his authority to prevent it; but Marshal Liniers had refused to interfere, saying that so long as the citizens obeyed him and paid the taxes they might meet as they liked in their own houses. Then Don Martin had sought the aid of Don Roderigo, and between them they had devised means for learning something of what should take place at this meeting. Now they came together to visit the Viceroy, and to lay before him the result of their enquiries.

" I think it strange of you, Don Roderigo, that you should move in this matter," said the Viceroy, after they had conversed with him for about an hour; "your son, your father-in-law, and some of your most intimate friends are those most deeply implicated."

An angry flush spread over Don Roderigo's face as he answered—

" Nothing has yet been done. I suppose men have a right to speak their opinions in their own houses, but it is always well for the authorities to know what are the ideas of the people."

" When these ideas are treason they have no right to give utterance to them anywhere," said Don Martin Alzaga; "and I call upon you, Don Santiago, to order the immediate arrest of Don Gregorio Lopez for holding a seditious conference."

" I hope you will do no such thing," said Don Roderigo.

" Why not?" said Don Martin.

" The Patricios would mutiny at once, and we should hurry on a catastrophe which it will require all our care to avoid."

" An example is necessary," said Don Martin.

" By due precautions we may avoid any such necessity, at any rate until we are strong enough to act with safety to ourselves. I have enquired into the particulars of this meeting simply as a precaution. In this idea of offering the sovereignty of the Viceroyalty to the Princess Carlota there is no danger whatever."

" I think it most dangerous," said the Viceroy.

" Where there is danger is in the growing arrogance of the Creoles," said Don Roderigo. " The first thing that should be done is to disarm the militia. We need them no longer, and so long as there exist in the city entire regiments of Creoles, commanded by Creoles, the arrest of any popular citizen would produce an outbreak."

" Which we would put down with our troops," said Don Martin Alzaga.

" And bring on the catastrophe at once. I know these men better than you do, Don Martin, and my knowledge tells me that we have need of the greatest caution. Miranda has his agents everywhere in South America."

" Evaña !" said the Viceroy. " He is the one man whom I consider dangerous. You did not mention him, Don Roderigo ; was he not at that meeting last night ? "

" He was," said Don Roderigo ; " but he spoke against this plan of inviting the Princess Carlota."

" He wants neither princess nor queen," said Liniers ; " he wants a republic."

" Arrest him, then, and let him have a republic all to himself within four walls," said Don Martin.

" I would advise your Excellency to avoid all extreme measures at present," said Don Roderigo. " Our power is falling away from us ; instead of exciting popular opposition, I think it will be necessary to make some concessions. The most enticing bait offered by Beresford when he came, was freedom of commerce. Let us grant it ; our treasury is nearly empty, the English merchants will fill it for us, and we shall take the most convincing argument out of the mouths of the demagogues of the city."

" And the Consulado de las Indias, you forget them, Don Roderigo?" said the Viceroy.

" The idea is perfectly inadmissible," said Don Martin Alzaga. " The first thing to do is to disarm the militia, then we can repress by force any attempt against our authority."

" The militia have done good service, and merit every consideration," said the Viceroy, "and they cost far less than the Spanish regiments."

" Then we are to do nothing, and let these Creoles conspire against us until some day they set up a government of their own," replied Don Martin, rising angrily from his seat. " Let us retire, Don Roderigo ; it is late, and here we do nothing."

The Viceroy rose from his chair, and bowing stiffly to both, dismissed them.

" With this man we shall never do anything," said Don Martin to Don Roderigo, as they crossed the Plaza de Los Perdices together.

"Whilst he is Viceroy the Creoles will keep their militia, and will do just what they wish. I should not be surprised some day to see them demand a 'Cabildo Abierto.'"

"Yes," replied Don Roderigo; "unless they send us another Viceroy from Spain we shall soon find ourselves unable to govern at all."

"We have turned out one Viceroy ourselves, and the result was good; we will see if we cannot do it a second time."

"Beware, Don Martin; the Patricios had more to do with the appointment of Liniers than we had."

"What matter to me the Patricios? With musketry we will teach them, if they want a lesson."

CHAPTER IV.

WINTER gave place to spring, spring ripened into summer, and everything in Buenos Aires seemed to go on unchanged, but in seeming only. As the suns of the spring-time covered the leafless trees with verdure, as the buds developed themselves into flowers, the flowers into fruit, so the thoughts of men developed themselves into distinct ideas, and these ideas grew and flourished till they were ready to become deeds.

Don Roderigo had spoken to his son, had told him that he knew of the idea he had brought back with him from Brazil, told him that it was folly, and counselled him to have nothing more to do with it.

"But, father," replied Marcelino, "can you not see why the idea pleased me? Do not you see that native Argentines are no longer the men they were two years ago, and that Spain is no longer the same Spain either? How can we accept Viceroys and laws from Spain, when Spain herself has no king, and when Frenchmen rule over half the country? There are men among us who speak of a republic, but most of us would be content with far less. With a queen of our own from the royal family of Spain, the government would remain in the hands of men such as you, who are accustomed to govern, instead of falling into the hands of inexperienced men, who would bring anarchy upon us.

"I will not argue the question with you, Marcelino," replied Don Roderigo, "but I merely warn you that so long as an armed Frenchman treads the soil of Spain the integrity of the dominion of Spain must be the first object with every true Spaniard."

Marcelino listened to his father unconvinced, yet stirred himself no further in the matter, leaving it entirely in the hands of his friend Don Manuel Belgrano, who, being a man of much greater experience and of higher position than himself, was more likely to be able to bring it to a successful issue. But he also refused to listen to the solicitations of his friend Evaña; returning to his post at the Consulado, he passed his days in the sedulous discharge of his duties, and his evenings in study, or in pleasant social intercourse. At least one evening every week he passed at the quinta of Don Alfonso, till Magdalen learned to look for his visits as one of the pleasures of her monotonous life. Sometimes Evaña accompanied him, but never did either of them speak a word to Don Alfonso on the politics of the day. He was invariably civil to them, but to him their visits gave no pleasure, and they could plainly see that it was often a relief to him when they took their departure.

To Evaña these visits were as a penance undertaken for the sake of his friend, but of Don Alfonso's increasing taciturnity Marcelino took no note. there was one there always ready to talk to him, or to listen to what he said, who took a deep interest in all his studies, and whose large gray eyes lighted up her plain features into a beauty all their own as he spoke to her. To him the months passed quickly, and happy in the present he gave but now and then a passing thought to the future.

As for Don Carlos Evaña, his thoughts were ever in the future, but his hopes, his fears, and his projects he kept all to himself, working continually with one object steadily in view, the overthrow of Spanish rule, but working in a way which appeared to none to be work. His estancia he but once visited all that spring, and then his visit was a short one, nearly all his time he spent in the city. Don Cornelio Saavedra, Colonel of the Patricios, offered him a commission in the first battalion, the command of the company formerly led by Don Isidro Lorea, which he declined, yet he practised fencing every day, and those of his books which treated of the art of war were those most frequently studied by him.

One battalion of the Patricios was known as that of the "Pardos y Morenos," being composed entirely of men of colour, liberated slaves, or the descendants of freedmen. At the head-quarters of this battalion Evaña was a frequent visitor. Don Cornelio Saavedra met him there one day and asked him somewhat scornfully whether he would prefer a commission in this regiment to one in the *corps d'élite*, but to him Evaña answered that as *yet* he had no wish to enter any regiment. Don Cornelio noticed the accent on the word "yet," and replied—

"It would be difficult for even a philosopher to understand you, Don Carlos; for me, I confess that I understand you not at all."

But the free negroes and mulattos understood something about Don Carlos, of which Don Cornelio knew nothing, which was, that if they required favour or assistance in any way, none was so ready to help them as Don Carlos Evaña, and that the only way in which they could repay him for any such service was to repeat to him all the tittle-tattle and gossip they could collect among their women-folk concerning the sayings and doings of certain of the chief men of the city who were Spaniards.

Don Manuel Belgrano entered eagerly into a secret correspondence with certain confidential friends of the Princess Carlota; despatched missives to trusty friends of his own throughout the provinces, advocating her claims; and kept alive the zeal of her friends in the city by frequent secret conferences, which were held in the guise of dinner-parties, or of excursions into the country, so baulking the vigilance of Don Roderigo, or of any others unfriendly to the project. So passed with him the spring very harmlessly, but his enthusiasm greatly subsided as he learnt that even American air could not liberalize a Bourbon of the royal house of Spain.

Don Martin Alzaga was looked up to by every Spaniard as the champion of what all Spaniards thought their birthright, the right to rule after their own fashion and their own will all the colonies of Spain. Don Martin knew himself also that he was their champion, and thought that he possessed every qualification necessary for a leader in such a cause. Tall, stern-featured, and spare of flesh, with a deep, harsh voice and an authoritative manner, his outward appearance gave the exact index to the man within. The events passing round him taught him nothing, the belief was innate in him that Spaniards were the natural rulers of America. He believed also that Napoleon was invincible, and that the Bourbons would never again rule in Spain. Acting upon these beliefs of his, he conceived the idea of erecting a new Spain in America, of which Buenos Aires should be the capital, and of which the government should be entirely in the hands of Spaniards, looking to Ferdinand VII. as their king, and acknowledging the authority of the Junta Central of Spain so long as any such Junta should exist.

Don Martin had devoted great attention after the defeat of White-lock to enrolling and equipping an artillery corps composed entirely of Spaniards. With this new corps and the Spanish infantry regiments previously existing, he considered that he might safely set the Patricios at defiance. So long as Liniers remained Viceroy, native influence was paramount in the State, and nothing could be done towards recovering the ground already lost. He took counsel with such of the leading Spaniards as were in his confidence, among whom was Don Roderigo Ponce de Leon. Together they wrote to the Junta Central of Spain, then established at Seville, advising the recall of Marshal Liniers.

After the despatch of this letter, Don Roderigo counselled patience, stating that with the arrival of a new Viceroy would come a fair opportunity for the adoption of severe measures of repression. But patience was by no means any part of the character of Don Martin Alzaga, he chafed at the delay, and purposed within himself to take the supreme authority into his own hands, until such time as a new Viceroy should make his appearance, to whom he could surrender his power intact.

Colonel Don Francisco Elio, at that time Governor of Monte Video, was a man of the same stamp as Don Martin Alzaga. To him Don Martin imparted his plans. The first result of their understanding was that on the 24th September Colonel Elio, justifying his proceedings by the friendly reception given by the Viceroy to the envoy of Napoleon, which he stigmatized as treachery to Spain, arrested the unfortunate envoy, who was then in Monte Video, and openly rebelled against the authority of Marshal Liniers, whom he denounced as a traitor.

Marshal Liniers took no steps whatever to crush this rebellion; the Spaniards of Buenos Aires hailed the event with joy, as a presage of what they would presently do themselves, and native Argentines were filled with well-grounded alarm. Don Martin Alzaga exulted at the success of his first step, and steadily prepared to follow it up.

Yet among the Spaniards there was one who felt alarm at this first success. Don Roderigo Ponce de Leon saw that the deposition of the Viceroy would be a much more difficult matter to achieve in Buenos Aires than it had been in Monte Video, and that any false step would bring on a collision with the people in which not only the power of the Viceroy but Spanish rule altogether, might be overturned.

And among native Argentines there was one who for precisely the same reason heard of the event with exultation. Don Carlos Evaña hailed with joy any event which might bring his fellow-countrymen into open collision with their rulers.

October passed over and nothing was done, so also November. Towards the end of November, one warm afternoon on which the sun shone down upon the city from a sky of intense blue, uncheckered by one white cloud, when the white-washed houses cast a glare upon the streets such that it was a torment to walk abroad, when steady-going citizens were just rousing themselves from their siesta in the coolest recesses of their houses, one man braved both the sun and the glare, left his house and walked slowly along the deserted streets till he reached the house of Don Fausto Velasquez. Entering by the open doorway, he crossed the first patio, passed through the zaguan into the second, and paused to clap his hands. A mulatta girl issued from one of the side rooms at his summons, smiled at him as she saw him, and came up to him, saying—

"At your service, Don Carlos. What may be your pleasure?"

"The Señora Doña Josefina; will it be possible for me to speak with her?" replied Don Carlos Evaña, for he it was who had thus come to disturb the siesta of Doña Josefina.

"Certainly it will, Don Carlos," replied the mulatta. "It is late already," she added, looking up at the sun. "If you will have the goodness to pass to the sala, in one moment she will be with you."

Don Carlos passed to the sala as he was requested, but the one moment had spun itself out to half an hour ere the folding doors opened, and Doña Josefina glided into the room. She was dressed in a flowing robe of some soft, white material, loosely girded below her ample bosom; the short, loose sleeves left nearly the whole of her plump white arms visible; the upper part of her dress was surmounted by a stiff sort of ruff about three inches deep, which rose from her shoulders almost to the level of her ears, and the dress itself was open in front to within three inches of the girdle. Her luxuriant black hair was simply plaited and wound round her head till it formed a sort of coronet, gold pendants hung from her ears, and in her hand she carried a large fan with which she fanned herself gently as she sailed down the large room to the obscure corner in which Don Carlos had esconced himself.

Don Carlos, reclining lazily in a low chair, was so absorbed in his own thoughts that her noiseless approach over the soft carpet was unperceived by him till she was close to him, when he started up from his seat and bowed lowly to her without speaking. Then as she stretched out her hand to him he raised it to his lips, an act of homage which the lady received with perfect complacency, after which, leading her to a sofa, he seated himself on a chair near to her, saying—

"With your permission, Señora."

"It is yours, Don Carlos," replied the lady, languidly leaning one

arm upon a cushion, and with her head slightly inclined to one side,
turning her lustrous black eyes full upon him; then as he returned
her glance she smiled and added—

"Do you know, Carlos, you are a perfect heretic. I was going to
deny myself, but when I heard it was you I knew it was no use, and
now your face is as solemn as if you were going to a funeral. I suppose you have something that you think very important to tell me."

"I have, Señora, or I should not have disturbed you at this hour."

"Well, I only hope it is not to recommend to me some other
protegé, for, frankly, he fatigues me, this Asneiros of yours. If you had
not come I was going to send for you before I went, to speak to you
about him."

"Before you went! then you are going? I only heard of it this
morning from Marcelino, and I have come at once to ask you not
to go."

"It is not quite settled yet, but I promised Constancia that I would
tell her certainly this evening. Constancia goes the day after to-
morrow and wants me to go with her. Justito has not been well
lately and the country air would do him good, but Fausto wants me
to put off my visit until the new year, why, I don't know."

"And I too want you to put off your visit."

"You! what interest can you have in keeping me in the city?" As
she spoke Doña Josefina leaned her head more to one side, and
waving her fan gently, cast a languishing glance above it, then suffered
the long lashes to fall over her eyes, veiling them.

"The interest is not mine, Señora, it is for the interest of the Patria
that I wish you to stop."

"Every one knows that to Don Carlos the interest of the Patria is
above every other consideration, so I suppose I must stop and suffer
another month or six weeks of this heat in the city. But what can
a poor thing like me do for the Patria, Carlos?"

"One thing that I cannot do, and I know that the Patria is as dear
to you as it is to me, else I had not troubled you, Señora."

"Yes, Carlos," replied Doña Josefina, straightening herself up,
dropping her hands into her lap, and in a moment throwing off her
usual languid manner; "yes, Carlos, the Patria is dear to me as you
say; though you care nothing for me, you appreciate me rightly.
You have confided to me your hopes and plans, in what I can do
you will find that I am as good a patriot as you are. And I know
that there is trouble before us; Fausto has told me that the Spaniards
will not be content until they have deposed the Viceroy here as they
have done in Monte Video. Deposed Liniers! do you hear me,
Carlos? These Spaniards are going to turn him out and send him to
Spain, perhaps in chains, because he is a Frenchman!"

"If that were all, Señora, it would be little," replied Evaña, "that
is nothing but the first step; the next will be to disarm the Patricios,
and then—— but it is not necessary to inquire what more."

"Disarm the Patricios! never!" replied Doña Josefina, closing
her fan with a click, as though she had quite made up her mind on
that point. "If such are their ideas we must keep our Viceroy at
any cost. We must prevent the first step, and all the rest is safe."

" Exactly so, Señora. I have spoken the same thing to many, but
you are the first to whom I have spoken who has seen as I do the
necessity of risking everything, of daring everything, rather than permit
the Spaniards to annul an appointment we originally made."

A pleased smile came onto the face of the lady as Evaña spoke,
then looking down at her hands as she twirled her fan between her
fingers, she said in a low voice—

" We are agreed then, Carlos ; tell me, what can I do ? "

" When the Cabildo publishes a decree deposing Liniers, which they
are sure to do before long, they will rely upon the Spanish regiments
to enforce it if necessary. If Liniers calls upon the native regiments
they will come forward to a man to support him, but they are fewer in
number than the Spaniards and not so well organized, the result of a
struggle would be doubtful."

" Not at all, Carlos ! You know not those young men how enthusiastic they are, and Liniers they will follow to the death."

" Liniers will never call upon the Patricios to support him unless he
feels certain of success ; he will yield without fighting. Now if we
can get one regiment of the Spanish troops to join us we shall then
have the superiority in numbers."

" And Gregorio's dragoons ? "

" Also I shall have them at hand when the day comes, and the
hussars of Don Martin Rodriguez, all the cavalry is ours. Have no
fear, Señora, with one of the Spanish regiments of infantry, our superiority in numbers and enthusiasm will secure us the victory. In the
Andaluz regiment nearly all the men are native Argentines, if one
officer pronounce in our favour the whole regiment will turn over
to us."

Here Evaña paused and looked steadily at Doña Josefina.

" Asneiros ! " ejaculated that lady, with a look of annoyance, then
leaning back again upon her cushions she commenced fanning herself.

" Yes, Señora, Asneiros. Among all the Spaniards there is no better
officer than Asneiros, and you can bring him over to us when the day
comes. I am sorry if he has given you any annoyance, but the kindness you have shown him for these months past will prove a great
service to the Patria."

" There is one can do much more with Asneiros than I can, Carlos,"
replied Doña Josefina, looking away from him with a fresh flourish of
her fan.

" Impossible, Señora," replied Evaña ; " any one to whom you show
favour is at once your slave."

" How the men are blind," replied the lady, turning her eyes again
upon Evaña. " Always that Dolores comes to see me then comes
Asneiros, and whilst she is here he has no eyes for any one else."

" Dolores ! " exclaimed Evaña, with a sudden start.

" Dolores ! yes, Dolores, Señor Don Carlos. Does it appear to you
strange that that barbarian of a Spaniard should think more of Dolores
than of me ? "

" But Dolores ! And she ? "

" What matters to you Dolores ? "

Then as Evaña leaned back in his chair with a frown on his face without answering, Doña Josefina bent forward and tapped him on the knee with her fan, saying—

"Ah! Carlos! you are a great politician, and very wise and very secret, but we ladies have our eyes and know how to use them. You are very astute, and think you can hide from us what you hope and wish for, but there are certain things that we know, and when the occasion comes, we discover them. But we, we are friends, Carlos; have no fear, there is one I know, for whose little finger Dolores cares more than for the whole body of that Asneiros."

Again leaning back upon her cushions, she turned her lustrous black eyes upon him, gently fanning herself the while.

"All the more necessary, then, for you to remain in town," said Evaña, after a pause. "Doña Constancia goes to the quinta the day after to-morrow, but she does not like Asneiros, she will not ask him to the quinta, but if you go he will visit you there, and he will be away when we want him, for we cannot tell when the day will come."

"Look you, Carlos," said Doña Josefina, interrupting him; "I had a plan for that Asneiros which would have suited us all very well. Every Wednesday I have two visitors, Dolores and Magdalen Miranda. They come to see each other, and are great friends. You have met them here on Wednesdays. Who you came to see you have never told me, but I am not one to whom it is necessary to tell things. I asked Asneiros to come that he might meet Magdalen, but when you are not there to make Dolores talk to you this gentleman can talk only to her, and for the Inglesita he has not one glance. Then when Marcelino can manage it, he comes always for at least one hour on Wednesdays, and has neither eyes nor words for any one but for Magdalen. These Wednesdays, which were to me a pleasure, are now the bane of my life, everything goes contrary, and I counted that by going out with Constancia I should put an end to them."

"You intended Magdalen for this Spaniard?"

"Precisely so, and she thinks nothing of him, and watches the door with all her eyes till Marcelino comes. That Marcelino should amuse himself with her is well enough, so long as it pass not amusement. Young men are not all like you, Carlos; they must have amusement, and with each new face they see they think they are in love. I wanted Elisa to come also on Wednesdays, and she came in the winter, but after Marcelino came back from Brazil she comes only in the evenings. That is all through Magdalen, the insignificant little creature; I begin to lose patience with her."

"Magdalen is a great deal too good for Asneiros," said Evaña.

"What an idea! Even he is good enough for that snub-nosed little thing. Think you what is her father? A miserable, without soul. And what has he? Just enough to live on. Not even presentable would Magdalen be but that we had befriended her."

"Possibly not, Señora; you have been very kind to her. But do not afflict yourself, let affairs arrange themselves. For Dolores there is not the slightest fear. She is kind to Asneiros, for he rings praises of Marcelino in her ear, and that is always music to Dolores; but more there is nothing."

"Ah! Carlos! with what confidence you speak," said Doña Josefina. with a toss of her head, and smiling.

"Let us leave that, Señora. What matters to us at present is that you keep, and increase if you can, your influence over Asneiros. How to do it you know much better than I can tell you."

"Do you want me to make love to him on my own account?" asked the lady, with a supplicating glance.

"Far be it from me to indicate the 'how.' One thing only I ask of you to promise me, which is that you do not leave the city at present."

"And when then will your lordship give me permission to go?"

"When we have tried our strength with the Spaniards, and have beaten them."

"Let it be so. I give you my promise."

"And the Patria will some day thank you, and know you as one of her most faithful children," replied Evaña, rising from his chair.

"Sit down, Carlos; do not go yet. Have you nothing more to say to me?"

"The object of my visit is accomplished."

"And already you go? Sit down again, Carlos. The Patria is your first love, and we are going to do what we can for her; but after her there is another love, come and talk to me of that."

"I have but one love, Señora," replied Evaña, standing before her, and twirling his hat round with his long, white fingers.

"Sit down, Carlos, and I will talk to you of Dolores," said Doña Josefina, with a full glance of her speaking eyes, before which his stern eyes sank abashed.

"Not now, Señora," replied Don Carlos, in a voice in which there was so clear an accent of pain that Doña Josefina. after looking at him for a moment in perplexity, insisted no longer upon his remaining, but rose herself from the sofa, and walked with him to the large folding-door which gave exit to the patio.

"Lose all fear. Carlos," said she to him, as he stepped out into the sunshine; "between the two of us we will arrange this barbarian of a Spaniard, and turn him into a patriot."

"That I fear we can never do," replied Evaña; "but if he serve us as we wish him the rest is no matter."

"If he serve us well we will give him the Inglesita as his reward," said Doña Josefina; then adding, with a laugh, "and a well-matched couple they will be."

To this Evaña made no answer, but with a low bow took his departure.

CHAPTER V.

HOW THE VICEROY TOOK COUNCIL WITH DON RODERIGO.

WEEKS passed till it was the third week in December. One evening in that week Don Carlos Evaña mounted his horse and galloped out to the Quinta de Ponce. The next morning at dawn he was again in the saddle, galloping over the level plains southwards to the estancia of Don Francisco Viana, where he purposed passing the noon-tide heat, and thereafter in the cool of the evening pursuing his way without halting till he should reach his own estancia.

While Don Carlos Evaña so rested at mid-day, Don Roderigo Ponce de Leon sat conversing with the Viceroy in his private room at the fort. Marshal Liniers had sent for him, telling him that there was matter of great moment on which he wished to consult him. Don Roderigo sat with an open letter in his hand, which he had just been reading; his face was very thoughtful, he seemed to be anxiously debating within himself how he should answer the Viceroy, who was speaking rapidly, and whose face showed evident marks of excitement and something of indignation.

"Do you know who he is, this Don Saturnino Rodriguez Peña?" asked the Viceroy.

"Perfectly. He is a brother of Don Nicolas," replied Don Roderigo. "He is the man who put that folly into the head of my son, of which I told you some months ago."

"But you have since told me that it remained there, and that nothing was done?"

"And so far as my son is concerned I know that nothing has been done."

"But she speaks most plainly of a conspiracy against me? I shall write to the Prince-regent and demand the arrest of this Don Saturnino."

"If there be any such conspiracy, the publication of this letter, written to you by the Princess herself, would at once put an end to it."

"The Princess Carlota warns me of a conspiracy, so there must be something."

"It may be; I too have heard rumours, but take little note of them. Your appointment as Viceroy can only be legally annulled by the Junta of Seville, and, failing that, your great popularity secures your authority."

"My popularity while it exists; but if the people themselves pronounce against me? Think you that I will uphold my authority by force against the will of the people?"

"Your popularity would vanish at once were you to do so."

"If because I was born in France the people trust me no longer, let them say so."

"Then if the people speak clearly their distrust of you, you will resign?"

To this Liniers did not answer, passing his hand across his forehead, leaning back in his chair with an air of great discontent, and Don Roderigo continued—

"Permit me to tell you, Don Santiago, that if you yield at once to a popular cry you sap the basis of all authority. If the people, applying through the corporations of the city, should request you to resign, I think you may take the matter into serious consideration, but not sooner."

"There is some secret conspiracy going forward; am I to take no steps to prevent it ripening into a rebellion?"

"Wait till we have more certain information, the Cabildo will advise you at once if there be danger of any attempt against your authority."

"How can I tell that the Cabildo itself is not in the conspiracy?" replied the Viceroy, looking sternly at Don Roderigo; "all are Spaniards. Elio and those who support him in Monte Video are all Spaniards. I distrust the Cabildo more than I do the people."

"You may have your reasons of which I know nothing," said Don Roderigo; "but the Cabildo would never venture upon any steps against you unless they were perfectly secure of the general acquiescence of the city."

"Then you acknowledge that you Spaniards would depose me if you were able to do so?"

"In the present state of affairs in the mother-country it is natural that a Frenchman be looked upon with jealousy, not only by Spaniards but by the Creoles also. The people murmured greatly at the friendly reception you gave to the envoy sent by Napoleon last August."

"But the people at any rate were satisfied when I ordered the proclamation of Ferdinand VII.?"

"It was on that very day that some of them discussed together the propriety of setting him aside in favour of his sister the Princess Carlota."

"True. I did badly in passing over that affair without notice. In that affair the first to move was your son, and because he was your son I consented to pass it over. See now your gratitude; without doubt, if there be a conspiracy he and his friend Don Carlos Evaña are the prime movers in it, and depend upon your concurrence and that of all the Spaniards."

"If there be any conspiracy I feel quite sure that neither my son nor Don Carlos Evaña have any part in it."

"I have heard Don Carlos speak freely his ideas years ago, and I have not forgotten it; I tell you that this Evaña is by nature a conspirator, and where he goes there goes Don Marcelino also."

"In this you are mistaken, I can assure you," replied Don Roderigo warmly. " Don Carlos left the city yesterday for his estancia, saying that it was uncertain when he would return, and Marcelino thinks of nothing but of his duties at the Consulado."

" But he has his ideas, which require checking. If it were not that he is your son I should arrest him and search his papers to discover what correspondence he has carried on with this Don Saturnino Rodriguez Peña, who has certainly, as you will have seen by that letter, some regular correspondents in this city."

Don Roderigo rose from his chair and walked several times thoughtfully up and down the room, then re-seating himself, he said—

" Do not let any regard for me keep you from any step which may be necessary for the vindication of your authority. I have months since spoken to my son, and I know that he has done nothing in this matter of the Princess Carlota since he first mooted it. Still his arrest may serve him as a warning not to meddle in affairs beyond his proper sphere."

" Thanks, Don Roderigo," replied the Viceroy with effusion. " This is a great sacrifice you make to me. I shall order his arrest at once, but to show you that I am actuated by no unfriendly feeling towards yourself I will entrust the examination of his papers to you together with my private secretary."

" That I must beg to decline. I can leave the examination of his papers with entire confidence to any one whom you may appoint." So saying Don Roderigo took up his hat from a chair near him and rose to go, then adding, " In anything that I can serve you always count upon me, Don Santiago," he went his way.

As Don Roderigo sat alone in his own room that evening, the door opened, and in walked Don Martin Alzaga.

" Now what do you say about our Viceroy, this Liniers?" said he.

" What has he done now?" asked Don Roderigo.

" Do not you know? He has arrested Don Marcelino and seized his papers."

" I knew it," said Don Roderigo quite calmly.

" You know it, and you sit there as if it were a matter of no importance! The news has spread through the city and has caused general indignation."

" So much the better, that was just what I wanted."

" The better! Then you are agreeable that this Frenchman shall do what he likes in our city, and put any one in prison as he chooses without consulting us?"

" He consulted me about it this morning, and I see that he has done perfectly well *for us*. To Marcelino a few days' imprisonment will do no harm. Marcelino is young, and has his ideas ; in case of any important event happening within the next few days he might be tempted to some course which would prejudice his future."

" I begin to understand you," said Don Martin thoughtfully. " Marcelino is very partial to the Viceroy, and some event may occur within a few days with which it is well for him that he should have nothing to do. You have asked the Viceroy to arrest him, what was your pretext?"

" You mistake ; the idea came from the Viceroy himself. He has some erroneous ideas in his head, and has acted upon them. If we make good use of this event it may produce some popular demonstration. Liniers values more than anything else his popularity, if we can persuade the people to cry out against him he will resign, and there will be no necessity for any Pronunciamiento."

" I see you always wish to go your own way about it. You want to turn the militia against him. Well, do what you can, but in this I cannot help you ; more dangerous than Liniers to us, is the pride of these Patricios."

" All that we have to do is to persuade the militia to keep quiet. Until the new Viceroy arrive I warn you, Don Martin, that any attempt at coercion will bring on a struggle with them which we must avoid at any cost."

" You always fear those Patricios," said Don Martin impatiently. " I came to speak to you about your son, but as you do not object to his imprisonment I see that it is a false step of this Liniers of which it is for us to take due advantage."

Later on that same evening, at the house of Don Fausto Velasquez, Don Roderigo complained bitterly of the insult he had received in the unwarrantable imprisonment of his eldest son.

Don Carlos Evaña did not make a long stay at his estancia this time, on the fifth evening from the day he left the city he was again at the Quinta de Ponce. Short as had been his absence, he had managed to spend one day at Las Barrancas with Colonel Lopez, and the very day that he left him, the Colonel sent out messengers right and left summoning his men to meet at the Barrancas on the 25th December for a fortnight's drill.

On the eventide of this day on which Don Carlos again visited the Quinta de Ponce, Dolores was seated under the front veranda of the house, holding on her knee a stout little boy, her cousin Justiniano Velasquez, who had been entrusted to her care by his mother until such time as she should leave the city and resume care of him herself. Dolores was very fond of her cousin, and was pleased to have the care of him. Her affection was fully reciprocated by the little fellow, who teased her and coaxed her to let him have his own wilful way in everything, was an all day long trouble to her, and rewarded her by an unlimited amount of caresses, and by screaming with all his might if he lost sight of her for an instant when he was awake. She called him the plague of her life, and was never so happy as when she was ministering to his manifold wants.

On this evening Dolores was somewhat pale and less cheerful than was her wont, yet as Don Carlos stepped into the veranda to salute her he thought he had never before seen her looking so beautiful. There was a pensive thoughtfulness on her face not often seen there, which added an indescribable charm to the smile of welcome she bestowed upon him.

" How soon you are back," she said ; " as you said your stay at your estancia was uncertain we did not expect you for a month."

"What has happened to you? You look triste, does that little rogue plague you?"

"Ah! Don Carlos, you do not know," replied Dolores, bending over the boy, and with difficulty keeping back her tears; "Marcelino is in prison, three days ago he was arrested by an order from the Viceroy and is in prison."

"Marcelino in prison!" exclaimed Evaña. "On what charge? what has he done?"

"Nothing. We know nothing of why he is in prison. Papa was here yesterday, you may imagine how angry he was, and he says all the city is indignant about it. But why he is put in prison no one knows. They went to our house and searched his room, and took away all his papers. Poor mamma, she wanted to go back to the city to see him, but papa would not let us go, and there he is with no one to speak to him, and he will think we care nothing about it."

"No, that he will not think, he knows you better."

"What a pity that you were away. Papa says that if you had been there you would have stirred up some demonstrations, and the Viceroy would have been forced to set him at liberty."

"Where is he imprisoned?"

"At the Cabildo. He is not in a dungeon; papa says he is only under arrest, but no one is allowed to speak to him. One has been very active and offered to papa to break into the Cabildo and rescue him by force—Captain Asneiros; his Andaluces would follow him anywhere, and there are some of Marcelino's Morenos in one battalion of the Patricios, who, he says, would dare anything for their old chief. But papa would not let him; he says that the indignation of the whole city will force Marshal Liniers to set him free. Ah! if you were only there, Don Carlos, you would do more than Captain Asneiros, and even than papa, for Don Cornelio Saavedra and the Patricios would all listen to you, and without them the Viceroy is nothing, papa told me so."

"Asneiros!" said Evaña to himself, rising from his seat and walking up and down the veranda, "Asneiros! I begin to understand. This is a trap, and if we are careless we will run our necks into the noose."

Then again he paused in front of Dolores and asked her—

"But nothing has been done, he remains in prison, and no one has spoken to him, not even Don Roderigo?"

"No one. Not even papa is allowed to speak to him, and nothing has been done, but to-morrow you will be there, and something will be done," said Dolores, looking up at Evaña with a flush on her cheek, and a trustful look in her gray eyes.

"Not to-morrow, but to-night I will go in, but I do not tell you that I will do anything to set Marcelino at liberty. Believe me, it may be best for him to remain where he is just at present, but not for long, not for long. This affair will not have the end which they think it will."

"Don Carlos!" exclaimed Dolores; "best for him to remain in prison! What has he done, Don Carlos? You know something."

"He has done nothing to deserve imprisonment, yet for other

reasons it may be best for him to remain where he is for a few days. He is innocent and therefore he is in no danger."

"Innocent! of course he is, and yet you would let them treat him as a criminal, and will do nothing to help him. Are you not my friend, Don Carlos? Are you not his brother?"

"I am your friend, he is my brother. Trust me, he shall not remain in prison longer than is necessary."

Up to this time little Justiniano had sat quietly on Dolores' knee listening to their talk, but at the word friend he started up, saying—

"You are Lola's friend? I have no brother, but I have a friend too. Tell me, Lola, again, where is my friend? Talk to me about my friend the Englishman."

A deep flush spread over Dolores' face as she clasped the boy in her arms kissing him.

"He is away over the sea, Justito, fighting the French for England and for Spain," she said.

"He is a soldier," said Justito. "When I am big I will be a soldier, and will go and fight the French for him, so that he may come back. He said he would come back, didn't he, Lola?"

"Yes, dear; and some day he will come," said Dolores, again kissing the boy and bending over him so as to hide her face from Evaña.

"Then you must not be triste, Lola; it makes me feel bad to see you triste, Lola; yesterday you were crying, and it made Justito sad to see you," said the boy, patting her cheeks with his two little hands. "Some day when I am big, then I will go and bring back my friend from away over the sea. Is it far to go, Lola?"

"Yes, dear, hundreds and hundreds of leagues, and all water, with the waves going up and down and tossing the ships about."

"Why did he go so far, Lola?"

"He had to go where the King of England sent him, for he is a soldier."

"Poor Lola," said the boy, again patting her cheeks, "again you are crying, Lola; who makes you triste, Lola?"

"A wicked man who has put Marcelino in prison. You love Marcelino, don't you, Justito?"

"Yes, oh so much! When is he coming again, Lola? Days that he has not been here."

But Dolores could prattle to the boy no more, her sobs choked her speech, and he threw his arms round her neck, kissing her and looking angrily back at Don Carlos, as if he thought he was the cause of all her sorrow.

"Come to me, Justito, and I will tell you about Marcelino, and about your friend," said Don Carlos, bending with one knee to the pavement and holding out his arms to the boy.

"No, no, go away," said Justito. "Are you the wicked man who has made Lola cry?"

"No, no, Justito, Don Carlos is not wicked; he is going to take Marcelino out of the prison, and then Lola won't cry any more," said Dolores.

Then Justito jumped from Dolores' arms and ran to Don Carlos Evaña.

"You will go, won't you, and bring Marcelino back with you, it makes Justito bad to see Lola cry?" said he.

"I will go, and will not come here again till I bring Marcelino with me," said Don Carlos, raising the boy up in his arms and kissing him.

Dolores rose from her seat with a smile on her face as Evaña spoke.

"Always my friend and his brother," said she, then taking the boy from him she led him away with her into the house.

Don Carlos Evaña only remained long enough at the quinta to speak a few words to Doña Constancia, and to learn from her all she knew concerning the imprisonment of his friend Marcelino. Then, declining her urgent invitation to pass the night at the quinta, he remounted his horse and galloped away through the darkness for the city.

CHAPTER VI.

THE EVE OF A GREAT EVENT.

It was nine o'clock when Don Carlos Evaña reached the city. Without stopping either to change his dress or to take food, he had no sooner dismounted than he went straight to the house of Don Gregorio Lopez. In the first patio he met Valentin.

"Don Carlos! Back already, I am so glad," said Valentin. "You know what has happened?"

"Marcelino has been imprisoned, that I know. Is there anything else?"

"That is enough, I think," replied Valentin. "He has been three days in prison, and nothing has been done. It is scandalous, but we will soon do something. There are some men here this evening in consultation with my father, pass forward, you will find them in the dining-room."

"Then nothing has been done?"

"Nothing."

"I am glad of it. There is more in this than you know of, my young friend, be content yet for a few days to do nothing."

So saying, Evaña passed on to the dining-room, where he found Don Gregorio Lopez in consultation with Don Fausto Velasquez, Don Cornelio Saavedra, Don Manuel Belgrano, and four others. Evaña joined them, and for an hour they remained talking earnestly together, then, as some of them rose to go, Don Manuel Belgrano said—

"Yet after all I do not like the idea of leaving my young friend in prison, when, if that be the crime charged against him, I am the real culprit."

"For many reasons I agree with Don Carlos," said Don Gregorio, "that it is the wisest course."

"Above all things it is necessary that they take the initiative," said Don Cornelio Saavedra. "The Señor Don Santiago Liniers is a man of no decision, and in order that he put full confidence in us we must show our acquiescence in any measure that he may think fit to adopt."

"We all know well what Liniers is," said Don Gregorio. "If we arouse in any way his suspicions, Don Martin and the bishop, between them, will persuade him to resign."

"If he resign we shall have in his place a Junta of Spaniards, and we all know what that means," said Evaña.

"I for my part assure you that we will have no Junta," said Don Cornelio. "Do you know, Señor Evaña, that if you had not fortunately returned so soon from your estancia I think we should have made some false step. Don Roderigo has infected us all with his own indignation; we must not forget that Don Roderigo is a Spaniard, and in these days it is not well to take everything that a Spaniard says, quite for what the words mean."

"Then let it be so," said Belgrano. "If Don Roderigo does not release him without our help he must yet remain some days in prison. Afterwards we will explain everything to him."

"I am sorry for him," said Don Fausto. "To pass these hot summer days shut up in a small room would kill me very soon, but when Don Gregorio and Don Carlos Evaña both say it is for the best, I say no more."

"One word more, Don Cornelio," said Evaña. "Have you not yet any idea when the Pronunciamiento is likely to take place?"

"It may take place any day," replied Don Cornelio. "But if nothing occurs to hurry it on, I expect we shall see something on the occasion of the municipal elections on the 1st January."

"The 1st January leaves not many days to wait now, and we are ready. In future years we shall look back upon that day as a great epoch in the history of the Argentine people. Upon you, Don Cornelio, depends the present welfare and the future greatness of a young nation; to you our country entrusts her destinies in the most critical moment of her existence." So saying, and looking fixedly upon Don Cornelio Saavedra, Evaña bowed to him with great solemnity and retired.

"The ideas of the Señor Evaña," said Don Fausto Velasquez, laughing. "When shall we see the end of them?"

"In this the Señor Evaña is not mistaken," said Don Gregorio Lopez. "May God help you, Don Cornelio, and remember that where you go you have an entire people behind you, who have placed their destinies in your hands."

Three days after this, as Captain Asneiros returned to his quarters after an early drill and inspection, he found a young slave waiting for him with a message from Doña Josefina Viana, who requested him to call upon her that evening without fail. The swarthy face of the Spaniard brightened with pleasure as he listened to the words of the little negro, but—

"It is well, you can go," was all his answer.

In the evening twilight Doña Josefina, dressed in a graceful negligée fashion well suited to the season, sat in a low chair beside one of the windows of her sala, which was thrown wide open, gazing out into the street. Young men as they passed doffed their hats, bowing lowly, and many of them paused, hoping that the graceful head which answered their salute with a gentle inclination might bend yet further forward and speak, and so give them an excuse for loitering there leaning against the iron bars, and talking for a few minutes. If any such favour had been granted to any of them they would have strutted off after exchanging a few conventional phrases, with the feeling that a great honour had been bestowed upon them, of which they might speak with great access of personal dignity in whatever social circle they might spend the rest of the evening. Men of mature years who passed that window were even more eager and obsequious than the young men in their manner of salutation, but after one glance at the figure reclining there behind the iron reja, enveloped in clouds of gauzy muslin, half shaded from view by the light curtains which draped the window, they passed on without any pause, perchance muttering to themselves—

"She awaits some one, our queen of the saloons, who may that fortunate be?"

To the salutations of both young and old Doña Josefina had but one stereotyped answer, a slight lowering of her fan, and a still slighter inclination of the head, with half-closed eyes. Thus she sat for about half an hour, when a man of medium stature, slightly built, but with square shoulders and very erect bearing, paused before the window. He was dressed in a coat of dark crimson velvet, embroidered with gold lace; his waistcoat, also richly embroidered, came well down over his thighs; his small-clothes were of black satin, and he wore black silk stockings and jewelled buckles in his shoes. The frill of his shirt-front and the ruffles at his wrists were of the finest lace. His hair was gathered together behind, tied with a ribbon, and powdered. In one hand he carried a thick golden-headed cane, and in the other his three-cornered hat, which he had removed as he performed an elaborate salute before the window. By his dress he was a dandy of the first water, but of rather an antiquated fashion, but his face and carriage were those of a stern soldier.

The large black eyes of Doña Josefina dilated with surprise and with something of amusement, as she looked at this finely-dressed gentleman who had paused before her window; for a moment she held her fan before her face to conceal the smile which played upon her lips, then bending forward she returned his salutation with great affability and said—

"Come in, Don Ciriaco, the hours that I have been watching for you."

"Then with your permission, Señora," replied Asneiros with another bow as he moved away towards the door of the house.

Springing lightly to her feet, Doña Josefina drew forward an easy-chair and placed it at the other side of the window opposite to her, in such a position that such daylight as yet remained should fall full upon the face of any one seated in it, and that he should be plainly visible to any one passing in the street, then she pushed her own chair further back so that her face should be quite shaded by the window-curtain, and a portion of her dress only should be visible to any one who might glance in at the window. Hardly had she reseated herself ere Asneiros entered the sala. Somewhat awkwardly he took her hand in his as she held it out to him in welcome; for a moment she feared he was going to raise it to his lips, however, he refrained, and seated himself in the easy-chair she had placed ready for him.

"How is this, Señor Capitan?" said the lady. "In moments so critical as the present can the Viceroy spare even for one day the services of one of his most trusted officers?"

"You advert to my gallop out to the Quinta de Ponce yesterday, Señora?" replied Asneiros. "Have then my movements so much interest for you?"

"You saw then my little Justiniano?" replied Doña Josefina, performing meantime some elaborate movements with her fan.

"Yes, Señora, I saw him, and he sends to you many expressions of his love. Better he could not be."

"Cruel! And you could remain a whole night in the city and yet not come to tell me of him!"

"It was late, Señora, when I returned, but even without your message I should have been bold enough to have presented myself to you this evening."

"And my good Constancia and Dolores?"

"Well, Señora, but sad, as you may believe, whilst the son and the brother suffers unmerited imprisonment."

"You went to speak to them of him, and to tell them what you are doing for him?"

"To speak to them of him, yes, Señora, without that I would never have had the temerity to present myself there. But yesterday Doña Constancia was all that the amiable can be, and the beautiful Señorita was if possible more of an angel than ever. Señora, yesterday I felt myself in Paradise, for the first time in my life I found myself admitted to the confidence of two angelic creatures, who wept as they spoke to me of their sorrow, and who looked to me with confidence and with smiles when I assured them that my own life should pay the forfeit for his liberty, if it were not otherwise to be achieved."

"And are they the only women who have ever treated you with confidence?"

"Ah! forgive me, Señora, but when I think of them and their sorrow I can think of nothing else. And it was sorrow to me that I could not tell them that I had done anything for him, I could only tell them what I wished to do."

"What did you wish to do?"

"Señora, you are cruel to me! Did not I offer to break into the prison at night with my own men and set him free, at any risk to myself?"

"You did, and I told you to do nothing till I had enquired further into the matter. You have done well to listen to me, for there is more in this imprisonment of Marcelino than I well understand even yet. Any ill-considered violence might have resulted in great disaster to us all, which Marcelino himself would have been the first to deplore. Now I have sent for you to know if you are yet ready to risk everything for your old chief?"

"Señora, you give me back my life, for I can obey you no longer if you tell me yet to do nothing. When I saw that angelical creature in tears for the sake of her brother, I could restrain myself no longer. I laid my hand on my heart, and swore to her that I would never see her more till her brother was free. Señora, I have listened to you and to Don Roderigo, and as yet have done nothing, but now I must do something. I have begun to-day. I have spoken to several of my men, all of whom will follow me. This night, if you wish it, I will seize the Cabildo, but I had planned to leave it for one day longer, as I have not yet spoken to any of my brother officers, and if they do not join me I must secure them."

As Asneiros spoke of Dolores, Doña Josefina leaned back in her chair, pressing her fan to her forehead, and so completely hiding her face. When he paused she still kept her face concealed, and did not answer. There was silence between them for a minute, then Asneiros resumed—

"You do not like to speak, Señora; there is no necessity that you should. It is not needful that you should know anything further of my plan. If possible I shall achieve the rescue without bloodshed. There is great excitement among the troops. I do not know if you are aware of it, but if I shout 'Down with the Viceroy' there is no Spaniard will raise his musket against me.'

Then Doña Josefina renewed her manœuvres with her fan, opening it and fanning herself gently, then shutting it again with a click. A girl entered the ante-sala with a lighted lamp, which she placed upon a small table in a corner, and then retired. Doña Josefina looked round at her as she moved about. Then, as she closed the door behind her, she again leaned back in her chair, gave two or three flourishes with her fan, and with a low sigh said—

"You think very much of my little niece, Señor Capitan?"

"How is it possible for any one to know a creature so amiable and not think much of her?" replied Asneiros.

"Then because she, an ignorant little girl, asks you to do something for her you will do it, even though I request you not?"

"Señora, what is this that you say to me? She has not asked me to do anything, but she weeps for her brother who is in prison, and I have sworn that I will rescue him. You have asked me if I am ready, do you yet want me to delay?"

"I want you to be ready, but to do nothing till I give you the signal. Now listen. You say they have placed confidence in you by telling you of their sorrows, I am going to put more confidence yet in you, for I am going to tell you my reasons, of which they know nothing. You think that it is the Viceroy who has put Marcelino into prison, and you are ready to shout 'Down with the Viceroy!'"

"And so is every Spaniard."

"And yet you know that the Viceroy and Marcelino have always been the best of friends. There is a conspiracy on foot. There are men here who dream of a republic. They have tried to implicate Marcelino, and make him one of their leaders. He is rash and hotheaded, as you know. The Viceroy has put him in prison until the danger has passed over, then he will let him go, and the real culprits will take his place. In this Marshal Liniers has shown himself a true friend to Marcelino."

"I know that there is some conspiracy, but I understood that we were to put down this Frenchman and name a Junta, as has been done in Monte Video."

"That they say to deceive you. While the troops remain faithful to the Viceroy these rebels can do nothing. The first step is to excite the troops to mutiny against the Viceroy. If they are successful all is lost, and we shall have a government of the Lord knows who." *

"And Don Marcelino knows of this?"

"He does. Don Roderigo pretends to be angry at his arrest, but he is well content that he should be out of this conspiracy. Who has more influence with Marshal Liniers than Don Roderigo? One word from him and Liniers would set Marcelino at liberty, for as yet he has taken no part in the conspiracy, and is quite innocent. The Viceroy expected to find some clue to the conspiracy among his papers, but I believe nothing has been found, and he would be set free to-morrow if Don Roderigo wished it. Now what I want you to do is to take care that these revolutionists do not tamper with your men, and when the Viceroy calls upon you, join him at once with all your battalion, then you can demand the liberty of my nephew, and all of us will thank you for the great service you have done."

"But, Señora, it may be days yet before they attempt this rebellion. What will the Señorita Dolores say if all these days I do nothing?"

"Dolores herself shall thank you; I will tell her what you have done for her sake."

"Why does not the Viceroy arrest the conspirators if he knows of the conspiracy?"

"As yet he knows but little. He wants to make sure of the leaders before he arrests any of them."

"I could put my hand upon one of them to-day," said Asneiros fiercely; "and here he comes," he added, in a low tone, as Don Carlos Evaña entered the sala.

Behind Evaña came Don Fausto Velasquez, who saluted the infantry captain with great cordiality, but Evaña, merely bestowing upon him a nod of recognition, seated himself beside Doña Josefina. Soon after, others dropped in. Among them came Don Juan Martin Puyrredon and his sister Doña Juana, the Señora de Sañez-Valiente, a tall, stately lady of very affable manners, who was an intimate friend of Doña Josefina. With her also came a younger sister, shorter in stature than Doña Juana, with large, dark eyes, luxuriant hair, brilliant complexion, and a face and figure said at that time to be unrivalled for beauty even in Buenos Aires, Elisa Puyrredon.

Among these, Asneiros would have felt himself strangely out of place, but Doña Josefina watched over him, and exerted herself so successfully to set him at ease, encouraging him to talk, that when, after a couple of hours, he rose to go, he felt as though he had never passed so pleasant an evening in his life, and was resolved that come what might he would let himself be guided by Doña Josefina, though he was too astute to believe all that she had told him concerning the conspiracy against the Viceroy.

Doña Josefina accompanied him to the patio as he went out, and said to him—

"Pass by my window every evening at sundown, I will call you in if I have anything to say to you. When you have anything to tell me come at any hour."

"What it is to give oneself to politics," said Elisa Puyrredon, as Doña Josefina returned to the sala. "Have you many paroquets like that to show us, Doña Josefina?"

"Picara!" said Doña Josefina; "this Asneiros was the Lieutenant of the 'Morenos de Ponce.'"

"I did not know that," said Elisa. "And this poor Marcelino, when will they let him go?"

"That is just what this Asneiros came to ask me," replied Doña Josefina.

"Asneiros makes no secret of his wish to break open the prison-door himself at the head of a party of grenadiers," said Don Juan Martin.

"Why does he not do it then?" asked Elisa.

"He would do badly to do so," said Don Fausto.

Every day for more than week Asneiros strolled at sundown past the window of Doña Josefina Viana, every day he found her sitting there watching for him. Sometimes she would rise from her seat and, leaning against the reja, would stand there for some minutes talking with him; sometimes she would invite him in, when if alone together she would listen in patience to his praises of Dolores and encourage him to think that he alone should have the credit of the release of Marcelino from prison; while every evening he had something to tell her of the progress he had made in re-establishing the waning popularity of Marshal Liniers, not only in his own regiment but also in the artillery corps which was supposed to be completely under the influence of Don Martin Alzaga.

So the days passed over till the morning of the 31st December, when he called at the house, and being admitted at once, was shown into the sewing-room of Doña Josefina, where she never received any but her most confidential friends. Nearly an hour he remained there talking with her, being on this occasion dressed in uniform, and speaking in a sharp, decisive manner which Doña Josefina had never before observed in him.

"Señora," said he, as he withdrew, "I know not whether you have been deceived, but I will delay no longer, and if Don Marcelino is not out of prison by this hour to-morrow I myself will head a mutiny against the Viceroy, in which case I can assure you that the whole of the garrison of the city will join me."

When he had gone Doña Josefina sat for some minutes very thoughtful, apparently far from pleased with the result of the interview, till with a start she exclaimed—

"To-morrow! that is the new year. It is done, he will be too late; now Carlos will acknowledge that I also have done something for the Patria."

Half an hour later Don Carlos Evaña was with her, summoned to a consultation by an urgent message.

Meantime, while Marcelino's friends were thus interesting themselves in his fate, there was one who was dearer to him than any other, who spoke of him not at all, but who thought of him every hour in the day, and wept for him and prayed for him in the solitude of her own room at night. A young girl who lived in great quiet with her father at his quinta at the Miserere. To her parent she had spoken of him, but he had chid her roughly, telling her that doubtless he deserved his punishment, and that she was not to speak of him any more. On one Wednesday only during this time had she paid her usual visit to Doña Josefina, who had laughed at her when she had timidly asked news of Marcelino, saying—

" What matters it to you?"

But as she sat sewing in Doña Josefina's own room there came in another lady, young and of radiant beauty, who spoke much of Marcelino, and to her Doña Josefina talked unreservedly, and spoke confidently of his speedy release. When she had gone—

" What think you of my friend Elisa?" said Doña Josefina; " Lola is very fond of her, but you and she seem hardly ever to speak to each other."

" She is very beautiful," replied Magdalen.

" Marcelino says she is the most beautiful girl in Buenos Aires," said the elder lady; "and he also so handsome. They are well matched, I do not know why they delay so long; Marcelino wants to amuse himself a little longer I suppose, young men are like that, and Elisa is not impatient, but if I were she, I should be jealous."

After this there was yet one Wednesday in December, but Magdalen told her father that she had a headache and would not visit the city that day.

During the last days of December there was much excitement throughout the city. Spaniards openly exulted in the speedy downfall of the Viceroy, under whose rule their monopoly of power was slowly but steadily slipping away from them. Quiet citizens, who troubled not their heads about politics, were tormented by vague apprehensions for which they could give no reason. Argentines of all ranks and ages, who had learned during the past two years to look upon their country as their own, fiercely determined that come what might, the leader they had chosen for themselves should not be thrust from his position if he would but call upon them for support.

Two men only fully appreciated the danger of the crisis, Don Roderigo Ponce de Leon and Don Carlos Evaña; each of these in his own way prepared to meet it.

On the morning of the 27th December, Don Carlos Evaña called his servant into his private room, and after a short conversation with him took up a sealed letter from his writing-table, which he gave to him. This letter was addressed—

Al Señor Coronel
Don Gregorio Lopez,
Comandante de los Dragones de Las Barrancas,
Su Estancia.

"Now away you go," said Don Carlos, "and neither rest nor sleep till you have delivered that letter."

"Before sunrise to-morrow he shall have it, Señor Don Carlos," replied the man.

On the morning of the 31st December, Colonel Lopez arrived at the Quinta de Ponce; he was dressed in uniform, and had two orderlies with him. He listened to all that Doña Constancia and Dolores had to tell him, but was very taciturn himself, and they were somewhat hurt at the small sympathy he expressed for his nephew in his imprisonment.

At sundown Evaristo reached the quinta, saying that Don Roderigo was not coming out that day, and that he himself was to remain there till Monday.

"We shall have plenty of room for you to-night, Gregorio," said Doña Constancia. "We have generally a house full on a Saturday evening. but it appears we are to have no visitors this week. Even Don Carlos has not been out to see us since he came in from his estancia."

"I shall not stop the night here," replied Don Gregorio; "I am going on after dark."

At ten o'clock Don Gregorio was still there, though he had ordered his horse to be saddled. They were seated under the veranda, looking out into the quiet night, talking little, for each one had his or her own thoughts, and none of these thoughts were cheerful. Evaristo was the most talkative, and his talk was of his brother or of the Viceroy, Marshal Liniers, and of whichever he spoke his words were words of anger. Suddenly he started to his feet.

"Hush!" he said. "Listen! who are these that come at this hour of the night?"

They stepped out into the garden, and from the south, through the thick foliage of the trees, and near at hand, there came the sound of the trampling of hoofs as of a multitude of horses at a quiet trot. Mingled with this sound came the jingling of sabres in steel scabbards, and the hum of many voices.

"Who are those, Gregorio?" said Doña Constancia, as a gruff voice shouted "halt," and the trampling and the jingling ceased. "They have stopped at the tranquera."

"They are my dragoons," replied the Colonel. "Sleep tranquil, Marcelino will not be many hours longer in prison."

"My God!" exclaimed Doña Constancia, clasping her hands; "what is it that you are going to do?"

"Who sent for you?" asked Dolores.

"Evaña," replied the Colonel; then kissing both of them he looked round to bid good-night to his nephew, but Evaristo was not to be seen.

Five minutes later Don Gregorio Lopez, at the head of a well-appointed squadron of dragoons, trotted down the road past the quinta gate, where Doña Constancia and Dolores stood watching them in silence. Beside him rode one who was not in uniform and carried no arms; this horseman, who was but a youth, turned in his saddle as they passed the gate and shouted—

"Good-night, mamita! good-night, Lola! to-morrow I will come back with Marcelino."

CHAPTER VII.

THE 1ST JANUARY, 1809.

IT seems to be a very old custom in Spanish-speaking countries to hold elections on the first day of the week, the day set apart by all Christian people as a day of rest. In these countries the right of all free-born men to choose their own rulers is not considered to be work, it is looked upon more as an amusement; the consequences of so looking upon one of the most important duties of a citizen are frequently disastrous.

This day, Sunday, the 1st January, 1809, was the day appointed for the election of the municipal officers of the city. The citizens of Buenos Aires on this occasion made no claim whatever to be admitted to some share in the election, being content that these officials should be selected, as they always had been, by the Cabildo, their attention being entirely engrossed by a subject to them much more momentous.

At sunrise on this Sunday morning the whole city was astir. Steady-going householders donned their uniforms and marched off to the barracks of the several militia corps, the Patricios and Arribeños. Shopmen, artificers, and peons left their homes all with one destination. Ardent young patriots of the more wealthy families buckled on their swords and proceeded to the head-quarters of their regiments. All were animated by one enthusiastic determination—to suppress by force, if necessary, any attempt against the authority of the Viceroy they themselves had chosen. All looked to Don Cornelio Saavedra as their leader.

At the same time, to the west of the city, on the wide, open space known as the Plaza Miserere, the suburban cavalry, composed of the butchers and quinteros who supplied the city markets, assembled under the orders of Don Martin Rodriguez, who had with him Don Juan Ramon Balcarce as his second in command. Most of these men had taken part in the defence of the city against Whitelock, the name of General Liniers was to them as a tower of strength.

The dragoons from Las Barrancas had passed the night encamped near to the Puente Galvès, at dawn Don Carlos Evaña was with them. Calling the officers together he spoke earnestly to them, commending the appearance of the men and the condition of their horses, telling them that they had not been sent for without deep necessity, that their country had need of them, and looked to them to vindicate her rights against the domination of foreigners.

"Have no fear, Don Carlos," said Don Gregorio. "My men will do their duty."

"What you or Don Cornelio Saavedra tell us, that we will do," said the others.

Among these dragoons there was one troop which excelled in efficiency and appearance, the horses all of one colour, dark bays, the men most of them of one family, brothers, cousins, or nephews of the wife of Don Francisco Viana. This troop was under the command of Venceslao Viana, all the horses were the property of Don Carlos Evaña. After speaking to the officers, Don Carlos addressed himself to the men of this troop, speaking to them one by one, and asking after their families, then he drew Venceslao Viana to one side and spoke to him alone. As Venceslao listened, his face showed signs of great perplexity.

"Without orders from the Colonel?" asked he.

"More than a year ago you promised me——"

"Say no more," said Venceslao; "I ask for no reasons. Give me the signal, and I see no other chief than you."

"If all goes well I shall not give it, then you have nothing to do but to obey the Colonel. But remember, if to-day pass without bloodshed everything is to begin again."

"Decidedly this Don Carlos is a man of few scruples," said Venceslao to himself as Evaña galloped away for the city. "But if he says it, it must be done; by the faith of a Viana, to-day we will do for him some service."

Soon after sunrise the trumpets sounded to saddle and mount, and defiling over the Puente Galvès, the regiment marched by the wide, sandy road to the city, passed the suburbs, and halted on an open space of ground near to the Residencia.

The Spanish troops were also early under arms, each corps in its own barracks, among them also there was much enthusiasm. In every quarter of the city armed men were collected together, and peaceably-disposed citizens shut themselves in their houses, fearful that the day would not pass without some great catastrophe.

At an early hour the members of the Cabildo met together, and were not long in deciding upon the list of municipal officers for the ensuing year. Having drawn up this list, a deputation from them, headed by Don Martin Alzaga, proceeded across the Plaza Mayor and the Plaza de Los Perdices to the fort, where they presented this list to the Viceroy. Few words passed between them and the deputation retired. In both Plazas hundreds of the citizens were walking to and fro, or stood conversing in groups, all anxiously waiting for what the day might bring forth. As the deputation left the fort after their interview with the Viceroy, passing through these groups of men, who gazed upon them in silence as though they would read their purpose in their faces, several of these Spaniards took off their hats, waving them in the air and shouting—

"Junta! Junta! como la de la España! Abajo el Francès Liniers!"[1]

Among the people this shout found no echo. Then began the church-bells to clang and the drums beat to arms in the streets.

---

[1] "Junta! Junta! like that of Spain! Down with Liniers the Frenchman."

Three corps of the Spanish troops left their quarters with their arms
and ammunition, and marching hurriedly to the Plaza Mayor drew
up on the west side the Plaza with their backs to the Cabildo, shouting as their leaders had already instructed them—

"Junta! Junta! como la de la España! Abajo el Francés
Liniers!"

As the bells rang out their peal, Marshal Liniers sent off a messenger to Don Cornelio Saavedra requesting him to garrison the fort.
As the Spanish troops entered the Plaza Mayor, the first battalion of
the Patricios marched through the Plaza de Los Perdices, crossed the
drawbridge of the fort, and occupied all the defences of this stronghold. At the same time Don Carlos Evaña, with a drawn sabre in his
hand, at the head of a strong party of armed citizens, entered the fort
by a postern gate, and placed himself and his followers at the orders
of the Viceroy.

Marshal Liniers in full uniform stood at the foot of the flag-staff on
the parade-ground, looking anxiously out towards the city, listening
to the clangour of the bells and the shouts of the troops in the further Plaza, when a Spanish officer in uniform and with his sword in
its sheath stood before him and saluted him.

"Asneiros! you here!" said Marshal Liniers.

"Yes, your Excellency," replied Asneiros, "I am here; my Andaluces are also close at hand, the Spanish artillery have not left their
barracks. It appears that there is some conspiracy against you; I,
my Andaluces, and the Spanish artillery all put ourselves under
your orders if you grant me at once a favour that I require of you."

"Speak," said Marshal Liniers.

"You have imprisoned an honourable gentleman, Don Marcelino
Ponce de Leon; I demand his immediate release."

"He is in the Cabildo," replied Marshal Liniers. "If to-day at
sundown I am Viceroy I will set him free."

"A thousand thanks, your Excellency; not to-day only, but many
days you will yet see yourself Viceroy."

Then as he turned away Asneiros looked around him, and his eye
fell upon Evaña, who, with his drawn sabre in his hand, was talking
eagerly with a number of militia officers.

"He here and armed!" said Asneiros to himself; "he then is
not of the conspiracy. Fool that I am, I have let myself be deceived
by the soft voice of a woman. But it is not too late yet; if I go and
shout for the Junta over there Don Martin will set him free for me."

But as he crossed the drawbridge, and looked to where he had left
his men, he saw a mounted officer sitting in his saddle in front of
them speaking to them. As he ceased, the men took off their round
caps and tossed them in the air shouting—

"¡Viva Don Cornelio!" Then as Don Cornelio, raising his hand
for silence, again spoke, they shouted even louder than before—

"¡Viva el Virey Don Santiago Liniers! Viva!!"

It was too late; to turn back now was impossible; he had nothing
left to do but to follow the lead of Don Cornelio and to trust to the
Viceroy.

During all this excitement one man stood quietly on the balcony of the Cabildo, watching everything, but since the selection of the municipal officers taking no part in anything, Don Roderigo Ponce de Leon. From his position he could see the sheen of the bayonets as the Patricios marched into the fort; he looked down into the Plaza below him upon the troops there assembled, he noted at once the absence of the artillery corps and of the Andaluces. None of his colleagues were with him, they had proceeded from the fort to the house of the Bishop of Buenos Aires, Monseñor Lue, who, with Don Martin Alzaga, was at the head of the conspiracy against the Viceroy. Unless some measures were immediately adopted to allay the excitement a struggle seemed inevitable; to this struggle Don Roderigo could see but one end, the total overthrow of Spanish authority. Hastily he descended from the balcony and walked to the house of the Bishop. His report considerably damped the enthusiasm of the conspirators; the Bishop consented to go alone to the fort to endeavour to prevail upon the Viceroy to dismiss the militia to their homes.

"Promise him anything," said Don Roderigo; but Don Martin Alzaga saw him depart without speaking, and with the rest of the conclave returned to the Cabildo.

As the Bishop presented himself to Marshal Liniers he was confronted by Don Cornelio Saavedra, and between these two there ensued a hot discussion. The Bishop protested that his only wish was to prevent bloodshed, and promised that if the Patricios would retire, the Spanish troops in the Plaza Mayor should be sent back to their barracks. To him Liniers seemed disposed to yield, whereupon Don Cornelio, still protesting against any attempt on the part of the Spaniards to depose the Viceroy, consented to retire from the fort with his troops, but declared that he should keep them under arms until such time as the Spanish troops had evacuated the Plaza Mayor.

Out over the drawbridge marched the Patricios in perfect order, the sun shining on the bright barrels of their muskets and upon their glistening bayonets. In one long column they crossed the Plaza de los Perdices, passed through the wide arch of the Recoba Vieja, and in imposing array marched straight for the artillery barracks, where the chosen Spaniards of Don Martin Alzaga joined them with acclamations, and with loud shouts of—

"¡ Viva Don Santiago Liniers ! ¡ Viva el Virey !"

Then came the second battalion of the Patricios, the "Pardos y Morenos," and the Arribeño regiment. Mounted messengers were despatched at speed to the Residencia and to the Plaza Miserere. The swarthy troopers, tired with long waiting in the hot summer sun, received the summons with joy, and noon was not long passed ere Don Cornelio Saavedra found himself at the head of a force nearly double in number to the entire force the Spaniards could bring against him, even should the Andaluz regiment, which remained under arms in the Plaza de los Perdices, ultimately declare for them.

Meantime Don Martin Alzaga and his colleagues, save one (Don Roderigo Ponce de Leon held himself aloof from them), determined upon a direct appeal to the people. Again the bells rang out their clang of alarm, and the royal flag of Spain, brought out from its seclusion, was displayed on the balcony of the Cabildo. Vain hope to excite loyalty to Spain in the breasts of men who already knew that they were Argentines. Few citizens responded to the appeal. Don Martin had none upon whom he could depend, save upon those three Spanish infantry corps which were still drawn up in the Plaza Mayor, underneath the balcony on which waved the proud flag of Spain, the symbol of the conquest.

Yet one other course was open to him. Sundry citizens who were well-affected to their Spanish rulers were summoned to the Cabildo, and incorporated with that august body, thus forming what was called in those days a "Cabildo Abierto," a corporation in which both Spaniards and Argentines were represented, and which might be thus supposed to embody the wishes of the people.

Then a deed of resignation was drawn up, by which the Viceroy resigned his office, and authorized the formation of a Junta, in which his powers should be invested. With this deed the whole of the members of the Cabildo, both Spaniards and Argentines, with the exception of that one man who still held aloof, crossed over to the fort and presented it to the Viceroy, notifying him that it was the will of the people that he should resign his office.

Liniers looked around him in surprise. All the ruling corporations of the city were represented in this group of men who presented this deed to him for signature. Among them were also several well-known citizens, Argentines by birth, and men of influence among their fellow-countrymen. It seemed to him that the voice of the people called upon him to resign; he took his pen and signed the document.

As Liniers gave his assent, and ere he had yet signed the deed of abdication, a messenger was sent across the two Plazas to the Cabildo, to the Spaniards who had remained there, telling them that their cause was won. Eager hands seized upon the flag of Spain, waving it triumphantly; eager voices shouted the pæan of victory, yet still Don Roderigo Ponce de Leon held aloof, leaning on the rails of the balcony and gazing out upon the Plaza, watching ever, but neither by voice nor sign showing that he had any part in the triumph.

Then from the Calle Defensa, memorable for the repulse and capture of General Crauford on the 5th July, 1807, issued into the open Plaza the firm array of the citizen-soldiers of Buenos Aires, with their trusted leader, Don Cornelio Saavedra, at their head. First came the Patricios, who ever claimed the post of danger, the post of honour; then came the Arribeños, the artillery, the Pardos y Morenos, and the Andaluces, who had last of all made up their minds to join the ranks of the patriots. The infantry with bayonets fixed, the artillery bringing their cannon with them, the gunners marching with the matches lighted in their hands. These drew up on the east side the Plaza in dense ranks, with the Recoba Vieja behind them, facing towards the Cabildo, where the three Spanish corps ceased their cries and jubilation as they gazed upon the formidable array so unexpectedly marshalled against them.

Behind the infantry and artillery there came yet two other corps, two squadrons of cavalry, the hussars of Don Martin Rodriguez, and the dragoons from Las Barrancas, dark-featured, long-haired men, who sat their horses as though they were parts of them, and whose bright sabres were held by brawny hands, wielding them as though they were toys. These two squadrons of cavalry, with the Andaluces, were drawn up behind the Recoba in reserve, but at the cross streets and at the central arch, spaces were left in the long line of infantry through which the cavalry might advance were there occasion for their services.

When all his arrangements were complete, Don Cornelio Saavedra glanced proudly over the serried files of men who obeyed his word, glanced indignantly across the Plaza at the troops still there in spite of the promise given him by the Bishop, then, deputing the command to Major Viamont, away he galloped to the fort. Followed by a group of his principal officers, he walked into the saloon of audience, in which the deed of resignation had just been signed.

The assembled grandees were struck mute at this unexpected intrusion. Monseñor Lue was the first to speak; turning to Saavedra he said:—

"Thanks be to God, all is finished. His Excellency loves the people, and does not desire that there be bloodshed for his sake. He has agreed to abdicate."

"Who has given his Excellency the power to resign the command legally conferred upon him?" asked Saavedra in reply.

"Señor Comandante," replied the Bishop, in a supplicating tone, "do you wish to involve this people in blood?"

"Neither I nor my comrades," answered the Commandant of the Patricios, "have caused this revolution. I have said, and I repeat it, that there is no cause for this violence."

Then hearing the Bishop say that it was the will of the people that the Viceroy should resign, Saavedra interrupted him, saying—

"That is a falsehood. In proof of it, let the Señor Liniers come with us, let him present himself to the people; if the people refuse him, and will not that he continue in command, then I and my comrades will sign the deed of abdication."

Then he and Don Martin Rodriguez took the Viceroy by the arm, saying to him—

"Descend with us, your Excellency, and hear from the mouth of the people what is their will."

It was already sunset when Liniers, surrounded by Argentine citizens and officers of the militia, crossed the drawbridge of the fort. The Plaza de los Perdices was full of people, beyond them were drawn up the dense ranks of the native troops. From all these there burst loud cheers and shouts of "¡ Viva Don Santiago Liniers! We will have no other to rule over us." [1]

Negro slaves, tearing off their clothes, strewed them on the ground before the Viceroy as he walked forth, so that he might not soil his feet with the dust. Behind this group came the discomfited members of the Cabildo, among whom walked the secretary of the Cabildo, carrying in his hand the deed of abdication. As he crossed the drawbridge, Don Carlos Evaña, who was close to Liniers, turned back, ran

---

[1] For this scene see " La Historia de Belgrano," by General Mitre.

to the secretary, and snatching the deed from him tore it into pieces,
and threw the fragments contemptuously into the air, at which sight
the exultant populace burst out again with shouts of triumph.

Meanwhile, at the first shouts of the people, the Spanish officers in
the further Plaza gave orders to their men to load with ball cartridge.
Don Roderigo Ponce de Leon, who still stood on the balcony of the
Cabildo, heard the order given.   Descending at once to the Plaza, he
ran along the front of the line of soldiery, shouting—

"To your barracks, Gallegos and Viscainos!   To your barracks,
Catalanes!"

At the same time an aide-de-camp from Marshal Liniers came to
them with an order from the Viceroy to lay down their arms.   Contradictory orders of all sorts were given by the officers, all was confusion; some of the men wheeled round and marched away, others
grasped their muskets and glared defiance across the Plaza at the
steady ranks of the citizen soldiers drawn up in defiant array in front
of them.

At this moment Don Carlos Evaña, standing under the arch of
the Recoba, shouted to the cavalry sitting motionless on their horses,
with sabres drawn in the Plaza de los Perdices—

"To me, muchachos! now is the moment!" at the same time
pointing with his sabre to the confused groups of soldiery who
occupied the far side the Plaza Mayor.

"Follow me, muchachos!" shouted Venceslao Viana, driving in
his spurs and dashing at full speed through the arch of the Recoba.

His troop followed him pell-mell, and the rest of the cavalry, supposing that some order had been given, charged through every opening
into the Plaza Mayor.

Don Roderigo ran frantically along the ranks of the Spanish infantry,
tearing the muskets from the hands of the men and shouting—

"To your barracks! to your barracks! Españoles!"

All was confusion and wild panic; the Spaniards broke their ranks,
and in headlong flight ran off up the streets abutting on the west side
the Plaza, throwing away their arms, many of them seeking refuge in
the open doorways of the houses as they passed.   After them came
the fierce horsemen of the Pampas, striking at them furiously with
their sabres, trampling them under-foot if they made any attempt to
resist.   Few of them reached their barracks, all over the city they
were dispersed, and the power of Spain was broken for ever in Buenos
Aires.

Then the royal flag of Spain, which had fluttered so proudly all the
afternoon on the balcony of the Cabildo, was withdrawn, never more
to see the light as an emblem of conquest and subjugation; when
again it was brought forth it was to grace some festival of a free people.

As the horsemen poured tumultuously into the Plaza, the native
infantry looked eagerly to Don Cornelio for a signal, but Don Cornelio
riding along the line called upon them to ground arms and not to
move; all obeyed, watching in silence the discomfiture of their
enemies, except a small party on the left flank where the "Pardos y
Morenos" were stationed.

During the whole day a slim youth of small stature, who by his dress evidently belonged to one of the principal families of the city, had hovered about under the arcade of the Recoba Nueva, absent occasionally for a short time while the patriot troops were concentrating under the orders of Don Cornelio Saavedra, returning with them to the Plaza, and resuming his former station under the arcade. As the horsemen dashed through the arch of the Recoba Vieja this youth ran towards the "Pardos y Morenos," waving his hat and shouting—

"Now, Morenitos! now!"

About a score of negroes obeyed his call, left their ranks, and, mingled with the horsemen, rushed across the Plaza straight for the main entrance to the Cab'ldo. The wide gateway and the courtyard beyond were crowded with panic-stricken soldiery, whose terror the sudden rush of the negroes yet further increased so that they fled before their levelled bayonets and left the way open to the main staircase. Up this staircase the youth, who was Evaristo Ponce de Leon, led the way towards a corridor where a sentry stood on guard.

"Back! back!" shouted Evaristo to this man as he levelled his musket. The negroes crowding up behind him gave a fierce yell; he dropped his weapon and fled.

"The key!" shouted Evaristo after him as he ran.

"The key!" said a stalwart negro, "I have key sufficient." And seizing the barrel of his musket with both hands he struck the side panel of the door as strongly as he could with the butt. The lock gave way and the door flew open.

Marcelino, pale with his confinement, and listening anxiously to the cries and shouts which he could plainly hear, but of the cause of which he knew nothing, stood in the centre of a well-furnished room as the door flew open. He gazed in wonder upon the joyful faces of the negroes, and the next moment was clasped in the arms of his brother.

"I have saved you, Marcelino, now you are free," said Evaristo, and without further explanation he snatched a hat from a peg, and a light poncho from a chair, saying—

"Put these on and come. It is sundown already, and I promised mamma and Lola that I would go back with you to-day."

Marcelino asked no questions, but put on the hat and poncho, and taking his brother by the hand went forth along the corridor, down the staircase, across the court-yard, and so out into the open Plaza. Here groups of excited men were talking and gesticulating together, troops were manœuvring on the open space in the centre, all the ground in front of the Cabildo was strewn with muskets and accoutrements, a body of horsemen with drawn sabres were stationed in front of the cathedral, and a party of the Patricios came along the side-walk, under the upper story of the Cabildo, carrying on their crossed muskets two men in the uniform of the Catalan regiment, whose heads were bound up with blood-stained handkerchiefs. Around him and behind him came the negroes who had burst open his prison door, their black faces shining with delight, and their white teeth gleaming between their thick brown lips.

"What has happened?" said Marcelino. "There is my uncle

Gregorio with a party of his dragoons ! There has been a fight ! What has happened, Evaristo ?"

" Never mind now, come along quick, presently I will tell you all," said Evaristo, hurrying him on past the cathedral and round the next corner.

Here Marcelino's own servant, the negro Manuel, stood holding two saddled horses by the bridles. The two brothers mounted at once.

" Now I am free !" said Marcelino with a shout of joy as he settled himself in the saddle. " I shall not forget this service which you have done me, Morenos."

The negroes answered him with a loud shout, "¡ Viva el Comandante Ponce !" and drawn up in line presented arms.

Both brothers touched their hats in acknowledgment of this salute, and then, slacking their reins, galloped away. Neither spoke till they had left the suburbs behind them.

" Tell me now what has happened, Evaristo ? " said Marcelino.

" I knew there was going to be something," replied Evaristo, " for Tata sent me out to the quinta yesterday and would not go himself. I found Uncle Gregorio there, and his dragoons came, Evaña had sent for them, and uncle said you would be set free to-day, so I came back. First thing this morning I went to the barracks of the Pardos y Morenos, there were some of your men there and they were glad enough to promise me. All day I waited but there was never a chance, there were the Catalanes and Gallegos right in front of the Cabildo. Suddenly the arch of the Recoba appeared a volcano vomiting dragoons with drawn sabres, the Spaniards were all in confusion, I saw that the moment had come. I called to the Morenos, they followed me like ' guapos ' and here we are."

" Yes, here we are, thank God, but why were the Spaniards there and the Patricios ? "

" It appears that the Señores the Spaniards took it into their heads to depose the Viceroy. That did not please Don Cornelio Saavedra, and the dragoons of Uncle Gregorio have trampled on them some little I warrant you."

CHAPTER VIII.

EVAÑA'S DREAM.

It was long past nightfall ere the Viceroy, wearied with the day's anxieties, returned to his official residence at the fort. As he crossed the drawbridge he was joined by Don Roderigo Ponce de Leon.

"I come to congratulate you, Don Santiago, on the happy result of the day," said Don Roderigo.

"Ah! Don Roderigo, is it you?" said the Viceroy. "I have looked for you several times to-day. How is it that you never came with the other members of the Cabildo?"

"I knew what they purposed doing and chose to take no part in it. I like not these popular demonstrations."

"But the people were with me entirely."

"By good fortune, and owing to the firmness of Don Cornelio. But after all we have only just escaped a great catastrophe."

"A catastrophe! Well, yes, if the Spanish regiments had stood firm there would have been bloodshed, but the end would have been as it is."

"If the artillery and the Andaluces had been against you to-day, you could only have crushed the conspiracy by great sacrifice of life, and the danger is merely postponed."

"I shall disarm all the Spanish regiments."

"Disarm the Spanish regiments! If you do that you are lost, you put yourself entirely in the power of these Creoles."

"The militia or the troops, I must choose between them," said Liniers.

"You do not see the danger from which both you and we have escaped to-day. Why did the cavalry charge the troops when all was over? I will tell you. There is a strong revolutionary feeling abroad in the city; there are many among the Creoles who supported you to-day who did so simply for the furtherance of their own schemes. They supported you for the sake of destroying the authority of the Cabildo, their next step will be to depose you. They seek to take advantage of the misfortunes of Spain to establish here a republic."

"Evaña?" said the Viceroy.

"I mention no names," replied Don Roderigo, "but I warn you that in the Cabildo only can you find a loyal and steady support to your authority."

"As I have seen to-day."

"To-day has been a foolish outbreak of Spanish pride and jealousy, of which I had forewarned you, but, as you know, all Spaniards did not go with Don Martin Alzaga. The artillery passed over at once when the Patricios went to them shouting 'Viva el Reconquistador.'

We Spaniards have not forgotten the 12th August and the 5th and 6th July. Whilst you hold your power by legitimate appointment from the supreme government of Spain we look to you as our chief and as our defence against revolution, there are not many of us who are hot-headed fools like Don Martin Alzaga. Beware of the revolutionary party, they are the men who are really dangerous. There has been bloodshed to-day, happily not much, not enough to satisfy those reckless revolutionists. The cavalry charged without orders from Don Cornelio, it was the last effort of the revolutionists to force on a conflict for the purpose of plunging us into anarchy and so making an opportunity for themselves."

The Viceroy listened attentively to Don Roderigo, but merely answered by inviting him to supper with him, and several others being present they had no more confidential talk together. As he rose to go Don Roderigo said—

"I think I have done your Excellency good service to-day, one boon I ask you in return, the liberty of my son."

"Pues!" said the Viceroy, with a look of surprise; "he is free hours ago."

"I did not know it," said Don Roderigo, "but I give you a thousand thanks, and also for the leniency with which he has been treated during his arrest."

"Then you knew nothing of it? I thought you had taken advantage of the confusion to release him yourself. When the troops dispersed, a party of negroes burst into the Cabildo and set him free by force, I thought you had sent them."

"This is the first I hear of it," said Don Roderigo.

"I am glad of that," said the Viceroy, "for this violence was quite unnecessary; I promised Captain Asneiros this morning that I would release him at sundown. To-morrow I will send you a formal order for his release, and his books and papers shall be returned to you."

Don Roderigo bowed and retired, feeling greatly disappointed, for he had planned to himself to end the day by bearing the order for his son's release, himself to the Cabildo, and by being himself the first to congratulate him on his liberation.

While Don Roderigo and the Viceroy sat at supper, the commandant of the dragoons from Las Barrancas and Don Carlos Evaña had a stormy altercation together at the house of the latter gentleman. They were in a large, plainly-furnished apartment, Don Gregorio seated in an arm-chair with his hat on, and his left hand resting upon the hilt of his sabre, Don Carlos walking excitedly up and down the room, while near the door stood Venceslao Viana, bare-headed and unarmed, his sword-belt and sabre lying on a side-table, near to which the Colonel was seated.

"Without doubt you are to blame, Don Carlos," said Don Gregorio, "but that in no way excuses the conduct of Venceslao. My officers are not to receive orders from any one but me, if they do they incur the extreme penalty of martial law. Your act, Venceslao, has cost the lives of six men, and there are some two score wounded; your act was in disobedience to my express orders, and your life is forfeit for the vindication of military discipline."

"To Don Carlos I owe my life," said Venceslao calmly. "If I lose it in his service, I do no more than pay my debt."

"Then that debt is paid," replied Don Gregorio. "If the Viceroy pass over this affair without enquiry I shall say no more about it. Take up your sabre and go."

Without the slightest change of countenance Venceslao buckled on his sabre, then with a low bow to both the others replaced his hat and left the room. In the patio outside the door of this room stood two dismounted troopers with their carbines; in the street outside half a troop were seated in their saddles with drawn sabres; one of these men held Venceslao's horse by the bridle, he mounted and trotted slowly away.

"It appears that I am to be a great warrior," said he to himself, as he trotted through the suburbs; "I am always just going to be killed, and away I go without a scratch. When I heard the order for my arrest I said to myself, 'Of a certainty he will shoot me,' I deserved it without doubt, yet here I am."

Without giving more thought to the matter he then commenced singing one of the monotonous songs of the paisanos, and so trotted on to a quinta beyond the suburbs where his regiment was encamped.

"Sit down, Carlos," said Don Gregorio, as Venceslao closed the door behind him. "Explain to me your ideas. Why did you seek to force on a conflict when all had ended as we wished it?"

"Because all has not ended as we wished it," replied Evaña, throwing himself upon a sofa. "We wished to break for ever the power of the Spaniards over us. What we have done is to secure the power of one who will maintain everything as it has been. I wished to force him into open collision with the Spaniards, as it is he has half the Spaniards with him. If I had succeeded he would have been forced to depend in everything upon native Argentines; until the government is in every department in the hands of Creoles we are not a free people, and that is the end to which you, I, and every true Argentine aspires."

"Truly it is so, but I like not your way of going to work. Liberty without strict discipline is anarchy, discipline is more necessary among a free people than among slaves."

Then there was silence for a space between them, till Evaña sprang from his sofa saying—

"Yet it is possible that we may do something. Promise me that you will return slowly, and not go further than the casa-teja till I see you or write to you."

"You have some fresh scheme in your head?"

"I have, and I may need your assistance."

"For three days I will wait, but no longer. Do what you can, and count upon me."

"I am going at once to see Liniers, to try what can be done with him. He must see by now what he can expect from the Spaniards. If he will but declare for us our cause is won."

Darkness shrouded the city which during the day had been the scene of so much tumult. It wanted but an hour of midnight, the moon had not yet risen, and the stars shining calmly down from the blue vault where they kept their stations, were the only lights which illumined the path of a tall man, enveloped in a large cloak, who picked his way carefully across the Plaza de los Perdices. He walked up to the drawbridge which crossed the dry ditch surrounding the fort on the land side. The bridge was down, but the gate beyond was closed, and on the bridge a sentry of the Patricios kept watch and ward.

"Good night, friend," said the tall man to the sentry.

"Keep back, whoever you are," said the sentry, bringing down his musket to the charge.

"Do not alarm yourself, Pancho, I am no enemy," said the other. "Who is the officer of the guard?"

"Back! replied the sentry. "Who are you? How do you know that my name is Pancho?"

But the tall man came still nearer, taking off his hat, and throwing back his cloak.

"Don Carlos Evaña!" exclaimed the sentry, recovering his musket. "What would you at this hour? Have you not the word?"

"No. But who is the officer of the guard?"

"The Señor Lieutenant Lopez y Viana."

"Valentin!" exclaimed Evaña; "it could not be better. Do me the favour to knock at the gate, and ask him to come out and speak to me."

The sentry walked back across the bridge and knocked at the gate. After a lengthened parley a sergeant stepped out through a wicket, and requested Don Carlos to come forward and step inside. Don Carlos walked across the bridge, passed the wicket, and found himself in the midst of an armed party of the Patricios, one of whom held up a lantern to his face.

"Ah! it is you, Don Carlos," said a young officer, stepping forward. "Excuse the delay, but after the affair of to-day no precaution is too much."

"You do perfectly right, Valentin," replied Don Carlos; then passing his arm over the shoulder of the young officer he whispered some few words in his ear.

Five minutes later Don Carlos was seated in the private apartment of the Viceroy, and with him held earnest converse for nearly an hour.

"Then your Excellency entirely rejects my proposal," said Evaña.

"I do," replied the Viceroy. "I hold my authority from the Court of Spain, and will suffer no innovations without consulting the supreme authorities, whoever they may happen to be."

"Think well what you do, Don Santiago. Such an opportunity as the present may never offer itself to you again. The people have to-day for the third time shown their power. Twice have they repulsed invasions of the English, to-day they have humbled the arrogance of the Spaniards. Put yourself at the head of this new power which has risen up in America, and a new career of greatness and of glory will open up before you. Attempt to arrest the progress of the people, and they themselves, who to-day have offered their lives for you, will crush you to the dust."

"You threaten me," exclaimed the Viceroy.

"I do not threaten you, I merely warn you. If I stand forth myself and proclaim the liberty of the people they will rise as one man to demand their rights. Who is there that shall say them nay?"

"The people would not listen to you," replied the Viceroy.

"I wish to avoid bloodshed and contention, therefore I ask you, who hold the power in your hands, to put yourself at the head of the people. Under your leadership there will be no contention, no bloodshed."

"Know you not that this is treason which you propose to me? What hinders me from ordering your immediate arrest as a conspirator against Spain?"

"Do it," said Evaña, rising. "Call in your guards, order them to arrest me. Doubtless they will obey you, but to-morrow's sun will see the last day of your authority in Buenos Aires. Shoot me if you like. I should die joyfully, for I know that my blood would purchase the liberty of my own people."

"No. You have come here unarmed and alone. I respect the trust you have placed in me, but give some attention to my words. I have long had my eye upon you as a man of dangerous ideas—ideas which you have now disclosed to me. Look well what you do, for whilst I hold authority as Viceroy I will maintain that authority intact, and will punish any revolutionary attempt with the extremest rigour of the law."

"And how much longer will you hold this authority?" asked Evaña. "Have not the Spaniards to-day shown you how little they respect it? I know it, if you do not, that months ago they sent to Spain for a successor to you, who may come at any time. What becomes then of your authority? Why should you submit to be deposed by the Junta of Seville? They did not appoint you. Your authority was bestowed upon you by the people; you retain it now solely by their will. I say no more, but I give you three days to consider of the proposal I have made to you. If at the expiration of that time you are silent, then I shall know that you have chosen your own course, and shall abandon you to your fate; but again I warn you, beware how you oppose the progress of the people. You, who are to-day their favourite, will be the first victim of their rage in the day when they rise up in their strength and seize those rights which you have conspired to keep from them."

As Evaña spoke he raised himself to his full height, looking with a stern, threatening gaze upon the Viceroy, who answered him not a word, but sat motionless in his chair, while the colour faded from his face and lips, and the sweat stood in great beads upon his brow. He forgot that he was in Buenos Aires, he forgot that he was Viceroy; in memory he stood again in the streets of Paris as he stood in his youth; again before his eyes there rushed a furious, half-starved mob, brandishing strange weapons and shouting fiercely in hoarse voices the refrain of that deadly song—

"Ça ira! Les Aristocrats à la lanterne."

Evaña saw the pallor in his cheeks, saw the vacant stare in his terror-stricken eyes, and waited for him to speak, half hopeful yet; but no words came, slowly the eyes recovered their usual expression and turned upon himself, their expression then becoming one of fierce anger. The Viceroy started from his chair, laying his hand upon the hilt of his sword, for one moment he stood irresolute, then his eyes shrank beneath the stern, threatening gaze of those dark eyes which confronted his so unflinchingly ; once more he sank back into his chair covering his face with his hands.

Evaña, taking up his hat and cloak, made a low bow to the unconscious Viceroy and left him to himself. In the ante-room he met young Valentin, with whom he spoke for a few minutes : crossing the parade-ground, where the guard drawn up presented arms to him as he passed, he stept out through the wicket, and folding his cloak closely round him went forth over the drawbridge and with long, rapid strides walked swiftly away for his own home.

His servant had supper waiting for him as he arrived ; he tried to eat, but it seemed to him as though his food would choke him ; he poured out a goblet of wine, drank it at one draught, and retired to his own room.

" Only six killed, and they men of whom no one thinks twice," said he to himself, as he paced up and down. " To-morrow it will be all forgotten, and we shall be as good friends as ever with our lords the Spaniards. That fool Liniers ! I have given him three days, but I know it will be all in vain ; to-morrow he will have some one else at his ear, he will do nothing. But can I do nothing ? He said they would not listen to me ; but many would, and lose themselves with me perchance. No, patience, patience yet, my day will come."

So he laid himself down to sleep, and in the visions of the night there came to him a dream.

Legions of red-coated soldiery obeyed his orders, encompassing his native city on all sides, assailing it with storms of shot and shell, laying the suburbs in ruins and advancing through streets of burning houses, slaying all who opposed them, till the city was won. Then he himself led the attack upon the fort ; forcing his way across the drawbridge, encumbered with heaps of corpses, he rushed to the tall flag-staff on which fluttered the standard of Spain. With his own hands he tore down this standard and set up another. Then as this new standard gave itself to the winds, floating high in air amidst smoke and dust, he turned, pointed to it with his drawn sword, and called upon his countrymen to acknowledge him as their liberator.

But when he looked around him he was alone, and there was none to answer him. Then from afar off there came to him an answer from the city. From amidst the crumbling walls and burning houses there reached him through the murky air the wailing voices of women and the piteous cries of children.

Then was he perplexed, and his heart smote him that he had done unwisely ; and as he thought of the desolation he had accomplished there rose up before him from a pile of mangled corpses one ghastly figure, covered with blood and wounds, which, frowning angrily upon him, rushed upon him with a dagger to stab him to the heart. Fiercely he struck at this phantom with his sword ; as he struck, another figure rushed in between them, the figure of a woman, whose long, dishevelled hair enveloped her with a radiance as of molten gold. His sword buried itself in her breast ; wildly she threw up her arms, gazing upon him out of a pair of large gray eyes, full of terror and reproach.

" Always my friend, whatever happens !" she shrieked out, then threw herself at his feet to die. It was Dolores.

With a loud cry Evaña started from his couch and woke

CHAPTER IX.

THE DAY AFTER.

MOTHER and sister received the rescued prisoner with open arms. Far into the night they sat together talking over the events of the last three weeks, while of the day itself the events were detailed to them by Evaristo after a fashion somewhat hard of comprehension.

When they separated, Marcelino retired to his couch with a heavy heart. During his imprisonment and since, he had learned sufficient to tell him that his father, though professing the greatest indignation at his arrest, had taken no one step towards his deliverance, and had rather hindered the plans of those who had interested themselves for him. During his imprisonment he had been subjected once only to a cursory examination, when the questions put to him showed him that the cause of his imprisonment was the scheme for inviting the Princess Carlota to Buenos Aires, which he had been the first to enunciate. In this scheme he had taken no further part, yielding to the wish of his father, though he still looked upon it as the only means of achieving independence without plunging the country into civil war.

That his father knew the cause of his imprisonment, and could have procured his release at any moment, he felt certain, yet he had neither written to him nor had been once to see him. The Viceroy would hardly have ventured upon such a step without consulting him, he must at least have consented to, perhaps even suggested, his imprisonment. So Marcelino pondered within himself, lying on his couch sleepless through the night until the dawn of another day, his mind filled with bitter thoughts and his heart with anger.

The next day Venceslao Viana, passing the quinta with the dragoons on the march outside, left a note from Colonel Lopez to Doña Constancia, telling her that if Marcelino was with her he need be under no fear of arrest, for the Viceroy had sent an order for his liberation to the Cabildo on the preceding evening.

The great heat of the day was past, the sun was already dipping towards the tree-tops, and the shadows were beginning to stretch themselves out over the broad walks of the Quinta de Don Alfonso. The wide porch, covered with honeysuckle, passion-flowers, and other creepers, was at this time of the day the coolest part of the house, here Magdalen sat alone in a low chair, sewing. She was dressed in a plain gown of dove-coloured muslin, fitting closely round the base of her neck, leaving her throat uncovered, girded round the waist with a belt of blue velvet, fastened by a silver buckle. Narrow straight

T

sleeves covered her arms down to the wrists, where they were confined by bands of blue velvet and terminated in little white frills. Her glossy brown hair was bound round her head by a fillet of blue silk, from which sundry stray locks had escaped, and lay in broad curls upon her neck and shoulders. She was not very diligently at work, every now and then she would pause, and laying down her task gazed with dreamy, far-looking eyes, out through the bright sunshine and through the foliage of the trees upon the white towers and domes of the city, so near to look upon, and yet to her so far off. For she knew hardly anything of what had happened there for two weeks past, she herself having never left the quinta and her father but once all that time, while the only visitor who had been with them was Don Fausto Velasquez. Since his visit her father had been very anxious and troubled, but of his trouble he had told her nothing. That morning his face had brightened, and he had gone into the city, from which he had not yet returned.

So she sat alternately stitching and gazing, watching the lengthening shadows of the trees, eagerly looking at any who passed on the adjacent road, listening to the sound of any footstep that came near her, waiting and thinking. Waiting for her father, who came not, thinking of many things. Waiting for her father, who had told her when he went that he hoped to bring her good news on his return ; thinking of what these news would be, yet doubting much that the news which would most please her would be but of small import to him.

As she sat thus she heard a footstep close to her, a footstep which she knew well, coming up the garden walk, close to the house. This footstep, light and quick, she had learned to know, for it had brought her joy many times, and now her heart bounded with a wild delight, and she whispered to herself—

" He is free."

Then a sudden pang shot through her and quenched her joy. The blood which had rushed to her face at the first sound of that footstep fled back again to her heart, and left her with pale cheeks and a nervous contraction of the lips, as she thought of some words which had been said to her days before by Doña Josefina, and of a girl of radiant beauty of whom he had spoken in terms of warm admiration.

The footsteps ceased, a figure stood in the entrance of the porch, and a low voice spoke to her in tender accents, one word only—

" Magdalen."

As she heard that voice, and that one word so tenderly spoken, the tremor of her heart ceased, the blood rushed back to her face, suffusing cheeks and brow, she started to her feet, stretching out her hand and trying to speak some word of welcome, but no word came. Marcelino took her hand in his own and raised it to his lips, then leading her back to her chair he seated himself beside her on a low stool, still holding her hand in his. So sat they silently for some moments, Magdalen was the first to speak.

" Papa is not at home," she said, drawing away her hand ; " all day he has been in the city."

" It is three weeks since I have seen you," replied Marcelino.

"They have been to me like three years. I have been in prison, I have been thinking of you all the time and wondering whether you would miss me. Have you been much in the city since I saw you last?"

"No, only once," said Magdalen. "Doña Josefina said that you would soon be free."

"I escaped last night, and am free, yet in great trouble; I cannot live here any longer, I must go, but I could not go without seeing you first."

"Going! Where are you going? Don Fausto said that it was a mistake, and that you had done nothing."

"Yes, I had done something, I had dared to love my country, and had dared to speak of a scheme which would free her from tyranny. To love one's country is a crime in the eyes of our lords the Spaniards, and my father is a Spaniard."

Then again there was silence between them for a space, till Magdalen spoke.

"Yesterday morning there was a squadron of horse here in the Plaza," she said; "all the morning they were there. Papa was very anxious and kept watching them, till in the siesta they marched away into the city. What happened there?"

"At sundown there was a fight in the Plaza Mayor. Evaristo with some Morenos of mine burst into the Cabildo and set me free. It appears that the Spaniards made a revolt against Liniers and failed. More I know not, but this is the beginning I hoped to have avoided, now I have to choose between my father and my country."

"Your father! But he was a great friend of the Viceroy, he would not join a revolt against him."

"My father is a Spaniard, what Spaniards do is always well done in his eyes, and without doubt he was with them."

"But you say they have failed; he may be in danger. When did you leave the city? What have you heard?"

"I left the city last night, and I have heard nothing more than I have told you."

"And all the day where have you been?" said Magdalen, looking at him in surprise.

"I have been all day at the quinta, I have just come from there. I could not pass the first day of my freedom without seeing you."

"And your father in danger! Oh, that is wrong, it is so unlike you."

"In danger of what? a prison? I have just escaped from the prison where he put me."

"He put you! It was the Viceroy put you in prison, and Don Roderigo was very angry about it; Don Fausto said so."

"The Viceroy does nothing of himself, he always consults some one, none more than my father. My father warned me of this conspiracy, and I told him that if the Spaniards here pronounced against Liniers, as Elio did in Monte Video, all Argentines would support the Viceroy against them. He wanted me to promise him that I would take no part either one way or other. I refused, and a few days after I was in prison. Do not you think that one word from my father would have set me free? That word he never spoke. None knew better than he that in the affair of the Princess Carlota nothing could be proved against me, and I fear that he himself suggested my imprisonment."

" Even if it be so it was for your sake he did it. If you had been with the Viceroy, and the Spaniards had been successful, no one knows what perils you would have run, in prison you were safe from all risk."

" Am I a boy, that my father must lock me up to keep me out of mischief? I gave up my scheme to please him, and see now how he trusts me."

" Oh! do not speak so, do not speak so, quarrels between Argentines and Spaniards are bad enough, but between father and son they are far worse. Your father has done this out of his care for you; perhaps he is now in danger. You must forgive him and help him."

" What can I do if he joins himself with the enemies of my country? Am I to be a traitor to my country for his sake?"

" Nevertheless he is your father. Where is he? Perhaps in prison."

" I wished to avoid this, he stopped me, and said my scheme was folly. They have commenced it, and now we shall have civil war here in America, with my father on one side, I on the other. I see nothing but misery in the future."

" Have you no faith in God? Mr. Gordon told me that you used to study the Bible, yet you seem to despair; he who has faith in God can never despair."

" For months I have not opened the Bible. I begin to believe that there is no God."

" But you did believe there was a God once. You read the Bible and learned lessons of faith from it, have you forgotten them already? When the English came you did your duty, though you said yourself that there was no hope of beating them. Have you less courage now than then? Can you not do your duty and leave the result to God?"

Then Marcelino looked up at Magdalen in surprise, he had never heard her speak so before; her voice was low, and there was a sweet tremulousness in her tones which showed that there was a deep earnestness in what she said. Again he took her hand in his, leaning upon the arm of her chair.

" Do you ever read the Bible?" he asked.

" Every day; my mother taught me when I was quite a little girl in England, and papa promised her that I should always read it. When I came here to live with papa he told me what he had promised my mother for me, and he gave me her Bible which he had kept for me. Every day I read it now."

" When I was at Chascomus with my Morenos I read the Bible every day."

" And when you read the Bible what did you learn from it?"

" Once Gordon told me that the great lesson of the Bible was faith, faith in God. I love my father, till now he has always been to me the best of friends, now we are separated for ever. Think you that I can have faith in God when my father becomes my worst enemy?"

" You have not read the Bible well or you would know that that is impossible. If you have faith in God you will do your duty now as you did before. You will help your father if he is in danger."

"I have to choose between my father and my country. Tell me, what is my duty?"

Magdalen was silent, and a troubled expression came over her face. She had admired the eager patriotism she had seen in Marcelino and in others, but of this sentiment she herself knew nothing, she had but one duty that she knew of in her life, her duty to her father, and she could not understand how any other duty could clash with that.

"Tell me, what is my duty?" said Marcelino again, looking earnestly at her.

"Where your father is, you will learn your duty," replied she.

Then there was silence between them for several minutes, and when they spoke again it was on other subjects, about Doña Josefina, about Lola, about Don Alfonso, but of whatever they talked both thought of Don Roderigo, though of him they spoke no more.

As the shadows deepened on the garden walks there came another footstep through the quinta towards the porch, a footstep very different from the one that had come before, a heavy, plodding footstep, as of one out of whose life the light and strength had departed, but Magdalen started up as she heard it, a smile beaming out from her eyes. That step, though so heavy, was lighter than she had heard it for many a long day, it was her father's step, and he was bringing her the good news of which he had spoken to her. She ran out to meet him with a flush of pleasure on her face.

"Ah! Chica," said he gaily; "how has the long day passed with you?"

And when he saw Marcelino, who stood on the step of the porch waiting for him, he stretched out his hand to him with greater cordiality than was his wont.

"Felicidades!" he said. "In the city every one is asking for you. The general idea is that you are with your mother at the quinta."

"I went there last night," replied Marcelino. "But what has happened? I hardly know anything."

"Then you had better return to the quinta, there you will learn all. A large party has gone out there this evening in search of you. Don't be frightened, Chica," he added, as Magdalen started while she clung to his arm, "all are now friends, and Don Martin Alzaga is in prison."

"And my father, what of him?" asked Marcelino.

At this question Don Alfonso frowned, but he answered gravely—

"Your father is more astute than I thought him; he has managed in some way to keep well with all parties."

"Did not I tell you so?" said Magdalen, with a bright smile. "Don Roderigo would never join a conspiracy against the Viceroy. Don Fausto said that he was his best friend."

"In the friendship of some men there is more danger than in the enmity of others," said Don Alfonso gruffly. Then leading his daughter into the porch, he added, turning to Marcelino—

"At the Quinta de Ponce there are many who wait for you."

Marcelino wished much to ask more, but after this he could remain no longer. Bowing in silence he took his leave of them both, somewhat repaid for the gruffness of the father by the sympathy which

looked upon him from Magdalen's gray eyes. He had left his horse
tied under the trees at the back of the quinta, thoughtfully he walked
from the house to where he had left him, mounted, and galloped away.

"How long has he been here?" said Don Alfonso to his daughter,
when Marcelino was beyond hearing.

"Nearly an hour," replied Magdalen.   "He said there was fighting
yesterday in the city. Something good has happened, I can tell that
from your face, Tatita."

"Yes, I can breathe freely at last, the danger has passed over, and
in no way am I compromised. But listen, Chica, I like not that this
Don Marcelino come here so often. The Señor Evaña is a friend of
mine, and for friends of his my door is open, but with the family of
Don Roderigo I want no friendship. Doña Josefina told me to-day
that you had frequently met his daughter at her house, this is bad.
Do not forget that such friendships are not convenient."

CHAPTER X.

AMERICA FOR THE AMERICANS.

THAT evening Doña Constancia could not complain of being lonely at her quinta. At sundown Don Fausto Velasquez arrived in his carriage, bringing his whole family with him, and attended by Don Manuel Belgrano and Captain Asneiros, who rode. Soon after them came Don Roderigo and Colonel Lopez. Don Roderigo asked at once for Marcelino, and was greatly chagrined when he heard that he had left in the afternoon for the city, as he had seen nothing of him there, but his annoyance was not of long continuance; before it was quite dark two more horsemen passed along the road by the quinta gate to the stables, and Evaristo, who had been on the watch, came running back to the veranda, announcing them to be his brother and Don Carlos Evaña.

As these two came up to the house after dismounting, both of them looked grave; on Marcelino's face there was even a deep shade of sadness. But Don Roderigo was in exuberant spirits, and warmly embraced his son.

"Evaristo was too quick for me," he said. "I had planned to set you free myself as the crown to the day's work. But you are free, and I have arranged it all; you will receive no more annoyance on that subject."

Then he gave his hand cordially to Evaña, saying—

"Ah! Carlos, at last you have emerged from your seclusion. I welcome you amongst us, we men of experience need the help of younger men like you. We will work together and between us raise up a new Spain in America, with laws and customs fitted to a new world, now that the old Spain is tottering to her fall."

Then Evaña, looking upon the smiling face, listening to the cordial words of Don Roderigo, felt for the first time doubt of the practicability of his own schemes, fear for the success of his darling project, a Republic of Argentines.

"A new Spain in America, with laws and customs fitted to a new world!" said he to himself, "what is this? Can Spaniards be freemen? Can Spaniards and Argentines live together as equals under the free laws of a new Spain?"

His heart was troubled; he walked away by himself under the trees, turning this matter over and over in his mind, and finding no solution to this fresh problem which was based upon the, to him, new idea, that tyranny and injustice were not essential ingredients in the charac-

ter of a Spaniard. As he walked to and fro in the dim twilight a
small hand was laid upon his arm, and a voice he loved to hear, spoke
to him in words soft and low.

"Don Carlos, what are you doing here all alone? You have not
been inside even to speak to us, and I have so much to say, so much
to thank you for, and mamma too, she has been asking for you. How
nobly you have kept your promise. We have heard all about it now,
Don Fausto and the Señor Belgrano have told us what you did
yesterday."

To all that she said Evaña answered not one word, but he took
her hand in his and side by side they walked together under the trees
in the dim twilight, she talking on, telling of her joy at seeing her
brother once more free, and of her certainty that now all would go
well, and that there would be no more talk of quarrels between
Spaniards and Creoles. Had not her father said so? And to Dolores
that which her father said was truth unquestioned. As Evaña listened
to her, her voice was to him as the rippling of waters, a music soothing the trouble of his soul, yet of what she said he knew nothing,
for his thoughts were far away peering into the dark future, which
seemed darker than ever from the veil which had been thrown over
it by the words of Don Roderigo.

As Evaña walked away Don Roderigo took his son by the hand
and led him inside, where his mother embraced him, chiding him
tenderly for having left her, and the others crowded round, overwhelming him with congratulations.

Eagerly they talked together recounting the events of the day past
and of the day now closing, of most of which Marcelino was entirely
ignorant. As they talked to him his sadness and his anxiety vanished, his face flushed with a proud joy, it seemed to him that the
work was already accomplished, that he was already a free citizen of
a free people, that the power of Spain was broken for ever in Buenos
Aires, that the bonds of Spanish rule were burst asunder, never more
to fetter the energies of a young nation.

Then as he looked upon his father, whose face and words were
joyous as those of the others, and to whom all ascribed the credit of
having by his foresight and intrepidity prevented a murderous struggle,
his heart smote him that he had been unjust towards him. His heart
yearned towards him, prompting him to confess his mistake and to
beg forgiveness. He rose from his seat beside his mother and went
to him, taking him by the arm and leading him out from the brilliantly-
lighted sala to the veranda.

"Forgive me, Tata," he said; "I have been unjust to you in my
thoughts. I looked upon you as one of them and you are one of us.
I even thought that it was to you that I owed my imprisonment, and
accused you of cruelty to me and want of confidence. Forgive me."

"Right willingly I forgive you, my son," replied Don Roderigo;
"your fault is nothing more than the inexperience of youth. I did
not imprison you, but I could have procured your release sooner had
I been able to trust in your discretion. You are an enthusiastic
partisan of Don Santiago Liniers, and if affairs had gone badly you
might have seriously compromised yourself for his sake, and all to no

purpose. I warn you that this Liniers is not the man you think him, but I tell you he will not rule much longer. The failure of this conspiracy will greatly increase my influence, and I trust that native Argentines will so support me that that influence may be exercised for the welfare of us all. We who are Spaniards must give up our old traditions of conquest and domination, and young Argentines must indulge no more in senseless dreams of republican equality. So, all may yet go well with us, and we may form a free and united people."

"Ah! father, that is just my wish, as I have said to you long ago," rejoined Marcelino. "If the Princess Carlota——"

"Do not speak to me of her," said Don Roderigo, interrupting him; "that scheme is quite inadmissible. Ferdinand VII., though in a French prison, is King of Spain and the Indies."

As Don Roderigo spoke his eye fell upon his daughter and Don Carlos Evaña, who passed near them walking side by side, the low murmur of the girl's voice falling indistinctly upon his ear.

"See," said he, "there is the master spirit of the new generation. He is your dearest friend, may he not also be to me a son? With two such sons to help me I have no fear of the future."

Then Don Roderigo laid his hand upon his son's shoulder leaning upon him, and Marcelino followed with his eyes those two forms which glided slowly along side by side under the trees, seen only by the light of the stars of heaven which twinkled down upon them through the overarching foliage. On the face of Don Roderigo there was hope and confidence, but on his son's there was doubt. His thoughts carried him back to an evening months gone by, when he had stood with Evaña and his sister at the end of the long avenue of the poplar trees, watching the setting of the sun, an evening on which he had seen sorrow and pity in his sister's face as she had looked upon his friend, an evening on which that friend had called him "brother."

As they stood there watching, Dolores saw them and, leaving Evaña, ran gaily towards them. Her father opened his arms to her, and kissing her fondly led her with him back to the sala, while Marcelino walked away and joined his friend under the trees. Passing his arm through his—

"Are you my brother?" he asked him.

"Most certainly I am," replied Evaña.

"And his son?"

"Never."

It was past midnight, most of the household lay asleep, but in one inner room lights were still burning, and the window and the door thrown wide open let in a constant draught of the cool night air, causing the lights to blaze unsteadily, and filling the room with flickering shadows. Here four men sat at a small table talking together in low tones. On the table stood a tall glass jug half full of claret, and several goblets.

"I knew nothing of it," said Don Carlos Evaña.

"Where have you been all day that at this hour you come to learn what is old news to all the city?" said Colonel Lopez.

"I remained in my room all day, and saw no one till Marcelino came."

"And the idea of last night, what came of it?"

"Nothing. It was a dream, and as a dream it vanished. I thought to do something with Liniers. I proposed to him to join us. With his great popularity to secure union among us, we might at once have declared our independence, and have achieved it without a struggle. He refused, and the victory of yesterday is sterile."

"From him we can hope nothing," said Marcelino. "Even my father says so, and my father says more yet—he says that his power is nearly at an end."

"Your father does not speak without knowledge," said Don Manuel Belgrano, who was the fourth man present; "without doubt they will send us a new Viceroy from Seville."

"The power is in our hands now," said Marcelino; "what we have to study is the means of keeping it. Such Spaniards as Don Martin Alzaga we can look upon in no other way than as enemies, but all Spaniards are not as he. Spaniards there are who would willingly join us in building up a new Spain, where the will of the people shall be the law of the State, and the welfare of the people the first object of government."

"Dreams!" said Evaña.

"A dream as yet, but it may become a reality," rejoined Marcelino. "To conciliate such Spaniards we must maintain our connexion with the Old World, and we must abstain from startling novelties and from rash experiments which may lead us no one knows where."

"Your love for your father blinds you to the truth," said Evaña. "If in all the Viceroyalty there were to be found six Spaniards like Don Roderigo I would support you. The Spaniards who come here, come with but one object, to amass wealth by any means in their power, and then to go back. For us Creoles or for our welfare they care nothing."

"You say true," said Colonel Lopez, bringing his fist down upon the table with a force which made the glasses clatter together. "Whilst Spaniards govern, we are slaves. Out with the Spaniards, and all is possible for men who know that their country is their own."

Marcelino looked up in surprise at his uncle; never before had he heard him speak thus. But Evaña smiled, and from him Marcelino turned away his eyes, for that smile was not one pleasant to look upon—there was no mirth, no joy, in it, nothing but fierce resolve.

"My correspondence with Rio Janeiro has not inspired me with any great hope of good from the Princess Carlota," said Belgrano, "but I would willingly make great sacrifices to keep among us such men as Don Roderigo, and I do not agree with Evaña that there are no other Spaniards like him, I believe there are many."

"There is but one sacrifice necessary," said Marcelino. "Some of us dream of an independent republic, we must give that up. When you write again to Rio state positively that we demand a 'Cabildo Abierto.' If the Princess yield that, all is possible. We shall have a new Spain, in which the majority of the citizens and all the troops will be Argentines. What would you more, Carlos? We shall have the liberty of a republic and keep the stability of an ancient nation."

"Dreams!" said Evaña. "The Princess is a Spaniard, her advisers are Spaniards and priests."

"We want no Spaniards and no Bourbons," said Colonel Lopez, "we want a government of our own. Spaniards such as Don Roderigo, who have married into our families, and have property here instead of sending it to Spain, are of us, concerning them there is no question. But Spaniards who come from Spain to rule over us and plunder us, what know they of us, or what care we for them? Out with them! We are no longer slaves that we should obey them!"

"As I have said already," said Evaña, "the triumph of yesterday is sterile, and we have need of all our vigilance to prevent the loss of everything we have gained since the victory of the 12th of August."

"Let us watch then," said Marcelino, "and from time to time let us meet together to consult upon the events as they fall out."

"At last then you see the necessity of adopting my idea," said Evaña, "a secret committee."

"I did not say so," said Marcelino.

"Nevertheless it is necessary, my friend," said Don Manuel Belgrano.

"If it has come to that it is time that I retire," said the Colonel; "with secret societies I will have nothing to do. But remember, prepare you everything, and when the day comes leave the work to us, we want no civilians interfering with the troops."

So saying the Colonel poured himself out a goblet of water and left the room.

"He says right," said Marcelino, as he went out; "it is for us to prepare the work, for others to do it."

"We must not only prepare, but much we must do also," said Belgrano.

"Without doubt," said Evaña. "The people are accustomed to look to one central power, we will destroy the Spanish power, but we must put another in its place, a central power ruling by the will of the people. This power we must guide ourselves, but we must also hold ourselves ready to act at times as its instruments."

"If we are not careful we shall but substitute one despotism for another," said Marcelino.

"Without danger nothing is done," replied Evaña. "To discuss fully all these points, and to provide as far as we can against all these dangers, it is necessary that we form a secret committee. A secret committee is irresponsible, and its members are pledged to nothing, we will have but one tie between us, that of nationality, we must all be Argentines. Each man will give account to the others of all that he does for the common cause, will consult with them as to what he may purpose to do, and will know where to look for aid in any event that may befall in which the co-operation of others is requisite."

"Who do you propose to invite to join us?" asked Belgrano.

"If you will both join me the committee is formed at once, then we may consult together as to whom we shall invite."

"I refuse no longer, I see that it is necessary," said Marcelino.

"I will join you also," said Belgrano.

"The first I propose to invite," said Evaña, "are Nicolas Rodriguez Peña, Francisco Passo, and Berruti."

"And Dr. Vieytes," said Belgrano; "his house will be a good point of reunion for us."

"And I propose Juan José Passo, Donado, and Miguel Yrigoyen," said Marcelino.

"I think all those will join us," said Evaña.

"All of them think as we do," said Marcelino; "all demand the liberation of our country from foreign domination; but even among so few there are many opinions as to the means of doing it. What plan of action do you propose in which we may all combine?"

"I propose nothing, the time has not yet come," replied Evaña. "One idea unites us, America for the Americans, let that suffice us for the present."

"America for the Americans," said Belgrano; "let that be our watchword."

Then the three stood up joining hands across the table, repeating together that watchword which expressed more fully than any other words could do, the crude plans and ill-defined aspirations of the new generation—

"America for the Americans."

BOOK V.

THE DAWN OF FREEDOM.

PART II.

THE MISTS OF THE EARLY MORN.

PROLOGUE.

THE vacillations of a youth are by no means a sign of instability. An unknown world opens up before him, at every step he meets some object, to him, full of novelty. When a prize seems within his grasp he draws back his hand and turns away to enquire into the substance of some fleeting shadow, which seems to him to have all the solidity of a grave reality. Disappointments fall upon him, and he loses much that was easily attainable in the pursuit of intangible myths. Yet are these disappointments no loss, they are the lessons by which his ignorance is cleared away, and he grows in knowledge as he grows in years. These disappointments are experience, without which no lesson is perfect.

When the beams of the yet invisible sun brighten the sky in the east, men know that the day is at hand. Yet do these beams often raise up mists from earth, moist with the dews of night, which cover their brilliance as with a veil, throwing out a new shadow of darkness; but that darkness is not of the night, it is the herald of the day. Behind that veil rises up the sun, soon to dissipate those shadows, bathing the earth in the full effulgence of his glory.

CHAPTER I.

THE TWO VICEROYS.

THE Señor Don Ciriaco Asneiros was far from satisfied with the part he had taken in the affair of the 1st January. To him there remained no doubt that he had been the dupe of Doña Josefina. On the evening of the 2nd January he rode out to the Quinta de Ponce, determined to come to some explanation with her. She, confident in her own power of fascination, was ready enough to give him the interview he sought, and soon succeeded in soothing his resentment. As they sat under the veranda together she spoke to him of Magdalen.

"Why do you not marry, Don Ciriaco?" said she to him; "if you were to marry your position would be secure."

"Señora, you know well——"

"Of folly I wish to know nothing, Don Ciriaco; be wise and listen to me. What you require is a rich wife; I can get you one. What think you of Magdalen Miranda?"

"The Inglesita!"

"Why not?"

"Think you that I have no eyes, Señora? For Don Marcelino there is no other in the world."

"Marcelino!" exclaimed Doña Josefina, interrupting him. "Have you also that folly in your head? Even though Marcelino worships the ground she steps on he can never marry her. I know you have great regard for Marcelino; believe me you would be doing him a service if you would help to cure him of that folly."

"You said to me, Señora, a rich wife; the old medico is as poor as a rat."

"So they say," replied Doña Josefina, "but I know that when Don Alfonso came here he was rich; it is only a few days since that Fausto told me so. You must not mention this to any one, but when his daughter marries, it will be found out what he has done with his wealth."

"The medico would not have me for a son-in-law, he hates Spaniards," said Don Ciriaco.

"Don Alfonso fears everything; every one who can protect him is his friend. Who can protect him better that the favourite of the Viceroy? Leave that to me." So saying Doña Josefina rose from her chair, and tapping her protegé on the head with her fan glided away.

Don Ciriaco gave but a passing thought to this proposition of Doña Josefina. The man in whose opinion he wished to stand high was Don Roderigo Ponce de Leon. He knew him to be a bitter enemy of Don Alfonso; no alliance with the medico could thus be thought of for one moment. As he so pondered, sitting alone under the

U

veranda, Don Roderigo came out from the house, and, seating himself in the chair lately vacated by Doña Josefina, entered into conversation with him.

"His Excellency the Viceroy has told me," said Don Roderigo, "that you led the Andaluces to his support solely for the purpose of procuring the release of my son."

"It is true," replied Asneiros.

"It was a mistake," said Don Roderigo; "but we will say no more of it. I do not doubt your loyalty to Spain, and I have come to put it to the proof. I have heard from Doña Josefina that you are on intimate terms with the family of Don Alfonso Miranda. Are you aware who he is?"

"I know nothing of him, Don Roderigo," replied Asneiros; "I have met him sometimes at the house of Don Fausto, that is all."

"I have been misinformed then, and I am sorry; your acquaintance with him might have been of great service to me."

"How? I will do anything I can to be of service to you, as you know, Don Roderigo."

"You can be of service only if you are intimate with him, and visit frequently at his quinta."

This conversation was prolonged far into the night, and resulted in the establishment of a complete understanding between the grandee and the soldier, one immediate result of which was, that Don Ciriaco Asneiros received his commission as major before a week had elapsed.

Don Carlos Evaña had received the congratulations of Don Roderigo Ponce de Leon upon his debut as a politican with great coldness. He seemed to have no wish to distinguish himself further in that way, but he surprised many of his friends by adopting a new pursuit, one for which he had in former years shown great distaste; he became a sportsman.

The one business of his life seemed to be to plan excursions into the country for shooting or fishing. On these expeditions he never went alone, Marcelino Ponce de Leon was frequently with him, Don Manuel Belgrano more frequently still, and there were others, such as the Passos, Don Juan José and Don Francisco, Don Nicolas Rodriguez Peña, Don Miguel Yrigoyen, Don Antonio Beruti, and Don Agustin Donado, some of whom were always of the party. Their favourite point of meeting when starting on these expeditions was at the house of Dr. Vicytes in the Calle Venezuela.

Often during the heat of the day when on these expeditions did they seek shelter under the hospitable roof of Don Roderigo at the Quinta de Ponce; not unfrequently, as the season advanced and partridge and snipe flocked to the "bañados de Flores," which are situate about two leagues west of the city, they would spend an hour or two on their return at the quinta of Don Alfonso Miranda.

These excursions seemed to afford to them all great pleasure, they looked forward to them and spoke of them with eagerness, as though they were events of the greatest importance, yet withal the trophies of their prowess were but meagre, and it was no unfrequent chance for them to return with empty bags. Partridges whirred up in front of them, the snipe piped his shrill cry and hovered before them, then flew away unharmed. If they went fishing it not rarely happened that some unlucky fish would hook and have full leisure to unhook himself again, ere the careless fisherman found that the bait was gone. They were but poor sportsmen after all, though so enthusiastic.

Dolores had many a laugh at them, telling them that she feared they would fare but badly if they had to depend for food upon their own exertions. And one day when Don Carlos took Magdalen a brace of snipe, after a long day's sport in the bañados, she held them up, one in each hand, saying merrily—

"Poor little things, how clever you must be! It took six men with guns all day long to catch you!"

In fact, during these excursions the shooting and the fishing occupied but a very small portion of their time, most of it was taken up in conversation. In knots of two or three, or all in one group, they would sit for hours by the side of a stream or under the shade of some clump of trees, talking together. Their talk was of the events of the day, and of the influence of these events upon the future. These friendly sportsmen formed in reality a secret committee; one watchword they had among them—

"America for the Americans!"

But of the meaning of this phrase there were as many opinions among them as there were speakers.

During the year 1809, to the end of which these sporting excursions continued, events succeeded each other with great rapidity. Each event as it fell out was followed by an excursion, during which all its bearings were discussed under the free air of heaven; if any acquaintance chanced to join them, discussion ceased, and their talk was solely of their sport.

Don Manuel Belgrano had taken a very prominent part in the affair of the 1st January, his conduct gained him the confidence of the Viceroy, who after that day began to consult him on many occasions. One of the chief difficulties of the Viceroy was the empty state of the treasury, the consequence of his lavish expenditure. For this Don Manuel Belgrano set himself to work to devise a remedy, and found it in free trade.

The restrictions imposed upon commerce by the Spanish colonial system paralyzed the productive industries of her colonies. Their trade was restricted to certain channels, marked out by the Consulado of Cadiz. The ports of Monte Video and Buenos Aires were closed to foreign merchants and to foreign ships.

Belgrano proposed to throw open the port of Buenos Aires to English ships and to invite English merchants to settle there, satisfied that a brisk trade would soon spring up, upon which a revenue might be levied ample for all the purposes of Government. With the approval of the Viceroy, he proceeded to draw up an extensive memorial on the subject. Previous to submitting it to the Viceroy himself, he wished to discuss it in detail with the members of the secret committee. In April a shooting excursion was planned to the neighbourhood of Quilmes; Don Manuel Belgrano was of the party, carrying his memorial with him.

It was evening, most of the sportsmen had returned to the city, but two of them, Don Carlos Evaña and Don Manuel Belgrano, rode off together to the Quinta de Ponce.

" Marcelino was not with you to-day," said Doña Constancia, as she sat with her two guests under the veranda.

" No, he could not leave the city," replied Don Carlos ; " I shall see him to-morrow, have you any message for him ? "

" You will not have to wait till to-morrow, for here he comes," said Dolores, jumping up from her chair as a horseman passed along the road, and walking away to greet him as he dismounted.

" Is Carlos here ? " asked Marcelino, as he walked with his sister to the house after giving up his horse to a slave.

" Yes, and Don Manuel Belgrano," said Dolores ; " they did not expect you, they said you were too busy to leave the city."

" I have news. I could not have slept to-night if I had not seen Carlos to tell him."

" It is good news, I can see that by your face. Is Juan Carlos coming back ? "

" No, but some one has come."

" Who ? "

" Guess."

" The Princess Carlota ? "

" No such luck. But what do you know of the Princess Carlota ? "

" Oh ! I know things. I know more than you think."

" Then as you are so wise I will tell you. A new Viceroy has come out from Spain."

" A new Viceroy ! " exclaimed Dolores ; then breaking from him she ran before him to the veranda.

" Mamma ! " said she, " great news, there is a new Viceroy, who has come out from Spain. Now we shall be all quiet again, there will be no more quarrels, papa said so, don't you remember ? "

As she spoke, Don Carlos started to his feet, and Don Manuel Belgrano, biting his lip, pressed his hand upon the breast of his coat, in the pocket of which there was a thick roll of paper.

Marcelino, bending over his mother, kissed her, and then turned to shake hands with his two friends, who stood silent, waiting for him to speak.

" It is true," he said, as he held their hands in his. " Last week Don Baltazar Hidalgo de Cisneros arrived in Monte Video, bringing his appointment by the Junta of Seville as Viceroy of Buenos Aires. When I tell you that Don Martin Alzaga is already his confidential friend I tell you all."

" Don Martin Alzaga ! But he is in Patagones," said Doña Constancia.

" He was, mamita," said Marcelino ; " but his exile was short. Elio sent an armed vessel to rescue him and the others ; he has been living at his ease in Monte Video for nearly a month now."

" My God ! Is there then war between us and Monte Video ? "

" Not now, Señora," said Evaña. " This new Viceroy of ours will doubtless soon bring us all to order and make us all good friends again."

As he spoke, another horseman came up the road, and, dismounting at the gate, threw his reins over a post, and walked up the narrow pathway to the house. It was Don Roderigo.

The three younger men stood in silence waiting for him, their anxiety visible in their faces.

"Ah! Marcelino has been before me," said Don Roderigo cheerfully. "You know the news already."

"Yes," replied Don Manuel Belgrano. "How long has this new Viceroy been in Monte Video?"

"A week. The north winds have kept the news from us till now. He was expected in Colonia to-day."

"Then to-morrow, or the next day, we may expect him here," said Evaña.

"And the Junta of Monte Video?" asked Belgrano.

"It is dissolved."

"And the members imprisoned for their rebellion against the legal authority?" asked Belgrano.

"No," replied Don Roderigo slowly; "they have not been imprisoned. Their proceedings were ill-judged, but they were actuated by a regard for the interests of their country, they cannot be considered as criminals."

"And now they will be the counsellors of our new Viceroy," said Marcelino. "That may not be, Liniers will not give up his authority to men who have shown themselves to be his enemies."

"Quietly, my son," said Don Roderigo, as Doña Constancia looked up in alarm at Marcelino's indignant words. "Liniers is a loyal servant of Spain, though he is a Frenchman; he will yield at once his authority to a successor legally appointed by the Junta Central."

"Liniers holds his authority from the King of Spain; when the Junta Central have re-established the King, then the King may cancel an appointment which the King made," said Marcelino.

"The appointment of Liniers came from the people," said Evaña. "Are the people to have no voice in this matter?"

"Liniers has told me of the memorial in favour of free trade, which you had promised to draw up for him," said Don Roderigo, turning to Belgrano, "it will now be useless so far as he is concerned, but if you will oblige me with a copy of it I will take care that it be submitted to the attention of the new Viceroy."

"With much pleasure, Don Roderigo," said Belgrano. "Within two days you shall have a copy, and believe me, that if this Don Baltazar de Cisneros seeks the real welfare of the country, he cannot inaugurate his rule better than by opening our ports to foreign trade."

"I am perfectly of your opinion, Don Manuel," replied Don Roderigo; "and with a Spanish Viceroy, reforms are possible which could not be entertained under the rule of a foreigner."

"You have probably seen Don Santiago Liniers to-day," said Evaña. "Does he himself announce his intention of yielding his authority into the hands of this new Viceroy?"

"He does. Of that there could be no question," replied Don Roderigo.

After some further conversation Don Roderigo and Doña Constancia retired into the house, and the three friends walked away from the veranda to the gate, where they paused, looking up and down the road and around them, to make sure that no one was within hearing. Evaña was the first to speak.

"America for the Americans!" said he. "Now has come the time, my friends, for us to put our principles to the test. If this Spaniard lands, we shall lose every advantage we have gained."

"I am not surprised that Liniers should declare his intention of yielding at once," said Belgrano. "He always yields to the first counsellor who gains his ear. He has shown great confidence in me for several months past, I will go to him to-morrow, and I think I can persuade him to put himself at the head of the people."

"You are aware that he rejected a similar proposal from me?" said Evaña.

"If he yield to Cisneros he signs his own death-warrant," said Marcelino. "He was in no such danger then."

"I shall show him his danger," said Belgrano, "and we must also devise means to prove to him that the people and the troops will support him."

"I can manage that easily, by a popular demonstration," said Evaña.

"I have also another piece of news to tell you, of which my father knows nothing," said Marcelino. "A gentleman, who is nominally travelling for amusement, has to-day arrived from Rio Janeiro, he has brought me a letter from Don Saturnino, his name is Don Felipe Contucci. He brings for you, Belgrano, an autograph letter from the Princess Carlota, he is in reality an emissary of hers."

"Bah!" exclaimed Evaña. "Unless we concentrate all our energies upon one object, we lose everything."

But Marcelino and Belgrano looked at each other, and each read the thought of the other in his glance. There was hope yet of reconciling all differences, and of founding a new Spain in America.

The news of the appointment and arrival of a new Viceroy spread rapidly through Buenos Aires, rousing in the Spaniards hope that their dominion had not yet passed away from them; awakening in the breasts of native Argentines something of fear, for the glamour of centuries is not to be effaced by a year or two of light.

Days of doubt and hesitation succeeded; the new Viceroy approached Buenos Aires with the greatest caution, sending emissaries before him to prepare the people for his coming, and to sound the disposition of the leading citizens and of the troops. When he at last reached Colonia it was with such an escort, as would have befitted a general advancing upon the capital of an enemy. Then Liniers declared openly that he had not the slightest intention of opposing in any way the will of the Junta of Seville and would himself aid the new Viceroy to establish his authority. These words of the Reconquistador were sedulously spread about the city and roused the indignation of the people. They thronged the street in which stood the private residence of their chosen leader, shouting that they would have none other than him to rule over them, and calling upon him to come forth and speak to them.

"You hear the shouts of the mob?" said Don Roderigo Ponce de Leon, who was at that moment with the Viceroy. "As loud as that will they shout '¡ Viva Cisneros!' when Don Baltazar thinks fit to cross the river."

Then went out Don Santiago Liniers onto his balcony and spoke to the people such words as seemed fittest to quiet them, caring nothing what pledges he might take in their esteem, thinking nothing of the trust they placed in him. To him they listened, and as he concluded by requesting them to disperse, they tossed their hats in the air, shouting again—

"¡ Viva Don Santiago Liniers! No queremos otro Virey. Viva!"
Then acceding to his request, each man retired to his own home.

Marshal Don Santiago Liniers standing on his balcony, looking at them as they slowly dispersed, listening to their shouts and cries of confidence and trust, words which he was never more to hear, was aware of a tall man leaning against a door-post some fifty yards off, watching him intently. From this man he could not withdraw his eyes, he felt attracted to him by some deadly fascination for which he could not account, yet there was nothing peculiar in the attitude of this man.

"Don Roderigo," said the Viceroy, stepping back into the room behind him, "look here one moment, tell me if you know this man?"

Don Roderigo stepped onto the balcony and looked over into the street, but the man had left his post and was walking slowly away with his back towards them.

"Is not that Evana?" said the Viceroy.

"Evaña? impossible!" replied Don Roderigo. "There is nothing for which Evaña has greater contempt than for the shouts of a mob." And so saying he went back and looked no more.

But Liniers lingered on the balcony, still fascinated by the slowly receding figure of the tall man who had looked at him so intently. He watched him till he reached a corner, turned it, and vanished from sight. But it seemed to the Viceroy that, as he vanished, he turned once more to look at him, and raised his hand in angry menace toward the evening sky.

Still borne on the evening air from neighbouring streets came the shouts of the citizens slowly dispersing to their homes—

"¡ Viva Don Santiago Liniers! No queremos otro Virey. Viva!"

Listening to these shouts, the Viceroy then turned his gaze to the evening sky toward which that figure had raised its threatening hand. To the west, where the sun had sunk below the horizon, the sky was covered by broad bands of scarlet and yellow, two of scarlet with one of yellow between them, and over these there hung a dark, black cloud, sinking lower and lower, till the crimson glories of the sunset faded away into the darkness. Over that dark cloud the sky was of the purest blue, and straight before him in the midst of it there shone one brilliant star.

Clutching the rail of the balcony with both hands, the Viceroy gazed upon this star, and as he gazed, again through the evening air there came the sound of voices shouting from far off, in accents clear and distinct, his own name. He thought of what he was about to do; again he thought of the people who had placed their destinies in his

hands, and a sort of dreamy hallucination fell upon ; he forgot that he
was in Buenos Aires, he forgot that he was Viceroy, again in memory
he stood in the streets of Paris as he had stood in his fyouth, and the
shouts changed from acclamations to yells of deadly menace—

"Ça ira ! Les aristocrats à la lanterne."

He shivered, an unknown terror seized upon him, he averted his rapt
gaze and turned back quickly into the room. Walking to a side table,
he filled a goblet with wine and drained it at a draught. As he filled the
goblet, his hand trembled so that he spilled some of the wine upon the
table, whence it flowed upon the uncarpeted floor; the rays of a lamp
falling over the spot lighted up the drops of wine as they trickled
slowly from the table, falling upon the floor in great red splashes like
drops of blood. Liniers started back covering his face with his hands.

" What is the matter with you, Don Santiago?" said a friendly voice
in his ear. " Let us dine, for all is ready and we have no time to lose."

Two hours after nightfall three men, muffled in large cloaks, left the
fort by the postern gate, and walked away towards the beach, where a
boat awaited them. He who walked in the centre was Don Santiago Liniers ; they who attended him were Don Roderigo Ponce de
Leon and Don Martin Rodriguez, confidential friends, who had
counselled him to set at nought the will of the people, who had made
him Viceroy. The three men reached the boat without molestation,
stepped into it, and were rowed to a small armed vessel, which immediately weighed anchor, spread her sails to the wind, and steered for
Colonia.

The next morning, as Don Baltazar de Cisneros, in a loose dressing-
gown, was imbibing his morning cup of coffee, an aide-de-camp came
hurriedly into the room, announcing the approach of the Señor
Mariscal Don Santiago Liniers. Cisneros started up from his chair,
in his alarm dropping his cup onto the floor.

" Liniers !" exclaimed he, " with what force ? "

"Two friends are with him," replied the aide-de-camp.

The next moment Liniers stood in the doorway, a smile curled his
lip as he saw the agitation of his rival, and the broken cup lying on
the floor at his feet. For a minute the two Viceroys stood looking
intently one at the other, then they mutually advanced, and opening
their arms embraced like brothers.

Some hours later Don Baltazar de Cisneros walked on the azotea of
his house in earnest conversation with Don Roderigo Ponce de Leon.

" I have been informed that I can place implicit confidence in
you," said Don Baltazar, "and that your counsel may be of great
service to me."

Don Roderigo bowed and replied—

"I trust I may merit your confidence, Don Baltazar, and it is not
unlikely that I may be of service to you. I have lived half my life in
Buenos Aires, and am intimately acquainted with most of the leading
citizens. In any way in which I can aid you, you may securely count
upon me."

" So I was given to understand before I left Spain," answered Don
Baltazar. " I will give you a proof of my confidence by telling you

my secret instructions and asking your advice as to how I can carry them out. In the first place I am instructed to send Liniers under arrest to Spain, and to disarm the native militia of Buenos Aires. I see great difficulties in the way of accomplishing either of these two clauses in my instructions."

"They are neither of them to be thought of at present," said Don Roderigo. "Don Santiago Liniers is immensely popular, not only in Buenos Aires, but throughout the provinces; his arrest would provoke an open rebellion against which we should be powerless. You must make use of his popularity to establish your own authority, and at the same time seize every opportunity of undermining that popularity, which is a great source of danger to us. To disarm the militia is at present a simple impossibility, thanks to the thick-headedness of Don Martin Alzaga."

"What steps would you then advise me to take? You say that the excitement of the populace in Buenos Aires is so great that it would hardly be safe for me to cross the river?"

"Your presence in Buenos Aires would ruin everything. I would advise you to send a delegate in your name to take command of the troops, and leave the nominal authority for a time in the hands of Don Santiago Liniers. In a month or two, when this excitement has cooled down, you may safely come to us, and you will find everything prepared for your reception."

"Ha! Don Santiago," said Cisneros, as Liniers ascended to the azotea and came towards them, "I have been talking with Don Roderigo, and find that his opinion is the same as yours, that it would be unsafe for me to cross over to Buenos Aires as yet."

"Your Excellency may have perfect confidence in the wisdom of any advice given you by Don Roderigo," said Liniers.

"Not less confidence than I have in your experience and loyalty, Don Santiago," replied Cisneros. "Your services are highly appreciated in Spain, and it will be a fresh claim upon the liberality of the Junta if you will consent to retain your office for a month or two longer, by which time you will be able to smooth matters sufficiently for me to assume the reins of government myself."

"I fear your Excellency overrates my influence with the citizens of Buenos Aires."

"Not in the least, Don Santiago," said Don Roderigo; "I have explained the matter to his Excellency, and we have both the fullest confidence in you. It is to you alone that the Junta can look for the establishment of its authority in Buenos Aires."

"The Junta will have no cause to find their confidence misplaced," replied Liniers.

Two days after this, Don Santiago Liniers returned to Buenos Aires, taking with him General Nieto, who held a commission from the new Viceroy as commandant-general of all the forces of Spain in the viceroyalty of Buenos Aires.

The two Viceroys separated with great cordiality on both sides, and with mutual expressions of esteem and confidence.

CHAPTER II.

THE return of Marshal Liniers to Buenos Aires, quieted the excitement of the people, which had risen to a dangerous pitch, but did nothing to allay the distrust of Liniers which was felt by the members of the secret committee.

A shooting excursion was at once planned by Don Carlos Evaña to the bañados of Flores. On this occasion not one member of the committee was absent. Seated under a clump of trees close to a deserted rancho, their guns unloaded, their dogs lying lazily stretched out in the sunshine, they discussed the topic of the day, the avowed intention of Marshal Liniers to surrender his power into the hands of Don Baltazar de Cisneros, the assumption by General Nieto of the command of the native troops.

The sun was sinking towards the horizon, when their dogs became uneasy, and, leaving them, went up to the deserted rancho, snuffing round the walls, some of them barking furiously.

" What is the matter with the dogs ? " said Evaña impatiently.

" An opossum or a skunk, or some such beast," said Belgrano.

" I'll have a look," said Beruti, starting to his feet.

Round the rancho he walked but could see nothing, while the dogs became more furious in their clamour. He tried the door but it was fast shut, and he could find no means of opening it.

" That door was open," said Marcelino, " when we came, for I went in and looked through the rancho, and it was empty."

" Let us go," said Dr. Vieytes. " It is late already, and I think we have decided that we can do nothing until we have secured the troops."

" I will first see what is in that rancho," said Evaña, taking up his gun.

Walking up to the door of the rancho he tried it, as Beruti had done before him. He could not open it, it was evidently fastened on the inside. He raised his gun in both hands and struck a furious blow with the butt upon the side-panel of the door. The stock of the gun broke short off. leaving a useless iron tube in his hands, but the door remained uninjured.

Perhaps it was as well for you, Don Carlos Evaña, that you did not succeed in bursting open that door. Behind it, in darkness, stood a man who held a cocked pistol in each hand. Had you crossed the threshold of that door, you would never have recrossed it alive.

"What are you doing, Carlos?" said Marcelino, seizing him by the arm. "Come, we have delayed here too long already."

"Come! come, Evaña!" shouted the others; "we may yet shoot a few birds as we go back."

"And we have need of special caution just now lest we excite suspicion," said Marcelino.

Evaña stooped, picked up the broken stock, and walked slowly away after the others, every now and then looking back upon the rancho, and never losing sight of it till they were free from the bañado and on the high road for the city.

"Do not let us go on to town yet; let us go to the quinta and see Magdalen," said Evaña to Marcelino, as they reached the Plaza Miserere. "I have forgotten how the tea tastes out of her porcelain cups."

"Let us go," rejoined Marcelino; yet his eye did not brighten as he acceded to the proposition of his friend, and something very like a sigh issued from his lips.

"My brother, you are sad," said Evaña, stretching out his hand and laying it upon his shoulder. "Do Magdalen's gray eyes look less kindly upon you than they did formerly?"

"Magdalen's gray eyes never look upon me now, Carlos. She shuns me; all our old intimacy is at an end. What I have done to offend her I do not know, for I have spoken to her and she refuses me any explanation."

"Let us follow the others," said Evaña.

"No, let us go on," replied Marcelino; "she will talk to you, and her voice is music to me still."

They found Magdalen alone, seated by the fireside, busily sewing. Her eyes brightened for a moment as they fell upon Don Carlos Evaña, who was the first to enter the room, but the light in them died away as she saw Marcelino enter behind him. In silence she stretched out her hand to each of them, without rising from her chair.

"Papa is in the quinta," she said, as they seated themselves without invitation. "Or perhaps he may have walked up the road to meet Don Ciriaco, who said he would be back before dark."

"Don Ciriaco comes very often to see you now," said Marcelino.

"He is more constant in his friendships than some gentlemen I know," replied Magdalen. "It is months since you were last here, Don Carlos."

"Not months, Señorita," replied Evaña, "but weeks; when I have been here I have generally met Don Ciriaco, who is a gentleman whose friendship I have no wish to cultivate."

"Papa and Doña Josefina think very highly of him, and they know him better than you do, Don Carlos. You have been out shooting to-day in the bañados, have you not? What did you shoot?"

"Nothing; I broke my gun, but the others have some birds in their bags."

"I was on the azotea, and saw you passing this morning. Did you not meet Don Ciriaco?"

"No. Did he go out shooting too?"

"Not when you did, but he came here in the afternoon, and when I told him I had seen you pass he said he would go and join you, but how he is to shoot without a gun I do not know. Papa offered to lend him his, but he went without it, and alone on foot."

To this Evaña answered nothing, but sat biting the ends of his moustache, while Marcelino twirled his hat round between his fingers, looking upon the ground in silence.

" If you had let me break open the door of that rancho we should have found a skunk inside," said Evaña.

" It is quite possible," replied Marcelino.

" A skunk !" said Magdalen. "And in a rancho ! If you had found one what would you have done with it ? "

" Shot him," replied Evaña.

Don Alfonso Miranda had walked up the road, but he returned alone, and Magdalen made tea for them in her porcelain cups. All the evening Marcelino and Evaña waited, at every sound they looked towards the door, and there was a constraint over them all, but Don Ciriaco did not come back, at which Magdalen expressed her surprise, but her father said nothing.

When their guests had at last taken their departure, Don Alfonso called to Magdalen to come and sit by him. She seated herself in her favourite low chair, and recommenced her sewing without making any remark. Presently her father spoke to her.

" This Don Marcelino does not often now trouble us with his presence, Chica," he said ; then he paused as though he expected a reply, but none came, and he continued—

" He seems almost as keen a sportsman as our friend Don Carlos, and when he is not shooting birds I suppose he has all his time pretty well taken up paying court to the fair Elisa. When a man chooses the prettiest girl in the city for his lady-love he does well to keep a strict watch on all rivals."

" Are they to be married soon ? " asked Magdalen, with the greatest composure.

" I know nothing about it, I never trouble my head with such matters," replied Don Alfonso. "Who told you that they were to be married ? "

" No one ; but Doña Josefina said one day——I don't know what she said, something, but what does it matter ? "

" It is about time for me to think of finding a husband for you, Chica."

" Oh ! don't say that, please don't, papa," said Magdalen, for the first time that evening showing any animation, " I don't want to marry."

" All girls say that," replied Don Alfonso, "but the most of them do marry for all that."

" Some don't," said Magdalen.

" And some find husbands for themselves, without waiting for their fathers to find them for them, as they ought to do. There is a gentleman comes here very often who does not come to see me. What do you think he comes here for, Chica ? " said Don Alfonso, with something of tenderness in his tone.

" I don't know what you mean, papa," said Magdalen, flushing scarlet.

" Ah ha ! Chica ! You think that we old folks have not our eyes about us. You know who I mean, you need not tremble, for I am not angry, for he is a gallant soldier, and if you would like him for a husband I should be proud to call him my son. You must not expect me to get a rich husband for you, for I am poor, very poor."

"But, papa, he does not often come here now, and——" here Magdalen stopped in confusion for she hardly knew what she was saying.

"Not come here often!" said Don Alfonso, laughing; "why he was here three times last week and again to-day. Do you want him to come every day, Chica?"

"Who are you talking about, papa? Here to-day! and three times last week, no one comes here so often but Don Ciriaco Asneiros."

"Don Ciriaco, the gallant major, who is winning his way up from grade to grade, who is the confidential friend of Marshal Liniers, and who will soon be one of the most powerful men in Buenos Aires. Of whom else should I speak but of him? Why does he come here so often if it is not to see you, and who is there that talks to you so much as he does?"

"Don Ciriaco!" exclaimed Magdalen, and she hung her head in bewilderment. It was true, as her father said, that he came very often, true also that when others were there he almost monopolized her conversation, but he had never given her the slightest reason to believe that he had any tender feeling for her, in fact he made no secret to her of his boundless admiration for her friend Dolores Ponce de Leon, and she had felt pity for him, and had shown it to him in many ways, for she saw that he had small hope that his love would ever be returned, and she thought herself that it was utterly impossible that it should be. So she had felt pity for him, and had shown him great sympathy and consideration, for was not she also indulging in a hopeless love. Now her father spoke to her of him as a possible husband. She thought of some jesting words which Doña Josefina had said to her not many weeks ago, concerning the success of a gallant soldier who both in war and in love carried everything before him. These words had dyed her own cheeks crimson, as she thought of a soldier who was to her the impersonation of all that was brave and noble, but could it be possible that Doña Josefina had meant quite another man, no other than this Don Ciriaco? Then she began to hate this Don Ciriaco, and to think of the awkward manners and of the rude speech which had made him a laughing-stock to the polished youth among whom she had first met him at the house of Doña Josefina.

Don Alfonso waited for a space to see what answer his daughter would give him, but as he got no further reply than that one exclamation, Don Ciriaco! he spoke again.

"And why not Don Ciriaco?" said he. "Why have you encouraged him to come here so often to see you if you are to be frightened when I speak about him?"

"Don Ciriaco, papa! Don Ciriaco never came here to see me. If no one else is here he always talks to you, and if he comes when you are out he always waits till you come back. He comes to see you, papa, he thinks much about you, he talks more to me about you

than about anything else. He seems never to be tired of listening
when I talk to him about you."

"About me!" exclaimed Don Alfonso, startled. "What can you
find to tell him about me?"

"Hundreds of things, papa. You have no idea what strange
questions he asks me at times."

"What questions? Tell me what questions he asks you?"

"If you are away he always asks me where you have gone to, and
how long you have been away, and when you will be back. And he
always wants to know all about every one who comes to see you,
especially about Don Carlos Evaña, and what he comes to see you
for, and what he talks to you about. Several times he has asked
me if you get any letters from Europe or from Rio Janeiro. I think
he is very rude to ask me such questions, I have told him so more
than once and have refused to answer him, but he will ask them, I
suppose he knows no better. Some of the young men at Doña
Josefina's used to call him the barbarian."

"And does he never speak to you about—about—does he never
talk love nonsense to you?"

"Never, papa, I assure you. If he had, I should have known
better than to listen to him."

Then Don Alfonso bowed his head on his hands and spoke no
more to his daughter, sitting motionless in his chair for more than an
hour, and when he at last raised his head, and rose from his seat to
retire to his own room, Magdalen saw again on his face that old
shadow of care and anxiety which had vanished from it during the
last few months.

"If not a tyrant, then a traitor, so is every Spaniard," said Don Alfonso, as Magdalen lifted up her face to his for a kiss before retiring.

As Magdalen lay down to rest, she buried her face in her pillow,
longing to cry, but the tears would not come. Her sleep was
troubled; in the morning she rose unrefreshed with a vague fear of
something dreadful impending. The day passed quietly, just as other
days did, and in the evening came Don Ciriaco, who was received
by Don Alfonso with more than usual cordiality, but Magdalen
pleaded a headache and hardly spoke to him at all.

A week after this, Doña Josefina Viana de Velasquez had one
evening a numerous company in her sala. The occasion was a
tertulia, an undress ball, given in welcome to her niece Constancia
who had returned to the city after spending the summer at her quinta.
At least such was the pretext announced for the tertulia, but Doña
Josefina and her husband Don Fausto were fond of indulging their
hospitable tastes and delighted to fill their rooms with young people,
and to give due scope to the flirting propensities of their friends,
flirtation being in the opinion of the lady the most important business
of life.

Some few days before this tertulia, she had paid a visit to Don
Alfonso Miranda at his quinta, and noticing that Magdalen looked
pale and out of spirits, had taken her back with her to spend some
days in the city.

This day of the tertulia was also the day for one of the shooting excursions of the secret committee, and Doña Constancia told her aunt that she did not think Marcelino would be there that evening. But Marcelino heard that day from Evaña that Magdalen was staying with Doña Josefina; he hurried back to town, determined not to lose such an opportunity of conversing at his ease with her, away from the watchful eyes and often sneering words of her father. For months he had missed the smile of welcome with which she had been wont to greet him, and report had told him that the heart which he had once fondly thought was his, had been given to another. He resolved to know all that evening, at the house of his aunt Josefina.

It was late when he entered the sala, the first person he met as he went in was Elisa Puyrredon. He and the fair Elisa had been play-mates together when they were children; his little playmate was now a beautiful woman, with whom romping games were things of the far-off past. Yet the frank cordiality of her friendship for him had left him nothing to regret.

One jesting compliment Marcelino exchanged with the fair Elisa, and then went up to salute his aunt.

"How cruel of you to leave Elisa to herself," said Doña Josefina; "do not you see they are just going to dance?"

"I have been shooting all day, aunt, I had rather talk to you than dance."

"Stupid!" said she.

But Marcelino hardly heard the remark, looking eagerly all round the large saloon for a face that he could not see, yet Magdalen, for whom he was looking, was close to him. She had seen him enter the room, seen him speak to Elisa Puyrredon, and had then retired into the deep recess of a window as he approached to speak with Doña Josefina.

"For whom are you looking? She is there where you left her," said Doña Josefina.

"Yes, I see she is, aunt, but she is going to dance with Valentin."

"With Valentin! I will soon arrange that for you. Give me your arm, I have been looking for Valentin all evening."

So Marcelino was walked off by his aunt, and presently found himself dancing with Elisa Puyrredon.

Don Ciriaco Asneiros had taken so much trouble to ingratiate him-self with Don Alfonso Miranda, and had succeeded so well by the as-sistance of Doña Josefina, that that lady made sure one of her schemes would end successfully. She was therefore greatly chagrined when she learned from Don Alfonso, on the occasion of her last visit to the Miserere, that her plan of marrying her protegé to Magdalen was likely to fall through. Don Alfonso had spoken to her vaguely of a certain distrust of the motives of Don Ciriaco for his repeated visits to the quinta, but Doña Josefina had found no great difficulty in laughing him out of his suspicions, she herself had no doubt whatever of the reasons which took that gallant officer so often to the Plaza Miserere. She had twitted him once or twice upon the subject, and all his answers had tended to prove to her, that he had quite given up any hopes he might ever have formed of winning the love of her niece

Dolores, and now thought only of Magdalen. Thus she treated him with greater favour than ever and began to take some real interest in him, for his manners had greatly improved under her tuition. He was high in favour with Marshal Liniers and with Don Roderigo Ponce de Leon, and General Nieto seemed to place great confidence in him; her pupil was evidently a man who would do her credit.

Of all this Doña Josefina was thinking to herself as she watched her nephew dancing with Elisa Puyrredon, flattering herself that she was managing very well for the happiness of all concerned.

"Once we dispose of Magdalen, all will come right," said she to herself; "even of Carlos I do not despair, though I confess both he and Dolores are a puzzle to me."

When this dance was over Marcelino left his fair partner and renewed his search for Magdalen, whom he found seated by herself, looking with lustreless eyes upon the gay scene about her. as though her thoughts were far away. His cordial words of greeting brought no smile to her face, to his questions she answered only in monosyllables, and when he asked her to dance she declined, saying that she was too tired. As he seated himself beside her, she rose, saying something about Doña Josefina, and went to where that lady was sitting and spoke to her.

"What nonsense, Niña," said Doña Josefina. "I did not bring you into town to mope by yourself in your room, you can do that at the quinta. Come, I know what you want, you have hardly danced at all, if you won't dance to please yourself you must dance to please me. Here is a great favourite of mine coming, I don't dance, you will dance with him for me, won't you?"

Before Magdalen could answer, Don Ciriaco Asneiros stood before her, bowing low and asking for her company in the next dance. Doña Josefina answered for her, and she felt obliged to go. As they took their place Don Ciriaco began talking to her of Dolores, a subject on which she was ever ready to listen, and more so now than ever, for she had not seen Dolores for months till that evening, and when she had met her, Dolores seemed strangely cold to her and had hardly spoken to her three words.

Marcelino remained in the dancing-saloon for some minutes exchanging salutations and compliments with such of his acquaintance as passed near him, but keeping his eye constantly upon one couple who were in earnest conversation together. He saw the dull, vacant look disappear from Magdalen's face, a faint colour came into her cheeks. and——he waited to see no more, he bowed his head as though in answer to some unspoken question, and with lips firmly pressed together left the room.

While the more youthful friends of Doña Josefina were amusing themselves by dancing, Don Fausto and some more particular friends of his, had retired to the dining-room. The large table running down the centre of this room was covered with salvers and dishes of sweetmeats, and with trays on which stood tall water-jars, surrounded by glass goblets of very varied design. Such was the refreshment provided by the abstemious Porteños for their friends on such an occasion as the present. In the intervals between the dances, servants waited upon the dancers, handing round these sweetmeats, which they eat from small plates with spoons, then other servants followed with the trays covered with goblets of water. Doña Josefina pressed the sweetmeats upon her friends, telling them that after eating they might drink water with safety. At one time during the evening chocolate was handed round, but there were no edibles of more solid description. On the dining-room table there were also jugs of claret, and bottles of the more fiery wines of Spain, but these were reserved for the use of such friends of Don Fausto as cared not for dancing.

When Marcelino entered the dining-room, Don Fausto with several of his friends were collected in a small knot at the end of the room; all looked round as he entered, and their conversation ceased.

"I give you welcome, Marcelino," said Don Fausto. "Shut the door and come here."

Don Fausto stood leaning against the table, in front of him sat Don Gregorio Lopez, beside him stood his son the Colonel, several others stood around. Don Juan Martin Puyrredon was speaking as Marcelino entered, and resumed as soon as the door was again closed.

"It comes to this," said he; "the excitement of the people has warned off our new Viceroy for a time, but that will pass. With the troops under the command of General Nieto, the influence of Marshal Liniers will be slowly undermined. Liniers himself has been cajoled by promises, the disorders in the interior will afford a pretext for the reorganization of Spanish troops. What say you, Señores? Are we to welcome this Cisneros amongst us, and give ourselves up again to the rule of such men as Elio and Don Martin Alzaga?"

"We have had enough of them," said Colonel Lopez. "Now has come the time for us to demand our due share in the administration. What want we with Viceroys who are sent from Spain? There are men amongst us who know well how to lead us if Don Santiago persists in retiring."

"Quietly, my son," said Don Gregorio, "without Spaniards there is no organization among us. Let us seek by every means in our power to conciliate such Spaniards as are friendly to us."

"We can do well enough without a Viceroy," said Don Juan Martin; "but we want experienced soldiers for our security, of whom there are many among the Spaniards; and we want a governing Junta, in which Spaniards of experience would naturally form the majority, but that the Junta of Seville should choose a Viceroy for us is, in my opinion, degradation to us."

"A Junta!" exclaimed Marcelino; "that was the idea of Don Martin Alzaga."

"And the idea was not a bad one if we had had no Viceroy, but at that time we had one," replied Don Juan Martin. "Don Santiago Liniers was then the legally-appointed representative of the King of Spain; but there is now no King in Spain. Each province in Spain has its Junta, we have an equal right to have a Junta of our own."

"Now that Liniers deserts us we remain without a legal head to the government," said Don Gregorio.

"In all the year of the English invasion we were in the same position, and it appears to me that we were none the worse for it," said Colonel Lopez.

Then others entered the room, and the conversation became more guarded.

When Marcelino returned to the sala he found his friend Evaña, who had told him that he was not going to the tertulia, standing in a doorway, strangely excited.

" I have been looking for you, I could not see you anywhere. Come with me, I have news for you, which I am afraid will pain you greatly, but I could not keep it from you." So saying Evaña led the way into a small ante-room where they could talk undisturbed.

" What was the name of the vessel in which our friend Gordon was about to sail for Lisbon, when he last wrote you?" asked Evaña.

" The sloop-of-war ' Petrel,' " replied Marcelino.

" I thought I was correct," said Evaña; then drawing an English newspaper from his pocket he added—

" I have just received this, read."

Marcelino took the paper and read the paragraph to which Evaña had pointed; as he read his eyes glazed over. He read an account of how H. B. M. sloop-of-war ' Petrel,' with a detachment of troops on board for the army then assembling at Lisbon, and with several officers, who were on their way to rejoin their regiments, had been totally lost on the coast of Galicia, two boats' crews only escaping. To this was appended a list of the names of the survivors. Eagerly Marcelino scanned that list, but the name of his friend Gordon was not among them. A strange calmness came over him; half an hour before he had felt wild and reckless under the pressure of a sorrow of his own, now he thought only of the sorrow this news would give to another, and that other, his own dearly-loved sister.

" Do not let any one see this paper, do not mention it to any one, it may not be true after all, he may have escaped."

Evaña tore the paragraph from the paper, and twisting it up, burned it in the flame of a taper.

In the ante-room Marcelino remained alone, moodily thinking of what he had heard and seen that evening; but Evaña returned to the sala, and seeking out Dolores was especially attentive to her, even once to her great surprise dancing with her. When he spoke to her his voice had a soft tenderness in it which she had never heard before. Don Gregorio Lopez and several others came and spoke with him, whispering to him that they had matter of much moment to impart to him, but he resisted all their attempts to draw him from her side. His thoughts were far from politics, far from all that had been hitherto the business of his life, he had given himself up to an intoxicating dream of love, he was a prey to the glamour of hope.

CHAPTER III.

LA JUNTA DE LOS COMANDANTES.

THE affair of the 1st January had resulted in giving Don Manuel Belgrano so much else to think of, that he left the project of inviting the Princess Carlota to Buenos Aires, very much in abeyance during the early months of the year, until the arrival of Don Felipe Contucci aroused his dormant zeal. He introduced Don Felipe to many of the leading citizens, and to such of them as were in his confidence, he unfolded the purpose of his visit. Above all he considered that it was necessary to gain the concurrence of Don Cornelio Saavedra, whose position at that time gave him an influence in Buenos Aires, second only to that of Marshal Liniers.

Many conferences had Belgrano and Saavedra together, in which the ideas of the latter underwent a gradual change, till Don Manuel became sanguine of ultimate success.

One evening in June Don Manuel Belgrano sat alone in his study, anxiously awaiting a visit from Don Cornelio, and prepared to concert with him some decisive step. His servant threw open the door, announcing—

"El Señor Don Juan Martin Puyrredon."

It was not he whom he expected, and his disappointment showed itself in his face.

"You are waiting for some one?" said Don Juan Martin.

"Yes, Don Cornelio Saavedra promised to visit me this evening," replied Belgrano. "I think I have at length persuaded him that the best solution of our differences will be to invite the Princess Carlota to take the supreme government of the Viceroyalty into her hands."

"There is no longer any question of the Princess," said Puyrredon. "At eleven o'clock this evening all the military commandants of the city, both Spanish and native, will meet at my house. It appears that this Cisneros will not much longer put off his arrival, Liniers will do nothing to hinder him. But he shall not come here, we have had enough of these Viceroys from Spain. To-night we meet to concert measures for a totally new order of affairs."

Belgrano started to his feet, his face glowing with animation. If the leaders of the troops were only united, there was no longer any impediment to the immediate assertion of independence.

"You invite me to join you?" he asked.

"I do. Your military rank entitles you to a place among us, and it is not sufficient that we have the soldiery with us, we also wish the concurrence of the people, in this you may give us most powerful aid. Marcelino Ponce de Leon has also promised to be with us."

"And Don Carlos Evaña, will he be there?"

"No, I have not asked him. There are many Spaniards with us, and Don Carlos will never agree cordially with any plan in which Spaniards are included."

Then the enthusiasm of Don Manuel cooled down considerably, yet he promised Don Juan Martin that he would be at his house at the hour he had named.

Puyrredon departed, and Belgrano was again alone, and so he remained, until it wanted little more than an hour of midnight, pondering deeply within himself. Native chiefs and Spanish soldiers, Evaña, who was as the soul of the fiery youth of Buenos Aires, shut out from the conference; from this what could result? Nevertheless, Belgrano had faith in the future of his own country, and having faith he hoped, and hoping he put on his hat and cloak and sallied forth through the darkness to the house of Don Juan Martin Puyrredon, who, as commandant of the cavalry on the 12th August, 1806, had won for himself a place in the first rank of the military leaders of Buenos Aires.

All the commandants of the city militia, many commandants of the cavalry of the campaña, several of the chiefs of the Spanish troops, which had been disbanded in January, and several of the leading citizens were there assembled; as also some whose only claim to be there was the distinction they had won during the two invasions of the English. Among these men were Don Marcelino Ponce de Leon, and his former lieutenant, Don Ciriaco Asneiros.

The presence of such Spaniards as Don Ciriaco introduced at once an element of discord into the conference. These men were ready to support any project, however extravagant, that might be proposed, but to the welfare of the country they gave not a moment's consideration; they thought only of their own advancement, and welcomed the idea of a civil war, in which they might sell their services to the highest bidder.

The conference had lasted two hours, and it seemed impossible for them to come to any understanding together, when Don Ciriaco stepped forward, and placing himself in front of Don Juan Martin Puyrredon said—

"Promise me the post of Inspector-general of arms, and I will guarantee to raise 2000 men in a week; I will cross over into the Banda Oriental, seize Monte Video, and will shoot Cisneros and Elio for you in the Plaza, then you can make whatever government you like."

Don Juan Martin started back as though he had been struck, and consternation was visible upon the faces of most of the native Argentines, but several of the Spaniards laughed.

"Traitor!" exclaimed Marcelino, seizing Don Ciriaco by the collar and drawing him back, "think you that we are assassins?"

The Spanish major laid his hand on his sword, but Don Manuel Belgrano stepped in between them.

"See you not, Marcelino," said he, "that this is a joke? This good gentleman wishes to show us that all the plans that have been proposed are alike impossible of fulfilment."

"A joke!" said Asneiros, turning sullenly away.

After this there was no more discussion, the conference broke up, and by twos or singly the members separated to their own homes.

Marcelino and Don Manuel Belgrano walked away together.

"If Evaña had been present we might have arrived at some resolution," said Marcelino; "but with these men of the sword it is useless to discuss anything."

"With Evaña it would have been impossible to come to any arrangement with the Spanish officers, and without their concurrence any plan we might devise would almost certainly entail a civil war," replied Belgrano.

"We might have striven to conciliate them, but to admit them to our conference was folly," said Marcelino. "What ideas have they but such as Don Ciriaco was bold enough to proclaim?"

"That was absurd; that was nothing but a joke," said Belgrano.

"A joke!" said Marcelino; "I fear me much some of us may find the whole affair something more than a joke."

When Don Ciriaco Asneiros left the conference he walked quietly away to his own quarters, but before sunrise, in the dress of a private soldier, he stood at the bedside of General Nieto.

The following afternoon Don Juan Martin Puyrredon was arrested in his own house and taken to the barracks of the Patricios, where he was placed in solitary confinement, and no one was allowed to visit him.

The news of this arrest spread consternation through the city, and brought sorrow and fear into many a household; to none more than into the household of the Señor Saenz-Valiente, whose wife, Doña Juana, was the sister of Don Juan Martin. That night and the next morning Marshal Liniers was besieged on all sides by applications for him to interfere and procure the release of the prisoner, but to all alike he turned a deaf ear. Even to Don Roderigo Ponce de Leon, who represented to him that he was likely to bring odium upon the rule of the new Viceroy, and so endanger the very existence of Spanish authority, he had but one answer, that the affair was none of his, and that doubtless General Nieto had sufficient reasons for what he had done, and would in due time declare them.

It was about two hours past noon when Don Roderigo left the Viceroy. Instead of going himself to tell Doña Juana of the non-success of his mission, he sought out his son, and commissioned him to tell her of it.

Marcelino found Doña Juana and her sister, with Doña Josefina and Doña Constancia, who had spent all the morning with them, sympathizing and encouraging their hopes, though every hour brought intelligence of some fresh failure. When Marcelino announced his message, their last ray of hope vanished, for if Don Roderigo could not prevail upon Marshal Liniers to interfere, they well knew that all other intercession was useless.

Elisa Puyrredon burst into tears, and Doña Constancia, bending over her, endeavoured in vain to soothe her, tears trickling down from her own eyes also, in sympathy. Doña Josefina clasped her hands tightly together, and composed herself into a most fascinating

attitude of despair, but Doña Juana listened as Marcelino spoke, in
tearless silence, as he paused she rose from her seat, tossing back
her head, and drawing up her stately figure to its full height.

"Now that the men can do nothing," said she, "it remains for us
to do what we can, and in our way. Will you accompany me, Marcelino?"

"With pleasure, Señora; it will be an honour for me to attend you
wherever you may choose to lead me."

Five minutes afterwards Doña Juana and Marcelino left the house
together. Three squares they walked in silence towards the Plaza
Mayor, then Marcelino made as though he would turn a corner,
saying—

"This way, Señora, is the shortest."

"No," replied the lady, "let us keep straight on."

"Are you not going to the fort?" said Marcelino.

"No, to the barracks of the Patricios."

The courtyard of the barracks was crowded with soldiers. In
addition to the detachment ordinarily on guard, nearly all the officers
of the regiment, and many officers from other native regiments, had
met there that afternoon to talk over the affair of the arrest, which
was the engrossing topic throughout the city. They were soldiers,
and were accustomed to obey orders without question. They had
lodged their prisoner in a strong room, posting sentries and guarding
him securely, nevertheless they liked not that their barracks should be
turned into a prison, and that they should be appointed gaolers over
one of the most distinguished of their fellow-citizens.

As they talked together, there stood in their midst a stately lady,
who looked round upon them with an air of great disdain. They
doffed their hats to her, and looked upon her with sympathizing eyes,
for many of them recognized her as the sister of the prisoner they
held in durance. But she still looked haughtily upon them and returned not their salutation, merely waving her hand to them to keep
silence.

"Fellow-citizens!" said she, "I have come among you to know if
that be true which men have told me of you. Men tell me that you
are no longer the gallant soldiers who in the day of danger stood foremost of all to confront the onset of a mighty foe, shedding your blood
and offering up your lives willingly in the defence of your homes and
fatherland. Men tell me that you are no longer the heroes on whom
your country can look with pride, to whom she may look with confidence for the securing of her rights and liberties. Men tell me that
you are now no more than the trained minions of a despot, and are
the gaolers of such of your fellow-citizens as dare to entertain the
thought of the complete liberation of their country. Can this be true?

"I look around me and I see in your faces the answer. You are
the same gallant soldiers that you were two years ago, you are not the
men to whom a despot can entrust the execution of his tyrannical
designs? You are Argentines, and are as ready as ever you were to
shed your blood in defence of the country which is equally dear to us
all. You are citizens as well as soldiers, and the rights and liberties of
your country are as dear to you as they are to any.

"How is it, then, that you allow your barracks to be turned into a prison? How is it that you, who are gallant soldiers, constitute yourselves the gaolers of the most noble amongst you all?

"He is your friend and your fellow-countryman, he whom you keep shut up within four walls, with barred windows shutting out from him the light of heaven, with a locked door and armed sentries shutting him out from all communication with those who love him. He is your friend and fellow-countryman, I say, whom here you keep locked up, over whom you keep watch and ward as though he were a dangerous enemy; he who in the day of danger was as forward as the bravest amongst you!

"What accusation, what charge has been brought against him? None that I know of, save that he has dared to love his country, and to plan how best to secure to you those liberties which you have won with your blood, and which are the inborn right of every freeman. Yet for this he is imprisoned, for this he may be brought up to judgment and sentenced to some fearful punishment, such as is reserved for those who are traitors.

"Citizens, will you consent to this? Will you consent that he, your friend, your fellow-countryman, be sacrificed to the cruel injustice of a despotic ruler?

"No, Patricios! I know you better, you will not permit that this eternal shame fall upon you. You will let my brother escape, so shall you preserve unstained those laurels which you have so nobly won."

Doña Juana paused and looked round her; no man spoke, but in the eyes turned upon her from all sides, in sympathy and in admiration, she read their answer, and knew that her brother was saved. She clasped her hands together in mute thanks, bowed her head courtesying lowly to them, then turned, and passing her arm through Marcelino's, walked swiftly away.

The tears stood in Marcelino's eyes, but he spoke not one word till he had conducted Doña Juana back to the shelter of her own roof, then as she, speechless also, stretched out her hand to take leave of him, he knelt down on one knee before her and raised that hand to his lips, paying homage to her as he might have done to a queen.

From the house of the Señor Saénz-Valiente, Marcelino went straight to that of Don Manuel Belgrano, and with him speedily concerted means for securing the safety of Don Juan Martin in case he should effect his escape.

Shortly before sundown that evening, the door of the room in which Don Juan Martin was confined, opened, and an officer walking in, told him that he was required to change his quarters. Don Juan Martin rose and followed the officer, who was attended by a guard with fixed bayonets, to another chamber far less comfortably furnished than the one he had previously occupied. He had no sooner entered than the door was closed and locked, and he heard the usual formula of the posting of a sentry outside. He glanced around the room somewhat discontentedly, hardly able to discern what was in it in the dim light, for the window-shutter was nearly closed. He walked to the window and set the shutter wide open, when to his surprise he

saw that the window had no bars to it. He looked out and saw a
small courtyard surrounded by high walls, in one of which there was
a wooden door. The courtyard was deserted, there was not even
a window in the blank walls which rose straight up before him and
on either hand. He stepped out of the window and walked across
the courtyard to that door which he saw in the further wall, it was
only closed with a latch, he opened it, and looking cautiously out,
saw a quiet street. Just then a young officer of the Patricios came
sauntering carelessly along, he recognized him as Valentin Lopez y
Viana, and made as though he would speak with him.

"Not yet, wait till dark," said the young officer, laying a finger on
his lip and passing quietly on, as though he had never noticed that
the door was open.

Then Don Juan Martin knew that he was free, and gently reclosing
the door he went back through the window to his prison-chamber and
waited, looking upward at the evening sky and watching the shadow
as it mounted higher and higher up the eastern wall, till there was no
flicker of sunshine left to tell him that it was yet day save from the
far-off reflection of the clouds. Then he watched the clouds till their
pink tints faded into one dull gray, then they disappeared, no longer
to be distinguished in the ever-increasing darkness from the deep blue
sky under which they floated. Then the stars came out, faintly shining
with their own pure light, and waxing brighter and brighter as their
great rival the sun sank further and further, down below the verge of
the black horizon.

When the stars twinkled brightly, Don Juan Martin stepped forth
again from his window, crossed the courtyard, and opened the
door. No one was near ; he walked out, closing the door behind him.
At the first corner he met two officers of the Patricios, who passed
him without a word ; further on he met two more, who, after he had
passed them, turned and walked slowly after him, but presently, as he
looked back, they were no longer visible ; unmolested and unquestioned
he reached the house of a trusty friend.

Three days afterwards he had said farewell to his native country,
and was on board a vessel bound for Rio Janeiro, bearing credentials
to the Princess Carlota, and charged by Belgrano and others to do
his utmost to prevail upon her to come at once to Buenos Aires,
where the advent of a Princess of the house of Bourbon was looked
upon by many ardent patriots as the only means of delivering their
country from the thraldom of Spanish domination.

CHAPTER IV.

MARSHAL DON SANTIAGO LINIERS felt his power and his popularity slipping away from him. The arrest of Don Juan Martin Puyrredon had injured the latter, his escape was a proof of the former. This escape was hailed by the citizens of Buenos Aires as a great triumph, but among their rulers it created consternation. A hasty council was convened, and General Nieto sent for Major Asneiros, whose evidence had caused the arrest of the Señor Puyrredon.

"As I told you before, my general," said Don Ciriaco, after his examination had lasted some time, "there is one man much more dangerous than the Señor Puyrredon, whom you refused to arrest, and whose arrest would not have occasioned such excitement in the city."

"You speak of the Señor Don Carlos Evaña?" said General Nieto; then as Don Ciriaco simply answered by an inclination of the head, he continued, "I have received from the Señor Don Roderigo the most positive assurance of the loyalty of the Señor Evaña."

"I have told you what I have heard and seen," replied Don Ciriaco, carefully avoiding the eye of Don Roderigo, who was looking at him intently.

"I know not what reasons the Señor Don Roderigo may have for placing such confidence in the Señor Evaña," said Marshal Liniers, "but I know him to be a man of the most dangerous ideas, and advise his immediate arrest."

"Without any specific accusation against him?" said Don Roderigo.

"Repeat the words you heard him say," said General Nieto.

"We can do nothing until we have secured the troops."

"And was that all you overheard of their conversation?" asked Don Roderigo.

"I heard nothing more," replied Don Ciriaco. "I had great difficulty in reaching the rancho unobserved, and had no sooner entered than their dogs began barking round the place."

"Did you recognize none of them except the Señor Evaña," asked Marshal Liniers.

"There was another came up to the rancho with the Señor Evaña whom I should recognize if I saw him again, but I do not know who he is."

"Don Marcelino Ponce de Leon very probably," said Marshal Liniers, with a distrustful glance at Don Roderigo.

" I am quite certain he was not Don Marcelino, I should recognize him at double the distance," replied Asneiros.

" Then the only thing certain is that a number of sportsmen ceased their sport to discuss politics," said General Nieto, "that this Señor Evaña was one of them, and that he made use of words which prove that he at least is engaged in some treasonable conspiracy, in which doubtless the next step was the meeting of the Comandantes at the house of the Señor Puyrredon."

Other members of the council concurred in this view of the case, and some spoke of Evaña as a dangerous man, against whose machinations every precaution should be taken.

" We need discuss the matter no further at present," said Marshal Liniers. " I shall at once order the arrest of the Señor Evaña. You will acknowledge the necessity of this measure, Don Roderigo ? "

Don Roderigo made no answer and the council broke up. Loitering in an ante-room some few minutes later, Don Ciriaco Asneiros was joined by Don Roderigo, who drew him into the recess of a window and said—

" My son Don Marcelino was with that shooting party in the bañados, are you sure you did not see him ? "

" See him ! Perfectly, as well as I see you now, but if you think I would bear witness against your son you do not know me, Don Roderigo," answered Don Ciriaco.

" The Señor Evaña is almost as a son to me, might it not be some other who said those words which you have reported ? "

" I am positive that it was he said them," answered Don Ciriaco. " He is at the head of a conspiracy, his arrest will put an end to all danger, but so long as he is at liberty it will never be safe for his Excellency Don Baltazar to come here."

" There is disaffection, but there is no conspiracy," said Don Roderigo. " His arrest will cause great sorrow to many of us and may occasion an outbreak, it must in some way be avoided, and I look to you to help me, Don Ciriaco. I cannot interfere myself to prevent the execution of an order issued by Marshal Liniers, but I wish you to inform Marcelino at once of it, he will warn Don Carlos to keep out of the way for a few days and so give me time to arrange the affair."

While Marshal Liniers and General Nieto so took counsel with their advisers, several members of the secret committee met at the house of Dr. Vieytes. Evaña had proposed to them some time before that the assumption of power by Don Baltazar de Cisneros should be resisted by force ; few of them were convinced of the necessity for any such extreme measure, but the excitement caused by the arrest and escape of Don Juan Martin Puyrredon was an opportunity not to be lost of making some popular demonstration which might deter the new Viceroy from crossing the river. Summoned by Dr. Vieytes, they met to consult upon this matter, when to the surprise of most of them, Evaña, who was commonly the most reckless of them all, now counselled moderation.

" We have the troops with us, what need we fear ? " said Beruti.

"I think also that we should do nothing at present," said Don Manuel Belgrano. "Liniers deserts us, we have no settled plan; unless the Princess Carlota makes up her mind to come at once, we have no visible head for any government we may establish."

"We want no princess or king," said Evaña; "what we do want is the co-operation of men already experienced in government, which we shall lose if we make any open demonstration against the new Viceroy. With the co-operation of such men as Don Roderigo Ponce de Leon, Don Baltazar will be forced to yield to our demand for a complete reform of the administration, and even under a Spanish Viceroy we shall establish a popular government."

Never before had Evaña been heard to speak such words as these, the listeners looked upon him with wonder, but further discussion was prevented by the sudden entrance of Marcelino Ponce de Leon, who walked hurriedly up to Evaña and laid his hand upon his arm.

"Carlos," said he, "Don Santiago Liniers has issued an order for your immediate arrest."

"Another prisoner for the Patricios," said Yrigoyen, laughing.

"No," said Marcelino. "It is a picket of the escort has the order, and his prison will be in the fort. There is no time to lose; hide somewhere, Carlos, till night, then we will get you away."

"Who told you this?" asked Evaña.

"Asneiros; my father sent him to me."

"Ha!" replied Evaña, taking up his hat; "I will enquire further into this."

"Where are you going, Carlos? The troops will be already at your house."

"Come with me, I will consult your father."

As Marcelino and Evaña went off together, the rest looked at each other in silence, then said Beruti—

"I cannot make out what has come over Evaña. I never saw such a change in a man as I have seen in him during the last two or three weeks. How has he come to have such faith in the liberal principles of Don Roderigo?"

"Don Roderigo is very astute, and has persuaded him that between them they can work out a pacific reform," said Dr. Passo.

"If an angel had told me I would not have believed Evaña capable of yielding to such counsel from a Spaniard," said Beruti.

"An angel has more to do with it than you think," said Belgrano musingly. "Let us go, we shall see no more of Evaña to-day, and without him we can do nothing."

"They may arrest Evaña but they won't keep him long a prisoner," said Beruti.

Don Roderigo returned to his house after the council at the fort, very thoughtful and somewhat sad. As he crossed the patio he was met by Dolores, who, noting the sadness on his face, leaned upon his arm praying him to tell her what had happened.

"I fear a serious misfortune has befallen a great friend of ours, Lola," said he.

"Have they caught Don Juan Martin?" asked Dolores, in alarm.

"No, it is another who is in danger, one who is very dear to me, Lola, almost as a son to me."

"Don Carlos?" said Dolores, in a faltering voice.

"Yes, Lola; Don Santiago Liniers has issued an order for his arrest."

"But, papa, what has he done? Tell me, he was not at that meeting, for he told me so."

"I believe he has done nothing, Lola, to merit imprisonment, but he has extravagant ideas, and sometimes he speaks them too freely."

"Ideas! so has Marcelino, you said so, papa; but you told me— Oh, papa! you will not let them keep him in prison."

As Don Roderigo entered his wife's morning-room, he had the same tale to tell over again to her, and looking upon them he saw wife and daughter gaze upon him with reproachful eyes, as though they thought that he could have prevented this great sorrow which was about to fall upon them. His heart sank within him, and he painfully revolved in his mind all the danger to his rapidly increasing power and influence, which would result from any open interference on behalf of a native Argentine charged with conspiracy against rulers of whom he himself was one. On the other hand, the power of Marshal Liniers was passing away, the post held by General Nieto was a mere temporary appointment, it was to the assistance of Evaña and such as he, that he looked, when he proposed to himself to obtain such influence over the new Viceroy as should leave the real power in his own hands. More still; he had said that he looked upon Evaña almost as a son, and such was the fact. Evaña's devotion to Dolores was no secret to any of them, and he waited in joyful anticipation for the day when he should ask him for his daughter and become his son in reality. The frank friendship which Dolores professed for Evaña, and her open admiration of his great talents, prevented him from feeling any doubt of what her answer would be, when he should propose the alliance to her; and the happiness of his daughter was as dear to his heart as his own ambition.

As these thoughts passed rapidly through his mind, sitting in silence, he saw Dolores hide her face from him on her mother's breast, while Doña Constancia bent over her soothing her, she was evidently weeping. He could bear it no longer, he started to his feet, resolving within himself to risk everything for the sake of the man whom his daughter loved. He was about to speak, when the door opened and gave entrance to Marcelino and the man of whom he was thinking.

"Don Carlos," said he, going to meet him with both hands stretched out in welcome, "never was I more glad to see you. In my house you are safe from arrest, and I know you can remove these unjust suspicions which have fallen upon you."

"I am perfectly ready to meet any accusation which may be brought against me," replied Evaña, placing his hands in those of Don Roderigo, but looking over his shoulder at Dolores, who had started to her feet on his entrance, and on whose face the traces of recent tears were but too evident.

"Come with me," said Don Roderigo, drawing him away, "we will talk over this matter quietly together."

In his own study Don Roderigo talked long and earnestly with his guest, but on neither side was there perfect frankness. Evaña did not deny that there had been talk of resisting the assumption of power by the new Viceroy, but he asserted that it had been merely spoken of in casual conversation, and that no one had the faintest idea of getting up a conspiracy for that purpose. He also denied that he had ever made use of the words which had been given in evidence against him, and had made no attempt whatever to secure the adhesion of the troops, which was partly true and partly false. On his side Don Roderigo refused to give up the name of the accuser, but Evaña learnt sufficient to confirm his suspicion, that he and his comrades of the secret committee had been watched, and their conversation partly overheard by Don Ciriaco Asneiros on the occasion of their expedition to the bañados of Flores. He learnt also that Don Roderigo was sincerely anxious to secure his co-operation in forcing gradual measures of reform upon the new Viceroy, but would resist to the utmost any attempt to dispute his authority.

Evaña was in a frame of mind which rendered him only too ready to give full weight to the specious arguments by which Don Roderigo sought to convince him that popular institutions might be established without severing the bond which bound her colonies to Spain; his heart for the time overpowered his reason, and made him willing to grasp at any chance which might permit him to work in concert with Don Roderigo for one end, the liberation of the Argentine people from the colonial system of Spain. This chance seemed now within his grasp, Spain might send Viceroys, but she was powerless to coerce her colonies; with the aid of such men as Don Roderigo the gradual introduction of salutary reforms was feasible, the ultimate end of such reforms would be the establishment of the Argentine Republic.

Evaña yielded, quieting his reason by saying to himself that he only rendered more certain of success the great work of his life by postponing for a time the execution of his designs.

All the time he passed listening to the arguments of Don Roderigo there floated before his eyes a fair vision, a sweet face looking upon him in tender sympathy; through all his reasonings there ran one thought, may not that gaze be yet turned upon me not in friendship but in love. So dear was this hope to him that he felt that for one glance of real love from those eyes, which that day had looked upon him in pity and in sympathy alone, he could even give up that purpose which had been the work of his life so far, and for the accomplishment of which, life itself had seemed to him but a small sacrifice.

Evaña yielded, and grasping the willing hand of Don Roderigo assured him of his aid and sympathy in every measure he might bring forward for the welfare of the people.

Night closed in ere their conversation came to an end, and darkness brought Marcelino, who announced to his friend that his house was occupied by a party of grenadiers under the command of Major Asneiros, and that it was reported in the city that he himself had fled to the campaña, where all knew that his safety was secure.

There were many anxious faces as they sat down to dinner that evening at the house of Don Roderigo, but Don Roderigo himself

was very cheerful, speaking of the danger to their friend as passed
over, while Evaña was in excellent spirits, talking much more gaily
than was his wont, surprising Dolores into many a laugh by his sayings,
but withal occasioning her some undefined uneasiness by the unusual
tenderness he threw into his manner when addressing her. As they
rose from table he said—

"Now, Don Roderigo, come with me. Let us go and visit this ex-
Viceroy, and I will ask him myself his reasons for sending a picket of
infantry to occupy my house. If Don Ciriaco Asneiros wishes to
inspect my papers in search of proofs of some conspiracy he is welcome to do so, but I should prefer to be present, he may mistake
a treatise on algebra for the records of some secret society.

"Now!" exclaimed Don Roderigo; "wait till to-morrow, then I
will see him myself, and I assure you I can arrange everything. I have
secret powers from Don Baltazar which I can use on an emergency. I
am even authorized to arrest Don Santiago and depose him if I find it
necessary."

"No, let us go at once," replied Evaña. "I intend to sleep under
my own roof to-night."

"The Señor Evaña has left the city."

Chafing angrily within himself at the trammels which bound him on
every side, trammels from which he might have freed himself by one
vigorous effort, which would have placed him at the head of a free
people; chafing angrily at his waning popularity, evidences of which
met him at every turn, the ex-Viceroy heard these words, telling him
that the man he dreaded had escaped him. Leaving his house he
returned to the fort to consult with his colleague General Nieto.

It was nine o'clock, steps were heard in the ante-room, the door
opened, the next minute Evaña stood before him. With head erect,
and dark flashing eyes, Evaña stood before him, demanding in stern
words the reason of the order which had been sent forth for his arrest.

"Two file of grenadiers and a priest, that would be my answer," said
General Nieto, springing angrily from his chair and laying his hand
upon a small bell which stood on the table.

Don Roderigo laid a hand upon his arm and drew him away.

"Señor Mariscal, I repeat my question," said Evaña. "Upon what
grounds have you issued an order for my arrest."

Still the ex-Viceroy answered not, but sat in his chair staring at him,
a strange fascination slowly creeping over him. Who was this man
who came again to him in the darkness of the night, as he had come
once before? A conspirator, whose life was forfeit, and who totally
reckless of danger again stood before him, looking down upon him
with fierce dark eyes. Who was this man that he should so persistently
defy him, and before whose gaze his own bold spirit quailed?

"Two file of grenadiers and a priest," said Evaña. "That butcher
who sat beside you just now, has repeated the sentence which
Spanish jealousy would pass upon yourself, but that they fear the
Argentine people, who are your friends; yes, Don Santiago, even
yet your friends. It is not too late, even yet you may save yourself
from the fate which looms over you. Choose now at once, will you

put yourself at the head of the people, or will you fall their victim. Choose now, for the time is short ; two file of grenadiers and a priest, such is your fate from Spanish jealousy or from the indignation of the people you have betrayed. That fate may yet be averted, but the time is short. What say you ? " added Evaña, stepping up to the ex-Viceroy and laying his hand on his shoulder.

That touch broke the spell ; Liniers sprang from his chair, pushed Evaña from him with such violence that he reeled backwards for several paces ere he could recover his balance, and seizing the bell rang it. For a minute there was silence ; to this summons there was no response, and Evaña, folding his arms across his chest, stood motionless in the centre of the room with a fierce glare in his dark eyes. Liniers strove to meet that glance with one of defiance, but his own eyes fell before it ; again he rang the bell, then as there was still no answer he walked to a door, opened it, and shouted—

" Officer of the guard ! "

In the ante-room all was darkness, no one was there ; he went on, opened another door, and found himself face to face with Don Roderigo.

" Did you call, Don Santiago ? " said Don Roderigo.

" The officer of the guard ; where is he ? "

" Beyond," said General Nieto.

" You do not want him," said Don Roderigo in a sharp voice, then taking Liniers by the arm he led him back to the further room, while General Nieto followed, closing the doors behind them.

In the further room stood Evaña, motionless, just as Liniers had left him.

Without a word Don Roderigo seated himself at a table, drew a sheet of paper towards him, and writing a few lines handed it to Marshal Liniers for his signature.

Liniers read the paper, it was an order to Major Asneiros to withdraw his men from the house of Don Carlos Evaña, and cancelling the order of arrest issued against that gentleman. Liniers looked in perplexity from one to the other, but General Nieto refused to meet his glance, and in the resolute countenance of Don Roderigo there seemed a consciousness of power to enforce his will which awed him into compliance. He took up a pen and signed the paper, feeling as he did so that he abdicated the last remnant of his authority.

General Nieto countersigned the order without a word, then Don Roderigo folded it up, put it into the breast-pocket of his coat, and turning to Evaña said—

" Let us go."

Evaña walked up to the ex-Viceroy, bent over him and whispered in his ear—

" Beware the day we meet again."

The next minute Liniers was alone, and alone he remained till near midnight, buried in gloomy reverie, when shaking himself free from his thoughts he rose to go to his own house.

" Two file of grenadiers and a priest, such is the reward of Spain for those who have served her too well," he muttered to himself as he threw his cloak over his shoulders.

On the 30th June, Don Baltazar Hidalgo de Cisneros, General of the Spanish navy, by the will of the Junta Central of Spain and by the tacit acquiescence of the Argentine people, Viceroy of Buenos Aires, arrived at the capital city of his Viceroyalty, landed and entered into the full exercise of his authority. The people of Buenos Aires, both natives and Spaniards, received him with acclamations, the Spaniards rejoicing that their former predominance would now be restored to them, the natives anxious to conciliate the good-will of their new ruler.

Many men looked on as he landed, who took no part in these acclamations, among them two fast friends stood side by side listening to the shouts of the people in far differing mood, Marcelino Ponce de Leon and Don Carlos Evaña. Marcelino's face was clouded over, he saw the last chance of freedom slipping away, he saw in Don Baltazar de Cisneros a triumphant agent of that ruthless despotism which had for so long crushed the young energies of his country, he saw in his enthusiastic reception the ruin of those high hopes he had dared to entertain. But on the face of Don Carlos Evaña there was no trouble or despondency, he looked upon it all as a pageant, meaning nothing. Marcelino looked at him in surprise as he saw the smile upon his lip.

"How can you smile, Carlos," said he, "when this man comes to undo all that we have gained during three years?"

"He will undo nothing," replied Don Carlos. "He comes to give stability to what we have already gained, and to help us on in our career of progress."

"He, Carlos! he is a Spaniard, and the nominee of Spain!"

"Don Roderigo is a Spaniard. Your father is his chosen counsellor," replied Don Carlos; Marcelino was silenced and spoke no more.

Then Don Roderigo, who was in close attendance upon the new Viceroy, perceived them and came up to speak with them.

"Ah, Carlos," said he, "those who stood forward in defence of the law on the 1st January have to-day reason to rejoice. Natives and Spaniards join to welcome our new ruler. There is now no longer division amongst us, once more we are a united people."

"And you know how our present union may be preserved," replied Don Carlos.

"I do, and I look to you both to assist me. Many reforms in the administration are of urgent necessity and are now possible, but of this we will talk later. At one o'clock his Excellency Don Baltazar will give a reception in the saloon of audience, I shall expect to see you there, and shall have the pleasure of introducing you."

Both the younger men promised to attend, and Don Roderigo left them.

"But, Carlos," said Marcelino, as his father walked away, "we must discuss this matter with our friends, from this, no one can tell what will result. If my father maintains his influence with the Viceroy, and has the real direction of affairs, all will go well, but his power depends upon the caprice of a man of whom we know nothing, and it may cease any day; we are in ignorance of the secret intentions of this Don Baltazar. There will be many wild-duck on the marshes now, let us go and shoot."

" With all my heart," said Evaña. " Whatever day will suit you, I will make convenient to me."

Marcelino soon found a day convenient, and a party which comprised all the members of the secret committee, sallied forth betimes to the bañados in the neighbourhood of Quilmes, where wild-duck swarmed by thousands. All looked to Evaña to fix upon some spot for a general halt ; the name of the new Viceroy had as yet not been mentioned among them. But Evaña, instead of seeking out some secluded spot and establishing himself there as was his wont on such occasions, split the party up into knots of twos and threes, which he despatched in different directions about the swampy plain, with instructions to concentrate towards one central point and to fire at any duck flying away from this point. His comrades looked at him in surprise, to reach this point would occupy the greater part of the day.

" They laugh at us, do our friends in the city," said Don Carlos ; " they say that such sportsmen as we are a disgrace to them, let us show them that we can do something besides talk of sporting. I think we have been sportsmen long enough to know how to shoot straight."

Then the same thought came to them all, their empty bags might well have excited suspicion that it was not for simple sport that these excursions were arranged, especially as they never took any servants with them ; the new Viceroy might well be suspected of special vigilance, after the caution he had shown in taking possession of his post ; it would be well, therefore, that they should do something to merit the name of sportsmen.

No man made any further observation, but each one went to his post as directed, and spent the entire day wading through swamps, scrambling across watercourses, crawling on hands and knees through the long grass to get within shot of their game. Of them all none was more indefatigable than Don Carlos Evaña. He had kept Marcelino with him, and rejected all his attempts to converse on any other subject than the sport on which they were engaged.

An hour before sundown the whole party met again at the place which had been fixed upon for concentration, with their clothes wet and covered with mud, their powder-horns and shot-belts empty, but their bags and pockets full of duck, teal, and snipe, and also with a few wood-pigeons, which Evaña had gone out of his way to shoot in a small plantation. Fatigued as they were, they yet found spirits to laugh at each other's draggled appearance, and to recount the misfortunes which had befallen them by falling into water-holes and so forth.

" But," said Marcelino, " there is yet an hour of sunshine, we have yet time to learn the opinions——"

" For my part, Señores," said Evaña, interrupting him, " I have but one opinion, which is not washed out of me by that last bañado, I never thought it was so deep or I would have gone round it ; my opinion is, that the sooner I reach home and change my clothes the better I shall feel to-morrow, and I think it is an opinion that you all share with me."

" At least it is also mine," said Don Miguel Yrigoyen.

" They can laugh at us no longer," said Don Manuel Belgrano. " We have earned our laurels to-day, let us be content with that, for the

Y

rest there is no great hurry. We have a new Viceroy, and it appears to me we shall have some years yet in which we may discuss his qualities. As for the Princess Carlota, I wash my hands of her."

"She has let the opportunity pass, and it will never return," said Marcelino.

Without further ado the horses were saddled, each draggled sportsman bestowing as best he could the unwonted trophies of his skill, and away they went for town, discussing among themselves no more serious subject than the weight of their respective bags.

That day's work quite redeeme l the reputation of these friendly sportsmen, and was for long after a theme on which they were wont to descant with immense gratification to themselves.

In spite of his exertions Don Carlos Evaña was not too tired to spend the evening at the house of Don Roderigo Ponce de Leon, which had of late been his great resort in leisure moments, and where he was always welcome. But before he even changed his clothes, he selected the finest birds from his bag and sent them by a servant to Doña Constancia.

"Now, Señorita, what do you say?" said he, as he sat near Dolores that evening. "Yesterday you laughed when I told you that Marcelino and I were going out shooting."

"I am sorry for the poor birds," said Dolores, "and I won't laugh again."

Months passed before Dolores had another chance of laughing at Don Carlos for his bad success as a sportsman. The wild-duck had flown back to their haunts in the icy south, and partridges were sitting on their dark-brown eggs, in nests hidden by the long spring grass, ere Don Carlos Evaña again shouldered his gun and went forth shooting with the members of the secret committee.

CHAPTER V.

HOW THE VICEROY PLACED A SWORD IN THE HANDS OF THE ENEMIES OF SPAIN.

THE first great difficulties which beset the new Viceroy arose from the same cause which had so greatly hampered his predecessor, the empty state of the treasury. The revenues of government from all sources little exceeded $100,000 a month, the expenditure was more than double, in addition to which there was a heavy debt incurred in repelling the second invasion of the English.

The Viceroy applied, in the first place, to the Spanish residents for a loan, his request was refused; in his perplexity he turned for counsel to Don Roderigo Ponce de Leon, who in reply laid before him the memorial on free trade, which had been drawn up by Don Manuel Belgrano.

" You think that by opening our ports to the English we shall increase the revenue sufficiently to meet all the expenditure ? " said the Viceroy.

" I feel sure of it," replied Don Roderigo.

" It is in direct contradiction to my instructions," said the Viceroy.

" I believe the main purport of your instructions is, that you put an end to these disorders that have broken out, and re-establish the full authority of government."

" Yes, and how I am to do it with native troops who release their prisoners and can't be punished, and without money, is to me a mystery. You see what has happened at Chuquisaca, the Audencia quarrelled with the President, and appealed to the people. The Creoles have set up a Junta of their own, now this Junta of Creoles overrides the decisions of all the Spanish corporations, and neither the President nor the Audencia has any power left. What is to be the end of all this ? Before long we may have a Junta of Creoles here in Buenos Aires."

" Your Excellency does not overrate the danger," replied Don Roderigo. " You want money ; open the ports to the English and you will have it. You want troops ; by establishing free trade [1] you will win the confidence of the people, and I engage that the Patricios themselves shall put down this Junta at Chuquisaca for you."

" I will think of it," said the Viceroy.

What the Viceroy did was to submit the memorial to the Cabildo

[1] This is a translation of the then popular cry, " Libertad de Comercio ! " and has not the thorough meaning of the English expression. It simply implies an open port.

and to the Consulado, both of which corporations were composed exclusively of Spaniards. Both returned the same answer, that the project was inadmissible.

Marcelino Ponce de Leon, as secretary to the Consulado, had the mortification of having to draw up the reply of that body himself, a work which clashed so completely with his own convictions that he was only prevented from throwing up his post by the earnest entreaties of his father.

To relieve his mind he organized a shooting expedition, in which the sport gave but a poor result in birds, but produced an idea which was carried out with great zeal by the various members of the secret committee. All the wealthy landowners were forthwith subjected to a vigorous canvass in favour of the project of free trade, and their interests were so plainly sacrificed to Spanish greed under the present system, that they were with no great difficulty prevailed upon to unite in support of the scheme of Don Manuel Belgrano. A number of them met at the house of Don Gregorio Lopez, and selected Dr. Don Mariano Moreno as their advocate to combat for them the arguments of the Spanish corporations.

The result was that Dr. Moreno drew up another memorial, dated 30th September, 1809, and entitled " La Representacion de Los Hacendados," in which occur the following remarkable words—

"The Sovereign did not confer upon Y. E. the high dignity of Viceroy of these provinces in order that you might watch over the interests of the merchants of Cadiz, but over our interests. It is a tyranny, that monopoly which the merchants of Cadiz have usurped, and the remonstrances of this city are echoed everywhere in bitter complaints, which are heard there only with contempt, expressive of the shamelessness with which they seize upon the wealth of a people in no way inferior to themselves. Y. E. rules over a great people, protect, then, with vigorous justice the development of the great wealth of which nature has been prodigal to us."

" At last, we begin to understand the meaning of the words, ' America for the Americans,' " said Don Carlos Evaña, as he read a copy of this memorial which Marcelino had procured for the secret committee.

In October the ports of Buenos Aires and Monte Video were opened to English ships, English merchants soon made their appearance, the empty coffers of the Viceroy were rapidly replenished, trade was developed to an extent never before known, and the increased value of their products doubled and trebled the wealth of the native hacendados.

Having resolved this matter, the Viceroy next turned his attention to the revolts in the interior. A strong detachment of the Patricios formed the nucleus of an expedition which, under the command of General Nieto, marched to Chuquisaca. With this expedition went as a volunteer Evaristo Ponce de Leon, the youngest officer in the regiment of the Patricios.

So under the rule of the new Viceroy, winter passed into spring and spring into summer, and the men of Buenos Aires saw the power which they had thought of as their own slowly slipping away from them.

But Don Baltazar de Cisneros distrusted their apparent apathy, he knew that any untoward circumstance might arouse the dormant spirit of revolution of which Liniers had warned him. Again he turned to Don Roderigo for counsel, and the result was that he determined to extend his influence over the people by means of an official newspaper.

This was not the first newspaper which had ever been published in Buenos Aires. In the first year of the century was published the " Telegrafo Mercantil," which was succeeded in the following year by the " Semanario." The English also, during their occupation of Monte Video, there published a newspaper, entitled " La Estrella del Sur," which was printed partly in Spanish, and partly in English ; both this paper and the " Semanario " ceased to appear during the confusion occasioned by Whitelock's invasion of Buenos Aires.

The editorship of the new newspaper was entrusted by the Viceroy to Don Manuel Belgrano, who at once convened a meeting of the secret committee at his own house.

" Señores," said he, when all were present, " there is no longer necessity for secresy ; I have invited you here to-day to assist me in conducting a newspaper, which his Excellency the Viceroy has commissioned me to publish, in order to teach the people by the writings of men of education and experience, the due appreciation of their rights and privileges. Every article before publication will have to be submitted to his Excellency for approval, the teachings of the newspaper will thus have official sanction and authority. The subject to which he desires me more particularly to direct attention is the necessity for union and public spirit. I think we may on these subjects easily devise such articles as may merit his approval, and at the same time may teach our fellow-citizens that the prosperity of our country depends upon our own union for the assertion of those rights which are most wrongfully withheld from us by Spain."

Before the end of January, in the year 1810, the prospectus of the new " Diario del Comercio " was published in Buenos Aires, and extensively circulated by viceregal authority throughout the provinces.

Through the summer and autumn the newspaper appeared at regular intervals, and in every number there was at least one article which in covert language was an attack upon the colonial system of Spain.

Long and weary were these months to Marcelino Ponce de Leon, the sweet voice of Magdalen Miranda no longer cheered him in his troubles, in vain he looked for sympathy into her deep gray eyes ; he seldom saw her at all, when he did there was a cold constraint in her manner to him, which more effectually kept him at a distance from her than would any outspoken anger. And of one great trouble he dared not speak even to her. Since the day when Evaña had shown him that fatal newspaper paragraph recording the loss of the " Petrel " he had heard no further tidings of his friend Gordon ; he had written to England, but communication was slow and uncertain in those days, he had received no answer to his letter, the fate of his English friend was yet in suspense, and suspense is more wearing than the most dreadful certainty. Sorrowing over the loss of the first love of his life, alternately hoping and fearing as the days wore on, the colour faded from his cheeks, and even faint lines of care began to show

themselves upon his smooth forehead. In vain his mother and Dolores
strove to cheer him, knowing nothing of the cause of his grief, or if
Dolores suspected somewhat of the cause, she kept it to herself and
never spoke to him of Magdalen Miranda.

Of his trouble he could not speak even to his friend Evaña, who
was to him as a brother, for Evaña had spoken to him scornfully of
Don Alfonso Miranda, and slightingly of her who was to him the one
pearl among women.   And in the face of his friend he had seen hope
and love softening the harshness of his features and infusing a gentle
tenderness into his dark eyes, he knew that the loss of that other friend
was to him great gain, he could not look to him for sympathy.

To Evaña this time had passed as one long holiday. As month
after month went by, and there came no news of Gordon, the thought
that he had perished in the wreck of the "Petrel" became to him a
certainty, yet of this certainty he spoke to no one, he dreaded what
the effect of the intelligence might be upon the girl he loved ; he
knew the firm constancy of her nature, firm even in faults, steady
with a steadiness which he had learned to look upon as a most unusual trait in the character of a woman.   Her constancy was itself
one source of the admiration he felt for her, even though her love were
lavished on another.   While Gordon lived he knew that her heart
would never swerve from its allegiance, and he disdained the thought
of seeking for himself the love of a heart which owned another master.
But if his rival no longer lived, then he thought that it might be his to
soothe the pain of a fearful wound and to win that heart wholly to
himself.

Yet he dreaded the day when this intelligence should reach her, he
knew that the pain would be all the more severe from the stern courage
with which she would hide it in her own bosom ; he loved her, and
her suffering, however bravely it might be concealed, would, he knew,
rend his own heart with fearful agony.   He dreaded the arrival of
every ship from Europe, yet every letter he opened, every letter he
saw opened by his friend Marcelino, awaked within him a wild hope
that his suspense was ended.

This time had been to him one long holiday, but a holiday to the
full as replete with alternate hope and fear, as it had been to him he
called his brother.   As the months passed on, hope grew stronger and
stronger within him, and as hope grew stronger so his love waxed
bolder, till he began to say to himself that he had no longer any living
rival whom he need fear, and that he might venture to seek for himself the love of a heart that might yet be his.

He talked much of the uncertainty of a soldier's life, spoke much of
the desperate fighting in the Peninsula, of which each ship from
Europe brought them fresh details, but as he did so, his heart often
smote him with bitter anguish as he looked upon the face of Lola
Ponce ; in the tightly-compressed lips and watching eyes he saw a
question which she never asked him ; he saw her ask herself, was there
any meaning to her in these words of his beyond such meaning as
they had to all.

The long summer days began to draw in, the wheat was garnered,
apricots glowed temptingly on the trees like balls of frosted gold,

grapes hung from the espaliers in great purple bunches, inviting the despoiler, and the peaches, losing their dull-green hue, began to deck themselves in scarlet and yellow, toned down with an exquisite bloom. The Quinta de Ponce looked more like an oasis than ever, the dark-green leaves of the trees contrasting strongly with the dry yellow grass of the Pampa, and with the arid hardness of the dusty roads, as Marcelino and his friend Evaña rode up to it, one evening in February. Evaña had been unusually silent on the way out; he had resolved that the time had come, for him to break as gently as he could the news to Dolores of the great loss she had suffered, and he had resolved to do it himself, for, as he thought, none but Marcelino and himself had penetrated her secret, and he sought to shield her as he could, even at the risk of bitter sorrow to himself.

Dolores came to meet them as they walked under the trees together, but no longer welcomed them with buoyant cheerfulness, there was a listlessness about her, as though she were a prey to some secret care. She laid her hand on Marcelino's arm and walked beside him, but her eyes looked searchingly into the face of Don Carlos Evaña. Few words they spoke together; as they neared the house Marcelino left the other two, and went himself to speak with his mother. Backwards and forwards paced the two under the trees side by side, saying little, but each with furtive glance watching the other. Evaña had said to himself that the time was come, but now that Dolores walked beside him he knew not how to commence, he knew not with what words he should prepare her and strengthen her, so that he might lessen the shock of the truth he had resolved to tell her.

"We have been friends a long time now, Dolores," said he, "and our friendship has met with no interruption such as I once feared."

"I do not know why it should," replied Dolores.

"At one time I feared much that there was great danger of an interruption to it, but the danger has passed over, and there is now no cloud between us. Shall I tell you what the danger was?"

"I know," said Dolores, "I have asked papa, and he has told me. Papa says that you learned many extravagant ideas when you were in Paris, ideas which might have been your ruin, but since then you have learned better, and papa says there is no other in whom he has such confidence as he has in you."

"Not only that," said Evaña, "Don Roderigo is now, next to Don Baltazar de Cisneros, the most powerful man in the city, and the system of government is completely changed. We Creoles can cheerfully submit to be ruled by men such as he, who will educate the people, till some day they will know how to rule themselves."

"That can never be," replied Dolores.

Don Carlos paused, the abruptness of the answer somewhat startled him; again they walked for a space in silence under the sheltering trees, again Evaña spoke—

"Your father has a hard task before him, Dolores," said he. "In some things I have been able to aid him; it has been a pleasure to me to aid him in any way, for my help to him brings me nearer to you."

"You come to see us much more frequently now than you used to do," said Dolores.

"I should like to come more frequently still; I should like to see you every day," replied Evaña.

"I fear the new 'Diario' would not have much help from you if you came galloping out to see us every day, Don Carlos," said Dolores, with a faint attempt at a laugh.

Again Don Carlos was silent, for this mention of the "Diario" brought a recent slight to his recollection, under which his proud spirit chafed. With great care he had written an article for the first issue of the "Diario," previous to sending it in he had shown it to Don Roderigo. Don Roderigo had read it carefully, and after drawing his pen through one sentence, saying but one word, "inadmissible," had handed it back to him without comment. This sentence contained the pith of the whole article, but Evaña had submitted; mutilated as it was, this article had appeared in the "Diario," and he never thought of it but with secret shame.

Again they walked on in silence, side by side, till Dolores asked abruptly—

"What is the matter with Marcelino?"

"I fear he is not well," replied Evaña.

"I am sure he is not," said Dolores. "But you see more of him than we do, what is to do with him?"

"I fear he is not happy," replied Evaña.

"I know he is not," said Dolores. "When any ship arrives from Europe he is miserable for days after."

"The news from Spain is continually worse," replied Evaña. "Even the English appear to be unable to do anything to stop the progress of the French armies."

"He has had no letter for months," said Dolores.

"Not from Gordon," replied Evaña. "But Gordon can have little time for writing if he is with the army."

"If! you say if; is he not with the army?"

"He was on his way when Marcelino last heard from him."

"But that is long ago," said Dolores sadly, then turning from Evaña, she left him and went into the house.

Evaña followed her, entered the sala, but found it vacant, seated himself, thinking over what he had said to Dolores, and telling himself that he had not said one word of what he wished to say, but had aroused in her mind vague suspicions of evil which in no way advanced his own cause. He had wished to tell her plainly of his own love first, asking nothing in return, but hoping everything, then gradually breaking the truth to her to make her feel the need of the sympathy he yearned to offer.

As he thus tortured himself, saying to himself that he had let the chance go by, Dolores entered the room. Evaña rose to meet her, but stopped as he saw the extraordinary pallor on her face, every shade of colour had vanished from it, even her lips were white and were firmly pressed together, while her eyes, looking straight into his, had a peering, anxious expression in them which caused his heart to cease for a moment its beating, too well he divined the reason of the change in her. She walked up to him and laid a hand upon his arm.

"I have been talking with Marcelino," she said, in slow, measured words. "What is this that you are hiding from me? He will tell me nothing."

"Hiding from you!" said Evaña; "Marcelino has no secrets from you."

"Are you not my friend, Don Carlos? Do you think I have no courage? Do you fear that I shall disgrace my name? Tell me, what is this that you are hiding from me?"

"Be sure that if we had any secret between us you should share it, were there any necessity that you should do."

Then the hand which lay upon Evaña's arm closed upon it with such force that the finger-ends buried themselves in his flesh, causing him severe pain, but he hardly noticed it, so fascinated was he by the determined eagerness of those gray eyes which so near to him seemed to defy him. The white lips parted once more, and through the half-closed teeth there came low but distinctly the question he dreaded to hear—

"Is he dead?"

For one moment there was wild conflict in Evaña's soul. He dared not tell the simple truth, though he had come there that evening to tell it, he dared not look upon the despair which that truth told bluntly would bring into the face he loved to look upon, he dreaded to see in that despair the ruin of his own hopes. But as he gazed down into the gray eyes which looked into his own defying him to attempt a falsehood, he could no longer pretend ignorance, and he answered rapidly—

"He has been in great danger, but the worst is over."

The next moment he would have given worlds to have retracted his words, but it was too late, she had believed him, the fierce grasp upon his arm relaxed, the defiant look of sorrow in those eyes melted into one of grateful hope, and Evaña learnt then what he would well-nigh have given his life to have never known, that in life or in death she had given her heart to one only, and that no other could supplant him even though fathoms deep under the sea.

"Always my friend," she said, then turning from him glided with slow step away.

Evaña saw Dolores no more that evening, Doña Constancia said she was unwell and had retired to her own room.

Long after nightfall, when the household had gone to rest, he paced in solitude to and fro under those trees, whose branches had over-shadowed him and Dolores as they had walked and talked together but a few hours before. But a few hours and yet how everything was changed to him! then with a heart full of hope and tenderness he had sought to tell her of the great blow that had fallen upon her, hoping that she might then turn to him for consolation, and that in the deep devotion of his love for her she might find solace, till her heart turning to him might forget its old allegiance and become entirely his. She had given him the chance he had sought, one word from him might have destroyed at once that hope in which her heart lived, that hope which was the barrier to his own happiness, for she trusted him so completely, she had never doubted him for one moment. And that word was the simple truth, "dead," yet he had not dared to speak it. He had bid her hope yet, when there was no hope, he had betrayed the confidence she had placed in him, he had shown doubt of her courage and strength of mind, some day she would learn the truth, then her confidence and her trust in him were gone for ever. And even though it were not so, had he not read in the grateful thanks which had beamed upon him from those gray eyes the baselessness of all his hopes.

"In life or in death, his only," he muttered to himself.

Then he thought of how he had sacrificed all for her, how he had sacrificed the creed which had been so far the guiding principle of his life, and had united himself with those who could never be other than the tyrants of his country, how he had sacrificed his ambition, perchance even the future of his country; for, as he now said to himself, the power of a man such as Don Roderigo could be but transient. He thought of the sentence in his article for the "Diario," through which Don Roderigo had drawn his pen, the only sentence in the whole paper which spoke plainly of the right of all men to think for themselves, which spoke plainly of some future day of freedom.

As he thought of all this, he asked himself why he had so forsaken his old creed, why he had forced himself to think that a republic of Argentines was a dream, practicable only in some remote future, in which he could have no part. To these questions his heart answered for him, that he had done it for her sake.

Then he pictured to himself what would have followed had he and his friends boldly resisted the assumption of power by Don Baltazar de Cisneros. He saw the country rent by civil war, himself and Don Roderigo, leaders on different sides; he pictured to himself this deadly strife, and as he did so his thoughts flew back to an evening on which he had dreamed a dream, a dream full of presage of future woe, a dream so bitter that its memory had been present with him ever since, a dream in which Dolores had fallen dead at his feet, stricken to the death by his own hand.

"It cannot be, it cannot be," he said to himself. "That fair young life sacrificed to a memory that is gone. Fool that I was not to tell her the truth at once!"

As he said this he struck himself fiercely on the breast with his clenched fist, and a sharp pang shot through his arm. Drawing up the cuff of his coat and unbuttoning the wristband of his shirt he turned up the sleeve; there on his arm, where her hand had rested, were four black marks corresponding to the four fingers of the tiny hand of Lola Ponce, four bruises inflicted by the pressure of those small fingers. Evaña walked into the moonlight and gazed long upon these four black marks, then raising his arm he pressed his lips upon them, muttering to himself with a deep sigh—

"In life or in death, his only."

CHAPTER VI.

¡ CADUCÓ LA ESPAÑA !

THE expedition to Chuquisaca met with no effective opposition. The Spanish authorities were reinstated, and many of the principal citizens of that far-off city were tried by court-martial and banished to Peru, there to languish in the stifling casemates of Callao. An expedition from Peru against La Paz, under General Goyeneche, was more stubbornly resisted. But the insurgents, badly organized and half armed, were routed with great slaughter, La Paz was taken by assault, many of the leaders perished on the gibbet, and their dismembered bodies were nailed on the sign-posts which marked out the public roads in Upper Peru.

The Patricios returned to Buenos Aires, but they cared not to speak of their exploits. Then men began to rouse themselves from their apathy and to murmur indignant words, whispering to one another with bated breath that Spain was ever the same Spain, that there was one law for Spaniards and quite another law for Americans. Elio and Alzaga and their companions, who had revolted against a Viceroy holding his appointment from the regal Court of Aranjuez, were held high in favour by the new ruler, who held his appointment only from the Junta of Seville. For Americans who had dared to revolt, there was the gibbet and the garotte, or imprisonment in a dreary dungeon.

The war in the Peninsula in the year 1809 was one long series of disasters to Spain, broken only by one or two insignificant triumphs, relieved only from utter disgrace by the heroic defence of Saragossa and that of Gerona, both alike unavailing.

The Sierra de la Morena stood as a huge, natural rampart around the ancient kingdom of Boabdil. Andalusia was as yet unsullied by the footstep of the invader, but to the north of the sierra, all organized resistance had ceased, the honour of Spain was upheld only by scattered bands of guerillas. Even the British allies of Spain, after their bloody but fruitless victory at Talavera de la Reyna, had retired to the frontiers of Portugal. Joseph reigned tranquilly at Madrid. All Spain, save that last stronghold of the Moors, lay prostrate at the feet of Napoleon.

Then the Junta of Seville determined upon one last desperate effort. Early in November an army of 50,000 men, with 7000 horse and sixty guns, issued from the defiles of the Sierra de la Morena, and marched upon Madrid. On the 12th November, on the wide plains of New Castile, they encountered their enemy at Ocaña. All that personal

bravery could accomplish was done, but military skill and discipline
were stronger than patriotism and fanaticism combined. The last
army of Spain was completely routed—20,000 Spaniards breathed
their last on that fatal field. The Sierra de la Morena remained, almost
undefended. the last bulwark of Spanish nationality.

Don Baltazar de Cisneros did all he could to prevent the extent of
this disaster from being known in Buenos Aires, but it was impossible
to keep it long concealed. In February, 1810, the minds of men,
already excited by the news from the interior, became still further
excited as they learned the full extent of the great defeat at Ocaña.

Men, no longer fearful of Spanish tyranny, thronged in the streets,
walking about in groups unchallenged, shouting boldly one to the other—
" Spain has fallen ! "

One day in the last week of February Don Carlos Evaña received
a letter, by private hand from General Miranda, who was at that time
resident in London, and who was more active than ever in his revolutionary projects, as he saw Spain daily sinking lower and lower in her
struggle against France. Enclosed in this letter came another for Don
Alfonso Miranda. Don Carlos had not been near the Miserere for
months, but on the evening of this day he walked out there. He
found Don Alfonso and Magdalen seated in the porch together. Don
Alfonso received him very cordially, and Magdalen, smiling upon him,
reproached him for his desertion of them.

" It is so many months since I have seen you, Don Carlos," she
said, "that I have almost forgotten the sound of your voice ; but I
went to see Doña Josefina last week, and she told me about you.
You have been spending these last months very pleasantly, no wonder
you forgot us. I did not think we should ever see you again."

" What nonsense are you talking, Chica ? " said Don Alfonso.

But Don Carlos did not seem to think it nonsense, and smiled
pleasantly upon her.

" There is some one who often speaks to me of you," he said.
Then noticing that Magdalen looked troubled at this, he turned to
Don Alfonso and spoke to him.

" To-day I received a letter from your brother the General," he
said. " Every letter is more sanguine than the one before. He sends
me an enclosure for you, which——"

" Go and walk in the garden, Chica," said Don Alfonso, interrupting
him. Then as Magdalen left them he signed to Don Carlos to follow
him to the sala, the door of which he closed before he spoke again.

Magdalen had not walked long in the garden before the gate opened
and Don Ciriaco Asneiros entered. She received him with much less
cordiality than she had formerly shown him. Even the name of
Dolores failed to arouse her to animation, but for some minutes she
walked beside him, listlessly attending to what he said, and answering
his questions at random.

" And the old man ? " said Don Ciriaco, tiring at length of this one-
sided conversation.

" He is in the sala," replied Magdalen.

" Let us go and talk to him."

" No, do not go in yet, he has a visitor with him."

"Who is it?"

"The Señor Evaña is with him."

Then Don Ciriaco, leaving her, walked softly up to the sala window, which was wide open, and bent down, apparently intent upon the examination of the flowers growing beneath it.

"Don Ciriaco!" called Magdalen, "come here, there are some much finer roses at the other side."

"The time has now come. The people that has not now the courage to strike for freedom is unworthy to become a nation."

Don Ciriaco had heard the rustling of paper, he had heard the above words read in a low voice by Don Alfonso. It was enough, he left the window and went back to Magdalen.

"Your uncle, Don Francisco, when do you expect him here?" he asked her bruskly.

Magdalen turned pale, looked at him with frightened eyes, and then said hurriedly—

"My uncle! I did not know he was coming. Papa never told me. My uncle never writes to papa."

"What is that you tell me?" replied Asneiros. "He is now reading to the Señor Evaña the letter he received to-day."

"You are mistaken," said Magdalen. "It is the Señor Evaña who has received a letter from my uncle. They sent me out here, I do not know anything of it."

Then twining her hands together and with tears of vexation in her eyes, as she saw him smile at her trouble, she turned from him and sought refuge in her own room.

Nearly a week after this, Don Carlos Evaña passing along one of the streets abutting upon the Plaza Mayor, paused to look upon a group of men who, standing in the open street in front of a large almacen, were discussing excitedly together, the latest news from Europe.

"I have said to myself that my work is all in vain," he said within himself. "In all that I have done I have done nothing, men have laughed at my words, and have scoffed at my ideas as at those of a dreamer. But has it been all in vain? who has given these men courage to speak such words as I hear now, in the open street? has not the day already come to put an end to this absurd farce of allegiance to Spain?"

As he so mused a hand was laid upon his arm, he turned and found himself face to face with Marcelino Ponce de Leon. In the face of his friend there beamed a look of pleasure such as he had not seen there for many months.

"You have heard the news of which those men talk," said Evaña, "and you are glad."

The smile faded from Marcelino's face, and passing his arm through Evaña's he led him away up the street. Turning his face from him and speaking in low tones he said—

"I have news which did make me very joyful, yet now I feel sad. Look——"

Putting his hand into his pocket, he drew out a letter and

showed it to Evaña. The letter bore an English postmark, the address was in a bold hand which Evaña recognized at once. For a moment his firm step faltered, and a deadly pallor overspread his cheek, but it was for a moment only, the next he asked calmly—

" How did he escape?"

" He never sailed in the ' Petrel,'" replied Marcelino.

For a minute or two they walked on in silence, then Evaña spoke again.

" But you have not answered my question," he said. " Is not the day at hand? are we not already a free people?"

"Alas! it is too true. Spain has fallen," said Marcelino.

Again they walked on in silence; again Evaña was the first to speak.

" I have been idle," said he, " but the work has been done for me, while I have been asleep, dreaming. The day has arisen, the dreams of the night have passed from me."

Then seizing the hand of his friend he pressed it fiercely in his own, and turning from him strode rapidly away towards his own dwelling.

For two days Don Carlos Evaña shut his door to every visitor, on the third day he sallied forth and took his way to the house of Don Manuel Belgrano. He found Don Manuel in his study, and drawing a roll of papers from his pocket he handed it to him.

Don Manuel spread open the roll on his desk, and glanced over the papers. They consisted of a series of political articles for the " Diario."

" It is too soon," said he, as he turned the last sheet and looked up. "They would not meet the approval of his Excellency Don Baltazar?"

" I dare not even submit them to his inspection."

"The day is at hand when the editor of the ' Diario' will scorn the approval of the nominee of Spain," replied Evaña.

Don Roderigo Ponce de Leon, walking through the streets of Buenos Aires, heard the careless comments of the people on the disasters which had befallen Spain, heard them as Don Carlos Evaña had heard them, but their effect upon him was far different.

" I have sought to raise this people from their ignorance," said he to himself; " I have studied their interests and welfare in every measure which I have adopted; I have even sought the aid of some of the most intelligent among them in the hope of inspiring them with the true spirit of patriotism, yet they can rejoice at the misfortunes which have fallen on my country, upon the country to which they owe the love and reverence of children to a parent."

So musing bitterly to himself he took his way to the fort. As he passed through the ante-room leading to the official apartments of the Viceroy, the door opened of a room in which Don Baltazar de Cisneros was accustomed to give private audience to such as were most in his confidence; from this room came forth Don Alfonso Miranda. Don Roderigo started, an angry frown spread over his features, he returned the obsequious bow of the medico with a haughty stare, and passed on into the presence of the Viceroy.

" Your Excellency is perhaps not aware of the character of the man who has just left you," said he to Don Baltazar, as he closed the door behind him.

"You speak of the Señor Miranda?" replied Don Baltazar.

"I do," said Don Roderigo. "I have just passed through the city, I have listened to the comments of the Creoles upon the disasters which have fallen upon Spain, I have come to warn your Excellency that we are on the eve of a catastrophe."

"And what has that to do with the Señor Miranda?"

"In admitting such a man to your confidence your Excellency runs great danger, if he visits you, he comes as a spy."

"Yes, but as my spy," replied Don Baltazar.

"You are acquainted then with his character, and employ him?"

"I seek to do so, for, before I left Spain, he was named to me as a man who might be serviceable in procuring for me secret information. I am as well aware as you that there are dangerous ideas abroad in the city, and there are some men upon whom I wish to keep watch. The Señor Miranda visited me at my own request."

"And what has he told you?"

"Nothing; but he has promised to report to me upon the movements of one man, of whom Marshal Liniers entertained great suspicions, the Señor Evaña. If this excitement of the people should culminate in any outbreak against my authority, I am assured that the Señor Evaña will be at the head of it."

"Do you know that the Señor Miranda is brother to Francisco Miranda of Venezuela?"

"Of Francisco Miranda! No, I did not know that."

"Your Excellency should enquire more carefully into the antecedents of the men you trust," said Don Roderigo, with something of contempt in his tone.

"I was informed that about ten years ago the Señor Miranda gave timely information to the Consulado of some conspiracy which was thus averted."

"Of a conspiracy invented in his own brain," replied Don Roderigo angrily; "his information averted no conspiracy, for there was none, but cast suspicion upon some most loyal Spaniards, and drove some of the best servants of Spain from her service. I was one of the conspirators he denounced; think you that I am a less trusty servant of Spain than a Miranda from Venezuela?"

"Yet you have your ideas," replied Don Baltazar softly, "and you had not then the experience you have now."

"The experience I have now, teaches me that the ideas I entertained ten years ago were correct. You have removed the restrictions upon trade, you admit Creoles to your counsels, such were the steps which I advocated in the year '98; for this I was denounced by your friend the Doctor Miranda to the Consulado of Cadiz, and lost my seat in the Audencia Real."

"You introduced the Señor Evaña to me on my arrival, he is an intimate friend of yours, but I believe him to be a most dangerous man."

"He is a man who may be of great service to us," replied Don Roderigo; "I have sought his friendship in order to wean him from the extravagant ideas he learned during his residence in Europe."

"I am informed that he is about to marry your daughter. You would not give your daughter to any man suspected of disloyalty?"

"Your Excellency is well informed," said Don Roderigo, smiling.

"Then I will accept your guarantee for the loyalty of the Señor Evaña, but General Miranda has agents in this city and I suspect that the Señor Evaña is in correspondence with him."

"The principal correspondent of General Miranda is his brother," replied Don Roderigo, "that I can prove to you by the testimony of Major Asneiros, who has been commissioned by me to keep watch on this medico. Major Asneiros surprised him not a week ago reading to the Señor Evaña a letter from the General, doubtless with the intention of drawing him into some conspiracy. If your Excellency were to order the arrest of Don Alfonso, we should certainly learn from his papers the real nature of the projects of Don Francisco."

After some further conversation, Don Roderigo took his leave, and an hour later Major Asneiros, sent by him, sought an interview with the Viceroy. The Major laughed heartily when he heard of the suspicions of Don Alfonso which Don Roderigo had excited in the mind of Don Baltazar.

"There is one man much more dangerous than the old medico ever can be," said Asneiros, "the Señor Evaña. He is the correspondent of General Miranda, that Don Roderigo knows well enough, and he overrates his influence with him if he thinks he can prevent him from engaging in any conspiracy against your authority."

"I have been frequently warned against the Señor Evaña," replied the Viceroy, "but without proofs of the existence of some conspiracy I dare take no steps against him, his arrest would only end in a fiasco like that of Puyrredon. How did you discover that he is in correspondence with Don Francisco?"

Then Asneiros recounted to Don Baltazar how he had surprised a confession of this fact from Magdalen Miranda, and continued—

"When she left me I went in after her and walked straight to the sala. Don Alfonso had an open letter in his hand which he crumpled up and thrust into his pocket. The Señor Evaña looked at me as though I were a wild beast, and soon afterwards put on his hat and went, but Don Alfonso kept the letter, and has it yet I don't doubt, for I know he has some secret hiding-place in his house. If we could get that letter we might find some proof against the Señor Evaña."

"I agree with you, in spite of the assurances of Don Roderigo, that Evaña is a most dangerous man," replied the Viceroy, "but I have every confidence in Don Roderigo himself, and shall entrust the management of this affair to him; if he instructs you to arrest Don Alfonso, do so, but remember, that what I want is a proof that the Señor Evaña is engaged in some conspiracy—proof such as I can show to Don Roderigo and to the Audencia Real, then I can proceed against the Señor Evaña without danger of having my orders set at defiance."

That evening Don Ciriaco set off alone on foot, for the Plaza Miserere. He reached the Quinta de Don Alfonso, opened the gate very cautiously, and walking to the sala window looked in. The medico was alone, seated in his arm-chair, buried apparently in deep thought, a shaded lamp burning on the table at his elbow. Don Ciriaco went back to the porch, and finding the house door open, entered very quietly and went on to the sala, treading softly and laying his finger on his lip. Don Alfonso started up with a faint cry, then sank down again into his chair, pale and trembling, as he recognized his untimely visitor. Asneiros went up to him, laid one hand on his arm, and whispered into his ear—

"Silence! all is discovered; but I have arranged a way for you to save yourself."

"What is discovered? I assure you I know nothing of it," answered Don Alfonso.

"I have come with the intention of helping you. If you wish me to be of any service to you, you must give me your entire confidence."

"But I assure you I refused to have anything to do with it, and would not listen to what he wished to tell me."

"The Señor Evaña spent the evening with you?"

"Yes, he did, but I kept my daughter with me, he could not speak with me."

"And the letter from your brother, did you return it to him?"

"What letter?"

"The letter he brought to show you last week."

"Mi Dios! Why should I return it to him? Why should I give him my letters? I burned it."

"You did badly, and you should have listened to the Señor Evaña this evening, he had something important to tell you."

"What matters to me that newspaper or the education of the people?"

"Look you, Don Alfonso, I did not come here to talk nonsense about newspapers or education. If you refuse me your confidence, I cannot help you. Your name is in the list of the suspected, but the head of the conspiracy is this Señor Evaña. Give me all the papers he has given you to keep for him, and I have a promise from the Viceroy that you shall not be molested in any way."

"The Señor Evaña has never given me any paper of his."

"Then I cannot help you at all," said Asneiros, rising from the chair on which he had seated himself. "Sleep well to-night in your own bed, to-morrow night you will sleep in the calabozo."

"Dios mio! Don Ciriaco," said Don Alfonso, seizing him by the arm, "what have I done? Why should they put me in the calabozo? I would not even listen to the Señor Evaña when he wished to speak to me of things."

"You did wrong not to listen, you might have learned something, and your evidence against Evaña would have saved yourself. But perhaps it is not too late, I will give you three days, after that I cannot protect you any longer; you will be arrested, your house searched, and all your effects confiscated."

"But, Don Ciriaco, do not leave me. Why do you say such things? You say there is some conspiracy, if there is I know nothing of it. The Señor Evaña has never spoken of it to me, how can I give evidence against him? Don Baltazar asked me———"

"A conspiracy there is, and we will know all about it very soon.

z

Don Baltazar de Cisneros is not like that Frenchman Liniers, the least punishment the conspirators may expect will be imprisonment and confiscation. Take care of yourself, you do not appear very rich, but everything you have will be confiscated."

Don Alfonso fell back in his chair with a groan.

"I am not a conspirator, and I am very poor. God help me!" he said. "But, Don Ciriaco, you have always been a good friend to me, even yet you may do something for me; even if they put me in prison you will not let them search the house, you will prevent that. Why should they, I have nothing worth the trouble of carrying away."

"You can prevent it yourself; if you have no papers belonging to the Señor Evaña, you can find them."

Just then the door opened and Magdalen entered the room. Seeing the miserable state of her father she ran to him.

"Papa! papa!" she said, throwing herself on his breast, "what has this man been saying to you? Do not believe a word he says, I know that he comes here as your friend to do some treachery to you. Pay no attention to him."

"Look you, Don Alfonso," said Asneiros, "I give you three days to find those papers. If you do not find them you will explain to the Viceroy, and not to me, why you have secret hiding-places cut in the walls of your house."

At that, Don Alfonso thrust his daughter from him, and gazing with terror-stricken eyes at Asneiros tried in vain to speak, but Asneiros, turning from him, went out through the door and through the porch and walked rapidly away.

Don Alfonso passed a sleepless night sitting in his arm-chair moaning and lamenting, Magdalen doing all she could to comfort him, till he sternly bade her leave him, saying that she had brought all this trouble upon him by attracting Asneiros to the quinta.

The next day Don Alfonso walked into the city, went straight to the house of Don Carlos Evaña, and told him everything that had occurred on the previous night, after he had left the quinta. Evaña listened somewhat scornfully, but looking at the haggard cheeks and blood-shot eyes of the old man, he felt pity for him.

"He wants proofs of a conspiracy? Pues! He shall have them. Here is all the conspiracy that there is," said he, taking up a copy of the "Diario" which lay upon the table, "and his Excellency the Viceroy is at the head of us. We are conspiring to educate the people, and I fully believe that the Señor Asneiros is correct in thinking that it imperils the existence of Spanish rule among us."

Don Alfonso looked helplessly at him, and answered—

"He spoke of a letter from my brother, how has he come to know of that? The letter you gave me from him I have burned, I kept it two days, then I burned it. I always do, I want no letters from Francisco. What matter to me his plans, all that I want is to live in peace. Cannot you help me in some way? You told me that the time of arrests and confiscations was gone, and I lived without fear, but it appears that all is to begin again."

"You think so! I can assure you that those times are gone, never to return."

"And he assures me that in three days I shall be put into the calabozo."

"That will not do you any great damage, and may help the cause of the people. It would be a scandal, for nothing can be even alleged against you, and we shall soon get you out again. Now that I think of it, it is well that you be arrested, the city is very quiet, and an arbitrary arrest might arouse a little excitement."

"Don Carlos!" exclaimed Don Alfonso, "what is this you say to me? They will search my house and rob me."

"Rob you! unless you have some treasure buried away under the flooring I don't think they will rob you of much."

"No, Don Carlos, no! I assure you I have no treasure. You know how poor I am. What can I have to bury under the floor?"

Don Carlos looked at him attentively one moment, then taking up the "Diario" he folded it carefully into a small oblong packet, wrapped it in a sheet of paper, which he carefully sealed with three seals, and drawing an inkstand towards him, endorsed it—

Proofs of the nefarious Conspiracy against the People of Buenos Aires, entertained by H. E. Don Baltazar de Cisneros, with the aid of Don Carlos Evaña and various others.

"I cannot compliment you on your choice of friends, Don Alfonso," he said, handing him the packet; "but when this distinguished major, the Señor Asneiros, next visits you, you can give him this as a proof of my treason. If after that he wishes to arrest me let him come, I am ready for him."

"But, Señor Don Carlos," said Don Alfonso, holding the packet at arm's length, "if I give him this he will say that I am mocking him, and then they will arrest me, and——"

"When do you expect him to visit you?"

"The day after to-morrow, in the evening."

"Then the day after to-morrow in the evening he shall meet me. If he should visit you in the mean time you can easily put him off."

The second day after this, about sundown, Don Carlos Evaña and Marcelino Ponce de Leon rode side by side through the suburbs towards the Miserere.

"You have judged rightly, Carlos," said Marcelino. "Any misfortune that might befall the old man would cause her great sorrow, and I thank you for asking me to assist you in anything that may keep a sorrow from her."

"Yet she has treated you very badly," said Don Carlos. "She led you to feel sure of her love, and then transferred her affections with the greatest ease to that traitor of a Spaniard."

"I do not think so, she loved me once. But her father wishes it, he never liked me, and she submits."

"It is strange, I always thought her a girl of much strength of character. Did you ever tell her that you loved her?"

"Not in so many words, but she knew it; an avowal of love needs no words. But it is now more than a year since I have had a chance of speaking with her, she shuns me. When we meet she will not let me pay her the simplest attention. She has not forgotten me, but she is trying to forget me."

"Perhaps we have been mistaken all the time."

"Oh no, I made sure, I asked my aunt Josefina, and she told me that they were only waiting till Asneiros got some settled employ which the Viceroy had promised him."

"That will all be at an end now."

"I suppose it will, but it will make no difference to me, her father will find another husband for her. When a girl once gives up her own choice at her father's command it matters very little to her whom she marries. You and I have seen many instances of that."

"Too many," replied Evaña.

After this they rode on in silence till they reached the quinta, where they dismounted, tying their horses under the trees behind the house.

In the porch they found Magdalen, sitting alone, with her face buried in her hands, weeping bitterly. From inside the house came the sound of a voice raised high in anger.

"Do not weep, Magdalen," said Marcelino, bending over her. "Don Alfonso has two fast friends here, who will see that no injustice is done him."

Magdalen's tears ceased instantly at the sound of that voice, and a thrill of joy shot through her as she looked up and met the glance of the dark eyes bent upon her in tender sympathy.

"Oh, help papa!" she said. "Do not let them take him, he has done nothing."

"I will remain with Magdalen," said Don Carlos, seating himself beside her. "You are more likely to arrange the matter amicably than I am, he always shows great respect for you. Go you and see what this is all about."

Marcelino went instantly to the sala, and, opening the door, saw Don Alfonso, hardly able to stand, clinging to the back of a chair, while Asneiros, standing in the centre of the room, was speaking to him.

"You are mocking me," he said. "I know where to find these proofs if I choose to look. If that letter is burned you can procure another, or you can make a declaration, which will do as well. I wished to give you the chance of setting yourself right with the authorities. You refuse; well go your own way, and do not blame me if your house is robbed while you are in gaol."

"Señor Asneiros," said Marcelino, stepping forward, "this is not the tone in which you should speak to a man whose hairs are white with age. Permit me, Don Alfonso," he added, turning a chair round and assisting the medico to seat himself.

"Señor Don Marcelino," said Asneiros, softening his tone considerably, "it is a fortunate chance that has sent you here."

"It is no chance at all, Señor Asneiros," replied Marcelino; "I heard that you were threatening Don Alfonso with imprisonment for complicity in some conspiracy which exists only in your own imagination. What may be your real purpose I do not care to enquire, but I insist upon it that you leave this house immediately."

"Señor Don Marcelino, I assure you that I am only acting under orders, and am actuated by the most friendly motives to Don Alfonso. There are grave causes of suspicion against him, and I have shown him the means by which he can set himself right with the authorities."

"You wish him to save himself by bringing a false accusation against some one else. Enough of that, Señor Asneiros. Don Alfonso knows nothing of any conspiracy, and can in no way assist you."

"You speak well, you speak well, Don Marcelino," said Don Alfonso, still in great perturbation; "there is no conspiracy, but do not speak harshly to this gentleman. He has been a good friend to me on many occasions, and will protect me. Is it not so, Don Ciriaco? You will tell his Excellency that you have made every enquiry, and have found that there is no truth in the accusations that have been laid against me."

"I shall have the honour of reporting to his Excellency what you have told me, but I hope that further consideration may induce you to take a wiser course."

So saying, Asneiros took up his hat, and with a low bow to Marcelino left the room.

In the porch he was somewhat startled to find Don Carlos Evaña in earnest conversation with Magdalen, but passed them without a word and walked away.

"He knows nothing, and cannot assist me in any way," he muttered to himself, as he slowly crossed the Plaza Miserere; "but I should like to have the inspection of that black coffer of his, he has some reason for keeping it so secret. Don Roderigo would be glad of any pretext for putting him in prison and looking through his papers. I'll give him one, who knows but I may do myself a service too?"

Don Carlos and Marcelino remained for two hours longer at the quinta, and had the pleasure of drinking tea once more from the porcelain cups of Magdalen Miranda, but the evening was not a pleasant one to any of them—there was a general feeling of constraint. Don Alfonso trembled at every noise, and was more than usually taciturn; Magdalen seemed confused, and spoke only in whispers.

As the two friends rode back to the city together through the darkness, Don Carlos spoke.

"I told her of the reports that are in circulation concerning her and this Señor Asneiros," he said. "It may be her father's wish but it is not hers, nor does she think that the major has any idea of it. She says that he has been a constant spy upon her father for more than a year past, and that she warned her father of him, but that he refused to listen to her."

"Poor girl!" said Marcelino, and then rode on in moody silence, hardly hearing a word of what Evaña said after that, till they reached the centre of the city and separated.

When Asneiros left the Miserere he walked straight to the house of Don Roderigo Ponce de Leon, with whom he had a long interview, the result of which was, that at midnight a party of soldiers, under the command of the major, proceeded to the Quinta de Don Alfonso, woke up the inmates by knocking at the door, and shouted to them to " open in the name of the law." Don Alfonso was arrested and his private room rigorously searched, but for some time nothing worthy of notice was found, till Asneiros, prodding the wall behind the bedstead with his sword, discovered a hollow carefully concealed by the wainscot. Not knowing how to open it, he ordered a panel to be wrenched away, and disclosed a small coffer of black oak, bound with brass and very heavy, which he took away with him, together with all the letters and written papers he could find, while Don Alfonso, more dead than alive, was lifted into a small cart and driven away to the Cabildo, where he was imprisoned in the same apartment which had formerly been occupied by Marcelino Ponce de Leon.

During the examination of Don Alfonso's room all the inmates of the quinta had been, by the major's command, imprisoned in the sala. When he had secured the black coffer he prosecuted the search no further, but proceeding to the sala, ordered Don Alfonso to come out alone. saying that he merely wished to speak with him for a minute. Magdalen appeared with her father, clinging to him, when Asneiros rudely pushed her back into the room and shut the door, placing a guard there with instructions to allow no one to leave the house before sunrise.

On the morning following this arrest Don Fausto Velasquez, who was an early riser, was walking about in his patio, wrapped in a loose dressing-gown, when a girl, enveloped from head to foot in a large shawl, came hurriedly in through the open doorway, and, throwing herself upon her knees at his feet, caught his hand in both her own, crying—

" Papa! Don Fausto, papa! They have taken him! Don Ciriaco——"

She could say no more, and would have fallen on her face, but Don Fausto, taking her in his arms, raised her up and saw it was Magdalen. He carried her inside into his wife's room, where she presently recovered sufficiently to give a clear account of what had happened, but it was a long time before Don Fausto could persuade her that her father was in no danger, and would very soon be set at liberty.

Don Alfonso was but little known in the city, and those who did know him had but small respect for him, yet in the then excited state of the public mind, a very slight circumstance was sufficient to create great agitation. Men enquired eagerly one of another who was this Don Alfonso Miranda, and what was the cause of his imprisonment ; and when they learned that he was the brother of General Miranda, whose exploits in Venezuela had caused him to be looked upon as the champion of liberty by all Spanish Americans, his crime became clear to them at once—he had dared to devise some scheme for liberating them from Spanish tyranny, and in their eyes he rose to be a hero and a martyr.

Groups of men paraded the Plaza Mayor and the principal streets, as they met they asked one another in loud voices—

" How long shall these things be ? "

And as some Spaniard high in office passed them, frowning angrily and chafing within himself at his impotence to put a stop to such disorderly assemblages, they would turn and shout after him as he went—

"Spain has fallen!"

Don Carlos Evaña, strolling through the streets of the city, heard these shouts and smiled, saying to himself—

"The day is at hand."

Marcelino Ponce de Leon, busy at his desk in the office of the Consulado, heard these shouts, and passed his fingers through his curly, black hair, saying resignedly—

"It is too late, America must be for Americans alone."

Don Manuel Belgrano, revising the proofs of his "Diario," heard these shouts, and turned over with his fingers the sheets of a series of fiery articles he had received some days before, saying to himself—

"I might almost venture them now; they do but say what men now shout aloud at the street corners."

Don Roderigo Ponce de Leon, in the quiet of his own study, heard these shouts and said nothing, for his heart was heavy with a foreboding care.

To the Viceroy, surrounded by his guards and sentries, came these shouts, and he shrugged his shoulders and thought nothing of them. To him they were but as the utterance of a fact, and conveyed no warning.

"Spain has fallen!" said old men, joining hands together, and reading each in the face of the other the realization of a hope long deferred.

"Spain has fallen!" shouted men in the vigour of life, throwing back their heads proudly, and striding through the streets of their own city, treading the soil of their own country with a joyful sense of freedom.

"Spain has fallen!" shouted young men, as they saw the world opening up before them with prospects of which their fathers had known nothing, and who saw themselves the centre of proud hopes, as yet but dimly discerned through the mists of the unknown future.

"Spain has fallen!" So throughout the great, straggling city was heard the voice of the people, asking nothing, demanding nothing, proclaiming only a fact known to all.

Yet was this voice both a warning and a menace to those who sought to rule the people for their own ends. Buenos Aires had looked to Spain as to a mother, yet in this voice there was no pity. Buenos Aires still looked upon Spain as a tyrant, yet in this voice there was no fear.

The hatred of an enslaved people against their tyrants, the jealousy of a dependent race against the race which has dominated over them for centuries, were both expressed in that one shout, which had in it nothing of love, nothing of fear—

"Spain has fallen!"

BOOK VI.

LIBERTY.

PROLOGUE.

The division of youth from manhood is marked by no fixed line established by law or custom. To each youth there comes a day when, without aid or counsel, he has to decide upon some important step which shall influence the whole course of his future life. According to the bias of his nature he ponders long upon this step, or he comes rapidly to some decision. The day he so decides, marks for him the end of his youth, the commencement of his manhood.

When a youth so steps into manhood, he meets the world face to face, and braces himself for the encounter. Hope, which is the dowry of youth, attends upon him; he puts forth all his energies, never doubting of success, and achieves that which is deemed impossible.

Buenos Aires, long impatient of Spanish tyranny, saw her tyrant helpless; she saw a continent around her, groaning with the slavery of centuries; she felt within herself the strength of a young nation, and asked herself whether the task were not hers to give liberty to these enslaved peoples, to achieve it for herself.

Long she pondered over this question, doubting within herself whether the day were come. Having decided, with resolute hand she cast aside the trammels which bound her, broke through the subterfuges of those who still sought to impose upon her ignorance, and stood forth, free herself, and the champion of freedom for all Spanish America.

As the sun, bursting through a veil of clouds, dissipates the mists of the early morn, rousing men from the slumbers of night to the active work of day, so Buenos Aires, bursting through the traditions of centuries, dissipated for ever the mists of ignorance, under which slumbered in ignoble servitude the colonies of Spain.

The sun of May, emblem of Buenos Aires, shone forth over the New World, rousing enslaved peoples to the bold assertion of their rights as men. In the struggle which followed, this emblem was ever in the fore-front of the battle, the rallying-point of a band of heroes, whose swords achieved the liberation of an entire continent.

Buenos Aires, free herself, became at once the apostle and champion of freedom for all Spanish America.

CHAPTER I.

HOW THE LAST TIE WAS BROKEN.

SPAIN has fallen! These words echoed through the city from end to end, but to the majority of men they were simply the proclamation of an acknowledged fact, an outburst of that jealousy of Spain, that fretfulness of Spanish domination, which had for years been growing up in Buenos Aires. But there was a minority in Buenos Aires, a minority ever increasing, a minority of men of cultivated minds, of men of far-seeing intelligence; to these men these words taught a lesson, in them they inspired a hope.

At the head of this minority were Don Carlos Evaña, Don Marcelino Ponce de Leon, and the other members of the secret committee. They consulted among themselves, asking one another, " Has not the day come?" " What shall we do?"

Then, true to their principle of keeping themselves as much as possible in the background, they decided upon requesting Don Gregorio Lopez to call again together a meeting of the chiefs of the militia and of the leading citizens, and to propound to them these questions, to which they themselves purposed to find an answer.

Yet March passed over and nothing was done, and all this time Don Alfonso Miranda lay in prison, and his daughter, who was not allowed to visit him, found shelter under the roof of Don Fausto Velasquez. Many efforts were made by Don Fausto and by Don Gregorio Lopez to procure his release, but in vain, and their enquiries as to the cause of his detention were met by evasive answers. Then as they insisted that they should at least have liberty to speak with him, the Viceroy referred them to Don Roderigo Ponce de Leon.

Don Roderigo answered his father-in-law and Don Fausto with great brevity, saying that he had long suspected Don Alfonso of treasonable designs, and had only acted upon receipt of positive information.

" Have you discovered anything in his papers to criminate him?" asked Don Fausto.

" Nothing. He either keeps his correspondence well concealed or has destroyed it."

" Then upon what pretext do you keep him in prison?"

" His examination is not yet concluded," replied Don Roderigo.

" And you still refuse us permission to visit him?" said Don Fausto.

" I can allow him to have no communication with any one. In

the present excited state of the city it would be unsafe to permit him
any chance of communicating with his accomplices."

"I compliment you upon your policy," replied Don Fausto. "It
may cause the death of a harmless old man, and can only tend to
increase the popular excitement, of which you seem somewhat apprehensive."

"His daughter spoke to me of a black coffer which was discovered
in his room, and by which Don Alfonso seemed to set great store,"
said Don Gregorio; "do you know what has become of it?"

"All his effects are in the hands of Major Asneiros, who had
charge of the examination of his papers," replied Don Roderigo.

"Asneiros has behaved like a brute," said Don Fausto.

"The Señor Major Asneiros has small sympathy for traitors,"
replied Don Roderigo.

Don Gregorio and Don Fausto returned to the house of the latter
gentleman but little pleased with the result of their interview. In
the ante-sala they found Doña Josefina with Magdalen and Elisa
Puyrredon; to them they recounted the ill-success of their errand.

"It is a barbarity," said Elisa Puyrredon. "Where are we going
to stop? Wait till my brother comes back. I cannot understand it
at all."

"Nor I," said Doña Josefina. "This Asneiros has not come to
see me for a month, why do you not go to see him, Fausto? He will
tell you more than Don Roderigo. Magdalen says it is all owing to
him that her father was arrested, and he was so great a friend of Don
Alfonso."

As Doña Josefina said this she looked sharply at Magdalen, who
flushed scarlet, and said—

"I do not think the Señor Asneiros was ever a friend to papa, he
was a spy."

"I know he did not go to the quinta so often to see Don Alfonso,"
said Doña Josefina.

At this moment Marcelino Ponce de Leon walked in at the open
door. His entrance caused no surprise for he had been a frequent
visitor at his aunt's house for a month past, but Magdalen rose from
her seat immediately and left the room.

"She is always so," said Doña Josefina, shrugging her plump, white
shoulders. "If any gentleman pays her any attention, from that
moment she abhors him. I can remember when Marcelino and she
were the best of friends, now see how she treats him, she will not
remain a minute in the room if he comes in. Without doubt it has
been the same with this Asneiros, you heard how she spoke of him
just now. He has resented her treatment of him, we have the old
man in prison, and the daughter——" here came another shrug of the
plump, white shoulders, then turning to Marcelino she asked—

"Are all English girls like that, Marcelino? The Señor Gordon at
any rate knew how to behave himself."

"The Señor Gordon was as polished as a Porteño," said Elisa
Puyrredon. "You thought he was drowned, Marcelino, and never
said a word of it for so many months. But I saw you were triste
about something."

" Where is he now ? " asked Don Gregorio.

" He was on Marshal Beresford's staff," replied Marcelino ; " but, as he can talk Spanish, he says they have set him to drill the Portuguese, from the idea that he can make them understand him."

" Well, Fausto, if you intend to see Don Ciriaco I think the sooner you see him the better," said Doña Josefina.

" We will go at once," said Don Gregorio.

When the two elder gentlemen had gone, Doña Josefina rose from her seat and went through the folding-doors into the sala.

" You are triste yet," said Elisa Puyrredon, drawing her chair nearer to Marcelino. " Have you some other sorrow than the supposed loss of your friend ? You might tell me."

" Think you it is no sorrow to me to see that when my father has the power he is a tyrant, the same as any other Spaniard ? In this imprisonment of Don Alfonso he has committed a great injustice. I have been told that years ago this Don Alfonso did him some injury ; now that he can he revenges himself, like a Spaniard. I thought him both too good-hearted and too politic to have taken such a false step in times so critical as the present."

" You take great interest in all concerns Don Alfonso ? "

" I think of my father and do not like to hear him accused of tyranny, and to be able to say no word in his defence."

" Magdalen is very unhappy. Have you no sorrow for her. As Doña Josefina said just now, once you were the best of friends together."

" Naturally I am sorry for her, I have done all I can for Don Alfonso for her sake."

" What have you done ? "

" I have used all my influence with Asneiros, who has the charge of examining Don Alfonso's papers, to prevail upon him to declare at once what he has found. But he refuses to examine them and says he has simply sealed them up until further orders."

" Have you not spoken to Don Roderigo ? "

" How can I go to my father and accuse him to his face of injustice ? "

" I thought that when men loved they would dare anything, even the anger of their father, for the sake of the one they loved."

" But if that love is slighted, and thrown aside as a thing of no value, why should I risk what is next in value to me for the sake of what is lost ? "

" Are you sure it is lost ? I have heard say that when a girl once loves she loves for ever. You once thought that you were loved."

" I more than thought so, I was sure of it. I have been told that girls easily love and easily forget. It is their nature to love something, but it is very little matter to them what they love."

" You heretic ! You never deserve that any one should love you, never."

" I do not care now if no one ever does love me. I am content with such love as I have. I love my mother and Lola, and I would give my life to preserve to its end my love and respect for my father."

" Don't tell me that, I know better. The love of father and mother and sister is never enough for any man. A man is not a man until he have some other love."

"And if he win another love, such a love as he has dreamed about, such a love as would make his life complete, only to lose it, what then?"

"The grave," said Elisa, in a very solemn voice, then bursting into a merry laugh she clapped her hands. "Mi Dios!" she exclaimed, "you have the face of a hero of tragedy."

"You have never loved or you would not laugh at me," said Marcelino.

"I never loved! I have been in love fifty times. Why the first time I ever met that Asneiros I fell in love with him at once. He was dressed in a gorgeous coat of crimson velvet, and had diamond buckles in his shoes; it was those buckles that captured me, the first glance at them."

Again she laughed, and this time Marcelino laughed with her.

"But I can tell you one thing I should not like," she said, after a pause; "if I were very much in love with any one I should not like to see him *very* friendly with some one very much prettier than I am."

"You need never fear that. Most men say that there is no one in Buenos Aires prettier than you are."

"Traitor! Is not the girl you love fairer to you than any one else in the world?"

"Dearer, yes. But beauty is to be admired, not loved. It is not essential to love that the loved one be beautiful."

"Yet the loved one is always fair?"

"Always."

"Even when she turns her back upon you and leaves you and smiles on some one else?"

"Even then."

"Then I retract my statement that I have been in love fifty times. I suppose I have never been in love, not even with the Señor Don Ciriaco Asneiros. I could never forgive a lover who was rude to me and had smiles for some one else—never."

"The love of women differs from that of men, it is more exacting," said Marcelino.

"I suppose it is," said Elisa, with something of weariness in her tone. "You and I have been always very good friends, do you know that there are people who say that there is more than friendship between us?"

"What matters it what people say?"

"Nothing to us, but if any one has said so to Magdalen it may matter much to her." Then Elisa looked down confusedly, twining her fingers together, and with a flush on her fair face.

Marcelino rose from his chair and went into the sala, where Doña Josefina was sitting out of sight, but within hearing of them.

"Aunt," said he, sitting down beside her, "was there any truth in what you told me, that Magdalen was going to marry Don Ciriaco?"

"I thought there was," replied Doña Josefina quietly. "I know Don Alfonso wished it, but Magdalen tells me it is quite false, and now I suppose it is impossible."

Marcelino remained talking with his aunt and Elisa Puyrredon for nearly an hour, when Don Fausto returned alone, saying that Don Ciriaco Asneiros could give them no help or information whatever, alleging that he was merely acting under orders and knew nothing of the cause of the arrest of Don Alfonso.

" You will speak to your father now, will you not? " said Elisa Puyrredon to Marcelino, as he took up his hat to go.

" I am going at once," said Marcelino.

" At last I shall believe that there are some men who know how to love," said she to him in a whisper.

It was late in the afternoon when Marcelino reached his father's house. Don Roderigo had left half an hour before for the quinta, where the family were then staying. He ordered his horse to be saddled and sent after him to the house of Don Carlos Evaña, whither he proceeded on foot. He found Don Carlos in his study, his table covered with sheets of manuscript which he was revising. Marcelino took up some of these sheets and glanced over them.

" If Don Ciriaco Asneiros still wants proofs of treason, you had better send him a few of these, Carlos," said he.

" Treason, you say," replied Evaña, " wait a month or two and you will call them patriotic."

" So soon ? "

" For what are we to wait? Everything is now ready, it wants but a spark and the mine explodes."

" Is this the spark ? "

" Scarcely so. This is the wind to keep the spark from going out."

" You seem to have done enough for to-day, a gallop would do you good. I want you to help me with my father as I helped you with Asneiros."

" You want him to set Don Alfonso at liberty. I tell you he will refuse."

" I hope not, it is a gross injustice."

" Then Don Roderigo is at the quinta ? "

" Yes, and I had rather see him there than in the city. He will not like my interference, and may say things which I should be sorry if any but ourselves were to hear."

Two hours afterwards Don Roderigo was seated in his sala at the quinta, his face was flushed as though something had angered him. Near him sat Don Carlos Evaña with a quiet smile playing upon his lips. Marcelino stood leaning against the window-frame, evidently suffering bitterly from some disappointment. Doña Constancia entered the room, and seeing the sorrow in her son's face walked up to him.

" Do you know, Constancia, what has brought these two young men out here this evening? " said Don Roderigo.

" They have come to see us, I suppose," answered the lady. " Don Carlos has been quite a stranger lately."

" Not at all; they have come to ask me to set that traitor Miranda at liberty."

"I can excuse Marcelino for that," said Doña Constancia. "Don Alfonso was very good to him when he was wounded."

"Don Alfonso is a physician, and found good practice in his broken ribs. He was well paid for his trouble."

"I did not know that you paid him," said Marcelino; "he refused any acknowledgment from me."

"You cannot think that I would accept a favour from a man like him. I can assure you he was ready enough to take my gold."

"I have no doubt he deserves his imprisonment or the Viceroy would not have put him in prison, so do not trouble yourself any more about him, Marcelino," said Doña Constancia.

"It is not about him that I trouble myself," replied Marcelino. "If he were justly imprisoned I would not say a word for him, but we have made enquiries and can hear of no accusation having been brought against him, merely suspicions. And men say——"

"Who are *we* that have made those enquiries?" asked Don Roderigo.

"My grandfather and Don Fausto as well as myself."

"They were with me to-day. In future you had better leave such enquiries to them."

"But, father, have not you heard how people talk about it all over the city? It has brought discredit upon the Viceroy, and upon all those who act with him. We all thought that the days of arbitrary imprisonments were gone by."

"What matters it what the mob says? You may be sure that the Viceroy has good reasons for what he does."

"Then why does he not bring him to trial? Why does he say that he does not know anything of the charges against him, and refer those who ask him to you?"

"I have given you my answer, and I request that you never mention the man's name to me again." So saying Don Roderigo rose from his chair and left the room.

As Don Roderigo left the room by one door Dolores entered it by another.

"What is to do?" said she. "Papa looked quite angry."

"There is this to do, my sister," said Marcelino; "that the cause of Spain is lost in America. There are many of us Creoles who would have gladly joined the Spaniards in raising up in America a new kingdom for King Ferdinand now that the French have taken his old one, but we demand equal rights and equal laws for all, and the best of the Spaniards will not yield that. There is one law for Spaniards and another law for Americans."

"What nonsense you talk, Marcelino. King Ferdinand will soon win his own kingdom back again."

"By the help of the English?" said Don Carlos.

"Yes, the English will help him. But what is it all about?" said Dolores. "Papa was angry."

"Marcelino wanted him to ask the Viceroy to pardon Don Alfonso Miranda, and to let him go," said Doña Constancia.

"No wonder then, that papa was angry. How could you think of making such a request, Marcelino?"

" I did not ask for pardon, my sister, I asked only for justice."

" Justice! of course he will have justice, he will be well punished."

" For what, fair lady?" said Don Carlos.

" They would not put him in prison unless he deserved it. I am not a bit sorry for him, but I am for Magdalen. Is she stopping yet with Aunt Josefina?"

" Yes," said Don Carlos, " the poor girl has nowhere else to go to."

" And I suppose the Señor Asneiros goes there every day to see her?"

" He has not been near the house since she has been there."

" Then do you think it is all over between him and Magdalen?"

" There never was anything between them. Magdalen merely looked upon him as a friend of her father's, but now she says that he only went to the quinta to spy upon him."

" That is strange; but Aunt Josefina is always trying to get people married who care nothing about each other. I thought it very strange that Magdalen should care anything for a man like Major Asneiros."

" Then we shall have another laugh at Aunt Josefina, she is always making mistakes of that sort, but she never tires of her amusement," said Doña Constancia.

" I fear it will be no laughing matter for Don Alfonso," said Don Carlos.

" I will tell you what I will do," said Dolores, going up to Marcelino and leaning upon his arm. " In a few days I will ask papa to speak to the Viceroy for Don Alfonso; but not yet, he is angry now, and no wonder, when you talk to him about justice."

Marcelino and Don Carlos remained that night at the quinta, the next morning, as they rode together to the city, Marcelino said to his friend—

" You think, then, that our errand has been successful?"

" I think it has," said Evaña. " Don Roderigo will yield to the prayer of his daughter what he refused when you asked for justice."

" From my father I hoped better things than that."

" Do not blame Don Roderigo, it is the Spanish system which makes such things possible. Unlimited power debases not only those who are subject to it, but quite as much, or even more so, those who exercise it. A few years of such power as he has at present, would change your father from a most liberal-minded man to a despot."

" We can only put an end to this system by establishing a government of our own," said Marcelino.

" Then let us do it at once. For what are we waiting? The people and the troops all anticipate a change, they wait only for the leaders to give the signal."

CHAPTER II.

SPAIN had fallen, but that made no difference to Buenos Aires,
all was apparently as it had ever been, Spaniards were the lords,
Americans were but vassals born to do their will. Yet in one respect
all was not as it had been, the troops who upheld the power of the
Spaniards were no longer Spaniards also, they were Americans.

Then was seen the anomaly of a small handful of men ruling over
an immense country, whose power was based neither upon the will of
the people nor upon brute force. Neither was there any external
power upon which they might fall back were their authority disputed,
their power rested solely upon an old tradition. They were men
born in the Old World, who upon this accident of birth based their
claim to rule in the New.

Again Marcelino Ponce de Leon urged upon his grandfather that
he should call together a meeting of the principal citizens, and ask
them this question which was in the mouths of every one—

" What shall we do ? "

It was a calm night in April, when men, singly or in couples, wended
their way through the streets of the city as they had done on two
former occasions, and sought the house of Don Gregorio Lopez.

One password, " Libertad," admitted them to the house and to the
large inner room.

Valentin Lopez y Viana, who had a list of those who had been
invited, and who had accosted each man on his entrance, announced
to his father that all were present, whereupon Don Gregorio took his
place at the head of the table, and when his guests had arranged
themselves round the room, rose to his feet and spoke—

" Señores," said he, " the question which I have invited you here
this evening to discuss, is one which occupies the minds of all. We
have no king, for our king is in a French prison ; we have no longer
a mother-country, the fall of Spain has been proclaimed aloud in our
streets. How, then, shall we submit any longer to be ruled by a
handful of Spaniards, who derive their authority from a power which
no longer exists ? We in no way disown our allegiance to Ferdinand
our king, if we assert our right to provide ourselves for the government of the country until such time as he may be able to re-assume
his authority over us.

" Señores, the idea of choosing from amongst ourselves the men who shall rule over us is now no novelty amongst us. Spain herself has set us the example. What we demand is a Junta. Among us there can be no question of our right to demand a Junta, the question I propose to you is this—"

"Has the day come for us to demand the appointment of this Junta?"

"Yes, yes!" shouted several of the younger men, as Don Gregorio paused and looked round him.

"A Junta! a Junta! we are free," shouted the others.

Then rose up Don Carlos Evaña from the chair on which he was seated, half way down the room.

"Junta! Junta! like that of Spain," said he. "We are a free people, therefore we must take example from a people who are not free, and must have a Junta to rule over us.

"What are these words that I hear? Have we not suffered long enough from the tyranny of Spain? Are we yet, when we cast from us the domination of Spain, to set her up before us as an example? Why should we take Spain as our example? We are a free people and demand a government of our own, but why look to Spain for a form of government suited to a free people. The history of the whole world is open before us, there we may learn how in ancient days free men have chosen their own rulers, and have been at once victorious abroad and prosperous at home. Let us not look to Spain for any guidance in the path before us, the example of Spain can be nothing more than a warning to us. Neither need we look far back into the history of the world for an example we may follow; in our own days a great people has risen against its oppressors, has stood forth as the champion of freedom to an entire continent, has fought unaided against the united strength of many despots, has triumphed over them and has given liberty to a multitude of peoples. France, emulating the most glorious days of Greece and Rome, freed herself from tyranny, and, as a Republic, gave to all the world an example of heroism such as even her enemies were fain to regard with admiration.

"Señores, let us talk no more of a Junta like that of Spain, or of a king, but let us concert measures for calling together a representative assembly of the people, and for proclaiming at once the Argentine Republic."

Opposite to Don Carlos Evaña sat Don Cornelio Saavedra, a handsome man with somewhat stern features, dressed in an old-fashioned uniform, and wearing his hair combed back and united in one broad plait which fell on to his shoulders, which style of dressing the hair was *de riguer* in the regiment of the Patricios, of which he was commandant. His face flushed with anger, and as the speaker sat down, he made as though he would rise at once, but Don Fausto Velasquez, who sat next to him, laid his hand upon his arm, saying to him—

"Cosas de Evaña! What matters it?"

Then several spoke one after the other, some saying a few words without rising to their feet, others interrupting those who spoke with contradictions, and there was much confusion. At length Don Gregorio Lopez leaned over and whispered to Don Manuel Belgrano—

"Speak you something, to you they will listen."

Then Belgrano stood up and there was silence.

"Señores," said he, "the idea of an Argentine Republic seems new to many of you, to others of us it is not new. We have thought of it years ago, but we thought of it then and we think of it now as a possibility, which may be considered of at some date far in the future. It is not for the consideration of any such matter that we have been invited to meet together this evening. We look upon ourselves already as a free people, while our present government is composed entirely of Spaniards, who are responsible to no one. The means of putting an end to this anomaly in the government of a free people is obvious, and being of Spanish origin will therefore be the more readily adopted by us; the appointment of a Junta of government, and the immediate abolition of the viceregal power. A Junta may not be the most perfect form of government, but it is the form which we can adopt at once, and which will secure to us opportunity for the full discussion of plans for some superior form of government."

The words of Don Manuel Belgrano, spoken calmly and deliberately, soothed at once the excitement which had been produced by the speech of Don Carlos Evaña; as he resumed his seat Don Marcelino Ponce de Leon rose.

"Señores," said he, "the only measure which is possible for us as an immediate step, is the substitution of a Junta named by the people for a Viceroy named by Spain; this I think even my friend Don Carlos Evaña will admit. Now the question before us is, not whether we be ruled by a Junta or an assembly, but whether we demand at once the resignation of the Viceroy and the vesting of his powers in a Junta. Shall we demand this at once, or shall we wait? If we must yet wait, how much longer are we to wait, and why?

"I say that the day has come, and that any longer delay in the assertion of our rights exposes each one of us to suffer from arbitrary acts against which there is no appeal."

As Marcelino sat down he was warmly applauded, and many shouted—

"The day has come! the day has come! Junta! No more of an irresponsible government; down with the Viceroy!"

Then Don Cornelio Saavedra rose to his feet and there was instant silence.

"Señores," he said, "it is not for us who are men of experience to give heed to the dreams of an enthusiast; let us look upon the peculiar circumstances in which we are placed with the sober eyes of mature reason. We are colonists of Spain, we are loyal subjects of King Ferdinand VII., but it is very just that we should not obey irresponsible rulers. If it were, as has been stated, a fact, that there exists no power to whom our present rulers are responsible, I should immediately concur with many here present in at once demanding the appointment of a governing Junta. But such a power does exist; so long as the Central Junta of Spain holds its position at Seville, the second city of Spain, that Junta constitutes in the absence of the king, the legal government of Spain and the Indies, and to its commands we, as loyal subjects of King Ferdinand, are bound to submit. Some of you have cried out that the day has come for the appointment of a Junta of our own; I tell you that so long as the Central Junta maintains itself at Seville, Spain has not fallen, and the day has not come. When the French force the passes of the Sierra de la Morena, when a French army chases the Junta from Seville, then Spain will have fallen, then may we with justice demand a Junta of our own, without violating our loyalty to our king. I pray to God that that day may yet be far off, that it may never arrive, but if it come then I will join you in demanding what will then be our right, a Junta of our own."

Don Cornelio was listened to with deep attention, and when he sat down men looked at each other, many seeming anxious to reply to him, more looking towards Evaña, as though they expected him to speak. Then Don Gregorio Lopez rose again.

"Señores," said he, "the question I have asked you has, I think, been satisfactorily answered by Don Cornelio Saavedra. Let us do nothing rashly; in so important a step as this we have discussed, it is of the first importance that we be all united. By many of us the establishment of a Junta of government may be looked upon as a first step only; be it so, but let them join us to accomplish this first step, there will afterwards be time enough to discuss what further steps the majority of us may think necessary. Let us await with patience the day when Seville shall fall into the power of the French, then we will look to Don Cornelio for that powerful assistance which will make the establishment of a governing Junta a matter of no difficulty whatever."

Don Juan Martin Puyrredon, who had returned from exile two days before, had sat near to the head of the table all the evening without speaking. As the door was thrown open, and the meeting commenced to disperse, he crossed the room and remained for some minutes speaking in low tones to Don Cornelio Saavedra, after which they left the house together.

Two days after this Don Juan Martin held another meeting in his own house, to which none were invited save military officers, both native and Spanish, above the rank of captain. To these he propounded the same question which had been proposed by Don Gregorio Lopez to his friends. The native officers were almost unanimous that the day was come for the deposition of the Viceroy and the establishment of a Junta Gubernativa, but many of the Spanish officers demurred, saying that they could see no present necessity for so extreme a measure.

After much time had been expended in useless discussion, Don Cornelio Saavedra rose and spoke to the same effect as he had spoken at the house of Don Gregorio. His words carried weight with them, and his proposal met with general acquiescence.

Throughout the city it soon became known that the principal citizens and the military commandants, had agreed together that the fall of Seville was to be the signal for the deposition of the Viceroy, and the establishment of a Junta Gubernativa, which should rule in the name of King Ferdinand over the whole Viceroyalty of Buenos Aires.

CHAPTER III.

was the first week in May, the family of Don Roderigo Ponce de Leon had returned to the city, Dolores had come to spend the day with her aunt Josefina, and was sitting with her and Magdalen Miranda in the ante-sala. The door opened, and in came Marcelino and Don Carlos Evaña.

Marcelino went at once to Magdalen and took her hand.

"I have come to bring you good news," he said, "Don Alfonso will be set at liberty to-day. Don Fausto has gone with the order to the Cabildo."

"Thanks, thanks," said Magdalen. "Poor papa! at last!"

"Do not thank me, thank Lola."

"I knew papa could, if he would only try," said Dolores. "The Viceroy will do anything that papa asks him. I made him promise me last night; you know I told you I would not rest until I had made him promise."

She could say no more, for Magdalen threw her arms round her neck, kissing her, and the two girls wept together, speaking to each other with many endearing words, till, becoming more composed, they sat hand in hand beside each other, waiting; Magdalen listening with all her ears for the sound of a footstep in the patio.

Half an hour they waited; then was heard the voice of Don Fausto. Magdalen sprang from her chair, and ran out into the patio. An old, old man, bowed with weakness, tottered towards her, leaning on the arm of Don Fausto, so old, so bent, Magdalen could hardly believe her eyes. With a cry she ran up to him, and threw her arms round him, it was her father.

"Chica!" said Don Alfonso, straightening himself a little, but he said no more, suffering himself to be led into the house and seated on a chair, where he looked round him with a bewildered gaze, apparently deaf to the welcome of Doña Josefina and to the congratulations of the others.

Magdalen drew a stool to his feet and seated herself upon it, leaning upon his knees.

"Papa, won't you speak to me?" she said. "You are free now, we will go back to the quinta and you will soon be quite strong again."

Don Alfonso laid his hand upon her head and smiled at her, then looking up with an anxious gaze at Don Fausto he said—

"And my coffer, where is it? Did not you tell me they would give me everything back?"

"Yes, I have an order to Major Asneiros that he return to you everything he took from your house on the night of your arrest."

"Give me the order," said Marcelino, "I will go and get them at once."

Don Fausto drew a folded paper from his pocket and gave it to Marcelino, who immediately left the house. During his absence Don Alfonso still sat in his chair with a vacant stare in his eyes, answering nothing to the questions that were addressed to him, and resisting every effort of Doña Josefina, who pressed him to eat something. Dolores placed a basin of broth in his hands; mechanically he took the spoon and stirred it, but put it away from him untasted.

Marcelino was not long absent. When his footstep was heard in the patio Don Alfonso pushed his daughter from him, and rising to his feet walked to the room door to meet him, with a firmer step than seemed possible from his former gait. Marcelino had with him two peons, one of whom carried a large package of books and papers, the other bore on his shoulder a small black coffer, bound with brass bands and with a brass lock. To one of the handles of this coffer hung a bunch of keys tied with a string.

"Bring it in, bring it in," said Don Alfonso to the peon who carried the coffer.

"Jesus! but it is heavy," said the man.

Then as he set it down roughly on the floor there came from it a jingling sound as of pieces of metal striking against one another. At this sound Don Alfonso's eyes sparkled, and he rubbed his hands together; then, stooping, he took hold of the coffer by one of the handles and tried to lift it, but it was too heavy for his wasted strength.

"Yes, it is heavy, it is heavy," he said, chuckling strangely to himself and again rubbing his hands together.

After this he took up the basin of broth which he had refused, and as he supped it he commenced talking, but when they questioned him of the lonely days he had spent in prison he shuddered and would answer nothing.

In the afternoon, Don Fausto took Don Alfonso and Magdalen out again to the quinta in his carriage, Don Alfonso insisting upon having the black coffer placed inside and sitting with his feet upon it. He seemed to have recovered strength surprisingly since the morning. Magdalen was in great spirits at finding everything at the quinta in good order, and that many needful repairs had been made during their absence, but she did not then know that this was owing to Marcelino Ponce de Leon and Don Carlos Evaña, one or other of whom had visited the place every day during the imprisonment of Don Alfonso.

Don Fausto left them at sundown, feeling no anxiety for Don Alfonso, whose prostration in the morning he attributed solely to the effects of solitary confinement upon one who was accustomed to live much in the open air.

Soon after dark Magdalen, who was setting out her tea-things, was startled by a shrill cry which came from her father's room. Running in she could see nothing, there being no light in the room, but she could hear a low moaning. She called aloud for her father, but there was no answer. Attracted by her cries, the single maid-servant who lived in the house with them came running with a lighted candle in her hand, to know what was the cause of the alarm, then Magdalen saw her father stretched, apparently lifeless, on the floor. Beside him stood the black coffer, open and with the lid thrown back; on the floor lay a small hand-lamp, broken; strewn about lay a number of silver coins, and under her father's hand there lay something which had been wrapped in paper, but from which the paper was partly torn away.

The two had great difficulty in raising Don Alfonso and laying him upon his bed, and for long all their efforts to restore consciousness were in vain. When at last he opened his eyes he gazed vacantly round him, answering nothing to Magdalen's eager questions, till he saw the black coffer which they had left untouched. Then he started up, and struggling from their hands staggered to it, throwing himself upon his knees before it, and groping with his hands inside of it. He pulled out handfuls of silver coins, throwing them on the floor, and several packages wrapped in paper, like the one Magdalen had noticed lying on the floor when she had discovered her father's state. From each of these packages he tore off the wrapper as it he took it out and threw it from him. Each package as it fell upon the floor gave a dull, heavy sound, as though it were a block of lead. As he threw from him the last package, he started to his feet, clutching his hair with both hands, and uttering a wild cry like that which had brought Magdalen to him.

Then he burst out with foul curses and imprecations, grinding his teeth and stamping his feet in his rage, while Magdalen and the maid both looked upon him in terror, thinking he had gone mad. When at last his rage subsided, he clasped his hands together and bent over the coffer once more.

"Not one! not one have they left me!" he exclaimed. "Fool that I was, ever to let a Spaniard inside my house!"

With a hollow groan he fell forward over the coffer, striking his head upon the floor. Again Magdalen and her maid lifted him up and laid him upon his bed, where for hours he lay insensible, breathing heavily, and when at last he began to speak it was in incoherent words, mingled with curses, which made Magdalen shudder as she listened.

So the weary night wore through, and with the day came more efficient help, but days and days passed ere Don Alfonso knew anything of what went on about him, or recognized his daughter. These days were a fearful trial to Magdalen, yet there was one who came to see her every day, whose loving words strengthened her and encouraged her in her arduous duty. Not a day passed that Marcelino Ponce de Leon did not sit with her for at least an hour, by the bedside of her unconscious father, telling her of all that was happening in those days, big with the destiny of a young nation, seeking counsel and solace from her in the sore struggle which was going on within himself. Years before he had thought of the day when he must decide between his father and his country, he had thought of it with trembling and dismay, and pondered long and anxiously of how he might avert it. Now the day was come, his resolution was fixed, yet it was none the less painful to him to array himself in direct opposition to his father, that his resolve was the result of mature deliberation.

Magdalen fully sympathized with him in his anxious wish, if it were yet possible, so to arrange matters that Don Roderigo might yield a tardy assent to a new order of affairs, and forget that he was a Spaniard for the sake of his children, who were Americans. But as she listened to the incoherent words and occasional curses which fell from the lips of her own suffering father, her heart refused to let her counsel Marcelino to give up one iota of what he considered his rights as a free-born citizen of Buenos Aires, or to shrink from any duty, however painful, which the assertion of those rights for himself and others might entail upon him.

And through all those days between these two there passed no word of love, yet were their hearts open to one another, the most simple words that all the world might hear, yet bore from one heart to the other a message of love, the most common act of politeness became a caress.

A week after the return of Don Alfonso to the Miserere, Don Baltazar de Cisneros, the Viceroy, gave audience in one of his private apartments, to two in whom he placed great confidence, Don Roderigo Ponce de Leon and Don Ciriaco Asneiros.

"I have brought the Señor Asneiros that he himself give you an account of this affair," said Don Roderigo.

"You opened the coffer yourself?" said the Viceroy to the major. "What was there in it?"

"Some few papers written in English which appeared to be bonds or titles, about $400 in silver coins, and some heavy packets wrapped in paper, what they were I did not look, I was searching for documents," replied Asneiros.

"And did no one but yourself examine the coffer?"

"No one. When I saw that there was nothing there of what I expected to find, I relocked it, and kept the keys in my own possession, till I received an order, signed by your Excellency, to deliver it and the other articles I had brought from the Miserere."

"But with false keys any one might have opened the coffer in your absence?"

In reply to this Asneiros merely shrugged his shoulders—

"And you did not open any of those heavy packages of which you speak?" said Don Roderigo.

"I pricked them with my knife and found them all solid metal, but I did not open one of them. They say now that they are ingots of lead, and that the medico expected to find them of gold and has gone out of his mind. There are men who will believe anything, and there are others who will say and do anything to throw discredit upon a loyal Spaniard."

"It is a most unfortunate affair," said Don Roderigo. "The people are in such an evil frame of mind at present that they lay upon us the blame for any unfortunate accident that may befall."

"It were easy to cure them," said Asneiros.

" How ? " asked the Viceroy.

" Shoot half a dozen men that I can point out to you."

" And bring on a revolution," said Don Roderigo.

" When men talk treason in their houses without hindrance, a revolution is not far off," said Asneiros. " Your Excellency thinks the troops will not support you, and whilst they are officered as they are at present they will not, but shut the troops in their barracks, arrest all the Creole officers, and commission me to raise a regiment for you, which I can do in two days, and I assure you these citizens will think twice before they will fight."

The Viceroy looked from one to the other irresolute. Asneiros was not the first Spaniard who had warned him of danger, and had counselled extreme measures of repression ere it was too late.

" There is at least one regiment upon which I can rely," said he.

" The Tijo," said Asneiros ; " it is little better than a skeleton regiment, but it would be easy to bring it up to the full complement, and there is only one regiment from which there is any danger, the Patricios. In the other regiments all you have to do is to change the officers, and they will serve you as well as the Tijo. There are scores of Spaniards unemployed, while these Creoles strut about the streets in uniform as if the city were theirs."

" Any extreme measure will force them into revolt and then the city will be theirs," said Don Roderigo. " Your Excellency would do well to shut your ears to such counsel, our only chance lies in temporizing. The misfortunes of our country have excited the most extravagant hopes in these insolent Creoles ; as you know, it has been actually proposed among them to demand a Junta Gubernativa."

" That was the doing of your friend Don Juan Martin Puyrredon," said the Viceroy. " It was false clemency on my part to listen to your request and permit his return."

" I think not," said Don Roderigo ; " he was not alone in proposing this Junta, and it is better that if any such revolutionary measure be forced upon us, we should have men such as he to treat with, and not men whose heads are full of extravagant French ideas. There are men in the city who look upon a Junta as only the first step to the establishment of a republic."

" The people generally will not support them," said the Viceroy.

" At present they will not ; but if we irritate them by measures of repression they will commit any extravagance."

" But we must repress with severity any such idea as the establishment of a Junta."

" Our best plan would be to forestall any popular demand by appointing a Junta ourselves."

" They will want a Junta of Creoles."

" They will ; therefore it would be wise to prevent all chance of their demanding a Junta by appointing one ourselves. If we set up a Junta half Spaniards and half Creoles, and appoint you President, all the moderate men among the Creoles will side with us."

" Well, I will take the matter into consideration," replied the Viceroy; " but I am not disposed even to yield so far as to appoint a mixed Junta, until no other course is left to me."

"Your Excellency does not fully appreciate the danger."

"I see no necessity for any immediate action, but you will do me the favour to advise me if you see symptoms of any increase in the popular excitement."

"When all remedial measures will be too late," replied Don Roderigo; then seeing the Viceroy indisposed to continue the colloquy, he took up his hat, and with a low bow retired.

Don Ciriaco Asneiros lingered till he had seen Don Roderigo pass through the first ante-room, then stepping up to the Viceroy he said to him in a low voice—

"Do not alarm yourself, your Excellency, at the warnings of this worthy gentleman. We all know him; though loyal, he is so intimately connected with Creole families that at times he forgets that he is a Spaniard. What want we with Creoles in a Junta, or a Junta at all? What we want are troops, troops, good Spanish soldiers, upon whom we can depend, and I assure you we will soon bring these Creoles to reason. When I told you that I could raise you a regiment in two days I did not speak without thinking, we Spaniards are tired of the insolence of these Creoles."

"You were not at that meeting at the house of the Señor Puyrredon?" said the Viceroy.

"These Creoles know me too well to ask me to talk treason with them."

"If they had resolved upon anything, we should know it?"

"According to what I have heard, the resolution is postponed until there come more certain news from Spain."

"Think you that this Puyrredon is a dangerous man?"

"Without doubt; but there are more dangerous. Whilst the Señor Evaña lives in Buenos Aires your Excellency is always in danger of some conspiracy."

"Evaña! But against him you have been unable to bring me any proof."

"Give me authority to arrest him and search his house."

"For the present there is no danger, this excitement will calm down, when something positive occurs, there will be time enough for severe measures." So saying the Viceroy bowed and dismissed the major, who left him at once and walked away to his own house in deep thought.

In an inner room of this house Don Santiago Liniers, ex-Viceroy of Buenos Aires and Marshal of the armies of Spain, walked restlessly up and down. Don Baltazar de Cisneros had not dared to send him under arrest to Spain in accordance with his instructions, but had exiled him to the learned city of Cordova, where he considered that his popularity would cease to be dangerous. Liniers, hearing of the excitement in Buenos Aires, had returned in secret, purposing to offer his services to the Viceroy for the preservation of the authority of Spain. Asneiros had been commissioned by him to speak to Cisneros, telling him of his arrival, if he found him disposed to adopt stringent measures of repression, but not otherwise.

As Asneiros entered the room Liniers paused in his walk, waiting for him to speak.

" Don Baltazar will do nothing," said Asneiros.   " Let us not think any more of him, he is lost.   Before many days we shall have a Junta of Porteños."

" And this Evaña, can you do nothing against him ? "

" Nothing.   He has always the protection of your friend Don Roderigo.   But have no fear, he will fall with the rest."

" When ?   A Junta is a revolution, and he will be one of the chiefs. He is a man of terrible energy and respects nothing."

" Without doubt he is our most dangerous enemy."

" Then you feel sure that we shall have a Junta ? "

" Or something worse, and without troops what can we do ?   Don Baltazar gives not the slightest attention to my offer."

" Then my journey here will result in nothing."

" Return to Cordova, it is the best thing you can do, but prepare at once for a second reconquest of this Buenos Aires.   Against a Junta of Porteños it will be a very easy matter to stir up the Provinces."

" To Cordova then this night," said Liniers.   " Adios ! Buenos Aires ; twice have I saved you from foreigners, yet once more will I come to save you from your own people."

CHAPTER IV.

DIAS DE LA PATRIA.

IN January the French armies forced the passes of the Sierra de la Morena, and poured like a deluge over the smiling plains of Andalusia, sweeping everything before them. Cordova and Granada fell, and on the 1st February King Joseph, at the head of his triumphant army, marched into the city of Seville.

Rumours of these events reached Buenos Aires in April, but till a month later there arrived no certain information. On the 13th May full details were received by a ship from Europe which anchored in the port of Monte Video. On the 14th the news reached Buenos Aires.

Don Manuel Belgrano had been for a fortnight absent from the city, recruiting his strength and refreshing his jaded energies in quiet solitude at a quinta he possessed at the little town of San Isidro, which stands on the banks of the river about five leagues north of Buenos Aires, leaving the "Diario" in the care of Marcelino Ponce de Leon. On the afternoon of the 14th he received a letter from Marcelino.

"Come at once, we have need of you. The moment has arrived to work for the Patria, and to achieve our longed-for liberty and independence."

Before nightfall Don Manuel was again in the city. A meeting of the secret committee was at once convened, not one of the brotherhood was absent, long and earnestly they discussed the measures they should adopt. The proposition of Don Carlos Evaña to appoint a committee of public safety with absolute powers, and to proclaim a Republic, was overruled. It was determined to call upon the Ayuntamiento of the city to appoint a Junta, elected in "Cabildo Abierto." which should unite the powers of the various corporations; that this Junta should invite the concurrence of each Province of the Viceroyalty for the purpose of assembling a Congress which should decide upon the future of the country; and that for the prevention of any attempt to oppose the authority of the Junta the first act of this body should be to despatch an army into the interior, the commander of which should be invested with ample powers for the repression of any hostile movement.

For three days the city was in a state of great agitation; Spain had fallen, the colonies of Spain were free.

"What shall be done?"

"What authority shall take the place of that which exists no longer?"

Every man asked these questions of himself and of his neighbour, and the members of the secret committee, spreading themselves through the city, did all in their power to increase the general excitement, and to prepare the way for such answers to these questions as should secure for ever the liberties of Buenos Aires.

Again the Viceroy sought the counsel of Don Roderigo, repenting him that he had not followed his advice, and prepared beforehand an answer to these questions which convulsed the city. In accordance with his present advice he now published a fly-sheet, giving in detail an account of all the recent events in Spain, which he followed up on the 18th by a proclamation, recommending the people for their own sake to preserve order and union, until such time as he, in concert with the other Viceroys of Spain in South America, might adopt such measures as were requisite for the public well-being, and for the due preservation of the royal authority in America.

That same day, the 18th May, Don Cornelio Saavedra and Don Manuel Belgrano applied to the Ayuntamiento in the name of the citizens of Buenos Aires that they should—

"Without delay convene a Cabildo Abierto, so that by a general assembly of the people it might be determined whether the Viceroy should resign his powers into the hands of a Junta of government for the better security of the public weal."

On the night of the 19th the Viceroy called together all the commandants of the troops quartered in the city, both Spanish and native, and announced to them that he depended upon them to put a stop to this demand for a Cabildo Abierto, and to maintain his authority. To this Don Cornelio Saavedra replied—

"Your Excellency cannot count upon me nor upon the Patricios for that purpose. Our future and that of America is in question, and we do not consider it secure in your hands. The time has come for your Excellency to resign your authority; the source of that authority no longer exists, therefore it also has ended."

With one exception all the officers present supported Don Cornelio, and the deposition of the Viceroy was thus virtually achieved.

During these days of excitement the secret committee had admitted several new members to their counsels. On the night of the 20th they issued orders to the native troops to remain in their barracks in readiness for any emergency. The troops obeyed, as though the committee were some recognized authority. At the same time they resolved that two of their number should wait upon the Viceroy, and notify to him that his authority had ceased. Dr. Don Juan José Castelli and Comandante Don Martin Rodriguez were chosen for this perilous mission.

The fort was that night garrisoned by a grenadier corps of native troops, the officers of which were for the most part Spaniards. With the two envoys went Comandante Terrada, who, entering the fort with them, took command of the grenadiers. Without sending forward to announce their visit, the envoys proceeded straight to the private apartments of the Viceroy, who, far from expecting any such visitors, was playing cards with some friends. Castelli spoke first.

"Most excellent sir," said he, "it is our painful duty to announce to you, that we come in the name of the people and of the army to notify to your Excellency that your authority as Viceroy has ceased."

These words caused the greatest consternation among those present, but Cisneros started angrily to his feet.

"What insolence is this?" said he to Castelli; "how dare you insult thus the King in the person of his representative? This is the foulest outrage you could commit against his authority."

"There is no need for anger, your Excellency," replied Castelli with perfect calmness; "there is no alternative."

"Señor, they have given us five minutes in which to return with your answer. Your Excellency would do well to think carefully what you do," said Don Martin Rodriguez.

Don Roderigo Ponce de Leon, who was one of those present, drew the Viceroy with him into an adjoining room, whence the latter soon returned.

"Señores," said he to the envoys, "I deeply lament the evils which will fall upon this country in consequence of the step you have taken. But if the people cease to respect me, and the army abandon me, pues! do what you will."[1]

Next day, the 21st, the Cabildo applied to the Viceroy for authority to—

"Convene a meeting of well-disposed citizens, who in public congress may give expression to the will of the people, so as to put an end to this state of dangerous excitement."

The Viceroy gave the needful permission, and the Cabildo, composed half of Spaniards and half natives, invited between four and five hundred of the leading citizens to meet the next morning in the saloons of the Cabildo.

On the 22nd, at nine o'clock, the citizens commenced to assemble; more than 250 accepted the invitation, while the Plaza Mayor and the approaches to it were filled with dense crowds of people, a detachment of troops being stationed at each corner to preserve order.

The place where this memorable assembly was convened, was a large saloon in the upper story of the Cabildo, to-day occupied by the Tribunals of Justice. Long straight-backed forms, borrowed from the churches, were arranged in lines down this saloon from end to end. At the head of the room was placed a large table covered with a crimson cloth, round which were seated in arm-chairs the bishops, the members of the Ayuntamiento and Cabildo, and other public functionaries, who presided over the meeting.

The discussion was opened by the following address from the Cabildo—

"Faithful and generous people of Buenos Aires, you are now met together, speak then with all freedom, but with the dignity which is natural to you, showing yourselves a wise, noble, docile, and generous people."

In this meeting three parties were represented. One, headed by the bishop and the Spanish employés, desired the continuance of the Viceroy in his office; the second, which included many Spaniards,

---

[1] For this scene see "La Historia de Belgrano," by General Mitre.

such as Don Roderigo Ponce de Leon, who preferred measures of conciliation, desired to invest the higher powers in the Cabildo, until such time as a provisional government might be organized, which should rule under the supreme authority of the government of Spain ; the third, which included all the more ardent of the patriots, desired the deposition of the Viceroy, and the establishment of a government chosen by the people.

Many speeches were made by the most distinguished orators of all parties, the discussion and the voting on many different propositions lasted all day, and the Cabildo clock sounded the midnight hour ere the meeting broke up. The resolution which was at length adopted by a majority of votes was proposed by Don Cornelio Saavedra, who was supported by Belgrano, by all the more moderate among the patriots, and by some of the Spaniards. It was as follows—

"The permanence of the Viceroy in his office and the continuance of the present system of government being incompatible with public tranquillity, the Cabildo is hereby authorized to appoint a Junta in conformity with the general ideas of the people and with present circumstances, which shall exercise supreme authority until a meeting of deputies from the other cities and towns of the Viceroyalty may be convened."

So terminated the first session of the first assembly of the Argentine people.

From this assembly Don Roderigo Ponce de Leon walked rapidly away to the fort, where the Viceroy had been for hours awaiting him.

"Then all is lost," said the Viceroy, as Don Roderigo read to him the resolution of the assembly.

"By no means," replied Don Roderigo. "Everything remains in the hands of the Cabildo, and I do not think it will be difficult to appoint a Junta which will keep the power in our own hands. You cease to be Viceroy, we will make you President of the Junta."

But as Don Roderigo walked away to his own house his heart was heavy within him, not from sorrow only, but from anger. That day one of the most violent speeches made at the assembly had been spoken by his own son, and Don Carlos Evaña, from whom he had hoped for aid in establishing a better order of affairs, though he had not spoken, had been incessantly active all day among the most determined opponents of Spanish rule, reconciling the varied opinions which prevailed among them, and at length uniting them to vote for the resolution which was carried.

The next day the sun shone gloriously upon an emancipated city. The bright but not scorching beams of the sun of May, shone upon a people who woke for the first time conscious that they were a people. In deliberative assembly they had decided upon the future of their own country, they had decided that they were no longer to be ruled by foreigners, responsible only to a foreign court, but were to be ruled by men chosen by themselves, by deputies from every city and town, by men who, representing the people, should be the exponents of their will, and should be responsible to the people alone.

The streets and public places were thronged with crowds of men, who greeted each other joyously, looking with a friendly eye even upon the Spaniards who passed among them, for Spaniards were no longer tyrants to be dreaded, and might be with them citizens of a new nation.

The Cabildo met at an early hour, and deliberated long with closed doors; hours passed and nothing was done, no new announcement was made to satisfy the eagerness of the joyous people. The Viceroy still occupied his official apartments at the fort, still the sentry paced to and fro before his door, to all appearance he was Viceroy yet, and the Junta was as yet but as a thing spoken of, as a thing which had no existence. So the day wore on, and the joyousness of the people disappeared and became impatience.

The secret committee had ceased to be a secret committee, its existence was known to the whole city, men spoke of it as the " Revolutionary Committee," and having none other to whom they might look, looked to the members of this self-appointed committee as their leaders.

·The meetings of the committee were no longer secret, many men of influence among the townsmen joined them on the 23rd May, many of the officers of the native regiments sought their advice on that day, and proffered their services for the enforcement of their resolutions.

At the house of the Señor Rodriguez Peña the committee was assembled, awaiting the announcement that the Cabildo had formally decreed the deposition of the Viceroy, awaiting also with anxiety the list of the members of the new Junta. No such announcement, no such list reached them. The delay roused in them suspicion, as it had aroused impatience in the people.

But, dreading the effect of a popular commotion, they determined to do all they could to allay the excitement of the people, and to demand from the Cabildo the immediate carrying out of the resolution of the assembly of the day previous.

Don Cornelio Saavedra and Don Manuel Belgrano were deputed to wait upon the Cabildo, and the rest of the committee dispersed about the city, where they soon calmed the agitation of the people and restored general confidence.

As the brilliant sun which had shone upon the city throughout this memorable day touched the western horizon, a company of the Patricios, with drums beating before them and bayonets fixed, marched through the streets, a guard of honour to a herald from the Cabildo, who at each street-corner proclaimed in a loud voice that the power of the Viceroy had ceased in the provinces of the Rio de la Plata, and that the Cabildo, by the will of the people, took the supreme authority upon itself.

The Cabildo met again early the next morning, and, warned by their experience of the day previous, proceeded at once to the election of the members of the Junta. They decided that the Junta should consist of two Spaniards and two natives, and should act under the presidency of Don Baltazar de Cisneros, who should retain the command of the troops. The two natives selected were Don Cornelio Saavedra and Dr. Castelli. At the same time they offered an amnesty to all who had taken part in opposition to the authorities on the 22nd.

" Don Cornelio Saavedra, always inclined to avoid extremes,

accepted in good faith the decision of the Cabildo, and his vote drew with it that of the other commanders of the troops, who pledged themselves to sustain the authority so established by the Cabildo." [1]

The Junta was proclaimed amid the ringing of the church-bells and the thunder of the cannon, the colonial system of Spain was re-established under a new form, and Don Roderigo Ponce de Leon, who had taken a leading part in this arrangement, returned to his house triumphant, doubting no longer of success ; Spaniards were a majority in the Junta, and the support of the troops was secured by the accession of Saavedra.

As Don Roderigo entered his sala he met Marcelino, who made way for him, bowing his head in silence.

" Ah, my son ! " said he, " we have seen nothing of each other for several days, except at a distance. I congratulate you on your speech the other day, it did you credit, but you see we have not yet arrived at the stage when such ideas can be more than dreams."

" I think that if you will walk through the city you will see that they are more than dreams already," replied Marcelino.

" Excuse me, I would rather not, it is raining steadily and there is a most disagreeably cold wind."

" Yet the streets are thronged with people as though it were as fine as yesterday. What, think you, is the reason that these people brave the weather in the streets instead of seeking the shelter of their homes ? "

" What matters it to me, the people ? "

" I am afraid it matters less to you than I once thought and hoped."

" This people was almost in open mutiny yesterday, as we did not appoint the Junta quick enough to please them. Now they have their Junta, what more would they ? "

" The people have been deceived and they know it. In the assembly on Tuesday it was resolved by the great majority of votes that the power of the Viceroy should cease, and that a Junta composed of men possessing the confidence of the people should exercise his powers, until deputies from the different cities and towns should meet to decide upon a new form of government for the whole country. Don Baltazar de Cisneros is no longer Viceroy, but he is President of the Junta, and Commander-in-chief of the troops, which comes to the same thing. What confidence have the people in such men as Salas and Inchaurregui ? To give us such a Junta as that is to invite a revolt."

Don Roderigo turned pale with anger, but ere he could speak in reply, Dolores, who had listened in alarm to this altercation between two of those whom she loved most in the world, ran up to him, and throwing her arms round him drew him away.

" Papa ! papa ! " she said, " do not look so at Marcelino, he does not know what he is saying. They have put quite strange ideas into his head in that committee."

" You love him, Lola, and he is your brother, he makes me forget that he is my son."

With this answer to his daughter Don Roderigo turned away, and Marcelino left the room and the house, and walked hurriedly to the Plaza Mayor.

[1] " La Historia de Belgrano," by General Mitre.

The wide causeway of the Recoba Nueva was covered with groups of excited men, other groups filled the roadway under the balconies of the Cabildo, shouting loudly their demand that the Cabildo should cancel the decree just published. Among these groups Marcelino walked, till he found Don Carlos Evaña declaiming angrily to a number of young men who were collected round him, calling upon them to resist to the last extremity, this fraud which had been practised upon them by the Cabildo. Taking him by the arm Marcelino drew him aside.

"Do not let us waste time in harangues in the streets," said he; "let us first secure the troops, all the junior officers of every corps are with us, through them we can secure the men, and, even if Don Cornelio still desert us, to-morrow we will upset this Junta by the bayonet, if no other course is open to us."

Evaña agreed with him, and separating they went among the groups, calming the excitement of the people by assuring them that next day they would secure the appointment of another Junta, composed of men in whom they might trust. Both of them were well known as prominent members of the revolutionary committee; men hearkened to them, believed in their assurance, and dispersed quietly to their homes. Before sundown the Plaza Mayor was tranquil.

Marcelino and Evaña then went to the barracks of the Patricios, where they found the troops under arms, and all the junior officers of the regiment collected in the guard-room, debating whether they should not at once march upon the fort and put an end by force to the authority of Don Baltazar de Cisneros. The great majority were in favour of this step and received Marcelino with shouts of welcome, calling upon him, as an officer of higher rank than any there present, to put himself at their head. Marcelino acceded to their request, but proposed the postponement of any active step to the next day, as night was already closing in, and it was necessary to concert measures with the rest of the native troops. After some warm discussion, the young officers consented to wait until Marcelino and Evaña could consult with the other members of the revolutionary committee.

Meantime the committee, convened at the house of the Señor Rodriguez Peña, also discussed the proceedings of the Cabildo with great warmth and indignation. Opinions were divided, but the great majority were in favour of an appeal to arms. As Marcelino and Evaña entered the room where they were assembled, the Señor Peña was speaking, calmly advocating the employment of all other means to procure the peaceful resignation of the Viceroy.

"But if he will not resign?" said Evaña.

Don Manuel Belgrano, wearied out with the anxieties of several days, lay on a sofa in an adjoining room; as Evaña repeated his question in a loud voice, Don Manuel, who was dressed in uniform as a Major of the Patricios, sprang from his sofa, and standing in the open doorway, his face flushed with indignation, his eyes flashing, laid his hand upon the hilt of his sword.

"I swear to my country and my comrades," he exclaimed, "that if by three o'clock in the afternoon the Viceroy has not resigned we will cast him out from the windows of the fort."

"Leave that to us, Don Manuel," said Marcelino, laying his hand upon the shoulder of Valentin Lopez y Viana, who had come with him from the barracks of the Patricios, and who with several other young officers there present had grasped the hilts of their swords as Belgrano spoke. "Leave that to us, the Patricios wait but the word and are ready to storm the fort at once, if it appear to the committee that such a measure is advisable."

There was great confusion and excitement as Marcelino told of what was occurring at the barracks of the Patricios, but the committee had already learned one thing, of which Marcelino was yet ignorant, which was that Don Cornelio Saavedra had reconsidered his hasty acquiescence in the decree of the Cabildo, and that they could count upon his support to a "Representation," which they had resolved to present to the Cabildo on the following day. Don Nicolas Rodriguez Peña with some difficulty succeeded in calming the excitement, and proposed that they should send a deputation to the Patricios, informing them of the change in the ideas of their commandant, and asking for their support to the "Representation."

This proposal was agreed to; two members of the committee left at once for the barracks of the Patricios, where they arranged that the men should remain in the barracks all night, and that the entire regiment should be under arms next day at an early hour, in readiness to support the people in case the Cabildo refused to listen to their demands.

After the departure of this deputation most of the members of the committee retired to their homes to recruit their strength for the next day; Marcelino Ponce de Leon threw himself upon the sofa where Don Manuel Belgrano had been lying as he entered, and fell at once into a sound sleep, but Don Carlos Evaña and a few others remained together and passed the night in endeavouring to draw up a list of names for the Junta, which should meet with general acceptance. All agreed that Don Cornelio Saavedra was the best man they could appoint as President, but, as the original members of the secret committee refused to allow their names to be proposed, there was great difficulty in deciding upon his colleagues. The discussion lasted till nearly dawn, many lists had been made out, but to all there were objections. Then Evaña, rising from his seat, went into the next room, and shook Marcelino by the shoulder.

"I am going home to sleep for an hour or two," said he. "Come with me."

Marcelino sprang up from his sofa, and he and Evaña walked away together along the muddy streets in the semi-darkness of the early morning, the morning of the 25th May. It had ceased to rain, but there was a cold wind, and the clouds hung heavily over the city. They reached Evaña's house, but the cold wind and the morning air had revived Marcelino from his sleepiness; he declined his friend's offer of a bed, and asked him for the loan of his horse.

"It is three days since I have seen Magdalen," he said. "She always rises before the day since her father has been ill. I will go and talk with her while you sleep; a talk with her always puts me into good spirits, and I have so much to tell her."

Evaña laughed, but lent him his horse, watched him as he rode away, awoke his servant, telling him to rouse him in two hours, and then throwing himself, dressed as he was, upon a sofa, slept soundly.

CHAPTER V.

OUT through the silent streets, out through the quiet suburbs, galloped Marcelino Ponce de Leon, arousing many an unquiet sleeper from uneasy slumbers, for few slept soundly in Buenos Aires on that night between the 24th and 25th May.

Spaniards cowered in their houses, mindful of the 1st January, 1809, dreading an explosion of popular wrath, which they knew themselves powerless to resist. Natives, indignant at the fraud which had been practised upon them, remembered also the 1st January, 1809, and looked anxiously for the day, resolute to overcome all obstacles to the full execution of their will.

Trampling through the mud, splashing through pools of water which lay in the unpaved roadways, Marcelino galloped on, heedless that many a window was thrown hastily open as he passed, and many an anxious eye gazed after him as he rapidly disappeared from sight; heeding no more the anxious looks of men than he did the angry snarling of the curs, who leaped out upon him from many a hedgerow in the suburbs.

He reached the Miserere, and, drawing rein at the quinta gate, looked over the hedge at the windows of the house beyond. That of the sala was thrown wide open, and the mulatta servant-girl stood there, staring with a bewildered look upon the clouds. Marcelino dismounted and, throwing his rein over the gate-post, walked up to the porch; the door was opened for him by Magdalen herself. She was dressed in a white wrapper with a frilled collar, and her hair was bound round her head with a fillet of blue silk. She seemed not in the least surprised to see him at that untimely hour, and her eyes spoke her welcome as she met him.

Marcelino took her hand, and she turned with him to go inside.

"I have not seen you for three days," he said; "I could not let another day pass without telling you what we have done, and to-day will be one which will mark an epoch in our history."

"I have heard something, but not all; you will tell me."

"Señorita!" exclaimed the mulatta girl, running out from the sala, "have you not seen the sky? In all my life I have seen nothing so strange."

Marcelino and Magdalen looked behind them through the open door of the porch. A bright light shone upon everything they saw, tinging everything with pink.

Then the two went out and stood in the porch, the young man and
the maiden, hand in hand together, speaking not, and in their silence
was there more eloquence than in many words.

Together they stood watching the dawn of the morning, their
hearts communing one with another in silent sympathy, the sympathy
of mutual trust and love. Together they watched the rising of the
sun on the morning of the 25th May, a sunrise which is now hailed
every year as the day comes round by the thundering salute of the
cannon of emancipated peoples, and by the voices of thousands of
children, who in every city and town throughout the one-time
colonies of Spain welcome with patriotic songs the rising of the sun
on the 25th of May.

Together they stood in the porch and looked forth upon the eastern
sky. The clouds which hung low over the city seemed to form but
one cloud, stretching from horizon to horizon in one dense mass of
dark gray, shaded with pink, which cast a bright pink reflection upon
the domes and towers of the churches, and upon the white-washed
walls of the houses in the nearest quintas. Then as they stood together and looked, the pink tints died out of the sky, and the dark
gray of the clouds changed to a brilliant orange. Far away on the
eastern horizon, just in the path of the rising sun, there was a break
in the vast uniformity of cloud, a semi-circle of deep blue; in the
centre of this blue sky, up rose the sun, launching his fiery beams
straight on the concave surface of the cloud. In an instant the orange
tints died out, and the whole cloud became one mass of brilliant
yellow, so brilliant and free from shades that it was impossible to tell
that there was any cloud at all. It seemed as though a noon-day sun
had spread himself over the whole sky, that the sky itself had become
a sun, bathing the world beneath in a flood of yellow light, which was
reflected from every object round, dazzlingly brilliant, but without one
ray of warmth in it.

As they gazed in silence, still hand in hand, from north to south
there darted a rosy streak of lightning, and the curtain of cloud sank
down over the blue space on the eastern horizon, shutting out the
sun. As the cloud descended the golden sheen faded away out of
the sky, and there came from far off in the north a clap of thunder,
which rolled and rolled away above the clouds, echoing and re-echoing
till it lost itself in the farthest south. Then the clouds were again one
mass of dull gray, hanging low over the city, and heavy drops of rain
fell pattering on the roof of the porch above them.

"What is this?" said Magdalen, drawing closer to Marcelino;
"never have I seen a sunrise like this."

"Nor I," replied Marcelino; "and if I mistake not, the day which
follows will be a day such as has never been seen before in Buenos
Aires."

"Saw you the sun, how brilliantly he shone out? Then there came
that angry flash of lightning, all the glory died out of the sky, and
there was a long roll of thunder. Do you believe in omens? Do you
not tremble?"

"I do not tremble," said Marcelino; "have you not taught me
faith? to do right and fear nothing? What can be more right or

more noble than to free one's native country from the slavery of centuries? The liberty we shall win to-day, may but give us the right to toil and labour for years to come, but is it not more noble to labour than to sleep?"

Then Magdalen leaned upon his arm and whispered—

"Yes, that is faith."

Marcelino, throwing his arms round her, pressed her to his breast and kissed her. For a minute there was silence between them. That kiss was the seal of a compact of which both had thought much, but of which neither had spoken until this day—a compact which bound them to each other so long as their lives should last, a compact which made the cares and toils of one, the cares and toils of both, a compact which blended their two lives into one life, and which death alone could cancel.

Marcelino was the first to speak.

"The presage of the rising sun," said he, "may be fulfilled. The liberty we shall achieve to-day may be soon clouded over, the storm may burst upon us, and all our efforts may be long unavailing to raise the people from the sloth and ignorance into which they have fallen under Spanish rule, but this sun over which the storm-cloud has fallen, this sun which is now hidden from us, will shine out again to-morrow when the storm has passed over. This storm is but the herald of the winter, which will tear off the last leaves from the trees, which will wither up the few remaining flowers. It is but the first of many storms, but they also will pass over. Winter will give place to spring. Again the genial sun will shine out, clothing the whole earth with verdure. The earth, refreshed and invigorated by the stern discipline of winter, will give new strength to the trees, fresh beauty to the flowering shrubs, and in the joyous spring-time we shall forget the storms of winter. Shall it not be so with us, Magdalen? Life has many storms in store for us, but we will not shrink from facing them. Shall we not walk together, cheering and strengthening each other, looking together in faith to the future?"

Magdalen's lips spoke no answer to his question, but her eyes looked up into his with a brave confidence, which was answer sufficient.

"Señor Don Marcelino, shall I not tie your horse under the shed, your saddle will be sopping wet in five minutes?"

It was the gardener who spoke, an old man with a face like a block of wood. How long he had been standing there neither of them knew.

"Leave it," said Marcelino, turning sharply on him.

"You must not go yet," said Magdalen, "I have so much to ask you. Papa is asleep, so I can make coffee for you myself."

Old Antonio got no further answer, and stood looking after them as they went back into the house together. Then, with a wink of his cunning old eyes, he hobbled to the gate, and taking the horse by the bridle led him away.

An hour later, Marcelino and Magdalen again stood in the porch side by side and hand in hand. Still the rain poured down, still the wind sighed mournfully among the trees, still the withered leaves broke

off from the swaying branches, and gathered in sodden masses on the
wet ground ; over all hung the leaden sky, and the far-off towers and
domes of the churches were invisible, shrouded in thick mist and
driving rain. The prospect as they looked out was dismal, yet they
looked upon it with cheerful eyes, the confidence which filled their
hearts made them oblivious to ought else than their own thoughts.

"Come to me when all is settled and tell me what you have done,"
whispered Magdalen.

"The knights of old went forth to fight with their lady's glove in
their helmet," said Marcelino. "There will be no shivering of lances
to-day, yet may I not carry with me some gage of love, to remind me
that I fight to-day not for myself nor even for my country alone ?"

As he spoke he looked at the fillet of blue silk which bound Magdalen's brown hair. She, with a smile, twisted it from her head and
unfastening it, passed it through the button-hole of his coat, tying it
there in a small bow from which hung two short streamers. Then she
stood off to look at him, but shook her head, and going back to his
side she untied the bow and pulled away the ribbon.

"Wait a minute," she said, shaking back the hair which hung over
her face, and then went off to her own room.

Some minutes she was away. When she came back her hair was
again bound up with a fillet, but the fillet was no longer a simple blue
ribbon, it was of two ribbons, one blue, the other white, twined together.
In her hand she carried a blue-and-white rosette, from which hung three
streamers, of which the centre one was white, the other two blue. She
brought also a needle and thread, and with active fingers stitched the
rosette with its three streamers to the lappel of Marcelino's coat.

"There," she said, as she finished her work and stood back to admire it, "there you take not only a gage but an emblem. The sky
in the spring-time is not blue only, it is blue and white. If you meet
with more difficulty than you expect, look on this ribbon, blue and
white, and think of the spring-time of which you told me."

As Marcelino rode away Magdalen stood in the porch looking after
him, till a tall aloe hedge shut him out from her sight, then she seated
herself in a low chair with her hands folded before her, gazing vacantly
at the rain-drops as they fell from the eaves, in deep thought, till the
sound of a bell called her to her father's room.

"You have had a visitor this morning, Chica," said Don Alfonso,
in a more natural tone than she had heard him speak in for weeks.

"Yes, papa," said she, what little colour she had in her face fading
away, and her lips closing firmly together.

"Who was it, Chica ?"

"Don Marcelino Ponce de Leon, papa," she answered.

"Does Don Marcelino love you, Chica?"

"Yes," she said, trying hard to answer in a steady voice.

Don Alfonso stretched out his hand, and drawing her down to him
he kissed her, and murmured in a low voice in English—

"Forgive us our trespasses, as we forgive them that trespass against
us."

Then Magdalen fell on her knees beside the bed and burst into
tears.

When Marcelino reached Evaña's house he found his friend already gone. On foot he followed him, not doubting that he would see him or hear of him on the Plaza Mayor. Neither here nor in any of the streets as he passed along did he see any troops, every corps was in its own barracks, under arms and ready to march at a moment's notice, awaiting orders only from the revolutionary committee to appear. But every street leading to the Plaza Mayor was thronged with groups of citizens, who, careless of the rain, wended their way thither. As Marcelino entered the Plaza he saw the wide causeway of the Recoba Nueva occupied by long lines of young men, all of whom were armed, some with pistols, some with sword-sticks. Among these young men Evaña walked hurriedly, striving apparently to establish some organization amongst them, which was each moment destroyed by the accession of fresh recruits.

"What is that?" said Evaña, as Marcelino walked up to him and he saw the blue-and-white rosette on the lappel of his coat.

"These," answered Marcelino, taking the streamers in his hand, "are the colours of La Patria."

"Viva La Patria!" shouted Evaña, taking off his hat.

The shout was taken up and echoed all over the Plaza, and in an instant all the organization which Evaña had been labouring to establish was destroyed. Each man after he had shouted turned to his neighbour to ask why? One only obtained a satisfactory answer, and he was Marcelino, who asked the question of Evaña himself.

"You have given me the idea I wanted," said Evaña. "There are of all sorts here, and we must have some means of knowing our own. Choose you pickets of young men we can trust, and station them at every entrance to the Plaza. I will procure blue and white ribbons for distribution to all patriots, your pickets will keep back any who seek to enter the Plaza who have not these ribbons."

Half an hour later the Plaza was crowded with people, but every man there, had in the button-hole of his coat two ribbons, one blue, the other white.

The Cabildo met at an early hour that morning. The first subject which engaged their attention was the resignation by Don Baltazar de Cisneros of the dignity of President of the Junta, which had been conferred upon him the day previous.

Don Cornelio Saavedra had been with Don Baltazar during the night, and, showing him that it would be impossible otherwise to preserve public tranquillity, had persuaded him to send in this resignation.

The second subject before the Cabildo was the "Representation" drawn up by the revolutionary committee, and signed by some hundreds of citizens, which formed a protest against their proceedings.

Don Roderigo Ponce de Leon exerted himself to the utmost in favour of moderation, counselling them to name Don Cornelio Saavedra President of the Junta in place of Don Baltazar de Cisneros, and Don Manuel Belgrano as the fourth member of that body, in the place of Don Cornelio. But Don Roderigo was feebly supported by the native members of the Cabildo, his proposal was scouted as an act of cowardice by the more violent of the Spaniards. He warned them that hundreds of the people, greatly excited, and most of them armed, patrolled the Plaza Mayor and filled the cafés. The answer of the Cabildo to this popular demonstration was to send for the commanders of the troops. As soon as these officers were assembled at the Cabildo they received orders to march their troops to the Plaza and disperse the people at the point of the bayonet. Most of these officers refused point blank to obey the command, the rest stated that any such attempt would infallibly produce a mutiny among their men.

The Cabildo thus found themselves powerless, but even then would not listen to the moderate counsels of Don Roderigo. Hours passed, and, as they debated the matter angrily among themselves, there came a violent knocking upon the outer doors, which were closed.

The people, wearied out by long waiting, had sent a deputation headed by Don Carlos Evaña and Don Marcelino Ponce de Leon, who demanded the immediate deposition of Don Baltazar de Cisneros. Don Martin Rodriguez, who was at the Cabildo with the other commanding officers, opened the door and went out to them. He was instantly surrounded by a number of excited young men, who asked him angrily what the Cabildo were doing, that for hours they kept the people waiting, instead of at once revoking their edict of the preceding day.

"Don Baltazar de Cisneros has sent in his resignation himself," answered Don Martin, "which renders necessary the appointment of an entirely new Junta. They require time to decide upon what men to choose for the Junta."

"Is that all?" replied Evaña. "We will save them the trouble of debating that question any longer."

So saying, Don Carlos drew out his pocket-book, and turning to a blank leaf wrote on it in pencil, seven names.

"There," said he, tearing out the leaf and presenting it to Don Martin, "there, give that list to the Señores of the Cabildo, and tell them that that Junta and no other will satisfy the wishes of the people."

"Come in and present it to them yourself," said Don Martin, drawing back.

Upon this Evaña and Marcelino Ponce de Leon followed Don Martin into the council-chamber, a large room in the upper story, lighted by windows which reached to the floor of the room, and opened upon the balconies overlooking the Plaza Mayor.

Evaña, holding the paper in his hand, strode up to the table round which the members of the corporation were seated, and laying it before the Alcalde de primer voto—

"Señores," he said, "you are but wasting your time here, the people have chosen a Junta for themselves, you have nothing more to do than to draw up an edict appointing this Junta according to legal forms, and then to retire and leave the power in their hands."

"The people!" exclaimed Don Roderigo Ponce de Leon, starting to his feet, "where is this people? and how have they chosen this Junta?"

"Step this way, Don Roderigo, and look upon the people," replied Evaña, drawing the bolts of one of the windows and throwing the window wide open.

Don Roderigo walked to the window and stepped out upon the balcony. Something more than a hundred young men stood drawn up in line on the roadway beneath him, the rest of the Plaza was nearly deserted; it was now an hour past noon, and the heavy rain had driven the greater part of those who had filled the Plaza some hours before, back to their own homes or to the shelter of the cafés.

"Do you call these boys the people?" said Don Roderigo.

"The people were here hours ago," said Don Carlos. "These only have remained, but they are sufficient to tell you the will of the people. Ask them."

Then as Don Roderigo looked back in indignation upon his colleagues, each man of whom still sat in his place as though stricken with fear, Don Carlos also turned to them.

"Señores," said he, "will you that I call all the people back, that you may speak to them? If you wish it I will do so. I will also send round to the barracks, and from each barrack there will march forth a regiment of patriots, each patriot with a musket on his shoulder. Will you that I send for them?"

But the Cabildo, especially the more violent members, were stricken with consternation, they cowered before the haughty bearing of Don Carlos Evaña, and looked in vain for hope into the quiet, resolute face of Marcelino Ponce de Leon. Round the door, which had been left open, there crowded other stern, determined faces. Evaña, Marcelino, and each of these men wore blue and white ribbons hanging from the lappels of their coats. The people who had thronged the Plaza two hours before had also each man worn these ribbons. These ribbons were the same colours which the Patricios had carried through smoke and fire triumphantly, on the 5th July, 1807. They looked at each other and their hearts quailed within them; they looked into the faces of the military commandants, who looked up at the ceiling or down on the ground, their hands playing with their sword-knots, or with the buckles of their belts, but who looked back at them, never at all. They fancied themselves the victims of some wide-spread conspiracy.

Then the Alcalde de primer voto, who was the President ex-officio, took up the paper which lay before him and read aloud the names which Evaña had there written.

"I see no objection to any of these gentlemen," said one, "they are all men highly respectable, and of influence among the people."

The rest murmured their acquiescence, all save Don Roderigo Ponce de Leon, who, coming back from the window, now even more vehemently opposed their timid yielding to dictation, than he had opposed their purblind obstinacy in the morning.

"Señores," said he, "if you appoint that Junta you endorse a revolution, you strike the first blow against the honour of the flag of Spain, you are guilty of treason to your legitimate sovereign."

"The Junta will rule in the name of King Ferdinand, and will be responsible to him for the use it makes of its authority," said Marcelino.

"I say nothing against the Junta," said Don Roderigo. "The Cabildo have the right to appoint what men they please on the Junta, but they have also the right of forbidding all intrusion upon their counsels, and when they submit to unauthorized dictation they are guilty of treason."

The members looked up irresolute, but behind Don Roderigo stood the tall figure of Don Carlos Evaña, leaning against the frame of the open window, twisting the blue and white ribbons which hung from the button-hole of his coat round his fingers. Their faces fell and they whispered one to the other—

"Why not? What better can we do?"

Then Don Roderigo turned his back upon them, and throwing his cloak over his shoulders, drawing his hat down over his eyes, left the room, elbowed his way through the throng of young men who crowded the staircase and the courtyard, and so out into the open Plaza, speaking no word to any, but walking rapidly away to his own house.

At three o'clock that afternoon, the Cabildo published an edict, appointing in the name of King Ferdinand VII. a Junta of government as follows :—

President.—Don Cornelio Saavedra.

Members.

Dr. Don Juan José Castelli.
,, ,, Manuel Alberdi.
,, Manuel Belgrano.
,, Miguel Azcuenaga.
,, Domingo Matheu.
,, Juan de Larrea.

Being a copy of the list which had been so hurriedly drawn up by Don Carlos Evaña.

No clangour of bells or roaring of guns hailed the publication of this edict, a solemn silence fell over the city, all felt that a great revolution had been accomplished, a revolution unstained by one drop of blood.

Buenos Aires made no noisy demonstration of joy over this great victory, she saw clearly the task she had undertaken, and, content that the first step was gained so peacefully, forbore to triumph over her fallen tyrants, setting her face steadfastly towards the great future now opening up before her.

The new Junta met the next day, the 26th May. Their first step was to appoint two secretaries—

Dr. Don Mariano Moreno

and ,, ,, Juan José Passo,

whom they incorporated into their body, thus raising the total number of the Junta to nine.

To this committee of nine men, Buenos Aires entrusted her destiny, the destiny of the Argentine people. They ruled Buenos Aires and directed her energies in the name of Ferdinand VII., King of Spain and the Indies. They styled themselves the Junta Gubernativa of the provinces of the Rio de la Plata ; they yet acknowledged as their King a Spaniard of the House of Bourbon, who lay in a French prison ; they yet considered their country as a part of the wide empire of Spain ; but they looked upon the men of Buenos Aires as the people from whom they held their authority and to whom alone they were responsible ; they were, although they knew it not, the founders and the first rulers of the ARGENTINE REPUBLIC.

CHAPTER VI.

LIONS IN THE PATH.

On the 26th of May Don Gregorio Lopez gave a dinner-party to a number of his friends to celebrate the installation of the new Junta. Don Cornelio Saavedra was there as the principal guest, also Don Manuel Belgrano, and other members of the one time secret committee; of course Marcelino Ponce de Leon and Don Carlos Evaña were present, but the chair which had been placed for Don Roderigo Ponce de Leon was vacant.

At the bottom of the table sat Colonel Lopez, who had only that morning arrived in town from his estancia, and was now eager to learn all the particulars of the events of the memorable days just flown.

Conversation was brisk during the whole time the dinner lasted, each man spoke proudly of the part he had taken in these events, every face beamed with confidence, none seeming to have any doubt of the prosperous future they had secured for their country, but the eye of Don Gregorio wandered now and then uneasily to that vacant chair, which had been placed for his son-in-law Don Roderigo, and which had been kept vacant, in the hope that he might appear.

The dinner concluded with a number of patriotic toasts, proposed in eloquent words, and honoured with enthusiasm, after which the company adjourned to the sala, where many ladies awaited them, among whom the eye of Don Gregorio sought in vain for his daughter Constancia, or for his granddaughter Dolores. The younger people soon commenced dancing, while the elders collected in groups in the corners of the sala, or in the ante-sala, talking; some remained in the dining-room, where coffee was served to them, of whom Colonel Lopez was one. As Evaña had risen from his seat to go to the sala the Colonel had stopped him, and Evaña had taken another chair beside him.

"So you have your republic at last," said the Colonel, after they had conversed some time together.

"Not quite," replied Evana, "but to this there can be only one end, a republic."

"Then there is work before us yet?"

"Without doubt. Here the Spaniards are powerless, but in the provinces they may yet raise opposition."

"And you wish me to join this expedition with my regiment?"

"I do, and more. You have no officer under you above the rank of captain, I wish you to take me with you with the rank of major."

To this the Colonel made no answer, but sat twisting his moustachios.

"I know why you hesitate," said Evaña. "You are accustomed to absolute authority in your own regiment, and do not like the idea of having another officer with you, so near to you in rank."

"And of all men you the least," said the Colonel bluntly. "I know you, Carlos, where you are, there you will have the command, and there are not a few men in my regiment who would be ready to mutiny if you told them. Besides, you have never served at all, how can you take rank at once as a major."

"I have arranged all that with Don Cornelio. Of course he would not give me such rank in an infantry regiment, but in the cavalry it is different."

"Hum!" said the Colonel indignantly, "you city men think anything is good enough for cavalry. I can assure you that if we have any fighting with the Spaniards it will be the cavalry that will secure us the victory. What would you do in a country which is one immense pampa, with infantry or artillery?"

"I thought you would feel flattered at my preference for the cavalry," replied Evaña. "But do not alarm yourself, I do not wish to interfere in any way in the management of the regiment, I merely wish to march with you and hold a definite rank."

"Look you, Evaña," said the Colonel, with a searching look in his eyes, "there is more in this than you tell me. Be frank with me, tell me what you want, and count upon me."

"I want nothing more than I have told you, but I will tell you why."

Evaña paused, looking round him to see that no one was within earshot, then drawing his chair closer to the Colonel and leaning his elbows on the table he continued—

"There is only one man whom we need fear, he is an able soldier and very popular. If he should pronounce against us, many even of the Creoles will join him, and among us there are few who will be eager to fight against him. If he rise, he must be crushed at once. I go to keep an eye upon the officers of this expedition and to ensure that there be no vacillation."

"Liniers?" said the Colonel.

Evaña nodded.

"I should not like to lead a charge against him," said the Colonel.

"If the necessity should arise I will be there and will lead the regiment for you," said Evaña.

"This Liniers, three years ago the 'Reconquistador,' to-day is a Goth, is he not, Señor Evaña?" asked the Colonel, stretching himself and leaning back in his chair. Then as Evaña looked at him in surprise without answering, he continued—

"What is this you have been telling Viana about Goths?"

"Ah! Viana, yes, I have told him about the Goths. Does he speak much of them among the people?"

"He does nothing else than talk about them. Goth now stands with them for everything that is bad. My little Ignacio was naughty the other day, and I heard Mauricia tell him that if he was not good the Goths would come and take him away. When I received your letter, telling me to come to town, the peons came crowding to the estancia to know if the Goths had landed. Why have you put such folly into their heads ? "

" It is no folly, Gregorio," said Don Carlos. "You understand the paisanos, it is of no use to talk to them about patriotism or about liberty. All their traditions and customs lead them to look upon Spaniards as their natural rulers ; if the Spaniards knew how to enlist their sympathies on their side, we might gain a transient victory in the towns and cities, but eventually we should succumb, for the main strength of every country lies in its peasantry. Fortunately Spaniards understand nothing of that, they look upon the paisanos as barbarians by whose labour they can amass wealth. Before they learn their error, I seek to forestall them by supplanting these traditions among the paisanos by a new idea, which they will comprehend very rapidly. We do not fight against Spaniards, who are very decent people, but against Goths, who are robbers and murderers ; in favour of the Goths there is no tradition among them. These tales that I have told Viana about the Goths are perfectly true, they will circulate from rancho to rancho all over the campaña, and if ever the day come that we are hard pressed, thousands of valiant horsemen will follow you against the Goths who would not move a finger to help you against the Spaniards."

" Then there really are such people as the Goths ? "

" They were barbarians who overran Europe in the time of the Roman Empire."

" And did they really sack the city of Rome and try to kill the Holy Father ? "

" They did."

" And they would do it again if they had the chance ? "

" There are no Goths now, but many Spaniards are descended from the Goths, therefore those of them who may refuse to obey the Junta, we can call Goths. There is much in a name, my friend Don Gregorio."

" Do you know, Evaña, you are a man who can see far," said the Colonel, "but there are men who can see almost as far as you. You say that the Spaniards understand nothing of the paisanos, I can tell you there are other men who are quite as ignorant as the Spaniards. What know these lawyers and shopkeepers of the city of the nature of the paisanos ? I tell you they know even less than the Spaniards. I know the Argentine people, and I know that they will never be content to be governed by lawyers and shopkeepers, so take care how you arrange this congress, for the danger is not from Spaniards alone, and will not be averted by telling extravagant tales about the Goths. Come, let us see what they are doing in the sala."

While Don Gregorio Lopez was in vain looking for his son-in-law among the many visitors who crowded his sala that evening, Don Roderigo was thinking of far other things than festivity and dancing. The first part of the evening he had spent at the residence of Don Baltazar de Cisneros in conference with the ex-Viceroy. About nine o'clock he left him and returned to his own house, walking with a firm, quick step, as though the result of his interview had been satisfactory. As he entered his sala he found there one visitor, talking with his wife and Dolores, Don Ciriaco Asneiros. Doña Constancia looked at him anxiously as he came in.

"Marcelino has been here," she said; "he wished to take us to my father's. They are all very much disappointed that you would not allow us to go."

"I am very glad papa would not," said Dolores. "I have no wish to dance with men who are traitors to Spain."

"There spoke my own daughter," said Don Roderigo, smiling.

"Marcelino is there and Don Carlos Evaña," said Doña Constancia.

"Marcelino does not know what he is doing," said Dolores; "and Don Carlos, we all know what ideas he has always had, but I never thought that he would do more than talk. Now I see that the Viceroy was right to put Don Alfonso Miranda in prison, and I am very sorry, papa, that I asked you to get him out."

"The Señor Evaña has been at the head of the conspiracy for years past," said Asneiros.

Doña Constancia glanced hurriedly at Don Roderigo.

"But, papa, I have something else to tell you," said Dolores. "Marcelino says that they are going to send an army into the provinces, and that Evaristo has volunteered. You will stop him, won't you?"

Don Roderigo started, and then walked up the room and back again.

"Cannot you prevent that, Constancia?" he said to his wife.

"I will try, but I am afraid he will not listen to me."

"Evaristo is always so obstinate, but if you order him not to go, papa, then he will not," said Dolores.

"When Buenos Aires revolts against Spain fathers need not hope for much obedience from their sons," said Don Roderigo; "I suppose Marcelino has persuaded him to go with him."

"Marcelino is not going," said Doña Constancia.

"I understood that he had been offered the command of a regiment."

"He declined it," said Asneiros. "I have been offered a command also, but not here, in Monte Video. I came to consult you about it."

"Elio is preparing in time. These patriots as they call themselves seem quite sure that all the cities and towns will join them, but they may perhaps find themselves mistaken," said Don Roderigo, with a significant glance at his wife, who took it as a signal to retire.

"Of course you will go to Monte Video at once," said Don Roderigo to Asneiros when they were alone.

"I do not know that, I have come to speak with you on the subject," replied Asneiros.

"It is from Monte Video that we must look for the reaction," said Don Roderigo. "If Elio remains faithful he will not have much difficulty in securing Monte Video, the fleet will obey him and will give us the command of the rivers, and I have persuaded Cisneros to apply to Peru for an army to secure the northern provinces."

"I was with Don Baltazar this morning; he then seemed quite cast down, and spoke of any attempt to upset the Junta as folly."

"We cannot do anything here at present, but I think we may soon reduce these rebels if we proceed cautiously. The provinces are all jealous of Buenos Aires."

"There is some one else thinks so," said Asneiros. "Don Santiago

Liniers was here in secret not many weeks ago. He hoped that Don Baltazar would have adopted severe measures to prevent this outbreak; when he went he thought only of a reconquest."

"Liniers!" exclaimed Don Roderigo, "I had not thought of him. Truly he is a man from whom at this juncture we may hope more than from Don Baltazar. Upon Concha and Bishop Orellana we may count with certainty."

" His name is alone worth an army," replied Asneiros. "He wished me to go with him, but I thought it better to remain here and watch the course of events. Yesterday I sent off a chasque to him. What say you? Should I not do better in Cordova than in Monte Video? In the provinces we may soon raise an army."

Don Roderigo hesitated, and Asneiros continued—

"What will give us difficulty is this, that as the Junta was appointed by the Cabildo it has the appearance of a legitimate government. What Liniers will require is the aid of some leading Spaniard from the capital, whose name alone will be guarantee for our loyalty."

"We want money and arms, in Monte Video we should have them."

"And be under the command of General Elio, who will have the credit of all you do. No, better join Liniers, and have the credit of what he does. I can procure arms and men too, if you will guarantee me payment of my expenditure when we retake Buenos Aires."

"Men you may persuade to follow you by promises, but arms you will have to pay for, I can assist you very little in that."

" I do not want any money from you, I merely wish your guarantee for the repayment, in the name of the first Spanish Viceroy who has the key of the treasury of Buenos Aires."

" I will give you that readily enough, but how can you raise money sufficient?"

" Have you forgotten the black coffer of that traitor Don Alfonso?"

"Three or four hundred dollars you said there were in it, but you returned them to him?"

" I thought you understood me," said Asneiros, turning aside his face to conceal his vexation. "Of course I gave him the money back, and his ingots too, but I gave him leaden ingots for his gold ones, they are quite as much use to him as the gold ones would ever have been, and now the gold will buy muskets and men to reconquer Buenos Aires for Spain."

" It was true, then, you stole the old man's gold?"

" It was no use to him, but it is rather a pity that it should turn out to be the dowry of your son's wife."

"The dowry of my son's wife! Marcelino's wife! What do you mean?"

" That Don Marcelino is going to marry Magdalen Miranda, the daughter of that old traitor, and that the ingots should have been hers. We will give them back to her if you like, when we retake Buenos Aires."

" Marcelino marry! I thought——leave me, I can talk no more."

" Come with me to Cordova. When you are president of a Spanish Junta you will have the remedy in your own hands."

To this Don Roderigo made no answer, and Asneiros, giving a fierce twirl to his moustachios, left the room.

CHAPTER VII.

By the second week in June the "Espedicion Auxiliadora," composed of 1200 volunteers, had assembled under the command of Colonel Ocampo of the Arribeño regiment. The force had been originally planned to consist of 500 men, but the first advices received by the new Junta from the interior, sounded a note of danger.

The answer of General Concha, Governor of Cordova, to the notification sent to him by the Junta Gubernativa of their assumption of supreme power, was a proclamation issued by Marshal Liniers and himself, in which they denied the authority of the Junta, and called upon all loyal subjects of King Ferdinand VII. to aid them in resisting its pretensions. Orellana, Bishop of Cordova, gave their opposition the sanction of his name and influence.

Instead of 500, 1200 volunteers were enrolled and equipped in little more than a fortnight, the whole of the preliminary expenses being defrayed by voluntary subscriptions. Ere they were ready to march, Colonel Lopez had already left the Barrancas at the head of 200 volunteers from his regiment. He proceeded to the north of the province, and encamped on the river Arrecifes, collecting horses for the force under the command of Colonel Ocampo. The entire troop commanded by Venceslao Viana had volunteered, on learning that Don Carlos Evaña would march with them as major of the regiment.

On the 10th June there was considerable excitement in Buenos Aires. On the preceding night, a number of the volunteers had left their barracks without leave, many of them having taken their arms and equipments with them; none of them returned to the barracks, it was evident that they had deserted. Some of the men began to talk of overtures which had been made to them by a certain Spanish major who had been greatly trusted by the ex-Viceroy, and it was remarked that all the men who had deserted, had formerly served in one or other of the regiments which had been disbanded on the 2nd January, 1809. In the afternoon it became known that at daylight that morning, a party of about eighty men, well armed and mounted, had crossed the river Las Conchas, apparently on the march for the north of the province.

Search was made everywhere for Major Asneiros, but he could not be found. Marcelino Ponce de Leon with a party of Patricios examined the house where he had usually resided, and was met by a finely-dressed lady, who told him that the Major had left on the previous night for Monte Video, and would not be back for some time. In his rooms nothing was found which could give any clue to the reason of his absence.

All that could be done was to send a chasque to Colonel Lopez, telling him to look out for and intercept these deserters.

Don Carlos Evaña had been one of the most active in prosecuting the search for Major Asneiros. In the evening he, with several other officers of the expedition, after dining with Don Cornelio Saavedra, strolled about the city paying farewell visits to their friends, for they were to march on the day following. The last house at which Don Carlos called was that of Don Roderigo Ponce de Leon, but he was disappointed there, not one of the family was at home. About ten o'clock he returned to his own house, at the door he found his servant Pepe waiting for him.

"Ah, Señor!" said Pepe, "for two hours I have been looking for you everywhere. There is a lady waiting to see you. She would not go till you came, and I could not find you. She is in the sala, Señor, and the girl with her."

As Don Carlos entered his sala he was met by a girl whose face was covered with a mantle. On seeing him she turned quickly towards another female figure, also muffled up, who was seated in an obscure corner of the room.

"Here he comes at last, Señorita," she said. Then stepping back so that Don Carlos might pass her, she went to the door and closed it, standing there as though on the watch lest any other should enter.

Don Carlos walked quickly towards the shrouded figure which he could dimly see reclining in a large arm-chair, when that figure started up, and throwing aside the heavy shawl which covered her from head to foot Dolores Ponce de Leon stood before him.

"Oh, Don Carlos! I thought you would never come," said she, and burst into tears, hiding her face in her hands.

Taking one of her hands in his, Don Carlos soothed her and led her back to the seat she had quitted, then drawing forward another chair he seated himself near her and waited till she was calm enough to speak.

"Papa! Don Carlos. Do you know where papa is?" she said.

"I have just come from your house; no one was there. I have not seen Don Roderigo for several days."

"Papa went away last night, I don't know where he has gone. Mamma has gone to see grandpapa, I have come to see you. Long ago you told me that perhaps the day might come when a friend—— when you might——"

"And you remember, and you have come to me. Thanks, thanks, it is so good of you. Tell me everything, your least wish is sacred to me."

Don Carlos moved his chair nearer her and tried to take her hand, but she drew it away from him, and folding her hands together looked straight at him.

"I knew you would," she said. "Yesterday Marcelino came to see papa, and papa was very angry with him. You know Marcelino wants to marry Magdalen Miranda, papa says the daughter of Don Alfonso cannot be fit to be Marcelino's wife. I did not hear all they said, for they were' in the ante-sala and the door was closed but not shut. But as Marcelino was going papa called after him, to beware, for though he was his own son he would never stir a finger to save the life of a traitor to his king and country. That I heard quite plainly, for papa spoke loud. I have not seen Marcelino since, but last night when papa kissed me and held me in his arms, there were tears in his eyes, and I could see that he was praying for me. When I went away he called me back and kissed me again, and I begged him to tell me what was the matter, but he said that nothing was the matter, and that I was to be cheerful and not to trouble my head about things which could not be avoided. I thought that he was thinking of Marcelino, but I don't know why, I was frightened, and I could not sleep, and long after that I heard the door of papa's room open, then the street door was opened very quietly and shut again, and I heard voices in the patio speaking, one of which was papa's, the other I am almost sure was Don Ciriaco Asneiros. This morning mamma said papa had gone and would not be back for several days, but told me I was to say nothing about it. In the afternoon Evaristo came, and said a number of the volunteers had deserted and were gone with Don Ciriaco Asneiros into the provinces to Cordova, to fight against the Junta, and that when they catch them they will shoot them all. For more than two weeks Don Ciriaco has been coming every night to see papa, after every one else was in bed ; Evaristo says that Don Ciriaco is a conspirator, and that they will shoot him too."

Don Carlos had listened to Dolores attentively, letting her tell her tale in her own way, but now she paused as though she expected him to speak.

"You fear that Don Roderigo has gone with these mutineers," he said.

"I am almost sure of it. Mamma tells me that it is nonsense, and that he has gone to Monte Video, but I know she thinks so too."

"I fear there can be little doubt of it," said Don Carlos.

Dolores covered her face with her hands and again burst into tears.

"Can you do nothing to help me, Don Carlos? I know you can. Think if they should fight, and Evaristo is with the volunteers."

"You wish me to stop Evaristo? If you and Doña Constancia cannot stop him what can I do?"

"No, no, Don Carlos. Do not be cruel to me, it is papa I wish you to stop."

"But he is gone, what can I do? If he has gone to join Liniers, if we fight I will make it my special work to save him for your sake."

Then Dolores sprang indignantly to her feet.

"I thought you were my friend, Don Carlos," she said. "He must not fight, they will shoot him, what can you do to save him in a battle? But you can stop him, I know you can."

"He is probably thirty leagues away by this time, how can I stop him?"

"I don't know, I don't know, but I know you can. How can I tell you what to do? Oh, Don Carlos! you are my friend, you said you were, do not be cruel to me. What matters Spain or the Junta if papa is killed?"

So saying Dolores fell on her knees at his feet, and seized his hand pressing her lips to it.

Don Carlos rose hurriedly from his chair, a thrill ran through his whole body at the touch of her lips, but she clung to him.

"Save papa for me," she said. "I know you can if you will. Save him for my sake."

Then Don Carlos bent over her and raised her to her feet.

"I will do what I can," he said. "Here I can do nothing, but if I start now I may reach Arrecifes to-morrow night ; my dragoons are there, I may perhaps overtake him on the frontier."

"I know you will, I knew you would if I asked you," said Dolores, holding his hand in both hers, and looking up at him, her thanks and her confidence, beaming upon him out of her large gray eyes.

"There is no time to lose," said she. "He left the house soon after midnight."

"I shall be in the saddle in half an hour," said he, as he took up her shawl and laid it carefully over her shoulders, but she raised it and threw it over her head, wrapping herself up so that it was impossible for any one who saw her to tell who she was.

"I will see you safe home, then I will go at once," said Don Carlos.

"No, no, not one step with me, I have Manuela." And stretching out her hand to him, and leaving it for a minute in his firm grasp without speaking, Dolores turned from him and, taking her maid with her, disappeared in the patio.

Evaña stood motionless, looking after her, listening to the light, rapid steps which passed along the side-walk outside his sala windows, till as he heard them no more he drew a deep sigh, then ringing his bell for Pepe he cautioned him never to mention this visit to any one.

Half an hour later, accompanied by two armed servants, he rode away, leaving a short note behind him for Marcelino, telling him, without any explanation of this hurried departure, that he had gone to join his regiment at Arrecifes.

Late the following afternoon, Don Carlos Evaña rode alone into the encampment of the dragoons, close to the small town of Arrecifes. His two servants had been unable to keep up with him, and he had only accomplished the journey so hastily by changing horses at different estancias on his way.

Colonel Lopez had marched with two troops, the day before, for San Nicolas, and no chasque had arrived from the city for several days ; such was the report of Venceslao Viana, who had been left in command with about 100 men.

"A party of mutineers left Buenos Aires yesterday. Send out scouts to make enquiries at every estancia for ten leagues to the east and west," said Major Evaña. "Two parties of three men each, with a sergeant, will do. Any intelligence they may learn must be reported instantly."

"Are they Goths, Señor Don Carlos?" said Venceslao.

"Yes," replied Evaña.

The news that Goths were in the neighbourhood caused great excitement among the men. In ten minutes a number of them had caught and saddled their horses, and before sundown the scouting parties were out of sight.

Close to the encampment there was a small rancho, where Colonel Lopez had taken up his quarters. There Evaña lay down on a catre to rest, but was too much fatigued and excited either to sleep or to eat.

At midnight one of the scouts returned, with the intelligence that about midday a party of eighty men, escorting a galera, had crossed the Arrecifes river, and was believed to have halted for the night at the estancia of Don Lorenzo Pico, some five or six leagues further on. Major Evaña rose at once from his catre, telling Viana to put his troop under arms, while he himself ate some food which had been kept in readiness for him.

In half an hour Viana's troop were in the saddle, mounted on picked horses. A corporal with two men were sent off to San Nicolas with a despatch for the Colonel; the rest of the command had orders to collect the spare horses at dawn, and march with all speed for the Estancia de Pico.

A countryman who had come back with the scout offered to lead Evaña, and performed his task so well, that at a quiet trot the Major with his one troop reached the Estancia de Pico before sunrise.

The estancia house was a large azotea, with a courtyard behind, surrounded by a low wall. There was no outer ditch or fence of any kind. In spite of the caution with which they advanced, their approach was perceived by the garrison. A few men whom Evaña sent forward to reconnoitre were driven back by shots fired from the barred windows, and the rising sun glinted on a line of bright musket barrels behind the parapet of the flat roof. Don Roderigo was evidently prepared for a vigorous defence, but it was not Evaña's purpose to fight with Don Roderigo if he could avoid it.

Halting his men at a distance of 200 yards, Evaña drew a white handkerchief from his pocket, and, waving it over his head, rode forward alone to attempt a parley. Standing close to the parapet with his back to him he saw a man of medium stature wearing a hat similar to one he had seen Don Roderigo wearing not many days before. He felt certain that this was Don Roderigo, and rode forward till he was within thirty yards of the house.

"Don Roderigo," he shouted, "I come to you as a friend."

Before he could say another word this man turned, took off his hat and bowed to him, disclosing the hated features of Don Ciriaco Asneiros, at the same time shouting—

"Fuego!"

Evaña had just time to drive his spurs into his horse's flanks and rein him sharply back. The animal reared up, received a volley of balls in his chest and neck, and fell backwards, Evaña only just saving himself from being crushed underneath him.

At this sight Venceslao Viana and his men rushed forward with furious shouts, and, surrounding their leader as he lay on the ground, poured a random fire from their carbines upon the windows and parapet of the house, after which many of them galloped closer and struck with their sabres at the garrison through the bars of the windows. But their fury availed them little. Asneiros kept up a steady fire upon them from the parapet, several of them fell from their saddles, and more of them had their horses shot under them. Evaña, staggering to his feet, shouted to them to keep back. They were too excited to hear him, but Asneiros saw him.

"C——jo!" he screamed; "not dead yet!"

Then, pointing to him, he shouted to his men to take good aim and pick him off. Venceslao heard the words and put himself in front of him, calling to his men to rally round him. Three more of the troopers fell, but the rest, re-forming their broken ranks, retreated beyond musket-shot, Evaña retreating with them on foot. Nothing more could be done than to keep watch on the house until the arrival of reinforcements.

Several of the men being wounded, Evaña applied himself to binding up their wounds, and had just cut out a ball from the shoulder of one man with his penknife, when an exclamation caused him to look round. A troop of about fifty horsemen were coming towards them at a rapid gallop from the south-west. Their wide-brimmed hats, striped ponchos, and long lances showed that they were not the dragoons. Evaña mounted at once upon a trooper's horse, and, wheeling his men round, waited for them. At a distance of 100 yards they halted, and one man came galloping forward alone. He was a short, stout man, with fat, red cheeks almost destitute of beard, with curly hair, and dark, piercing eyes. In his hand he carried a long Indian lance, decked with ostrich plumes.

Reining up his fiery steed with the ease of a consummate horseman, he looked eagerly at Evaña. Then changing his lance to his bridle-hand, he removed his hat and bowed, saying—

"Have I the honour of speaking with the Señor Major Don Carlos Evaña?"

"Your servant, Señor," replied Evaña.

"I call myself Andrès Zapiola, I am an hacendado of Arrecifes. Last night some scouts of yours came to my estancia and told me you were in pursuit of some mutineers. I have collected what men I could, I have the honour of placing them at your orders."

"Never could you have come at a more opportune moment," said Evaña, shaking hands warmly with his new ally. "We have had a skirmish with them already."

The men of both troops were ordered to dismount, while Major Evaña and Don Andrès carefully reconnoitred the house at a safe distance. Don Carlos was much perplexed as to what he should do next, for he wished at all hazards to ensure the safety of Don Roderigo, and desired if possible to conceal the fact of his being with the mutineers. Don Andrès advised him to give up all idea of attacking the place, assuring him that hunger would soon compel them to surrender.

"But then," Evaña thought to himself, "the delay may bring me more allies such as this, and it will be impossible to secure the escape of Don Roderigo."

As he thus thought, scanning eagerly the defences to the rear of the house, where the low wall round the courtyard offered no great obstacle to a vigorous assault, Asneiros solved his perplexity for him. The men were withdrawn from the azotea, and the courtyard, which appeared full of horses, became the scene of busy preparation.

"They are going," said Evaña.

"Let them go," said Zapiola; "it may cost us some lives, but in the open camp we shall have them all the sooner."

Evaña looked on every side for the galera, it was nowhere to be seen. He turned rein, and they rode back to their men, telling each man to take his horse by the bridle and be ready to mount at the first note of the bugle. They had not long to wait, the iron gate in the low wall was thrown open, about forty men rode out, and formed in column of march on the green sward outside, many of them led a second horse by the bridle. Behind them came the remainder of the small force on foot, with shouldered muskets and bayonets fixed.

"They have not horses to mount them all," said Evaña, "therefore we can overtake them when we please. If you will spread your men over the camp in front of them, Don Andrès, and prevent them from catching fresh horses, I will follow you as soon as I have provided for my wounded and made some enquiries here."

Don Andrès bowed, and taking up his long lance, which quivered like a reed in his grasp, he started off with his men at full gallop in pursuit. Evaña followed him as far as the house.

Asneiros halted as he saw the horsemen in pursuit, and facing round with his infantry, prepared to give them a warm reception, but instead of charging him, the Señor Zapiola and his horsemen galloped past him with wild shouts of defiance, and, spreading over the camp on his line of march, drove off all the cattle and horses from before him.

Asneiros again put his men in motion and marched steadily on for about a league, when he re-halted, and, mounting several of his infantry on the spare horses, ordered the rest to get up behind such of the others as were best mounted ; he then gave the word to trot, and resumed his march at a much quicker pace.

Meantime Evaña had dismounted a number of his men, and had sent them round to the front of the azotea, where a number of his troopers lay wounded. Four of them were found to be dead, seven more were removed inside the house.

In the principal room of the house one man in the uniform of the grenadiers was found lying, shot through the heart. The house had been thoroughly ransacked, and not a living creature was to be found inside of it. In the courtyard were several horses lying about in the last stage of exhaustion.

Leaving a sergeant with three men to take charge of the wounded, Evaña, after remaining half an hour here, started in pursuit at a quick trot, but the march of the Spaniards was so rapid that it was two hours ere he rejoined Don Andrès Zapiola. About a league further on there was a large estancia.

"Let us charge them at once," said Don Andrès.

"Collect your men and support me," said Evaña. "We must not give them time to dismount."

The dragoons, who were marching four abreast, wheeled quickly into line, and led by Venceslao Viana dashed at full gallop upon the enemy, with uplifted sabres and a wild cry of "Death to the Goths !"

Evaña, galloping behind them with his sword drawn, had left the lead to Venceslao, so that he might devote his attention to protecting Don Roderigo in the mêlée.

But, quickly as the dragoons had performed their change of front, Asneiros had seen his danger. He halted at once, and ordered every man to dismount and form up in front of the horses. His men had not been drilled to these manœuvres, and, being unaccustomed to riding, were sore and stiff with the rapid marches of the last two days. Before he could get them clear of the horses the dragoons were upon them. In vain he shouted to them to close up and fire, a random volley did not stop the dragoons for an instant; bending low on their horses' necks, so that they could hardly be seen, the shot flew over them; the flankers on both sides of the short line of infantry were swept away and trodden under-foot; a small knot in the centre alone stood firm, beating off the horsemen with their levelled bayonets.

Asneiros, who had remained on horseback, was carried away by the rush and separated from them. As soon as he recovered command of his horse, he turned rein and tried to cut his way through the disordered dragoons, coming, in the midst of the tumult, face to face with Evaña. Muttering a fierce execration he struck at him with his sword, but Evaña parried the blow, and Venceslao Viana, spurring his horse between them, clove him to the teeth with his sabre.

"Venceslao," said Evaña, "have you seen Don Roderigo, he was with these yesterday?"

"Don Roderigo! I have not seen him. If he is with those," said Venceslao, pointing to the small knot of infantry who yet stood firm, "we must be quick to save him."

A number of the dragoons riding round this group were firing upon them with their carbines, every shot telling on the close rank. Evaña galloped up to them, shouting to them to lay down their arms; a number of them did so; the next moment the horsemen of Don Andrès Zapiola poured over them like an avalanche. Behind the rush of the partidarios the dragoons closed in, cutting down without mercy any who yet kept their feet.

With an aching heart Evaña rode over the field, while Viana called his men together by the bugle and so put a stop to the slaughter. Evaña searched among both dead and wounded, frequently dismounting to turn over one lying on his face, but saw nothing of Don Roderigo.

The dragoons had taken some few prisoners, he inspected them, and casting his eye upon a young man who was not dressed in uniform he called him to him.

"What is your name?" he said.

"Joaquin Saurez, Señor, at your service."

"How do you come among these mutineers, you do not seem to be a soldier?"

"Señor, I had urgent necessity for money, and the Señor Major Asneiros gave me two doubloons to enlist in the regiment of Cordova."

"Well, Joaquin, you are mixed up in a bad business, but will you swear to me that you are not a deserter from some regiment in Buenos Aires."

"By the Holy Virgin Maria and by all the saints I swear it to you, Señor. I never was a soldier, I do not know how to handle a musket. Señor, I will tell you how it was I came to enlist."

"I have no time to listen, but if you will answer me my questions, and I find your information correct, I will give you your liberty and a good horse, so that you may go where you like; if you deceive me,

with your life you will pay for it. Now listen ! was Major Asneiros
your own leader ? "

" He was the only one who gave any orders ? "

" Were all here to-day who left Buenos Aires with you ? "

" No, Señor. There was a gentleman with two servants who rode
with us the first day, but we stopped that night at an estancia where
there was a galera waiting for him."

" And he came with you in this galera yesterday as far as Pico's
estancia ? "

" Yes, Señor, we reached there soon after midday, and the men refused to travel any further. He picked out the best of the horses and
went on."

" How many men went with him ? "

" Four postilions and his two servants who were in the galera with
him."

" Do you know who this gentleman was ? "

" I heard his servants speak of him as Don Roderigo, and I have
seen him before in Buenos Aires. I think he must be some powerful
Señor, from the respect that the Major showed to him."

" Did you hear where he was going ? "

" To Cordova, Señor. He was very angry that we would not march
on yesterday, but some of the men could not sit their horses any longer."

As Evaña finished his examination the second party of the dragoons
came up, driving a mob of horses before them. The whole of the
dragoons dismounted and stood in a circle round these horses, while
each man in his turn caught one. When all were supplied they turned
the horses they had previously ridden adrift, and saddled these fresh
ones.

Meantime Evaña had walked to where the body of Asneiros lay
stretched on the ground in the charge of a dismounted dragoon. This
man he told to search the pockets and give him all the papers he
could find. The man found few papers on the body, but he found a
leather belt round the waist, filled with gold coins. Evaña took the
papers, but handing the belt to Viana told him to distribute the money
among the men of both troops. He did not think it necessary to give
any of it to the men of Don Andrès, for they were busy plundering the
slain for themselves.

Evaña was not long in making up his mind what to do. Stiff and ·
fatigued as he was, and sore with the bruises he had received when his
horse fell back with him, he yet determined to carry on his pursuit
himself. Telling Viana to select twenty men from his troop, he gave
up the command of the rest to the captain of the other troop ; then,
with many thanks to Don Andrès Zapiola for his opportune assistance,
he turned his horse's head to the north and galloped away, attended
only by Viana, and a guide well acquainted with all the roads through
Santa Fè, who had been found for him by Don Andrès.

After them galloped the twenty picked troopers without any attempt
at military array, driving before them some two score spare horses.

CHAPTER VIII.

HOW GENERAL LINIERS LOST AN IMPORTANT ALLY.

It was an hour past midday when Don Carlos Evaña galloped from the scene of the skirmish. Judging that Don Roderigo would proceed by the high road for Cordova, he cut straight across camp for the town of Pergamino, where he halted for half an hour to make cautious enquiries. His uniform and his announcement that he was on government service, procured him every attention from the townspeople, who were eager in their offers of assistance, and he soon learned, without exciting suspicion, that the galera had arrived there late on the preceding night, and had started again at sunrise.

Onwards he galloped, and soon after sundown reached an estancia near to the Arroyo del Medio, which divides the province of Buenos Aires from the province of Santa Fè. Here he found it was useless for him to attempt to go any further, as, though a good horseman, he was quite knocked up, not having galloped for any distance for several months. The estanciero pressed him to remain, and at once sent some peons to slaughter a cow for his men.

" I am dead beat," he said to Venceslao, taking him to one side ; " I must trust to you to catch this galera for me and bring it back."

"Pues ! that is not strange, Señor Don Carlos," said Venceslao ; "but you know you have only to tell me what to do and I will do it."

" The gentleman who is in this galera is Don Roderigo Ponce de Leon. He is on his way to Cordova to join Don Santiago Liniers in raising an insurrection against the Junta. All who join this insurrection will be shot, so we must stop Don Roderigo at any cost."

" Have no fear, Don Carlos, even if I have to go to Cordova I will bring him back. I do not forget that he is a relation of mine, and you know that the family has its obligations."

" You must stop him before he reaches Cordova, or it will be too late, and above all you must let no one know who he is. I shall wait here for you."

" And if he will not come ? " said Venceslao thoughtfully.

" If the men he has with him resist, shoot them, but do not touch him on any account. He does not anticipate pursuit, so I do not think he is prepared to resist. You have nothing to do but to turn the galera round when you overtake it, and drive back. Speak to him as little as possible. Everything depends upon your speed ; if you start at dawn you may catch him to-morrow."

Evaña asked the hospitable estanciero for a bed, and, in spite of the fever of fatigue, was soon in a dreamless sleep; but soon after midnight he woke and heard the jingling of spurs and the rattle of sabres in their iron scabbards, as Viana with his men mounted and rode away.

Viana took fifteen men with him, leaving the other five behind in charge of the spare horses; by sunrise he had reached the first posthouse in the province of Santa Fè on the main road to Cordova. All day he travelled rapidly, changing horses at the post-houses as he went on, encouraged by finding that the roads were heavy, and led through many swamps and bad passes, which would seriously impede the progress of a wheeled vehicle. At every post-house he heard that the galera was before him, at the place where he halted at sundown he learned that it had passed about two hours before.

Mounting again at midnight, he reached the next post-house at dawn, just as the galera was leaving. Don Roderigo, supposing his party to be a detachment of Asneiros' men, waited for him to come up. Venceslao rode alone to the galera.

"You have mistaken the road, Señor Don Roderigo," said he.

"Are not you Venceslao Viana?" replied Don Roderigo.

"Your servant," replied Venceslao. "The Señor Major Evaña has detached me with this escort to secure your safety, there are many bad characters about."

"Evaña!" exclaimed Don Roderigo; "I thought he was in Buenos Aires."

"He left the day after you did, Señor Don Roderigo. The day before yesterday we arranged those vagabonds, so now with this escort you need fear nothing."

"And the Señor Major Asneiros, what of him? Where is he?"

"He died, Señor."

"And the Señor Major Evaña, where is he?"

"He was tired and could come no further, he is waiting for you at an estancia on the Arroyo del Medio."

Don Roderigo looked fixedly at Venceslao, asking with his eyes a question he did not care to speak. Venceslao bowed his head in reply.

"Carry out your orders, whatever they are." So saying Don Roderigo shut the window of the galera through which he had leaned during this colloquy, and, seating himself in a corner, wrapped himself in his cloak.

Viana then rode up to the postilions, telling them to turn and go back the way they had come, silencing their objections by throwing back his poncho and laying his hand on the butt of a pistol.

On the afternoon of the day following Don Carlos Evaña, now quite recovered from his fatigue, sat talking with the estanciero who had given him shelter, when one of his troopers came to the door of the room and announced that a galera had crossed the arroyo, and was coming up towards the estancia, escorted by a party of dragoons. Don Carlos sprang joyfully to his feet, and went out with his host to watch the galera as it came swiftly towards them. At the tranquera it stopped, Don Carlos himself opened the door.

"My friend," said he, "I am rejoiced to see you in safety."

"I am your prisoner I suppose, Señor Don Carlos?" replied Don Roderigo, stepping out, but refusing the hand which Evaña stretched out to him in welcome.

"My prisoner, no," said Don Carlos ; "I shall be happy to escort you to Buenos Aires, or any other place to which you may wish to go."

"I am on my way to Cordova and have lost four days by your interference."

"To Cordova! that is impossible, Cordova is in the hands of a party of rebels against government."

"Cordova is the present station of the only legitimate government of the Viceroyalty of Buenos Aires. I see what you wish, Don Carlos, I see that you wish others to believe that I have taken no part in this insurrection as I suppose you call it. You have not introduced me to this good gentleman, who is, I presume, the owner of this estancia."

"The Señor Don Luis Peña," said Evaña, on which the estanciero stepped forward, raising his hat.

"I have much pleasure in welcoming you to my house, Señor, and put it and all I have at your service," said Don Luis, shaking hands with Don Roderigo.

"Peña!" said Don Roderigo, "I know your father well, and a worthy old gentleman he is, but I fear me infected with the disloyalty of the present time. I am Roderigo Ponce de Leon, Señor Don Luis, I am a member of the Cabildo and of the Audencia Real of Buenos Aires, and I am on my way to Cordova to join Marshal Liniers and to concert measures with him for the upsetting of this rebel Junta which has been established by the mob in Buenos Aires. If you still offer your services you can aid me very much, Don Luis, by raising the partidarios in this district and liberating me from these dragoons."

"I am sorry, Don Roderigo, to have to refuse your first request," replied Don Luis ; "we all here recognize the Junta of Buenos Aires as the only legitimate government of the Viceroyalty."

"Then, Don Carlos," said Don Roderigo, turning bruskly away from Don Luis, "I am your prisoner."

"If you think well over it," said Don Carlos, "you will see that in turning you back on your journey I have been actuated only by a desire to prevent great unhappiness to your family."

"And have acted as a traitor to your country," replied Don Roderigo, then turning his back upon him he walked with Don Luis up to the house.

Don Luis Peña strove by every means in his power to render the compulsory visit of Don Roderigo pleasant to him, but Don Roderigo declined to look upon himself in any other light than as a prisoner. He absolutely refused to return to Buenos Aires, although both Don Carlos and Don Luis gave him every assurance that he should suffer no molestation ; he considered that to reside quietly in Buenos Aires, taking no part in public affairs, would be equivalent to acknowledging the authority of the Junta.

Thus two days passed ; on the third Colonel Lopez arrived with the rest of his regiment and encamped near to the estancia. In company with the Colonel came Don Andrès Zapiola and several other wealthy hacendados from Arrecifes and Pergamino. To many of these Don Roderigo was known personally, to all he was known by repute.

Don Carlos Evaña was sorely perplexed; some of these new arrivals spoke of Don Roderigo as the man who had induced the desertion on the 10th June from the "Espedicion Auxiliadora." This expedition had already left Buenos Aires, and might probably reach the frontier in a day or two. He himself was now under the orders of a superior officer, on the arrival of the expedition both would be under the orders of Colonel Ocampo, who would unquestionably send Don Roderigo to Buenos Aires as a prisoner, for trial on a charge of treason. He consulted with Colonel Lopez, who had declined to visit the estancia.

"Do what you will, Don Carlos, and lose no time," said the Colonel; "I do not require your services with the regiment for a day or two, and if you wish to go anywhere you can take an escort. In your report to me of the defeat of Asneiros you have mentioned that you started at once after the action in pursuit of a detachment which had gone in advance. Since that you have made no further report, I suppose the other party escaped, but I have instructions from Buenos Aires to arrest Don Roderigo Ponce de Leon if he is in the neighbourhood; if I see him I shall carry out my orders, but I have also letters which inform me that he is in Monte Video."

Don Carlos returned to the estancia, and offered to escort Don Roderigo to San Nicolas if he would promise him to go thence by water to Monte Video, and give up all thoughts of joining Marshal Liniers. For long Don Roderigo refused, the news of the approach of the volunteers under Colonel Ocampo had no effect upon him, and it was only when Don Carlos entreated him to secure his safety for the sake of his wife and daughter that he at last consented.

As soon as it was dark that night, Viana's troop of dragoons left the encampment and marched away eastward, passing close to the estancia of the Señor Peña, where they were joined by five men well mounted, who rode with them through the night at a rapid pace, and left them at dawn near to the frontier town of San Nicolas. The dragoons encamped till the next morning, when they were joined by Don Carlos Evaña and Don Luis Peña; returning immediately to the estancia of the latter gentleman, they were there met by the intelligence that the "Espedicion Auxiliadora" was encamped near at hand on the Cañada de Cepeda.

CHAPTER IX.

LA CABEZA DEL TIGRE.

THE Spanish adherents of Marshal Liniers, had done their best to excite enthusiasm for the cause of Spain, in the hearts of the citizens of the learned city of Cordova, a city of which it was said at that time, that even the waiters in the cafés talked Latin, and that the favourite amusement of the peons at the street-corners, was to discuss among themselves the most abstruse questions of philosophy and metaphysics.

Among other reports which were diligently circulated, was one that a great part of the troops in Buenos Aires had mutinied, and were on the march to join Marshal Liniers under the command of Don Roderigo Ponce de Leon, who had been appointed by Cisneros as his delegate in the provinces. The news of the skirmish on the Estancia Pico, in which these troops were stated to have been cut to pieces, consequently produced great consternation among these Spaniards, but made little impression upon the good citizens of Cordova, who for the most part heard of all these events with indifference, not considering matters of government to be any affair of theirs.

Marshal Liniers was better informed concerning the particulars of that skirmish. The aid he looked for was not from Buenos Aires but from Peru, yet still he lingered at Cordova, hoping to be joined by Don Roderigo, of whom he had heard nothing, save that he had left Buenos Aires for the purpose of joining him. So passed the month of July, his adherents falling away from him, till he lost all hope of making any effectual stand where he was against the patriot army.

Meantime the patriots had met with great difficulties on their march across the Pampas of Santa Fè, and it was already August when they ascended the high lands which surround the city of Cordova, marching with great precaution, for they knew not what resistance they might meet.

It was a fine morning, it seemed as though the spring had already come, the air was so balmy, the vegetation so luxuriant, when on the 5th August, Don Carlos Evaña with a troop of dragoons, which formed the advanced guard of the patriot army, debouched from a thick wood, and looked down upon the pleasant city of Cordova, snugly nestling among the hills in the valley below him ; upon Cordova, the city of churches and convents, the city of monks and nuns, the city of learned doctors and of eager seekers after a knowledge void of all practical value ; upon Cordova, a city of which no native

was ever known to be in a hurry, and where men were well content
to sleep away their lifetime, sheltered from the storms of nature by
those encircling hills, sheltered from the storms of men by their ignorance of all those varied aspirations, which make life in other climes a
never-ending race after prizes for ever vanishing away ; upon Cordova,
the peaceful and the learned, where Spain was thought of as the
empress of the world, and where more was known of the history of
Carlo-Magno and his Paladins than of that of Frederick the Great or
of Napoleon, where the greatest war that the world had ever known
was supposed to be the war against the Moors waged by Ferdinand
the Catholic and his Queen.

Upon Cordova looked down from those wooded heights, the vanguard of the patriot army; upon Cordova looked down Don Carlos
Evaña, a man to whom the learning of Cordova was but as an idle
dream, a man in whose eyes its peacefulness was sloth, and its religion hypocrisy.

But no thought of all this passed through the brain of Major Evaña
as he gazed upon the learned city, whose white domes and towers
filled up the small valley beneath him ; he thought but of that one
man whom he considered as the most dangerous enemy of the Argentine people ; he had determined within himself to crush this man, and
as he looked down upon the city, where he had set up the standard of
Spain, he thought only of how best that standard might be trampled
in the dust, he dreaded only lest his foe might have escaped him by
timely flight.

As his men cleared the wood, he gave the word to trot, and with
much jingling of spurs and clattering of iron scabbards, each man
with his loaded carbine resting on his thigh, the little force wound its
way rapidly along the tortuous path, and, descending the hill without
meeting a foe, trotted swiftly up the main street of the city to the
Plaza.

Men standing in doorways, gazed curiously upon them as they
passed ; between the iron bars of many a window peered many a fair
face, looking upon the rough soldiers as though they formed part of
some unwonted pageant.

Both men and women looked upon these swarthy troopers, and
women looked much upon the pale, stern face of him who rode at
their head ; but the men spoke no word of welcome, and the women
gazed after them with foreboding hearts. The steady tramp of the
horses, the clattering of the iron scabbards, were sounds unfamiliar to
their ears, they recognized intuitively that these men were the heralds
of a new era, and that there was little in common between them and
the black-robed priests and bearded monks who were the more usual
occupants of their streets.

Major Evaña drew up his troop across the sandy Plaza in front
of the cathedral, and himself rode up to the hall of justice. Here he
was met by a group of the civil authorities, who stood in the sun before him bareheaded, and invited him to dismount. Evaña replied
by asking them a question.

" Where is the Señor Mariscal Don Santiago Liniers ? "

" Marshal Liniers had left the city on the preceding day."

" What troops had he with him ? "

" None. Only a few friends had accompanied him."

" What road did he take ? "

" The northern road."

As the last question was answered, the great doors of the cathedral were thrown wide open, a procession of priests issued forth, bearing an image bedecked with jewels, seated on a throne under a canopy heavy with golden fringe. In front walked a number of boys bare-headed, dressed in white robes, with long hair which flowed down over their shoulders. Some of these boys carried censers, which they swung to and fro, filling the air with perfume, others carried small silver bells, which they shook as they walked, producing a medley of sweet sounds which announced the approach of the procession. Immediately before the canopy, walked a young priest bearing a tall crucifix of massive silver, behind came other priests bearing a crozier and crosses of silver, while on either hand, and further behind, came a number of citizens, bare-headed and in long white robes, carrying immense wax candles, which were lighted and burned in the bright sunshine with a dull, yellow flame.

Evaña, with a gesture of impatience, wheeled his horse round, and placing himself in front of his troop drew his sword, while Viana shouted the word of command, " Present arms ! "

Straight for the centre of the troop marched the procession, but Evaña stirred neither foot nor hand, each swarthy trooper sat motionless on his horse. An aged priest, with an angry scowl at the dragoons, spoke a word to the boys, they turned to the right, and the whole procession passed on in front of the line of horsemen and took its slow way down the main street by which the dragoons had come, bells tinkling, and censers swinging before it. The citizens in their doorways, and the women-folk behind the barred windows, who had gazed so apathetically upon the dragoons, now kneeling down with uncovered heads, devoutly crossed themselves, muttered an " Ave " and a " Credo," and gazed with admiring eyes upon the gorgeous canopy and upon the jewelled figure beneath it.

No sooner was the front of his line free than Evaña, sheathing his sword, gave a signal to Viana, the troop wheeled at once into column, and trotted swiftly away by the northern road, watched by many a wondering eye as it crossed the Rio Primero and wound its way up the steep hill-side, till it was lost to view among the abrupt peaks of the sierra.

As simple shepherds tending their flocks by night gaze wonderingly at the track of some fiery meteor, so the simple citizens of Cordova gazed wonderingly at the cloud of dust which marked the track of the fast-receding soldiery. They were accustomed to think of Spain as of a great nation, empress of the world ; they had heard of revolution as of a deadly sin, as of a whirlwind sweeping over the earth, destroying nations in its course, and inflicting unutterable woes upon the people ; now the whirlwind had descended into their peaceful valley, the deadly sin had passed along their streets, the authority of Spain was uprooted from amongst them.

Cordova was as the heart of the southern continent, her universities were renowned teachers of theology and jurisprudence, and to her flocked students from all the Spanish colonies of South America. Of late there had come among them, men telling them that their learning was folly, talking to them of the right of men to make their own laws, and to worship God according to the dictates of their own conscience. These men had spoken of the revolution of the 25th May as of a glorious event.

The townsfolk had looked upon Marshal Liniers as the man who was to vindicate the authority of Spain, who was to uphold the integrity of those laws and religious customs, the teaching of which was the glory of their city. But Marshal Liniers had fled from among them, and now came this troop of horsemen pressing after him in pursuit, passing through their midst and injuring no one, neither halting to eat nor to drink, but pressing on with the steady purpose of a relentless fate.

The genius of liberty rode unseen at the head of that small party of dragoons, and, passing through Cordova, brought the knowledge of a new era into the heart of South America.

Leagues beyond the sierra, on the road to Tucuman, there stood a large estancia, used also as a post-house, which went by the name of " La Cabeza del Tigre." About noon, on the day after Evaña with his dragoons passed through the city of Cordova, Marshal Liniers with General Concha, Bishop Orellana, Colonel Allende, and two others, were seated at dinner in the principal room of this estancia. The faces of all present were clouded and anxious ; news had been received that morning that it was not safe for them to proceed on their way to Tucuman, that province, the garden of South America, had pronounced as one man in favour of the Junta of Buenos Aires ; the route to Peru was closed. San Juan and Mendoza, lying at the foot of the Andes, had also declared in favour of the Junta, barring the way to Chili. On every side there were enemies, wide desolate plains, or impenetrable forests.

As they conferred together, there came a sound through the open doorway of the galloping of horses, then came hoarse words of command, and the jingling of spurs, as of horsemen dismounting.

"See what it is, Anselmo," said Marshal Liniers to the serving-man, while his companions looked upon him in consternation.

Anselmo went out a handsome, smooth-faced mulatto, he came back at once, his face of a pale-green colour, his eyes almost starting from his forehead with terror.

"Señor ! Señores ! my General ! the revolution !" he gasped out.

Then there came a heavy step with the jingling of a spur, a hand was laid upon his shoulder, he was pulled roughly back, and Don Carlos Evaña strode into the room.

"Señores, all of you, surrender yourselves prisoners to the orders of the Junta Gubernativa."

Liniers started to his feet, stared wildly at Evaña, then turned deadly pale and sank back into his chair, muttering between his teeth—

"It is he. All is lost !"

"What is this? who are you?" said the Bishop angrily, while Colonel Allende drew his sword.

"It is madness to think of resistance, the house is surrounded," said Evaña.

"Promise us our lives," said General Concha.

"I promise nothing. Give up your arms," replied Evaña, stamping his foot.

At this signal, in at the doorway came Venceslao Viana with his drawn sabre in one hand and a pistol in the other, behind him filed into the room a strong party of dragoons. Marshal Liniers, unbuckling his belt, handed his sword to Viana.

It was the afternoon of the 25th August. The large dining-room of the Estancia "La Cabeza del Tigre" was the scene of a court-martial.

At one end of the room, at the head of the table, sat Dr. Don Juan José Castelli, member of the Junta Gubernativa, who had come express from Buenos Aires on learning the capture of Marshal Liniers in order to preside at this court-martial. On each hand sat several field-officers of the patriot army, who formed the court. At the other end of the room, and facing the President, stood Marshal Liniers, General Concha, Colonel Allende, and two civil officials named Rodriguez and Moreno, who had been captured at the same time. Behind them stood a party of the Patricios, with grounded arms and bayonets fixed. Several other officers of the patriot army, who had not been summoned to sit on the court-martial, stood grouped about the doorway.

About half-way down the table stood Don Carlos Evaña, in full uniform as a major of dragoons. He had just concluded his speech as public prosecutor, demanding in vehement language, that sentence of death should be passed upon the five prisoners who stood before them, as guilty of treason against the legally-constituted government of the provinces of the Rio de la Plata; warning the members of the court not to permit their private feelings to interfere with their duty to their country, for if they allowed the authority of the Junta to be set at defiance with impunity, they would deliver their country over to anarchy, entailing upon it greater evils than had ever been inflicted by the tyranny of Spain.

As he sat down a deep silence fell upon all present. Then Dr. Castelli addressed the prisoners, calling upon them for their defence against the charges which had been brought with sufficient witness against them, charges of attempting to foment rebellion against the royal authority of King Ferdinand VII., and against the Junta governing in his name.

"If my acts and services do not attest my loyalty, I have no other defence to offer," replied Marshal Liniers.

General Concha and the others denied the authority of the court, and demanded to be sent for trial to Buenos Aires.

When the prisoners had been removed, many of the officers who had served under Liniers, and were anxious to save him, demurred to the sentence of death, but the influence of Dr. Castelli, seconded by Don Carlos Evaña, overcame all opposition. It was determined that the five prisoners should be shot on the following day, and buried with military honours, in consideration of the past services of Marshal Liniers.

The prisoners being recalled, the sentence of the court was read out to them by Dr. Castelli. General Concha and the three others protested against the sentence as unjustifiable, but Marshal Liniers had given up all hope of life when he surrendered his sword.

"What would you from the agents of a revolutionary Junta?" said he to his fellow-prisoners; then turning to the court, he added—

"To one only of you have I a word to say—to you, Don Carlos Evaña. My fate I have brought upon myself, by listening to the words of those who induced me to spare you, when I had you in my power. I have long known you as a dangerous conspirator. I have known you as one of those reckless men, who care nothing what evils they bring upon a people in the prosecution of their own extravagant ideas. But beware! this people whom you have led to rebellion against their legitimate rulers, will learn quickly the lesson you would teach them. As ruthlessly as they now cast aside that authority and allegiance which has for centuries watched over them, so will they trample underfoot any such ephemeral government as you may attempt to set up. The people know no gratitude for past services, and the day will come when they will turn upon you and destroy you, in payment for the lessons you have taught them.

"Beware, Don Carlos Evaña! Here in America you have raised up the fiend of revolution. You, and those who work with you, take to yourselves pride, in that you have liberated a great people from the power of a crushing despotism. You have done no such thing. You have but raised up among them an evil spirit whom your puny efforts will be powerless to curb. This people, this Argentine people, will themselves destroy the work which you labour to accomplish. You are to-day the murderer of five innocent men, condemned to death for no crime but because they stand in the way of your own insensate ambition."

Here Marshal Liniers was interrupted by Dr. Castelli, who commanded the officer of the guard to remove the prisoners.

"I pray you, Señor Presidente, to let him speak," said Don Carlos Evaña. "We, conscious of the rectitude of our own hearts, may well suffer our motives to be impugned; it is but another sacrifice we make upon the altar of our country."

"You are to-day my judges, to-morrow you will be my executioners," continued Marshal Liniers, looking haughtily round him, heedless of the interruption; "but I tell you that the day is not far distant, when the Argentine people shall themselves call you to account for the blood so unjustly shed, and shall deliver you over to be torn in pieces by the evil spirit you yourselves have raised—a spirit which will soon deluge in blood those same streets of Buenos Aires in which I have twice led you to victory—you who are to-day my murderers."

He spoke no more, but, with a proud inclination of the head, retired, surrounded by his guards.

Many efforts were made during the night by inferior officers who had served under Liniers to procure a commutation of his sentence, but after this farewell address the members of the court were more convinced than before, of the necessity of ridding themselves of so dangerous an enemy.

On the following day, the 26th August, a volley terminated the existence of the man who had first led the people of Buenos Aires to victory, of the man who had first organized their militia into an effective force, who had first taught them their strength, and had so made liberty and independence possible to them. Marshal Liniers fell before the fire of a platoon drawn from the ranks of a volunteer army, the offspring of his own exertions, which Buenos Aires had sent forth to vindicate in the provinces, the liberty she had already achieved for herself.

CHAPTER X.

ONCE more, in the balmy spring-time, they stood in the porch together, Marcelino and Magdalen. The storms of winter had passed over, again the trees clothed themselves in brilliant green, again the shrubs decked themselves with flowers, and all nature rejoiced in the renewal of life and strength. Together they stood in the porch, looking out into the mellow sunshine, she leaning upon his arm with happy confidence, with a sweet sense of ownership, for she was his wife.

Seated in an easy-chair under the shade of the trees, with the soft wind playing round him and tossing lightly about the scant white hairs which lay upon his temples, sat an old, old man. Don Alfonso had survived his illness, but he rose from his bed older by apparently twenty years, since the night when Magdalen had found him lying on the floor of his room beside the brass-bound coffer, from which his treasure had been stolen. He might yet live long, although the zest of life had gone from him, leaving him only a monotonous, aimless existence, but he had now both a son and a daughter to watch over the comforts of his declining years. He accepted their attentions, passively submitting himself to their care, and seeming happy, though taking no interest in anything that went on around. Still his eye would brighten as they spoke to him of the devastation and ruin which had fallen upon Spain, and of the success which attended the measures of the new Junta of Buenos Aires. One day he asked Marcelino for $1000, a sum which it was no easy matter for Marcelino to procure, and he was curious to know what it was required for, but for days the old man would do nothing except repeat his demand, till Marcelino promised him that he should have the money. Then he rubbed his hands together, saying—

"Such a good stroke, it should be well paid."

"What stroke, papa?" said Magdalen.

"That man who saved Don Carlos and killed that traitorous Spaniard."

Then Marcelino gave him the money, and he locked it up himself in the black coffer, till Venceslao Viana should come back and receive the gift from his own hands. Magdalen sighed as she saw that her father had not yet fully learned the lesson of forgiveness, but to Marcelino she spoke only of his gratitude.

Together they stood in the porch, watching the old man as he sat under the trees, looking out into the mellow sunshine, thinking of troubles past, fearing little for troubles to come, confident that their mutual faith and trust, would bear them through whatever trials might yet be in store for them.

"You have not told me if you have been successful," said Magdalen.

"I have had no difficulty at all," replied Marcelino. "My father can come back and remain here as long as he chooses, but I fear there is little chance of his remaining long, I fear he has made up his mind to return to Spain, and will take my mother and Lola with him."

"And is Doña Constancia willing to go?"

"Yes, she is even anxious; she dreads nothing so much as that my father should take an active part in the hostile measures of the Spaniards of Monte Video. Dolores rejoices at the idea."

"That I can understand very well," said Magdalen, smiling.

"She was always more a Spaniard than a Porteña," said Marcelino. "Though she does not say anything to me, yet I know she sorrows over me as a hopeless rebel. When my father returns I think that both she and my mother will come to see you."

"Does she ever speak of Don Carlos Evaña?"

"Yes, and you would be surprised to hear her. She will not allow any one to say a word against him. She calls the execution of Marshal Liniers a foul murder, but is angry when any one says that he had anything to do with it. She says she knows that it was for quite another purpose that he joined the army."

"Yet every one says that he went only to pursue Marshal Liniers. Don Fausto says that when he marched from Arrecifes he was not in pursuit of Major Asneiros, but of some one else, and that he had false information that Don Santiago Liniers was with the mutineers."

"One thing is certain, that he went away after the fight on Pico's estancia with twenty men, and that nothing was known of him for more than a week after, but Marshal Liniers was at that time in Cordova."

"Do you think it is true that he sat on the court-martial?"

"Of that there is no doubt. My uncle Gregorio refused, and they named him instead. Dr. Castelli told me that, when he returned."

"Is that the reason why Don Gregorio came back and left the command of the regiment to Don Carlos?"

"I believe so, but I have not seen my uncle since, he only remained one night in the city."

"When you write to Don Carlos do not forget to tell him that Don Roderigo is going to Spain, and will take Doña Constancia and Lola with him," said Magdalen.

"I will not forget," replied Marcelino.

Spring drew on towards summer; everywhere the patriot arms carried everything before them. Goyeneche, general-in-chief of the Spanish armies of the Viceroyalty of Peru, maddened by repeated defeats and the loss of some of his most trusted officers, gathered his forces together for one last effort to retrieve the cause of Spain in the late Viceroyalty of Buenos Aires, of which he, a Peruvian, was the champion. The fight was fierce and bloody; the cavalry of Diaz Velez, charging with true Argentine impetuosity, broke through the lines of the partidarios of Peru, and scattered them in hopeless confusion ; the infantry of Buenos Aires, pressing on through showers of grape and musketry, stormed with the bayonet the centre of the Spanish position, but, broken by their rapid advance, their ranks in disorder, they here found themselves opposed by a regiment of Spanish infantry, which had been kept in reserve, and whose steady fire mowed down their men by scores. Diaz Velez was far off; to retreat was utter ruin, to re form the column under this murderous fire was impossible. Already the signs of panic were visible, soldiers throwing down their arms and seeking shelter, officers running wildly about, striving to collect their men and make some reply to the volleys which shattered each rank as it was formed. One young officer seized a standard, and waving it over his head, calling upon his men to follow him, rushed upon the levelled muskets of the Spaniards, who, in close ranks and steady as on parade, loaded and fired with the rapidity only acquired by long practice ; alone he stood unflinchingly, under a tempest of balls, which tore the flag he held into streamers, and shattered the shaft till it fell in pieces in his hands. Other Spanish corps began to rally on the flanks of the patriot column ; all seemed lost, when through the smoke and dust a small band of horsemen came rushing at full gallop, and hurled themselves upon that serried line of infantry. At their head rode a tall man with pale olive features and high square forehead, who neither waved his sword nor shouted, but, taking his bridle in both hands and plying his spurs, forced his horse into the thickest of the levelled bayonets ; he never looked behind, but rode straight on, knowing that those who followed his lead, would follow it to the death. With wild shouts his troopers galloped close behind, and their sabres drank deep of Spanish blood that day.

The murderous fire was stopped, the panic was at an end, his men answered to the voice of the young officer, who again called upon them to rally to the standard, the ranks were re-formed, the patriot column rushed on, and the field of Suipacha was won.

"Major Evaña," said General Balcarce, as he strained that officer in his arms, when covered with blood and dust he retired from the hard-fought field, "to you our country owes the greatest victory she has yet achieved. The enemy is totally routed, to-morrow there will not remain one armed foeman on Argentine soil."

"Not to me alone," said Evaña ; "let me ask you a favour for a young officer, who did even more than me to-day."

Evaña stepping back laid his hand upon the shoulder of a young officer of the Patricios, and continued—

"You have granted me leave of absence, let Don Evaristo Ponce de Leon accompany me, he will be back ere you have need for him again."

"He shall carry my despatches for me to the Junta," replied General Balcarce, "and shall carry his shattered flag-shaft with him as a proof of the gallantry of the youth of Buenos Aires."

The year 1810 drew near to its close ; a few days more and 1810 was merely a date in the past, a date replete with memories both sad and joyful to many of those whose lives and deeds have furnished the materials for this book.

In the roadstead of Buenos Aires there lay a noble ship, with anchor apeak, sails hanging in the brails, the blue-and-white flag, signal of departure, flying from the truck of the fore-mast. On the quarter-deck of this ship were collected several of those of whom we have just spoken. Over them floated the flag of England, under whose shelter political animosities were forgotten, and the close ties of relationship and of friendship were once more acknowledged.

Don Roderigo Ponce de Leon had settled his affairs in Buenos Aires, and shaking off the dust from his feet, was on his way to Europe; rending asunder the liens which bound him to the country of his adoption, he turned himself again to the country which had given him birth, determined to devote the rest of his life to her service. But he went not alone, with him went his wife and daughter, and he said to himself that he had yet a son left, who, uninfected with the heresies of the present age, was still a loyal child of Spain. Yet as the moment of departure drew nigh his heart yearned towards the son who had at one time been his pride, his anger towards him melted away, and forcing himself to forget the present and the immediate past, he talked only to him of the future; talked to him of the day when Ferdinand of Bourbon, reinstated on the throne of Spain, should re-establish his authority over his subjects in America who yet acknowledged their allegiance to him, and, grateful for their past loyalty and devotion, should forgive their present disloyalty to Spain.

Side by side he and Marcelino paced the deck together. Marcelino, deeply grateful for the love his father yet displayed to him, seizing eagerly at any topic of conversation in which he could agree with him, and speaking confidently of the day as not far distant, when Spain and her colonies should again be united under one sceptre.

"You have forgiven me, my father," said he. "God bless you for it. When you are far away, and in your own country are striving to substitute the will of an entire people for the tyranny of a few, when you establish a cortes at Cadiz, and so direct the valour of a noble people, fighting for rulers in whom they can trust, that this unbroken series of defeats shall be changed into one of victories, till not a Frenchman tread the soil of Spain, then, father, you will do me justice. Buenos Aires is my country, as Spain is yours; what I have done for Buenos Aires you will do for Spain, and under free institutions, Spain and her colonies shall all acknowledge one king."

Then as Don Roderigo answered nothing, but paced the deck with a flush of pride on his face as he thought of down-trodden Spain, and of the future which lay before him, should he contribute to her certain triumph, Marcelino continued—

"You have forgiven me, my father, there is one here to whom you owe no forgiveness, who has never wronged you, and who, if you love me, has every claim upon your love also, for she is your daughter. Father, you have never spoken to Magdalen, she is my wife, and only waits permission to share with me, all the love and respect I have for you. Father, will you not speak to Magdalen? May I not bring her to you, and will you not bless her for my sake if not for her own?"

"Magdalen! Your wife! Yes, let me see her," replied Don Roderigo.

Apart from the others, sitting by Doña Constancia and soothing her sorrow with many gentle words, was Magdalen Miranda, who had already found in Doña Constancia a second mother, and had learned to love her dearly, only to lose her. Marcelino went up to her, and taking her hand in his said—

"Come, Magdalen."

And Magdalen knew why he spoke, for her eyes had followed him wherever he had gone, and her heart was with him in its one hope, that Marcelino's father might yet bless her and call her his daughter ere they parted, never to meet again.

She rose, and with her hand in his, walked with him to where Don Roderigo stood awaiting them. Don Roderigo raised his hat, bowing to her with courtly politeness, but without speaking, till seeing the yearning look in her gray eyes, eyes which reminded him so much of those of his own daughter, Lola, he forgot that she was the daughter of the man whose life he had blasted, of the man who had ruined for him his hopes when life was at its brightest, he saw in her only the wife whom his son loved; opening his arms he took her to his breast and kissed her, then raising his hand he laid it upon her head and blessed her, calling her his daughter, and thanking her for the happiness she had brought into the life of his son.

Taking her hand he led her to a seat, and seating himself beside her began talking to her, questioning her much concerning herself, and listening with ever-increasing pleasure to the sound of her voice, which fell upon his ear with the melody of soft music.

Marcelino sat beside his mother with her hand in his, trying to speak cheerfully to her of the future time when they should meet again, and Dolores, flitting to and fro, kept the others from approaching these two couples, so as to prolong for them the few minutes they might yet have together.

"Here he comes at last," said a voice.

It was the English captain who arrived in a boat from shore, for his arrival alone the ship was waiting. As he set his foot upon the deck, the boom of a gun drew all eyes towards the distant city, then there came the boom of another gun, then another.

"The guns are firing from the fort, papa," said Dolores, and as she spoke, the continued roar of the guns came to them mingled with the joyful clash of bells, coming to them with a softened sound across the wide waste of water which separated them from the land.

"What is it?" asked several, of the English captain.

"They have just received news of a great victory somewhere in the north," replied he; "they were making no end of a hullabulloo about it when I left."

"Oh! my son! my son!" cried Doña Constancia, when these words were translated to her, "I shall never see Evaristo again; but he could not know, poor boy!" and she covered her face with her hands.

But her son was nearer to her than she thought. In the wake of the captain's boat came another, swiftly propelled by six stout oarsmen. As it drew near, it was seen to contain two passengers, whose eyes eagerly scanned the row of faces peering over the bulwarks at them. Both were in uniform, but in uniforms travel-stained and sun-browned.

"Evaristo!" said Dolores, with a cry of joy.

"And Evaña," echoed Marcelino.

Hardly had the boat touched the side, ere the younger officer, springing lightly up the ladder, stood on the deck looking eagerly about him, then bursting from those who pressed round him with congratulations and many questioning words, he ran to where his mother sat, even yet barely comprehending what she heard.

"Mamita!" he said, clasping her in his arms.

Leaving mother and son together, the rest crowded round Evaña, pressing his hands and listening eagerly, as he told them of the great victory which had freed Argentine soil from the footstep of a foe. Even Don Roderigo, forgetful of all else, came up to him, and taking his hand, listened with a father's pride, to the words in which Evaña spoke of the gallantry displayed by his youngest son, attributing to him more than to any other, the glories of Suipacha.

Evaña spoke with head erect, he stood among them with the bearing of a conqueror, he felt that the dream of his life was rapidly approaching its full accomplishment. Though he spoke but little of his own deeds, he knew that had he not marched from Cordova with the army of the north, the victories which had crowned the standards of the patriots, had never been won. He it was who had infused determination into the counsels of the chiefs; he it was who had set his foot with ruthless energy upon every attempt to shackle in any way the authority of the Junta; he it was who had interpreted to them the orders of that Junta, and had dared to trample in the dust the standard of Spain, when upheld by those who equally with the Junta claimed to rule by the authority of King Ferdinand.

Evaña spoke proudly and haughtily as a free citizen of a free people, but as he spoke, his eye wandered from them who hung upon his words, wandered unceasingly, till his gaze fell at last upon her he sought, his eye had found Dolores, seated at some distance from him with her mother and Evaristo; then his voice faltered, and he answered at random the questions which were put to him.

"And General Nieto, is it true that he fell in some action?" asked Don Roderigo.

"No," replied Evaña fiercely, "I took him prisoner. Two file of grenadiers and a priest, you remember his counsel to Marshal Liniers, such mercy as he would have shown to me, such mercy I gave to him."

Then, heedless of more questions, he made his way through them, and walking up to Doña Constancia took her hand and raised it to his lips.

"Oh, Carlos, how good you have been to my son," said Doña Constancia. "If you had not brought him, he could not have come, and I should have gone away without seeing him."

"He might have been here before," said Evaña, "but Evaristo is a brave soldier, and his country could not spare him on the eve of a battle. I never told him you were going till the fight was over."

"I never saw any one in such a hurry to finish a fight," said

Evaristo; "but for Viana he would have been killed twice over. Then when all was over he told me and we have galloped ever since."

"Don Carlos, I am so glad you have come," said Dolores, putting her hand in his.

Evaña drew her away from the others to a vacant corner behind the wheel, where they stood side by side, looking together at the shore.

" You are glad to see me, Lola," said Evaña.

Dolores started and her face was troubled as he spoke to her by this name, which he had never used but once before during all their long friendship, but quickly recovering herself she answered—

"Yes, so glad. You have been a true friend to me and mine, I have so much to thank you for, you managed it all so well. No one knows here that papa went with the mutineers, no one, not even mamma or Marcelino."

"I told you that I would be your friend, Lola, I have kept my word and you have kept yours. I have left the army and come here on purpose to see you once more, I have come to ask you to give me yet one promise."

"Tell me, you have only to ask me, I will promise what you wish."

"Listen first. You see that fair city stretched white and smiling, with its towers and glistening domes, before us on the shore. That city is the city of your birthplace, this country which you leave behind you to-day is your country. You are going to Spain, you love Spain because Spain is your father's country, when you have lived in Spain you will know better what Spain is. I am glad you are going, but some day you will come back, and to make sure that you do come back, I want you to make me one promise, the promise I have come here to ask from you. Promise me that you will never forget the land of your birth, promise me that you will never forget that you are a Porteña."

"I will promise," said Dolores, "I can make that promise very easily, for I am a Porteña. I love Spain as you say, because it is papa's country, but I am a Porteña."

"Away across the ocean in the land to which you are going there is a gallant soldier, whose heart will beat with a wild joy when he hears that you tread the same soil as he. Some day you will be his wife, Lola, remember then that your country is his also. He has promised us, he has promised me and Marcelino, that when his own country no longer needs his sword, he will come and join us, and will fight beside us till the independence of your country and my country is secure."

Dolores flushed scarlet, her hand trembled as it lay in Evaña's firm grasp, and she answered hurriedly—

"But the war is over, is it not? After this great victory there will be no more fighting?"

"The war is but commencing," replied Evaña; "so long as Spain holds one foot of ground on American soil, our independence is not secure."

The white sails came fluttering down from the brails where they hung in festoons, the monotonous clank of the capstan ceased, the cheery cry of the sailors announced that the anchor was aboard, and the noble ship, swinging round, spread her wings to the wind. No longer an inert mass lying lifeless on the waters, she became a thing of life, and cleaving her way through the dancing waves, began her voyage back to Europe, bearing within her the mingled joys and sorrows, hopes and cares, which make a ship a small epitome of the world.

"Remember!" said Evaña to Dolores, then bending over her he pressed his lips upon her forehead and so left her.

Again they stood in the porch together, Marcelino and Magdalen. Evaña had just left them, and the evening breeze tossed about the branches of the trees which had waved over him as he disappeared, going from them with his heart full of proud hopes of which he had eloquently spoken to them, going forth into a life such as he had planned out for himself long ago, a life full of proud hopes and high resolves, a busy, turbulent life, the life of a politician in a young democracy. They stood in the porch together, and through the evening air came again to them, as it had come to them in the morning across the waste of waters, the loud boom of the cannon, the joyful clangour of the bells.

"Again!" said Magdalen. "Have they not made noise enough over Suipacha?"

"Again," replied Marcelino, "but for another cause; this is to celebrate another victory. Belgrano has forced the passage of the Paraná, and the army of Velazco has fled before him. Everywhere the Junta is victorious."

So joyously and gloriously ended the year 1810, with the booming of cannon and the loud clangour of the bells. So, decking her brows right early with the laurel leaves of victory, there rose up in the New World a new nation. As a young man, glorying in his strength, rejoices in the difficulties and dangers which beset his path, so Buenos Aires, recking nothing of the toils and dangers she entailed upon herself, set her hand zealously to the task she had undertaken, scorning to count the cost of the great work she purposed to accomplish. Manumission from the thraldom of a tyrant is purchased by the lives of men, and Buenos Aires sent forth her best and her bravest to bear the standard of freedom in the fore-front of the battle. Over the whole continent of South America the sun of May rose resplendent, awakening enslaved peoples from the sloth in which they wallowed, calling upon them to claim their place among the nations.

"Then there will be no more fighting now," said Magdalen; "the authority of the Junta is established."

"That I cannot tell," said Marcelino; "but one truth I know, which you have taught me, that he who works out zealously the life-task which God gives him to do, need fear nothing that may befall him in the future—as his day is so will his strength be."

GENERAL EPILOGUE.

GENERAL EPILOGUE.

I.—THE VICEROYALTY OF BUENOS AIRES.

THE Spanish colonies of La Plata were, from the conquest up to the year 1776, annexed to the Viceroyalty of Peru, but in that year, the same in which the revolted colonies of Great Britain declared themselves an independent republic, King Charles III. of Spain created by royal edict the Viceroyalty of Buenos Aires.

"Its limits extended from ten and a half degrees south latitude to Tierra del Fuego, and from the Cordillera of the Andes to the hills from whence flow the upper affluents of the Paraguay, Paraná, and Uruguay; this immense line terminating at the opening where the Rio Grande de San Pedro falls into the sea. This territory, equal to a quarter part of the whole of South America, comprehended the most beautiful fluvial system of the world, and might compete in fertility, riches, and natural beauties with the finest empire of the universe. It contained within its limits six out of the seven climates into which Humboldt has divided the globe—from the region where bloom the cinnamon and the spice-trees to far beyond the agricultural countries; thus it produced all that man requires for his sustenance, comfort, and delight." [1]

The first Viceroy, Don Pedro de Ceballos, landed at Buenos Aires on the 15th October, 1777; the last actual Viceroy was deposed by the people of Buenos Aires on the 25th May, 1810.

The Viceroyalty of Buenos Aires was divided into several provinces and "intendencias," which later on became provinces. Of the Viceroyalty Buenos Aires was the capital city, being the seat of the Viceregal government, and the general residence of the Viceroy. The province of Buenos Aires was thus under the immediate rule of the Viceroy. The other provinces were ruled by governors appointed by him, but were in their internal administration, completely independent of Buenos Aires.

The Spanish colonial system, not only prohibited direct commercial intercourse with foreign nations, but also imposed great restrictions upon the intercourse of the several provinces with each other, the aim of Spanish rule, being to secure the dependence of each separate colony upon herself.

The whole of these provinces were independent colonies, bound together only by their common allegiance to Spain, under the rule of one Viceroy. The conquest of Spain by Napoleon destroyed the only bond which held these provinces together.

[1] "La Historia de la Republica Argentina," by Don Luis José Dominguez.

The several events which followed the capture of Buenos Aires by
Beresford in the year 1806, and which it is the object of this book to
elucidate, gradually raised the citizens of Buenos Aires from a state
of blind subservience to Spanish rule, taught them their strength, and
accustomed them to criticize the acts of their rulers. Thus the revolution of the 25th May, 1810, was nothing more to them than the
spontaneous outburst of popular will, a will which they had already
exercised on previous occasions with most glorious results. But the
provinces had undergone no such training. Thus, when the conquest
of Spain was apparently complete, and the whole Viceroyalty was left
without any legal authority, the citizens of Buenos Aires did not hesitate as to what they should do. They saw at once that the appointment of a new government rested with themselves, and, taking such
means of expressing their will as they had already in other cases found
efficient, they named the Junta Gubernativa. But upon the provinces
the news of the conquest of Spain fell as a thunderbolt. The fall of
Spain left them at the mercy of any ruler who should call upon them
to obey.

Such was the condition of the masses of the Argentine people on
the 25th May, 1810, but both in Buenos Aires and in the provincial
cities, there was a small minority of educated men who had learned
and had accepted with eagerness, the principles inculcated by the
revolutionary leaders of France. "Le Contrat Social" and "Les
Droits de l'Homme" were for these men the gospel.[1] It was they
who directed the popular enthusiasm of Buenos Aires to one definite
object, the establishment of a Junta composed for the most part of
men of Argentine birth; it was they who throughout the provinces
echoed the cry of "Liberty" raised by the patriots of the capital.

II.—THE YEAR 1810.

"The new government lost no time in propagating the revolution
throughout the Viceroyalty, inviting the towns to follow the example
of Buenos Aires, to appoint popular assemblies, and to name deputies
to form a congress, which should decide their future fate. Where the
people were free to express their opinions the vote was unanimous.
Maldonado and Colonia, in the Banda Oriental; Las Misiones and
Corrientes, La Bajada and Santa Fé, along the rivers; San Luis, in
the interior of the Pampas; Mendoza and San Juan, at the foot of
the Andes; Salta and Tucuman, on the confines of Upper Peru,
answered the call of the capital; Chili soon afterwards following the
same example."[2]

The revolution of the 25th May, 1810, was the work exclusively of
the citizens of Buenos Aires. Buenos Aires took upon herself the
responsibility of the step, and spared neither blood nor treasure to
secure to herself and to the Argentine people, that liberty which she
was the first to proclaim in South America as the birthright of man.
Throughout the provinces there were many friendly to the cause, but

[1] Mitre.
[2] "La Historia de Belgrano," by General Mitre, from which work the dates and
facts of this Epilogue are chiefly taken.

there were also many who were not so, and more still who looked on with perfect apathy, and were ready to accept as their rulers any who might claim the sceptre which had fallen from the hands of Spain.

To secure the triumph of her friends, Buenos Aires fitted out an army composed of volunteers, equipped by private subscription, and despatched it into the provinces. From Cordova this army marched to the borders of Upper Peru, under the command of Don Antonio Balcarce, defeated Goyeneche and other Spanish generals in several actions, shot General Nieto and other chiefs, and completely freed the Arribeño provinces from Spanish rule. The revolution advanced in every direction, Chili entered into strict alliance with the Junta of Buenos Aires, and sent a contingent of troops, and the auxiliary army, again victorious at Suipacha, menaced with destruction the last remnants of the Spanish army of Upper Peru.

A second expedition was also depatched to Paraguay under the command of Don Manuel Belgrano, who received the grade of general. Belgrano crossed the Paraná on the 19th December, putting to flight a small force under Colonel Thompson, which opposed his passage, and occupied the town of Itapúa.

But there was one exception to this general success which attended the first measures of the Revolutionary Junta. General Don Francisco Elio, Governor of Monte Video under the late Viceroy Cisneros, was appointed in his place Viceroy of Buenos Aires by the new Regency of Cadiz. Until the receipt of this appointment, Elio had given a favourable hearing to the emissaries of the Junta Gubernativa, but he now insisted upon their recognition of his authority, and, finding his friendly overtures rejected, declared war against Buenos Aires, and despatched the Spanish squadron to blockade that port. The authority of Spain was for a time re-established throughout the Banda Oriental, but the blockade of Buenos Aires, after lasting three months, was raised in November, through the intervention of Lord Strangford, who considered the Junta Gubernativa, who ruled in the name of King Ferdinand, as the allies of Great Britain.

So ended the year 1810. During the seven months which had elapsed since the revolution of the 25th May, many reforms had been introduced into the administration, chiefly through the influence of Dr. Don Mariano Moreno, secretary to the Junta Gubernativa, but even his far-seeing intellect did not fully comprehend the magnitude of the task Buenos Aires had taken upon herself.

The first aim of the patriots was to procure the concurrence of all the different provinces of the Viceroyalty. The next necessity was to organize some entirely new form of government, which should amalgamate these different provinces into one people. The history of the Argentine Republic for the next six years, is the record of struggles for these two objects, and of resistance against the attempts of Spain to re-establish her authority.

The cry of " Liberty " raised in Buenos Aires on the 25th May, 1810, had resounded throughout the Western Hemisphere, awakening responsive echoes in the hearts of the down-trodden colonists of Spain. Venezuela and Mexico had arisen against their oppressors, Chili had declared for the revolution, Peru alone remained faithful to

Spain, and Peruvian troops marched under the Spanish flag against the patriot armies of Buenos Aires. But in Buenos Aires only had the champions of liberty any secure footing, to Buenos Aires alone could the enslaved peoples of America look for the full achievement of their freedom.

III. PARAGUAY.

Paraguay had suffered more than any other province of the Viceroyalty from the tyrannical exactions of Spanish rulers, but the rule of Velazco, the then governor, was extremely popular, and General Belgrano with his small army, instead of meeting with a friendly reception, found the whole country in arms against the Porteños; the country people fled before him, driving off their horses and cattle, leaving nothing behind them that could in any way assist his progress, but without venturing to molest him.

Through forests and swamps Belgrano forced his way with infinite labour to within eighteen leagues of Asuncion, where, at Paraguay, on the 19th January, 1811, he with 800 men attacked the Paraguayan army under Velazco, which numbered 9000. The impetuous valour of the volunteers at first carried all before them, but, disordered by success, one part of them was surrounded by overwhelming numbers and cut to pieces, and the rest under the immediate command of Belgrano were forced to retire. On the banks of the Tacuari, Belgrano halted with the remnant of his small army, was there attacked by a pursuing column of 3000 men, repulsed them, and then offered to retire across the Paraná if allowed to march unmolested, saying it was not his object to conquer Paraguay.

In a lengthened conference Belgrano fully explained his views to the Paraguayan generals and officers, his proposition was accepted, he recrossed the Paraná, but the object of his expedition was achieved. Soon after his retreat the Paraguayans rose against their Spanish rulers, deposed them, and placed the government in the hands of a triumvirate of natives. Of this triumvirate Dr. Francia, a lawyer of Asuncion, was the leader, a man of considerable mental attainments and of great suavity of address, but withal of an iron will and of a most ruthless disposition. Before long he had made himself the sole ruler of Paraguay, and presently, seeing that anarchy was gradually spreading over the other provinces of the late Viceroyalty, he cut off all intercourse between Paraguay and the rest of the world.

IV. THE BANDA ORIENTAL.

Early in 1811 the campaña of the Banda Oriental rose in rebellion against the Spanish Viceroy; the Junta of Buenos Aires sent an army to aid the movement. To Belgrano, recalled from the frontiers of Paraguay, was entrusted at first the command of this army, but he was soon superseded by General Rondeau, who was by birth an Oriental.

José Artigas had commenced life as an estanciero, and had obtained great fame and influence among the paisanos of the Banda Oriental, till the Government of Monte Video, finding themselves unable otherwise to put a stop to depredations upon the revenue, entrusted him with the task of suppressing contraband trade ; his influence with the paisanage became greater than ever. In February, 1811, he put himself at the head of the popular outbreak, marched with his "gauchos" upon Monte Video, won the first victory of the war at Las Piedras, and then, joining the army of Rondeau, assisted him in laying siege to Monte Video.

The Princess Carlota of Brazil sent an army of 4000 Portuguese in aid of the Viceroy. Then peace was made in November, 1811, but was of no long duration. José Artigas took umbrage at the slow retreat of the Portuguese, and made war upon them with his light cavalry on his own account. Again the Government of Buenos Aires sent an army to aid him, and secured the retreat of the Portuguese by concluding a separate peace with them, after which, in October, 1812, Rondeau again laid siege to Monte Video.

On the 31st December the garrison sallied out, under the command of Vigodet, who had succeeded Elio in command, and attacked the principal position of the besiegers at the Cerrito. The sortie was at first successful, but the day was retrieved by the gallantry of Colonel Soler, who with the 6th regiment recaptured the Cerrito at the point of the bayonet, and drove the garrison back with heavy loss into the city.

After this, Artigas left the whole work of the siege to the Porteños, named himself the military Governor of the Banda Oriental, and sent deputies chosen by himself to the "Constituent Assembly" of Buenos Aires. The assembly refused to admit his deputies, on the ground that they were not legally elected ; whereupon Artigas declared war against Buenos Aires, and sent emissaries into Entre Rios, Corrientes, and Santa Fè, seeking to stir up the people of those provinces against the "Government of the Porteños."

At this time, the Government of Spain sent out to Monte Video a reinforcement of 2200 men. Thus, when in January, 1814, Don Gervacio Posadas was appointed Supreme Director of the united provinces, he found himself with two wars upon his hands in the Banda Oriental. The Argentine army, aided by Artigas, had been unable to capture Monte Video, the garrison of that city was now much stronger than before, and Artigas was actively engaged in cutting off the supplies of the besieging army. Don Juan de Larrea, a Spaniard by birth, and one of the members of the Junta Gubernativa appointed on the 25th May, 1810, was the man to whom belongs the credit of overcoming these difficulties. Up to this time the Spanish fleet had held the command of the estuary of La Plata ; the Government of Buenos Aires, inspired by Larrea, now fitted out some small merchant vessels as men-of-war, and, placing them under the command of an Irishman named William Brown, determined to dispute this supremacy.

The Spanish fleet was at that time divided into two squadrons, one stationed at Martin Garcia, an island which commands the entrance to the rivers Uruguay and Paranà, the other stationed at Monte Video. Brown sailed in the first place against Martin Garcia, but was beaten off by the Spanish squadron with heavy loss. He returned to Buenos Aires for the purpose of refitting and procuring reinforcements, after which he again approached the island, and, landing his crews, captured it on the 16th March, 1814. The Spanish squadron fled up the Uruguay, and placed themselves under the protection of José Artigas.

Brown then sailed for Monte Video, attacked the Spanish squadron there on the 14th May, and after a desperate conflict against very superior numbers, gained a complete victory, and blockaded the city.

On the 8th May General Alvear crossed the river from Buenos Aires with 3000 men, and with this reinforcement took command of the besieging army. On the 20th June Monte Video, closely invested by land and sea, surrendered. The trophies of this victory were 3500 prisoners, eight standards, 545 guns, and 8200 muskets.

Artigas, on hearing of the surrender, immediately advanced upon Monte Video, but his lieutenant, Otorguez, a caudillo of infamous repute, was twice defeated by a small force detached against him under the command of Colonel Dorrego, but Dorrego was in his turn completely defeated at Guayabo by Don Fructuoso Rivera, in consequence of which, the Government of the united provinces entered into an arrangement with Artigas. On the 24th February, 1815, Artigas took peaceable possession of Monte Video, the Argentine army returned to Buenos Aires, and the Banda Oriental became an independent state.

V. THE ARMY OF UPPER PERU.

The auxiliary army of the north after its first successes, took the name of "the army of Upper Peru," and, under the command of Colonel Diaz Velez, penetrated victoriously to the confines of the province of Cuzco, but was on the 20th June, 1811, surprised by Goyeneche at the Desaguadero and totally routed. The remains of the army, under the command of Don Juan Martin Puyrredon, made good their retreat, in defiance of all the efforts of the Spaniards to stop them, to the city of Salta. Here Puyrredon and Diaz Velez again attempted to make head against the enemy, but their vanguard was defeated at Nazareno and they were compelled to retreat upon Tucuman. On the march they were joined by General Belgrano, who had been recalled by Government from the Banda Oriental and appointed to the command of this army, at the request of General Puyrredon, whose health was much shattered by the hardships through which he had passed.

On the 26th March, 1812, Belgrano took the command of the army of Upper Peru, which was no longer an army but a disorganized, half-armed mob, with a very small supply of ammunition, consisting of barely 1500 men, one fourth of whom were sick. The retreat of Goyeneche gave him time to form an army on the basis of this remnant; again he advanced into the neighbourhood of Salta. Government, too much occupied by the war in the Banda Oriental to send him any effective reinforcement, sent him positive orders to retreat to Cordova. To these orders he paid no attention, till Goyeneche, after quelling an insurrection in Cochabamba, despatched General Tristan with an army of 3000 men to attack him.

In August Belgrano commenced his retreat from Jujui, closely pursued by the Spanish vanguard, till on the 3rd September they drove in his rearguard under Diaz Velez at Las Piedras, upon which he turned on them with his whole army and totally routed them. The success of this skirmish so greatly encouraged his men, that Belgrano, disregarding renewed orders to retreat to Cordova, determined to halt at Tucuman. The inhabitants of this city received him with acclamations, and some of the principal citizens raised a contingent of "gaucho" cavalry among the paisanos for his assistance.

On the 24th September Tristan marched past the city of Tucuman with the idea of cutting off the retreat of Belgrano and compelling him to surrender. Belgrano sallied out and attacked him; he himself at the head of his gaucho allies broke through the Spanish line and assailed them in the rear, while his infantry completely routed their centre, capturing five guns and three standards. The left wing of the Spanish army stood firm, but the next day Tristan beat a precipitate retreat, having lost 450 killed and 700 prisoners; the loss of the patriots was 80 killed and 200 wounded.

The news of this victory excited the greatest enthusiasm in Buenos Aires; then in January, 1813, came the news of the victory of the Cerrito, and in February the victory of San Lorenzo. Fortune seemed again to smile upon the patriot cause.

Colonel San Martin, since his arrival in Buenos Aires in 1812, had been actively engaged in organizing a regiment of cuirassiers, known to history as the mounted grenadiers, famous in the campaigns of Chili and Peru. Their first exploit was the affair of San Lorenzo, where they cut to pieces a detachment of Spaniards who had landed from the squadron.

After the victory of Tucuman, Belgrano received reinforcements until he had 3000 troops under his command, exclusive of the gaucho cavalry of Tucuman, who scoured the whole country round, and greatly harassed the Spanish general, Tristan, in his endeavours to reorganize his routed army.

Up to this time the patriot armies had fought under the Spanish flag. Previous to taking command of the army of Peru, Belgrano had been for a short time stationed at Rosario, where he had adopted a new flag for his troops, two horizontal stripes of blue and one of white, with the national arms embroidered in the centre of the white stripe. For this proceeding he had incurred the censure of the Government, and had withdrawn his flag, saying that he should keep it concealed until he could adorn it with the laurels of victory.

In February, 1813, Belgrano marched from Tucuman; on the banks of the Rio Pasages, in the province of Salta, he halted his army on the 13th February, and hoisting the blue-and-white flag upon a flag-staff, administered to the whole army an oath of obedience to the "Sovereign Assembly," from which imposing ceremony that river bore afterwards the name of the "Rio del Juramento." Belgrano stood beside the new standard, and drawing his sword held it across the staff, while every officer and soldier of the army came up and kissed this military cross as he took the oath. This standard was afterwards adopted by the nation, and is to-day the national flag of the Argentine Republic.

From the Rio del Juramento the patriot army marched upon Salta, where Tristan was then stationed with 3500 men. In the neighbourhood of this city the two armies met on the 20th February; the battle was hotly contested, but at length the Spaniards were driven in disorder back into the city, where the whole army surrendered that afternoon, but after laying down their arms were permitted by Belgrano with misplaced generosity, to retire to Peru.

The losses in this battle were about equal, 600 killed and wounded in each army. The trophies of the victory were three standards, ten guns, and the whole of the arms and baggage of the royal army.

Goyeneche, who was at Potosi with 4000 men, retired precipitately on the news of this disaster, and throwing up his command was succeeded by Pezuela.

Belgrano made but slight use of his victory, and spent months at Potosi organizing schools, while the royalists recovered from their panic and organized an army. Of his supineness Pezuela took every advantage, and, having assembled about 4000 men, advanced in the spring upon Potosi. Belgrano awaited him on the table-land of Vilcapugio, where he was attacked by Pezuela on the 1st October. The patriots, advancing with their usual impetuosity, at first carried all before them, but through an ill-understood order were seized with a sudden panic and suffered a total defeat. Belgrano lost the whole of his guns and baggage, but saved his standard, and four days afterwards established his head-quarters at Macha with a remnant of his army.

In a month's time Belgrano had succeeded in again assembling about 3000 men, while the victorious royalists were held in check by the gaucho cavalry, which swarmed all around their position. In November Pezuela again advanced and again defeated the patriots at Ayouma, Belgrano retiring from the hard-fought field with only 400 infantry and eighty cavalry.

Belgrano retreated to Jujui, where he succeeded in collecting 1800 men, but on the approach of Pezuela he evacuated that city, and continued his retreat to Tucuman, where he was met by considerable reinforcements, including the mounted grenadiers of San Martin, who was named second in command.

Worn out with sickness and reverses, Belgrano applied to be relieved of his command, and in January, 1814, resigned it into the hands of General San Martin, who, establishing his head-quarters at Tucuman, applied himself diligently to reorganizing the army, and constructed an entrenched camp to the north of the city. Pezuela reoccupied Jujui and Salta, but the two victories gained by Belgrano had so roused the spirit of the people, that the paisanos rose in mass against the invaders, and under Arenales and Güemes prevented any further advance of the royalists.

In this year 1814, the revolution in Chili was completely crushed by the defeat of the patriots at Rancagua. San Martin gave up the command of the army of Peru to General Rondeau, and, marching with his mounted grenadiers and a small force of infantry to Mendoza, set to work to collect and organize the immortal "army of the Andes."

Rondeau, advancing from Tucuman, retook Salta and Jujui, but was afterwards totally defeated at Sipe-Sipe by Pezuela, on the 29th November, 1815, and retreated to Jujui.

VI. THE SOVEREIGN PEOPLE.

Such is a slight sketch of the military achievements and reverses of the Argentine patriots, during the first six years of the era of liberty. But not against external foes alone had they to contend, even yet a more formidable foe, was the ignorance of the most enlightened among them of the first principles of popular sovereignty. The principles of representative government, then but partially understood even in England, were by the Argentine people understood not at all. Further, the Viceroyalty of Buenos Aires comprised a host of discordant elements, which only the most consummate skill could weld at once into one homogeneous people.

The Junta Gubernativa had not been long in power before it became divided into two parties, Conservatives and Democrats. The latter, under the leadership of Dr. Moreno, represented the revolution; they were for completely changing the whole system of government, and to themselves made no secret that their ultimate aim was the establishment of an independent republic on the democratic basis of the sovereignty of the people. The Conservatives, of whom Don Cornelio Saavedra was the head, aimed at nothing more than continuing the government under the old forms, but independent of Spain, until such time as Ferdinand VII. might again exercise his royal authority. Such reforms as were forced upon them they accepted, but they made no attempt to direct public opinion to any definite end, they had no fixed policy whatever, and thus the measures of the Junta were directed exclusively by the more active Democrats, until in the month of March, 1811, twelve deputies named by the Cabildos of as many provincial towns arrived in Buenos Aires.

These provincial deputies, in spite of the opposition of Dr. Moreno, were incorporated with the Junta itself, and gave an overwhelming majority to the Conservatives, who, not content with this triumph, stirred up a popular commotion for the purpose of crushing the Democrats. The result was the expulsion of four of the leading Democrats from the Junta, after which the provinces were directed to form Juntas of their own.

In September the form of government was again changed by the authority of the Cabildo. The Junta was resolved into a deliberative assembly, whose functions were very obscure, and the executive was entrusted to a triumvirate, Chiclana, Passo, and Sarratea. To this triumvirate Don Bernardino Rivadavia acted as secretary, and his clear intellect infused itself into every measure adopted.

The provincial Juntas and the Junta of the capital were abolished, and the triumvirate, under the name of "The Superior Provisional Government of the United Provinces of the Rio de la Plata." commenced a vigorous policy of centralization, with a view to putting an end to the disorder which had crept into every branch of the administration. Among other decrees was one establishing liberty of the press.

The only check upon the power of the triumvirate was an assembly of "Notables" chosen by the Cabildo. This assembly had the right of appointing a successor to an outgoing triumvir every six months.

On the occasion of the first election their choice fell upon Don Juan Martin Puyrredon, who was at that time absent in the interior. The triumvirate denied their right to appoint a deputy to represent him until his return to the capital, they insisted, the assembly was dissolved, and the whole powers of government were assumed by the triumvirate.

But the Argentine people, in accepting the revolution of the 25th May, had delegated their power to an executive, only until the meeting of a sovereign congress. The triumvirate convened a new assembly elected by the Cabildos of the capital and of the provincial towns, which was far from representing the people, and was in no sense a congress.

At this time there existed in London a secret society, composed entirely of men born in Spanish America, organized by General Don Francisco Miranda of Venezuela, with the object of working out the independence of the Spanish colonies of America. Three members of this society, José de San Martin, Carlos Maria de Alvear, and José Matias Zapiola, all Argentines by birth, arrived in Buenos Aires on the 13th March, 1812, in the British ship "George Canning." They at once proceeded to form a branch of this society under the name of "Los Caballeros Racionales," and found many eager adherents among the more advanced Democrats of the capital.

Taking advantage of the popular discontent with the measures of the triumvirate, the "Caballeros Racionales" stirred up a commotion, and a fresh revolution in September placed the executive in the hands of a new triumvirate, consisting of—

> Dr. Don Juan José Passo.
> Don Nicolas Rodriguez Peña.
> ,,   Antonio Alvarez Jonte.

all of whom belonged to the Democratic party.

"The eternal captivity of Ferdinand VII. has destroyed the last rights of Spain."

Such were the words with which the new Government commenced their first address to the Argentine people. They cast aside at once the fiction of loyalty to a foreign king, and claimed to govern only by the will of the people.

In accordance with this programme they devised a new plan of electing the deputies to the assembly. Each town or city was divided into eight electoral districts; in each district the citizens voted "viva voce" for an "elector;" the eight "electors" so chosen by each city named the deputy or deputies who should represent that city. Buenos Aires, as the capital, had the right of sending four deputies to the assembly, the capital of each province two, and all other towns one each.

This was an immense advance upon the old system of leaving the right of naming deputies to the Cabildos, and produced a very fair representation of the urban population of the united provinces, but the rights of the rural population were entirely overlooked.

"The General Constituent Assembly" was inaugurated on the 31st January, 1813. Without proclaiming the independence of the united provinces, they yet took to themselves the supreme power, substituting the national arms for those of Spain; a national flag for the flag of Spain; suppressing all laws and customs which in any way recognized

Spanish tribunals as courts of appeal; abolished the Inquisition and judicial torture; gave liberty to all children born of slave parents after that date; and in the service of the Litany substituted a prayer for the "Sovereign Assembly of the United Provinces" in place of the one previously offered on behalf of the King. Further, they decreed that all Europeans, whether ecclesiastics, civilians, or soldiers, who should not within fifteen days become citizens should forfeit any employment they held under Government.

In January, 1814. the assembly determined upon another great step, they abolished the triumvirate and placed Don Gervacio Posadas at the head of the state, with the title of "Supreme Director of the United Provinces," but after holding office for one year Posadas resigned, and Don Carlos Maria de Alvear was named Supreme Director.

Alvear owed his election to the influence of the "Caballeros Racionales," of which secret society he was President, but he was disliked both by the mass of the people and by the army.

The position of the united provinces was at this time very critical; the fall of Napoleon had set Ferdinand at liberty, he was again King of Spain, and was preparing at Cadiz an expedition of 15,000 men for the purpose of reconquering the revolted colonies of La Plata. Alvear despaired of securing the independence of the united provinces, but five years of revolutionary rule had inspired the entire Argentine people with a hatred of Spain; he determined to place them under the protectorate of Great Britain. With this object he chose two ambassadors, Don Manuel Belgrano and Don Bernardino Rivadavia, whom he despatched to London with credentials to the Court of Saint James, and with a despatch addressed to the Secretary of State for Foreign Affairs, in which, after describing the disorder into which everything had fallen from the inaptitude of the people for self-government, he said—

"These provinces wish to belong to Great Britain, to adopt her laws, to obey her Government, and to live under her powerful influence. They deliver themselves unconditionally to the generosity and good faith of the English people."

The two ambassadors reached London in March, 1815, only to find Europe in a fresh commotion produced by the return of Napoleon from Elba. This unforeseen event, put an end to the expedition in preparation at Cadiz; greatly improved the position of Charles IV., ex-King of Spain, who still asserted his right to the crown of Spain, and was then living in retirement at Rome; and utterly precluded any hope that the British Government would adopt any policy in opposition to the interests of Ferdinand.

The two ambassadors never presented their credentials to the Court of Saint James, and, in conjunction with Sarratea, who was at that time agent in Europe for the Government of the united provinces, addressed themselves instead, to the ex-King Charles, offering to bestow the crown of Buenos Aires upon his adopted son the Infante Don Francisco de Paula. Waterloo put an end to this negotiation, Rivadavia went to Spain to endeavour to treat with Ferdinand, and Belgrano returned to Buenos Aires.

Belgrano was no great genius, either as a military man or as a politician, but he was a hard-working, honest patriot; loving his country, and ready to make any personal sacrifice in her service, he aspired to no dignities and was careless of all emolument ; he devoted his life and his energies to securing the independence of the Argentine people. But he was also a deep thinker, and foresaw that the anarchy which was spreading over the united provinces threatened evils even worse than the tyranny of Spain. During his residence in England, he had seen that the liberty of the people was perfectly compatible with monarchical institutions ; he returned to Buenos Aires, convinced that the establishment of a monarchy was the only means by which order and liberty could be at once secured to the Argentine people.

During the campaign of Tucuman he had entered into friendly relations with various Indian chieftains of the interior, among them he now proposed to search for a lineal descendant of Atahualpa, for the purpose of re-establishing the Empire of the Incas. In this purpose he found many willing to join him, but the Argentine people, jealous of their new-won liberty, looked upon the project as a dream.

The necessities of Government had compelled them to many extreme and arbitrary measures for the replenishing of the exhausted treasury. Of these measures the Spanish residents of Buenos Aires were the especial victims. Early in the year 1812 the capital was almost drained of troops by the large reinforcements despatched to the army in the Banda Oriental, and the Spanish residents, headed by Don Martin Alzaga, entered into a conspiracy together, their object being to seize the city, put to death all the principal Argentine leaders, and to set up a new government in connexion with the Spanish Cortes then assembled at Cadiz. To further their scheme they entered into a correspondence with the Princess Carlota of Brazil, and the Portuguese army, which had received orders to retire from the Banda Oriental, delayed its retreat in pursuance of secret instructions, and was held in readiness to support the conspirators if they should succeed in gaining possession of the capital.

Until the eve of the outbreak, the Government was in complete ignorance of the danger, but immediately on the discovery of the conspiracy adopted the most vigorous measures of suppression. Thirty of the principal conspirators, including Don Martin Alzaga, were shot, and their bodies hung upon gibbets, seventy-eight of less note were condemned to minor punishments, and the danger was thus averted.

The authors of the revolution of the 25th May, 1810, had sought to establish a new government upon the democratic basis of the sovereignty of the people. Many of them were men of great intellectual attainments, but they had adopted the ideas of the revolutionary leaders of France, in the full persuasion that that form of government, which is in theory the best, must necessarily be the best in practice. The failure of democracy in France had not opened their eyes to the fact that a government, to be securely based upon the will of the people, must be constructed in conformity with the traditions, circumstances, and instincts of the people.

The first five years of revolutionary government were thus a series of political experiments, a series of abortive attempts to govern a number of distinct provinces by schemes of administration, which might have been fully adequate for the government of the small republics of ancient Greece, or of the Italian cities of the middle ages, when each city was a separate state, but were totally inadequate for the government of an immense territory, peopled chiefly by herdsmen and shepherds. They totally failed to give the people any adequate means of expressing their will, and the result was that during these years the people, who had responded eagerly to the cry of liberty, interpreted in their own way the theory of popular sovereignty.

The nature of the country and the traditions and instincts of the people all inclined them to an aristocratic form of government; the attempt to form an administration on a democratic basis was consequently a complete failure.

The mass of the Argentine people were herdsmen and shepherds, who lived scattered over immense plains, who were yet in a state of semi-barbarism; the theory of the sovereignty of the people was interpreted to mean that each man had a right to choose his own ruler. The qualities which they could most fully appreciate were dauntless courage, a strong seat on horseback, and a ruthless will. Men possessed of such qualifications were those to whom they would naturally look as their leaders, and to whom they were ready to yield the most unquestioning obedience; but men like these were not the men to work cordially with the authors of the revolution in the regeneration of their country. Thus the leading Democrats, almost ignoring the existence of the mass of the people, except when they looked to them for aid against the Spaniards, sought only the co-operation of the towns and cities in their attempts to form a national government.

The revolution of the 25th May, 1810, was exclusively the work of the citizens of Buenos Aires. The nucleus of all the armies which fought in the subsequent campaigns was formed of the militia of Buenos Aires; the Patricios, and other regiments levied in Buenos Aires, bore the brunt in every conflict. It was the militia of Buenos Aires who marched with Belgrano through the dense woods and endless swamps of Paraguay, and held their own against the overwhelming odds of fourteen to one. It was the militia of Buenos Aires who kept the Portuguese armies in check in the Banda Oriental, laid siege to Monte Video, where the garrison outnumbered them three to one, gained the victory of the Cerrito, and eventually compelled the surrender of the city. It was the militia of Buenos Aires who penetrated with Balcarce, Diaz Velez, Puyrredon, and Belgrano to the confines of Upper Peru. It was the militia of Buenos Aires who decided with their bayonets the fields of Suipacha, Tucuman, and Salta; they stood round Belgrano and the blue-and-white standard among the rocks on that dismal night which followed the rout of Vilcapugio; they retreated with him from the still more disastrous field of Ayouma. Argentines from other provinces, Paz, Arenales, Martin Güemes, and many others, vied with their comrades from Buenos Aires in gallantry and endurance on many a hard-fought field; on two occasions Belgrano saved the remnant of his army solely through the devoted bravery of his "gaucho" allies of the interior, but in every conflict the brunt fell upon the infantry of Buenos Aires.

Buenos Aires not only furnished the nucleus to every army, but her citizens impoverished themselves to provide by voluntary contributions for the support and equipment of these armies, while her trade was harassed, and at times destroyed, by the hostility of the Spanish cruisers. Of all the cities of the interior, Tucuman alone displayed equal patriotism, equal zeal for the cause of all.

But Buenos Aires in return for the great sacrifices she made, claimed for herself the chief place in the direction of affairs. The Cabildo of Buenos Aires took upon itself on more than one occasion the right of nominating the Government which ruled in the name of the Argentine people. The "Constituent Assembly" of the year 1813 was the first legislative body which in any degree represented the united provinces. This assembly soon fell under the influence of the secret society, then known as "Los Caballeros Racionales," and later on as "La Sociedad de Lautaro."

᾽ The provincial jealousy of Buenos Aires, which almost disappeared in the first burst of enthusiasm that welcomed the cry of "Liberty" raised by Buenos Aires on the 25th May, 1810, soon revived; the provincial cities began to ask themselves whether the domination of Buenos Aires, the domination of a secret and irresponsible society, was not worse than the domination of Spain. The disastrous issue of some of the campaigns, and the continued demands upon them for supplies, exhausted their patience. Then rose up a new power in the state, to which both the provincial cities and Buenos Aires, had hitherto given but slight attention—the people.

The army of Peru under Rondeau, the army of the Andes under San Martin, refused to obey the orders of a Government which was merely the mouth-piece of a clique. In their dilemma the citizens of Buenos Aires looked about for a deliverer who should free them from a despotism which threatened them with the loss of all for which they had fought. Their gaze fell upon the new power which had risen up amongst them, they appealed to the people.

In the year 1815 José Artigas stood forth prominently as "the man of the people." The people were in a state of semi-barbarism. He himself was little better, but he understood them, knew how to attract their sympathies to himself, and how to rule over them. The Banda Oriental, Entre Rios, and Corrientes obeyed him. In answer to the appeal of the citizens of Buenos Aires, he crossed the Paraná into Santa Fé with the pompous title of "Chief of the Orientales and Protector of the Free Peoples." The men of Santa Fé received him as their deliverer. Cordova declared herself independent of Buenos Aires.

The people, knowing nothing of representative Government, chose for themselves their leaders, and prepared to yield them unlimited obedience. In every province there rose up petty chieftains, ruling with absolute sway over their followers, ready for any sacrifice to defend their country against Spain, equally ready to defend their provincial rights against the domination of Buenos Aires. These popular chieftains throughout the provinces hailed Artigas as their champion.

Alvear bestirred himself against this new enemy, and despatched an army to drive him from the province of Santa Fé. But on the frontier of Buenos Aires this army joined the popular movement, and fraternized with the barbaric hordes of Artigas. Then the citizens of Buenos Aires arose and decreed the downfall of the Government, the assembly was dissolved, and Alvear took refuge on board a foreign vessel anchored in the roadstead.

The Argentine people was left without a government, and, in presence of the anarchy which prevailed, without any legal means of appointing one. Again Buenos Aires put herself forward as the arbiter of the destinies of the nation. The Cabildo of Buenos Aires resumed to itself the powers of government, and decreed the election by the citizens of Buenos Aires of a "Junta de Observacion," which should form a provisional government until the convention of a sovereign congress. This Junta named General Rondeau, then in command of the army of Upper Peru, Supreme Director.

The new Government found itself face to face with three distinct enemies, Spain, the provinces, the people. Two provinces of the old Viceroyalty of Buenos Aires, Paraguay and the Banda Oriental, were now completely independent of Buenos Aires; every other province had an equal right to such independence; Cordova and Santa Fè utterly refused to recognize the new Government; Entre Rios and Corrientes had chosen a ruler for themselves, and obeyed the orders of Josè Artigas. The people everywhere, weary of the exactions of the nominees of the capital, looked to Josè Artigas as their champion.

Artigas, obeying the universal law which impels "the man of the people" to become a despot, sought only to consolidate and extend his own power.

The Government, after a vain attempt to come to some definite arrangement with Artigas, concluded a truce with him. He retired across the Paranà, and they despatched an army to occupy Santa Fè. But this army was compelled to capitulate to the "Montonera," or "gaucho" cavalry of Santa Fè. A second army, stationed at Rosario, revolted, and demanded the resignation of the Supreme Director. The Government yielded, the "Junta de Observacion" named General Antonio Gonzalez Balcarce, Supreme Director, and the army of Buenos Aires was withdrawn from Santa Fè.

VII. THE CONGRESS OF TUCUMAN.

The only hope now of putting an end to this anarchy lay in the assembling of a sovereign congress, in which all the provinces should be duly represented.

On the 24th March, 1816, this congress was convened at Tucuman, the mass of the Argentine people looking on with supreme indifference. At the same time Artigas amused himself by convening a Federal congress of his own at Paysandù in the Banda Oriental.

Each province sent deputies to the Congress of Tucuman in proportion to its estimated population, and some attempt was made to procure the representation of the campaña. Buenos Aires sent seven deputies; Cordova, five; Chuquisaca, four; Tucuman, three; Catamarca, Santiago del Estero, Mendoza, and Salta, two each; La Rioja, San Luis, San Juan, Misque, Cochabamba, and Jujui, one each. The

Banda Oriental, Entre-Rios Corrientes, and Santa Fè sent no deputies, Paraguay was by this time completely isolated from Argentine affairs.

The Congress of Tucuman did not fully represent the Argentine people, nevertheless it was a more exact representation of the popular will than any assembly which had yet been convened. Upon one point only had the Argentine people as yet made up their minds, they looked upon themselves as an independent nation, and were ready to assert that independence before the world. To this resolve of the people, the Congress of Tucuman gave full expression.

The first measures of Congress were marked by great timidity, as though they feared to measure the extent of their power, but on the 3rd May they appointed Don Juan Martin Puyrredòn Supreme Director, thus annulling the appointment of General Balcarce by the Junta of Buenos Aires.

VIII. INDEPENDENCE.

In June Belgrano and San Martin arrived in Tucuman; neither of them were members of Congress, but their personal influence had great weight in the decisions of that body. In pursuance of their counsels, on the 9th July, 1816, a day ever memorable in the annals of the Argentine people, the secretary of Congress proposed this question to the deputies—

"Do you desire that the provinces of the union form a nation free and independent of the kings of Spain?"

"Yes," answered every deputy, springing to his feet.

That answer was the true, outspoken will of the Argentine people, and has been maintained by them with unshaken heroism ever since. By that answer the Argentine people took their place in the world as an independent nation. Nothing less than that answer would have justified the revolution of the 25th May, 1810. That answer was the seal to the liberties of the New World, it carried with it the independence of all the infant peoples then groaning under the tyranny of Spain.

The Act of Independence was then drawn out as follows—

"We, the representatives of the united provinces of South America, invoking that eternal Power which presides over the universe, in the name and by the authority of the people we represent, protesting before Heaven and before all nations and men of the globe, the justice of our vote, solemnly declare before all the world, that it is the unanimous and undoubted will of these provinces to break the chains which bind them to the kings of Spain, to reassert the rights of which they have been despoiled, and to take upon themselves the high character of a free nation. In consequence of which they remain with ample and full power to adopt such form of government as justice and their circumstances may require. All and each one of us so publish, declare, and notify, binding ourselves to the fulfilment and support of this their will, under the security and guarantee of our lives, fortunes, and good name."

Twenty-nine deputies signed their names to this Declaration of Independence. To maintain this independence the Argentine people, by their deputies and their authorities of every class, devoted themselves, their lives, and their properties, and amid all the convulsions through which they have since passed they have never faltered for one moment in their adhesion to this solemn declaration which was made for them by the Sovereign Congress of Tucuman on the 9th July, 1816.

Since then the anniversary of that great day has been yearly welcomed with rejoicings throughout the length and breadth of the land. Amid the vineyards of Mendoza, on the sunny plains of Santa Fè, in the peaceful seats of learning at Cordova, and amid the busy hum of commerce at Buenos Aires, the yearly recurrence of that day has been welcomed ever since. Arribeños, Rivereños, and Porteños, whatever their passing differences, alike look back in boastful pride to the day when their forefathers boldly asserted their right to a place among the nations of the world.

Through much turmoil and sorrow, through anarchy, tyranny, and bloodshed the Argentine people have struggled since the day when Buenos Aires first raised the standard of freedom. For six years they laboured before they could unite to declare themselves a nation, even to the present day their efforts to form themselves into one homogeneous people have not met with full accomplishment. But the Argentine Republic now exists, she holds her acknowledged place among the nations. The dream of those gallant men who, on the 25th May, 1810, shook themselves free from the traditions of centuries, is fulfilled.

In many of the events which we have so shortly chronicled in this epilogue, Don Marcelino Ponce de Leon and Don Carlos Evaña took their share, playing their parts, each according to his several character. Both of them sprang to their feet and responded with an enthusiastic "Yes" to the question proposed to the deputies by the secretary of the Sovereign Congress of Tucuman, on the 9th July, 1816, both of them signed the Declaration of Independence. Yet if you read that document you will not find either of those names there written. They represent two great sections of the Argentine people, differing widely in their principles, more widely yet in their modes of thought, who joined cordially together, to overthrow the domination of Spain, to establish the Argentine Republic.

THE END.

www.ingramcontent.com/pod-product-compliance
Lightning Source LLC
Chambersburg PA
CBHW030942110726
47900CB00004F /1100